JACOB'S LADDER

BOOKS BY DONALD McCAIG

Novels

The Butte Polka
Nop's Trials
Nop's Hope

Entertainments

Stalking Blind
The Man who made the Devil Glad
The Bamboo Cannon

Nonfiction

Eminent Dogs, Dangerous Men
An American Homeplace

Poetry

Last Poems

JACOB'S LADDER

A STORY OF VIRGINIA DURING THE WAR

Donald McCaig

W. W. NORTON & COMPANY

NEW YORK · LONDON

For information about permission to reproduce selections from this book, write to
Permissions, W. W. Norton & Company, Inc., 500 Fifth Avenue, New York, NY 10110.

The text of this book is composed in ITC Garamond
with the display set in Vineta, Copperplate 31bc, and English 157.
Composition and manufacturing by The Haddon Craftsmen, Inc.
Book design by JAM Design

Library of Congress Cataloging-in-Publication Data

McCaig, Donald.
Jacob's ladder: a story of Virginia during the war/by Donald McCaig.
p.   cm.
ISBN 0-393-04629-X
1. Virginia—History—Civil War, 1861–1865—Fiction. 2. Virginia—History—Civil War,
1861–1865—Afro-Americans—Fiction. 3. Afro-Americans—Virginia—Fiction.
4. Gatewood family—Fiction.
I. Title.
PS3563.A255J33   1998
813'.54—dc21   9731165
CIP

W. W. Norton & Company, Inc., 500 Fifth Avenue, New York, N.Y. 10110
http://www.wwnorton.com

W. W. Norton & Company Ltd., 10 Coptic Street, London WC1A 1PU

2 3 4 5 6 7 8 9 0

CONTENTS

And Jacob went out from Beersheeba, and went toward Haran. And he lighted upon a certain place, and tarried there all night, because the sun was set; and he took of the stones of that place, and put them for his pillows, and lay down in that place to sleep.

And he dreamed, and behold a ladder set up on the earth, and the top of it reached to heaven: and behold the angels of God ascending and descending on it.

And, behold, the Lord stood above it, and said, I am the Lord God of Abraham thy father, and the God of Isaac: the land whereon thou liest, to thee will I give it, and to thy seed; and thy seed shall be as the dust of the earth, and thou shalt spread abroad to the west, and to the east, and to the north, and to the south: and in thee and in thy seed shall all the families of the earth be blessed.

And, behold, I am with thee, and will keep thee in all places whither thou goest . . .

—GENESIS 28:10–15

PART ONE

Antebellum

Everything is founded on the death of men.

—*Captain Oliver Wendell Holmes,*
20th Massachusetts

1

—

COX'S SNOW

WINTERS WERE COLDER in those days; they remembered that. And the apples were smaller and tart and some of them so orangy they were more orange than red. And every plantation, even the poorest hardscrabble place, grew its own seed corn, so everyone's corn was different—some plump-eared, some long and narrow; some flourished on the wet clay ground beside the river, some did best on the dry limestone hills. The sermons were longer in those days; those Baptist preachers could get to rolling at daybreak and never miss a lick until suppertime. Nobody went hungry—at least not anybody anybody knew. There were plenty of chickens and hog meat, and what Master didn't provide, they could take out of the woods—possum and raccoon and squirrel.

It was a long time before anybody got around to asking them how it had been in those days, seventy years, and the young people who came around with their spanking new notebooks to ask questions came, often as not, from the big house up on the hill and bore the same names the old masters had.

One remembered seeing the butternut soldiers that first time they crossed into Maryland. She said they looked lean and dirty. She said they looked like wolves. Another remembered Confederate cavalrymen with dead horses' hooves slung around their horses' necks. She understood right away that they cut them off and kept them for their shoes and never forgot the way the bloody things bounced and spattered the living horses' necks.

Nobody remembered the day the war started but some remembered the day they hung John Brown because all the coloreds were locked up from dawn to dawn.

The WPA interviewers were young, many fresh out of college, and their own beliefs about the war were so strong they found it hard to credit the memories of the ancient black people who'd lived through it. "How about Lincoln's inauguration? You remember when Lincoln became the President?"

"No, Miss."

Some of them remembered the day the general surrendered—how subdued and lost the white folks seemed. And they remembered Cox's snow.

"I was three years old, the winter of Cox's snow," or "That year I was working at Edgeworth Plantation, the year after Cox's snow." Most of them had never learned to read or write and that was how they remembered things. They remembered that the apples were tart and people prayed longer in those days and they remembered Cox's snow.

The girl was tired and her feet hurt and she thought she might as well leave her pumps at home and buy a pair of shoes like nurses wore. The heat shimmered over the James River and the air was so thick it was like breathing through wet cloth. The family had gone to the mountains as they did every summer and she surely wished she was with them. She would have lain down flat in the pine needles and looked up through the trees to the pale blue sky and been happy.

Interview number three this morning and nothing to show for it. It was awfully easy to understand why people called them stupid. Couldn't remember a thing. "Missy, that was a powerful time ago!" Except for the apples. Her last interview had insisted that the apples had been "the most tart I ever seed." Now there was useful history—to a pomologist.

The car Daddy gave her when she graduated from Sweet Briar was an elephant-back coupe, the sort of car salesmen drove. "Plenty of room for your samples," her brothers had joked, but it was a Chrysler Airflow, at least.

Things had been getting awfully serious between her and Phil, and she thought a summer apart might give her some breathing room. When Uncle Harry told her about this writer's job with one of President Roosevelt's new "alphabet soup" agencies, she jumped at the chance. But was any job worth August in Richmond?

Perspiration crept down the back of her neck and the leather car seat scorched the back of her legs and would probably leave red marks—not that her interview subjects would notice or care. Her previous interview had taken place in a shotgun shack down the River Road in a room so powerfully "negroid" she'd sat beside the open window so she could breathe. The creature on the bed was so wizened and so swaddled in quilts she wouldn't have known its sex except for the name on her inter-view list. The woman had remembered apples. All she could talk about was apples.

She'd told her supervisor, "How can I write their stories if they have nothing to say?"

Her daddy had asked: "If those government people are so all-fired cu-rious about what happened on the plantations, why don't they ask the people who knew what was going on? Why inquire among the servants?" Daddy said it was scandal-mongering, just like that Scottsboro business.

But the old negroes she'd interviewed weren't eager to repeat those awful stories. Yes, they knew there were whippings and wicked goings-on, but those things went on at other plantations, no'm, never happened to me. Truth was, the girl's own Uncle Harry told more horrible stories than the coloreds did. Uncle Harry relished recounting tales of rapes and whip-pings and outright murders. But then, Uncle Harry had spent an awful lot of time up in New York.

The onetime capital of the Confederate States of America dozed in the sun. Single-story unpainted clapboard buildings lined avenues broad enough for triumphal parades. So much of the city had been destroyed in the evacuation fire. Only here on Shockoe Hill had the grand old town-houses survived.

She drove past Mr. Valentine's house—Mr. Valentine had made his money in tinned meat juice—and the big white mansion Jefferson Davis had lived in. They'd wanted to tear it down but the Daughters of the Con-federacy had stepped in and bought it. Fashion had abandoned Shockoe Hill decades ago, and most of the surviving mansions were rooming houses now.

She parked in the shade of an enormous elm tree which filled most of the tiny front yard of 376 Clay Street. The iron gate dragged as she pushed it open, the sidewalk was cracked, and weeds flourished at the verges. The porch was a pinched vestibule—wood, painted gray—but she could see where they'd removed a wider, more generous veranda. The doorbell was encrusted with dried yellow paint, and she poked at it without confi-dence. The house felt like "nobody home" and she was surprised when the door opened.

The servant was elderly, black, hunched. She wore a faded green print housedress.

The girl said, "I am with the Works Progress Administration. Are you Marguerite?"

"No'm, I ain't. I'se Kizzy. Miss Marguerite inside." She squinted against the noontime glare. "Powerful hot today," she observed. "Powerful."

The girl checked her clipboard. "This is 376 Clay Street," she said. "We are collecting recollections of negroes who were once slaves."

"What you want to do that for?"

A trickle of sweat ran down the girl's spine. It was unpleasantly inti-mate. "Marguerite's on my list. Apparently she has agreed to cooperate."

Grudgingly the old black woman stood aside. "You wait in the garden room. I fetch Miss Marguerite. Don't you go stirrin' up no trouble."

Clipboard tucked under her arm, the girl passed through the long dim hallway. The rooms on both sides were closed off and the hall chairs shrouded in gray muslin. It was so cool goose bumps rose on her arms. At the back of the house she came into a long room facing the garden. The wide French doors stood open and the scent of climbing roses perfumed the air. A carpet of primroses bordered the brick path. The sun didn't penetrate the canopy of tremendous old trees, and the room—done in shades of pale blue—was cool and comfortable. Unlike the front of the house, this room was lived in. Maritime lithographs were grouped on the walls: feral blockade runners plowed through crashing seas, pursued by angry vessels whose decks were wreathed in cannon smoke. Magazines were stacked on the table beside a plump couch: chintz patterned in over-sized flowers. Reading glasses of a severe old-fashioned style peeped be-neath a clot of blue yarn in a wicker sewing basket.

Idly, the girl leafed through the magazines—Virginia Cavalcade, The Saturday Evening Post, Collier's, quarterlies of modest size but rigorous typeface from university history departments. Perhaps her hostess was the wife of a retired professor—or his widow—made comfortable by family money. The girl rather looked forward to meeting her. Afterward, of course, she'd have to interview the subject: Kizzy, no doubt.

Who poked her head through the door. "Miss Marguerite wants to know, do you want tea? She say she's having some."

"Tea would be nice, thank you." The girl pictured a tall glass, full to the brim with icy tea. Perhaps a sprig of mint.

The room was quiet. Though traffic passed on the streets outside, the loudest sounds that penetrated here were polite birdsongs from the gar-den. The perspiration dried on the girl's forehead and her underarms were unpleasantly sticky and she hoped she didn't know the hostess, that there was no family connection. It was one thing to traipse off for a bo-hemian summer interviewing negroes and quite another to do so in the presence of one's respectable connections.

The woman, ancient and no taller than a child of ten, was dressed sim-ply in a silk wrap. Both hands gripped a gnarled black walking stick which preceded her every step. Her hair was wispy and white. The knuck-les that clasped the head of the stick had been thickened and twisted by arthritis. When the girl rose to her feet, the woman motioned impatiently for her to sit. Her skin was yellowish-gray, like medieval parchment, and the bones of her skull were visible just beneath the skin.

Kizzy brought in a tray: a tea service, and two frail porcelain cups. Hot tea. The thought of it brought fresh perspiration to the girl's brow.

"I have never become accustomed to tea with ice in it," Miss Marguerite said. *"During the War, coffee was scarce, but tea was practically unobtainable. We had our last cup of tea the week the* Wild Darrell *went down. After we fled Wilmington, there was nothing but sassafras."* She arranged herself at the end of the couch and leaned her stout stick against the arm. *"I am told the government is interviewing those who were once slaves. That is correct?"*

The girl made a face. *"I don't make much progress, I'm afraid. The ex-slaves still alive are not always—well—*compos mentis.*"* She laughed. *"Perhaps they don't wish to speak frankly to a . . . a . . . white person. We haven't always treated them with kindness, you know."*

The old woman produced a parsimonious smile. *"I believe I've heard something about that."*

The girl wondered why people shrank when they got old. She poured plenty of cream into her tea.

"Most of those who knew slavery best have passed on," the woman said. *"And many others speak only negro patois. It is useful if you are a slave to have a language to which the masters do not have perfect access. There is some slight advantage to understanding them while they cannot understand you."*

"Has Kizzy been with your family long?"

The old woman smiled. *"Patience, child. As you grow older you will appreciate its merits. After my son finished Harvard, he went west. Los Angeles. I intended him to stay in Richmond with the bank, but try and tell him anything. My grandson Joshua does something with the Los Angeles Water Authority. What do you know about water authorities?"*

"Not much, I'm afraid."

The old woman drew a shawl about her shoulders. *"I see you find the day uncomfortable. Would that I did. Children, you know, can abide the most daunting cold. I fear my plumbing is clogged with scale. I dread the winter."*

The girl's Longines had been a graduation present, and each time she consulted it, she felt newly important. *"This tea is refreshing,"* she said. *"Who would have thought it—hot tea on a hot day."*

The old woman set her cup on its saucer without a clink. *"What is the purpose of your inquiry?"*

The girl lifted her shoulders. *" 'Government make-work,' Daddy calls it. All through the South, WPA writers are conducting interviews. There are so few written records."*

"I suppose," the old woman replied distantly. *"And once the WPA has this information, what does it propose doing with it?"*

"One day it may be of interest to historians." She gestured at the stack of university quarterlies. *"Was your husband an historian, by chance?"*

"Oh, no. My husband was a gentleman."

"I'm sure, ma'am. I had noticed your historical interests and thought . . . Might I . . . Perhaps I could speak to Kizzy?"

The old woman's sigh emitted no more air than a bird's. *"My doctor tells me I shan't survive much longer and I'm not certain I wish to. We've had a death in the family."*

"Oh, I'm sorry."

"Yes." The old woman's milky eyes were blank. *"Most unexpected."* The birds sang their self-involved tunes. The woman's voice strengthened. *"My family lives on the other coast and can no longer be hurt by the truth. When I read of your project, after due consideration, I wrote the Senator and asked to be included."* She cleared her throat. *"Would you ask Kizzy to bring me a glass of water? The other homes on this street are on municipal water, but we have always had our own well."*

As they waited the old woman remarked, *"Although we have many negro depositors, our bank is not known as a negro bank. Virginia's negro banks failed to reopen after President Roosevelt's bank holiday, did you know that?"*

"No, ma'am."

"Insufficient capital, too many small loans." She drank the water and dismissed Kizzy, who seemed inclined to linger. She rubbed her high forehead. She said, *"I became a woman the year of Cox's snow. I don't know how old I was, twelve or thirteen, I suppose, and when I had my first effusion, I mentioned it to no one. The whites believed that we primitives matured younger than white girls, and their theory was of economic benefit to them, since a negress's greatest value was her ability to bear children. We were bred as early and frequently as could be managed within the decencies of Christian convention. . . ."*

A chill raised goose bumps down the girl's neck and arms. She was suddenly nauseated. *"Excuse me,"* the girl whispered. *"Do I understand you correctly . . . ?"*

The old woman looked into her cool, orderly garden. *"My mother was light-skinned, and of course my father, the Reverend Mitchell, was white. It is curious, is it not, that the lighter-skinned we are, the more anxious the dominant race is to mate with us. Those first white men to sleep with the dark-skinned daughters of Africa were such bold pioneers!"* She raised her invisible eyebrows mockingly. *"I suppose it is more agreeable to make love with creatures that closely resemble oneself. Narcissism is one of the South's notable frailties."*

The girl wanted to leave this place. Surely she could leave.

The old woman sipped, then swallowed, her throat clenching painfully. *"The city wishes me to cap my well and accept their water, which, I believe, they pump from the James. I tell them I have lived beside the James for too many years to have any great desire to drink of it.*

"*That January it started snowing on Thursday afternoon and contin-ued through Sunday—the winter had been uncommonly mild and we had no reason to anticipate harsher weather. As I have told you, I had re-cently become a woman but was determined to conceal my new cir-cumstances. I was a house servant, Mistress Abigail's personal servant, and intended to retain my position at any hazard. Mistress Abigail's chil-dren were grown, her daughter, Leona, married with two children of her own. Her son, Duncan, was her husband's confidant and favored com-panion, and I expect Miss Abigail was lonely. I was a clever child and un-usually confident. I thought I was 'the cat's pajamas.' " The old woman paused. "You young people still employ that expression, do you not?"*

The girl felt trapped. "*I don't know.*"

"*My grandson William was annoyingly fond of it. He owned a Stutz roadster. I haven't seen a Stutz in some time. Do they still manufacture them?*"

"*I don't believe so, no.*"

"*My grandson was fond of his.*"

"*You . . . you are a negress?*"

"*When I was young, as I have said, I was unusually self-possessed. I had a gift for mimicry and could imitate the nuances of my employers' speech as well as my fellow servants' patois. I could read—a little—and later, Jesse Burns taught me sums. I was good at sums. My education*"—she gestured at the periodicals—"*has been irregular. Bits and scraps.*" She paused. "*I suppose I know as much about those days as anyone. Mr. Free-man is forever after me to write something for the Historical Society, though he would be astonished, I imagine, at what I might say.*" She struck the edge of the coffee table with her tiny soundless hand. "*Think of what I might have become given a fair chance at life!*" She looked around the sunny room with angry satisfaction. "*Still, I have made the best of whatever opportunities presented themselves. I did nothing to benefit my-self. Nothing.*" Her age-spotted hand waved away that possibility. "*Are you a Christian, my dear?*"

The girl stuttered that she was an Episcopalian . . . St. Paul's . . . she at-tended St. Paul's.

"*Not exactly what I meant. President Davis learned Richmond must fall while attending services at St. Paul's. Did you know that?*"

The girl said she had never asked questions about the War. Staunchly she added, "*General Lee told my grandfather that the War was over and we must rebuild the South. That we should no longer discuss the War. In my family, we haven't.*"

"*Oh? The reticence of Virginia's gentlefolk never fails to astound me.*" She held the cool water glass against her cheek. "*As Miss Abigail's personal servant I slept in the loft over the kitchen house, beside the cook. In the* cold months I banked my bed against the warm bricks of the kitchen chimney and slept snug as a dream. When the other coloreds went out into the fields for wheat harvest or cutting corn or the January threshing I remained indoors with Miss Abigail, Master Samuel's spinster sister, Kate, and Grandmother Gatewood, who retained great influence with her son. Her husband, Thomas Gatewood, died under a cloud, and mother and son spent their life overcoming the scandal. Lord, how the Gatewoods yearned to be ordinary!

"I used the same necessary the white folks used, though I had to finish before they rose up in the morning. Oh, I was full of myself. Some afternoons, while Miss Abigail was taking her nap, I'd stand before her pier glass: I looked like white folks. I was learning to talk like white folks, and I was smarter than most white folks. From this I concluded that I was just like white folks, an error which later caused me much pain.

"Miss Abigail loved me as her own. Her first infant, Leona, had been followed by a stillborn baby. Then infant Samuel, who died before his second birthday. Duncan was next, and fourteen years later Miss Abigail had the twins. The twins were born dead, and the midwife said it was a miracle Miss Abigail didn't die from blood evil. She was desperately ill, and it was to care for her that I was brought up to the main house. The midwife said Miss Abigail's twin boys had been dead for days. Miss Abigail insisted on holding a boy—she may have been unconvinced of his death—and the skin slipped off his body like skin off a dead rabbit. They buried the twins in a single coffin, foot to foot, in the cemetery on the hill back of Stratford House. The colored burying place was behind the Quarters.

"I spent my hours with Miss Abigail. Grandmother Gatewood prayed all day and Sister Kate did her level best to keep out of everybody's way, which was no simple task, since she shared a bedroom with Grandmother. It was no life of ease. Not for me. Not for any of them. Sister Kate watched over the servant babies when their mothers were out in the fields, Mistress Abigail sewed and knitted. When Grandmother Gatewood wasn't praying she was at the wheel or loom. Although she could buy ready-made cloth she swore by homespun for the servants. Miss Abigail's daughter, Leona, had made a good marriage to Catesby Byrd, a promising lawyer in Warm Springs, the county seat.

"Catesby Byrd had an agreeable disposition, but was fond of card-playing, a vice viewed more seriously then than it is today, when every grandmother sits down for her afternoon canasta. The courthouse card-players were not of the better class, and I believe Byrd failed to get an anticipated judgeship because of his associations. Though Stratford Plantation was a three-hour ride from Warm Springs, Catesby Byrd visited regularly and closeted himself with Samuel Gatewood.

"In those days, at the peak of his strength, Gatewood was an impressive *man, and his son, Duncan, followed him like a dog. Summer evenings the two would carry chairs out onto the porch roof and sit side by side while the father pointed at this or that and determined what work was to be accomplished on the morrow, the boy drinking in every word. Duncan wasn't clever, but he was one of those fortunate lads whose cleverness doesn't matter. He could shoot well enough, speak well enough, wrestle well enough, and he was brave. Virginia was filled with boys like him, but most were killed in the war.*

"Everything came so easily to Duncan he was puzzled by those who had to work for what they got. His perfect ears hid under his auburn curls like seashells. He was such a beautiful boy. Unblemished by life or sorrow or thought, he was so smooth it made you want to touch him." She cackled a dry cackle. "Certainly it made me want to touch him." Her smile was reminiscent. "His only evident knack was for horses. When he climbed onto the back of his mare, Gypsy, he and animal were transformed into a centaur. That ability to be one with animals is one sort of intelligence, I suppose.

"Cox's snow began falling, as I was saying, on a Thursday. I was in Miss Abigail's first-floor bedroom when the first flakes drifted past the windows. The snow was driving from the east instead of the customary west, and I expect I said something about it to Miss Abigail. From the start, it was a most unnatural storm."

She stared out into her summer garden, her old eyes focused on the swirling snowflakes of years ago. "They called me Midge in those days. . . ."

STRATFORD PLANTATION,
VIRGINIA JANUARY 22, 1857

The snow obscured the summit of Snowy Mountain and whitened the Jackson River Valley. It sifted into the village of SunRise, dusting the chapel and MacIver's forge. It swirled westward, softening the ruts in the stage road, enveloping Uther Botkin's modest homestead.

The Botkin place was as neat as a poor man's homestead can be. Although the hames dangling in the horse barn were worn, they were recently oiled and each hung in its proper place. The dirt path from the house to the milking barn was neatly lined with stones, the interior of the springhouse freshly whitewashed. The house was small when Uther inherited it—one large room—but since he contained so much space within his own mind, he had not thought to enlarge his domicile. Thirteen years before, when Uther received news of his legacy, he was a sixty-five-year-old itinerant schoolmaster whose wealth consisted of a one-volume edition of Shakespeare, works of Mr. Jefferson and Mr.

Paine, saddlebags to protect these books, and a mule which transported him and his capacious understanding to rural communities seeking to improve their young. Uther hadn't seen his Uncle William since childhood. Uncle William, a Presbyterian elder at SunRise Chapel, had his only son caught up in the "Businessman's Revival," which was subsequent to and only slightly less influential than the "Great Awakening" earlier in the century. These revivals emptied established congregations in favor of the Baptists, and Uncle William's son was among those who repented and was duly immersed. In their infrequent, dutiful correspondence, Uther and Uncle William had never touched upon religion. Doubtless Uncle William would have found his nephew's Deism as offensive as his son's vigorous evangelical Baptism, but Uncle William never thought to inquire. If a schoolmaster wasn't Presbyterian, what was he? Therefore, in his last will and testament, Uncle William bypassed his own issue in favor of his nephew, Uther.

Uther Botkin's legacy was eighty acres of limestone ledge and shallow topsoil bordering Stratford Plantation. The property was conveyed with three milk cows, a team of horses, half a dozen sheep, and twice that many hogs. Chickens and guinea hens scratched in the dirt and roosted in trees. The barn's feed room contained basket beehives, scythes, wheat cradles, hay forks, and those small tools necessary to a plantation of modest size. Uther Botkin also inherited a servant: Jesse Burns. Jesse was ten years of age, already unusually strong.

Uther Botkin had been a thoroughgoing schoolmaster, instructing his charges in arithmetic, geometry, spelling, rhetoric, and his special pleasure, history. The rapid changes sweeping the South greatly affected Uther's students. Sequential generations were invigorated by religious revivals, frightened by Nat Turner's uprising, and engrossed by the arguments of the Nullifiers. They admired John Calhoun over the nation's founders, Washington, Jefferson, and Adams.

"Calhoun would destroy the country," Uther once complained.

One of his pupils, a planter's son, retorted with a citation from that senator: "Duty is ours. Events belong to God."

The old schoolmaster sighed.

Upon the news of his unexpected legacy, Uther resigned his post, proposed marriage, and with his new wife perched on the mule he walked beside, made his way toward distant blue-tinged mountains.

Had Uther Botkin more practical experience of the world, he might have wondered why his bride's family was so willing to match an eighteen-year-old maiden of good character with a man so much older whose prospects were entirely an attorney's letter promising a legacy of unknown value. A more experienced man than Uther might have noticed Martha's pallor, her frail arms, the telltale crimson spots of the consumptive in her cheeks, but Uther was a mental virgin as surely as he was a physical one, and in this instance, ignorance was bliss. The unlikely couple fell deeply in love. If either noticed the shabby condition of the one-room cabin where they spent their first nights of connubial joy before the fire, neither ever remarked on it.

Perhaps the fields were stony and the fences in poor repair. Perhaps the south end of the barn canted alarmingly. Perhaps the chimney smoked and perhaps the team had been foaled in 1826, that sad year when Thomas Jefferson died. Uther Botkin had never been happier.

Because of his learning, which the mountain planters thought deep, pleasantly old-fashioned, and (if the whole truth be told) inconsequential, Uther and Martha were invited to balls at Warwick and Stratford. Mrs. Dinwiddie of Hidden Valley thought these considerations too nice, and neither the old schoolmaster nor his bride were ever invited to view "the finest balustrades west of the Blue Ridge."

Uther was far too happy to be snubbed, wouldn't have recognized a snub if it smacked him in the face. Martha, Uther, and the boy, Jesse: in the twilight of his life, Uther had found the family he'd always yearned for, and those who might have wished to humble him were deterred by the radiance of his countenance, his gentle speech, the unassuming nature of his learning. Why, certainly he would instruct the Gatewood children—most happy, most happy, your humble and most obedient servant, sir.

Uther and young Jesse hacked out a garden and planted it. They cut the scrub brush from ten acres and fenced the pasture with chestnut rails exchanged by Samuel Gatewood for his children's education.

Uther's wife sang as she weeded her garden and tended the pinkish Globe and early Danver tomatoes. She sang as she scrubbed Uther's Sunday shirt and his woolen socks. She sang all through her pregnancy. And six months after Baby Sallie was born, she sang no more.

An old man and a boy tended the baby, changed her, soaked a handkerchief in milk to give her suck. The boy, Jesse, did what heavy work got done.

If Samuel Gatewood hadn't supplied provender—hams, corn, oatmeal, beans—the little family might have starved. If he hadn't brought in hay and grain, their few animals certainly would have. Next spring, Gatewood's servants plowed and planted the little garden. They completed the rail fence around the new pasture.

In May of that year, Samuel Gatewood arrived, a colored woman of indeterminate age in the back of his farm wagon. Samuel Gatewood announced that he was offering the woman for rent at half the usual terms, just forty dollars per annum, payable at Christmastide, plus a pair of good leather shoes to be supplied the woman annually. The woman, Gatewood averred, would make life easier on Botkin's plantation.

Uther demurred. Like Mr. Jefferson, he said, he wished an end to slavery and meant to emancipate Jesse Burns when the boy attained his majority.

Samuel Gatewood replied that whatever his qualms, Mr. Jefferson retained his slaves, all of whom were pledged against extensive debts and sold within a month of the great man's death. He noted, further, that Virginia laws had hardened and emancipation was not the simple matter it had once been. Master Botkin could pursue whatever course he desired, but the servant woman in the wagon, Opal by name, was barren and of a shrewish disposition, and if Botkin didn't wish to rent her, Gatewood intended to offer her for sale—the slave speculator Silas Omohundru being in the neighborhood. Uther's eyes toured his dirty cabin, the mound of unwashed clothing, yesterday's grease congealing in the frypan, his sleeping daughter, and the twelve-year-old boy his only helper. "I accept your generous offer, sir," Uther said.

After Gatewood left, Uther welcomed the woman to his plantation, humble though it was.

She said, "Don't know if I 'barren' or not. Never met no man ever made me care to be fertile."

"I shall endeavor to treat you fairly," Uther said. "I pray we can lessen the inherent awkwardness of this situation."

"I wash your dishes and I cook your meals," Opal said. "But I ain't no good at it. You a hand with livestock?"

"It is a skill I admire in others."

The woman grinned a gap-toothed grin. She wasn't as tall as the schoolmaster but possessed more girth. "Then maybe we get along after all."

Every morning, Samuel Gatewood's daughter, Leona, arrived for instruction, and his son, Duncan, came too when he turned six, and Botkin's daughter, Sallie, toddled onto the porch to be with the others. On the porch in warm weather, by the fire in winter months, the children puzzled over their slates and calculated sums. Uther was a teacher again and knew it was for the last time.

Duncan was a harum-scarum boy who had to be persuaded away from his horses in favor of learning. Leona prayed she was pretty but feared she might not be. She learned because the others learned. And, to Uther's unconcealed delight, little Sallie loved learning—especially natural philosophy. After Jesse finished morning chores, he joined them, and though he rarely volunteered a question, he was soon able to read. This peculiar school seemed perfectly natural because to Uther Botkin it was perfectly natural.

Cox's snow was named after its best-known victim, a Lynchburg doctor, who returned home that night late, and some said drunk, and froze to death when his horse and buggy stalled in snowdrifts a scant half mile from safety.

At Botkin's plantation, Opal was first to notice the snow. Seated at the table, she slurped tea cooling in a saucer. Uther was at the dry sink, washing his cup and bowl.

From the first, Uther and Opal had adopted a division of labor: she did the livestock work and cooked, he advanced his studies and tidied up. Uther never complained about her cooking, which he accepted as his lot. Every year at Christmastide after he paid rental to Samuel Gatewood, ceremoniously, Uther presented Opal with a pair of new shoes. The cabin wasn't exactly spotless, but was orderly enough. Sometimes a person looking to perch upon a chair or settee must needs remove an article of clothing, but Opal's dried herbs hung from the ceiling beams in cheerful confusion and along the cool back wall, farthest from the fire, dangled hams cured last November and onions braided into ropes.

Light streamed through the two windows—it was thirteen-year-old Sallie's task to keep them washed—and dull coals glowed in the fireplace.

Opal said, "We're in for bad weather."

"Opal, it is a mild winter. Every day I expect to see the first spring crocuses pop through the earth."

"Snow about to cover them again. I tell Jesse bring the hogs down off the mountain. He shoo 'em into that lower lot, toss 'em some corn, keep 'em busy. I goin' to fetch the cows and the horses. The sheep can manage. They got their wool on 'em."

Sallie set her book aside. "I'll help, Auntie Opal. The cows will be over by the woods fence corner."

"And," old Uther suggested, "I'll heat milk for hot cocoa upon your return."

When Opal and Sallie stepped onto the porch, a gust of wind smacked them hard. That gust continued down the valley, skimming the frozen ground, skittering ice crystals against the dead broom sedge, turning the stolid sheep's faces away from the storm.

A half mile later, it reached Stratford Plantation, where it dropped into the valley the Jackson River had created, forming the alluvial subsoil that was Stratford's best cropland.

Samuel Gatewood's father, Thomas, had created Stratford. The Gatewood's original grant had been awarded to Samuel's grandfather (another Samuel) in 1768, but Thomas had tripled his family's holdings along the Jackson by purchase, exchange, and more imaginative means. Eighteenth-century surveyors had so muddled the original settlers' land grants and warrants that a determined man backed by a clever attorney (and Thomas Gatewood employed such a fellow) could claim land everyone thought had been granted years ago. Thomas Gatewood swore he didn't covet all the land in the county—only what was adjacent. The plantation he created was five thousand contiguous acres—the finest land between the Shenandoah Valley and the Tygart River Valley, three mountain ranges to the west. Alluvial fans at the foot of Snowy Mountain produced the plantation's fine oats. Although the river fields sometimes flooded in the spring, they grew fine wheat and better buckwheat, and the river never removed more topsoil than it deposited. Corn followed clover in the clay soils. A stone-lined millrace sliced through the river bend to power Stratford's overshot mill. Here, under Jack, Samuel Gatewood's excellent driver, fulltask hands ground corn, rolled oats, mashed sorghum, sawed logs, and, in winter months when no other work was available, crushed limestone rocks into particles fine enough to sweeten the croplands.

Stratford's wheat, sawn planks, and railroad sleepers traveled by wagon south to Millboro Springs, where the western ambitions of the Virginia Central Railroad had been checked by the impassable mountains.

Excepting the few weeks in winter when the race froze, the creak of that tall mill wheel and the growl of millstones were the living breath of Stratford Plantation. Day started when Jack the Driver opened the floodgate and stopped when he dropped the heavy gate into its slots again.

Forge, granaries, corn cribs, fowl house, and dairy clustered near the mill. Next came two great barns, each bulging with feed. Between the barns and the great house were the Quarters, a narrow street lined with one-room log cabins, each with its own wattle-and-daub chimney, each with a garden plot behind. The house and its dependencies stood on a low rise, facing south.

Meathouse, root cellar, and kitchen were behind the plantation house. The kitchen house was connected to the main house by a covered passageway—the "hyphen."

Twenty-eight colored servants lived at Stratford. Children and elderly milked the cows, made the cheese, slopped the hogs, gathered eggs, killed and plucked chickens, and tended the kitchen garden. One very ancient servant, Agamemnon, had no assigned tasks, though he sometimes made up potions and salves. Middle-aged men and women worked the fields, and two gangs of timber cutters—"Rufus's gang" and "the old gang"—lived in the woods, visited weekly by Jack the Driver. House servants included Pompey, the houseman, a scullery girl, the cook, and Miss Abigail's personal servant, Midge, who looked out the window and shivered. "There's Master Duncan ridin' out. I expect he's goin' out to warn the woods gangs."

Miss Abigail clipped a pattern from *Godey's Lady's Book.* "If you wish to improve your speech, dear, you mustn't drop your 'g's."

Midge flushed. "Yes ma'am. I forget myself."

"Modest and pleasant speech always produce a favorable impression.

Midge, I feel a headache coming on. If you fetch a cool cloth, I shall lie back and you shall read to me. When you encounter a novel word, spell it for me."

Midge took up the lady's magazine reluctantly. Speaking correctly was easier than reading. She had a knack for imitating speech, and last Christmas when Cousin Molly visited, Midge soon had Cousin's Molly's Tidewater drawl duplicated perfectly. The snow pelted the bedroom windows of Stratford House as the young Midge read aloud an account of a fancy dress ball in London, which, *Godey's* noted, Prince Albert had attended. A draft brushed the crystal pendants dangling from the lamps, and light sparkles danced across the veneered mahogany wardrobe and the settees commodious enough to seat three males shoulder to shoulder or one lady in hoops. Several treasured articles—Miss Abigail's dressing case, a hat box—rested on the stairs to the nursery on the second floor. These stairs were three-quarter-size, the latticework balustrades too close for a child to slip through. No child had used them since Duncan.

Abigail's husband, Samuel, slept in his spartan office. Every morning, Abigail Gatewood dressed carefully before passing through the parlor and across the hall to the dining room, where Pompey had her breakfast.

"Master Gatewood already out?" she'd ask, surprised. Though he invariably was, Miss Abigail was always surprised.

The afternoon of the snow, Samuel Gatewood was at his mill.

"Comin' down hard, Master Samuel," Jack the Driver said.

"The last time a January storm came from the east was in '35—the year before my father died. I don't care for it. Send boys up the mountain after the hogs. Toll them in with corn. We'll want the big barn prepared to receive the milk cows and horses. See to the partitions. We'll feed more than customary ration tonight. Send Franky through the Quarters. She must ensure all have sufficient meat, cornmeal, and beans. Many woodboxes are nearly empty. Set some hands to the slabwood pile—it may not burn long, but it burns hot. After the firewood is cut, close the millrace—I misdoubt we'll be milling tomorrow. If this storm is less severe than it appears to be, our precautions will appear foolish, but . . ."

"Master Samuel, look yonder. Cows all lying down. Critters know better'n we do what's coming."

The Botkin plantation was ready before its downriver neighbor, but doubtless that was because there was less to ready. By four o'clock, when falling snow was precipitating the night, Opal, Jesse, Sallie, and Uther were seated at the pine table with their hot cocoa and a stew warmed by the fire. There was a chicken in it, and potatoes and carrots, and it smelled rather wonderful, but that may have been due to their exertions and the snugness induced by wild weather outside their plank door.

At Stratford, in the last minutes before darkness was complete, Jack said, "Master Samuel, if you don't leave for the big house this minute, I believe you'll spend the night with me."

The lantern in Stratford House's parlor window blinked through the blizzard. Samuel Gatewood trudged home through foot-deep snow, aware, suddenly, how weary he was.

Although Rufus had offered a bed in the woods cabin and begged him to stay, young Duncan hadn't. Emergencies pleasure young men, and at four o'clock, just as the Botkins were settling in, Duncan turned Gypsy's head back down the mountain. In the hollows and the west-facing ridges the horse could still find good footing and Duncan's eyes were young and sharp, and it wasn't until they reached the wheat bottom that Duncan lost track of everything. His hair was frozen, his eyelashes stuck to his face, the thick reins stiffened in his hands. Gypsy shifted her feet. Duncan's heart jumped and he could not seem to catch his breath. He waited until panic subsided before saying, in almost his normal voice, "Well, girl, I hope you know the way because I surely do not." He loosed the reins, gave Gypsy her head, and clucked. The horse stayed still for a moment before turning her head sharply left and proceeding. When she stopped of her own accord, Duncan dismounted to open the gate; a gate Duncan prayed opened into the lower barn pasture. When Gypsy stopped again, Duncan could see no better, but he heard animals inside the barn chewing and belching. A horse nickered, and Gypsy nickered back.

When Duncan slid the door open, a single lantern glowed outside the tack room. Insulated by the hay floor overhead and heated by a dozen horses and as many milk cows, the barn was yeasty, a little moist, and warm enough that he couldn't see his breath. Duncan led Gypsy down the aisle to an empty stall and found rags to rub her down. When Duncan had Gypsy dry, fed, and watered, he leaned against the stall door, his knees shaking.

"Bet you wish you hadn't been so bold," a girl's voice said.

"Who the devil . . . ?"

The colored girl was in the manger above the stalls, among tomorrow's hay, her feet dangling. "I ain't no devil," she said.

"It was you lit the lantern!"

She turned and hang-dropped into the aisle. Rubbed her hands clean. "Weren't no cow lit it. Dark in this old barn. Rats and bats and goodness knows what-all else."

"Midge, why aren't you in the house?"

She put her hands on her hips, a skinny child with lank black hair, all long bones and elbows and taut skin. "Because your mama was afeared for you and ask me go to the barn and see is you back but you ain't so here I waits and when I sets to leave I can't see three feet through that snow, nary three feet. I don't want be in no smelly barn I want to be in the kitchen house in my warm bed."

"That's where you sleep?"

"My bed next the chimney. Sometimes cook says she might take my bed. Reckon she'll have it tonight. You get any supper?"

Duncan wiped moisture off his face. "No."

"Me neither. They be eatin' in the kitchen house, Jack and cook and that old conjure man, Uncle Agamemnon, all of them. Cut up possum this mornin'. Be potatoes and carrots and cook's got a big onion . . ."

"Will you hush? Why talk about what we aren't about to have."

"Not much else a colored girl can talk about. Want to talk about the River Jordan or gettin' to the Promised Land? I was readin' Mistress Abigail about some fancy ball in London, maybe you like me talk 'bout that?"

"I didn't know you could read."

"Lot you don't know, young Master Duncan."

He was clumsy and tongue-tied and didn't want to look into her flashing eyes, so he turned to give Gypsy a pat. "She found the way home. Even when I couldn't see a darn—damn—thing, Gypsy found the way. Aren't horses amazing?"

The girl nodded solemnly, "Oh yes, Master Duncan, you right there: horses mighty amazin'." In a voice that sounded remarkably like his mother's, Midge said, "I cannot begin to name the amazements provided by our magnificent horses."

A shiver went down Duncan's spine. "Where'd you learn to do that?"

She shrugged. "That Franky say I'ze witchy," and she rolled her eyes.

Duncan went to the barn door and pressed his ear against the wood. "Still howling," he pronounced. "No telling how long this will continue."

"We be hungry. Maybe you kill a cow?" She had her head cocked slightly and her eyes wouldn't stop flashing.

"We won't get that hungry," the boy said scornfully.

"You sayin' that 'cause you can't do it," she said. "Here we be in this ratty barn with no food and snow blowin' all around and lots to eat—" this time in Cousin Molly's cool Tidewater drawl—"were there merely a gentleman to provide it."

"I don't like you doin' that," he said.

"I don't care what you like."

The moment came for Duncan to rebuke his servant, but Gypsy arched her tail and passed manure and it fell plop plop to the floor and the two giggled. "Whew," Midge said, "What you feedin' that horse!"

"Rose petals," Duncan said, and they giggled again.

When they ran out of giggles, tension returned, but it was a different tension: friendlier.

"You got no more clothes than that?" Duncan asked.

Outside her short-sleeved cotton shift the girl's arms were goose-pimpled.

For reply, the girl sneezed. "Duncan . . .—I" She sneezed again.

He fumbled along the stall partition for a dry horse rag, into which she snuffled. She threw it down. "Now I don't smell no better than that horse," she wailed, and Duncan was rendered helpless by her tears. "Account of you, I'm cold and I'm hungry and now my face stink like horse sweat. You got any more notions, young Master?"

Duncan took a sudden dislike to a title he'd heard all his life. "Don't call me that," he said.

She judged him with her eyes, valuing him as if he were on the auction block. At last she said, "You got any more of them rose petals?"

Their smiles were remarkably like.

In the tack room they found a chunk of cheese meant for the rat traps, but Midge wrinkled her nose. When she wrinkled her nose, her entire face became her wrinkled nose: nothing halfhearted.

Duncan forked straw into an empty stall and laid a horse blanket atop. A torn gray-green buggy robe served for a coverlet. "You'll be warm here," he said.

She took off her shoes and wiggled her toes. She said, "It's a mighty big stall. Might be room for two."

That night Duncan slept curled against a girl so light he dreamed she was slipping through his fingers.

In the morning, a curious gray light filtered through the barn walls, but out of doors was a howling white wilderness. They spoke a few words, but not many, because words would have led them where neither was ready to go. They fed and watered the animals and twice milked all the cows, and excepting what warm milk they drank, emptied their buckets out in the snow.

By next morning, Cox's snow had deposited seventy inches of snow on Stratford Planation, seven and eight feet where it drifted. Jack and a gang dug a path from the Quarters to the main house before digging to the barn, where they hoped to find Miss Abigail's young servant.

The big double doors were drifted shut, so men boosted Jack in through the loft door. On hands and knees Jack said, "That you there, Master Duncan? Praise the Lord! We powerful feared for you!"

When little Midge stepped out from behind Duncan, Jack fell dumb.

2

JOHN BROWN'S BODY

Charles Town, Virginia
December 2, 1859

AS IT HAPPENED, nearly two years later Cadet Duncan Gatewood guarded John Brown's gallows the night before Brown's execution. Hoarfrost diamonded the dead grass, frost whitewashed the planks of the gallows floor, and Duncan wondered what they'd do with the lumber after this machine had satisfied its purpose and been disassembled. Although the planks were clear yellow pine, the milling was imprecise. Duncan was Jack the Driver's principal assistant at Stratford's sawmill, and in the young man's critical judgment, these boards were barely suitable for rough siding.

Picket fires blinked on the Blue Ridge, and from time to time Duncan heard faint challenges from the ford where Captain Ashby's cavalry was stationed. The dome of the Charles Town courthouse glowed in the moonlight. That's where they'd condemned him. The jail across the street—that's where they'd imprisoned him. That light in the second story window—it was his light.

Mr. Poe was Duncan Gatewood's favorite poet, and he loved Walter Scott's romances, and he believed that this ordinary grassy meadow at the edge of this village was kin to other blood-haunted places where men had done bold deeds. He hoped Charles Town might enter the noble list that included Hastings, Agincourt, Vera Cruz, and Crécy. Duncan was not deluded by his own part in this, a part he correctly deemed slight: second watch at a gallows guarded by two thousand Virginia troops who'd swiftly waylay any abolitionists intent on mischief. If Duncan's post had been important, an older cadet, an upperclassman, would have filled it.

In the grandeur of the moment, he made a pledge to his lover. "I pledge you," he prayed. "My sacred honor." Sixteen-year-old Duncan Gatewood couldn't pledge anything less precious. He owned only his horse and clothing. Prospects of one day becoming master at Stratford had dimmed when a furious Samuel Gatewood learned of their affair. Duncan ached to give Midge something, and honor was all he had to give.

Back at the Institute he often put himself to sleep remembering their lovemaking. The gentle underslope of her small breasts, the way she stood splayfooted when she was naked. Her elbows, she had solemnly assured him, were too big. And so he kissed each elbow and one thing led to another.

"You fancy." Midge had laid her smooth wrist against his cheek. "You my fancy man."

A gaunt figure startled Duncan from reverie. "Halt! Stand still a minute till I get a look at you!"

It—he—was a cadet. Well . . . almost. A charade of a cadet; his gray overcoat broomed the dirt, his dashing, braided kepi perched on streaky-gray hair. As if a cadet had moldered overnight, a Rip Van Winkle cadet who'd awakened after twenty years.

Duncan drew back his musket's hammer. "If you don't quit coming, I'll put a ball through your gut."

"Sic Semper Tyrannis, son. That's the countersign, and had you proffered the proper challenge, I'd have returned it to you. Please set aside that blunderbuss before you do something that'll leave Mrs. Ruffin grieving."

The oldster's sliding steps kept his greatcoat off his heels.

"You're no Institute cadet. What're you doing wearin' our uniform?"

"Craved to be a soldier since I was a lad digging mud forts in the flats of the James. Son, I told you about that musket! Colonel Preston himself located this proud uniform. A cadet captain had forethought to bring a spare. Pay no heed to his badges of rank. I am an honorary cadet private, nothing grander."

"Yes, sir. But since you haven't any business here, I'll ask you to repair to the bivouac."

Ruffin flapped both arms like a disturbed hawk pumping for altitude. "Son, I am come here to see and see I shall."

If Duncan raised the alarm, there'd be soldiers here on the instant, displeased to be so summoned. "Your word of honor then," Duncan said. "Your word of honor you are not an abolitionist."

The old man had muttonchop whiskers, flat cheeks, a tiny sharp nose, but when he grinned he opened a frog's mouth from jawhinge to jawhinge. His teeth perched on the red ridges of his gums like coracles on a wave. "I've been accused of many sins, but of that particular wickedness I am innocent as this moonlight here. I am Edmund Ruffin."

"I know no Ruffins. No Ruffins in my home county."

"Your father—is he a planter?"

"We thresh some wheat. Cattle. Been a good year for cattle. I been sent away from home since spring. To the Virginia Military Institute."

"Does he subscribe to the *Farmer's Register?*"

From the way the man spoke, Duncan surmised that Edmund Ruffin and the *Farmer's Register* were one and the same.

"No, sir," he said.

"Does your father manure?" Ruffin flipped his coat and set his hands on his hips. Cadet Spaulding's trousers yawned at his waist. "Calcareous manures, sir: marl, plaster, carbonate of lime. Does your father marl his fields?" The old man shook his head. "Sometimes I despair for agriculture in the Commonwealth."

The moon slid behind a cloud and blackness chased across the commons, and Ruffin clutched his coat about him. Nodding at the solitary light in the jail's second-story window, he said, "He'll be busy this night, I'd venture."

"I hear he does right smart of praying."

The old man's grin yawned like a trap. "There's not hours enough left to him to undo the damnation he has merited."

"Sergeant Colley—Colley's with the regulars—says he's all the time writing letters."

The moonlight washed so strongly it dimmed the picket fires on the Blue Ridge. "I suppose," Ruffin said, "we are fortunate to have had him."

"Sir?"

"Clarity, son. Brown has provided clarity. Have you inspected the pikes he intended to distribute to our servants that they might employ them upon our sleeping wives and children? Pikes eight feet in length with a double-edged spearhead honed and stropped keen as your razor."

Duncan, who was not a regular shaver, nodded.

"Only a fool can mistake that murderous yankee steel. Recently I had despaired of secession's prospects, but Mr. John Brown has made me glad. Now, sir . . ." And with that, as if he'd given himself leave, the old man darted up the thirteen steps onto the gallows platform overhead.

Thumb hooked around the hammer of his musket, Duncan followed. On each stair the old man's footsteps had scuffed frost.

Edmund Ruffin stood at the rectangular trap, boot toes at the crack. He said, "Don't fret, son. For the certainty of heaven I wouldn't disturb these arrangements." When he turned, his eyes were wide as a child's. "You ever consider how it feels?" Unerringly his left hand located the overhead beam, the hook over which they'd pass the rope; he gave the hook a jolly tug. "Imagine such a thing. Everything you've done in your life, all the wonders you've seen, why, the very way you clasp your pen or button your britches, all come together here." He stamped. "And after they mumble a few hypocritical prayers, ohhhh . . ." His free hand gripped his throat and his tongue spurted out, dark as blood, and his head canted to the side.

Duncan backed from Ruffin's mime, and the old man returned to life. "You ever wonder what remains of us, son?" He jutted his jaw toward the jail. "I imagine yonder fellow has some acute thoughts on the subject."

"Don't!"

But it was done. The old man had hopped on the trap. He flexed his legs, trying the hinges and bolts that held it fast. "Ahh," he said.

The commons below were washed by the moon and the picket fires high on the Blue Ridge were diamonds forming the limits of the known world. " 'I do not wish your comfort,' " he said in a voice not his own. " 'I die in my faith.' A queen said that, son. How about 'It is a far, far better thing I do now than I have ever done'?" Ruffin spat. "Mr. Dickens vilified us after his American tour. We in the South were not nice enough for him. Uncommonly fastidious, Mr. Dickens, for a scribbler. Should he return to Richmond, I believe he would find the climate disagreeable. Step up here, boy. Go ahead. Standing on a gallows trap will flush the cobwebs from your brain."

Duncan stepped beside the older man.

"There now, doesn't that make you want to produce an oration?"

Dry-mouthed, Duncan shook his head.

"Look out there: two thousand men gathered in your honor. Not many deathbeds, I think, boast such a show of martial ardor. The Brigade of Cadets, the Virginia Grays, United States troops under Colonel Lee. Oh, we think high of you, boy. What have you to say for yourself?"

Duncan's head shook no, no, in dumbshow.

"I ask you, sir: why did you wish to arm our servants against us? Why did you conspire to murder our families in their beds? Why did you invade a sovereign state to such bloody and terrible purposes?"

Duncan blurted, "I'm not him."

With a sweep of his hand, Ruffin dismissed the waiting troops, the dignitaries. "You've no imagination. And we ask why the South has no profession of letters. Do you think he'll falter, son? Refuse the noose?"

Duncan eased off the trap as if it were hair-triggered. "Just who the dickens are you?"

"Edmund Ruffin, agriculturalist, editor. Present occupation: firebrand."

Duncan said who he was: "From Stratford Plantation, south of here. We come here by train, the Brigade of Cadets, first time I was ever on one of the stinkers and it like to made me sick, the cinders and smoke and swayin' from side to side . . ."

The ancient cadet wasn't listening. "I believe our John has come too far to show the white feather. If his life has been precious to him, none of his previous adventures have proved it so. Mr. John Brown will wear his noose like a riband of honor. Sometimes courage is easy. Have you ever seen the moon so near to the earth? What do you fear, Duncan Gatewood?"

It was getting on toward three and Duncan had been on duty since midnight. He would have scant sleep before morning muster, and the hanging was scheduled for nine. "The loss of honor," Duncan said, and it was true what he said despite its nearness to his tongue. If the old man had pressed him, Cadet Gatewood might have admitted that he preferred honor to love, to country, to, even, the safety of his own soul. Such preferences were not too rare in the Cadet Brigade. Many a young man will go to the devil gladly if honor's intact.

"This will be a tale to tell your grandchildren . . ." Ruffin began.

Annoyed by Ruffin's probe, which had taken unfair advantage—Duncan thought—of the natural respect accruing to his gray locks, Duncan asked, "And you, sir; what do you fear?"

Ruffin was silent.

"It's only fair, sir, that you answer as I answered."

Ruffin's sharp eyes weighed the young man. "One day, Cadet, you will say you were here where it began, you were present at the birthplace of a new republic."

"Your fear, sir."

"When Andrew Jackson fought Lawyer Dickerson, allowed his foe the first shot, suffered his wound and then coolly shot and killed his man, honor was satisifed. Honor can be satisfied by a pistol ball, a rapier thrust. The loss of honor, sir—and I intend no disrespect—is a young man's fear. We old men fear falling upon the mercy of others."

The moon slipped behind a cloud and darkness chased the sparkle from the dead grass. In the jail behind the gallows, the condemned man's lantern gleamed, unwavering as a star.

3

JUMPING THE BROOMSTICK

Until death or distance us do part.

—*Slave marriage vow*

"IT WON'T BRING five bushels." Samuel Gatewood crushed the wheathead in his hand. "Last week's storms lodged and ruined it. This Mediterranean wheat may defy Hessian fly but I believe it produces a weaker stand."

Uther Botkin (who knew nothing about wheat) crushed a wheathead and was rewarded by chaff fluttering onto his pantlegs. Old Uther's black suit served him equally for occasions of celebration and mourning. An oversized, old-fashioned silk foulard drooped across his shirtfront. "Surely," he said, "if one man can pluck the wheat upright again, another can scythe it."

"A slow process, my friend. And the rain will have stripped the stalks. Flour is bringing record prices in Richmond. Those unpropitious thunderstorms may well have cost me a hundred dollars."

"So much? Goodness. I had no idea."

Stratford's prime bottomland stretched out at their feet. Jack the Driver's gang was hoeing corn. Two women switched milk cows into the woods to graze. Behind the big barn, a servant was emptying the slops barrel into the hog pen.

"I never tire of looking at it," Samuel said. "Excepting my years at

Washington College, I've never been away for more than the two weeks I visited my wife's family home in Chesterfield County." He smiled. "They were two painfully long weeks. My Abigail's kinfolk were unimpressed by a crude backcountry planter. Excepting dear Cousin Molly, my wife's family have never visited Stratford."

"If Mahomet cannot go to the mountain, the mountain must come to Mahomet," Uther said happily.

"You have received a letter from your daughter, Sallie," Samuel Gatewood speculated.

"I have indeed." The old man's pleasure was extreme and even a little comical. "I have boasted, neighbor, of my Sallie's good fortune securing admission to Augusta Female Seminary. I should say, sir, I believe your kind intercession with Dr. Timberlake weighed strongly in Sallie's favor. Of a hundred thirty girls, my Sallie is one of three scholarship students. I had worried she would be restricted to the 'womanly' arts: decorum, music, a little French. But the Seminary, Sallie writes, boasts a Latinist who has taken an interest in her. My Sallie quotes Cicero! Two quotations in a single letter! Oh, I am beside myself!" Uther loosed his reins, fluttered his hands. Luckily the antique beast he was astride was indifferent to his rider's behavior. "But I forget my manners. What news have you of Duncan? I do not know that your son is the cleverest boy I ever taught, but he is blessed with frankness and generosity and uncommon grace. Nature has been kind to him."

"Duncan does not understand where his interests lie," Samuel said roughly. His big roan shifted his feet and Samuel jerked the bit, and it was a moment before the horse settled again. Samuel said, "You will have heard of Duncan's grandfather, Thomas Gatewood."

The most venerable local scandals reliably produced headshaking at every hearth in the county. Uther's silence was as close to a polite lie as the old schoolmaster could manage.

"Like my son, sir, my father loved ladies. I turned a blind eye to his transgressions until, on an occasion when my mother was away visiting her people, my father installed his slut from the Quarters in my mother's bedchamber. When I remonstrated, he spoke to me as no gentlemen speaks to another."

"Samuel, perhaps . . ."

Samuel Gatewood's eyes wandered over his plantation. "I departed for Washington College and did not return here until my father's funeral. Once he was buried, that very afternoon, I purged the Quarters of my father's mistresses. You are a learned man, my friend. Do you think these vices follow the blood, recurring again and again, skipping one hopeful generation only to manifest themselves in the next? Duncan . . . is my Duncan beyond hope?"

"Samuel, I . . ." Uther took breath to give the matter thought. "Sir, I cannot believe in such inheritances, dreadful or benign. Like Mr. Jefferson, I believe reason the grandest of our faculties. Reason is available to every intellect."

Samuel Gatewood shifted in his saddle and wouldn't meet his neighbor's eye. He twined his reins. "Our neighbors expected me to challenge the cuckold who shot my father. But why should I duel someone for resenting acts I despised myself?"

With nothing to say, old Uther was wise enough to say nothing.

Jack the Driver had concluded the hoeing and dismissed the hands, who hurried toward the Quarters to prepare for the celebration. Samuel said, "How they enjoy an occasion. How they love to dress in their Sunday best. They are children, my friend."

Old Uther shook his head. "Jesse is no child. Had he been born white, any man would be glad to claim his acquaintance. We are mistaken about our coloreds, Samuel: if the abolitionists exaggerate their accomplishments, we diminish them. Had it not been Jesse's express wish, oft repeated, I should never have sold him to Stratford. But poor Jesse is as smitten with Midge as I was with my own dear wife."

"Neighbor, I wish you had accepted a fair price for the boy. Ten dollars!"

"A sop to my conscience, sir. And I am in your debt for many kindnesses. Samuel, you promise Midge has consented?"

"She is young. She will learn to care for Jesse in time, and, in any event, they are of my family now, Uther, and you must trust me to do what is best for them."

"I suppose . . ." Uther began cheerfully, but subsided to a quieter note. "We all do what we can."

"My wife is partial to Midge and plans a nuptial feast in our dining room. It is Abigail's fancy, and I can't see how it can do harm. The couple, Jack the Driver, Abigail, myself, and you, when you join us, my friend, we will create a happy occasion."

The rap at the door was Sister Kate's diffident appeal. When Abigail removed the cloth from her eyes and sat upright, a bolt of pain shot to her forehead. "Yes?"

Sister(-in-law) Kate peeped around the door, her watery eyes bulging like the eyes of an aging feist dog.

Kate Gatewood had been fifteen when her father was killed, just a child really. Her mother's acolyte from that day forward, she had never known a man.

"I come seeking counsel, sister," Kate Gatewood said in her thin, cheerful voice. In the winter months Sister Kate spent her days indoors with Grandmother Gatewood. In warmer weather she tended the garden and seemed healthier. She inspected Abigail anxiously. "Sister, are you well?" Worry lines pinched Sister Kate's forehead. "Poor dear. You shoulder so many burdens."

"No more than I ought," Abigail replied dryly. "I was lying down. These headaches rack me terribly." Abigail poured fresh water into the broad porcelain bowl and dabbed at her cheeks. What would she do without Midge? Midge had begged to retain her position, but her baby was already showing and mistress and servant alike must acknowledge that Midge was a grown woman whose proper place was in the Quarters with others of her race.

Though Samuel had never berated her, all this unpleasantness was Abigail's fault. Why had she indulged the child? Why had she made a colored servant her confidante?

Two decades ago when she met Samuel, Abigail had been summering in Lexington, Virginia, with distant kin. Since a throng of wellborn, unattached young men attended college in that town, handsome girls like Abigail were courted to distraction. "Do come to the ball, dear Abigail," and "Do ride out with me along the canal."

Abigail had judged herself fickle and too proud until she met Samuel Gatewood. She never afterward looked at another man, and the day Samuel came into his competency, he proposed.

She had loved Samuel—loved him still—though they had not shared a bed since the twins . . . she dared not think of the twins. The palms of Abigail's hands tingled remembering how the skin had slipped off her dear baby's face. She dared not remember the twins. She would make a pleasant ceremony for Midge and Jesse, and in time, all things would be forgotten.

"I fear Grandmother Gatewood is dissatisfied with our plans for Midge's levee, sister. She opposes our nicer touches."

Abigail thought to say, "It is a near certainty Grandmother will be dissatisfied." But as ten thousand times before, Abigail held her tongue. "Oh," she said. "That is too bad."

Kate looked doubtful.

"I mean to do what I can to make this day as agreeable as circumstances allow. Midge is a confused child. One minute she intends to marry within her race, the next she expresses the most unsuitable ambitions. Jesse dotes on her. The other evening, after day's work was done, I surprised him waiting at the kitchen-house door with a bouquet of wildflowers. Jesse has a way about him, a strength, that will tame Midge's excesses."

"Would you please come to the dining room, sister?" Kate asked. "Grandmother Gatewood is in one of her humors."

. . .

Midge and Jesse would be married on Stratford's front porch, Samuel Gatewood officiating. Samuel asked Jesse if he wouldn't rather be married by Preacher Todd, but Jesse said no, they'd just jump the broomstick in front of the master like the other coloreds did. He said Midge would come to love him and he'd care for her and her baby. He said he'd care for her baby as his own.

Grandmother Gatewood was laying out the cheap tinware they brought to the fields for the harvest gangs.

Abigail did not quite sigh. "Good morning, Grandmother. I trust this weather is agreeing with you."

The older woman looked her reply. Scarlet fever had taken her three youngest children and a babe in arms. John Dinwiddie's .58-caliber ball had taken her unfaithful husband. After her husband's death, she never left Stratford except for worship at SunRise Chapel. After services, while other parishioners exchanged the week's gossip, Grandmother Gatewood and Sister Kate waited in the carriage, side curtains drawn. Grandmother Gatewood had worn pride like a mask for so many years the mask had become her face.

"Samuel intends Midge's wedding feast to be uncommonly nice," Abigail said. "Jesse is a valuable hand, and Midge is dear to me."

Mother Gatewood's knowing glance meant, "Not so dear to Jesse as to your son, Duncan," and Abigail flushed to the roots of her hair.

"It was Samuel's express wish this wedding be dignified," Abigail said.

Grandmother Gatewood went to the sideboard for a basket of tin forks and spoons. She upended the basket in the center of the table, meaning, "This is the dignity they deserve."

"Grandmother, although our best china and silver were your dowry, surely we must respect Samuel's wishes."

Grandmother Gatewood's satisfied smirk meant, "He may be master of Stratford Plantation but he is still my son."

"Perhaps we could use the better candlesticks," Sister Kate whispered. "They are too large to steal."

Grandmother Gatewood's sly grin meant, "Niggers can steal anything!"

"Grandmother, I shall have to speak with Samuel!" Abigail said.

When she closed Samuel's study door behind her, her hands were shaking. Why was malice so powerful? Samuel was an honorable man trying to guide his family. Why was he thwarted?

Her husband's room was spartan: desk, pine wardrobe, camp bed—perhaps the same sort of bed Duncan had at the Military Institute. Although every servant coming into the house passed through this room, Samuel made his own bed, swept his own bare floors, and carried his own firewood.

His modest library lined one wall, and agricultural periodicals lay on the commode beside the bed. Abigail adjusted them, tenderly. She would go to the Quarters to fetch Midge. What more can we do than our duty?

When Samuel Gatewood came into the kitchen house, Rufus was perched on the cook's table. Rufus chewed fast and swallowed hard. "Cook give me this stale cornbread before it go to the hogs. I come in here for the broomstick, Master. Me and Jack gonna hold the broomstick for Jesse and Midge jump over. They got to hop right smart if their marriage be lucky. Yes, sir, me and Jack, we make 'em hop."

When Rufus was in the woods with his gang of timber cutters, he was a first-rate hand. Up close, he was an irritant. Samuel said, "In the meantime, perhaps you'll take this tea to Master Uther in the parlor."

In his study Samuel washed his face and hands and combed his hair. He tied a pale blue neck scarf. "Come in," he said, and Jack the Driver entered the room where, every morning, he received the day's instructions.

Jack's forehead shone with perspiration. "Master, I been asked to talk to you."

"Take a chair, Jack. We needn't stand on ceremony today."

Jack perched on the rim of his seat and he set his hat on the floor beside him. He said, "Master Samuel, Midge won't have it."

"Jesse is willing?"

"Jesse 'bout as willing as he can get. He crazy 'bout that gal since first time he see'd her when we all plantin' oats this spring. I could see that day how it was with Jesse. Midge say she don't want Jesse."

"Jesse is a man of constant affections. He will treat her kindly."

"She say . . . she say he too black!" Jack's work-thickened hands kneaded his thighs.

Samuel Gatewood's friend Uther dismissed every distinction between the races. But every so often one of Samuel's servants demonstrated to Samuel Gatewood's entire satisfaction that the white and black races had been engendered on different planets. "Jack . . ."

"Oh, I know, Master, I know. I know you tryin' to help her. I know you get Master Botkin to sell Jesse to Stratford so Midge could take herself a husband and not get into no more trouble. Midge know all that too, but she . . . she . . ."

"Go on." Samuel readjusted his neck scarf.

"She say she won't lie with him. She say Jesse too black."

Samuel opened a drawer for his razors and laid them neatly on his washstand. He hummed a few bars of "Camptown Races." "I am certain Midge will do a wife's duty," Samuel said. "Sometimes I am at a loss to know how to treat you people. You are my family and precious to me, but sometimes . . ." He shook his head. "When I first discovered my son's unfortunate dalliance with this servant girl, I was angry. I sent Duncan to the Military Institute hoping they would instill the self-discipline he lacks. After six months and creditable soldiering at John Brown's execution, I believed I could trust Duncan home with us for our Christmas celebrations. I so looked forward . . ." Samuel paused for a moment and spoke more harshly. "The consequences of my son's Christmas festivities are apparent in Midge's swelling belly. So. Again I exiled my only son, because of a colored servant girl whose sole distinction is the inappropriate mimicry of her betters. It is not amusing when a colored house servant's mocking speech is indistinguishable from speech employed by the first families of Virginia. If that is a joke at all, it is a joke in the poorest taste."

Jack hung his head.

"Jack, most Virginians would have resolved this difficulty by selling the girl south—a solution, I believe, that would be more approved than the one I have elected. Instead, at some inconvenience, I have provided Midge a fine husband of her own race, a good man who adores her. Jesse will take her as she is, sullied, bearing another's child. Jack, if Midge will not lie with Jesse, she will sleep tomorrow night in the slave pen behind the Wayne Tavern in Staunton where at auction I will sell her to Silas Omohundru or any other speculator who can meet my price. On my honor, I swear it."

After Jack left, Samuel shaved. When he nicked his chin, he stanched the flow with a liberal application of alum. Now that Midge was to be a respectable married woman, she would need a new name. They would name her Maggie.

HALFWAY HOME

THE FINEST STRETCH of the journey home was a mile past West Augusta where the turnpike surmounted a rise below Cross's plantation and the blazing panoply of fall leaves came into full view. Mrs. Sallie (Botkin) Kirkpatrick clucked the horse on. Alexander would be so enchanted.

When Alexander laid his *Harper's Weekly* aside, Sallie longed to converse but held her tongue. Her husband's pleasure would be enhanced by woman's silence when the sublime prospect presented itself.

Though low on the horizon, the sun was still strong enough to transmogrify the maples and oaks, whose scarlets and golds pronounced the death of one season and the dormancy to come. Sallie, whose life had changed as dramatically as those trees, was in a philosophical humor meditating on the end of her prior life and the small new life within her.

Oh why won't the horse hurry!

At fifteen years of age, Sallie Botkin Kirkpatrick was delighted with her discovery that life could be beautiful and simple. Married women, when they said, "Child, you'll understand better when you've a husband of your own"—how wise they were—how much they understood!

The vista was Sallie's happy secret. In a few moments her Alexander would be delighted and (she dared to hope) awed by her beautiful mountains. She so wanted him to love her home. Grumpy dear Opal and her sweet father: how she wanted those she loved to love one another!

She wouldn't contemplate Uther's reaction to the news of her expulsion from the Female Seminary and that Sallie's new husband had been invited to seek other employment. From an early age, Sallie had been able to steer her thoughts toward agreeable prospects, and now she exercised this useful faculty. She was the daughter of one educated man and wife to another. How elevating it would be when the two men met.

Sallie, who ordinarily had a rather good opinion of herself, had of late been chastened. Mrs. Kirkpatrick wondered what value was one's own head when one could marry a man with a greater one and all the knowledge of Rome, Caesar, Cicero—even Catullus (Sallie blushed)—stuffed into it? It was one of Sally's charms, Alexander had told her: how readily she blushed.

Her Alexander had graduated—with the highest honors—from Yale College and afterward taken a position with a great banking firm in New York City. There Alexander met Dr. Timberlake when the Seminary's president traveled to that city to discuss school finances. How sorry Alexander's firm must have been to lose him (how fortunate for Mrs. Alexander Kirkpatrick!). Alexander was far too fine for commerce.

Until Alexander, Sallie had thought her womanhood an encumbrance: something that kept her from doing those interesting things boys did as right. As a child her nearest female model had been Auntie Opal, who'd rather foal a mare than keep house. Two summers ago, Sallie awoke with her thighs drenched in blood and ran to Aunt Opal. "It's nothing terrible, child. Pin a rag in your underthings. No different from cows coming into season."

The thought horrified her. "Am I going to be like that, 'bulling' after every man who comes near?"

"Honey, I pass blood like you're doin' and never let no bull near me. Some girls like that foolishness, some girls don't. Get back to the house and tear yourself some rags."

From Opal, Sallie had learned how to pull lambs and calves, how to treat foot evil in sheep and nosebot in cows. This evening, thus, it was Sallie's second nature to spare the old mare which had been all Alexander could afford.

At last they arrived at the vista Sallie had been anticipating, and it was grand indeed. Feminine ridges comforted her, brilliant colors enlightened her: truly, God had been gracious to this part of the world. The ugliness of the past week, the angry angry men—all behind them. Safe in the bosom of these mountains, she and Alexander would rear their baby and not care a jot for the world's opinion. Sallie's eyes welled with tears. "Look," was all she said.

"What?"

Alexander had been dreaming.

"The mountains," she breathed. "Their colors."

"I was remembering," he said, "that damned Olden. Such effrontery: I 'betrayed his trust'! I trifled with the affections of 'a scholarship student of superior faculties but inferior background.' You know perfectly well it was you who came to my rooms that night. To return my Catullus, you said.

"But . . . !" Alexander could be so unjust! The first time Sallie read Catullus, how her virginal ears had burned.

"You may be one who'll find this amusing," Alexander had said when he gave her the poems, though he must have known simply possessing that book would endanger his position at the school.

Amusing? Hardly. By candlelight, in her room, the beginning scholar had translated the ancient poet of Eros. She guessed at some of the Latin. Those words were not to be found in any dictionary belonging to the Augusta Female Seminary.

Catullus's poems made Sallie's life seem flat and uneventful. Six months before, the scholarship girl from the mountains had thought Augusta Female Seminary a cathedral of the intellect. Now it seemed shabby and provincial, a school to instill nice manners in stupid country girls.

Sallie Botkin had allowed Alexander Kirkpatrick to make love to her because she thought he was her new life.

The poor old horse trudged along. The sun dropped behind the mountains, outlining the ridgeline trees like bristles. "Do you have such colors in yankeeland?" she asked.

"I believe so. I am recalling a disagreeable exchange I had earlier with Trustee Olden—this was at one of Dr. Timberlake's insufferable garden parties. Olden was trying to impress me, quoting Cicero's *'Aegroto, dum anima est, spes est'* as 'While there is spirit, there is hope'—mistranslating *anima*, thus making a medical opinion a religious one. Of course, I corrected him. . . . "Olden asked me, 'Don't you think your previous employer . . . generous, sir, to set our poor needs before his own?' The overbearing fool! Sally, Trustee Olden took my modest correction as an excuse to berate me. Even then I had fallen from Olden's favor. Even then he looked upon me with a cold eye. . . ."

In the distance, Sallie saw the lights of Halfway House, whose owner claimed it was the finest inn this side of Parkersburg. Though the old mare was awfully tired, Sallie urged it to pick up the pace.

Alexander droned on, "When your . . . difficulty . . . became known, Trustee Olden thought marriage an unsatisfactory remedy. 'Marriage would reward this scoundrel.' He spoke thus in my presence! What reason had Olden for hating me so?"

"There's Enoch Cross, Alexander." Timidly, Sallie waved to the figure outside the inn. Suppose Staunton gossip had traveled faster than they had? "Mr. Cross's establishment is well regarded in the mountains."

On the flat across the road were cattle pens where drovers held their charges overnight, and even in this cool weather, the smell was pungent.

"Oh, hello, Sallie Botkin. Hello. We're a little rough tonight—all men, all drovers. But they're a good lot—don't go mistaking the heart for the manners."

"Not Sallie Botkin any longer, Mr. Cross. As of yesterday forenoon, I am Mrs. Alexander Kirkpatrick, and the handsome fellow here beside me is my husband. He is a professor of Latin. We go to bide with my father for a spell."

The bald plump innkeeper took her arm and afterward stuck out his hand to Alexander. "Glad to make your acquaintance, sir. I am Enoch Cross, and my family owns the valley you entered when you put Deerfield behind. So you have plucked the fairest of our mountain flowers. You are a happy man, sir." The innkeeper pumped Alexander's hand. "I don't believe there is a perter girl west of the Blue Ridge. I have known Miss Sallie since she was a babe in arms, making the Staunton journey with her father and his nigger, Jesse." To Sallie: "A child is born of Jesse's wife, Maggie, that girl they used to call Midge. The baby is said to be whiter than her mother, and she is whiter than some immigrants coming into Richmond." Cross rubbed his hands briskly. "But we'll gossip later. I'll have the boy unload your luggage and care for your horse. Do come in, do come in. Last night we had a prodigious frost—did you feel it in Staunton?"

"I didn't take particular note," Alexander said.

"My husband is a scholar, Mr. Cross. Only we plantation folk are creatures of the weather. Some of your corn is not yet cut?"

"Oh, we cut as we go. We cut as we go."

Halfway House was a large one-room log house improved by an addition in the rear and a second identical log house attached to the first. Oddly angled roofs ran hither and thither and gray cedar shakes made the roof appear mossy in the dusk.

The original cabin served as the inn's keeping room, and the wide-throated fireplace at the end of the room threw reddish light and welcoming heat over Sallie's pale, weary face.

While the travelers hung their wraps, the innkeeper related a tale about Aunt Opal. "In September it was, a drover came in this very room and warmed himself before this fire." He indicated the fire in question as proof of his words. "After a time, he is describing a homestead, in the mountains, not far from SunRise." Mr. Cross winked. "Hadn't thought to waste my time at such a place,' the drover says, 'but I heard they had likely steers and I was looking for such.' The drover continued never guessing I am familiar with that very homestead! 'Mr. Uther Botkin did have some steers to sell, red polls, and they were the finest damn animals I seen this journey.' Excuse my language, Miss Sallie, but those were his words. 'Best damn steers I seen in five trips through the county.

Would they make the drove to Baltimore? Oh, I'll say they would. And would they bring top dollar in that city? I'll say. But Mr. Uther Botkin who is selling them acts like he can't tell the tail of a steer from the snout and I ask him how much they weigh and he says he don't know so I ask how much does he want for them and he excuses himself to go inside his house, and when he comes out Botkin says, "They're eight hundred pounds and I'll have eight dollars seventy-five for each of them," and he won't come down on his price no matter how I dicker, not even when I pretend I'm so disgusted I'll seek elsewhere and mount my horse as if I would. How in tarnation that man knows to a nickel what them cattle is worth without telling one from another I can't tell you but I give him his price and they are down in your pens, right now, Mr. Cross, if you wishes to see 'em.' And I say I don't because I've seen Uther Botkin's cattle before and though they are not numerous, they're prime red polls, none better. I don't tell him it's Auntie Opal that's reared them and priced them because I figure the joke's on him. How is Auntie?"

"My father writes Opal is in good health." Sallie paused. "Our marriage is not yet known to him."

Mr. Cross eyed Alexander. "I see."

"But Father will be pleased, I just know it. Two educated men in one household. Mr. Cross, I anticipate so many learned conversations between them." She took the innkeeper's arm familiarly. "Dear Mr. Cross, I have not thanked you for your news about Jesse's wife's newborn. Jesse is almost a brother to me."

She turned to Alexander. "Dearest, Mr. Cross's cook came to him from Philadelphia and is famous the length of the turnpike."

Cross said, "Here, Miss Sallie, you're shivering. This won't do. We'll move these rough fellows back from the fire. You see they've made camp and blocked the heat from the rest of the room. Move aside there, boys. Can't you see a lady is with us this evening, her and her husband? Here, I'll pull this table to the fire and you shall sit, Miss Sallie, so the fire warms your back and you can look upon your husband instead of these rascally countenances. Now, Professor . . . Kirkpatrick, did you say it was?"

"Yes."

"I don't recall any Kirkpatricks in this county. There were Kilmartins down by Dayton. Two brothers. In the miller's trade."

Alexander brushed the wood table as if it were littered with invisible debris. "I suppose the beef will be juicy?"

"Yes, sir. Juicy as you like."

"Thank you. I prefer my meat juicy."

The drovers removed from the fireside were dressed in canvas pants, heavy shirts, and vests. Most wore short overcoats and none had removed his hat. Their talk was of cattle and markets and prices, and scraps of that conversation slipped though the crackle of the fire: "Knacker up by Broadway will take any beast can't make the drive . . ."

"Fifteen heifers and that damned Brown swore wasn't none of 'em in calf . . ."

"Philadelphia's good but Baltimore's better. They ship salt beef from Baltimore. Brothers, some of our good mountain beef travels all the way to the South Americans. I 'spect they don't have beef cows of their own."

Sallie so enjoyed watching her husband eat; each neat cut of his knife, every fork motion brought her pleasure. Although she would have averted her eyes had he raised his, Alexander concentrated on his meal. It was one of the things she so admired about him: how he could lose himself. She admitted no doubts. Alexander would find a new position, and until that happy day, they would live on love. In her father's house, they would travel the byways of history, politics, and poesy. Sallie smiled. Alexander would introduce ancient Rome to Mr. Jefferson's most ardent disciple. What a convention of ideas!

Seeing Mr. Cross's inn through Alexander's eyes reduced it somewhat in Sallie's estimation. The drovers hadn't washed too recently and they would spit their tobacco juice into the fire, punctuating conversation with explosive hisses. Dusty cobwebs swathed the rafters, and Sallie sensed a host of small red eyes in the dark gaps between the chinking. Mr. Cross's Philadelphia cook had overdone the beef.

Alexander pushed his plate away and in the same motion rose to his feet. "Come, my dear, didn't you say we had to be away at dawn?"

Their chamber was tucked away under the eaves where three of Halfway House's eccentric roofs met. The room had a sloped ceiling here, a tucked-in corner there, and a window that was no more rectangular than it needed to be. Three beeswax candles cast a soft glow. The new Mrs. Kirkpatrick had never seen anything so delightful.

Apple wood crackled on their fire and apples perfumed the air. The quilt on the high bed was cross-and-crown pattern and the bedposts were topped with pineapples carved from black walnut. It was cozy, the kind of room a child dreams about.

"Oh, Alexander," Sallie said, "I am so happy. I know you are not pleased matters . . . turned out a they did. You are a splendid teacher and I am certain Dr. Timberlake and Trustee Olden will altogether regret their decision to dismiss you. Where will they find another man of your accomplishments?"

"As Cato said, my dear, 'Wise men profit more by fools than fools by wise men, because the wise man avoids the faults of fools while the fool cannot emulate the wise man's good example.' " Alexander beamed. "I am glad you are happy." He sat on the corner of the bed and proffered his boot, and she clamped it between her knees and tugged. His stocking had a hole through which his toe protruded. How glad Sallie would be to mend it! She had never admired the matrimonial state and as recently as this spring had disparaged other girls' efforts to attain connubial bliss. Hoops and crinolines had seemed more encumbrances for active limbs than honey traps for a gentleman's glance. The conversation encouraged at the Female Seminary (where a girl's every other sentence must lift the heavy burden of embellishing some man's quite ordinary accomplishments) bored Sallie to distraction. She'd rather describe the wildcat Aunt Opal had trapped or dispute Mr. Gibbon's opinions about the Emperor Hadrian. And here was Sallie positively yearning to mend a man's sock! She giggled as she tugged at Alexander's boot.

His raised his eyebrows.

"Oh, nothing. I was just thinking how meeting you, dear Alexander, has altered my little world."

He blinked rapidly. "You are a curious child. I breach your virginity and compel you to a hasty marriage. Together we are exiled into a country where wolves may howl. And for this, you thank me." Alexander's eyes were softer than she'd ever seen them. Sallie knew he could say nothing that wasn't true, honorable, and fine. His eyes changed; grew vague. "Dear Sallie, our child may be the sort of man other men look up to, perhaps a senator."

"I am only sure that he will be beautiful as you, my dearest."

And in this apple-scented admixture of ignorance and hope, the pair spent their nuptial night.

5

CHRISTMAS GIFT?

Stratford Plantation
December 25, 1860

IT WAS WHITE, so glaringly white Sallie Botkin Kirkpatrick shaded her eyes to make out the welcoming silhouette of Stratford House while they swept up its drive as grandly as their old horse and positively older wagon could manage. Between the wheel ruts, the snow was tender, virginal. The weight of her baby was great in Sallie's belly. She had hoped, by now, to feel its kick. She would be happy. She would.

Jesse had come to drive them, and it was almost like old times. En route to Stratford, beside Jesse on the wagon seat, Uther chattered happily, explicating Mr. Madison's and Mr. Hamilton's disagreements and urging Jesse to read *The Federalist Papers*. "A young man cannot obtain too much education," Uther opined.

"I don't know, Mr. Uther," Jesse drawled. "It hasn't done me much good so far. Look, there's Mistress Abigail at the door."

"Education is undervalued in Virginia," Alexander pronounced. "Scholars of antiquity are deemed no better than clodhoppers who sign their names with an X."

Uther nodded vigorously. "There are times when I, whose education is so inferior to yours, think Virginia a too-perfect democracy."

Jesse drew up precisely at the dismounting step and hurried around to assist his onetime master. He cradled Uther's foot in his hands until it was safe atop the granite block.

"Shun strong drink this day, Jesse." Uther waggled his finger. "We expect you to return us home and we may be in our cups."

Jesse, who had taken the temperance pledge as a boy, grinned at

Uther, who never took strong drink. "I try to watch myself, Master Uther. Don't you get too rambunctious."

Opal shifted her bulk. "Boy, you gonna help me?"

"Yes'm." When Opal was established safely on flat ground, she gave him the parcel she'd been carrying in her lap.

"Don't you get no grease on this," she said.

The shirt she'd made for Jesse was white canvas, wrought more thoroughly than delicately, seamed with green thread.

"Why thank you, Aunt Opal."

"Don't you go dirtyin' it." She sniffed and set off toward the Quarters.

Uther fumbled in his pocket for a dime. "For the baby," he said.

"Happy Christmas, Master." It wasn't Jesse's baby, and Maggie was barely Jesse's wife, but the gesture was kindly meant. "Happy Christmas, Happy Christmas." Jesse followed in Aunt Opal's wake.

Alexander Kirkpatrick uncoiled himself from the cask which had served as his seat and inspected Stratford Hall's colonnades as if he might take a notion to buy, provided the present owner hadn't exaggerated its value.

Although Stratford contained more cropland than the valley's other big plantations, Warwick and Hidden Valley, its principal residence was smaller than theirs. Samuel Gatewood's father, Thomas, had moved the family from the log cabin his own father had built into a one-room brick house with sleeping loft overhead. That single large room was now Abigail's bedroom. Five years later, when Thomas Gatewood started sawing sleepers for the Virginia Central Railroad, he added the front portion: parlor, dining room, and office downstairs, two bedrooms above. From the drive the house was plainly and rigidly symmetrical. Its front door with attendant window lights was echoed by a second-story door opening onto the porch roof, a roof supported by four hand-molded cement columns, the center two topped by wooden Corinthian scrolls. Since its ground-floor windows were tall and the second-story windows short, the house seemed a toothy smile under a lowering brow. Christmas smoke lifted from chimneys at the gable ends as well as from the kitchen house out back.

Happily, Sallie took her husband's arm. "Since I was a little girl, every year we've come to Stratford on Christmas Day. That's Preacher Todd's horse tied to that maple, and look, Daddy, there's Elmo Hevener's buggy."

"Mr. Hevener can do considerable harm to a joint of beef or a smoked ham," Uther remarked with satisfaction.

In a white gown trimmed with gold brocade, the mistress of Stratford Plantation waved from the doorway. "Welcome, Uther, Sallie, Mr. Kirkpatrick. Make haste! It's so much nicer indoors."

As they proceeded down the hall, Pompey, Gatewood's houseman, collected their winter wraps and mumbled something which—had anyone bent low enough to hear—was his inquiry "Christmas gift?"

It was Abigail's Cousin Molly's custom to visit Stratford Plantation over Christmas. Molly Semple's home was Richmond, and most unmarried respectable women would have preferred the high social season in Virginia's capital—the gala balls, witty charades, dinner parties which tried the strength of their hosts' cellars and their cooks' prowess, the amateur theatricals—all the town fun which filled the days when there was no work on the outlying plantations. But every December, without fail, Cousin Molly made the uncomfortable rail journey to Millboro, where Abigail's servants would convey her (and many many trunks and portmanteaus) into the tall snow-covered mountains. When Cousin Molly's friend Governor Wise asked her why on earth, she replied, "Christmas— I mean the real Christmas—comes so much nearer in the mountains." Cousin Molly's most treasured gift was gossip of kinfolk and the Tidewater gentry Abigail Gatewood grew up with, but Molly also brought pattern books with the newest fashions (seen no later than the previous spring at the Court of St. James's), as well as new-fangled manners and speech. Last year Cousin Molly introduced the "German tree," which the Tidewater plantations had taken up so eagerly. This year she proposed the custom of distributing small money to those servants alert enough to cry "Christmas gift?" before the gentry wished them the felicitations of the season. "It's a game," Cousin Molly explained. "And the servants enjoy it."

"An idea worthy of Mr. Dickens," Abigail agreed and asked Jack the Driver to instruct the servants. Jack did as bid but couldn't explain the game, exactly, nor just how they might sing out with the proper admixture of enthusiasm and respect. Most of the servants discarded the idea as soon as it was mooted, except for Pompey, who had learned to take his mistress's whims seriously.

Unaware of all this, a smiling Uther Botkin replied to Pompey's unconvincing murmur, "Yes, Pompey, and a Happy Christmas to you too."

"Yes sir, Master Uther." His arms full of coats and cloaks, Pompey backed into Master Gatewood's study.

With its corniced ceiling, high windows, and blue-gray walls, Stratford's parlor was pleasant in the summertime, but wine-dark winter drapes, dancing fire, evergreen garlands across the mantelpiece, and a German tree glowing with candles transformed the room into a convivial winter snug.

His face flushed with kindness, Samuel gripped his old friend's arm. "We are honored, good sir, honored. You will recall General Washington's enthusiasm for this season. In our rustic fashion, we emulate his noble example. Can I find you some punch? Will you take a cup of eggnog?"

Sallie was so happy. How good it was to forget her troubles! The tears that leapt to her eyes were tears of pleasure.

Gatewood's spectacles quivered on the bridge of his nose. "I particularly commend the eggnog. A tidewater recipe which originated with the Carter family. Mr. Kirkpatrick, delighted you could join us today, though doubtless you will be accustomed to more sophistication than you will find here. Mr. Botkin assures me your learning is profound. Did you not graduate at Yale College? I had some college myself, but abandoned my studies upon my father's demise. Now I study my plantation."

"No doubt an improving study." Kirkpatrick bowed.

Gatewood, the agricultural improver, cocked his head. Had this stiff young man made a pun? "The eggnog, friends! The eggnog!"

Ornaments glistened: blown glass balls of silver and gold and blue, strands of plump popcorn, and colored paper silhouettes.

Sallie exclaimed, "Dear Samuel, the tree is beautiful! I have read descriptions of German trees in the *Richmond Whig,* but hadn't ever expected to see one in our valley. Lovely!"

"Pompey is convinced its candles will set the house afire, and the water bucket doesn't reassure him. Whenever my back is turned, he slips in with that candle snuffer, and whup"—Samuel pinched his fingers—"another flame is gone."

A full score of neighbors and kin thronged the parlor: the Botkin-Kirkpatricks mingled with elderly Gatewood cousins come out from Warm Springs for the day. Preacher Todd, who disapproved Sallie's hasty marriage, found more congenial souls to talk to: Grandmother Gatewood particularly. Andrew Seig's kindly wife found something to say to wan Sister Kate. Uther gravitated naturally to the hearth: contented. Cedar wood in the fireplace, evergreen boughs, cigar smoke and heated spiced wine, ladies' perfumes: these scented the room.

When Andrew Seig and Elmo Hevener discussed the thrilling news of South Carolina's secession, Samuel Gatewood took the horse breeder's arm. "Andrew, Andrew. It is Christmas—the one day of the year we are positively forbidden to discuss weighty matters. In my home, sir, please indulge me."

When the Byrd carriage clattered up, the Gatewoods and Pompey hurried to meet them. With a grand flourish, Pompey opened the door, murmuring "Christmas gift?"

"Meemaw," young Pauline shrieked, and young Thomas's voice broke from excitement. "Oh Happy, Happy Christmas. I'm so happy I could burst!"

"May God bless you, you silly boy!"

Catesby Byrd bowed deeply. "All the felicities of the season, ma'am."

Byrd was a knobby man, more bones than flesh, and how her daughter Leona could lie beside him, Abigail Gatewood couldn't imagine. Might as well lie down with a sack of barrel staves!

"Leona, my dear. How fetching you are."

In her flounced yellow gown, with her lily-pale complexion and vermilion lips, Leona Byrd strongly resembled one of her daughter's dolls. Leona's smile was so hopeful and so timid it invariably took Abigail's breath away. Abigail thanked God her daughter had married Catesby. Leona needed a strong man to take care of her.

His father-in-law took that worthy's hand, beaming. "Good to see you. Isn't it all . . . ?" Samuel admired the mountains, the snow-covered pastures, the neat negro cabins with their chimney smokes, the barns, his grandchildren, his wife. "Well, isn't it?"

"Yes sir. It is. It certainly is!"

Yes, everything had been going well with Catesby. Always plenty of law work in the county seat. "We're more disputatious than you good country folk!" No, Catesby's selection for the bench was just rumor. Several other men had as good a chance, nay better, when Judge Ayres retired.

"Oh, I'm sure you should get it," his wife, Leona, cried, "if the courthouse loafers would hush up for one minute!"

A grinning Pompey ushered them into the hall, and when pretty Leona Byrd passed, he muttered, "Christmas gift?"

"But Pompey, the children's gifts will be under the tree, I'm sure."

And so it proved. Firecrackers banged in the Quarters while the Byrd children received their gifts and Pompey kept a wary eye on the candles. Little Pauline got a huzzit—the thinnest cunningest sewing kit—as well as two dolls, one handmade in the Quarters, the other pink glossy porcelain whose tiny gown had been in vogue last summer in Richmond. Accompanied by many solemn warnings, Thomas was given his first hunting rifle.

Samuel Gatewood filled his son-in-law's cup and took another himself. Wordlessly the two men toasted this gathering, so precious and so fragile. They did not speak of the terrible storm gathering beyond the peaceful boundaries of Stratford Plantation.

When servants came to receive their annual issue of clothing, poor Pompey was torn between duties. He was wanted in the front hall, but daren't abandon a tree that looked mightily like a lit bonfire.

"I'll keep an eye on it, Pompey," Catesby volunteered. "Give me that snuffer before you impale yourself." Byrd dug in his pocket for a two-bit piece, said: "Happy Christmas, Pompey." And Pompey left, not knowing whether this was "Christmas gift?" or not, whether the new magical charm was efficacious.

Bundles of clothing were stacked on a long table in the front hall, and as the servants filed past, Jack the Driver addressed them, "Master and Missus be givin' you new clothes. Finest blouses, finest pants, best-quality linsey-woolsey. All year Grandmother Gatewood spun and loomed so you'd not traipse into the New Year naked. And whenever Mistress Abigail be havin' time, she knittin' your socks. Wool socks from Stratford Plantation, big ones for the mens, medium ones for the womens, and little ones for the children. You know that Mistress Abigail, she cast off a strong stitch, and these socks they last until next year if you treat 'em right, wash 'em every Sunday, don't put 'em on when you can go barefoot. Shoes made by a German shoemaker in Lexington, big ones for the mens, mediums for the womens and the children what's old enough. Master Samuel say we had a good year at the plantation, the railroad bought every sleeper we sawed and his calves fetch a good price. So inside your sock you like to find a silver coin, yours to keep. And Master and Mistress wishin' all their colored family Happy Christmas."

The two-bit piece Abigail Gatewood had inserted into each pair of thick woolen socks was half a day's wages for a free white, and some of Gatewoods' neighbors would have disapproved. Miss Dinwiddie had been heard to complain that Gatewood "spoiled his niggers," and it was partly for this reason that the money was discreetly delivered. Discretion came naturally to the servants, and they did not inspect their bonus until they were well clear of the house.

Mistress Abigail smiled. "Odona, how is your ague? All the damp we've had! I trust you are using the comfrey poultices I gave you?"

"Oh yes, Mistress."

"And Rufus, your hand is still swollen."

"Rufus be a little more careful jerkin' them logs downhill, he don't get run over by them," Jack the Driver said.

Rufus grinned. "Had me a driver's job where I wouldn't do no work, I'd heal quicker."

"Come to the kitchen house tomorrow and I'll have another look."

"He don't be so full of himself, Mistress, he don't get hurt," Jack muttered.

"I'm sure that's true, Jack. But we can't help that, can we?"

Some of the younger women unrolled their new clothing before they were out the back door.

Mistress Abigail gave Jesse the largest socks she had. "Happy Christmas to you both," she said gaily.

The parade snaked past the table to the rustle of new cloth and Abigail's inquiries. "When we broach the keg, don't you act up as you did last year," she admonished ancient Uncle Agamemnon, who sixty years ago had been a Bakongo sorcerer before he was sold into slavery.

·   ·   ·

Duncan reined in his mare, Gypsy, at a bend where he could see all Stratford at his feet.

He hated refusing his roommate Spaulding's Christmas invitation: two weeks in the Piedmont—horse races, hunting, gala balls, people who didn't know Duncan Gatewood from Adam—but Duncan could not deny his father's stiff, courteous summons. "Your dear mother would be so pleased . . . You will be interested to see the wonderful wheat crop we have put up. That servant marriage in which you had some interest seems satisfactory. I pray you and I might resume more congenial relations. . . ."

Thank God South Carolina had seceded! Thank God Duncan had something to think about besides his own misery!

As a boy, Duncan had been good-natured and natural—nothing had prepared him for desire, he never imagined that anything could set him and his father at loggerheads. He had tried to be an obedient son, but Midge, she . . . Duncan's hands trembled, and Gypsy stirred restlessly. Gypsy knew she was home.

Smoke lifted from Stratford's chimneys. A wagon rumbled across the plank bridge over the millrace. How small everything seemed. How could this mountain plantation have been his entire world?

Samuel, the thoughtful master, had provided Maggie with a husband and father for her baby. Duncan's old schoolmate, Jesse. Duncan himself could not have chosen better. But awake, late at night in the Institute barracks, listening to Spaulding's snores and the soft pad of a sentry's footfalls in the hall, Duncan tried not to think of Maggie with Jesse. Duncan tried not to think how Jesse would be learning Maggie's ways. Oh, she had her ways!

To make this day bearable, Duncan vowed to shun her. He vowed to shun her baby. Some cadets joked about slipping down to the Quarters for a taste, but no cadet ever joked about the babies.

Samuel Gatewood's guests' servants were celebrating with their fellows. At the end of the lane, one of Andrew Seig's field hands was inspecting the hog slow-roasting over a bed of coals. He kept his hands folded behind his back, ostentatiously resisting temptation. Aunt Opal visited from cabin to cabin. Franky and Dinah Williams perched on the seat of a worn-out dump rake. Though all the cabins had wooden floors, only Jack the Driver's cabin, at the head of the lane, boasted a modest front porch, where Uncle Agamemnon sat rocking. Uncle Agamemnon claimed to be a hundred years old and maybe he was, because he remembered Africa and could talk to you in its language.

Jesse Burns said, "How you gettin' on, Uncle? I'm Jesse, Maggie's husband."

The old man was dark skin over skeleton. His tiny black eyes sparked. "Come up and sit, son."

"Thank you, Uncle."

In his twenty-sixth year, Jesse Burns was muscled like a bull calf, veins and sinew prominent, each in right proportion. It graveled some white men the way Jesse stood as though he had an absolute right to take up the space he took, to breathe the air he breathed.

When he was twelve years old, Jesse was already doing a man's work. By eighteen some SunRise sports wagered that Jesse could outpull a light drafter and would have put the matter to the test had not Uther Botkin forbade it. The irises of Jesse's large eyes were light tan, and though he neither dipped snuff nor touched liquor, the whites were yellowish.

Uncle Agamemnon occupied the Quarters' sole rocker, which had adorned the Gatewoods' porch until it wore out. Mended, it sufficed to hold one frail old man who didn't weigh as much as his years. Jesse sat on the crackerbox beside him.

"You seek something of me," the old man said. "The name of something, *nkisi,* to help you."

Jesse lowered his head. "Yes, Uncle," he said. Jesse had been taught by rationalist Uther Botkin, and asking this old conjure man for help shamed him. Two women waited, out of earshot, in the street with letters they had brought for Jesse to read. Jesse spoke softly. "Uncle . . . can you help me? My woman, Maggie, she will not come to my bed."

The old man's toothless smile. "Grow old, you will no longer want her," he suggested. "Can't you wait?" After a pause, the old man relented. "Bring me red flannel and four new needles and I will make you a charm." Loudly, and with audible satisfaction, the old man called to the waiting women, "What do you want? Why have you come? To read white man's marks?" He snorted and spat and rather grandly drew a feed sack over his shoulders and closed his eyes.

While the old man dozed, people brought Jesse their letters. "Dear Ellie, I am still at this place . . ." "Darling husband, I have not heard from you in such a spell. Are you still with Gatewoods?" "My dearest, we have been so long separated that today I jump over the broomstick with Dell a woman on this plantation. She is carrying my child. She is a hard worker. She is plain-featured, and a good Christian."

"I'm sorry," Jesse said.

"What you got to be sorry about?" The woman snatched her letter back.

When bid, Jesse replied in his florid hand, on cheap paper which could be folded to serve as its own envelope.

Children ran hooting and hollering between the cabins.

Jack the Driver gave a gaily painted tin box to Rufus. "You let the young'uns fire these off, but Rufus, have a care."

Rufus dipped into the box for a string of ladycrackers and flipped it into the hog fire, where it exploded coals and soot into the air, to the children's delight and the hog cook's indignation.

"I'd like to talk with you, Jesse," Jack the Driver said.

Jesse patted the porch where his letter writers sat, but Jack shook his head no. "Inside," he said. He called, "Franky, you bring us some of that tea you got brewin'."

More ladycrackers chittered as Jack ushered Jesse into the cabin. It contained a straw pallet against the back wall, rolled up so you could sit on it, a chifforobe (doors missing) beside the sprung thirty-gallon cask which served as a table, and two handmade wooden stools, legs guyed by rawhide. The wool jacket hanging in the chifforobe was Jack's now, but had been Catesby Byrd's. Jack took a stool and waited until Jesse took the other.

Franky presented battered teacups as if they were finest china. "These mine. Don't you bust them now."

After each man took a suitably cautious sip, Franky left.

Jack the Driver said, "I ain't never had no young buck who worked better'n you or mooned around so much neither. What's the matter with you, boy?"

"I expect you know."

Jack did, but didn't intend to have that knowledge thrown up to him. "Master Duncan comin' home today."

"I wish to hell he'd stayed away."

"Don't you go blaspheming, boy. Ain't no blaspheming in my house."

Jesse stared into his handleless teacup.

After a time, Jack the Driver began, "I come here with Maggie when she come to this place. She weren't nothin' but a pickaninny then. The Mitchells in Warm Springs was where we was before. Me and her and Auntie Opal. I sleep in the horse barn with the bridles and saddles. Maggie's mamma sleep in the big house, which is how she gets into trouble."

"What trouble?"

"Trouble with the master. For a colored gal, worst trouble there is!"

The tea was mostly hot water, but Jesse took another respectful sip.

"You see that hog out there?" Jack said.

"Fine hog, mighty fine hog."

"And we got deer hams for tomorrow which Master Gatewood and Master Byrd hunted on the mountain. Great big ol' deer hams!"

Jack was making Jesse nervous. When people beat around the bush, usually they want you to do something that doesn't make good sense.

Jack smacked his lips over his tea. "How many drivers you know don't carry no bullwhip?" he asked. "That's 'cause Master Gatewood don't care for no whip. Been two years, more, since the bullwhip come out at Stratford."

"I never had no man lay a whip on me. I don't know how I'd take it," Jesse said.

"Then you one lucky nigger," Jack said. "You want more tea to drink?"

Jesse stood up. "Thank you for your kindness, Mr. Jack. People outside waitin' on me."

"Sit down, boy. I ain't done." Jack wiped his lips on the back of his hand. "You see this sock? Knit by Miss Abigail her ownself. Look at these nubbins on the outside—outside—so they don't rasp at my feet. And you know what I find in the toe of this here sock? A silver dollar! The master he just give it to me."

"What was you wantin' from me?"

"That you keep yourself from bein' foolish. That you don't lose the chance you has here. Colored woman not like white woman. Colored woman got no choice who she take up with."

"Maggie's my woman. We jump the broomstick together."

"But you ain't happy and she ain't neither. Why you don't take up with some other woman? That Franky gal ripe as a new peach."

When Jesse went blank, Jack realized that Jesse's face was just as big as the rest of him.

"Maggie'll come to care for me bye 'n' bye," Jesse said carefully. "I'm good to her all the time. Baby Jacob, he's not mine but he will be. Your daddy's whoever decides to be your daddy, not the fellow sowed the seed. Hell, I never knew . . ."

"Don't allow no cursin' in this house."

"I never did know who my daddy was. Old Uther's been as much daddy as I have, and he's white. I'll be Jacob's daddy one day. Don't tell me about that Franky gal. I don't want to lie with her. I lie down with Maggie when she's willin'."

"Don't you go spoilin' things. Ain't been no servant sold from Stratford Plantation since I been here. Master got work for all of us—more work 'n he got hands to do it. Time Master Duncan comes into his own, I be like Uncle Agamemnon on the porch, rockin' and snorin'. I gonna die right here on Stratford Plantation. Uncle Agamemnon don't work no more, but he get a shirt every year, same as me, and he eat hog meat, same as me, and some of the womens they cut it up small for him."

"Stratford's a fine place to be a nigger, all right. Mr. Jack, you're a fair driver, and you set me a task, I do it. But me and Maggie, we are man and wife, and the Bible says that no man comes betwixt us." He stood.

"I believe I got more letters to write. Maggie be along directly. She's restin' with the baby."

Jesse marched outside. "How many of you want somethin' writ? I don't do love letters. You want love letters, you got to ask somebody else."

Later that afternoon, from the head of his dining table, Samuel Gatewood inspected his guests with eyes softened by his own excellent eggnog. This was what it meant for a man, by dint of his labors, to have created a competency. So many nights he had lain awake worrying: would the railroad be satisfied with his sleepers, would the crops come, might he and his son reconcile?

Samuel Gatewood felt like a mariner who'd charted a course through perilous seas and brought his boat, almost, into safe harbor. Stratford Plantation was prosperous, and necessary improvements would occupy him until his dying day. His family, white and black, hummed with contentment. His only daughter, Leona, was safely married. Although upon his arrival today Duncan had seemed sullen, he had obeyed Samuel's summons to come home for Christmas. Surely Samuel could take that as a favorable omen. Surely Duncan could be persuaded of his own best interests. Samuel was willing to forgive everything. The gift he'd ordered for his son had arrived at the Millboro depot just last week, just in time!

Soft winter light cast its benison on kinfolk and friends. Samuel Gatewood swallowed the lump in his throat and tapped a spoon against his glass. "Ladies and gentlemen," he said, "I've never heard a nobler toast than George Washington's: 'Our friends!' "

"Our friends!"

"Samuel, our friends!"

His son got to his feet. Duncan said, "And I offer a second toast. Ladies, gentlemen—to South Carolina, the world's newest and bravest independent nation. May Virginia soon follow her lead!"

Andrew Seig and two other men stood. After glancing at Samuel Gatewood, Catesby remained seated.

The hand with which Duncan offered his glass tremored.

Deliberately, Samuel Gatewood rose. "My son's new fervor for politics distinguishes him." He lifted his glass. "To our friends and kinfolk in South Carolina. Let us pray they have made a wise decision."

"And so say all of us." Andrew Seig gulped his brandy.

"Hurrah for our dear hostess, my mother-in-law, Abigail Gatewood," Catesby cried. "Now where is that scoundrel Pompey?"

With prodigious ceremony, Pompey ferried a roast of beef from the sideboard, and conversation resumed while his master carved.

As swiftly as Pompey removed a dish from the sideboard to the table, other servants replaced it. A roast goose nestled between a brace of ducks, the smoked ham had hung in Gatewood's meathouse since the year of Cox's snow; there was a venison tenderloin baked in red wine and juniper berries, scotch eggs, a lamb fricassee, and two pork pies. There were white potatoes, sweet potatoes, dilled cucumbers, an apple-and-carrot casserole, baked squash, pumpkin soup, diced turnips in butter, winter spinach, and cress gathered just that morning from Strait Creek spring. There was light bread and cornbread and biscuits. There were pies: apple, mince, pumpkin, buttermilk, pecan. And there were more cakes than pies! Ten of the best beeswax candles were pickets of light down the dining table, and each piece of Grandmother Gatewood's silver shone like a new sun.

During Christmas mouth, the valley plantations paid calls. Stratford visited Warwick Christmas Eve, and Samuel Gatewood was the first across the door lintel at Hidden Valley (that front door kept bolted to hold good luck in until the Gatewoods' arrival) on New Year's. But Christmas Day was reserved for family, white and black, unto the fourth cousin once removed and the lonely spinster aunt who must have been related to Cousin Edward but nobody remembered exactly how.

Stratford's dining table had been increased by six leaves, so that Mistress Abigail Gatewood, seated at the foot, had her back scant inches from the front window, and Samuel Gatewood, at the head, was pressed against the china closet, which would have made serving impossible had not every last piece of silver been exhausted from its drawers, every plate previously laid out. The door through which the servants brought dishes from the kitchen house swung open and closed, open and closed.

Catesby Byrd sat at Samuel Gatewood's right hand. Duncan, in uniform—white trousers, dark gray jacket, black stock at his throat—was farther down the table. To Duncan's left was Aunt Sadie, who, having lost hearing at the advanced age of eighty-one, had abandoned speech as well, and hovered over her plate of soft vegetables as if only her strictest attention would prevent their flight. Duncan turned to his other partner. "You'll be Alexander Kirkpatrick. Congratulations on your marriage, sir. Sallie's a fine girl. I've known her all my life."

"Ah yes, young Gatewood. Your attire, sir. Do we fear military alarms?"

"This rig?" Duncan grinned. "This was to show Father his money wasn't altogether wasted. Likely to be plenty boys in uniform before long. Boys at the Institute expect Mississippi and Alabama to secede before the year is out."

Kirkpatrick lifted a slice of beef, inspected it, replaced it to pare away a scrap of fat. "You favor secession, sir?"

"I figure we came into this union voluntarily and we can come out of it should we choose to." He took a roll. "You're a professor, I hear."

"I am not presently employed. As you may know, your father had our modest home built. Since I have no practical skills, I am grateful." Kirkpatrick speared a roasted potato.

"You're educated! Just the sort of man we need in Virginia. Why, old Tom Jefferson thought so high of education . . ."

"I am acquainted with Mr. Jefferson's views. My father-in-law is his devotee."

Heedlessly, young Duncan rushed on. "There are civilians who teach at the Institute. Old Gummy Stewart, he teaches French and German; he's never fought a war. And Washington College down the road, there aren't any soldiers at that school. That was Father's college. Why, I bet he'd recommend you. Father's fond of Sallie. So are we all. If you were to come to Lexington, I'll bet you could find a position."

"I have not found that Virginians, as a people, appreciate a superior education. Not only do they shun it themselves but they reproach their children should the poor creatures incline toward acquiring one. They disdain those who, like myself, have taken the trouble to complete a course of studies. Virginius Rusticus prefers unlettered traditions to knowledge."

Duncan put down his fork, and a cool smile fastened to his mouth. "You are my father's guest, sir," he said.

Across the table, Elmo Hevener and Andrew Seig were arguing the merits of a horse the latter had at stud. Seig had bred Duncan's Gypsy, and Duncan turned to their congenial conversation.

Roast followed roast, and then the Christmas pastries were succeeded by a plum pudding. Dusk smote at the windows, helpless to dim the cheer inside. Mistress Abigail's cheeks bloomed, and she wouldn't have traded places with any of her Tidewater kinfolk; no, not with any fine lady in the Commonwealth. She and Mrs. Hevener debated the proper amount of sherry to flavor a Christmas cake (Mistress Abigail: two gills; Mrs. Hevener: a Methodist pint).

Duncan Gatewood had no more than two glasses of wine. His father, Samuel, had drunk more than his accustomed portion. Afterward everyone agreed about that.

Long shadows darkened Stratford's fields when the gentlemen stepped onto the porch. Andrew Seig saluted the season with both barrels of his shotgun. Honest Uther Botkin piped a cheer and contributed a shot from a pistol which had begun life as half of a dueling set but had fallen on hard times.

Samuel Gatewood balanced a mahogany box on the porch rail before extracting a square-framed blue-black revolver from the box's velvet interior.

Smoothly he aimed, and BOOMBOOMBOOMBOOMBOOMBOOM and the thump of each ball striking the white oak fell hard on the heels of its discharge.

"This is one of Mr. Colt's Hartford pistols." Gatewood's soft words filled the aching silence after his fusillade. From the Quarters (which had gone still) came a single bitter yell.

"What a splendid, terrible instrument," Uther Botkin exclaimed. "What a century we have made."

Samuel Gatewood latched the case before presenting it to his son. "May you never require this weapon. But if you do, may you use it in defense of home, family, honor . . ." Samuel groped for more graceful words but failed to find them. ". . . and Virginia's hallowed traditions," he concluded.

Duncan also did the best he could. "Thank you, sir. Few cadets possess anything so fine."

Another whoop from the Quarters rang off the mountain.

"The attachment between a Christian father and his son must outweigh every other," Samuel Gatewood said.

Catesby Byrd frowned.

Samuel paid him no heed. Turning to his guests, he said, "Gentlemen, though I discourage strong spirits amongst my servants, in my experience denying spirits entirely is more disruptive than a modest holiday issue. Now we must broach their holiday cask. Duncan, you will accompany me."

"Sir?"

"Come."

In the Quarters, children were tossing inflated pig bladders hoarded all year for this occasion.

In swap for his letter writing, Jesse had a one-pound sack of best ground cornmeal, a pair of handmade suspender tabs, and a woman's promise to mend any shirt he might need mended. Maggie sat beside him on the porch, chin in her hand. The dress she'd fashioned from Miss Abigail's drapes dragged in the dirt, but she paid no mind. Baby Jacob lay flat in her lap, washed, swaddled, and wrapped against the cold. "You takin' the Botkins home after?"

"I expect so."

"They gonna pay you?"

"Christmas gift, Massa? Christmas gift?"

She wrinkled her nose. "Why is Rufus scorchin' that hog? That scorch make my teeth grate."

"Your tastin' been funny since Jacob's born," Jesse said. "You want, I'll go up to kitchen house, fetch you some of the Gatewoods' Christmas."

"You see Mistress Abigail this mornin'? She looked right through me.

Like it wasn't me had brushed her hair every mornin', a hundred strokes, way she liked it." She paused. In another woman's voice Maggie said, "Dear Maggie. You know how I care for you, child. But there is nothing, absolutely nothing, I can do. You do understand!"

Jesse shivered. When Maggie talked like this, Jesse felt there were two women living inside of his wife and one of them would remain a stranger.

"Mistress using that Franky for lady's maid. Franky—straight out of the kitchen house into Mistress's boudoir. You think Mistress ever give me my job back?"

Jesse shrugged. Had any man ever been asked so many questions he couldn't answer?

Jesse gave her his gift: a six-inch slippery-elm tube. Maggie's face lit up briefly.

"What's this?"

"Whistle. Rufus showed me how to whittle it. Took me three nights whittlin' it while you and baby Jacob was sleepin'."

Jesse blew a high trill. "Shapin' that wooden ball inside without bustin' the outsides, that was the sly part," he said.

Jack the Driver slashed into the thickest part of the hog and twisted his blade to see the juces run. "He ready," he cried. "And he prime."

Men slipped poles under the carcass and hoisted it onto the plank-and-barrel table. Aprons shielding their faces, women raked blackened yams out of the coals. Iron frypans filled with green kale fried in fatback were set on the table. Some celebrants owned plate and fork, others only spoon and wooden bowl. Jack ran his butcher knife over his whetstone, whisk, whisk, whisk, and tested the edge on the hair of his arm.

"Driver," Rufus called, "we don't need for you to be shavin' that hog. We just want you cuttin' him up."

The children went to the head of the line. If the food ran out, it wouldn't be the children who suffered.

Someone said, "Praise the Lord for His blessings."

Someone else said, "Amen."

"You want me to fetch your dinner?" Jesse asked.

"Why you want to be with me?" Maggie stirred a circle in the dirt with her foot. She changed to her white-lady voice. "Jesse, I am not intended for you. No doubt you are an excellent man, but when I look, I see nothing I desire. I cannot make you happy."

Jesse's voice was hoarse. "You make me happy, give me what you can."

Her dark swimming eyes turned away. "But I ain't givin' you nothin'. I lie down with you and I don't feel nothin'. Nary a itch!"

Jesse swallowed. "That child wrapped warm enough?" He tucked cloth under the sleeping infant's cheek.

The hog was speedily reduced. Rufus waved a ham hock. Grease streaked his chin.

Gunshots roared from the big house as the masters celebrated the birth of their Prince of Peace. When Mr. Colt's pistol boomed its shots, all the coloreds fell silent except Rufus, who howled like a dog. "Master got one of them guns you load on Sunday and shoot all week," he whispered.

"Master! Master!" children called as Samuel and his jolly guests came into the Quarters. Samuel put hard candies in every child's hand.

"Evening, Uncle Agamemnon. Hope you got sufficient to eat. Rufus, Ellie. I'm pleased that your new clothing fits you."

Rufus stepped out to shake Duncan's hand. "Young Master, welcome home. Ain't no good sawmill work goin' on since you gone away. We loafin' all the time."

Franky curtsied sillily. "Master Duncan, you right fetchin' in your soldier suit. Was that you shootin'? Scared me half to death." With focused concentration she aimed a mock rifle right at Duncan's heart. "Bang! Hee!"

Samuel said, "Jack, you've a grand bonfire and Hevener's George has his banjo tucked under his arm, so perhaps we could broach the Christmas cask?"

Though Jack was tone-deaf and indifferent to dancing, he said, "Master, you sure right there," and sent Rufus for the whiskey.

As if it were everyday business, Samuel beckoned Jesse. "Jack says you are making a good hand. I trust you are content."

"Land of milk and honey, Master," Jesse said.

"Uther taught you to read. Though your reading violates Virginia law, it speaks well of your urge for self-improvement."

"Oh, it were right hard to get words through this nappy skull," Jesse said, rapping his head. With his mouth open his knuckles produced a hollow "tunk," and kids giggled but older folks looked at their feet.

"Duncan, feel this man's arm."

"Sir? May I ask . . ."

"His arm. Can you encircle his arm with your hands?"

Duncan formed a circle with his hands but did not apply it to Jesse's arm. "No, sir. I believe I could not."

"Jesse, how much corn can you cut in a day?"

Jesse shook his head. "I ain't no great shakes at corn cuttin'. Ten, eleven acres 'twixt can and can't."

"From can see at sunrise to can't see at dark," Gatewood translated. "Rufus here, a reliable man, can't cut eight."

Rufus called out, "I ain't no worker, Master. I was born for love."

Gatewood froze for an instant. Rufus slipped into the darkness. "Jesse, remove your shirt."

"Samuel, my friend . . ." Catesby cautioned.

"Do you question my management of my property, or the instruction I intend for my sometimes wayward son?"

Catesby's face emptied. He turned on his heel and walked away.

Jesse eyed the Gatewoods, father and son, for a fat moment before he moved slick as a snake shedding his skin and his shirt came over his head and onto the ground.

"Sir?" Duncan said.

"Now, Jesse, turn away, if you please."

Jesse's black skin glistened and his shoulder blades were smooth prominences in the lift of his back.

"Note his musculature," Samuel Gatewood said, his finger not quite touching, tracing muscles from the shoulders to where they bunched above his hips. "Short-coupled and thick in the withers. Like one of Alex Seig's Percheron stallions. And nary a mark on him. Planters who rely on the whip are fools. A whipped servant can't work, and if time comes to fetch the speculator, a scarred man won't command a good price. Thank you, Jesse."

Samuel's guests, who'd only come to wish their own servants a Happy Christmas, stirred uneasily. Andrew Seig called, "Samuel, if you were to broach their cask, we could return to the comforts of your parlor."

Master Gatewood's raised hand commanded silence. "And this is Jesse's woman, Maggie."

"Master . . ." Jack the Driver warned.

"Duncan, you are acquainted with Maggie."

Maggie broke into a luminous, tremulous smile as she took a step forward.

With his finger, Master Gatewood turned Maggie's face, one profile, then the other. She had the features of a pharaoh's queen. "Servants like Jesse and Maggie are the firm foundation of Stratford Plantation. That's right, isn't it, Jack?"

"Master, there's folks waitin' on that cask. Old George's banjo anxious in his hand."

"Your child, Maggie—what do you call the boy?"

She whispered, "Jacob. I call him Jacob because Jacob got to see the gates of heaven."

"Duncan, take the infant."

"Sir . . . I cannot."

"Maggie doesn't object, do you, Maggie?"

Silently, Maggie extended the infant toward the young white master. Maggie's eyes cast Duncan adrift. His body felt light as down. The baby stirred and put his tiny fists to his innocent eyes. Baby Jacob was just as white as he was.

"It is not unknown for a young man to succumb to temptation," Samuel droned on. "We pray that error, repented, may be converted into useful knowledge: the master's assumption of his duties. Son, take this child who will one day be your servant: a field hand perhaps, a woods worker like Rufus or a house nigger like Pompey . . ."

Duncan jerked his fist into the air and (Elmo Hevener said, afterward) his father flinched. But instead of striking a blow, Duncan pressed his hand to his mouth and bit down, his teeth sinking into the heel of his hand, and a fine spatter of blood sprayed Maggie and the infant and the boy growled the way a bulldog growls when it's taken hold. Still growling, hunched over his hand, Samuel Gatewood's son lurched up the lane toward the house. Frightened, the infant began to wail.

In a strangled voice, Gatewood said, "Jack . . . Jack, you may broach the cask."

Maggie's eyes flooded with tears. "Master, why are you doing this to us?"

Samuel wiped his face with his linen handkerchief. He said, "You are unaccustomed to strong drink. Use a little sense, will you?"

"Yes, Master," Rufus called in the deadest voice imaginable. "We use all the sense we got."

"Pray put away your wraps," Catesby Byrd urged Samuel's guests. "I'm certain the Gatewoods intend you to stay for the dancing. They will rejoin us directly." He spoke confidentially. "Please. It will demonstrate respect for the family."

Reluctantly, Andrew Sieg unbuckled his fiddle case. An oblong leather case another opened contained a harmonium, and Leona Byrd seated herself, with a childlike air, at the pianoforte.

Sister Kate dozed in a wing chair.

With Pauline against her knees, Cousin Molly read from Mr. Dickens's "A Christmas Carol."

Having done his duty by fire hazards and extinguished every candle on the tree, Pompey was sitting upright in the corner, feet stuck straight out, fast asleep. Though she usually retired when dancing began, Grandmother Gatewood perched on a straightback chair, hands folded patiently in her lap, eyes glittering.

When Leona Byrd struck the first chords of the somber. "Lorena," her husband cried, "Come, dear, this is Christmas. *Tempo vivace* if you please!"

Elmo Hevener proposed to call figures and urged the gents to select their partners. Uther Botkin and Sallie were first on the floor.

Though at first the music was ragged, it soon hit its stride and was at a racehorse clip when Abigail returned and motioned Catesby into the dining room. The house servants had hurried to the celebrations in the Quarters and hadn't cleaned up. Ruined cakes slumped on the sideboard, platters were yellowed in congealed grease.

"Dear Abigail . . ."

"Oh, Catesby. I can do nothing with my husband or son. They are in Duncan's room, Duncan crumpled on his bed, Samuel pacing! Samuel will have the filial obedience that is his due, and Duncan, poor Duncan, has taken leave of his senses. He begs him to rear that negro infant as his in the house."

"Duncan is young, too imaginative, he . . ."

"He is confounded, Catesby. Entirely confounded. Duncan freely acknowledges his transgressions but will not see his plain duty. Catesby, both of them trust you, won't you . . ."

The tune "Leatherbritches" jangled from the parlor, and the floor vibrated from dancing.

"Abigail, I cannot interpose myself between father and son."

"Catesby, Duncan dares to speak of matrimony!"

Catesby had a headache behind his eyes and knew he had drunk too much. The road home would be snow-dusted and vacant, the harshest sound the jingaling of harness bells. "Dearest Abigail, may I find you a restorative?"

She clutched him so close he could smell sweat under her perfume. "Catesby, I never have seen Samuel in such a state. The day his father was buried, Samuel went into the Quarters, accompanied by Omohundru the slave speculator, and banished—nay, sold—every one of his father's concubines. The poor souls wailed and begged, but what else could Samuel do? Samuel despised his father's lusts. He loves Duncan but would see him dead before he assented to any further improprieties."

A cry, a blow, an outraged shout, and Catesby Byrd jerked the hall door open as young Gatewood reeled downstairs, while his father bellowed from the landing above him, "Hell, boy, you might as well breed with that mare of yours!"

Duncan bore the unmistakable mark of his father's blow on his cheek. Samuel Gatewood cried, "That impudent slut has soiled my honor . . . your honor! She is your dependent! Your chattel!"

Grandmother Gatewood peeped from the parlor, but Catesby shut the door firmly in her face.

Snow blew across the lintel where Duncan had left Stratford's door open wide, and Gypsy's hoofbeats fled into the night. Samuel Gatewood descended clumsily, stupefied. No music came from the parlor. Samuel licked his lips. He said, "Wife, our son has returned to the Institute. Now I must be rid of his slut."

"Dear Samuel . . ."

"Abigail, you would oblige me if you troubled me no more this night. I am a damnable fool. Perhaps you can reassure our guests."

Abigail took a deep breath and disappeared into the parlor, and moments later the two men heard Leona Byrd's tinkling rendition of "Dixie."

Samuel inspected his puffy right hand as if it did not belong to him. He said, "My friend, I will thank you to fetch my driver, Jack, to my study. I have an ugly duty to perform."

Older guests murmured their goodbyes to Abigail—"We'd love to stay longer but ours is such an arduous journey . . ."—but younger spirits determined to see the evening out. Their midnight gaiety was feverish and promised headaches on the morrow. Gentlemen danced flamboyantly and visited the punch bowl as if they were thirsty. On the next day, some ladies were ashamed to recall their extravagances.

Only Grandmother Gatewood was refreshed, her smile a bright gash.

Two hours later when Catesby Byrd came back into the parlor, Leona lifted her hands from the piano keys and let go the pedal, which twanged.

"Samuel Gatewood offers you his sincerest apologies, but believes it would be best if you were to repair to your homes. Uther, Jesse cannot take you home tonight. Rufus will drive in his stead."

"Jesse? Where is Jesse?"

"Sir, I needn't remind you that Jesse Burns is no longer your servant."

"Of course, of course. I must speak to Samuel. Samuel has always been a friend to us . . ."

"As a precaution, Jesse has been placed under restraint. Samuel cannot allow Jesse to protest this . . . disagreeable business. Rufus will take you home."

"I will speak to Samuel Gatewood. I will."

"Master Gatewood is no longer at Stratford House, sir. He's gone to fetch Omohundru."

6

THE FEEJEE MERMAID

NEAR SUNRISE, VIRGINIA
MARCH 10, 1861

Veritas odium parit.

—Ausonius

A WIFE'S SILENCE can ring louder than the clapper of a bell. Alexander Kirkpatrick's wife hunched herself into the corner farthest from the fire and clamored soundlessly. The fire popped and a barrage of sparks exploded onto the new floor of the first house Alexander Kirkpatrick had ever owned, and he wondered if they might set it afire. The planks at the hearthstone's edge were pockmarked with black scars where other embers had flared and died while Alexander considered them. He wondered what flooring wood Samuel Gatewood had installed. On the single occasion Alexander visited the cabin during construction (it went up in two weeks in November), Gatewood wasn't present. Jack the Driver was directing the gang, and Jack was patient with Alexander's questions; oh yes, he was.

Sallie said Gatewood was settling a moral debt: when Gatewood needed Jesse, Uther sold him; when Uther's daughter and new son-in-law needed a place of their own, Samuel Gatewood had it built.

Alexander shifted in the rocker—the cabin's only chair—and turned the page he hadn't read. From the stillness of her corner, Sallie made it too noisy to read.

How long must he bear this contemptuous silence? Two days after she lost his baby, in retaliation for one idle remark, Alexander's wife lost her tongue. He wondered when she'd recover it. Daily, she toted kindling from the stack Gatewood had provided. In the morning she cooked oatmeal, in the evening ham and beans or beans without ham. She washed their plates. She drew water and scrubbed their clothes. Sometimes when she was busy, he was able to read his Juvenal, sometimes he could daydream his way back to Juvenal's sordid, bitter ancient city, Roma Aeterna—but usually Sallie was too noisy.

How much better it would have been had she brought the baby to term. A new Alexander, a second chance! Alexander had hoped for the best! He had! Assuredly he would have been a better father than his own. Was he a drunkard? Did he beat his wife—even when she provoked him terribly?

How his mother had cosseted him, sharing bright daydreams whenever his father was out of the house. His mother was educated—youngest daughter of a Boston clergyman. In poetic revery, Alexander imagined her as a fragile china cup which by ill fortune found itself in some low waterfront saloon. Alexander did not know how his father had been employed, only that his work was sporadic and never provided for clothes or enough food for their table. When his father came home, reeking of spirits, and removed his belt, Alexander made himself invisible. Children can do that. While his mother cried for mercy, Alexander was under the table playing with his hands. His busy fingers were warriors or the chariots Mother told stories about; Roman soldiers' chariots, colliding, upsetting, wrecking one another.

Alexander preferred a life of dreams, not this: a one-room cabin in a rude country whose roads—mere traces really—positively deterred visitors. It had been two weeks since Sallie's nattering father paid a call. Oh, Sallie talked then. So long as Uther was in their house, Sallie pretended all was well, conversing even with Alexander. As they stood on the porch waving Uther goodbye, Alexander said, "That was pleasant. I do enjoy a chance to exchange ideas with an educated man, even though he does not possess a first-rate mind." Why hadn't Sallie understood his nervousness, how he had to say something even though it might not have been precisely the right thing to say?

Sallie hadn't answered him. Had not answered his subsequent query—some minor domestic detail—had instead resumed her thoroughgoing noisy silence.

Mrs. Gatewood had come during the February thaw—a woman come to mourn another's baby. That day, Alexander took a long walk. When one doesn't know how to act, the wise man makes his excuses. Of course he had wanted the baby! And when it was dead, he couldn't think what to do or say. One had to make the best of things.

Here, miles from any civilized establishment, enclosed by giant snowy mountains, in the depth of winter's frozen silence, Alexander's dumb spouse made so much racket he might as well have been back in Manhattan's hurly-burly. Indeed, peace had been easier to find on Broadway than here. For the first time in his life, Alexander Kirkpatrick was unable to remove himself from the world, to find his way into his still and private safety.

The fire snapped. No, that was some creature outside, some wild beast slaying smaller creatures by starlight.

Alas, it was too early to go to bed. When he retired to the pile of quilts his wife would usurp this chair. The rocker squeaked. All night long he would hear it squeaking.

It wasn't his fault she had lost the baby! He had wanted it as badly as she. Young Alexander! Through that tiny, helpless life, the father might have lived anew, might finally have comprehended. For isn't it said that a little child shall lead them?

How he envied simpleminded fellows: their ease, their intuition of emotions he'd studied in detail and shammed as best he could. Alexander wasn't arrogant because he felt superior to other men, he was arrogant because he must not be found out. During his brief sojourn at Yale College, Alexander learned one valuable lesson: arrogance kills questions. The humble man invites conviviality: that jostling Alexander dreaded.

Alexander's smiles were smiles he'd seen on the faces of others, his pretensions those he'd observed in senior faculty, men assured of gravity and power. Seducing Sallie had been, for Alexander, an act of bravery. He had never been with a woman he hadn't paid, and Sallie's vigorous aptitude for love terrified him. She wanted so much! True, sometimes he lashed out at her, but couldn't she surmise how frightened he was?

He leaned forward to set another stick on the fire. Of course he complained about the cabin, but surely she could have guessed that this new, bare log house was finer than the cramped rooms in shabby boardinghouses where he had previously resided. In this place, with her, Alexander had dared to hope—dared to imagine himself as husband, father, a man not unlike other men.

When Sallie regained her senses he would tell her these things, avail himself of that intimacy husband and wife are meant to share. Perhaps one day he would tell about the mermaid. No doubt Sallie would be amused at the fright it had given him.

"Did you hear a sound?" Alexander asked. "I thought I heard something. Oh, ha, ha. I suppose it is some wolf come down from the mountain to devour us. I am certain I heard a sound."

When he threw the door open, he saw nothing, no swift shadow on the hard snow. The moon had not risen and the mountains were dark jagged silhouettes. There was nothing out there for miles in every direction, and nothing inside but a woman who hated him. How had she learned to hate him so thoroughly?

Alexander had been so careful to keep from her all that was discreditable: his failures, his weaknesses, his inability to comprehend. If Sallie once learned how lost he was, she would flee.

Alexander was six when his mother died, and his father readily relinquished the boy to his elderly uncle. The afternoon they buried her, Alexander, wearing the clothes he'd worn to her graveside, accompanied his uncle onto the Hoboken Ferry for the first stage of their journey to New Haven, Connecticut, where his uncle had his ministry. Alexander's bachelor uncle was vaguely good-hearted, unaccustomed to children, and had no notion how to divert the boy from recent sad events. At the ferry slip, a hawker sold pamphlets of a curiosity even the unworldly minister had heard about, so he bought one for the boy.

The Feejee Mermaid had woman's torso and fish's tail. The pamphleteer rhapsodized about this scientific marvel, its capture by Japanese fishermen and subsequent embalming by a Hindoo of scientific bent. The remains had been obtained by a sea captain (at considerable expense to himself) and delivered to the United States, where enthusiastic scientists were to study this link between man and sea creature.

It was a brilliant August afternoon and waves sparkled and seagulls squabbled in the ferry's wake and the Hudson was cluttered with ballooning white sails. Sailors dotted a brigantine's rigging and seine fishermen hauled nets and the ferry chuffed through it all like a pug-ugly. His uncle was enraptured, but the boy, who had never been on the water before, kept his eyes affixed to the flat black words, the engravings of mermaids and Japanese fishermen and a bare-breasted wonderful sea creature who bore an unmistakable resemblance to his mother. If it was true there were mermaids, life might be all right. If it was true— if a boy's yearnings had any authority—then unloved, baffled Alexander's dreams might come true. The boy prayed that anything was possible.

His uncle had engaged a room at the Astor Hotel, but for economy they supped in a small café down the street. After their meal, man and boy climbed to the fifth floor, and after recovering his breath the minister prayed for his new ward and the repose of his sister's soul, removed his teeth, climbed into bed, and soon was snoring. The boy crept to the window, dazzled. From Barnum's American Museum, kittycorner across Broadway, a brilliant white light glared, lighting the bustling street for blocks north and south. Flags of every Christian nation lined the rooftop. Vivid paintings of elephants, kangaroos, and cobras plastered the facade.

Although a living panorama of nightlife passed along the street below—Manhattan's whores, loafers, hackmen, pickpockets, coppers, and swells—the boy saw nothing but the museum and its amazing promises.

His uncle had allowed some time for sightseeing, and being assured by Astor's desk clerk that Mr. Barnum's cabinet of curiosities was improving and not unsuitable for young minds, he acceded to Alexander's plea. First they breakfasted at the modest café, though the boy ate little. He kept the pamphlet in his lap; it reassured him. Already down the street a crowd was gathering.

Alexander towed his slow uncle toward the exhibition. Close up, the wild animal paintings were awe-inspiring: elephants, tigers, bears!

Anything might be inside this storehouse of wonders, perhaps even a creature that looked much like his mother, alive again and swimming happily through the sweet blue sea.

They paid the small admission, and though his uncle was entranced by the curiosities assembled in the cavernous three-story hallway—the eagle skins, the panoramas, the models, exact in miniature detail, of Dublin, Paris, and Jerusalem, the boy was impatient.

Up the stairs they proceeded, through rooms crammed with scientific exhibits: a stuffed buffalo, a towering brown bear, a live anaconda in one cage, live crocodile in another; passing at last into a vestibule where a floor-to-ceiling flag depicted the mermaid in nature's colors, a golden-haired creature rising through gentle waves.

The crowd pressed through into the room beyond, and Alexander Kirkpatrick gripped his uncle's hand tightly as they approached the open casket.

Inside was a wizened, hairy, blackened creature no more than three feet long. It had a fish tail. It had small furry dugs with hard black nipples. Its gums were drawn back over its sharp teeth in a plea for mercy. Thin arms, long-fingered hands had defended the creature's face in its final urgent moment. The Feejee Mermaid had died in agony.

The boy screamed and screamed, and though he would have run he had nowhere on earth to run to.

Years later in his wilderness cabin, Alexander Kirkpatrick said to his wife, "I told you I heard something outside. Listen, there is some animal scratching at our door."

Obeying their own mysterious law, great changes always come swiftly and without warning.

7

A RUNAWAY SLAVE

Near SunRise, Virginia
March 18, 1861

HORSES' HOOVES THUDDED in the snow and the iron shackles clinked over the withers of Jack the Driver's mule. Late-winter stars whirled overhead, and Samuel Gatewood thought he could pick out the curve of Orion. The moon was making its last stand over the mountain. Things didn't always turn out the way they should. A man can do what is honorable and things get worse instead of better.

The slave hunter's voice rambled among the patrollers like poison ivy through a thicket. "Ohio," he said. "That's prime. They get across that Ohio River and they sing their hosannas and they're thinkin' that's the end of it. Why, they got no more caution to them than guinea hens in a tree. Any man can walk through an Ohio darktown knockin' runaways on the head. Me and Nate—Nate partners me some—we plucked fourteen of those birds in one week, drug 'em down to our bateau, and except for one what jumped into the river and drowned himself, we brought each and every one of 'em back to his rightful master. Niggers got no sense."

Catesby Byrd rode at Samuel Gatewood's side. An hour ago, both men had been awakened by a hullabaloo outside Stratford's front door. Hullabaloos were no longer rare in Virginia. Even before Abraham Lincoln was inaugurated President, rumors and portents troubled the night air, sharp and angular as bats. Last month while the Confederate states were holding their first convention, Catesby heard unexcitable men swear—on a Bible—they'd heard cannonfire somewhere deep in the mountains.

Would Lincoln try to relieve Fort Sumter? Would the South Carolina firebrands dare to attack a federal fort?

Samuel Gatewood was the best-regarded citizen in the upper Jackson River Valley. His essays on deep plowing and improved negro hygiene had been published in the *Southern Planter*. Surely, Byrd thought, Virginians like Gatewood would find solutions to Virginia's dilemma. Secession or subservience: surely there was some other way!

At two in the morning, Byrd and Gatewood had been awakened and admitted three men to Stratford's front hall: two patrollers known to them and a slave hunter with a distressing tale.

Samuel Gatewood's lips had narrowed to white lines. "Are you entirely satisfied that the Kirkpatricks—Sallie and her husband—are harboring my runaway servant?"

The slave hunter just grinned like the devil.

Jack the Driver had begged to be excused from the hunt. "This's white man's work, Master." But when Gatewood placed a hand on Jack's shoulder, the black man went to saddle his mule.

Soft snow over frozen dirt. The road curved along the Jackson River running dark between snowcapped boulders.

"Cap'n, this sure is fine country you got." Pierce—the slave hunter's name was Pierce. "Looks like good oat ground. You grow oats?"

Samuel Gatewood wished he'd thought to wear his overcoat. He couldn't remember the last time he'd been out so late. Snowy Mountain loomed over them like some bulky, primitive god. He'd cut timber off that mountain for thirty years and his father before him and the trees still darkened the coves and you'd never know men had ever tried to civilize it.

The patrollers, Billy Stuart and Amos Hansel, rode to the rear, keeping a gap, as if they weren't really part of this and left to their own devices might have done things differently.

"How long you been seekin' this boy, Cap'n?"

"Jesse ran the day after Christmas," Samuel Gatewood thought, but didn't say. His stomach lurched unpleasantly and he didn't trust himself to open his mouth. He kneed his roan and showed Pierce his horse's tail.

Like ravens' cawing you can hear for miles, the man's voice was unaffected by distance. "I'm born on the Tidewater. Buxtons of Boxwood Plantation, they're cousins of mine, though they don't claim kin. I was raised amongst some of the finest gentry in the Commonwealth. Oh, them boys could chase the fox all day and dance all the night. Wasn't nobody get one up on the Buxtons.

"Ever time I get toward Ohio, I got to pass through these damn mountains, in and out, up and down, and don't look down into the gorge lest you'll want to puke. Not here, Cap'n. I mean this is good crop ground. Can grow anything in ground like this—oats, anything.

"Three months—that's a good while to be a maroon in the wintertime. 'Course, the other niggers feed 'em. Maroons sneak into the Quarters after dark. They slip past the patrollers. Maroons got too many places to hide. This country'd be considerable improved if you was to cut those damn trees."

"Didn't slip by us," Amos Hansel said in his deep voice. "That boy crept onto that mountain and denned up."

"Oh, they sneaky, Mister. If they wasn't supposed to slip around in the night, why you think God made 'em black, ha-ha?"

"It's winter," Amos said. Amos was the bigger patroller and the younger. He had a reputation among the colored. Sometimes a young buck slipping around when he shouldn't, if it was to visit his gal, why then Master Amos sometimes he understood that. "Snow leaves tracks," Amos said, settling himself deeper in his saddle.

The patrollers rode solid horses, beasts that wouldn't shy or balk, but wouldn't win races either. Every night the patrollers went out, dollar a night, dangling their lanterns in the faces of colored women and boys. ("Passes, let's see your passes!") Didn't need a fast horse for that work, needed a comfortable one. Under his oilskin slicker, Amos wore a jacket, woolen vest, woolen socks—two pair. Riding all night, that's where the cold bit. Feet didn't get a chance to wiggle around and warm up, so Amos Hansel wore two pair of socks.

"Tracks," Amos's partner, Billy Stuart, added. "Runaway slippin' around the plantation in wintertime, a blind man can see where he's been."

Jack the Driver had fed Jesse Burns three times from the porch of his own cabin, last time a slab of hogmeat and a cornmeal pone, but Jack wasn't the man to correct a patroller.

Jack was driver over twenty-eight men. Jack got logs to the mill at the right time and carted sleepers to the railhead before they turned blue in the stacks, and timed sawing so it didn't interfere with grinding cornmeal in November, or milling the wheat. He drove all types of men: young men, crazy as buck lambs; fulltask hands; old men who couldn't hit a lick anymore, but needed to make a show.

Jack was thinking that hunting a man was simpler than his usual work, that hunting a man was no harder than hunting a possum.

"How much farther?" Pierce asked.

"We ain't left Stratford Plantation yet," Jack said. He shouldn't talk to this man, but words escaped his mouth.

The slave hunter slowed so Jack just naturally had to come up beside him. "You the driver, boy?"

Jack's mind went blank. "Yes, Master," he said.

"You the boy supposed to know everything what's goin' on? Tell me somethin'. How come I can come here, a stranger, and set 'round Sun-Rise store for a couple hours, just chewin' the fat, and somebody says there's this Jesse who has run from the biggest plantation in the valley, and I ride around one afternoon, and directly I learn where he is, this boy who's been runnin' since Christmas?"

"It ain't our line of work, Master."

"Pierce!" Samuel Gatewood turned in his saddle. "I'd thank you to not interfere with my servants."

"Just talkin', Cap'n. Just tryin' to get the lay of the land. These fields yours too, Cap'n? Was they mine, I'd plant buckwheat in these fields. Hell, I was just wonderin' how come nobody in these parts knew where that nigger was hidin', and me, I come in here, no kin to nobody, it takes me but two days to find him. I could understand were this some no-account nigger, old or sick, but this supposed to be a prime buck, fetch eighteen hundred at Wayne Tavern's auction block, any Tuesday you bring him there. They say this buck reads and writes. Cap'n, how come a nigger can read when many a good white man can't?"

"He belonged to a schoolmaster." Catesby Byrd spoke for the first time.

"Agin' the law, teach a nigger to read."

"My wife and brother-in-law did their sums under that schoolmaster's guidance."

"Man taught niggers and whites?" Pierce shook his head, disbelieving.

Catesby Byrd had two healthy children, a frame house in the county seat, and a pretty wife he adored. Excepting only his cardplaying, Catesby was a fully domesticated man. Tonight, plucked from his warm bed, riding a frozen, moonlit road, Catesby was surprised how natural it felt. In these times, nothing was more natural than what was unnatural.

"Heard the nigger run when the cap'n sold his wench," Pierce continued. "Anytime you split buck and wench or mama and pickaninny, you never, never let 'em see the speculator till it's too late, and soon as they're away, you jail the one that's left, a week, two weeks, and don't give 'em no meat ration neither. Feed 'em porridge and dry peas, corn mush. Couple weeks, they'll forget. No different than a cow what's had her calf weaned away. Did I hear talk about the cap'n's son?"

"Mr. Pierce," Catesby said, "we are grateful for the information you have provided and you stand assured of that reward for which you bargained. We will do our duty by you, sir. Do you understand?"

Pierce muttered, "Yes, sir."

"Mr. Gatewood's son, Duncan, is a cadet at the Virginia Military Institute. I pray the Commonwealth will not require his martial skills."

"Think we'll go out, do ye?" Pierce sought safer ground.

"Most Virginians would rather stay in the Union," Catesby said stiffly.

"Naw," Pierce said. "We'll go out. You can bet on it."

The road lay blank and white beside the lightly dusted fence rails. The field between road and river was smooth as an ironed shirt. The road climbed onto the mountain and paralleled a wide bend in the river.

"This begins Uther Botkin's land," Samuel Gatewood said. "It was Kirkpatrick you said? Alexander Kirkpatrick?"

"Uh-huh. The nigger's sleepin' right in the house. Hell, everybody knows." He spat.

The patrollers' faces were stone. "Never heard a word," Amos mumbled.

"Let us be about our business," Samuel said. The road zigged up a dry wash hummocked with old snow.

The cabin was set against a clay bank. The log-and-stone structure next to the cabin was the root cellar, and the kitchen garden lay uphill, between the cabin and the springhouse. Broken cornstalks crossed the top of the garden like a religious procession. Frozen britches and a quilt hung rigid from the clothesline.

"Leona told me Sallie lost her baby," Catesby said.

"Yes, poor dear Sallie. Abigail said the poor child was crazed with grief."

"Abigail saw no sign of Jesse?"

"None."

"Nearly daylight, Cap'n." Pierce found a pepperbox pistol in his saddlebag.

"Master," Jack said. "Don't harm that boy. He big but he ain't got ary meanness in him. I never seen Jesse lift his hand to any man."

Most of the stars had been washed out by gray light on the horizon. Heat blurred the blackness above the cabin's chimney.

"Shot nigger aint' no good to anybody," Pierce said. "What you think your master'd say was I to shoot you? Think he'd thank me? Pistol's just to affright him. Cap'n, I ain't tellin' you your business, but in my experience if you jump 'em when they're asleep, they don't act up."

The cabin logs were new, the chinking smooth as pottery. Its single window faced the shallow front porch and boasted four panes of real glass. The door was rough-hewn oak.

"Amos. Billy. Do your duty," Samuel Gatewood said.

The two patrollers dismounted, and Billy passed his horse's reins to Jack. "If she ain't tied to something," Billy whispered apologetically, "she starts for home."

Both patrollers held the short bullwhips that were their badges of authority, and Amos used the butt of his to bang on the door.

"Alexander Kirkpatrick! Patrollers to inspect your premises! Alexander Kirkpatrick!"

Pierce moseyed around the side. Most of these mountain cabins didn't have a back door, but you never could tell.

"Alexander Kirkpatrick!"

A thump in the cabin—in the loft maybe. Sounded like a cat jumped off a chair.

"Bust out the window," Pierce shouted. "That'll fetch 'em."

"We wait," Gatewood said. "I have waited three months already and am no worse for it."

Amos drummed on the door. "Mr. Kirkpatrick! If you don't answer, by God I'll bust your window!"

"What do you want of us?" A man's muffled voice behind the rough-hewn door.

"Kirkpatrick, this is Samuel Gatewood. We are searching for my servant, Jesse. For God's sake, sir, open the door and let us get this disagreeable business concluded."

"This is a white man's home," the voice replied. "You have no rights here."

"Kirkpatrick, let us search and we will trouble you no further."

A hissed exchange of words inside, and a lantern flooded the window with light. The door jerked open to reveal a woman dressed in a patched blue flannel nightshirt, barefoot. In her arms she held a short-barreled flintlock musket. She dragged back the hammer with both thumbs.

"Sallie!" That was Samuel Gatewood.

"Ma'am!" That was Amos, stepping backward.

When Samuel Gatewood regarded this scrawny girl, he was ashamed. He might have stopped by this lonely cabin to see her, should have come by to mourn her baby. When Sallie was expelled from the Female Seminary, President Timberlake had written Samuel of her fall from grace. The planter had said nothing, not even to Abigail, nor had he exposed Sallie's seducer—her husband now. But Samuel should have visited. He should have. "Sallie," he said, "I must speak to your husband."

"Samuel? What brings you out so late? Night air can bring on the ague. Aunt Opal nailed Father's window shut, so deleterious is night air." Absently, she leaned her musket against the wall. "Alexander is dressing. Alexander is particular about his appearance. It is admirable in my husband, his particularity."

Samuel Gatewood handed the musket to Amos. "Let us step inside. Child, you'll catch your death."

The cabin was rectangular, low-ceilinged, a ladder to the loft overhead, fireplace on the weather wall.

Alexander Kirkpatrick was stretched out in the only chair, pants beneath his nightshirt, feet stuck out to the fire.

Coats, pants, shirts, and dresses hung on pegs. Their table was stacked with the household tinware: knives, forks, and spoons in a stoneware crock. An iron kettle and frypan were overturned on the hearth, their blackness flecked with ash. The Kirkpatricks' bed was a heap of quilts in the corner.

"First time you've honored us, sir." Kirkpatrick said. "If you'd arrived at a more civilized hour I'd have offered refreshment." He was smiling, but Samuel couldn't tell what he was smiling at. He gestured at the stout log walls. "Welcome to the home you built for us."

Samuel Gatewood said, "I did what any neighbor would."

"I should be grateful for this hovel, and damn it, Gatewood, I am. I can't tell you how disagreeable it was to sleep in my father-in-law's house: one small room with that gentleman snoring, Auntie Opal passing gas, and a wife with bony elbows. Damned if I'm not . . ."

"Your language, sir. The presence of a lady," Samuel Gatewood murmured.

"Sallie? Sallie doesn't mind. Sallie's studied Catullus. I tell you, sir, if you can read Catullus, you needn't shrink at simple hells and damns. Isn't that so, dear wife?"

Plain and quiet as a woolen cloak, Sallie held her hand to her mouth.

Samuel Gatewood pulled an overturned washtub beside the rocker and put his hands toward the dying fire. "Mr. Kirkpatrick, you were not born in Virginia? You came to us from the North?"

"I was a clerk at Buell & Peters, New York City. Export, import, letters of credit. An ill-paid clerk, I might add."

"Sir, you are not native here and cannot understand our ways. Please indulge me when I assure you that customs which may to the naive eye appear harsh are necessary for the management of our domestic institutions. Men as wise as Jefferson, Calhoun, and Clay have contributed to our debate. Better minds than yours or mine have wrestled with it. There are, if you'll permit me the term, 'Yankees' who simplify our concerns. Theirs is a world of vivid blacks and whites, ours is swirling gray."

"I have studied the Romans, sir."

"Then you will understand Virginians' willingness to defend our mores against those who would destroy them. Sir, do you require proof of my affection for Sallie?"

Alexander stretched and yawned. "Our present domicile is proof enough."

When Samuel tried to hold the younger man with his gaze, Alexander's eyes roamed, darting from lamplight to shadows. For a moment Samuel wondered if the arrogant whelp wasn't, in fact, scared out of his wits, and he spoke deliberately, as if overloud expression, might drive the man into trembling panic. "For Sallie's sake, let me construct a theory. Suppose a young couple were living in the back country in winter. If a colored man came to their door begging sustenance, should they in conscience refuse him? Perhaps they knew the man from happier times.

Perhaps he failed to confess his fugitive state and the samaritans knew nothing of it. Suppose the couple fed and housed him of Christian charity."

Alexander Kirkpatrick's dark brown hair fell down one side of his face. He steepled his fingers like a cleric. "Suppose they were wearied of each other, this hypothetical pair? Suppose the wife had nothing to offer the husband but angry silence? Tell me, sir. What can a husband do with a wife who despises him?"

Samuel Gatewood spoke as to a slow-witted child. "It is for the wife I speak, sir. It is in her that our affection resides. The husband is nothing to us." His weary voice rasped on, "In Virginia, sir, harboring a fugitive slave is a felony—a theft of valuable property. Although Mr. Jefferson designed our penitentiary, its accommodations are not salubrious and its regimen is punitive by design. Sir, am I plain?"

"You could not be more so, sir."

"This pitcher—it is drinking water?"

"Mr. Samuel," Sallie said timidly, "it will be stale. Let me fetch fresher from our spring."

Samuel poured, took a long swallow, and turned the earthenware cup in his hand as if it were fine Venetian glass. He spoke as if each word were a bomb fused and sputtering. "After I sold his . . . mate, my servant, Jesse, ran from Stratford Plantation. Since Christmastime, Jesse has been a fugitive—a 'maroon.' Pursuit was perfunctory: I trusted that when time had healed Jesse's heart, he would return home to Stratford. Provided Jesse is repentant—nay, provided he merely promises to run no more—Jesse need fear no punishment. If my servant is restored to me, nothing more need be said."

Samuel Gatewood extended a hand to Sallie, but she was shaking her head, mute, desperate, implacable. "Understanding that the matter can be treated as simple misplaced kindness, I ask you: Is Jesse beneath your roof?"

Alexander Kirkpatrick shrugged. "You must ask my wife. She may speak to you."

"Sallie, is Jesse here? If you say no, I shall be satisfied and depart. By the time I reach Stratford the cook will be bringing the cornbread from the oven. How an early-morning ride improves the appetite. Why, it is the finest thing, quite the finest thing . . ."

"Tell him, wife! Having lost my child, certainly you can lose another." Kirkpatrick yawned prodigiously.

In her dull voice, Sallie said, "You dreamed of a child as if it were salvation. A child couldn't have satisfied you any more than I can.

"Mr. Gatewood, are you sure you wouldn't prefer fresh water? It's only a moment to fetch it."

Samuel Gatewood looked down at the floor and whispered something—the word "duty" was audible. He went to the door and threw it open.

Amos Hansel was bulky with winter garments, and those garments were none too clean. A shabby, comfortable young man, Amos. His bullwhip dangled from his hand. "Ma'am," he said.

Gatewood said, "Mr. Hansel is a duly appointed officer of the county. It is his duty to regularize servants' movement, to enforce the curfew and apprehend runaways. Mr. Hansel may enter any domicile in pursuance of his duties, and in the execution of his duty Mr. Hansel may use what force he deems necessary. Once Mr. Hansel takes action, matters are out of my hands. I ask you a final time: Is Jesse in this house?"

Sallie turned to the wall.

"Very well. Amos, search the house."

"Billy," the patroller bawled. "Fetch me that bull's-eye."

Amos used his broad shoulders to lift the loft trapdoor aside, and Billy handed the lantern up to him. Clumsily, they climbed through the trap; their bootfalls and lantern light through the ceiling cracks marked their progress.

Sallie's tears washed her cheeks. The patrollers' boots clumped overhead. The first feet back through the trap wore heavy boots, the second were black and bare.

Jesse's good body was starved. His ribs stuck out, his skin was more gray than black, and his feet were cracked and raw.

"Jesse, you look like you could use some breakfast," Samuel Gatewood said quietly.

Jesse's eyes were empty. His hands were clasped in front of him.

"He was hidin' behind an old trunk," Amos said.

"He didn't give us no trouble," Billy Stuart piped.

"We were concerned about you, Jesse," Gatewood said. "It has been a bitter winter."

Jesse licked his lips. His yellow wool jacket had once belonged to Samuel Gatewood. Years ago, Samuel had worn it to a ball at Warwick. How glittering that evening, how charming the ladies! His Abigail had been the most widely admired woman there.

Pierce came in. "That your nigger, Cap'n? Big son of a bitch, ain't he? Auctioneer be glad to see a buck like him. Them Mississippi plantations got more gold than they know what to do with. All their agents be bidding for a boy like him. I heard tell of a hand just last week brought two thousand dollars. 'Course, that boy hadn't ever run away and he couldn't read nor write. They discount for writin'. Cap'n, you want, I take him with me. I keep five percent of his price and his feed comes out of my own pocket. Silas Omohundru won't do you no fairer'n that. Five percent and I'll forget the reward."

"Well, Jesse, what about it? Do you wish to be sold south?"

The black licked his lips. After wait enough to make the white men impatient he said, "No."

That quick, the haft of Billy Stuart's bullwhip tapped his cheek. "Show respect, boy. You ain't up the mountain no more."

Jesse put a hand to his face.

"What do you say, nigger, when you're talking to a white man?"

"Master," Jesse said, like they'd dragged it from his gut.

"Thought you said this boy was smart," Pierce said. "Couple days walkin' after my horse into Staunton, I venture he'll be smarter." Pierce's eyes had the hot look men's eyes get when the dogs have treed a coon and there it is, frozen in the lantern light.

When Samuel Gatewood stepped toward him, Pierce involuntarily retreated. "Mr. Pierce. As you see, your information has born fruit. You shall have your reward from Mr. Byrd."

"In gold. No shin plasters."

"Fifty dollars in gold as agreed." Gatewood called to his son-in-law. "Catesby, please settle with Mr. Pierce."

Jesse's chest rose and fell.

"Jesse, will we require shackles?"

Jesse did not respond, and Samuel's voice betrayed irritation when he summoned his driver.

Jack was the best driver in the valley, but this morning, he was just a gray-headed colored man with heavy shackles draped over his arm. He kept his eyes fixed to the floor and shuffled.

"Oh, no!" Sallie cried. Alexander Kirkpatrick uncurled himself from the rocker. The tips of his ears were red.

"Say nothing, sir!" Gatewood commanded.

The driver knelt at Jesse's feet. "I surely do hate to be doin' this, son," he said. "But you been caught fair, and now you got to make the best of it."

Each shackle clicked shut on an ankle. The short chain connecting them permitted Jesse short clumsy steps.

"Wait! Oh, wait!" Sallie rushed to her knitting basket. "He cannot go out in the snow. His feet, can't you see his feet?"

"I fell into Strait Creek and lost my shoes," Jesse said dully. "Bark tied 'round my feet do pretty good but snow gets in."

Sallie brought a pair of woolen socks, one completed, the other lacking only the toe, and knelt at the prisoner's feet. "I was knitting these for him. These are all I can do."

The shackled black supported his weight on Amos Hansel's shoulder as Sallie fitted a sock on one foot, then the other.

In the dawn light, the snow seemed dingy and gray, the horses smaller and dingier too.

Catesby Byrd's breath puffed short frozen clouds. Leafless oaks and maples seemed unwashed, the pines looked black. One last star in the west. Catesby thought it might be Venus.

They unshackled one of Jesse's ankles to lift him onto the mule, and reshackled under the mule's belly. Jack sat behind, fed the reins around the prisoner, and clucked softly. The burdened mule started down the hill.

"Thank you, gentlemen," Gatewood said to the patrollers. "I am obliged to you for this night's work."

"What about them two?" The slave hunter grinned. "Them that hid that boy? You bringin' 'em to jail?"

Samuel Gatewood rubbed his eyes. Stiffly, he mounted his gelding. "Is there nothing that can be done?" he asked Catesby.

"These patrollers—these witnesses—are officers of the court," Catesby Byrd replied. "As am I."

Samuel turned toward the modest cabin, its gaping doorway. "Catesby, I am sick at heart. Do what you must."

His son-in-law shook his head. "They have brought this on themselves, Samuel. You did all you could. Go home, friend. It has been a hard night for younger men than you."

Amos Hansel had stationed himself before the cabin door, feet stolidly apart, bullwhip clasped behind his back. Samuel Gatewood set his face for home.

8

SO GALLANTLY STREAMING

LEXINGTON, VIRGINIA
APRIL 1, 1861

FOUR HEFTY UNIONISTS strained as the tip of their flagpole soared skyward and its base slipped into its socket with a thump. One wiped his forehead on his sleeve, another rubbed his hands together: job well done.

Dr. Junkins, Washington College's president, waited calmly on the courthouse steps, speech in hand. Other Union sympathizers flanked him: storekeepers, two doctors, a cluster of lawyers, mechanics uncomfortable in their Sunday suits, half a dozen foundrymen, arms crossed over thick leather aprons.

It was a beautiful Saturday afternoon, and the plump clouds that streamed unconcernedly overhead were casting swift shadows over the United States of America, the Confederate States of America, and those states, like Virginia, that hadn't decided. The Stars and Stripes of the federal government dangled lifelessly from the brand-new thirty-foot white pine flagpole.

Lexington, Virginia, was the prosperous terminus of the James River/Kanawha Canal. Its foundries manufactured iron pots and firebacks, Monmouth Mill wove woolens for the Richmond market, potters produced salt-glaze vessels, local plantations thrived, and two colleges added a cosmopolitan air to the town. Students at Washington College and the Military Institute were fighting a war of flags. One night, some miscreant climbed Washington College's roof and replaced the Stars and Stripes with the bonny blue flag of the Confederacy. At Dr. Junkins's direction, workmen undid the exchange, only to have their federal flag stolen again two nights later. Dr. Junkins made an impassioned speech to his attentive students, but not three nights later the banner of the

Confederate States of America flew again over a college in a state which did not belong to the Confederacy. Union sympathizers now guarded the college flag at night and took up a collection for a new flagpole and flag for the courthouse.

Cadet Captain Spaulding jogged Duncan Gatewood's elbow. "Oh, they're proud of the damn thing, ain't they?"

Spaulding was a fourth-year man and Duncan's roommate at the Military Institute. A dozen of their fellow cadets—Confederates all—sprawled on the courthouse lawn. Spaulding passed Duncan a flask.

Duncan Gatewood was no prize cadet. He was unexceptional at drill and not punctilious in religious observances. His mathematical skills were modest, his computations delivered with the desperation of a commander who has just committed his last reserves, and his recitations before Major Jackson were painful to the cadets who witnessed them.

On the other side of the ledger, although he was no adept at parry and riposte, his determination at saber drill often defeated stronger opponents, and it was said that Gatewood gave as good as he got. He was a noted horseman, in Virginia where fine horsemen were commonplace. His nickname was Wheelhorse. Although the Virginia Military Institute possessed six batteries of guns, they had horses enough for only one, and during gunnery practice cadets were pressed into service in their stead. The cadets would detach the gun from its two-wheeled wooden limber cart, pretend to bring powder and shot from the limber chest, pretend to load, ram, set the elevation, prime, and pull the lanyard, then hitch to the limber again and pull the combined four-wheeled rig to a new location. One spring day, emboldened by strong sunlight and new life in the air, Duncan Gatewood began to prance and nicker. Their dour artillery instructor, Major Jackson, didn't turn a hair, "Put that wheelhorse on report," Jackson had said.

By dint of great effort and Spaulding's tutoring, Gatewood had survived the rigors of Institute education until this term, when his recitations collapsed and his maneuvers on the drill field befuddled the first-year men he commanded. Duncan became comrade to those cadets who bought whiskey from the liverymen and played cards until dawn. Not two weeks ago, Duncan had been called before the commandant, Colonel Smith, who warned him bluntly that he was risking expulsion, that only his prior record had averted that drastic step. "Sir," Smith said, "would you care to explain yourself?"

"Colonel, I am honor bound to silence." Duncan paused. "It is . . . a family matter." His face twisted painfully. Colonel Smith was a big man, ruddy-complected, equable, happiest on the drill field, tongue-tied when he delivered homilies in chapel: a man of honor. What would Smith say if Duncan told him the truth?

Colonel Smith would be shocked, disgusted, appalled—as Duncan was. Colonel Smith would find Duncan's behavior dishonorable. Colonel Smith could have no advice except that Duncan ought not to have done what he had done and could not undo. Duncan's lips were dry. "Sir, I shall endeavor to be more attentive to my duty."

The colonel drummed his fingers on his desktop. "In these times, Gatewood. In these times . . ." He looked as if he meant to say something about the looming war but contented himself with a sigh. "No more demerits then. Eh, Gatewood?"

On the courthouse steps, Dr. Junkins prepared to speak, Duncan took a jolt of raw whiskey and coughed. "Spaulding, God damn you and your popskull. I thought you Piedmont boys drank good whiskey."

"Same whiskey we've been drinking all night, Brother Rat," Spaulding observed. "You didn't object to it before. Didn't pay for any of it either." Spaulding gave him a broad wink. He turned to another cadet. "You applaud my jest, Cooley?"

"Let us pray the wind increases. We didn't come to listen to jests." Cooley said.

Spaulding lay back on the grass and watched the clouds scudding overhead.

In his shrill voice, Dr. Junkins began, "Fellow Virginians, patriots, loyal citizens . . ." A gust of wind lifted the federal flag off the pole and snapped it open. Like the pole, the flag was overlarge, as if Lexington's Unionists were countering Confederate sympathies by sheer size. The flag fluttered and popped, and Dr. Junkins looked up and produced a brisk, somewhat unmilitary salute. Other Union men uncovered. Pale faces uplifted.

When the flag put its full strain on the pole, it broke at the two-thirds mark and the top third, with flag, folded like a jackknife, then the overburdened second third snapped, and finally flagpole and flag fell on the heads of its adherents leaving only a vibrating stump.

Duncan was laughing so hard he was rolling on the ground, and Spaulding's guffaws could have been heard in the next county.

Men had been injured, and friends helped them away. Mechanics were at the broken pole examining the saw cut, three-quarters through, disguised by beeswax and sawdust. Dr. Junkins reverently bore his fallen flag indoors to safety.

"It was them," one foundryman cried, and a hundred Unionists rushed the laughing cadets. A blow took Duncan in the left eye, and black-and-red stars shot through his head. His uniform jacket tore at the shoulder.

"Cadets, form on me!" Spaulding cried. "Damn you ruffians to attack without warning!"

A gun was fired. One of the Unionists had a revolver.

"Oh Christ, Gatewood! Back to the Institute!"

The clot of Unionists and cadets rolled down Main Street. One boy was jammed into a doorway and worked over thoroughly. One excited citizen fired a revolver into the air.

"Run, you toy soldiers!"

"Traitors! Cowards! Stand like men!"

At the Institute's gates the Unionists abandoned pursuit. Cadets carried two beaten boys toward the barracks. Somebody was banging the fire bell.

"You all right, Wheelhorse?"

"Spaulding, tell me, do I still have my left eye? I pray I have my eye!"

"God yes. Damn thing's swelled shut. What did he hit you with?"

"Those cowards. Attacking unarmed men!"

Blue-and-white cadets disgorged onto the parade ground, where officers' commands and cries—"D Company!" "To me, Company B!"—might have been crows cawing, so little were they heeded while cadets gawked at their bloodied fellows.

"Oh, those traitors! Those damn traitors!"

"Unionists are murdering cadets! Turn out! Brigade of Cadets, turn out!"

More cadets poured onto the field. Some fetched ammunition from the armory. As quickly as they armed themselves, in twos and threes, they double-quicked across the parade ground toward town.

Spaulding was so excited he shook.

"Oh, I hate them! I'd use my bayonet on them!" Duncan cried.

Although staff officers were urging restraint, the cadets ignored them as they stuffed handfuls of cartridges into their pouches.

"Those bastards! Those black Republican bastards!"

"Can you see well enough to fight, Wheelhorse?"

Despite his pain, Duncan Gatewood was pleasured, as if some benefice had descended from heaven. He might kill someone. He might even be slain. What a splendid afternoon!

He and Spaulding raced after their fellows gathering in Wilson's Tavern's horseyard. A staff officer shouted, "For God's sake, boys, haven't you learned anything? These Unionists are armed and have climbed onto the rooftops. They've baited you and you have fallen for their trick."

Cadet officers took their posts and called their men into ranks. "A Company, fall in on me!"

"C Company . . ." That cadet lieutenant's voice broke. He was just sixteen.

Keen as a greyhound, Cadet Captain Spaulding peered down Main Street. Duncan clutched a cloth to his hurt eye. Spaulding pivoted to face his company. "Cadets! In nine steps, load!"

Each man bit a cartridge open, dropped it into the octagonal muzzle, ramrodded it home with a thump. Next, bullet. Ramrod again. Pointed muzzle to the sky, inserted brass cap, eased hammer to half cock.

"Fix bayonets!" Spaulding ordered, and with a slithering metallic clatter, the cadets complied. "Right shoulder shift!" The air above their ranks shimmered as the sun danced off their triangular bayonets.

Duncan was so very happy. Honor would be put to the test. Honor might be retrieved. His body was cooled by gratitude.

Colonel Smith galloped up before his bristling youthful brigade and dismounted on the tavern's mounting stile. His face was pale.

It became so quiet Duncan could hear a bee buzzing and wondered whether a bee flying so early would survive the spring night. The bee zipped and soared among the immobile ranks. It hovered at one cadet's red kepi, inspected a second. Duncan fancied he heard annoyance in the bee's buzz.

Colonel Smith stretched his hand out over the cadets. "Young gentlemen, you have received a great wrong and you have my sympathy. But this is not the way to right it. I appeal to your reason and better natures."

The bee zoomed through the sparkling forest of bayonets. Duncan knew that if one lad yelled "Forward!" or "Let's get the bastards!" the cadets would charge and nothing old Smith could do or say would stop them. He yearned to cry the fatal command but choked.

Colonel Smith repeated, "I appeal to your reason and better natures. A moral victory is finer than a bloody one. Virginia has not yet seceded, and these townspeople are fellow citizens! Follow me. I will see that you get redress."

The commandant got back on his horse and started for the Institute.

For a long hesitation, the cadets held fast. Duncan felt like vomiting. A handful fell out of the back ranks, and then the ranks crumbled entirely.

"Come on, Wheelhorse!" Spaulding threw his arm across his friend's shoulder. "It ain't so bad as all that." Spaulding backed, repelled by Duncan's futile rage. "We'll get our chance at 'em, my friend," Spaulding predicted. "All the chance we want." He offered his flask, but Duncan pushed it away.

When the cadets filled into the Institute, Colonel Smith's face had recovered its customary red hue. He fired barrages of homilies, and told them that war was likely. The cadets should save their courage for worthier opponents.

At that moment, Duncan could have killed anyone, Unionist, old Smith, anyone. Death seemed rich in opportunity.

Major Jackson made an uninspired speech, but he concluded, "If we have to fight, let us draw the sword and throw away the scabbard," and the cadets cheered until the rafters rang, including, though he was weeping too, the dishonored Duncan Gatewood.

9

A HIGH-HEADED SHEEP

SunRise, Virginia
April 7, 1861

And ye shall hear of wars and rumours of wars;
see that ye be not troubled.

—*Matthew 24:6,*
text for Preacher Todd's sermon

ALTHOUGH THE WHITE congregation of SunRise Chapel was not lacking in Christian devotion, neither was it numerous, and only the larger planters' generosity made a preacher possible. To augment his income, Preacher Todd made cabinets, pie safes, and coffins. He was not a very good cabinetmaker but he was the best in SunRise.

Gangs from Warwick and Stratford had built the chapel three years before, replacing the log house on Pheasanty Run where Presbyterians worshiped when Captain George Washington was building forts against the Indians. It was square and brick, with a squat wooden steeple and two cement columns which filled most of the vestibule. Enclosed stairwells mounted into the servants' garret, which overhung the sanctuary. Although the pews in the sanctuary had been bought in Lexington, Preacher Todd himself crafted the backless oak benches in the garret. The pulpit was carved black walnut. The piano Sister Kate Gatewood played had been donated by the Dinwiddies, though its tone (Grandmother Gatewood often stated) was not refined.

On this Sunday, Preacher Todd descanted on rumors and alarms. He reminded his congregation that Virginia remained in the union and prayed that the federal government would peacefully relinquish Fort Sumter to its rightful master, the sovereign state of South Carolina. Anxiety and distress among the parishioners were remarked. Specifically, it had come to Mr. Todd's attention that some in the congregation—even, he believed, some elders—had entered into contracts for life insurance on rented negroes. The preacher deplored this practice, inquiring, "How can we ask God's help, if we do not trust His Providence?"

His parishioners seemed contrite, so the preacher moved into his closing prayer, wherein he prayed for the congregation's sick or grieving, all magistrates and county officials, and the governor of the Commonwealth of Virginia. Missing from his petition was the President of these United States, dropped from the prayers of the SunRise congregation when Abraham Lincoln assumed the office.

Sister Kate shifted from pew to piano and, with as much flourish as she permitted herself, struck up the recessional.

Several servants in the hot, badly ventilated garret cleared their throats. Gatewood's Pompey hummed a C, and Warwick's cook laid in the harmony.

Since no Christian could object to praising the Lord, the coloreds did so with a will. Their praises overwhelmed the white congregation and the piano itself. Colored singers relished every verse, extended every harmony, and determined Sister Kate's tempo.

When their last note was sung, they remained standing while the preacher led his white congregation out, then filed down the narrow stairs.

The whites gathered at the door, the coloreds in the new graveyard. Just three stones had been emplaced thus far, and the almost empty graveyard seemed like an ill-sown field.

"Ah," Jack the Driver said, "Aunt Opal. So glad you could come here today."

In Sunday finery which squeezed her where she wasn't used to being squeezed and itched her where she wasn't used to being itched, Aunt Opal made a face.

"Is Master Uther well?" Jack inquired.

"Last I seen of him he was," she said. "More'n a fortnight past."

Jack shook his head sympathetically. "You farin' well?"

"I got myself used to that old fool bein' underfoot." She coughed. "He in Warm Springs, at Master Byrd's house, until court day." Opal inspected the throng of brightly dressed negroes as if they were strangers. "I come today to beg you to ask Master Gatewood keep Miss Sallie safe," she confessed. She added, "Generally on Sundays I washes clothes."

"Master Gatewood has already spoke up for Miss Sallie," Jack the Driver said. After a pause he added, "Course I'll talk to Master."

On the church steps, Preacher Todd and Samuel Gatewood were in serious conversation. Preacher Todd was a founder of the county militia, which Samuel Gatewood had denounced as inflamatory.

Jack said, "Auntie, I was meanin' to come see you anyway. We won't start plowing in the river bottoms until Monday next, and we can spare hands to put in your oats and corn. Is you gonna work the same ground as last year?"

"That five acres below the barn and the three acres beside the creek." She turned, "This headstone. Who is it?"

"Jim Ervin. He weren't no old man, neither. Was the bloody flux killed him. If you lack seed, we . . ."

"Why do white folks write on their gravestones? They afraid folks forget who they are? Ain't nobody write on colored gravestones."

Jack the Driver said, "Master Gatewood was thinkin' you might want somebody stayin' with you until they have the trial and Master Uther comes home."

"Jesse," Opal snapped. "He can send me Jesse. Jesse already knows where things is."

Not far away, Franky Williams was flirting with Rufus, who had a foot propped on a gravestone and was chewing on a straw. The straw bobbed up and down when he chuckled.

"Jesse locked up in the root cellar. He's run twice already."

"You ever wonder why I never took me a man?" Opal asked. "I couldn't bear it was they to sell a child of mine. Better not to have no child. This fool white child—Sallie—break my heart. I told her to her face in that jailhouse, 'Miss Sallie, you got to humble your pride. You got to get down on bended knee. You tell 'em how you and Jesse was raised under the same roof and Jesse cared for you when you was a tiny baby and when Jesse came knockin' on your door, middle of the winter froze near to death, you let him in, just couldn't help yourself. Tell 'em you know you done wrong, you're sorry and won't ever do it again, and likely they'll turn you loose.'"

"What she say?"

Opal shrugged and traced the letters on the headstone. "I don't care if I never be in no jailhouse again, 'deed I don't. They keep man and wife apart. Only one to look in on 'em is Old Uther."

"White folks scared. In Warm Springs they holdin' torchlight parades and marchin' around like soldiers. And Franky's sister, Dinah, who was give to Master Byrd when he married Miss Leona, Dinah says the white folks talkin' hard talk about Miss Sallie and that husband of hers. Miss Ophelia Simmons so feared her servants goin' to murder her in her sleep she lock them in the coal cellar every night before she goes to bed. You know Simmons's Billy? Billy a godly, cleanly man. Billy a Baptist church deacon, and he plumb hate to sleep in that filthy cellar."

Franky mock-slapped Rufus, pretending offense at Rufus's remarks. Her girlfriends raised eyebrows and giggled.

Jack shook his head. "White folks sayin' Miss Sallie and her husband are abolitionists like Mr. John Brown."

"You think my Sallie gonna stay in jail?"

"Master Samuel say they done 'felony,' same as if they was to steal Master's watch or pocketbook."

"How can you steal a person?" Aunt Opal glared at Jack until he had to look away. She muttered, "Well, it's nothin' to me. She's just a white child, none of my own."

"Sallie's husband, Master Alexander, is harmin' them; aggravatin' people the way he does."

"He plumb ruined that girl," Opal said. "Master Alexander he take up more space just sittin' than any man I ever seed. Don't know how to milk a cow, can't pour oats to the horses without spillin' 'em. Old Uther ain't the handiest man ever walked the earth, but Uther always willing. Old Uther, he pull up a chair by the fire and talk educated talk, all about Mr. Jefferson and such. Do you think that Alexander said a word? Talk goes on long as Uther is moving his mouth. Minute he quits all his fine words fall on the floor lay there looking foolish."

"I never heard anythin' good about Master Alexander. Nary one good thing."

"Sallie, she saw somethin' in that boy nobody else can see. Might be if their baby was born, it would have been different. Some men like havin' somethin' more helpless than theirself to care for. Baby'll take some men that way."

"And some men run from 'em." Rufus had his arm around Franky's waist and was whispering in her ear. Franky had carried two babies to term but neither had lived. It was supposed that Rufus had been the father, but popular opinion credited Rufus with many infants he did not deserve.

Brow furrowed, Aunt Opal considered Master Alexander. "I had a buck sheep once, called him Henry. Handsome, high-headed sheep. Oh, he was skittery—hated to be touched, and when the other sheep came to the grain he'd hide on the fringe of the woods and wouldn't come out so long as I was near. September—was a full-moon night—and them no-count Stuart boys came down the bottoms coon hunting and their dogs got in the sheep. Next morning there's three sheep tore to pieces and Henry, soon as he sees me he runs down into the corner and tries to bust through the fence. That fence is new chestnut rails six high and when he runs at 'em, he gets knocked back onto his haunches. Makes an awful sound. I can see him thinkin', 'Should I try that again?' And 'deed he does. Oh, he must have run at that fence eight or ten times tryin' to get away from what wasn't chasin' him before he broke his neck. Oh, he was a good-lookin' buck. High-headed."

The Gatewood buggy drove away. Pompey, the driver, did not deign to notice lesser mortals.

"Scared out of his wits," Jack the Driver opined.

"I don't know he was scared. I think something was wrong in his mind. I swear I could see that sheep take thought, makin' up his mind each time to try one more time what hadn't ever worked before and didn't make no sense anyway."

10

AT NIGHT THE COFFLE RESTS

BLACKS FORD, TENNESSEE
APRIL 8, 1861

THEY WERE THREE days east of Memphis on the Big Sandy River. Ellam wanted to see Memphis. He'd heard things about Memphis. Wasn't anything you couldn't find in Memphis. Ellam smacked a mosquito on his cheek. You'd think bugs'd learn that it didn't pay to fool with Ellam Omohundru.

The light was yellow over the Big Sandy and the sky was big, and Ellam wondered why it was so big here and not so big back in Virginia. Already, the slave jail was lost in shadows.

Uncle Silas wanted to get to Vicksburg before the cotton planting. Prices were lower in the winter, when you had to feed a slave and you couldn't get much work out of him, and they'd drop later in the summer, after the Delta planters had all the hands they needed. Ellam belched. Brown beans and cornbread. Wasn't much better than what the niggers ate, except niggers didn't get no ham and they sure as hell didn't get no brandy. Ellam scratched a lucifer across the doorpost and waited until the sulfur stink burned itself out before he lit his cigar. He put a thick boot on the bench set outside the inn for travelers to wait for the ferry or simply admire the sweep of the river, whence the bugs were coming. Cigar smoke helped some.

Ellam Omohundru was a young man with an untested conviction that men of quality would rise naturally in society and that he was among their number. He identified his wishes with needs and needs with rights. Let that goddamned Lincoln try to relieve Sumter. Boys like Ellam Omohundru would give him what for!

Uncle Silas and the others were still inside, digesting politics with their dinner. When you did something—like those South Carolina boys were doing—you pulled all the politics along behind you. Politics was what filled the time between doing something.

Ellam was twenty-two. He wanted to see Memphis. He'd wanted to see Richmond too, but Uncle Silas said they'd get a better price in Tennessee. Uncle had spent the winter putting this coffle together, fifteen prime hands, not one of them over thirty. No lungers, no runaways, no whip scars. Only three missing fingers and one missing eye among them. Uncle Silas walked them across Tennessee like they were on a Sunday picnic: twenty miles a day, meals morning and evening, and under roof any night it threatened rain. It wasn't going to rain tonight, Ellam could tell that, but there they were in the slave jail, which had been a horse barn from the stagecoach days. Now the railroad was putting paid to that line of work. One day they'd have slave jail cars on the railroad and the coffles'd be a thing of the past too.

For two weeks, Ellam had been eyeballing that high yellow girl with the baby. Watched the way she moved, how she held her head so high. Saw her breasts when she gave her baby suck. He liked it and didn't like it: liked the breasts, didn't like the way they were being used, no different from a milk cow's udder. Today, she caught him spying on her, and when the baby was done, she took forever to cover herself. Maggie was her name. Colored girls started younger than white girls did, on account of being more primitive, with stronger animal natures.

The jailer had carefully combed gray hair, a neatly patched vest, and braces embroidered with yellow and black squares.

"They ain't doin' nothin'," he said, gesturing to the judas hole in the door. "One of 'em's prayin', but most the rest are just lyin' in the straw. Last week I watched a pair of them doin' it in there. They was just walkin' from Clarksville to Memphis, so they had plenty of strength. Didn't take long, no longer than a stallion on a mare, just five minutes or so, and I couldn't see much on account of the lantern light don't hardly reach, but I could tell they was doin' it. People on all sides of them, but they didn't care. They was married and goin' to different masters, maybe that's why they didn't care. I'm Oliver. Mighty pleased to meet you." The gray-haired simpleton stuck out his hand.

Ellam kept his hand in his pocket.

"Less'n I let you, you can't watch 'em," Oliver said. "They might be your niggers, but this is my brother's jail."

"I'm Ellam," Ellam said, looking down to the river, where clouds of bats were sweeping the water. "This is my Uncle Silas's coffle. He brings a big coffle every spring. 'Buy in the fall and winter, sell in the spring,' that's what my uncle believes. This is my first trip. I was hoping we'd sell 'em in Memphis. Forrest and McMillan has the biggest slave and horse auctions in the west, and I'd surely admire to see 'em. But Uncle Silas says no, we'll get a better price in Vicksburg. I got to inspect them every night. It's my job." He laughed. "I tuck them in just like they was babies."

Oliver lit a lantern, and the two went inside. The jail was squat and sprawling. The square openings cut in the stone to pass air and light to horses were barred with iron rods.

Ellam wrinkled his nose. "God," he said. "God damn."

"They get new straw in here once a week, and there's a thunder jug every three rings."

"It's them," Ellam said. "It's just them."

Oliver giggled.

One side of the jail was a forty-foot pen bedded with straw. At intervals, rings in the stone wall anchored the blacks' chains. The other side was horse stalls, piled high with broken hubs and axles. A lantern hung from a low beam.

"We didn't want too many lanterns for fear of fire," Oliver whispered.

A young black was kneeling, facing the stone wall, praying. Every evening, indoors or out, after supper, before he slept, he got on his knees for praying. Never gave any trouble, never talked back, never bucked or tangled his chains. He'd come from Fluvanna County.

Those that weren't asleep eyed the two white men. None of them said a word, but their eyes followed every move. A woman was squatting on a chamber pot. When she finished, she shoved a handful of straw underneath her skirt to wipe herself. She replaced the chamber pot against the wall and lay down on her side.

The high yellow sat back to the wall, baby swaddled in her lap, legs stuck out in the straw. Ellam wondered why she had such skinny legs. "What's this?"

Oliver swung a door open. "Was a tack room. Now we just use it case one of 'em's sick so the others don't catch it. Sometimes when we got a runaway we keeps 'im in here." The room had a high barred window, and a straw pallet on the stone floor.

Ellam took the lantern from Oliver's hands. "That's all I'll be needin' you for."

"You intendin' to stay in here? With them?"

"For a little while."

The young-old man's pale eyes wandered the shadowy room. "You're gonna do it? Which one you gonna do it to?"

"Go on, now. You can see your way to the door. Plenty of light."

"I'm supposed to stay right here. Particular if anybody's with 'em. We had one to run away once and it was a good thing the patrollers caught him or brother would have had to pay for him."

Ellam turned his back before rummaging in his pocketbook for a dime. "Here. I won't be but half an hour."

Solemnly Oliver turned the dime in the lamplight. "Some fellows can do it two or three times."

"Go on. Get out of here. Close the door behind you."

No sooner was the door pulled shut than the judas hole opened and darkened as Oliver pressed his face against it.

Quietly, Ellam detached the high yellow's chain. The woman looked at him.

"You'll want somebody to care for the baby," Ellam said.

Her eyes were big, and in the lantern light, black as well holes.

Wordlessly, a woman held out her arms, and Ellam passed the baby to her, careful not to step on anyone's legs. He could have sworn the baby was awake, but it didn't cry. It smelled cleaner than he expected. The woman cradled the baby in her arms and crooned as Ellam tugged on the high yellow's chain and she came to her feet, all in one motion. He held the door of the tack room open, and when he closed it behind them, he set the lantern on a high shelf and wrapped his end of the chain around his wrist.

"I'm Ellam," he said.

"Yes, Master."

"And you're Maggie."

She had her fingers laced in front of her. Long, delicate fingers.

"Why you lookin' at me like that." She looked down at her feet. Her feet were pretty good-sized and flat.

"How old are you?"

"I was born the year before the railroad came to Millboro."

"Where the hell's Millboro? I never been to Millboro."

"Millboro, that be where they ship our flour, and we saw up a mess of sleepers for them too. Stratford Plantation, that's my home." A tear started down her cheek, and she sniffled.

"Stop that. You're goin' to have a new home now. You and your baby."

"They gonna sell us together, Master? I'd be ever so grateful was you to sell us together. I'd fetch a better price too, on account of everybody know I'm a breeder."

Ellam smiled a tight smile. "Woman for one price, infant for another. Might fetch more that way."

"Master, that'd be hard! Little Jacob here is all I got to remember his father by!"

Ellam held his key ring to the light to select the key that released her chain. There was a scurrying outside the barred window, like a possum scratching around.

"I might ask Uncle Silas to sell you together," Ellam said. His throat was curiously tight, and he swallowed. "Uncle Silas, he ain't so wellborn as me, 'n' he'd do most anything to please me. He's teachin' me the business now, but one day I'm gonna run it by myself. Buyin', sellin', travelin' everywhere I want. Hell, maybe I'll get up to Millboro."

"Stratford's only a half day farther. First there's Warwick Plantation and then Dinwiddie's and then Stratford. After Stratford there's nothing but Snowy Mountain. Stratford last and the best. Oh, you'd want to stay at Stratford Plantation once you got there, Master."

"Maybe I would and maybe I wouldn't," Ellam said. "I don't suppose you been to Charlottesville."

She shook her head.

"Bridgewater? New Market?"

She hadn't.

"Well, there's plenty of towns and plenty of goings-on. Two days hence we'll be passing near Memphis. I might just tell Silas to walk the coffle by himself while I go in for a time. I just might do that."

"What's gonna happen to us, Master?"

Ellam shrugged. "Most will sell as field hands. Some of those Mississippi plantations got two hundred servants planting and hoeing and picking cotton. Cotton's the South's biggest crop!"

"I'm a house nigger," she said brightly. "Ever since I was a pickaninny, I served Mistress Abigail Gatewood. I can wash and iron, I can brush a lady's hair, a hundred strokes. I can help her to dress, and while she's out I can clean her boudoir so it looks like nobody's ever laid down in it. I know which are First Families of Virginia and which ain't. I can sew and do fancy work."

"Can you cook?"

"No, Master," imploringly, "but I can learn. Miss Abigail many time say she never knew no gal to learn so quick as me."

"You're pretty."

Another thud outside the window. Awful big for a possum.

She stared at her feet. She scuffled her feet. She fixed her eyes to his. "That may be so, Master, but it's never been anything but sorrow to me. Many a time I wished I was born with a cast in my eye or a twitch in my shoulder or a foolish look." And as she described these maladies, she acted them out, casting a bad eye, twitching at will, grimacing like a fool.

Her mimickry of a demented woman was so accurate Ellam found himself grinning. He hadn't come to laugh. "Oh, you're right pretty all right. Light as you are, you're prettier than many a white girl." His ears tingled. He licked his lips. "You want two bits?"

She looked around the walls of the room as though the walls had messages. Her eyes roamed from the ceiling beams to the straw-strewn dirt floor, never once looked at the pallet on the floor. "I brush Miss Abigail's hair a hundred strokes every morning. Miss Abigail say she never had anybody like me. One night, after a ball, two years ago, she come upstairs and I help her into her sleeping things and Miss Abigail said she cared for me same as a daughter. 'Course the gentlemen always drink a little at a ball, and I expect ladies do too."

"You ain't her daughter."

"No, Master. But Auntie Opal says I'm the daughter of Reverend Mitchell, who was drowned when he ordered his buggy drove into the Jackson River when it was in flood."

"You got a preacher for a pa?"

"I'm not sayin' he was, and I'm not sayin' he wasn't. It's what's been told to me."

"Preacher lyin' down with a nigger slut. Think of that."

She was examining her hands, as though surprised at her pale translucent skin. "Master, I don't need a quarter dollar. I got nothin' to spend it on."

"Two bits is the highest I'll go. I don't got to give you nothin'."

She was looking at her feet again. "Master," she said softly, "I got me a husband."

"You jumped the broomstick with some buck. That don't make him your rightful husband."

"It wasn't him I was thinking of. Please, Master."

"You mean you got two sweethearts? Well then, Missy, you're about to get you a third one. And this one might do you some good. Might be I could tell Uncle Silas to sell you as a house servant. Might be you could keep your baby."

A clattering sound outside, a scrape against the windowsill.

"Well then," he said, taking a step to her. "Well then."

Out of her clothes she was pretty enough, but she didn't hold herself like she was pretty and didn't lie like she was pretty either. She was dry, and she kept her eyes closed until Ellam told her to open them and then she fixed them somewhere overhead. When he was done, still kneeling between her legs, he had an uneasy feeling, and goddamned if that fool wasn't peering at him through the window, where he'd piled boxes on top of an old whiskey barrel so he could see everything. The fool was grinning to bust.

Next morning Ellam woke with a powerful erection and it seemed his member was longer than it had been before. Maybe doing it stretched your member. He hadn't heard about that, not even from the Summerfield boys, who had girls in the Quarters and used to describe everything they did and how it was when they did it. Uncle Silas was already up. The sun poured through the windows and scrubbed the room. Ellam yawned enormously. The sun said it was half past six. Uncle Silas would be out feeding the niggers. He always fed the niggers before he ate himself. When Ellam sat up he could smell her on him, kind of a fishy smell. He wondered how long that'd last.

He clumped down the narrow stairs into the ordinary, where a long table was set with tin plates and coffee mugs. Platters—already considerably picked at—held ham and bacon. Another platter had a half-eaten chicken. Cornbread still in the pan, jugs of water and coffee. Most of the plates were dirty. Drovers were always in a hurry to get on the road.

He'd loaded his platter before his Uncle Silas came in, so skinny that from a distance you'd swear he was just a boy. His hair was combed straight back off his head and fastened behind in an old-fashioned queue. The spectacles he'd taken to wearing jutted out of his vest pocket.

Ellam was lifting a forkful of ham to his mouth when Uncle Silas smiled at him, laid his hand on the back of Ellam's chair, and upended it. One second Ellam was at table, next second he was flat on his back with an aching head where he'd knocked it against the wall and Uncle Silas had dumped his plate on him, ham, cornbread, and all.

Ellam was so confused, he thought, "I can't eat that now."

Deliberately Uncle Silas lifted up the pitcher of coffee, dunked his finger in it, testing for heat, and finding it tepid enough for his purposes, poured it over his nephew's head.

"What the hell, what the hell!" Ellam sputtered.

Uncle Silas's smile returned. Things had been pleasanter without it. "You look like a fool, boy. Hell, you are a fool. Have more breakfast." He dumped the cornbread on his nephew.

"Now wait a damned minute, Uncle Silas. What's gone wrong with you?" Ellam scuttled into a corner as the smaller man stalked him.

Silas said, "Have I got your attention?" His voice was so mild. "That was your father's trouble. My brother, my wellborn, legitimate brother, ran good businesses into the ground. And it wasn't for lack of sensible men, including myself, warning him to watch his step, that people weren't as witless as he thought they were; they expected value for what they bought and a fair price for what they sold. You'd think that wouldn't be beyond a grown man's powers of comprehension. But, by God, your father sold shoddy and paid late in Virginia and he did no better in Tennessee and God knows what he's doing out in Missouri, because I surely do not. My poor bankrupt brother never could pay attention. Oh, he was kind enough, kind to his servants, kind to his wife, the only Omohundru who ever claimed kinship to me. My legitimate brother's creditors never thought he would cheat them until he did. I cannot count the times I sat down to explain matters and your father'd smile and say, 'Yes, Silas,' and in that moment perhaps he did understand. In the next instant, sir, the cloud would lift from the sun or a pretty girl would walk by and he'd forget every word I ever told him. I trust you will show more improvement."

"Yes, sir, Uncle Silas."

"Now, pay attention." Ellam cautiously dropped his hands from his face. A servant wench came in and knelt to clean up the mess. "I am a slave speculator. Do you know what it is I do?"

"Yes, Uncle Silas."

"The hell you do!"

Ellam clapped his hands over his face and peeked through his fingers.

"I ride the backroads of Virginia and North Carolina and I let it be known that I'm seeking prime negroes, and I wait. I wait until word gets around that I'm in the neighborhood in a buying frame of mind and I wait until somebody's banker says no, no, he can't lend any more money on the mortgage. Or the new heir, who is feeling his oats on account of he hasn't distinguished between what he has earned himself and what someone else has given him, that heir gets to playing cards with fellows who are older than he is and have seen his like before. After dark, comes the knock on my door and there's this young gentleman who I never saw before and might not see again, and Christ, he's got to have a thousand dollars then and there, because he's got to get back to the game, and he points to his carriage and he says, 'You see my coachman?' "

Uncle Silas spoke to the servant wench. "Bring more hot coffee. My clumsy nephew has spilled it.

"Now, it would be easy to inspect this prime negro and offer half what he's worth, and you know that heir would curse me, take the money, and get back to his game. You'd take that advantage, wouldn't you, boy?"

"No sir, Uncle Silas."

"Yes, you would. Yes, you would. Your father he would have too. Your father would have bragged on it. And the young fellow he beat, when he wakes up in the morning and is grabbing his head, which is fat as a slaughter hog, you think that young fellow's going to say, 'I brought that on myself,' or 'I would have lost that money anyway'? No. He will cry out to any man who will listen, 'Silas Omohundru has cheated me.' Because, boy, it is a sight easier for a man to admit to being robbed than admit to being a fool. And when I come back into that neighborhood next year to buy, well, what do I find? *What do I find, boy?*"

"Nobody'll sell to you?"

The servant set one jug of coffee close to Uncle Silas, and he thanked her and said no doubt she'd wait to clean the table because they weren't quite finished with their business.

"What's a negro wench, boy?"

"Sir?"

"We got eight wenches, fourteen bucks, two infants. What are they all?"

"They's what we buy and sell?"

Uncle Silas sighed and poured himself a cup of black coffee, and Ellam kept his eye on it for fear it'd be flung at him.

"They're human beings, boy. They can smile and they can frown. They get angry as we do. They can grieve. God said there should be the white man and the black man and the white man should have the care of the sons of Ham, because they can't look after themselves. Some idiots look at that fact and conclude, 'Niggers just another beast in the field,' but, boy, they're not. Some can read and some can preach and some play banjos and jump Jim Crow. And some of their women are the prettiest things a grown man ever saw. Many white gentlemen see no harm in lying with a negress, since if she gets a baby, it'll be lighter than the mother, and if it's a girl, perhaps even light enough for the fancy trade, like that Maggie woman you were diddling last night."

Ellam opened his mouth to deny everything but closed it again when he saw Uncle Silas's eyes.

"Good," Silas said, setting his cup down. "Might be you can learn. What will that wench bring in Vicksburg, herself and the child?"

The boy shook his head.

"Twenty-four hundred dollars, maybe more. Man buys her, sets her up, and she brings in ten dollars a night, every night except when she's bleeding and Sundays. Fancy woman costs two hundred a year to keep, so after one year, he's got his money out of her and he's still got the pickaninny if it lives. Now, boy, pay attention! Suppose you're a buyer for the fancy trade, what do you want?"

"Pretty. Light-skinned. Young."

"Anything else?"

"I don't know, Uncle Silas."

"You are looking for a girl who is pert and gay. What kind of girl is Maggie?"

"Sir?"

"You diddled her. What's she like?"

"Like you said, sir. Right pert."

His uncle shook his head. "Did you talk to her or just stick it into her?"

"She seemed pert to me," Ellam said stubbornly.

"That girl hasn't known more than one, maybe two men in her life, and she's got a way of speaking sometimes you can't tell if she's a white woman or not. You're lucky you caught that girl young. Two or three years hence, if you try to stick it in her, she'll cut it off and hand it to you. Until we get to Vicksburg, you chain Maggie every night and don't come near when she's got anything sharp in her hand. You gave her something to think about, boy, and I'll not thank you for that. In Vicksburg, when we put her on that block and tell her, 'Sing and dance, Maggie, so you fetch a good price,' you know what she'll be thinking? 'Why should I dance and act pert when some stupid white boy stick his thing in me anytime he want?' She'll stand on that block like she's cross, and you know what the buyer for the fancy trade will be thinking? He'll think that maybe she won't bring ten dollars a night, and if some customer acts up with her, maybe Maggie will scratch his eyes out. That buyer will say to me, 'Silas, that's a fine high yellow you sellin' there, Silas, but she seems a handful. I'll give you fifteen hundred for her.' "

"Oh hell, Uncle. I didn't mean nothin' by it. I didn't hurt her any."

Silas rubbed his forehead. "God forgive you, you're no smarter than your father." He thought for a moment. "What did I promise you for coming with me and helping me?"

"Hundred dollars."

Uncle Silas smiled, and Ellam sort of wished his uncle hadn't smiled. "What's that wench worth?"

"Twenty-four hundred dollars."

"That's right. And in lieu of paying you, I'll give you every cent over sixteen hundred dollars she brings, herself and the baby. Nephew, you might get rich. Boy, you might just change your luck."

11

THE PLUNGER

GOSHEN, VIRGINIA
APRIL 18, 1861

"GENTLEMEN," PROVISIONAL THIRD Lieutenant Duncan Gatewood exclaimed. "Thank God for secession. We live a new life."

Catesby Byrd interlaced his fingers behind his head and cricked his neck from side to side. "I'd rather have new cards," he said. "Spaulding, what time do you show?"

The florid-faced young man extracted a silver hunter. "I fear we are in violation of the Sabbath. It is ten past four—if the watch keeps good time."

"It did when I last wound it," Catesby muttered. "You military gentlemen have cleaned me out."

Duncan grinned. "What's mere wealth compared to our prospects? Catesby, the prospect of military glory invigorates a man."

Catesby eyed him somewhat sourly. "A king of hearts would have invigorated me wonderfully. He or his diamond brother. Lord knows there were two of them in the deck, unemployed."

"Catesby," his young kinsman objected, "our Commonwealth of Virginia has seceded and is the brightest star in the new Confederate Nation. Like our forefathers, we create a new nation. Patriots are rushing to the colors throughout the South"—he gestured solemnly at the invisible host—"while you fret about a game of cards."

Three men, two in cadet uniforms, lounged in the empty saloon of the hotel that served Millboro passengers of the Virginia Central Railroad. They'd been playing cards since Catesby Byrd made his surprise appearance last night after dinner.

"I'd not fret," Catesby said, "if you returned my watch. I had no notion your studies included the mechanics of gulling kinfolk."

"Wheelhorse and I did play some cards at the Institute," Spaulding said, smiling. "I've many a demerit for cardplaying. How innocent that all seems—demerits! How we shall miss the dear old Institute."

Duncan stretched. "I believe there's daylight in the sky. Remember that damn train when we went to hang old John Brown? It was my first train ride, and I was devilish sick. I remember when we finally reached Relay House, a hundred cadets rubbed the sleep from their eyes and dined on tea and hot bread. And afterward, when we huffed and puffed along the Patapsco: the sun burned the fog off the river and none of us knew whether a thousand armed abolitionists were coming to free Brown. Spaulding, that was the finest morning of my life."

The older youth yawned. "Railroad journeys can be tiresome. Richmond isn't a hundred twenty miles, but my Christmas travels took every bit of thirteen hours."

Duncan's face darkened. "God, how I wish I had accepted your invitation. I wish . . ."

Spaulding waited for more, but Duncan fell silent.

"Why not travel to Richmond by canal?" Catesby asked. "You could float majestically down the James while ladies on shore wave lacy handkerchiefs and swoon at your martial splendor."

"The best regiments are filling up," Spaulding said briskly. "I'd hoped to join my cousin A. P. Hill, but his regiment is already chock-full. Duncan, you'll remember I attended Cousin Hill's wedding. Lord, how those regular officers can drink! Cousin has commended us to the 44th Infantry—its adjutant and lieutenant colonel are Institute men."

"Such laudable ambition," Catesby drawled. "Duncan, wouldn't you rather exercise your appetite for mayhem in the company of your familiars? I'm sure Spaulding here is a good fellow, but the regiment he hopes to join will be strangers, none from our mountains."

"Catesby, I damn well will not ever again have aught to do with my previous acquaintances!" Duncan's young face was cold. In a lower tone he added, "You know my reasons."

Catesby coughed. He shuffled the cards, once, twice. He turned to Spaulding. "Do you think this war will last long enough for you to get into it?"

"God, I pray it will! General Johnson has already seized Harpers Ferry, cut the National Road, the canal, and the Federals' rail link from the west. I worry he will take Washington before we get a chance at them!"

Catesby sighed. "Duncan, you're a horseman. Why not the cavalry?"

Spaulding answered for his friend. "Oh, the cavalry's the place for a swaggerer. If a man wants to cut a figure, there's nothing like a fine horse to help him do it. But battles aren't decided by cavalry. The infantry carries the day. Our regiment will want good noncommissioned officers, too. You are a patriot, Mr. Byrd. Why not accompany us?" Spaulding consulted his new watch. "Our train departs in a quarter hour."

"My wife and two children are hostages to fortune."

"Catesby, surely you'll sign up! The enlistment is only a year. Think how awful you'll feel afterward if you miss the fun."

A shadow crossed Catesby's face. "You think so, Duncan? Wars have a way of getting away from men."

"Well, this war is going to get away from Mr. Lincoln. The Federals can't whip our gallant boys."

Spaulding slapped the table and upset his tumbler. "Duncan, that is the spirit!" He pushed his bench from the table and swept spilled whiskey onto the floor with the edge of his hand. "Is that the locomotive bell? I thought I heard a bell."

Duncan went to the door and leaned into the darkness.

"Yesterday," Catesby noted in his quiet voice, "I came hoping to dissuade my young kinsman from rashness. When we met, at this place, I found him already celebrating the rashest thing imaginable. . . ."

Duncan said, "I cannot go home to Stratford, Catesby. You know that."

"I know that you are young and occupy a place in my affections!"

"And you do like to play cards. Admit it, Catesby—you do!"

"Yes, young friend, I am partial to cardplaying. Cardplaying promotes conviviality. Tonight I am fortunate I didn't wager my horse."

Spaulding laughed too loudly. "Mr. Byrd, your horse is happy you haven't wagered him! You are a plunger, sir. I know you because I am a plunger myself. Wager on anything and devil take the hindmost, eh?"

"Sir, risk makes the time pass faster."

"Catesby . . ."

Catesby raised a hand. "One last entreaty, Duncan. If you can't think of me, won't you consider your sister and mother?"

The younger man placed his hand on the older man's shoulder. "Catesby, I am thinking of them, can't you see? Surely you can understand! If I go away, they will forget me. I will no longer shame them."

Spaulding was listening somewhat distractedly as he went into his pockets and plucked banknotes from here and there. He dipped into his purse for two gold coins, which he employed to weight the bills. He added watch and chain. He shuffled the cards and pushed the deck toward Catesby, where it sat, smug and mysterious as a heathen idol. "Sir, in the course of this evening I have satisfied myself as to Gatewood's good opinion of you. I think I could enroll no better man in our new regiment. Let us decide the issue by wager. Win, and this"—he gestured at the money contemptuously—"is all yours. Lose, and you're in for the fun. Let a single card decide."

Attorney and responsible family man Catesby Byrd felt a spasm of loathing for Cadet Spaulding. Catesby considered that Cadet Spaulding resembled a white Leghorn rooster which had once tormented his daughter, Pauline, rushing at her whenever she went with her basket for eggs. He'd made, Catesby recalled, a rubbery supper.

The locomotive bell was drawing nigh. Its clatter was unmistakable. Carelessly, Catesby Byrd reached out and revealed the fatal card.

12

CONSCIENCE

RICHMOND, VIRGINIA
APRIL 24, 1861

ON APRIL 22, in Warm Springs, Virginia, Judge Robert Ayres sentenced Sallie and Alexander Kirkpatrick to terms of five years in the state penitentiary in Richmond. Nine days previously, Fort Sumter had surrendered, and shortly thereafter, Virginia joined its fortunes to the new Confederacy.

Dismissing Uther Botkin's heartbroken pleas for leniency and Samuel Gatewood's stated conviction that the Kirkpatricks had acted from Christian motives, the judge observed that neither felon demonstrated contrition and Mr. Kirkpatrick had, throughout the proceedings, treated the court with grave disrespect. Furthermore, although, since legally he was a nonperson, Jesse's testimony could not be taken, Judge Ayres understood that the slave was also unrepentant. "These times do not permit mercy to those who, if not abolitionists themselves, are the abolitionists' willing accomplices," Judge Ayres said.

Since the county possessed no adequate conveyance for transporting felons to the penitentiary, the sheriff hired a closed carriage, with a canvas partition between the seat where Alexander Kirkpatrick and his warder sat and that of Sallie and the warder's wife.

Under command of silence, the warder's wife read her Bible and dozed. Below the curtain the men's footwear could be seen: Alexander's dress shoes, his laces clumsily spliced, next to the warder's blunt brown boots. Sallie avoided looking at them; their mute testimony distressed her. Sometimes Sallie wished she'd been less defiant, had uttered mealymouthed lies in the courtroom; but when she'd wavered, a hot coal at her core whispered that betraying Jesse was to betray herself, to betray the sweet hopes she'd had for her own poor infant.

At the trial, Alexander had shown his customary contempt.

The streets of Lexington were thronged with men in bright militia uniforms. Had Sallie not been making this melancholy journey, she would be knitting socks for soldiers or piecing brave new flags. She smiled, at her own foolishness: the quality of her needlework restricted her to sock patriotism.

The warder's wife pulled down the shade, so they traveled in musty dimness. What was the woman thinking—that Sallie would cry for rescue?

As the carriage rolled south, the seasons accelerated. There'd been redbuds still on Warm Springs Mountain; in Lexington the dogwoods were in flower. Outside Buena Vista they passed through lilac groves aromatic and spicy, and in Lynchburg peach trees were faintly pinked with blossom.

They tarried overnight in that city's jail.

The roads were dry. They crossed the James at Scottsville and again at Bremo Bluff. Sallie felt like a chip upon the current, willy-nilly in the spring flood. She had always been busy and had no knack for indolence, but now her only duty was obedience—"Step out, here, ma'am," or "My wife will accompany you to the johnny house."

The carriage rattled past red clay soil, turned and glistening, awaiting the transplanting of tobacco. In the warm and hazy afternoon, Sallie remembered the baby she had hoped to bear. Alexander had wanted the baby as much as she. The baby was perhaps the only thing Alexander wanted. He had neither sought a new position nor embraced his new circumstances. She did the chores, she brought in the firewood. If Sallie took the trouble to command him, Alexander obeyed—but nothing called to him. Sallie had come to think their baby would disappoint him no less than she had. Alexander expected something . . . extraordinary, a baby who'd give a grown man everything he lacked. Alexander had been so certain the infant would be a son.

Sallie Kirkpatrick had loved her husband for one year and six months. From that day she first heard him speak so brilliantly about the Roman poets until the day after she lost their baby.

As was her custom in those winter days, Sallie had been taking a thoughtful walk beside the Jackson River puzzling about Alexander. That he was intelligent she didn't doubt, but if he was learned, he kept his learning hidden. Ardent in their first weeks together, Alexander was ardent no more. Sometimes Sally fancied he'd simply forgotten marital pleasures were possible.

When the great pain hit her belly, Sallie dropped to her knees, and when bloody fluid started running out of her, she was terrified. She stumbled home quick as she could, trying to hold the wetness inside of her.

The first day Alexander kept her in bed, brought her broth and wash water, helped her to the chamber pot. That night he sat up, staring into the fire. The morning of the second day, Sallie was overwhelmed by a wash of grief so strong it almost choked her. It was her fault: she had failed to eat properly, should have shunned exercise. She said, "Alexander, I should never have walked so much. I should have known better."

He had looked up from his book with an odd smile. "What would we have done with a baby?" He never mentioned the baby again; and from that moment, Sallie's husband was a stranger to her.

The James was blue-green before it tumbled white through its rapids, and in the soft light of a spring rain the prisoners' carriage rolled across Mayo Bridge into Richmond. When the warder's wife reached to tug down the blind, Sallie gripped her wrist with such ferocity that the woman gasped and rubbed her wrist. Sallie ignored her glare. That river, the rain falling on the canal barges, it was so beautiful Sallie thought her heart might burst. On Cary Street they fell in behind a procession of conveyances: goods wagons loaded with young men, some uniformed, some not, many armed, some not. The young men viewed each other expectantly, and spontaneously one or another wagonload would raise a hurrah. The boardwalks near Capitol Square were jammed with men indifferent to the light rain, curious about each other and every passerby. Although Richmond's homes were shuttered tight, their balconies were filled with gawkers, and the veranda of the Spottswood Hotel couldn't have held one more soul.

"Hurray for Jeff Davis! Hurrah!"

"The Constitution, hurrah!"

Cries rose here and there like the first tremors of a volcano, venting steam, toss-potting rock: anticipating the greater crisis to come. At each hurrah's conclusion, those who'd cheered would shake hands all around as if congratulating themselves upon their invention.

Bold youths dashed into the street to peer through the carriage windows. Surely such a stately conveyance must bear persons of importance, another brave general coming to fight for the Commonwealth, a senator perhaps, resigned in Washington to take up his post with the brave new government. Though the Confederacy's official capital was still in Montgomery, soldiers and office-seekers made their way to Richmond, knowing already what was bound to be.

The rain washed the new green of the leaves and the brownstone housefronts and made the cobblestones glisten. When Sallie shut her eyes her captor's hand flashed to the shade and drew the coach into dimness.

Smoke from Tredegar's ironworks lay low in the gutters and was stirred into full pungency as the carriage trundled toward the stone-and-red-brick prison on its solitary eminence above the James. The blind face of the prison fronted the river. The driver answered a challenge and his horses clopped through the sally port into the courtyard like a birth reversed—out of the daylight and air into the darkness of dependency, unknowing, and fear.

The door jerked open, and Alexander and the warder stepped down. The warder's wife parted the canvas curtain, and the women faced the empty bench where their husbands had sat. Like their own bench, it was slightly softened with thin black cushions.

They have me now, Sallie thought. I am theirs.

13

"REMARKS BY A MOUNTAIN AGRICULTURALIST (SAMUEL GATEWOOD)"

as printed in the *Southern Planter,* April 19, 1856

IN MANAGING HIS fellow negroes, the first aim of the driver should be to obey the master's orders, the second to satisfy his fellows that he is doing so. Naturally jealous of his superiors, as men of a lower rank whether white or black always will be, the common negro cannot be expected to yield that willing obedience which is necessary to his own happiness and the driver's comfort unless he is certain that he is not oppressed or imposed upon. It is evident to all that know negro character that the slave when satisfied as his master proscribes, is in better temper and more submissive. Let him go freely to the master if he has a complaint. If the master is fit to own slaves, as some "good masters" are not, and the driver be a man of good character, no harm can come of it.

The manners of a driver to other negroes should be kind. Kindness, and even gentleness, is not inconsistent with firmness and inexorable discipline. If they require a reprimand, give it privately and in a low tone of voice. Whether it be "mesmeric" I cannot say, but I have noticed that a loud and angry tone, whether addressed to man or beast, excites corresponding emotions, or scares away the wits. The best ox-driver I ever saw only said, "Come boys, go it." The best wagoner never scolds his team. The best rider never frets at his horse. Our best driver has never lost his temper. A mild expostulation is better than a fierce rebuke, a deliberate warning more effective than a hasty threat.

Nor should a driver ever fret at other negroes. It injures their capacity for work. If they are working wrong, show them how to work right. Have patience and they will soon learn, or if they are too stupid, put them at something else. We have seen negroes injured in value by being fretted at and terrified when young.

The habit of swearing either at or before negroes a driver should never indulge in. If the negro is not allowed to swear because it is disrespectful to the driver, the latter should not swear because it is disrespectful to his Maker. Besides, it shocks some pious negroes, and sets a bad example to all, and is provocative of the very habit of anger and petulance we have been arguing against.

The driver should also aid in promoting cleanliness in the negro cabins, and he should see that their clothes are washed and patched, and their shoes kept in good order. On Sundays he should see that they come out cleanly clad, and if they dress themselves in the ridiculous finery which they sometimes display, and which will often provoke a smile, it should never be made a subject of derision or scornful remark. Rather encourage than repress their taste in dress. It aids very materially in giving them self-respect.

Nothing more reconciles the negro to his work than the driver sharing it with him. If they shuck corn late into the night, let him be present until the last moment; if the sun shines hot, let him stand it as much as they do; if it rains, let them stake his share of it; if it is cold, let him not go to the fire oftener than they do.

We have known drivers to declare that a fellow negro should not complain of them to the master, and they would whip him in spite of the master if he did. This is simply brutal and no man of spirit will permit it. When the servant comes within the general rule which prescribes his punishment, let him be punished, and appeal to the master afterward, if he chooses.

If a negro requires whipping, whip him and be done with it.

The third time Jesse Burns ran away and was retaken, Samuel Gatewood asked what he could amend to guarantee his servant's better conduct.

"Bring Maggie and Jacob home," Jesse said.

"I cannot. Her presence tears my family apart. I must have your word you'll not run away again."

"It's a big mountain up there," Jesse said.

When Gatewood ordered Jack the Driver to punish Jesse, Jack refused, so Samuel Gatewood ordered Rufus, who also refused, which put Samuel Gatewood out of temper, and he whipped Jesse until the man swooned and even for a time afterward.

PART TWO

The Bonny Blue Flag

"These men are not an army.
They are citizens defending their country."

—*R. E. Lee*

14

LETTER FROM CORPORAL CATESBY BYRD TO HIS WIFE, LEONA

CAMP BARTOW, VIRGINIA
SEPTEMBER 16, 1861

DEAREST HEART,

Though we have been damp and moldering these last weeks, I am dry at last, feet before a fire. While Duncan and other officers of the gallant 44th are quartered with families in the village, Corporal Fisher and I have a nearly weathertight shed to ourselves and the amiable Private Ryals totes our water and hews our wood. The steaming socks dangling before our fire are a perfect reminder of the tired feet that have inhabited them during painful marches through these weary western mountains.

Your brother, Duncan, is an indifferent correspondent but promises he wrote you while in the hospital in Staunton. The measles that afflicted him sickened a good many others, and cholera has plucked several boys from our ranks—boys latterly so hearty and patriotic. Few avoid "soldier's disease": the desperate quickstep to a necessary or the sinks we've dug. With sickness and desertion, our numbers are half those we mustered in the gay days in Richmond. How we paraded! What figures we cut! How jolly war seemed! The man who enrolled me in our country's service, Duncan's friend Spaulding, has departed for the army outside Washington. Though Spaulding's kinsman Colonel A. P. Hill did not distinguish himself at the battle of Manassas, when Hill wrote of a vacancy on his staff, Spaulding abandoned the gloryless 44th with no visible regrets.

Doubtless my ill humor will depart me after my socks dry and the sun plays once again upon the western mountains. When food was plentiful and meals regularly presented, I was an indifferent eater. Darling, I am cured! Hardtack soaked in coffee seems ambrosia to me now, and tonight when four of us devour a commandeered rooster, it will be a feast fit for a king.

Though these mountains are the same range that buttresses Stratford Plantation, extreme western Virginia is unlike the soft valleys of home. Here, instead of broad, fertile river valleys are hard ridges which climb sharply from narrow brush-choked bottoms. Instead of fat cattle and thick-fleeced sheep, starved creatures. Instead of plenty, poverty. Here are no enthusiastic patriots but sharp-featured men who shoot at our columns from the safety of the woods and slatterns who do not answer when we ask directions. Some of our soldiers mutter that we should let the Federals occupy all this land—that our Confederacy can do quite well absent western Virginia's wilderness.

Despite the success of Confederate arms at Manassas (why didn't Beauregard crown his victory by capturing the federal capital?), in these mountains we are everywhere routed. Our new commanding general, Robert Lee, designed a grand strategy which less failed than fizzled. Our regiment, I regret to say, got itself lost en route to the battle and was forced to hear the distant engagement from the wrong side of the mountain, our wagons, ambulances, and guns so deeply mired in the mud they skidded on their bottoms like children's toboggans.

That night, our morale already pretty well sunk, we bivouacked on a steep mountainside in the rain. About midnight a bear blundered into our encampment, smashing shelters and tents, entangling himself in tent ropes, and waking every sleeper with colossal roars. It was pitch-dark and pouring rain, and had the enemies of our new Confederacy been present to witness our brave boys rushing to and fro, lighting up the night with musket flashes, which proved more hazardous to ourselves than the bear (two men wounded—the bear escaped unhurt), I cannot doubt they should have taken great comfort from the sight.

I was so happy to come home and be with you and our children. Last month's idyll seems a lifetime ago. I trust that by now you know pretty well how things will be in nine months. Colonel Scott is reluctant to grant furloughs. The Tidewater boys hate all mountains, and after they go home to their loved ones, they find desertion more appealing than a return to this country of mildew and misery.

I know how much you hated closing our own dear home and returning under your father's roof at Stratford. I suppose it must seem as if you, our children's mother, have become once again your father's child. But I am not certain this war will end as swiftly as our patriots hope, and if it goes on longer the Federal blockade of our ports must start to bite, and you and the children will be better off where food is plentiful. Stratford has many hands to lighten your burden and look after you if you fall ill or must endure a difficult pregnancy.

I pray you seize an opportunity to speak with your father on Duncan's behalf. If Duncan sinned—and doubtless he did—his sin was no worse than the sins of countless other young boys faced with that temptation and no very strong proscription against it. Although I never took a servant wench, some of my young friends did, and I believe my chastity was less from better morals than lack of temptation—none of our house servants was as handsome as Duncan's inamorata. Duncan is punished not for what he did but for the sin of owning up to it, which, if we were honest, we would admire rather than deplore. Your father's actions caused Duncan great distress, though I cannot think what else Samuel might have done. Should he have let the two marry? I do not know if there is anywhere in either nation that would have accepted their union. And Maggie's child (I do not call it Duncan's child because it cannot ever be his child), what will become of him? Poor infant, so innocent of the world!

Your father sometimes has a blinkered view of what is best for his family, but he loves us all. Should you persuade Samuel to write, I believe Duncan would be happy to resume more familiar relations. Perhaps Abigail can put in a word with Samuel.

Though your brother lost flesh during his illness, he is improved and in good spirits. The most junior of the regiment's second lieutenants, Duncan is popular with the men, and his previous military training is of advantage. All this drill, this military punctiliousness, allows men who know each other only slightly to perform complex maneuvers in the fierce confusions of battle. (Though I confess I don't understand why we must as cheerfully obey a fool's orders as those produced by a man of sense.)

Duncan has just now come in, streaming wet, and is backed to our fire. He is damper than a raincloud come indoors! Duncan is eyeing our rooster with more avidity than seems proper.

Your brother sends you his affection. Please remember me to our children, and your mother and father.

I sign myself, your Devoted Husband,
Catesby

15

COUSIN MOLLY

RICHMOND, VIRGINIA
NOVEMBER 12, 1861

SALLIE'S PENITENTIARY LIFE was fragments overheard, dreams of the past, and her fingertips, adjusting the warp of her strands of wool. Forty warps, then five wefts; forty and five, forty and five.

Twelve hours at the loom, forty minutes for each meal, seated beside other silent women, the scrape of tin on tin, the relentless mastication of jaws; no more conversation than cows at a manger. Sallie sometimes thought to whisper to the wretch seated next to her—a pale-faced fat woman who mashed her food with blunt, toothless gums. Sallie might say, "Did you sleep well last night?" or "My home is in the mountains— where is your home?" But Sallie had learned a few things and would not give way to momentary satisfactions. If she broke her silence, warders would bear her from the room and take her to her the punishment cell, and there she would sit while eternity played itself out.

The warders talked as freely around the convicts as if the convicts had lost hearing as well as the exercise of speech. According to the warders, the confederate victory at Balls Bluff was a salutary check on the Federals' pride, but Sallie detected wishful thinking in their confidence.

Sallie's whitewashed cell was tall and airy, with a wooden hook to hang her dress. When the sun disappeared over the James, the barred window that was her sole source of light went to black. In the spring it would be warmer.

She had done more harm than good; she had held her head too high.

Thrice daily she saw Alexander when the women filed into the eating room the men were vacating. Alexander wore that look: that blank childlike expression—nothing could hurt him because nobody was at home. Wearing his slight smile, he marched mechanically, one hand upon the shoulder of the prisoner ahead. Alexander might march that way forever.

"The Professor," the warders called him.

Most prisoners were mulattos or Irish from Richmond's Shockoe Bottom, imprisoned for assault, highway robbery, burglary. The women prisoners were passers of counterfeit or confidence tricksters, or accomplices. There were two murderesses, a tall gray-skinned mulatto from Norfolk who'd stabbed her lover as he slept, and the toothless woman who ate beside Sallie every meal. Who she'd killed Sallie never did learn.

The warders' talk fell upon Sallie's ears like the gossip of kings, each word cherished, to be examined in privacy afterward. The acting keeper, Mr. Tyree, was said to be a "hincty nigger," which phrase she turned over in her mind for an evening. The prison was "lousy with Micks." Jefferson Davis was "crazy as a bedbug." (Once a month, she emptied her straw tick into the heap for burning, and she thought of Jefferson Davis while the bedbugs hopped and crackled in the flames.)

One afternoon, at her loom ("forty and five"), the workshop warder touched Sallie's shoulder and beckoned her to accompany him, which she did, made fearful by the novelty.

The keeper's house faced the sally port like a sentry's challenge. New prisoners were delivered to its whitewashed prisoners' parlor to become acquainted with the venerable traditions and mores of prison life. There a warder issued clothing with the alternating black and white stripes that had given the prisoners their nickname: Zebras. There were no female warders: a wizened black trusty found rags for their monthlies and attended to their complaints. The acting keeper, Mr. Tyree, was a free black who never made an appearance without his brushed homburg and ironed sleeve protectors. Mr. Tyree was invariably present when new prisoners were welcomed in that stony room, but he neither lifted a hand nor passed out clothing.

After the rules had been explained (ten lashes for disobedience, two weeks in the punishment cells for breaking silence), Mr. Tyree spoke his welcome. "I am Acting Keeper Tyree. If you repent, reexamine your conduct, and obey without exception those regulations to which your crime has made you subject, I will not speak to you again. If I speak to you again, you will wish I had not."

Mr. Tyree's superior, the governor's appointed keeper, Mr. Blackwell, listed penitentiary duty among many other duties of a mercantile and governmental nature. The first Sunday of every month, Blackwell attended the penitentiary chapel, where he produced a homily for the prisoners' edification; day-to-day matters were left to Mr. Tyree.

Whenever Blackwell entered the penitentiary the smile wilted from his face, and Mr. Tyree's somber attitude did nothing to restore it. In truth Blackwell had no occasion for complaint: no drunken warders, no offenses to morality, and no escapes. The penitentiary books were exact and scrupulous: the income from the clothing woven for the madhouse and orphanages had produced a profit of some ten thousand the year before, and the present work manufacturing blouses for the Confederate army promised even better returns.

The penitentiary did not intrude upon Mr. Blackwell's attention, and he had Mr. Tyree to thank. Indeed, why should a penitentiary be merry? It should be a solemn place, officiated over by solemn men like Tyree.

If Mr. Tyree had a first name, the keeper didn't know it. If Mr. Tyree had a home in Richmond, a family, Mr. Tyree must have visited them on Sunday afternoons, which were the only hours he could not be found at his duties.

Sallie's warder banged the brass door knocker, which was shaped like a crouching lion. "Peters, sir," he bawled, "with Female Convict Kirkpatrick."

The entry hall had the smell of a room that wasn't often used, and moisture had invaded the glass that framed the lithographs. They were "Wolfe on the Plains of Abraham," "Old Ironsides," "Lafayette Arriving at Mount Vernon." Sallie stood downcast and demure.

When Mr. Tyree stepped into the hall, he pulled the parlor door shut behind him.

"You are satisfied here?" His voice was austere.

"Sir?"

"Your treatment has been fair? You have received adequate nourishment?"

"Oh. Yes sir."

"See that you say so. Are there signs of discontent among the other convicts?"

"I cannot speak for those to whom I do not speak."

"And I will not abide insolence."

"Having no knowledge of the overall management of this institution, I can hardly remark upon it."

Mr. Tyree's eyes were black as hard coal, as if all the blackness in his chalky complexion had drained into them. His eyebrows were so thin Sallie wondered if he plucked them. He templed his fingertips. "If Jefferson Davis's daughter had been remanded into my care, she would receive treatment no different from, neither better nor worse than, that received by the bastard daughter of a scullery maid."

He seemed to expect comment.

"In Keeper Blackwell's absence I am responsible," he continued.

Sallie kept silence.

"A man who fails his responsibilities is a low creature."

Sallie could think of nothing.

"Very well," Mr. Tyree said. "Just so we understand each other."

The unofficial parlor of the keeper's house was identical in size, though not in furnishings, to the grim parlor where prisoners were welcomed. The woman beside the inadequate fire was round on the bottom and round on top. She was round in the face and her arms were round and her hair was pulled back in a round bun. "Good afternoon, dear," Cousin Molly said in a cheerful tone. "My, we have got ourselves into difficulties, haven't we?"

And that quick Sallie's eyes filled with tears and she couldn't do a thing to stem them.

"You may reply, Female Convict Kirkpatrick," the acting keeper said. "Mrs. Semple has come to the penitentiary especially to interview you."

"Why did you locate so near Tredegar's?" The round woman made a face. "The smoke is dreadful. Just dreadful."

"I believe we predate Tredegar's, ma'am," the acting keeper said.

"Can't you ask Tredegar's to smoke less? I know they must be forging guns and swords, but must they be so smoky about it? You'll have your share of respiratory diseases, I'd venture." Her eyes were oval, brown, and shrewd.

"Why, I . . ."

"All these people in your care. Malefactors, to be sure, but none of their sentences include death by asphyxiation." The round woman extracted a silk square from her half-moon recticule and coughed into it. Twice. "Never you mind," she said, suddenly gay. "I suppose we must all make sacrifices. Now, Keeper, I would not detain you for another minute. I know you have important responsibilities. So many lives in your hands, just imagine. I am sure General Johnson has no greater responsibilities."

"Well, I did think I might . . ."

"And I am certain you shall, Acting Keeper! I am certain you shall!" She held her beaming smile on Tyree until that worthy closed the door behind him. Cousin Molly took a deep breath. "You do remember me?" she asked in a kinder tone.

"From Christmases at Stratford, yes, ma'am. You always accumulate the children."

"Say rather that the children accumulate me. They know a sentimental, childless fool when they see one. I am first cousin to Abigail Gatewood, on her father's side. He was a Semple from Southside. I have always thought Christmas is for children. We adults relive our joys through theirs."

"Yes, ma'am." Sallie looked at the floor.

"Well, dear. You have got yourself in a fix, haven't you?" She gestured at the shabby gentility of the keeper's parlor. "I mean, all this."

Sallie looked up. "If you have come to condemn me, madam, there are others with prior claims."

"Child, I . . ."

"Having no personal or familial acquaintance with me, you have satisfied your duty to your cousin and need not trouble yourself to visit again."

Cousin Molly laughed, a round woman's laugh. "I begin to understand how you find yourself in this predicament. Abigail wrote and asked that I look in on you, but at the time we were overwhelmed by the Manassas wounded—I will not describe our confusion, crossed purposes, the needless suffering. By the time we put things right, it was October, and then we moved to Camp Winder and . . . Oh, dear, where was I?"

"I fear I don't know, ma'am," and tears began leaking from Sallie's eyes, and she was ashamed.

Cousin Molly dove into her recticule for a fresh silk square. "My dear, my dear . . ."

While Sallie dried her eyes, Cousin Molly extracted neat packages from that recticule. "I am informed there is no prohibition against supplementing the Commonwealth's provisions," she began, "and have provided you with the same parcel we provide to wounded soldiers: some good soap, a square of cheese, a huzzit for repairing one's garments. I have not included tobacco. You don't use it"—her eyes grew serious—"do you?"

"Oh no, ma'am."

"Abigail writes that your father, Uther, is well, though not in the best of spirits. Abigail makes a point of speaking with him at church. Quite a pleasant chapel, SunRise's, so airy and light. And the singing from the colored loft, how unusually vigorous. In his sermon last Christmas, your Preacher Todd"—she glowered—"heaped overmuch praise on predestination. If a person cannot effect her own salvation, then what is the point of ironing her underthings?"

"Suppose, madam, one were suddenly upset on the street?"

Cousin Molly contemplated the imagined spectacle. "There is that. I suppose one must put a good face on things. Though one's face might be one's bottom."

The two women eyed each other in silence for seconds before Sallie entrusted a timid smile.

"There is always a crowd of men outside the Exchange Hotel. The gentlemen, one hopes, would avert their eyes. One fears laughter. Or worse, applause."

Because Cousin Molly visualized the scene so clearly, Sallie, who had never seen the Exchange Hotel in her life, nor its gentlemen, began to see it too. And it was Cousin Molly she pictured, upended, presenting her hind parts to their gaze, and Sallie smothered her giggles in her palm as Cousin Molly beamed.

Sallie begged for news. Cousin Molly said her nephew Duncan had been ill but had recovered. She said there was little war news, but the government had high hopes of British and French recognition. "Since the armies are in winter camp, things are quiet at the hospitals, and I shall certainly find occasion for visits. For my dear cousin's sake." She paused. "It is a dreadful fix you find yourself in, but there's no use complaining. God did not grant us strength because He thought we wouldn't require it."

16

BULLWHIP DAYS

*The Spirit of the Lord came mightily upon him,
and the cords that were upon his arms
became as flax that was burnt with fire,
and his bands loosed from off his hands.*

—Judges 15:14

THE THIRD TIME he ran, Jesse packed his waist bells with tallow to silence them. When he was caught, Samuel Gatewood ordered a copper rod riveted to Jesse's iron belt in the back so he couldn't reach the bells. The copper rod curved over his head like a buggy whip. The waist bells had been sheep bells, but a cow bell dangled from the new copper rod.

"I intend to waste less time hunting you should you run again," Master said.

Jesse said nothing.

Jack the Driver set Jesse to feeding logs into the sawmill and locked him to the log carriage with a light chain. "I'll unchain you when you promise you won't run no more," Jack said.

Jesse looked at Jack as if Jack were riffraff.

Jesse guided logs to the blade, flopping them to this side and that as the sawyer commanded. At that time they were sawing white oak.

When it got too dark to work, around five o'clock, Jack led Jesse to the root cellar, which was his jail. When Jesse dipped his head to go underneath the low doorframe, the cowbell clanked and everybody knew Jesse was in his jail until morning. Jack brought supper in a tin pan, and sometimes Jesse ate it and sometimes he didn't.

The root cellar was beneath the curing house, where hams hung until they took the salt. The cellar was stone, eight by ten, with a dirt floor; dug into a rise behind the big house's kitchen garden. Since only the ceiling was above ground level and since that ceiling was packed with sawdust, the cellar stayed at forty-five degrees, and Jesse was warm enough under a wool blanket. His bed was a wide plank laid across the potato bins, and his mattress was the same plank.

Chilly air came right through the pocketbook-sized ventilation hole in the door, but Jesse left it open because hunkered down, with his cheek pressed against the door, he could see the stars.

Where was Maggie?

Could she see the stars?

That awful night last Christmas, before Omohundhru seized her, Master Samuel himself had decoyed Jesse down here, and when Maggie shrieked out Jesse's name, called it again and again, there had been nothing Jesse could do but hurl himself helplessly at the thick door clawing until his fingers bled.

After they turned him loose, soon as he could, he ran.

He didn't run to get away, he ran to be with Maggie, who was somewhere among the stars. Jesse puzzled out which one; it was that bright star just below the cup of the Little Dipper, that star which has a smaller star tagging along with it, which must be Baby Jacob.

Maggie came to love Jesse more as a star than she'd loved him as a woman. Maggie told Jesse all her secrets. Her and the young master. Didn't mean a thing. Both just children first time it happened, and the pure delicious deliciousness of it. What about us? Well, what about us? We wasn't the same. It was grown-ups doing it, as man and wife. For us it was just duty.

His first runaway, Jesse found himself a den on Snowy Mountain which might have belonged to a wolf once, only the wolf was gone and Jesse lay under his coat and a mound of dead leaves and he'd talk to the Maggie star, pour out his heart.

Somewhere below, down the mountain, was Stratford plantation.

When he got so hungry he couldn't tell one star from another, and couldn't know which was Maggie, he came down to the Kirkpatrick cabin, where Miss Sallie fed him and warmed him by the fire until the slave patrollers came. Jesse knew Miss Sallie and her husband had been jailed on his account, but he didn't care. They weren't any worse off than he was.

Second time he ran he'd been harrowing oat ground. Jack found

Jesse's abandoned team grazing quietly at the base of the mountain. Master set ten men to looking, and a week later they found Jesse. That's when Master had an iron belt fabricated for Jesse and sheep bells attached to it.

Third time was in September, when they were cutting corn. Jesse packed his bells silent with tallow and ran again. Jesse figured Master wouldn't stop harvest work to hunt a runaway, but Jesse was wrong. The corn got cut late that year, but Jesse was brought home to Stratford.

The whip didn't cut Jesse sharp as he expected. After the first few slashes, each additional cut was a broad stroke, like a deathblow applied to his whole back at once. Jesse would have screamed but for the rag between his teeth. It hurt him worse than he'd expected, because he didn't lose his senses until the end.

Jack the Driver stayed the master's hand, and for an instant it seemed as if Jack might be next. "He ain't no use to you dead," Jack said softly.

Panting, blood-spattered, Master Gatewood threw the bullwhip into the dirt. "He's no use to me alive," he said. He stepped to the bushes and vomited, which none of the servants were supposed to see, so they didn't.

Miss Abigail treated Jesse's wounds with clean water and soft cloths and comfrey poultices, but Jesse wasn't aware of her, because of the fever that set in. Miss Abigail wanted Jesse moved back to the Quarters, where he could be looked after properly, but Master wouldn't hear of it.

Corn and wheat prices were double a year ago, but the new money wasn't as good as the old money. One afternoon at the mill, Master told Jack the war would be over before spring, "soon as Mr. Lincoln knows we mean business," and Jack said, yes, sir, surest thing in the world. That very night in the Quarters, Rufus said the blacks were like the Israelites in Pharaoh's day and Father Abraham was going to set them all free. Jack the Driver didn't like that kind of talk but didn't know how he could stop it.

"Until that day of Jubilo we all got to work," Jack said. "And until the quittin' bell rings on that day, you gonna live by the sweat of your brow, and don't be gettin' notions otherwise."

A Confederate commissary man came out from Warm Springs to buy twenty of Master's prime cows, and when Master said he didn't want to sell, the man said the time would come when he'd sell whether he wanted to or not, and Master got hot and said no matter whether tyranny bore the name "Federal" or "Confederate," it was tyranny all the same. The commissary man said he'd be back.

Local young men signed on with the Highland Mountaineers or the Bath Cavalry, and when the Federals surrounded Colonel Pegram at Rich Mountain, most of those same boys were captured. Masters Gatewood and Byrd had enlisted with a Richmond regiment which missed that fight. The servants didn't want any harm to come to them and hoped Father Abraham wouldn't feel it necessary to lay them low. Many heartfelt prayers were uttered in the negro garret of SunRise Chapel on the two masters' accounts.

One Sunday late in the year, Aunt Opal and Uther Botkin returned to Stratford with the Gatewoods after church, and while Master Uther sat with Master Samuel in the parlor, Aunt Opal went to the root cellar. "Go inside," Jack the Driver said. "I don't reckon Jesse'll hurt you."

"Wasn't that gave me pause," Aunt Opal sniffed. "Was the stink."

Jack the Driver took away the slop jar, though that wasn't his task.

Jesse perched on the edge of his plank bed, blanket draped around his shoulders.

"I heard you got skinny," Aunt Opal said. "I brought you a pie." When he didn't reach for it, she set it beside him. "You always was a stubborn boy, but you wasn't no fool. Why you keep runnin' away? You know Master's sworn to bring you back."

"I don't care about him," Jesse said in a dull voice.

"Old fool Uther at the big house right now, tryin' to buy you away. Brought every dollar he got."

"His ain't my home either," Jesse said.

"Don't talk foolishness," Aunt Opal snapped. " 'Course it is. Whatever other home you ever knowed? Uther's too old for this trouble. I want you promise you won't run away no more."

Jesse didn't say anything.

"I won't have that. I ain't no white master. I ask you a question, I'll have an answer."

Jesse licked his lips. "I'll run till I die."

Opal pushed her face right up to his and examined his eyes. "Weren't your baby," she said.

"I made him mine."

"Your woman always yearned for another."

"I got my share of faults."

"God knows where your family is now."

Jesse knew perfectly well where they were. Every clear night he pressed his face to the splintery plank door and found the patch of stars and talked to Maggie.

Jesse's dreamy smile fetched a tear from Aunt Opal's eyes. She rubbed the tear from her cheek with her apron. "They feedin' you all right?"

"Oh, I got everything I'm needin'. It's astonishin' how much I got."

In Samuel Gatewood's parlor, Uther Botkin sat with his hat in his lap. "I have brought a fair price for Jesse," he repeated.

A wan Samuel Gatewood sat in the window seat, the thick drapes drawn. "After the triumph of our arms at Manassas, I expected Mr. Lincoln to abandon his invasion. Surely he knows he cannot force a sovereign people to submit."

"Have you received news from . . ."

"My son-in-law writes frequently. Catesby's has not been a bloody war, thank God. My daughter, Leona, could wish no better news. Leona is with child, and as you know, she has always been delicate. I pray she receives no shock before her delivery. I will not sell Jesse."

"Samuel, why torment yourself? Jesse will never be happy here."

"Mr. Botkin, we are not put on earth for happiness but to fulfill our Christian duty. Jesse is my chattel. If I fail in my resolve, what will my other servants think? One man's rebellion may well become general."

"But Samuel, surely Jesse's circumstances are . . . unique."

"It is, alas, not uncommon for servant families to be separated. Who will do our work? Orphans? Bachelors? Those with no family connections at all? Now, Mr. Botkin, if you will excuse me."

Uther stood, gripping his hat in his hands. "Is there no end to this suffering? My Sallie . . ."

"As you know, I did everything in my power for your daughter and can do no more. I am grateful for your neighborly concern, sir, but this affair is between Jesse and me, and until he accepts his lot, it will go hard with him."

Prior to November 26, 1861, the nearest free state was Ohio, two months' hard walk over the mountains, and few runaways completed the journey. But western Virginia voted to secede from Virginia, and Federal troops were making its secession good. That Jordan River so many slaves yearned to cross had come nearer.

Mrs. Dinwiddie took up a subscription to increase the slave patrollers, no easy task with so many men with the army. Some nights elderly planters made rounds, Samuel Gatewood among them, and hardly a week went by without their capturing some runaway. One young servant had walked all the way from Georgia.

"Where're you going, boy?" Gatewood inquired.

"North," the boy answered.

And one morning when Rufus's gang formed to go out in the woods, two men were missing. Gone.

"How I'm gonna get tasks done without hands to do them?" Jack the Driver asked.

Patrollers caught the runaways. When they were returned, all the servants were turned out and Jack did the whipping.

"This is what happens to runaways," Samuel announced. Then his face contorted, "What do you people want? Do you want my family to starve?"

That night after dark, Rufus slipped up on Jesse's cellar; he snuck down the stairs quiet as a cat and set his butt on the lowest step. "It's me. Rufus. Cold out here, yes, sir."

Rufus heard a sound between a whisper and a sigh.

"Stars bright on the colder night," Jesse breathed.

"Yeah. Goose bumps bigger too."

They sat for a time before Rufus ventured, "Jesse, when you run, why you run up the mountain instead of north? If you run north, maybe you be free by now."

"I knowed that mountain all my life. Never been to the North."

"Past Strait Creek, everything's changed. Past Strait Creek it ain't Confederate no more. Nigger get across Strait Creek and don't get caught, he a free man."

"Look! One of them fallin' stars. Wonder what makes them fall that way? You think they lonesome?"

"Jesse, how long I been knowin' you?

"Long time. Been a long time."

Rufus drew his jacket up around his shoulders. "You gone mad, Jesse? I got to know if you took leave of your senses."

Another silence then, plenty of time for Rufus to roll his head around on his stiff neck.

"Rufus, I don't know whether I'm crazy or not. Most of what used to fret me don't fret me no more. I wonder why there's so many stars."

"Before I come to Stratford, I belong to that Dr. Willoughby, down by Staunton. You know where the American Hotel sets? We was in a big house next door. Dr. Willoughby promise he gonna set me free, just like old Uther promise you."

"Master Uther he tried to buy me back. Aunt Opal told me."

"Oh, them white folks they hate ownin' niggers. It be wrong and not Christian charity, and besides, we be too much damn trouble. But as many as I heard talkin' about settin' this one free or that one free, I never heard of nobody to do it. Dr. Willoughby took the smallpox and died and wasn't in his grave three days before I belongs to his nephew, and I wasn't with him no longer'n it took to sell me off to Stratford. I was just a young'un then."

"Rufus, why you tellin' me all this? Why you sneak 'round in the night pester a man can't keep you from pesterin' him?"

"Jack whipped Jim and Yellow Billy for runnin'. Laid that bullwhip on their flesh! Patrollers caught them down by Millboro. They two got turned 'round someways and went south instead of north and they was fixin' to slip aboard a train goin' direct to Richmond, thinkin' it was goin' to Philadelphia." Rufus spat.

"I went to Staunton once," Jesse said dreamily. "I was bringin' Miss Sallie in to the Female Seminary. Oh, she was so excited and pleased. First girl from this part of the country to go so far with education. She had a scholarship! I had me a load of maple sugar from Master Botkin to sell and at McGrory's Mercantile they wouldn't give me but five cents a pound. Staunton a mighty big place. No end of people in Staunton."

Rufus rubbed his head. "Look, Jesse, I got to ask. Is you the man you was?"

The root cellar was illuminated by the slot through which Jesse searched the night sky. Had he changed so much? Maybe so. His family was up in the stars. "Depends," he said thoughtfully.

"Jesse, I been thinkin' to be free. Ain't a bad life here with Master Gatewood, but I'm thinkin' I want to be free. I been studyin' horseshoein' so I can live on my own."

"Why you askin' me? I run three times, never got nowhere. I can tell you where the springs is on Snowy Mountain, where you can lie out of the weather, but Master Gatewood he follow you with dogs. Master not allowin' runaways these days."

"I been studyin' the forge too. I shape a horseshoe good and I fit it on the hoof. You reckon there be any need for a man can do horseshoein' up north?"

"They don't like colored any better'n they do here."

"But Father Abraham he king and tell 'em what to do."

"Rufus, we're born black and I reckon it's the same wherever we go. Preacher says we ought to put our faith in the life to come."

"I'm thinkin' to put my faith in horseshoein'. Can't be too many who'll shoe cheap as me."

"Go at night, soon as the Quarters asleep, and you'll be a night's run ahead when they start lookin'."

"I been thinkin' you might be showin' me the way."

Silence locked their conversation for a time, and when Jesse spoke his voice was kindly. "Rufus, nobody ever laid a bullwhip across your back. That bullwhip, it's not what you think. It'll change your mind. I swear it'll change your way of thinkin'."

17

LETTER FROM SERGEANT CATESBY
BYRD TO HIS WIFE, LEONA

CRABBOTTOM, VIRGINIA
JANUARY 1, 1862

DEAREST HEART,

How I dream of home, how I yearn to see you and our dear children again. Crabbottom is a wretched place, unimproved by days of freezing weather. Our Tidewater boys are unaccustomed to this harsh climate and suffer dreadfully. Colonel Scott has taken advantage of a flattering newspaper account of his military accomplishments and has returned to Richmond to sit in the legislature. Many of us pray he does well there and does not return. In the army our regiment is known as the Retreating 44th, having attended several battles but fought none. Having escaped our desolation, our Colonel Scott has determined no other soldier should follow his example and ruled there are to be no more furloughs, none until spring; so here we sit in our miserable huts, watching the snow blow in through the cracks in the door.

Our eccentric General "Allegheny" Johnson's winter quarters are east of us on the turnpike. The Federals are holed up to the west along that turnpike in the newly seceded West Virginia. When the Federals resume their drive in the spring, we will be first to face them.

Though you and I are not a day's ride apart I cannot travel, and, in your delicate condition, you must not. Samuel and Abigail do not visit because they are unreconciled with their son. Perhaps Jack the Driver can be prevailed upon to call upon me!

We eat, we sleep, we play cards. When the weather permits we drill. Details forage for firewood. Men line up before the surgeon's hut to complain of their ills. Our officers hatch plans to escape this place, and more than a few have succeeded, some by transfer, some by feigned illness, one or two by desertion.

Like me, Duncan has the soldier's disease, but not severely. He is in better spirits than I.

I pray this confinement is easier than your last. I especially pray that you are less bothered by stomach complaints. Daily, I think of you and the little being we are bringing into the world. How I wish it were a better world!

I cannot but compare this dismal holiday with those we enjoyed at Stratford in years past. This year I will be thirty-six years old. Will we ever see happiness again?

I hope you were able to find oranges for the children. The blockade has made such treats rare and expensive. Our provisions have been adequate, but only because the poor citizens of these parts are much pressed by us. We are an army of patriotic locusts.

You write that our son, Thomas, is rebellious. Ill manners, sloth, and rebellion are common faults of boys his age, and there is only one cure: discipline properly applied. If you do not feel able to apply this necessary discipline, ask Samuel to intervene. Your father is head of his family, and any misbehavior reflects upon him.

I am pleased to learn our Pauline is making herself useful to Abigail.

I prefer that all my family keep a distance from Grandmother Gatewood. She is a strong woman but not a charitable one, and her overt and constant supplication to the Deity is offensive to me. Since, presumably, an omniscient God can identify our needs, why pester Him with endless tiresome entreaties?

If you can find and send me a warm wool overcoat, please do so. You must pay for it out of your money, as we patriots have seen no pay since August.

Kiss the children for me and tell Thomas that I expect better reports of his behavior.

Your Loving Husband,
Catesby

18

INAUGURATION DAY

RICHMOND, VIRGINIA
FEBRUARY 22, 1862

Hath not the morning dawned with added light?
And shall not evening call another star
Out of the infinite regions of the night,
To mark this day in heaven? At last we are
A nation among nations; and the world
Shall soon behold in many a distant port
Another flag unfurled!

—*Henry Timrod*

ALEXANDER KIRKPATRICK SAT on a hard-backed chair in the prisoners' parlor of the keeper's house. As instructed, he sat still. The prison's rule of silence so hated by other prisoners was a positive pleasure to Alexander, and though he'd been waiting in this cold room for more than two hours, he was not distressed. In Alexander's daydream he swam with mermaids in the sunny green sea. On shore, his friends the poets Catullus and Lucretius were preparing a feast, but the water was so warm, the shimmer of the mermaids so uncannily beautiful . . .

Mr. Tyree entered the parlor like the breath of the storm, and when he hung his oilskin on its hook, a puddle formed beneath. His trouser cuffs were dark with moisture and his felt hat was shapeless as a feed sack. He reformed the hat and laid it on the windowsill, all the while staring at Alexander, whose own eyes were fixed on the wall opposite.

"Mr. Davis would hold his inaugural out of doors." Tyree's voice was soft but exacting. "Bareheaded, too. What should we do if the President were to fall ill? You may speak, Convict Kirkpatrick."

"Sir?"

"If President Jefferson Davis were to become enfeebled, which statesman would guide our new nation?"

"Sir? I don't know, sir."

Mr. Tyree removed his damp jacket, tapped a bell, and passed the garment to his servant. Within a minute, the man returned with a fresh jacket, identical to the first.

Mr. Tyree shot his cuffs, plucked at his trouser knees, and sat on his tall oaken stool. "Do you think General Beauregard might be persuaded to accept the post of commander in chief? Perhaps Mr. Benjamin. He is a Jew. In perilous times we might look to the Jew."

"I wouldn't know, sir." Calm was receding from Alexander's's mind and too familiar panic tightened his throat.

"But you are an educated man? It is written, in the book." Tyree tapped his ledger.

"Only in inconsequential matters." Alexander made himself speak. "Ancient Rome is more familiar to me than our modern world."

The pupils of Mr. Tyree's eyes were hard as dried beans. He drummed his fingers. "Education is the most valuable of possessions," he pronounced.

Alexander opened his mouth slightly to take a breath.

"Your wife has made a poorer adjustment to her imprisonment than yourself. How do you explain that?"

Alexander snatched at a theory. "Her people are mountain people. Such people are independent, sir."

"The coloreds as well?"

"Sir, I have no means of comparison. I am originally from the North, where there are few of your race."

"My race?" Mr. Tyree leaned forward.

"Am I mistaken, sir? I took your complexion for . . . an Indian's, perhaps?"

"I am an octoroon," Mr. Tyree said. "Tainted in my ancestry to one-eighth degree. Should I marry a woman with no deeper taint, my own children will appear white. Such a woman is rare, sir, and greatly in demand."

Alexander's mind fluttered. "You could marry a white woman, sir."

"The white woman who would take a colored man is no better than a . . . trollop!" Mr. Tyree's fingers flipped furiously through his ledger. "Who owns the largest cartage in Richmond?"

"I don't know, sir."

"Tredegar's superintendent on the night shifts—what is the color of his skin?"

"Sir?"

"When was the first negro Baptist church built in Richmond?"

"I did not, I do not . . ."

"How come you by your education, Convict Kirkpatrick?"

"My uncle was a Congregationalist minister. He was chaplain at . . . at Yale College, which I subsequently attended. I . . ."

"School came naturally to you? You took to it as a duck takes to water?"

He had, he had. Even as a child, the rigors of study were nothing to the hazards of the schoolyard: all that shouting, his schoolmates demanding he play some game he neither understood nor cared for. For Alexander Kirkpatrick, learning was a variant of his daydream.

"You are defiant, Convict? You do not elect to answer?"

Alexander came within an ace of blurting out the truth, telling this keeper of his confusion, his estrangement from the world of men.

"You will know of Mr. Darwin's work, Kirkpatrick?"

"Sir, I am not acquainted . . ."

When Mr. Tyree set his hands flat, his fingers seemed uncommonly long. "You were convicted for abetting the escape of a servant from his lawful master, is that correct?"

"Yes, sir." Alexander licked his lips. He thought he saw an escape. "One of your fellows had been badly mistreated by . . ."

"My fellows, Kirkpatrick? Am I a servant then?"

"Why no, sir . . ."

"I am the acting keeper of the Commonwealth's penitentiary, the duties of which I perform with due diligence. Like Mr. Robert T. Cahill, who owns the cartage service, and Mr. James Washington, Tredegar's furnace foreman, I was born free but impoverished, and owe everything I am to my own efforts. My uncle, Convict Kirkpatrick, was not the chaplain of Yale College. If Mr. Darwin is correct, people who prevail against great odds are more likely to pass on desirable characteristics to their offspring."

"But where to find a wife?" Alexander mused.

Mr. Tyree's lips pressed together and the veins stood out on his forehead, and Alexander's fumbled apology—"I'm sorry, sir, I didn't mean . . ."—did not improve matters.

"All that you have has come easily to you," Mr. Tyree said in a choked voice.

Alexander wanted to say it was not true—wanted to say that after his elderly uncle died, he'd had nothing except a failed career at Yale College, his silver watch, and an introduction to Buell & Peters, New York, New York. When he arrived in New York, Barnum's museum had been closed, and for all Alexander knew it might have been another day-dream—there was no way to tell! No way to tell!

Mr. Tyree enumerated Alexander's advantages, educational and racial, which Alexander, in the name of mistaken philanthropy, had discarded. "Do you think that your colored runaway was helped by a white man's compassion? Would it not have been better for him to fail or succeed on his own? Why would you enfeeble my race?"

Last winter, when he found Jesse on the doorstep, Alexander had thought he was dying. He had wanted to return Gatewood's slave to Gatewood, but, wordlessly, Sallie ignored him. Sallie laid Jesse before the fire, wrapped him in their warmest quilt, and fed him cooked pap, a spoonful at a time.

Now, Alexander wanted to cry that it hadn't been his idea, that his wife had insisted, that he'd been as willing as Tyree to let Jesse succeed or fail on his own, but Mr. Tyree had moved on another matter. "You know that our young nation is gravely threatened, that our recent defeat at Roanoke Island has alarmed the capital."

Alexander Kirkpatrick cared nothing about Roanoke Island. What did this war have to do with him?

"Our army is composed of volunteers. Enlistments are expiring and new soldiers must be found. My superiors, Keeper Blackwell, and Governor Letcher are agreed that prisoners willing to serve with Confederate arms may be pardoned. I am to decide who is worthy of this mercy."

Alexander's brow furrowed. He could not fathom what Tyree was driving at.

Mr. Tyree flipped open his ledger and dipped his pen. "You, Kirkpatrick."

"Sir?"

"You do wish to serve our country? You do wish to expunge your shame?"

Alexander's heart fluttered in his breast like a panicked sparrow. "Shame?" he said stupidly. "What shame?"

19

ELEMENTARY ARITHMETIC

MCDOWELL, VIRGINIA
MAY 8, 1862

If one Confederate soldier can whip 7 yankees,
how many Confederate soldiers can whip 49 yankees?

—*An Elementary Arithmetic Designed for Beginners,*
Raleigh, North Carolina, 1864

THAT SPRING THE armies in the western mountains fought like black
snakes bumping noses. Tap, and the Confederates slithered east, abandoning the hamlet of McDowell. Another tap and they snaked rearward
over the mountain into the Shenandoah Valley, pursued by cautious
Federal cavalry.

Something big in the wind. Far to the north, Stonewall Jackson's army
had dropped off the map. Two additional Federal armies were rumored
hurrying toward the scene. Allegheny Johnson's Confederates blocked
the Parkersburg–Staunton Turnpike at Staunton, and the Federals held
the passes. Toward Parkersburg, the turnpike passed through mountain
ridges close as fingers laid flat.

On May 4 at its Staunton Depot, the Virginia Central disgorged train
after train of Jackson's veterans to swell General Johnson's army. The
VMI Brigade of Cadets arrived from Lexington.

The newly fattened Confederate snake faced west and extended
its snout. Tap, the Federals recoiled up Shenandoah Mountain. Tap, they
abandoned their provisions train. Tap, back over Shaw's Ridge. The

Federal army had coiled back upon itself and would withdraw no farther.

At sundown the pursuing Confederates made a misery bivouac. The night was frosty and the stars were remarkably bright. The body of the Confederate snake stretched eight miles along the turnpike.

At dawn, Johnson's men were glad to be up and building fires. "Black walnut is just the thing for a coffin," Second Lieutenant Duncan Gatewood opined. "Tree off a backslope, stunted tree. Water won't make walnut wood swell and crack. You'll see to it, Catesby?"

"Anything you say." Catesby Byrd was devoting his full attention to a tin cup boiling upon a precarious triangle of stone, bayonet, and ramrod—the coffee was real, never before used, and with the entire brigade stumbling around any fool might kick it over.

"I suppose you'd prefer oak?" Duncan perched on the stone wall that funneled turnpike travelers into Marshall's Tollgate. Duncan's hands were tucked into his sleeves, his legs clamped together for warmth. "Suppose we're among the fellows killed in this fracas and we get buried in oak coffins. Burial parties aren't overparticular which army a man fought with: they lay everybody in one hole. Soon enough, the oak'd start coming to pieces and directly all the coffins'd burst and what with frost heaving, corpse'd get jumbled so there'd be a Federal skull on a Confederate chest and a rebel leg hooked to a yankee hip. Now, when Gabriel blows his horn and the earth is rent open to give up its dead and we present ourselves before Saint Peter, it'd be a hellacious mixup. Walnut coffin for me, Catesby. It is but simple prudence."

"Indeed." Catesby's pursed lips touched the hot cup. "That good farm wife said this was good coffee, and she didn't lie. Let us give thanks for patriotic southern women." After two sips he passed the cup to Duncan, who warmed his hands with it.

"Damn if I didn't think I was going to freeze to death last night. What did ol' Allegheny think he's up to? The Federals know we're coming, and we've got to come at 'em up this turnpike. Why wouldn't Allegheny Johnson let us light campfires? Until my blood warms I am no soldier."

Catesby retrieved his cup. "You're still meaning to reenlist?"

"Thought I might."

Catesby peered into the black liquid as if it contained his future. "Leona puts a brave face on it, but things are not well at Stratford. The government has requisitioned so many blacks to build fortifications in Richmond it is difficult to get plantation work done. Our baby is due soon, and doubtless Leona would prefer me home."

"Hell, Catesby. You're not gonna quit now? Ain't you having fun?"

A slight figure came up the road and presented his musket to Duncan. "Sir?"

Private Ryals was the youngest man in the regiment, just fourteen, and he carried a Kentucky rifle so venerable Daniel Boone might have known it. A previous owner had sawed it into carbine length and installed a percussion lock. "I got fast nerves, sir," the boy explained. "Last night, I was sittin' with Private Saunders and we was talkin', wonderin' what would happen today, and I wasn't thinkin' at all, so I kept on pourin' bullets into it."

The boy had stuffed so many cartridges into the weapon that the ultimate glistening ball was perfectly visible four inches from the end of the muzzle.

"Tell you what, Ryals," Duncan said solemnly. "What you want to do is charge into the biggest bunch of Federals you can find, and you pull the trigger. Won't matter what you shoot at, you'll kill everybody."

"But Lieutenant . . ."

"I'm just foolin', Ryals." Duncan returned the useless carbine. "Take this to Corporal Fisher. He has the worm. Don't shoot until you've wormed every cartridge out or this gun'll do you more harm than the Federal you're shootin' at. Soon as we lay into the Federals, keep your eyes peeled and snatch yourself a better gun."

Duncan opened his hand, but closed it again. You don't tousle a soldier's hair—not even a fourteen-year-old soldier's hair.

As Private Ryals went after the corporal, Catesby said, "Just a damn farm boy. Never been anyplace before, never did a thing. Never knew a woman. Only time he was in a city was when we paraded through Richmond. And today he'll fight a Federal army. Dear God. . . ."

"Catesby," Duncan said seriously, "sometimes it doesn't pay to think about things."

Catesby was framing his reply when Colonel Scott galloped by shouting orders, and the brigade fell into line of march.

Bullpasture Mountain was steep, and a few officers rode on ahead and waved handkerchiefs at every switchback, signaling: so far so good, no Federal bushwhackers.

March a hundred yards march and wait twenty minutes and officers and couriers raced along the narrow road and the Confederate army took six hours to gain the summit and start downhill toward the town of McDowell.

Duncan showed a hand-drawn map to Catesby. "The Federals are holed up in McDowell. Our scouts found a way to the top of Sitlington's Hill, which looks down on them. If we get guns up there before they do, we can knock hell out of 'em."

The Confederates turned into a steep westerly ravine and the lead Virginia regiment clambered for the top of Sitlington's Hill.

While the 44th waited its turn, men fell out and boiled water for coffee. Others dipped into their haversacks for hardbread. Duncan wished he had an apple. In Stratford's cool springhouse, apples kept until March, and they'd broach the last barrel of cider for the haymakers. When Duncan recalled the taste of that fine cider, his mouth seemed bone-dry.

At the first spattering of gunfire, men looked up at the woods as if they could see through all the way to the top of the hill. When the musketry died, shoulders relaxed, and jokes were told. Scattered shots were followed by intense rolling volleys, and the Federal guns started to boom.

"Damn," Corporal Fisher cried. "Now why'd we have to go and make 'em mad at us."

"Stay in ranks there," Duncan growled. "We go in after the Georgia boys."

The 44th Virginia jammed into the fan-shaped meadow at the foot of the ravine as the Georgia boys ascended two by two, clutching at saplings and roots.

Catesby's face had been weather-roughened since the days when he was a householder and county lawyer. He fanned his face with his hat. If Catesby lives, Duncan realized with a shock, one day he'll be bald.

"No way to get our guns up this ravine," Catesby said.

"Don't believe there is."

"Then what in hell are we doing? I thought our intent was to get above the Federals and rain hellfire on their pernicious heads."

"I'm not General Johnson. And I certainly ain't General Blue Light Jackson. You're asking me does this make sense?"

The gunfire above grew more insistent—a percussive clatter as if hundreds of china plates were hitting the floor.

It was two in the afternoon. The way was steep, and wherever men could slip they had, creating greasy slides for those coming after.

The Virginians clambered through a light rain of spent balls and broken twigs pattering to the ground. Corporal Fisher found breath for steady monotonous cursing. At last they surged onto a hogback ridge above the valley. "Line of battle on the right! Forty-fourth to the right! Shake a leg now, damn it!"

Bent over and gasping, the Virginians scurried along the crest wincing when minié balls zipped over their heads.

The valley below the hill was smoky from Federal guns, and of the village only a church steeple could be seen. But the distance was too great for artillery, whose rounds exploded short of the Confederate line.

The hogback was open ground thirty yards wide. Two hundred yards downhill, Georgians held a rail fence, and below that fence a woodlot wreathed with Federal rifle smoke. Bullets buzzed like yellow jackets.

Colonel Scott cried, "Spread out! Two men every five yards. One man to fire. The other to load."

Men in blue charged uphill from the woods and tumbled over the rail fence and hit the Georgians hard. Federal and Confederate were so intermingled the Virginians couldn't shoot. The hot swarm of men rolled toward the crest, receded, rolled again, until, sullenly, the Georgians withdrew. Gray and blue figures slumped lifeless as laundry across the rail fence.

"Fire! Lie down to reload!" Colonel Scott commanded. A sergeant stood to relay Scott's order and a bullet hit him with the tunk a hatchet makes going into soft wood and he dropped to his knees, mewled, and fell on his face.

The Federals fixed bayonets and cheered as they came. Duncan swallowed hard, strolled behind the Confederate line, calm as Sunday, though his knees were shaking.

"Bullets go high firing downhill! Aim for their knees. Their knees, damn it! You there, Private, haven't you reloaded yet?! Hurrah for General Johnson! Hurrah!"

A volley roared from the Federal line. A weaker volley from the Confederates.

Some Virginians lay flat, hands clamped over their ears.

Colonel Scott raged, "Get up, damn you! Get up!"

The Federals came on in a rush.

"Damn you for cowards!" Scott bellowed and booted his horse down the line of prone soldiers, taking no particular care where the animal stepped.

The Federals were at point-blank range: a smoke cloud through which silver bayonets protruded, backed by dim blue shapes.

"Retire two steps and fire!" Scott ordered. "Retire and fire!"

A step back, another. They backed toward the ravine they'd come from.

Private Ryals had a new rifle, an Enfield, and he was loading it fast as his hands could fly and firing it straight up into the air. Reload, fire into the air. Reload, fire.

"Ryals!" Duncan yelled. "There are no Federals up there!"

"No! And I'm afraid there never will be!"

Waving his walking stick and cursing, General Allegheny Johnson rallied the beleaguered Confederates. "Stop the bastards! You must stop these goddamned son-of-a-bitching bastards! Stop them! Cut them down!"

Deep within the Federal ranks, a cry rose: "That's Allegheny Johnson! Let's take him!"

"Oh you will, will you? You will? The hell with you! The hell!" Lifting his walking stick like a saber, the general demanded: "Cut those Federals down!"

Duncan laughed from pure joy. Bullets snapped by his ears, tugging at his clothes; Duncan didn't know when he had been so happy. He thought: So this is why men go to war—because they are so tender and it doesn't matter. Because men die and that's how the world has been, always, and it makes not the least difference what day you die so long as you die honorably, facing your foe. Your cause doesn't matter, nor whether you conquer or are defeated, only that you lift your Colt's patent revolver and select a man from the charging blue, a man like you, a blond-haired sergeant carrying a flag, and that you squeeze off one, two, three shots until suddenly he is fallen from your V-notched sights, fallen below your shimmering barrel, and perhaps you slew him, and his wife and children may grieve, his mother mourn, but like you he has elected to be on this field, and moments before he was as elated as you are.

The Federals fell back. Time passed. Men drank water. The Federals charged. They fell back. An hour passed. They attempted to turn the Confederate right, but a fresh Virginia regiment repulsed them.

Colonel Scott's horse was killed.

The sun dropped lower, balanced on the rim of the western mountains. On the slope below, the Federals were only musket flashes and smoke, but on the crest the Confederates were silhouetted against the sky.

Accompanied by fresh blue troops and vigorous hurrahs, a Federal flag emerged from the smoke. Confused Confederates started to retreat. Colonel Scott waved his hat and cried, "Do you intend to let these damn Federals drive Virginians from their own soil?"

The Virginians lifted their rifles and a bright bolt of fire crashed into the Federals. They quit.

Private Ryals was aiming carefully now, firing at flashes in the Federal smoke. Catesby Byrd tossed Duncan his canteen. Duncan swallowed warm water gratefully.

The sun disappeared. The Georgians ran out of ammunition and withdrew down the ravine. The 10th Virginia took their place and another Virginia regiment filled in behind them. VMI cadets were pressed into service as litter bearers.

General Johnson climbed a rock pile to see better. His stick twisted and he fell face forward into a stump hole. "God damn you men, drag me out of here. Drag me, you hear?"

The general's legs were waggling in the air like an upset beetle's and Duncan was running to help when the Federals volleyed. Duncan sat. It felt like somebody had smacked his right leg with a singletree. When he tried to stand, his leg buckled. "Oh," Duncan said. "So this is what it's like."

He pushed his revolver into his holster and fastened the flap and started crawling. His leg didn't hurt but wouldn't support his weight. He didn't want to inspect his leg closely because he didn't want to know. He hunched along toward the rear. Bullets flew high over his head.

Private Ryals put his rifle down and pulled Duncan by his armpits, but Ryals was too slight to do much good. "Wait a minute, sir!" he cried. "I'll get help."

Duncan thought but didn't say, "I won't go anywhere," and slumped onto his arm, his cheek in his hand.

He emerged into partial consciousness on a litter halfway down the ravine. He gripped the litter rails to steady himself. Lanterns held high marked the worst spots, but sometimes litter bearers slipped and wounded men shrieked when they crashed to the ground.

"Watch your feet! Damn it, have a care!"

The stars swirled safely overhead, but on earth it was dark and crowded and dangerous.

A young voice reassured Duncan he'd be all right, he'd be fine, it was only a short distance to the field hospital. "The surgeons will care for you, sir," the young voice said. Duncan opened his eyes. The boy at his head was a VMI cadet, high-collared jacket, stock; apparently he'd lost his kepi somewhere.

That'd mean demerits, Duncan thought.

"Only a little farther, sir," the boy said. "Just hold on a little longer."

"They called me Wheelhorse," Duncan whispered.

20

NOTE FROM CATESBY BYRD
TO SAMUEL GATEWOOD

HEADWATERS, VIRGINIA
MAY 9, 1862

SAMUEL,

I regret that your son Duncan was wounded during our signal victory over the Federals during the battle for McDowell. Duncan is shot through the upper leg but Providence has spared both his life and his leg, since the bullet missed the bone. He is weak from loss of blood and will require patient nursing while he recovers. Please come yourself or send Jack with a wagon to Wilson's Hotel, which, to Mr. Wilson's distress, has been converted into our hospital.

I send this by James Cleek, a reliable man, who will be scouting with the cavalry. Despite our severe losses, General Jackson has us formed into line of march to pursue the Federals.

Bless you,
Catesby

21

AN ABOLITIONIST

RICHMOND, VIRGINIA
MAY 25, 1862

SALLIE SAT IN the window seat of the keeper's parlor, mending a stocking. Her striped convict's shift was neatly patched and clean. Her long hair lay on top of her head in two braids tied with strips of rough cloth.

Conversing with a convict is like speaking to an inhabitant of a country one never wishes to visit, but Cousin Molly, who had commenced her visits with the expectation of uplifting Abigail's imprisoned neighbor, had come to rely on them for an opportunity for candor her work customarily forbade. "I have never seen our soldiers in such low spirits," she admitted. "They straggle into the city in twos and threes and find some inconspicuous place in the alleyways or Capitol Square, and sprawl—silent, unwilling to meet anyone's eyes. We have suffered too many grievous defeats.

"New Orleans is now under the heel of that Federal beast Ben Butler. How gallantly the Louisiana regiments paraded through Richmond last spring. How bravely their General Beauregard fought. Now his home is confiscated, his family subservient to Federal rule. Dreadful."

The younger woman listened from a new deep calm. Disgrace had strengthened her.

"Our hospital is a machine to treat wounds. We are to heal the injured and return them to duty. But too many of our patients are malingerers, lightly wounded men using their wounds to shun danger, strapping soldiers who'd rather sweep ward floors than return to their regiments. General McClellan's inexorable advance has snatched the heart from them. First Norfolk falls, then Williamsburg, then Yorktown. Federal divisions are at Seven Pines! In the summer we would picnic at Seven Pines, it was so pleasant and convenient. Now those same woods swarm with Federal cavalry, and our President has evacuated his family from Richmond. I try to present a good front, for nothing is more injurious to a sick or injured man than a matron's mournful countenance, but child, if matters do not improve, the Federals will be in Richmond before the Fourth of July. General McClellan has siege guns so tremendous they must be shifted by railroad. That has slowed his progress—as he advances he builds a railroad for his guns!"

"But if McClellan captures Richmond, the killing will stop."

"At the cost of the subjugation of our people who ask nothing but to go our own way in peace. . . ."

Sallie smiled.

Cousin Molly lifted a round hand. "But dear, I haven't given Cousin Abigail's news. My nephew Duncan has come home to Stratford. He is furloughed to convalesce from his wound."

Sallie's calm toppled to the floor with her mending. "Duncan? Wounded?"

"Child, his wound is not grave, and he is mending. He was wounded during the battle at McDowell, where General Jackson first demonstrated his remarkable abilities. General Jackson's campaign in the Valley is the only bright news in our Confederacy. Dear Cousin Abigail feared Duncan's wound might become corrupt, but her prayers were answered. Take my word, child, young soldiers who do not sicken from their wounds almost always recover. Duncan will be fit for duty by fall, and meantime is enjoying civilian existence at Stratford.

"Abigail worried the conflict betwixt husband and son would reignite when they were once again under the same roof, but to her satisfaction, the men never discuss old differences, and excepting inevitable awkward silences when tender subjects are inadvertently touched upon, father and son are reconciled. Daily Duncan rides out to visit your esteemed father and his servant . . ."

"Aunt Opal isn't a servant . . . exactly."

Cousin Molly raised one eyebrow. "I think it advisable to keep these matters clear: that a person is or is not a servant, is or is not a master, is or is not a Christian, is or is not an abolitionist."

The thought came to Sallie's mind unbidden: And me? But she didn't utter it, knowing that Cousin Molly's practical goodness far outstripped her theories.

"Aunt Opal is dear to me," Sallie said. "She reared me."

"Why of course she is, child. My Amelia has been with me since I was a girl at Madame Talvande's School for Young Ladies in Charleston.

Amelia kept me in frocks then and keeps me in dresses today. I surely don't know . . ."

"What news have you of Father? He seldom writes. I think all this"— she gestured at the walls—"it is too disagreeable to him." A tear started down Sallie's cheek. "I so wish I could see him. I so wish he could come to Richmond for a visit, but at his age . . ." She blew her nose. "I suppose it is best. He has always loved the nobler edifices of man's reason. It would shatter him to see me here!"

"And how are you faring, dear?"

"Perhaps you noticed the chained negroes in the yard. Runaway slaves kept here until they can be returned to their masters. Such were housed in the city jail, but the war has crammed that institution with riffraff, gamblers, and women of the streets. Our prison population of Irish highwaymen and mulatto murderesses is topsy-turvy. I owe my disposition to your visits, ma'am. It seems that one day a week where I can speak openly is all I require." Sallie set down her mending. "I would like to have other books in addition to the Bible they allow us. If you would suggest it to the keeper, I would be grateful."

A diffident knock interrupted. Mr. Tyree held his hat in his hand. "I am so sorry to disturb you, madam."

"Is my visit terminated, Keeper?"

"Tyree, madam, acting keeper. No, ma'am. I must speak to Convict Kirkpatrick."

With a look that queried his entire value, "Surely you mean Mrs. Kirkpatrick?"

Tyree drew himself up. "Ma'am, those in my charge are convicts. Now, I must speak to Convict Kirkpatrick privately."

Elaborately, Cousin Molly consulted the delicate watch pinned to her bosom. "Child, count on my return seven days hence." A sharp look at Tyree. "Keeper, how do you justify the presence of so many colored males amongst white women?"

"We are overcrowded, ma'am."

"I can see that. Does Governor Letcher know of this overcrowding?"

"I am not in regular communication with the governor."

"No, I suppose you wouldn't be." Bussing the younger woman on the cheek and bestowing the severest glance upon Mr. Tyree, she departed.

Sallie sat demurely, eyes downcast, hoping to outwait the storm. Mr. Tyree and humiliation did not agree with each other. "Mrs. Kirkpatrick . . ." he croaked. "You must dissuade your husband from a course which will produce the gravest consequences."

"Sir?"

"Convict Kirkpatrick, he . . . is much encouraged by the approach of the Federal enemy to our city. He finds political issues in the crime that brought you here. Your husband intends to communicate with President Davis."

"I fear I do not follow; what has Alexander done?"

"Convict Kirkpatrick seeks to be treated as a prisoner of war."

Sallie drew breath.

"Convict Kirkpatrick demands to be transferred to Belle Isle, there to await parole with the Federal prisoners of war. He says that you and he must be treated under the conventions of war."

"You wish me to dissuade him from this course?"

Keeper Tyree's face wore a sheen of perspiration. "This prison is not what it was. In happier times, it was quieter. I cherish quiet, Mrs. Kirkpatrick. I owe my position to the quiet my presence inspires. As you may appreciate, my post as acting keeper is coveted by jealous men. I remind you, Mrs. Kirkpatrick, within these walls, my gratitude is valuable coin." With a not especially convincing smile, Mr. Tyree backed out the door.

Thumbs hooked into his wasitband, Alexander strolled into the keeper's parlor. "Hello, Sallie. You're looking well. I see you are making the best of it."

Like a sudden immersion in ice water, Alexander's familiar arrogance shrank Sallie's heart. "I miss Uther terribly. Aunt Opal is well. I hear nothing of Jesse."

"Ah yes, poor Jesse. The runaway we tried to help."

"We would have sheltered anyone, a dog, under those circumstances."

"We were convicted because we opposed the 'peculiar institution,' and when George Brinton McClellan occupies this capital city of traitors, we shall be liberated. Sallie, I am overjoyed!"

"Alexander, the Federals have no reason to free us."

"They are fighting slavery!"

"If that is so, Alexander, they haven't openly confessed it."

"Like some great snake, the Federal army slides toward its mesmerized prey. And then the dreadful bite!" Alexander gripped his own arms and shivered dramatically. "Sallie, we shall be the heroes of our reunited nation. I shall give credit where credit is due: you, Sallie—you were most insistent. But we both, by helping Jesse, struck a blow for freedom!"

"Alexander, we are convicted felons."

He clasped her hands in his and smiled knowingly. "Dearest Sallie. Were our pathetic circumstances known to General McClellan, it would spur his advance."

"Alexander, we are not persons of consequence, we . . . ."

"Does that mean we cannot act for the right? *Alea iacta est!* This very morning, clear as a bugle, I heard cannonfire—McClellan's guns. The rebels have nothing that can stand against McClellan's mighty engine of war." Alexander's grin was boyish, triumphant.

"You have lost weight," his wife murmured.

"I have no appetite for the slops they feed us. When we are freed, dearest . . ." He tried to embrace her, but Sallie stiffened. "After we are freed, I shall return north. Some respectable institute of learning. Will you accompany me?"

"Alexander, Virginia is my home."

"My uncle—my uncle always hoped to be invited to preach, just once, at Yale College. But he was too humble for the likes of them! Now his nephew will speak on that platform, sharing honors with Emerson, Garrison, and Thoreau. Have you ever wished to visit Boston? Chicago?"

Sallie had thought Alexander's uncle had been chaplain at Yale College.

Alexander expanded his impromptu gazetteer: "Cleveland, New York, Hartford. Perhaps one day, after the rule of law has been reestablished in the South, we can return to Richmond, this seat of our present humiliations, to instruct our repentant enemies."

Sallie was heartsick. What could she have seen in this poor sad fool? "Alexander, I am not with you."

"Perhaps President Lincoln will invite us to his White House. I believe others have been so honored." Alexander summoned his most powerful persuasion. "Sallie, you are my wife."

"If this painful experience has proved anything, it is that I am not your wife. Alexander, I was young . . ."

Although his raised eyebrow had often silenced her, she continued. No man would command her silence again. "Alexander, I wish, nay I intend, legal dissolution of our marriage bonds, and should you refuse, I shall effect a practical severance of our union."

"You would quit me now, when our troubles are almost over?"

"I do quit you, Alexander."

He shrugged. He smiled. He looked away. "As you like. If my stratagems prove to your benefit as well as my own, I would be much pleased. I never wished to misuse you . . ."

"Alexander, you will not be accepted as a prisoner of war. 'Abolitionist' is a word—merely a word."

"And 'wife,' dear Sallie. Is that merely a word?"

"Alexander, I will not be berated by you. I will not! You sat in that courtroom wearing that insufferable smile, treating everyone, even those who might have helped us, with disdain. What could you have been thinking of?"

"I suppose . . . I suppose I was thinking of nothing. I recall wondering if the long-dead jurist whose portrait hangs over the bench ever enjoyed the loving to which we were at first addicted. Sallie, after my beloved mother died, my uncle took me in. Uncle's musty library was a warmer conversationalist than he. Sallie, believe me: I have tried. On his deathbed my uncle bequeathed me an introduction to an old friend at Buell & Peters. Picture me copying correspondence, letter after banal letter, ten hours a day, Sundays excepted. Picture an impoverished clerk walking the streets of Manhattan until weariness permitted sleep because strolling costs no money. Oh, Sallie, I had so hoped you and I . . ."

"Alexander, I will not be your wife from pity."

"Pity?" His yearning dried. "Are you so educated then? Do you read Virgil? Caesar? The immortals? Sallie, once you failed to produce our son, the affection I had for you dwindled immeasurably. It's right in the penitentiary regulations: any prisoner has the right to petition the highest official for redress of grievances. As a convicted abolitionist, I shall demand to be treated as a prisoner of war. If President Davis fails in his duty, he will answer to General McClellan upon that gentleman's triumph." Alexander flung his arms apart, welcoming McClellan's army of hosts.

Sallie swallowed. "But, Alexander, can't you wait? Everyone says the Federals will be in Richmond before the month is out."

His words tumbled over one another in his eagerness. "Don't you see? That's the cunningest part. If I take a principled stand, and am confined with the other Federal prisoners, my story will be credited. If I wait too long, I am merely another convict with a complaint!"

For the first time in her life, Sallie Botkin fainted.

Two warders came to Sallie's cell on the morning Alexander was to be flogged. One offered to read from the Bible, but Sallie said no. Perfectly composed, she sat on her stool, hands folded in her lap. She did hope Alexander might not scream.

Even while they tied him to the whipping post, Alexander remained confident reason would prevail. When the fire of the first blow reached his lungs, his bellow was less pain than astonishment. With no defenses prepared, no stoicism at hand, he begged and shrieked like a child. Life proved so much worse than he feared.

The flogging was done by an Irishman who, offended by Alexander's unmanly noises, laid on worse than he otherwise might have.

Of course, Mr. Tyree could not flog a white man.

22

LETTER FROM CATESBY BYRD
TO DUNCAN GATEWOOD

BEAVERDAM, VIRGINIA
JULY 2, 1862

DEAREST KINSMAN,

In the past seven days I have witnessed sights I had not thought to see in this life. Of dead men and dead horses and swamps and gunpowder I am heartily sick.

After our bungled attack at Gaines Mill, Corporal Fisher (who regularly cleans me out at poker) and I had picket duty in a copse of sycamore trees which had been splintered and shredded by the day's cannonades. At dusk, when the wounded earth was steaming and the night fog rose from the streams and swampy places, we heard a noise. It was a single soldier: a corpulent Federal private in a uniform so fresh he must have donned it for the first time that evening. When he espied us he stopped, uttered a cry—half alarm, half moan—before extracting a horse pistol his parent may have carried during the Mexican war. The Federal's shape was deformed, his breast sharpish as if a rooster's breastbone had been grafted onto a man.

"I won't kill you if you don't kill me," he said, his pistol wobbling from one of us to the other.

Corporal Fisher, who earlier had pillaged rations from one of this figure's deceased countrymen and was desirous of putting those rations to good use, replied, "Son, why don't you walk back in that fog and leave us patriots in peace."

"I'm lost," the Federal confessed.

"Well, son," Corporal Fisher replied, "from our uniforms you can presume we ain't the folks you're lookin' for. Fellows you want wear blue."

Duncan, I swear the fellow had a tear in his eye. "If I turn my back, you gonna shoot?"

"Naw," Fisher said. "You ain't no use to us. Why, you wouldn't even make a good prisoner. Now, you are interruptin' a repast I have been long anticipatin'. Why don't you sound retreat? Follow General McClellan's sterling example and change your base."

Then, Duncan, the fellow thumped his chest with the barrel of his pistol and it gave off a hollow sound, like someone beating an iron bucket. "I got no protection behind," he complained.

Duncan, that Federal was wearing a steel breastplate some rogue of a sutler had sold him.

Corporal Fisher leaned his Enfield against a tree, perched on a downed sycamore, and began to unwrap his supper. "I ain't gonna take you prisoner and you ain't takin' me prisoner. Army you seek is somewhere behind you." with no more ado, he began sampling Federal hardtack, which is, in every respect, quite as loathsome as our own.

Seeing that he was getting nowhere with negotiations, the Federal withdrew, facing us every cautious backward step. Since the ground was littered with shattered trees, his retreat was extremely tedious. Before he had quite disappeared, Fisher called out to him, "Yank, if you're gonna fight General Lee again it'd be well to put your armor on backward. It won't do you no good while you're runnin' away."

So we have our jests even as dead men grin at us beneath the bushes where they crawled to die.

I am sorry to give news that Private Ryals was taken to the hospital suffering from cholera and he succumbed to that disease.

You are not a good correspondent, Duncan my friend. And since you have seen my infant son, Willie, I would welcome any word of him, his surprising beauty, intellectual prowess, etc. None but shameless flattery of the little creature will be permitted! I am so grateful that Leona has recovered from her delivery. Sometimes when the interlude between infants is too long, childbirth is dangerous.

I must tell of the Strasburg farmer who produced a fine wedding celebration for his daughter. When the bridal party exited the church, our quartermaster's men were leading their horses away. Carriages of the wedding processions stood unhitched and, so far as I know, still stand outside the church. Our quartermaster notices all weddings in the countryside. He avers he is beginning to notice funerals too.

Of Jackson's troops, only Burke's regiment fought at Mechanicsville. Although the very air roared with battle, the 44th was never summoned. The next morning we were ordered to scavenge the battlefield. We heaped rifles, haversacks, shoes, and foodstuffs on our commissary wagons. Though my son Thomas would appreciate some souvenir of our victory, I took nothing, fearing the example I might set. Some of our men—Corporal Fisher among them—needed no example and happily pocketed valuables from the Federal dead. Our officers could not halt the pilferage.

Leona writes that you are reconciled to your parent. He is as good a man as I know and oft times when I am in doubt or confused I resolve the issue by asking what Samuel Gatewood might do in my place. I was glad to learn that Stratford's wheat crop is promising. Until this war is over, our provender will come from our domestic economy. I count my family fortunate to abide at Stratford, where food is plentiful.

General Jackson shattered the Federals in the Valley and now Lee shatters them on the outskirts of Richmond. Surely they must sue for peace!

Although I confess to a stirring in my heart when the yell goes up and our brave banners start forward, these battles in the swamps below Richmond have impressed me with the awfulness of war. Horses scream, wounded men weep all night. Only the crash of great guns drowns out these terrible commonplaces.

Since we are so near Richmond, President Davis sometimes pays us a call. Yesterday afternoon, he and his entourage arrived where General Lee was directing operations. Lee inquired, "Sir, who are this army of people?" Davis replied that he did not know.

"Well, sir," Lee stated, "they are not my army and I do not want them here." And so our President was driven away by his own general.

The Federals abandon prodigious stores, and we are eating like Turkish pashas: hams, salt beef, an immense herd of cattle captured on the hoof. And these are the mere residue of the tons of foodstuffs the Federals burned during their hasty retreat. The combined stink of unburied dead and scorched bully beef is unforgettable.

Tuesday our line formed along the railroad, where it crossed the Chickahominy on a trestle. Because of the high banks we expected a peaceful bivouac and were resting, smoking, writing letters home, until the Federals, despairing of withdrawing an ammunition train, set it afire and throttled it toward our lines. The cars bulged and thrashed and streamed white smoke, and the entire train shook as if palsied as it hurtled toward us. The locomotive failed to negotiate the final curve before the trestle and dove like an iron arrow to the mud flats below, and the subsequent explosions made my ears ring. Duncan, what shall we do when this war is over? We shall never see these sights again in our lifetime. There is something truly glorious in this prodigal waste.

General A. P. Hill has distinguished himself in battle, and though his kinsman Spaulding must have been at Hill's side, I have no news of him.

I am gladdened to learn that your wound is knitting. A modest limp conveys distinction upon a young man. When will you rejoin us? Although Lieutenant Bartles has your old company, I am sure the men will be happy to revert to your cooler leadership. Stonewall Jackson is so successful every junior officer is imitating his habits. Since Stonewall sucks on a lemon for refreshment during battle, so do they. Our quartermaster cannot keep a supply.

Your Obedient Servant and loving brother-in-law,
Catesby

23

RESPECTABLE WORK

RICHMOND, VIRGINIA
JULY 4, 1862

THE AMALGAM OF metals ideal for casting church bells is identical to the formula armorers prefer for cannons, and a good many of Richmond's bells had been melted down for that purpose. After General Lee's guns had done their duty, driven the invader from the city and ceased their thundering, the victory peals in Richmond were faint—victory was celebrated in the Confederate capital by a municipal buzzing like a hive of especially satisfied bees.

Men who'd known Richmond in Patrick Henry's time couldn't recall a warmer June, and the air had been thick as a wet glove. Citizens had stayed up half the night to the flash and rumble of guns, and fell gratefully into bed at dawn. Cary Street and Broad Street were jammed boardwalk to boardwalk with carts of wounded, and beside the carts walked dirty, bloodstained men. Though men in the carts cried out, the walking men were uniformly silent.

It was a foggy morning, cooler, the sun a pale coin in the east. Dew glistened the grass as Cousin Molly's barouche turned into the penitentiary's sally port. A brief pause, a murmur, and the clop-clop-clop across the cobblestones until it drew up before the keeper's house.

The coloreds were lined up against the outer wall, chained to a chain that might have hauled an anchor. Some had erected scrap-canvas shelters, some had strung blankets on poles, most sat against the cold stone and wrapped their arms around themselves. While waiting return to their masters, they marched out to dig fortifications. Each morning, Keeper Tyree's manservant made him one small pot of coffee and these men could smell it. Their nostrils twitched.

The cellblocks were brick above stone. The yard cobblestones were perfectly regular. The roofs of workshops and warders' quarters were cedar shakes, long faded to undifferentiated gray. The old cellblocks were capped with roofs of slate.

Cousin Molly's barouche was done up in the grand style, blue with gold trim for the footboard and door, and Cousin Molly's driver's faded uniform was of the same color scheme. He rapped the keeper's door more sharply than any prisoner would have dared.

Abruptly, the door swung open, and the driver recoiled slightly before proffering the message that had been entrusted to him. The door thudded shut.

A streamer of thick fog drifted into the yard, clammy on the skin. A raven cawed somewhere. Cousin Molly's driver returned to the barouche, ducked under its formal black canopy, and spoke. The keeper's side door banged open, and Tyree's servant hastened across the yard to the female cellblock, up the stairs to the second floor.

Men make drama of the material available to them: the acting keeper's vanished servant, the barouche waiting quietly in the fog, Mr. Tyree's window curtains suddenly swept apart and his sallow face pressed to the glass, the girl hurrying across the yard behind Tyree's servant, wearing her prison shift belted with dark cloth.

Even the colored prisoners knew about Cousin Molly. They knew that Convict Sallie Kirkpatrick shared Cousin Molly's food parcels with other female prisoners. When Tyree intercepted Sallie and reproved her, and Sallie threw her head back, proud and defiant, the coloreds shook their heads: even with Mistress Semple on your side, it didn't do to cross Mr. Tyree.

Cousin Molly dismounted from the barouche: a round, respectable women dressed entirely in brown. Her smile was below freezing.

"You'll pardon me, madam," Tyree met her, "if I cannot find these circumstances amusing."

Cousin Molly's bright blue eyes narrowed down to slits, her lips tightened, and she grew several inches taller than her statutory five feet two.

"Nor do I, Acting Keeper Tyree. Camp Winder's beds are full, badly wounded men lie on the floor in rows, the surgeons operate until they drop in their tracks, I haven't slept in seventy-two hours, and you delay me. You have seen Governor Letcher's order. Must I interrupt the governor for another?"

"But madam, nursing is not respectable work."

"Do you presume that I am not respectable, Acting Keeper Tyree? Who are your people?"

"No, no, you misunderstand." The keeper ran his hand over his hair. "Mrs. Kirkpatrick . . ."

"Are you concerned for Mrs. Kirkpatrick's respectability? In her circumstances? Acting Keeper Tyree, you are pleased to thwart me. I assure you such is not in your best interests."

A bitter smile fastened itself to Tyree's mouth. "I am awfully pleased to know that you have my welfare in mind, ma'am. For my own trivial purposes, I shall require a receipt for Convict Kirkpatrick."

"Of course," Cousin Molly said indifferently. The acting keeper retreated into the prisoners' parlor, opened and slammed drawers.

Ignoring his clatter, Cousin Molly turned to Sallie. "Our victories, child, use us up more than our defeats." She unfolded a handkerchief and blew her nose. "I am not certain I do you a service employing you. Many who volunteer to assist at Camp Winder cannot stomach the work."

"I am of no use in this place," Sallie said simply. "I cannot promise that I will be equal to the task, but I am willing to try."

When Tyree proffered his receipt, Cousin Molly signed it carelessly, without reading.

"And Alexander . . . ?" Sallie looked at the older woman.

"Alexander is thrown upon his own resources, my dear. I pray he will make the best of them. Child, time is of the essence. You will be outfitted from my wardrobe. Good day, Mr. Tyree."

Every eye in the prison yard yearned after them.

As the barouche clattered out of the yard, Cousin Molly chattered breathlessly. "What a sullen fellow! Perhaps his post makes him so. Your new clothing, dear, will not gladden your girlish heart, for we Camp Winder matrons are garbed in dowdy, uncomfortable brown. Your garments will be warmer than you might like, and you must keep them buttoned up to the neck. You will be spared hoops. There are Confederate prigs—though not one is a Confederate surgeon—who would dispense with our services."

Sallie's head was whirling, and though she heard words embedded in Cousin Molly's chatter—"brown," "neck," "surgeons"—their meanings were lost. She understood that her life had changed again and that she would be asked to do tasks other women found repellent. She'd grown accustomed to the prison's smoky sour stench, and now when fresh air hit her lungs it was almost painful, like a draught of too chilly spring water.

At Cousin Molly's fine house on Broad Street, Sallie changed her garb under the watchful eyes of an elderly servant, who picked up her prison dress with reluctance.

"Do be careful," Sallie said cheerfully. "You'll not find my lice agreeable companions."

·　　·　　·

Early in the war, wounded soldiers were segregated by state and rank—Tennessee officers to Chimborazo Hospital, Virginia privates to Camp Winder—but as the number of wounded swelled, many nice distinctions were discarded and families seeking their son or father or brother made a melancholy tour from one hospital to another.

Chimborazo was the largest—some said it was the largest hospital in the world. Camp Winder, under Chief Surgeon Lane, was built to accept Chimborazo's overflow, and when Winder could take no more, wounded men were placed in tobacco warehouses and private homes.

"I do not know how many wounded soldiers are in Richmond," Cousin Molly confessed tiredly. "When melancholy overcomes me, I fear we will fight until every young man in the South comes under the surgeon's knife."

Camp Winder was a rectangle of rough pine buildings on Richmond's north side. Water tanks towered above its whitewashed buildings. Within its perimeter fence, behind the wards, plump shorthorn cows grazed.

"Our own bakery, gardens, dairy; we are a complete island. Chief Surgeon Lane is a most dedicated organizer."

Although Malvern Hill had been fought three days ago, wounded men were still coming into Richmond, many already stinking with infections that would kill them. A very young boy with a blood-soaked bandage around his forehead made a deep bow as the women passed through Winder's gate, and Sallie drew breath.

The ward had beds along both walls and at one end a small storeroom, which had been converted, at Cousin Molly's instructions, for matrons' use. It contained a camp bed, a chest (which doubled as a table), and one window (curtained).

Three brown-clad matrons came to Cousin Molly's elbow seeking instructions, passing on surgeon's orders, asking advice. Cousin Molly dispatched the pair to assist surgeons and requested the third stay on the ward. "That Kentucky boy is dying," she noted matter-of-factly. "See if he wishes a letter written home."

By now, the sun had got up in the sky. The ward stank of rot and the slightly sweeter smell of flesh trying to mend itself. The flies were everywhere, thickest on the bloody rags and lint bandages heaped beside the door. "Remove those," Cousin Molly told Sallie. "Throw them into the ravine."

The flies were angry at being disturbed and buzzed Sallie's face. The rags reeked of old blood and pus and feces and corruption. Sallie made a sack of a torn blanket and slung it over her back like a peddler.

The ravine was a deep ditch from the hospital grounds to the James which the water towers flushed every other day. The ditch was full of objects Sallie's eyes didn't care to identify. Some of the objects shimmered with maggots.

• • •

Men sat or lay on stretchers until convalescents carried them in to the surgeons.

"Must I lose my leg, sir?"

"It is your leg or your life."

The matron presses the chloroform-soaked rag over the man's nose and mouth until his eyes roll back, the surgeon wipes his bloody saw on his apron front, and the saw bites and the hot stink of cutting bone, rick, rick, rick, and the fine-toothed saw jerks through, and the surgeon's swift knife finishes the job. The flap is sutured over the stump, the limb tossed into the tub of unnecessary human accouterments. Some limbs are small, some long, some short, some plump, several have been so shattered it is impossible to guess at their original shape or whether they were once arms or legs. The surgeon wipes his forehead with the back of his forearm. "How many more?" he asks.

When he is told there are another fifty waiting outside he closes his eyes for a moment and sways.

Cousin Molly touches Sallie's arm. "Child, you said you wished to be useful."

"Yes, ma'am," Sallie says. "It is not what I expected, that's all."

"It will soon seem like all the world."

24

THE HIGH LIFE

IT HAD BEEN Captain Sutterfield's mansion, the ornament of the S&S Riverboat Line until the Federals cut the Mississippi at Corinth and stopped its mouth at New Orleans and Memphis's riverboats rotted at the Memphis docks and Captain Sutterfield was killed when the Confederate rams were defeated by Federal gunboats. Mrs. Sutterfield, who had watched her husband's fatal action from the bluffs above the river, still lived in the back of the captain's house in what had been the nursery and Captain Sutterfield's library, but the doorway between front and back was bricked up and only Mrs. Sutterfield's oldest friends came to call, from the rear, through the garden.

The Federals who occupied Memphis wanted cotton, the Confederates in the hinterlands wanted medicines and other supplies, so an uncomfortable, thriving trade commenced. Some men grew rich.

Mrs. Davis (no relation to the President) let the front of the mansion. Respectable citizens crossed to the other side of River Street when they passed, their servants likewise. An unusual number of carriages at night for such a respectable neighborhood, a ship's lantern in a front window, its bull's-eye painted red: these were the only signs.

Small boys were amazed at how late the house arose. They were surprised at how many wine bottles found their way into the household trash, how many torn ribbons and solitary silk shoes.

At noon, the colored man with the scarred face opened the front door and toured the property. He carried two buckets, an empty one for the bottles he'd find tucked under the bushes and flowerbeds, and a bucket with sand to cover the vomit and, twice, blood.

Inconsequential visitors dropped by during the long afternoon, and sometimes a piano could be heard playing Chopin half badly. In the evening the carriages came, parking along the street once the drive was filled.

Fashionable Memphis ate late in those days, and only after the Gayoso Hotel dining room closed, near midnight, did the tip-top clientele arrive at the Captain's House, as it had come to be called. "Let's go up to the Captain's House," some wag would cry, pulling the cord of an imaginary steamboat's whistle. "Choo, choo."

A particularly fine carriage paused long enough for its two occupants to descend, before proceeding down the street, where the flare of sulfur matches and glowing cigars marked other coachmen.

As was her policy, Mrs. Davis met the two at the door. "Why, Mr. Turnbull, do come in. And Mr. Omohundru, we've not had the pleasure lately. . . ." Mrs. Davis was unknown in Memphis before the war.

Wordlessly, the scarfaced negro took their wraps. Off the hallway, the piano tinkled "Camptown Races." Turnbull—who owned the Gayoso and never tired of company—started toward the parlor, but Omohundru hesitated. "It has been a demanding day, Mrs. Davis. Perhaps you could bring me a brandy—in the private room?" Ahead laughter burst, intertwined with a girl's shriek of amusement. To Turnbull: "There will be Federals in there. I began my day dealing with Federaldom, and I'll be damned if I'll end it in the same manner. I am to have a new pass, you know. Apparently the old pass no longer serves. I report to their provost marshal tomorrow at eleven. Damn them. God damn them."

"Those Federals are paying a dollar a pound for cotton. In gold, Silas."

"They will extract their pound of flesh, rest assured. My new pass, I am given to understand, will cost fifty dollars. And the provost accepts only gold. What sort of sovereign power, John, does not accept its own currency?"

Turnbull winked. "I am told Mrs. Davis has offered a place to a Cajun girl, young, accomplished in the French arts. I hope to impose my sovereign power upon her."

Returning with Omohundru's brandy, Mrs. Davis caught the last of this. "You speak of Minette. What a spirited creature! When the Yankees occupied New Orleans, she fled north—for all the good it did her. Yankees here, Yankees there—all the same after they have their trousers off."

It was one ribaldry too many, and with a vague smile, Omohundru retired to the private room, where a wall sconce gleamed dimly. "Let me turn up the gas," Mrs. Davis offered.

"No," Omohundru said. "This well suits me. My eyes . . ." He rubbed his forehead, and closed the door—himself in and Mrs. Davis out. Omohundru set his brandy on the table, sprawled upon a settee, and closed his eyes. The room was damp, its drapes pulled shut, and cool. The furniture was dark mahogany. In the hall outside, footsteps passed and wisps of conversations.

"George McClellan retreated down that peninsula a damn sight faster than he went up it. . . ." (Federal officer, likely.)

"If we don't sell our cotton to them, we cannot buy the provisions our beleaguered armies require." (Confederate.)

"Grant ain't nothin' but a damn drunk." (Hard to know which party.)

Silas shouldn't have come out tonight, he should have gone directly to his hotel room. He'd not slept in two days. But Turnbull was so useful; without Turnbull, Silas couldn't get his goods onto the Memphis & Jackson, the only railroad in the South which passed goods through the lines. When Silas became aware of breathing he sat bolt upright.

"No need to turn up the light," a soft voice said. "I intend no harm."

"What the hell!" A jab shot through his forehead.

She whispered, "I came here for the quiet. Maybe you don't want people finding you either?"

Silas's body lost tension and sank back into the cushions. "I sometimes think . . ." he murmured tiredly.

A smile in her voice. "Sometimes I think that way too."

She was well-spoken, a lady, but no lady ever crossed the lintel of the Captain's House, only girls. "It is the war, this . . ." Silas swallowed his curse. "This unfortunate war. Why did they invade us? Why did we go out? We cannot hope to win. Already they are too strong for us in the west and soon they will be too strong in the east. I am an ordinary man of business . . ."

"Silas Omohundru, 'ordinary'? You're reputed the most successful cotton broker in Memphis."

"I am as good as my word."

"Oh, I meant no offense. I never heard criticism of you. Not like some other traders. I do believe the Federals aren't overly fond of you."

The girl was partly concealed in a wingback chair. Silas could see she was slight, but nothing more. He closed his eyes. "We make our market of necessity, not affection. The Federals treat us with contempt and we cut them socially. No doubt Federal officers with whom I do business are in Mrs. Davis's parlor, but should I go in, we would not speak. Confederates and Federals find opposite corners, and excepting those inevitable occasions when they dispute a girl's affections, we ignore one another. Gold for cotton: that is our entire relationship."

"How did you come to the cotton business?"

Silas shrugged. "Only blockade running offers a better return. Although it does not always gratify me, I am a trader. I find it easy to assess a man's fears and greed, his concupiscence and conscience. Today I shipped chloroform, horseshoes, and shoe leather for our armies. And how do you come here?"

"My son will sleep the night through, thank God. There is a linen room, no more than a closet, where I set his bed. My Jacob may wake during the night—from time to time he must—but he never cries out."

"I don't understand children. I am quite confirmed in the bachelor's ways."

"Many of the men who come to this house are married, I think."

"Won't you be missed . . . in there?"

"Mrs. Davis despairs of me. She says if I don't try harder, I'll have to go. She threatens one of those riverfront places. I try to act gay and carefree, but I've been a married woman and I've been a mother and I've seen some things. Did you ever meet Lieutenant Malone, that Irishman? A little fellow, no bigger than I, stabbed Lieutenant Malone with a knife, and our carpet was ruined and Paulie—he's the houseman—scrubbed and scrubbed to get the stain out of the flooring. The murderer escaped through the window, and I don't know what they did with Lieutenant Malone's body, but Paulie said his family was told he was killed in action."

Mrs. Davis stuck her head in. "Here you are, dear. Some gentlemen were asking after you."

"Yes, ma'am." The girl got to her feet, a lithe shadow.

Silas squinted. "She will remain with me, Mrs. Davis, if you please."

The woman's irritation was poorly concealed. "Of course, Mr. Silas. Should I have Paulie fetch champagne?"

Silas winced. The light framing Mrs. Davis in the doorway was painfully bright. "Some cool water. A pitcher of cool water, please."

He didn't open his eyes when Paulie brought his water, nor did he overhear what the houseman said to the girl. She laid a cool damp cloth over his forehead and eyes. It was delicious.

He licked his lips. "I didn't have these headaches before the war. The cannonade at Fort Sumter brought them on." He smiled thinly. "I understand that President Davis suffers too."

"You take a drink of this water. They've good water here: well water. I hate that smelly cistern water."

"What did he say to you?"

"Paulie? He wanted to know if you were drunk."

"And?"

"Patience has her time of the month, Minette's sulky. Baby Bear's favorite, Captain Olsen, wants her to himself. Paulie says I should finish you quick."

He smiled. "I believe this cool cloth has finished me. How long have you been in this house?"

"When I came to Memphis, I stayed with James Shelby, the banker. He wanted me to keep to my little room downtown. I said I've got to go out sometime, but he was jealous, thought I was seeing a younger man. One afternoon I wasn't home when he came by—I was promenading Baby Jacob along the riverside—and when I got home he hit me as hard as he could, which wasn't as hard as he'd intended, but I pretended great distress, so he fled. That night a big blond-headed fellow came and threw me down on the coverlet, in front of Baby. Then he brought me here."

"Have you nowhere else to go?"

Her fingertips rubbed his forehead. Delicious.

"You don't know who I am, do you?"

Silas's head throbbed. Had she been last week's girl? The girl from the week before? Most times he came to the Captain's House, he didn't feel quite so low. "Did I . . .?"

"No, Master Silas Omohundru, you've never been with me that way."

He plucked the cloth from his eyes. She had skin the color of almonds, a long aquiline nose, long slanted Mediterranean eyes. Her smile was calm and kind. "Yes, you seem familiar," he said. "Where . . . ?"

She replaced the cloth. "Never you mind," she said. "I don't want to get you too stirred up."

"I didn't mean . . ."

"I know you didn't, honey. When you came in, what was bothering you?"

Thumps on the door. Turnbull's voice. "Silas, you got more stayin' power than I gave you credit for. You comin' out of her anytime soon?" Laughter.

"Well," Silas drawled falsely, "I believe I'm set for the night. You tell Mrs. Davis her girl . . . has as much as she can handle. Tell her I'll settle in the morning."

"I thought you were feeling poorly."

"I was!" Silas's guffaw shamed him as he uttered it. In a whisper he began an apology to the girl, "Please don't think . . ."

"Hush now. I am greatly pleased to have you spend the night." She stroked his temples gently and drew an afghan over his chest.

Silas's voice tiptoed through the dimness. "Confederates think me a traitor for profiting from the enemy—though they must have the medicines and weapons I buy here in Memphis. I swear there are times I wish I'd been born a Yankee. They do not despise traders!

"Southerners of the better sort snub me. Yes, I speculated in slaves, but when I gave up that business nothing changed. Nathan Bedford Forrest was the greatest damn slave dealer in Memphis, and there is no bigger market in the west. Today Forrest is the great cavalry commander, his name on every man's tongue!"

She patted his hand, stroked his wrist.

"Forrest is legitimate. His parents may have been backwoods bumpkins, but he is legitimate."

She said, "I hear you're awfully rich."

"I suppose so."

"I always wondered if there was anything a rich man couldn't buy."

There was an edge in her voice that hadn't been there before, but he was too weary to ask about it. "I'm a bastard and you're a nigger wench," he said. "Money seems like everything, until you've got it."

He didn't know when she fetched him a coverlet, but when he woke, he was warm and early summer's dawn light slashed a vertical gap in the heavy drapes and on the opposite wall framed a lithograph of a bird, one of Mr. Audubon's birds. The wallpaper was in the French mode, pale green stripes with regular white borders. The woman had slept sitting on the floor, her head resting against his thigh. His hand happened on her head, stroked her hair.

She stretched then, lifted her long arms, and his hand fell naturally upon her breast.

"I know who you are," he murmured. After a long minute, he said, "Jesus Christ, I'm sorry."

"It wasn't you caused my troubles," she said. She nestled herself into his hand.

When Silas Omohundru departed Memphis for Wilmington, North Carolina, most of Omohundru's cotton trade accrued to Turnbull, and because he knew his enhanced prosperity was due less to his own efforts than to the withdrawal of a better man, Turnbull joked that Omohundru had got out while the getting was good. And when word came that Omohundru had purchased a blockade runner and had married a strikingly beautiful Bahamian girl, Turnbull joked about that too: "They call them girls 'conks,' you know, on account of they been conked by that ol' tar brush. . . ." Shrewder men thought Silas had judged it right, got his money out when the markets were at their peak. U. S. Grant took over Federal command in Memphis, and though his factors kept on buying Confederate cotton, they paid for it in scrip.

25

THE GRANARY OF THE CONFEDERACY

THE CRADLERS SPREAD along a golden wall of wheat like skirmishers. A step forward and whiss the sharp blade slices the standing grain; on the backswing, twist the cradle so it deposits it in the swath: step and cut, an easy motion that let a man enjoy the small clouds scudding overhead, the trickle of sweat down his brow, his hickory snathe smoothed by other hands, other harvests. Step and cut. The Jackson river bounded this field, and over the whiss of his blade, a man could dream of that water's sweetness.

The field was ten acres: longer than deep. The wheat was the new-fangled Mediterranean variety. The field was the last the gang would cut, the farthest upstream, highest elevation, last to ripen and dry. They'd worked Hidden Valley and Warwick Plantation and Stratford's lower fields and the sun had stayed bright and the courteous rains came on Sundays when they wouldn't interrupt the work and the harvest promised to be bountiful.

It had been hard on the older men, and every morning they rose stiff from their beds and toppled gratefully into them at nightfall. But the work peeled years away, and as their muscles lengthened and suppled, they joked more and grew easy with each other.

A man could dream fantastical dreams while the wall of wheat receded before him. Duncan Gatewood dreamed of horses: fast horses, sleek-sided mares, foals dancing in the pasture.

Beside Duncan, Rufus watched barn swallows wheeling after insects dislodged by the cradles and the ground-dwelling insects exposed when their wheat roof was suddenly removed. The swallows were conducting their own harvest.

Cradling alongside Rufus, Samuel Gatewood was calculating profits. A barrel of prime flour was bringing forty dollars at Richmond, and since there were ready buyers at the Millboro Springs railhead, a man didn't have to wait for his money. Private buyers bid against the government, and some paid in gold.

Samuel was working tasks he hadn't since he was Duncan's age.

Beside Samuel, a colored man from Warwick Plantation; next Thomas Byrd, his first year with the fulltask hands; and finally, at the verge of the plowed ground, big, pleasant, simple Joe Dinwiddie. People worried what would happen to Joe if he was conscripted.

The rakers followed the cradlers. Pauline Byrd, Franky and Dinah Williams, and four children from Warwick Plantation who never spoke except to one another.

Pompey veered from swath to swath, binding sheaves. He'd strip wheat into cords, knot it, loop it around a fat sheave, and knot again. When Jack the Driver called "Shock!" the children dropped their rakes and fetched armloads of sheaves. Since the shocks must defy the weather for weeks, only Jack built them. Eight sheaves formed a shock's walls, and Jack flattened two sheaves for the roof. "A good hudder makes a good shock," Jack frequently remarked.

Day after day each cradler cut his bushels, and day after day, over rough ground and smooth, the rakers raked their swaths, Pompey bound his sheaves and Jack cried "Shock!" They started as soon as the dew was off the wheat. Same sun every day: it felt fine in the cool of the morning but turned cruel before noon. Waves of grain receded before the skirmish line of cradlers, and the barn swallows swirled and cried overhead.

When the sun stood directly overhead, Samuel Gatewood lodged his cradle, wiped his forehead with his kerchief, called out, "Take your ease!" and excepting Jack and the children, who were finishing a shock, everyone shouldered tools and ambled to the riverbank where the great elms distributed shade. Rufus found a low spot on the grassy bank and lay flat on his belly and splashed cool water on his head and neck and ducked his face under the water and drank that way. He shook his head like a dog. Sweaty, chaff-covered, Duncan slumped against a tree. Although new skin closed his wound, pallor was just beneath Duncan's tan; he worked awkwardly, disjointedly, and his swaths were no broader than young Thomas Byrd's. Samuel Gatewood uncorked his flask, swallowed, and offered it to his son, who shook his head no.

Rufus looked at the ground as Gatewood pocketed the flask.

"Jesse Burns the best cradler I ever seed," Rufus said. "Jesse cut seventy bushels at Warwick barn field last year and day's end he was still rarin' to go. Jack, you recall when Preacher Todd broke a wheel fording Strait Creek? That water was over my waist, and Lord! Cold? Jesse lift that whole wagon and hold it up while we pry the old wheel off the hub and hammer a new wheel on. I wish we had Jesse on the cradle. That man make short work of a field of wheat."

"He not much help in leg irons," Franky Williams giggled.

A wagon bumped across the field where yesterday no wagon could have passed, rattling over ground that had been hidden by tall golden grain. In a cool calico dress, her face shaded by an oversized bonnet, Miss Abigail rode beside old Uther. Feet dangling over the tailgate, Aunt Opal was in back.

Young Thomas Byrd brought a water dipper to his uncle. "Duncan, when they were comin' at you, the Federals I mean, were you scared?"

The water tasted fine, and Duncan knew he would cherish such memories after he returned to his regiment. "If you get to thinking about it, sure you're scared. Thing is—mostly you're too busy to think. Fighting a battle is hot work."

Samuel Gatewood accepted the dipper from his son. "The post rider reports that when our army fought that fearful battle at Malvern Hill, Reverend MacDonald of Mint Springs could hear cannon fire from the direction of Richmond, and others attest to the phenomenon. My God, sir. Richmond is more than a hundred miles from Mint Springs."

"My father wrote," Thomas added, "that G'nrl Lee whipped the pants off 'em. I wish I could have seen it."

"Thank God Catesby is spared," Samuel said.

Thomas refilled the dipper for Jack, who rested against the back of Duncan's tree, feet stuck out straight.

"Thank you, son. I gettin' too old for real work."

"How old are you, Jack?"

"Don't rightly know. My mother was servant to Robert Obenchain outside Harrisonburg. Cattle he reared, and hogs. When the drought took his crops I was sold to Reverend Mitchell in Warm Springs. That was the year after Nat Turner got to killin' planter folks."

"Jack . . ."

"Uncle Jack," Duncan corrected.

"Uncle Jack, why'd he do such a thing? Was Nat Turner one of John Brown's men?"

"Before Mr. Brown's time, I 'spect," Jack said. "I believe we shocked a mess of wheat this morning."

"Was he a madman, Uncle Jack? Why'd Nat Turner want to kill planters? What'd they ever do to him?"

"Thomas," Duncan said, "go and help your grandmother unpack our dinner. Looks like she brought that blueberry shrub you're so partial to."

Supported on Aunt Opal's arm, Uther Botkin came near. "Good day, Duncan. You seem much improved."

"Considerable, sir. I have another month furlough before returning to duty. I can't leave Catesby to fend for himself amongst those Tidewater men. They think we mountaineers talk funny!"

Samuel asked, "May I offer you brandy, sir? Or would you rather Abigail's shrub? Most refreshing." He turned to his son. "Duncan, have you been reading my Tom Paine? I couldn't find it the other night." Perplexity troubled Samuel's face. "I'd swear someone is rearranging my books. Twice this week I searched for a volume only to have it turn up the next day."

"Maybe Pompey gettin' himself some education," Rufus joked.

Thomas set the basket (cornbread, ham, roast beef, piccalilli, mustard, pickled horseradish) on a broad stump where all the workers could help themselves. Everybody ate the same food. Excepting Jack, the coloreds sat farther down the riverbank.

Infant Willie Byrd was sick with fever again, and the crisis was upon him. All through the night, Abigail and Sister Kate took turns bathing his tiny body and Mother Gatewood prayed ceaselessly. The infant's mother, Leona, was beside herself with worry.

"It is hopeless then?" Samuel asked his wife.

"The issue rests with God."

In previous summers Stratford had had a dozen fulltask hands for the wheat harvest. These days Samuel was lucky to find five. The Richmond government had conscripted fifteen of his servants ("rented" was their word) from the plantation. Others had run away.

Most of the runaways were returned after Samuel Gatewood put out the advertisement and offered the reward. West Virginia was seceding from Virginia, but that didn't make it a haven for runaways. West Virginians might not care for the Confederacy but that didn't mean they embraced the negro.

The ones brought back were the lucky ones. Yellow Billy and Pompey were heading north and Billy had been fording the Cheat River when a couple white boys on the bank shot him to pieces for the hell of it. Hidden in the brush on the riverbank, while Billy begged for his life, Pompey had a change of heart and came directly home. Master Samuel told Pompey he could continue as houseman but he'd help with the field work too. Jack the Driver asked Pompey why he'd run.

"I run because Billy run," Pompey said. "And Billy run 'cause he was foolin' with buckra's woman and buckra found out about it and was gonna kill Billy. Billy said when we get north, Master Lincoln give us a pillowsack full of gold."

"And you believe him?"

Pompey hung his head.

Stratford quit sawing timber. Women could milk cows and shock hay and women could bring the hogs out of the woods and tend to the horses. But women couldn't fell and limb sawlogs.

Samuel Gatewood complained to Abigail, "Government rents my servants whether I wish to rent or no. And the Lynchburg Fire and Hose Company won't insure them because they're on public duty. Thus if my servants are injured or fall ill through neglectful treatment it is my duty to restore them to health, and should they die it is my loss."

Auntie Opal removed the basket from the stump, sat old Uther down, and stood before Samuel Gatewood. "Master, they after our cows," she said. "Government after our cows. Already took six."

"You sold willingly?"

"Us? Them? Hah!" Aunt Opal spat. "They took half what we got, said they'd be back for the others. What we gonna do, Master Samuel, without those cows? Where we gonna get money from?"

Uther cleared his throat. "They mentioned . . . my daughter and her husband. They said that we of all people should be glad to contribute to the Confederate effort."

"Specie," Opal snapped. "They pay us in specie. Those cows was in calf, due in September, and now they be slaughtered for beef, and we never took specie for a cow before, never once."

Samuel Gatewood pinched the bridge of his nose. "When next I'm at the courthouse, I'll speak to the commissioners. I can't restore your cows but may prevent future takings."

Uther said, "The Confederate government conscripts men as the Federal government does. The Confederate government confiscates what it needs from its citizens as the Federal government does. Tell me, Samuel, what are our people fighting for?"

Duncan said, "Because we never asked the Federals to come here and tell us what to do and we're gonna make 'em go back north where they came from."

For a moment, the old man contemplated rebuttal, but a softer light came into his eyes. "I beg your pardon, sirs. I did not come to Stratford today to dispute but to offer you, Samuel, and dear Abigail, my profoundest gratitude. My Sallie has written me, sir." He extracted a much-read letter from his breast pocket and handed it to Abigail. "It is to your offices Sallie owes her freedom from . . . that place. My daughter is conditionally pardoned, Samuel. . . ." The old gentleman did not conceal his tears nor his trembling when he touched his neighbor's hand. "Samuel . . ."

Samuel nodded, "My wife's cousin Molly wrote us of her regard for your daughter and her intent to ask Governor Letcher to intervene. I do not doubt that practical considerations have influenced the governor's decision. If we will fight wars, we must have those to care for our wounded. Letcher is no fool, he . . ."

"Sallie does not mention Alexander," Abigail returned the letter.

Old Uther stowed it in pocket and patted the bulge. "That my daughter is impetuous, I'll allow, but from her dear mother she has inherited her heart. My Sallie is a good girl."

"Once Molly's mind is made up, not much deters her." Abigail smiled. "You remember, Samuel, that summer we were courting? At Warm Springs, all the young people, oh what a gay time we had! It was the time I remember most fondly from my youth. Mischievously, we brought silly people into Molly's company to see what she would make of them. One Baptist preacher—a man from Georgia, I believe—was particularly aggravating. Every evening he took a central place on the veranda, lecturing those who were scarcely acquaintances about the evils of cards and drink and the all too numerous flaws of the younger generation. Finally, Cousin Molly had had enough. 'Sir, complaints of elders about the young are not unknown in the Bible. As I recall, the philistines made a dreadful fuss about young Jesus.' "

Uther tried to smile, but he was thinking about his daughter; tears spilled again, and he faced away. Aunt Opal stared at the sky as if something novel might occur in that firmament.

Thomas and the younger boys were inspecting the rock circles of last spring's fish nests in the diminished river. His mouth open, arms spread, Joe Dinwiddie dozed in the shade. Aunt Opal and Miss Abigail gathered the food, offered a last glass of shrub. Samuel took a thoughtful pull on his flask, and his face grew slightly redder. The wagon horse's foot was tucked under Rufus's arm while he picked at its hoof. Rufus constantly practiced his horseshoeing.

Duncan laid his cradle blade on a pocket anvil and hammered an edge into the soft metal.

Directly, other cradlers got to their feet and the ching, ching, ching of their hammers marked the sleepy afternoon. Ten minutes later, the skirmish line was athwart the wheat, and by four that afternoon, the last wheat was in shocks and the workers were finished.

Samuel Gatewood and his son went directly to the barn and saddled their horses. They had resumed their familiar twilight ride, with altered details. Previously they had ridden side by side while Samuel explained fine points of plantation management—grasses, livestock health, negro care, the training of a first-rate driver—while his son asked respectful questions. Nowadays Duncan showed no interest in these matters, so they rode single-file.

Gatewood followed the trail his timber gangs had created. Already the track was grown up in grass, the wagon ruts nearly invisible. There were more deer in the woods since the timber cutters weren't hunting them. The horses climbed above the hot still valley. The wheat fields were as bare as a bearded man fresh-shaven. Along the track, butterflies darted among purple thistle flowers. Wherever man disturbs the earth, thistles remark it.

Duncan came beside Samuel's stirrup. "Father, let's ride to the Blue Hole and bathe."

The Blue Hole was a deep pool where the Jackson River slowed and swirled beneath a brow of limestone cliffs. It was shady on the riverbank and the water ran cold. Duncan tied Gypsy to a skimpy redbud and stripped off his shirt and trousers. His wound was a pucker on his right thigh with a broader pucker behind, where the bullet had exited.

His son glowed in Samuel's eyes—young and fragile and precious.

When Samuel folded his clothing, Duncan avoided staring at his father's graying pelt and poorly fleshed body. He is not the man he was. Duncan dove from the thought, the water a green shock sluicing over his body, and went deep enough that he was glad to return to the warmer layers near the surface. When Duncan shook his head he flung sparkles in the dappling sunlight.

The current was swift under the cliffs. Duncan jackknifed and dove, his white buttocks flagging the air.

As Samuel tired the water seemed colder, and he picked his way to shore across sharp stones. Duncan climbed a smooth limestone slab familiarly and eased onto the bank. Samuel pulled his shirt over his shoulders and sat on his folded trousers while his son dried himself, oblivious to his father's gaze. He was here with Maggie, Samuel Gatewood thought. This is where they came, and this is where he made love to her.

Almost, Samuel Gatewood could picture Maggie. Almost, he could see her lithe, laughing figure.

Duncan stretched his arms over his head as a cat stretches, pleasured by the day.

My seed became him, Samuel thought. His seed is my seed.

Our servants are always with us. They take up habitation in our intimacies, collect our dirty undergarments; they wash bedding still damp from our lovemaking. We have no secrets from them.

A breeze shivered the leaves. Above the cliffs somewhere, a woodpecker battered away.

Duncan said, "Beautiful, isn't it."

And his father said, "Yes," including the river, the limestone cliff, Snowy Mountain, his son, the whole of Stratford Plantation. "This is what we are fighting for."

26

CAN YOU RUN?

Trans-Allegheny Virginia
August 21–September 18, 1862

TEN MINUTES AFTER Jack the Driver made his bedtime check, Rufus removed the boards he'd previously loosened from the root cellar and burrowed through the sawdust that insulated the ceiling, about two feet of it, and set his prybar to the ceiling planks, jerking back and forth until tongues broke and grooves split and the boards tore longwise to make a ragged hole.

"Jesse, you here?"

"Been in Memphis earlier this evening but I back now."

"This ain't no time for foolin'." Rufus dropped down. "Don't you ever wash?"

"How we gonna get these shackles off me?"

"First we gonna get on out of here. You climb up on my back and pull yourself through."

A stream of sawdust funneled through the hole onto Rufus's neck and shoulders when Jesse wriggled upward.

Outside, Rufus had a five-pound hammer, a cold chisel, and a steel plate he'd stolen from the forge.

Rufus hadn't counted on Jesse getting tangled in every fox grape and vine. He hadn't thought how Jesse's muffled fool's bell wouldn't pass under low branches.

Jesse perched on one stump and dragged his chain atop another, positioned the chisel on a link, and smacked it sharply.

"Damn Driver done too good a job," Jesse said. Jack had used a steel chain from kindness, steel is lighter than wrought iron, but it is stouter too, and by the time Jesse finally got the link opened, pinkness glowed on the horizon. "We fix my bell tomorrow night," Jesse said, standing and stretching. "Can you run?"

And they ran. Up Snowy Mountain until the cattle trails became sheep trails and the sheep trails became hog trails and the hog trails deer trails and the blurry hot sun's circle was peeping over the Blue Ridge. Jesse flopped down, sucking air like a winded dog. Rufus didn't have enough breath for speech. They'd made eight miles, most of it uphill, making no attempt at evasion. When they planned this escape, Jesse prophesied, "Master Gatewood not gonna hunt us. Won't have heart for it since his son is home."

Now Jesse pointed at a screen of red maples at the foot of a ledge. "Mama bear use that hole in the wintertime, but she gone out of there now. We sleep there."

The den was half as tall as a man, just enough to crouch in. Floored with leafmold, it smelled powerfully of animal wastes.

"Master put dogs on our trail he'll have us by noon," Rufus said.

"Driver, he don't like to whip a man," Jesse said solemnly. "If you cry out loud he might give it up."

Maybe Jesse was right. Maybe Samuel Gatewood had lost the will to pursue; certainly no patrollers came up the mountain after dogs straining at their leads. They slept until nightfall.

In his bindle Rufus had beef jerky and fishing line and hook. Rufus had two rasps, shoeing hammer, clippers, and hoof knife. He also had two dollars and twenty-five cents in silver, a two-blade Barlow knife, a tin cup, rawhide laces for snares, needle and thread, and a wool hat in case it got cold.

Uncle Agamemnon had fashioned Rufus's amulet. It contained a tiny rock crystal to catch a spirit eye and grave dirt from Thomas Gatewood's grave, because Samuel Gatewood's father had been powerful and to possess a man's grave is to possess the man.

Though Pompey couldn't read, he'd searched the master's books for a map for the fugitives.

"Map be what?" Pompey had asked Jesse.

So every night before he locked up the house, Pompey stole books from the master's shelves and passed them to Rufus, who slipped them to Jesse. Most nights, the books were back before morning, but Pompey removed *Notes on Virginia* from Master's desk while Master was reading it, and Master turned the house upside down searching. When Mr. Jefferson's treatise mysteriously reappeared, Master worried he was losing his wits.

No map in that book. "Look to see where Master puts Jefferson's book on his shelf," Jesse said, "and fetch the books on either side of it."

Jesse'd guessed right. Samuel Gatewood's systematic mind placed Jefferson's commentary next to *Mason's Traveler's Map of Virginia* (complete with a glossary of manufactures).

"We goin' up the Cheat River?" Rufus asked.

"That's where they catch coloreds that runs." Jesse pushed his finger across the map. "We climbin' out of the Cheat Valley, over the mountain. Tygart River's on yonder side."

Rufus wanted to cut away Jesse's fool's bell, but Jesse thought no, they'd better put distance between themselves and the plantation before slave hunters learned about their flight. Master Gatewood might not come himself, but he'd offer a reward.

"You been studyin' the white man's mind," Rufus said.

Jesse said. "Can you run?"

Despite severed chains which flailed against Jesse's ankles and the fool's bell rod which dipped and swayed like a bad joke, they half jogged, half trotted until at dawn they crossed a thigh-deep stream and red blood billowed away from Jesse's ankles. Jesse led them to a cave, another animal den, damper and colder than yesterday's.

"This was as far as I come last time I run," Jesse said. "Yonder is new country to me."

Rufus lay flat on his back sucking air and watched the sky spin overhead.

By nightfall, they'd cut the rivets out of the fool's bell harness, broken the shackles, bathed Jesse's sores in the creek, and wrapped his ankles with Rufus's shirtsleeves.

"Can you run?" Jesse asked.

That night they ran more easily, jogging through the woods, pausing like spooky deer at every trail broad enough to accommodate a man on horseback.

Near midnight they crossed a broad valley of crops and hayfields. Using every fence row and hay stook for concealment, they scooted across. Once, they laid flat and still as mounted men passed silently, masked lanterns hanging from their saddles.

They couldn't chance the Cheat River fords, so they wallowed across hip-deep rapids, clinging to slick lichen-covered river rocks. Safe on the far side, Rufus shivered and vomited. "I can't swim," he explained.

By dawn they were through the cultivated land and climbing another unfamiliar mountain. Rufus pointed back at the quiet valley. "Got a jail at Marlinton big enough for a hundred runaways, and fortnightly they make up a coffle and march 'em back to Virginia. If they ain't got rewards out for them, they sell them in Staunton. Better money than farming."

The hayfields were lovely in the dew, smoke lifting in straight columns from the farmhouses, cattle grazing in the fields they had crossed so furtively. A rooster crowed and another accepted the challenge.

"You ever wonder what it'd be like to be white?" Rufus asked.

"I know what it's like," Jesse said. "It'd be like me—the meanest part of me."

"Those people down there: they risin' up, eatin' they corncakes and fatback, thinkin' on the day's work. Youngest ones blinkin' sleep out of they eyes."

"Don't get on like that. We ain't got no home until we make us one."

Cheat Mountain lifted into the clouds, the trees crouched to bush size, the deer trails narrowed on slopes of sharp, sliding shale. To spare the soles, Rufus carried his shoes. Jesse didn't have shoes. They ate the last two cobs of the field corn they'd picked that morning. They traveled in broad daylight and saw half a dozen chipmunks and some big rabbits and once a pair of hawks climbing high above them. Rufus envied those hawks.

They didn't dally at the summit but pressed on through the night and by dawn were down where trees grew taller and birds sang. Farmers had cleared these pastures a fair way up the mountain and fenced them with chestnut rails. The cows were not, Rufus noted, near so fine as Stratford cows.

"Some white folks poor too," Jesse said.

"Yeah, but they got cornbread to eat. Jesse, what was the best corn-bread you ever ate? Remember Franky's cornbread, you ever eat behind that woman?"

"I never did nothin' with her."

Rufus laughed. "Well, you missed out there, too. Spend the night with Miss Williams, and in the mornin', Sunday mornin', you take your ease while she fixes cornbread. When I get to heaven, that's how it's gonna be."

"How you know you gettin' to heaven?"

"Because I already done my sufferin'."

"Lookee there."

A rickety milk cow with her new calf eyed them from locust trees along the fence line. The ground was pounded hard and dotted with cow droppings. Despite his mother's anxious shufflings, the calf paid the men no mind.

"Look at her bag," Jesse said.

"Oh, she's right. Calf just born. She got plenty of extra."

Jesse angled on down the hill so the cow couldn't bolt that way. Rufus eased along the fence line and mama cow dropped her head and pawed the earth.

"Ain't nothin' gonna hurt you, honey," Rufus said. "We just want what you ain't got no use for anyway."

She stepped left, ready to dodge, but Jesse blocked her. Again she pawed, again she dropped her head, and Rufus flipped his neckerchief in her face and she backed up, exposing her calf, and Rufus pounced. He tried for the calf's neck but it ducked and Rufus wrapped long arms around its middle and the calf bucked and Rufus's grasp slipped down the ham to the hock and the calf let out a bleat and lunged after Mama. That calf was dragging Rufus and the back foot Rufus didn't have hold of was peppering his head and Jesse was laughing so hard he almost missed his catch.

"Weren't nothin' funny about that," Rufus said, when the calf was flat on its side and bawling.

" 'Course not," Jesse snickered.

Mama cow circled worriedly until she got near enough for Jesse to grab her neck. When Rufus loosed the calf it scrambled to its feet, darted to Mama's offside, smacked Mama's udder with its head, and sucked. "Easy," Jesse said.

Rufus was busy on the other side, squeezing spurts of hot milk into his tin cup, and as soon as he had it filled he drank it; the blood-temperature liquid was powerfully scented as new earth.

"She's been in the wild onions," Rufus said, not missing a squirt.

The calf was slobbering the teats on its side, and when it tried for Rufus's teats, Rufus smacked its hard rubbery nose and the calf pulled back bewildered. Again it butted Mama's bag.

Second cup, Rufus handed to Jesse. They took turns until Rufus announced, "That's what there is. We could kill the calf, carry hams with us."

Jesse burped a white frothy burp. "Farmer won't miss this milk. Kill his calf, he'll hunt us down."

Cow and calf wandered down the hill, the cow plucking grass clumps resentfully.

Rufus hunkered on his heels surveying the wide valley, the small farms, the meandering river. "Where this Tygart River go?"

"Up to the Ohio. Ohio goes on to the ocean someplace."

"Maybe we should make a raft," Rufus said dreamily. "Just drift away to freedom."

"You can't swim," Jesse said. "Let's run."

Milk was what they ate that day, the fifth since their escape. The sixth day they ate nothing. The night of the seventh day, they ate an opossum whose feigned death after they snared him soon became real enough. "I wish we could cook him," Rufus lamented.

The eighth day they hid in a tumbledown shed behind a burned-out log cabin. On the shale bank behind the ruin were a dozen apple trees, young trees not more than eight or ten years old. The fruit was sparse but full and perfectly formed, and that evening they rested beside the orchard spring chewing on apples.

"What you fellows want with Grady's apples?" The tatterdemalion white woman had a basket in her hand.

"Looks like you were after Grady's apples your own self," Rufus replied. "Go 'head. We ain't took them all."

"I got a right to those apples," she said hotly. "Grady was second cousin to me and I've sat on his porch many a time eatin' apples. He'd be glad to know I had them. Where you thievin' niggers come from?"

Wordlessly Jesse pointed to the south.

"Figured. Where you goin'?"

Jesse pointed toward the north.

All the bristle went out of the woman. "Well, I suppose I can't blame you. You comin' up on Philippi. Was Federals there until May, but ain't none there now. They off chasin' the rebs. Some say it was rebs that burned Cousin Grady out, but some say it was Federals. Don't matter to Grady, he's burned out whoever done it." She cackled. Her hands were cracked, her nails black and broken. Jesse borrowed her basket and picked apples.

"Cousin Grady was a fool, but he knew where to plant an orchard. I'll wager these trees will be here in a hundred years. You ever wonder what it'll be like then? Of course some folks say the world is gonna end."

"I think it's ended," Jesse said.

"Well maybe it has. But if you two boys stroll through Philippi yours will. Folks in Philippi don't want to see no niggers. Don't fill that basket plum to the brim, you'll spill it." Speculation flared in her eyes. "Got any money?"

"Might, might not," Rufus said.

"You got cash for a hot meal? Can you keep a secret?"

"Ma'am?"

Her forehead puckered with the effort of deciding. "Silver coin," she said. "We don't take no scrip."

They followed her into thickets and brush on a trail she could see but they couldn't. Half an hour later it got darker and low branches whipped Jesse's face and vines caught at his legs and the sullen sky overhead was the only light in the world.

They smelled cooking meat before they spotted the fire at the base of an overwhelming pale boulder. Ruddy light reflected over the black men in the clearing. A pole laid between uprights kept the meat above the fire. The largest man went three hundred pounds and his bare gut hung over the rope that encircled his trousers and his hair was slicked straight back off his head with grease and his eyes glittered like eyes glitter from dens within the earth. "Who you?"

"I brought 'em, Ezekiel. They mine."

"Two more goddamn runaways. We got enough mouths to feed."

"They can pay for it. In silver. Can't get whiskey without silver."

Ezekiel extracted an old horse pistol from the back of his pants. "You gonna give me your silver?" Suddenly he heaved with silent mirth. "Old Master Colander weren't gonna give us his mule. Said he needed it. Mule's on the fire. You got silver?"

"Give you ten cents for supper and a safe place to sleep."

"They's six of us not countin' the white woman. Little Toby's the youngest and he's got a man's growth. This pistol is loaded. I loaded it myself. Master Colander said he wouldn't part with that mule. Lucky we don't eat Master Colander too." Though he shook with hilarity, not a sound came from him, and Jesse could hear the crackling of the fire, the spatter as grease flared up, a hoot owl in the forest behind. The old white woman hunched beside the fire gumming an apple. Men circled and those that didn't have knives in their hands had clubs. Little Toby waggled his club.

Rufus counted coins. "Here's a dollar six bits," he said. "I keepin' four bits in case we get hungry again one day."

Ezekiel frowned but then he grinned and stuck out his hand and ceremoniously bit each coin, after which he made a sweeping gesture of welcome. "Come set," he said. "How long you boys been runnin'?"

Weapons were put away, and Jesse sat beside the white woman even though turning his back on Ezekiel raised his hackles.

When the meat came off the spit, Ezekiel laid it on a flat rock and divided it into portions, one for each man, one for the woman, two for himself.

Little Toby hunkered beside Rufus and asked where they'd come from and didn't wait for his answer before saying that he, Toby, had belonged to a Master Talbott until the Federals came down from Philippi and Master Talbott ran and then white folks from yonder burned Master Talbott's house and took everything they could carry including Master Talbott's best rocker, so Toby wandered through the woods near starved until he met these maroons. "I stayin' here till white folks quit killin' each other. Then I go back, find Master Talbott. I never hungry a night when I was with him." Little Toby said Ezekiel never killed people unless he had to, that they hadn't killed old Master Colander, but they surely took his mule.

"Not much different than beef," Jesse said. "Sweeter, maybe."

"He were a young mule," Little Toby said. He added that pickings were good on account of all the white folks going around burning each other out. He hadn't gone to sleep hungry since he joined Ezekiel, and they could do worse to do the same. "We'd had to kill you if you didn't give up your money," he added solemnly. "We got to do what Ezekiel wants. He master here."

After they finished eating, Ezekiel produced a stone jug, which went around the circle until each man had taken one swallow. Ezekiel himself passed the jug to Rufus. Rufus wiped his mouth and shook his head. "That's somethin'," he gasped. He coughed. "God damn, that's somethin'!"

When Jesse said, "I don't drink liquor, I took the pledge," the smile fell off Ezekiel's big face and he took two swallows and set the jug at his feet and glowered at Jesse.

Little Toby started in with his harmonica, quavering notes, "Turkey in the Straw," and though Ezekiel kept glowering, a couple men started dancing and pretty soon most were. The white woman was asleep against a tree.

Ezekiel heaved his bulk around and abstractedly took two more measured swallows of the whiskey.

Some of the maroons had partners, others danced alone, but other than Little Toby's plaintive harmonica and the rhythmic thud of feet, the dancers made no sound. Finally, they threw themselves down by the fire. Again Ezekiel passed the jug for their single swallows and his two. Again he was angered by Jesse's refusal. When the jug completed its rounds, Ezekiel set it between his thick feet.

"Now if I was a young fellow," he said, "runnin' through the woods and breaks, hidin' by day and runnin' by night, if I was to come up to that mighty River Tygart where it rolls through Philippi and where there ain't no ford, neither above the covered bridge nor below the covered bridge and always patrollers at that bridge, always, I'd lose hope. And if I was to happen to fall in with maroons, kindly-disposed outlaws of the wild woods, I'd think about joining them. I'd ask, 'What you gonna eat tomorrow, Master Ezekiel?' and he'd say back, 'Mule hocks,' and I'd ask, 'What you gonna eat the day after that?' and he'd say, 'There's a widow woman by Parnassus got a couple fat ewes hid in a shed. And maybe some gold too if we was to ask her right.' I'd say to myself, 'Hmmm . . . these maroons are right and I might could travel with 'em for a spell. No more freedom anywhere than here in these wild woods.' "

"Amen," Little Toby said. Everybody looked around with satisfaction. The woman snorted a snore and somebody kicked her foot. After a pause which neither Jesse nor Rufus filled, Ezekiel shut his eyes and seemed to settle into himself, but he wasn't sleeping, he was drawing attention. When he talked again he talked soft, almost womanly. "You all know how God made the heavens and the earth and the beasts of the field and the birds of the air and he made 'em all in seven days, but he weren't done creatin' until he made him a nigger. Birds was hard to make and fish was hard to make and Adam was hard to make, but hardest of all was that nigger."

Although Ezekiel's eyes stayed shut, his hand found the jug. The cork squeaked when he pulled it, tumped when he drove it home. "Until them Israelites got out of bondage there wasn't no need for niggers. You remember how the pharaoh's daughter found Baby Moses and when Moses growed to be a man he lead his people out of Egypt and across the River Jordan into the Promised Land?"

"Oh, I remember," someone said.

"And he lead them into the land of milk and honey?"

"I remember."

"And them Israelites they all work in they fields and they all milk they cows and all shuck they corn and preacher just as quick to hoe a row as sing a hymn."

"Milk and honey."

"They go on that way and they go on that way, long time. But directly some fellows lyin' under a shade tree when everybody else finish they supper and go back in the fields, these fellows just wave and say they rest in the shade a mite longer. And some of the women discontent on account of how if they got a red scarf, all the other womens got red scarves too, and if they got a ham hock for soup, everybody else got one. Some of the women start to foolin' around with them fellows under the shade trees. Preacher, he's heard how Moses used to go up on the mountain and talk to the Lord, so he figures he'll talk to the Lord too. He climbs all day and he climbs all night but that mountain lift up forever. No water to drink neither. Wasn't no water on it. He gets to this big limestone ledge looks out over everything below, fields and cattle and houses and people, and he prays to the Lord, says how his people gettin' unhappy because everybody's got the same identical possessions and because nobody feelin' bad, there ain't nobody feelin' good.

"Well, a big black cloud covers the sun and rainstorm chase everybody out of the fields below but the sun keeps shinin' on that ledge and Preacher hears this mighty voice louder than a railroad train. 'All right,' the Lord says, 'but this the last thing I'm ever gonna do for you.'

"And when Preacher come down the mountain, he finds half the people been turned into niggers. And from then on everything just fine. The masters happy because they got nothin' to do except practice with they swords and shields and make war on each other. And the wives happy because not everybody got that same scarf, and maybe if they husbands do good in the war they might own everybody else's scarves, and they get more milk and honey than they need or they children need so they pour it on the ground and pretty soon the master with the biggest mess of milk and honey outside his kitchen door, everybody start sayin' what a great man he is and listenin' close to every word he say. Whole world get divided into what's nigger and what's not. There's nigger work, which is plowin' and shockin' and milkin' and butcherin' and scrubbin' and carin' for the children. And there's masters' work, which is dancin' and racin' horses and squabblin' with each other. There's nigger names like Mingo and Jim and Franky and Ezekiel and there's master names like James B. Stoddard and Robert E. Lee. And worst thing can happen to a master is he lose his name so he become a nigger. He'll fight to the death so that don't happen: 'Give me liberty or give me death,' that's what Master say. What he mean is: 'Please Lord, don't make me no nigger.'

"Now it ain't so bad for that nigger either. He got to carry the water and tote all the wood, but he never have to fight in the wars. The masters afraid if the nigger learn to fight', instead of killin' the other masters' niggers, he go crazy and start killin' masters too. So when the fightin' start, the niggers stay at home with the womens and children. And since the nigger ain't a master, nothin' that happen to him is his own doin'. He got a pain, Master make it to be. He work too hard, Master make it to be. He get sick and die, Master make it to be. Bein' a nigger sets you free. You already the worst thing they is."

A log broke into the fire and flared up and Ezekiel got to his feet and farted a thunderclap fart and scooped up his blanket and jug and retired under the biggest tree. Everybody else stretched and yawned and followed his example.

Four hours later, Jesse crept to Rufus and touched his shoulder and the two slipped away. It was slow going through the brush, but they were miles from the maroons by daybreak.

All the next day and most of the night, they waited outside Philippi, and the moon was sunk in the west when they slipped through the town, flitting from shadow to shadow. They hesitated at the covered bridge until they were sure it was unguarded before they crossed.

They stole through fields and woodlots. Sometimes dogs set up barking and twice lanterns blossomed in farmhouses and once a man came onto his porch and called, "Who's there?" By dawn they dropped down beside the river where the walking was rougher. At first light Rufus put out a line and caught two rock bass and a smallish trout. "I ain't gonna eat no fish raw," Rufus said.

Jesse said they should wait until night when nobody would see smoke, that they were too near Philippi, that from the alders where they were hid they could see men in a field just upstream picking corn. "Just a small fire," Rufus pleaded.

The wood was dry, the fire hot and quick, and they smeared the fish with mud and laid them in the coals. Scraps of steam issued from the mudpie they'd created.

They lay quietly in the thicket. From time to time they heard a voice from the harvest field, once or twice horses' hooves, and each time one particular wagon filled and drove away, they heard the squeak, squeak, squeak of its bad wheel. Crows cawed overhead and a buzzard circled until Jesse flicked a hand. Rufus shuddered. "I hate them things."

"Buzzards like the undertaker. Nobody's glad to see him come but things be worse without him."

After dark they struck the railroad line.

With the quarter moon on their shoulder they walked the pale trackbed. The stars were bright and Jesse searched among them for Maggie but he didn't see her. Maybe he had to be quiet to see her. Maybe he had to be in chains.

"Wonder why they ain't no trains?" Rufus said.

They crossed the river on a trestle, and a couple miles later they crossed again. A scattering of houses on the hill above them, none lit.

"What's that?"

"That" was a wooden signal tower on the edge of Grafton's railyards. Its signal blades hung down like a dispirited windmill.

One track became two tracks became three tracks and the third track split in two.

"How many trains they run at one time?" Rufus whispered.

"Halt! Give the countersign!"

Both men froze as a Federal soldier stepped from beneath a water tower.

"We don't know no countersign," Rufus called. "But we ain't no enemies of yours. We just followin' these tracks to freedom."

"You swear you not rebs?"

"You ever seen any colored Confederates?" Jesse drawled.

The soldier was young and his rifle muzzle wandered nervously across their midriffs. A cloud choked the moonlight. "Well I'm damned," the soldier said. "Now don't you get to wiggling. Far as I know you might be scouting for ol' Stonewall himself."

"We see General Jackson, we run like hell," Rufus asserted.

"You won't be the first man to adopt that course." The soldier relaxed. "You don't run and I don't shoot you. Sound all right?"

"We been walkin' long time to get here. . . ."

"Yeah. I'm from Minnesota myself. Railroad to Baltimore and railroad to here and on my feet ever since. Suppose I'm lucky. Least I ain't been killed."

The soldier led them past silent trains. Grafton Station was a square marble structure with an Italianate tower beside the somewhat larger and equally ornate Grafton Hotel. Every hotel bedroom was crammed with stranded passengers, lobby couches and settees were reserved for women and children, and when Jesse and Rufus passed through the station waiting room, they stepped over sleeping men's feet.

"Ain't been no train in three days," their escort explained. "Trains keep gettin' here from the west, but they can't go ahead on account of Stonewall Jackson."

In his smoky office, the telegrapher hunched over his brass instrument evaluating clicks and pauses, head cocked skeptically. "That's not Lewis's hand," the telegrapher said. "I'd swear to it. Whoever it is says Jackson has loaded three trains with troops and sent them west to Grafton, says J.E.B. Stuart is coming up the Tygart to take us from the rear, but it's not Lewis's hand. He says he's Lewis, but he ain't."

The Federal captain was young, prematurely bald, sweating. "Oh God, we can't fight Jackson." He looked at Rufus. "Where you come from?"

"We come from Stratford Plantation, biggest plantation on the Jackson River."

"We were below Philippi yesterday," Jesse said.

"Have you seen Confederates? Troops? Cavalry?"

"No, Master."

"I'm not your master. I'm from Vermont. We don't keep slaves."

Rufus grinned. "Then you just the master for me."

The officer hurried right past Rufus's joke. "Have you seen cavalry in the Tygart Valley?"

"Nary a one. Seen plenty farmers, plenty burned-out farms, but nary a Confederate."

"He's telling you the truth, Master," Jesse said.

The captain calmed. To the telegrapher: "Send a message that five Federal brigades are expected in Grafton within the hour."

"Master," Rufus said, "we're hungry. We work for a meal, sweep up, polish your boots, clean your saddle, anything."

When the telegrapher's fingers quit, the officer leaned forward into the silence. "There. That's given the lying bastards something to think about." He motioned to a pasty-faced sergeant. "Bennett, get these men some rations. They've done a service for us tonight."

"Begging your pardon, Captain. These niggers ain't told us anything we don't already know."

Rufus said, "I'm a farrier. I'll bet you gentlemens don't care to be shoein' your own horses. Any of you bettin' men, I can do racing shoes so neat and small, horse don't think he wearin' anythin'."

The captain's attention was riveted to the silent telegraph. "Uh-huh . . ." he said vaguely. "Get them fed."

"You brung 'em," the sergeant said to the sentry. "You feed 'em."

Rufus "Thank you, Master'd" all the way to the rations shed, where the sentry gave them hardtack and salt beef.

"You got any shoes in there?" Jesse asked. "Think you could let me have a pair of shoes?"

"Naw. Sergeant Bennett'd skin me alive. Track goes east and west. West is Ohio. East is Washington."

"Be fightin' to the east," Rufus said.

"McClellan and Lee are lined up for a hell of a fight. Old Bobby Lee will whip Mac again and he'll retreat and lick his wounds."

"What if Gen'r'l McClellan wins?"

"Well, then, this war is over and we can all go home."

Jesse said, "Ain't got no home." He started down the track, and Rufus hurried after.

"Why we goin' this way?" Rufus asked.

"We go ask Master Lincoln what to do."

Rufus walked for half an hour thoughtfully. "What if he won't talk to us?"

On the gray gravel right-of-way, they walked through that night and into the next day, the rails stretching ahead, two rusty promises that joined at the horizon. The telegraph line which paralleled the track might have been carrying encyclopedias of talk but they never heard one word. The gravel abraded Jesse's feet and by noon he was limping. After they rested and ate, Rufus took off his shoes and passed them over.

When the rails divided they knew they were nearing a town and swung wide, taking to the rough country to pass.

The morning of the second day out of Grafton, the railroad tracks disappeared into a hole.

"You think there's railroad wagons in there?" Rufus asked.

"No tellin' what's in there." Jesse slowed his pace. "We ain't seen no trains since Grafton."

There was enough light in the hole they could see to walk.

"How come this hole twice as wide as the track?" Rufus asked.

"Might be they puttin' in another track later."

"Two tracks? Can't be enough trains in the world to keep two tracks busy."

It was cool in the tunnel and damp. Seeps darkened the rockface and trickled toward iron grates set in the floor. The spot of light at the far end swelled into a circle and redefined itself as a half-oval; the tunnel floor was the base. The tracks leapt out into space.

The trestle arced away from the tunnel, clinging to the bare rock cliff before hurling itself over a roaring river. The river was vigorous and murky, smashing into great boulders, throwing spume into the air.

"I can't . . ." Rufus said.

Jesse, who'd stepped on to the crossties, paused. "You want to wear the shoes?"

"Come back for a minute, let me catch my breath. I can't bear it, you standin' over the air."

"You sick? You look awful pale."

"What happens a train come along while we out there?"

"I suppose we'd grab one of these upright timbers and swing out until the train passes."

"What if the bridge fall down?"

"If it'll hold a whole railroad train it won't have trouble carryin' two niggers. Rufus, we can't stick here. There's nothin' for us here."

White-faced, a step at a time, with never a downward glance, Rufus followed Jesse across the six-hundred-yard trestle until they entered the tunnel on the far side, where he crumpled, his trembling back and hands pressed against the stone.

"Jesse," Rufus gasped. "Maybe the masters right. Maybe whites ain't the same as us. What nigger could've built that thing?"

Jesse walked back out on the trestle and set his hands on his hips. "Me," he said out loud.

Two days later, outside Cumberland, when the tracks made a loud random click it startled both of them. Dark smoke pillars rolled at them from the east, and they lay down in the bushes.

Two trains, one on the heels of the other—furred with soldiers: soldiers in the cars, on the roofs of the cars, on the platforms between cars. There were soldiers on the coal car and lying in rows on flatcars. Many were bandaged, some were shirtless, most didn't have hats. Jesse lifted his hand in silent greeting. A knapsack toppled off a flatcar, maybe intentionally.

"They look like they been in a fight," Jesse said.

The knapsack held a spare shirt, two days' rations, and a packet of ground coffee. Rufus hefted the empty knapsack and grinned. "This just the thing for my horseshoeing tools. Just the thing."

That night, on the banks of the Cumberland, they boiled coffee in their metal cup. Holding the cup with a bit of rag, Rufus said, "If I knew this was goin' to be so fine, I'd've run last year."

"We ain't there yet."

"What you gonna do when we get north?" Rufus asked.

"I been studyin' on that. I don't know as how I want this war to pass me by."

"Hell, Jesse. They ain't no colored soldiers."

"Maybe not. But I can tote for the soldiers and bring their firewood and drag 'em off the field when they're shot. I can do some good."

"You still hate the master for sellin' Maggie?"

"I don't think I ever did. He didn't have no more choice than I do. For a master, he wasn't so bad."

"Then why we runnin'?"

"When God told Moses to bring His people out of Egypt, you don't think some of the Israelites didn't have good jobs under the pharaohs? Good many were drivers, some overseers too. But they all packed up and left, just like Moses said. Probably some of 'em were married to Egyptians. Probably some had Egyptian children, but that didn't matter. Sometimes you don't have any choice. When it's your day to run, you run."

Through wild country that day, the track clung to the river, but finally it veered south again.

Jesse consulted his map. "We'll be near Martinsburg by night. Next day, Harpers Ferry. That's where John Brown tried to set us free."

"Was he crazy like they say?"

They were in flat country and it was near dark when they spotted the horsemen, a dozen of them, silhouetted on the horizon. "Step like you got no care in the world," Jesse said. "We belong to Master Williams in Martinsburg."

The riders trotted along beside the tracks and onto the railbed. Some wore homespun jackets and cavalry boots, others horsemen's dusters. One man had a black silk stovepipe set square on his head.

That man had plump dirty cheeks and a twinkling expression in his tiny eyes. "Where you boys headed?"

Jesse jerked his head. "Martinsburg, Master. We been to visit our gals and now we goin' home to Master Williams, just where we belongs."

"Baxter, you lived in these parts. Anybody named Williams in Martinsburg?"

"Three or four of them, Cap'n."

"Which Williams you goin' to, boy?"

"Master Jack Williams, Master. He be expectin' us before dark. He don't like his servants out after dark, no sir."

The man who drew up beside their interrogator was as thin as the first was plump. His hat boasted a turkey feather.

"You be Master Stuart?" Jesse asked tremulously.

The thin man was startled but recovered with a grin. "You think I'm Stuart?"

"If you not Master J.E.B. Stuart, you his spittin' image," Jesse said. "Lord, you have made some rides!"

The thin man produced a flask from his saddlebag, sucked it, and tossed it to another. "Come on, Cap'n," he said. "I don't like to come into the picket lines at night."

"Just rest yourself, Ollie," the twinkling man said. "Don't make overmuch difference if we come in today or tomorrow in the full glare of daylight. If Gen'r'l Lee wants the services of Cap'n Stump's Partisan Rangers, by God he'll sign us on. If he don't we keep on going it alone. Plenty of Federals for everybody."

"I was thinkin' pickets might pick us off, we come in at night," the thin man drawled.

Fiercely hot, abruptly: "Well, there's two can play at that game."

Thin man laughed like the cawing of a crow. "Ain't you the one. Cap'n Stump. Ain't you the one."

There wasn't a blade of cover for five hundred yards, and Jesse's knees were trembling. He hoped his pantlegs weren't quivering. "Master Jack Williams, he waitin' on us, Master Stump."

"If we hold you up we'll inconvenience him. That right?"

"No, Master. Nothin' you do incon . . . veyance anybody." Deliberately mispronouncing a word he could spell, goddamn spell, so a man who probably signed his name with an X could be comfortable in his superiority.

Suddenly bored. "Don't lie to me, boy. Look at yourself. You been on the road as long as we have, and there ain't no Master Williams in Martinsburg, not that we'd give a damn."

A couple riders dismounted and led their horses to the creek to water them.

"Oh, Master Williams, he's a hard master, but he fair, he . . ."

"Oh, shut the hell up, boy. Don't matter if he's real or not. Not now." A smile dawned on his face. "You mean you ain't heard? Hell, I thought nigger telegraph would have give everybody the news. By Jesus, you really don't know?"

Jesse was tired but he wasn't foolish, and the first word out of his mouth was, "Master . . . heard what, Master?"

"Why you're free, boy. That Black Republican Abraham Lincoln has e-man-ci-pated your black ass. You just as free as me and Ollie here. You want my horse?"

"Master?"

"I mean, hell, it ain't like it belongs to anybody. Courier who used to ride it won't be needin' it no more. Belongs to any free man who can take it." He extended the reins to Jesse.

"Master . . ."

"So, we free men," Rufus said. "And that a free horse, no strings to it."

"Nope."

"Old Master, he used to ride a horse like that. Great big damn horse. Wouldn't want to go messin' with Master's horse, no sir." Hands clasped behind his back, Rufus walked around the horse inspecting it. "This here horse branded 'US.' I don't read so good but I'd venture that how they mark them Federal horses. And I see this saddle blanket is spankin' new and blue and gold. And I see here down the bottom of the saddle a stain in the leather turnin' red-brown here at that girth strap. Master, I don't believe this horse always a Confederate. Horse be a convert, praise the Lord."

A couple riders grinned and Cap'n Stump showed his teeth, but Ollie's brow wrinkled in irritation. "I always did enjoy a smartass nigger," he drawled, slow as he could.

The grin dropped off Rufus's face and fell to the sharp gravel.

"You free now," Cap'n Stump continued. "Ain't there anything you want to do?"

His sidekick lifted himself in his stirrups. "Cap'n, we better get a move on."

"Hush. I'm learnin' what a man wants when he's free."

"I want to be a farrier, Master. Want to shoe horses." Rufus unslung his knapsack and took out his hoof rasps. "Master, I shoe all you horses. Won't be chargin' nothin' either."

Cap'n Stump nodded. When he slung a leg over the saddle horn, his saddle creaked. "Last week we run into you two, we take you down to the slave pen in Winchester. Jim there give us twenty dollars a head for runaway niggers. Jim takes all the newspapers, *Staunton Examiner, Winchester Star, Harrisonburg Herald,* and sorts out which niggers belong to who, sends 'em up the valley and collects his reward. But soon as the niggers got emancipated Jim closed up his jail. How much your master pay for you, boy?"

Despair changed to defiant pride in Rufus's face. "Eighteen hundred dollar. In gold. I can fell, limb, skid logs, operate a sawmill, plow, do farm work. I'm a good farrier. I got most my teeth."

Stump shook his head sorrowfully. "Yeah, but you free. Don't belong to nobody but yourself. You're worthless." And with his sudden pistol he shot Rufus in the chest and Rufus sat on the gravel leaning against his hands.

"Master."

"I done told you, you ain't got no master." At the second shot Rufus jerked stiff for a moment before he fell onto his side and his feet commenced drumming.

"Boy been runnin' so long he's runnin' after he's dead," Ollie said.

Jesse wanted to bolt, to dodge, to hold Rufus's feet from that terrible kicking, but he could do nothing but watch the black hole of Stump's gun muzzle.

"If I shoot you, who's gonna bury your friend?" Stump complained. "I don't mind killin' but anytime I get a whiff of that death stink, I lose my victuals. I never got no nearer to the Sharpsburg battle than a mile, but I upchucked till my gut ached. Christ, what a slaughter pen! Nigger, you gonna bury that boy?"

Jesse nodded until his neck hurt.

And that quick, everything was different; like quicksilver they were riding off and Jesse was alone on the railbed with the stink of the gunpowder, the stink of Rufus's bowels, and the spasmodic jerking of Rufus's heels.

"I'm going away now, Rufus," Jesse said. "But I won't go far. I need to find dirt soft enough to dig with our cup. I won't put you in the ground until you're quit running."

27

A LETTER FROM SERGEANT

CATESBY BYRD

TO HIS WIFE LEONA

CAMP NEAR OPEQUON CREEK, VIRGINIA
SEPTEMBER 20, 1862

MY DEAREST DARLING,

Although we have fought a fearful battle at Sharpsburg, I am by God's
mercy unwounded. Your brother, Duncan, rejoined the army in time to
march with A. P. Hill's division. Hill's footsore men arrived on the field
late in the day when the Federals had broken our lines and our cause
seemed lost. I am told Duncan distinguished himself in sharp fighting.

Our brigade was posted to the extreme left of the line, supporting
J.E.B. Stuart's horse artillery, in woods behind the Hagerstown Pike.
When the Federals charged the woods, we caught them enfilade, with
volley after volley, broke them and pursued through the smoke and
crash of musketry. Excepting the pungency, I might have thought we
were fighting in a fog, so dense was the powder smoke. Our company
blundered into a clearing which the Federals were vacating. The farmer
for whose land we contended had cut his winter's firewood and stacked
it. When a cannon shot struck one woodpile it hurled sharp wood splinters into our ranks and cut down our captain. Undaunted, we rushed forward and delivered a devastating volley into unsuspecting Federals who
had not realized their flank had been turned by Virginians. Determined
to hold their ground, the Federals returned our volleys with interest,
and their fire grew so hot that I lay down in a depression behind fence
rails. I was joined in my refuge by a Texan who had survived the fighting across the turnpike. If we lay absolutely flat we were safe enough but
could hear minié balls chunking into the fence rails just at our head. In

our forced intimacy, his face next to my ear, he cried his name. He was E. P. Hagwood from Galveston, Texas. He shouted his wife's name, it might have been Linda, though I cannot be sure I heard right on account of the roar of guns and musketry. He shouted the name of his regiment and his regimental colonel who'd been slain and the names of his comrades, one after another: all slain. I suppose we had lain there for ten minutes though it seemed like hours before an officer rode by crying we should fall back to regroup. I never saw that officer again but the instant we stood, my acquaintance took a bullet in the throat. He tried to say more, more names of those he loved, but could not. His blood gushed from the horrible hole.

Providence spared your husband. I ran to our regiment through a positive hail of musketry, and though my sleeve was plucked twice by importunate bullets, I was unhurt. One of our batteries was withdrawing when a shell felled an artilleryman and cut the leg from a horse. The surviving gunners cut the horse out of its traces, but the horse hobbled after them on three legs.

Our regiment tried to go forward anew but were confounded by overwhelming Federal fire. We took up a position behind a ridge and our sharpshooters exchanged rounds with their sharpshooters. Every hour of that awful day was filled with musketry, cannon blasts, faint cheers, and the shrieks of dying horses and men. The Federals tried our center, which held firm. Finally they tried our right, which was having severe difficulties until General Hill's fortuitous arrival.

Not long after dark the cannons stopped thundering and litter bearers from both armies came unchallenged onto the field, freely intermingling, directing one another to fallen comrades. In one forty-acre cornfield the dead lay so thick I might have walked across on men without once touching the ground.

We waited the next day for the battle to resume, so weakened from our efforts that had the Federals tried us again, we surely should have been overwhelmed. The following morning, my regiment withdrew across the Potomac onto Virginia soil.

In the weary quiet that follows a great battle, I thought about geometry. I fear that Mr. Euclid's discoveries have had too slight a hold on our son Thomas. Thomas takes more delight in boys' games than rigorous theories, and I deplore his laxity. I pray you urge Tommy to be a better student. I deeply regret that old Uther is too unwell to take on another generation of scholars.

Dearest Leona, if one has lost everything—property, friends, perhaps even honor—one retains the furnishings of the mind. Many of my fellow soldiers find consolation in religion, the road from Sharpsburg Ford was littered with discarded playing cards, and many a man spent the night before the battle thumbing a Testament whose flyleaf bore his mother's most pious hopes. Old Blue Light Jackson is a beacon for these men, for he is as fierce a prayer as he is a fighter. Dear wife, though I admire the faith of these fellows, snatched from their families and placed in the fore of this sanguinary conflict, I cannot share it. I am no atheist. I believe that purpose, frequently benign, guides all things, that no sparrow falls unnoticed by God. I have had the thought, perhaps a blasphemous one, that when we fought at Sharpsburg, God and His recording angels had their hands full.

Although we Confederates prevailed, it was a near thing. The Army of Northern Virginia is a great bear lying in its den licking its wounds.

If our Thomas will study and learn and take his lessons to heart he will be rich in goods none can ever snatch from him. If he is blessed with the faith so many of my comrades exhibit, so much the better, for there is nothing finer than an educated Christian.

Dearest, with our army I have passed through great destitution: ruined plantations, shattered granaries, homes whose fire-scorched foundation stones testify to happier times. None of the good citizens of Sharpsburg or Kernstown or Winchester or Front Royal thought, when first this struggle began, that they would be asked to give more than their lives to this conflict. None thought they would have their property confiscated, homes destroyed, their children starving. This is war unlike any that has ever been fought.

I entreat you to remember our daughter, Pauline. Some think it unwise for young women to have much education, and there are those who cite Sallie Kirkpatrick's imprisonment as evidence for that proposition. Many of my fellows believe not much is changed, that life after this war will resume as before. Alas, that cannot be. The world which Uther Botkin knew, that generous span of time from Mr. Jefferson to General Lee, will remain enshrined in memory, but I fear tomorrow. Neither Thomas nor Pauline is prepared for a life that might include poverty, subjugation, and sorrow. Stratford's isolation may not keep it from battles to come, and Samuel Gatewood's barns will burn as well as any. When I imagine the worst—and on the battlefield the worst seems too plausible—I torment myself with the vision of Thomas and Pauline with no dower except that which they can carry on their backs, their family destroyed and family competence dispersed to the four winds.

I am glad to be serving with Duncan again. Though I would not tell him so, I wish his wound had been a trifle worse. Men can recover from the most appalling injuries, and many who survive this war will be those with wounds severe enough that they can, with honor, quit the battlefield.

You may accuse me of being ungallant. An army is a clumsy device:

it kills. An army that is compassionate or tender is no army at all. We Confederates have disguised bloody slugging behind gallant scrims and charades. There is nothing gallant about case shot nor canister.

I do not know how General Lee perseveres. Our numbers are half what they were, and we are filling our ranks with conscripts. When we have exhausted our able men, will we turn to the oldsters, to the boys? Will we draft our Thomas?

Though visibly worn and aging, General Lee remains confident. Can the heart ever be too strong for the body? Can too tenacious a love of freedom destroy everything freedom holds precious?

This has been a morose communication, but I come at last to the matter I least wished to touch upon. I can scarcely think upon it. I am devastated we have lost our blessed infant Willie to fever. Our dear babe was so ill for so much of his brief, brief life. I am only consoled by your report that in his final hours relief came swiftly to him. God sometimes does intervene, I believe, to show mercy to the innocent. I love little Willie as I do our other children, though I shall not in this mortal life once see his dear face.

My religious comrades assure me we will all be united on the other side: you, me, little Willie, E. P. Hagwood of Galveston, Texas.

> *I can write no more,*
> *Catesby*

PART THREE

The Year of Miracles

"They called for water as all wounded men do."

—*Private Benjamin A. Jones,*
F Company, 44th Virginia Infantry

28

THE OUTSIDE WIFE

NASSAU, THE BAHAMAS
NOVEMBER 6, 1862

"CALM SEAS, DARK moon!"

The governor's guests cried, "Hear, hear!" and Captain Horner, who was elderly for a blockade runner, responded stoutly, "Confusion to the Federal fleet!"

Glasses flashed in a crystal salute, and Marguerite clenched hers betwixt thumb and forefinger exactly where stem met bowl and set it, just so, on the snow-white linen tablecloth, and that quick, the dark servant behind her chair refilled it, and Marguerite hadn't yet learned how to tell him to stop. She didn't like the sharp bubbly wine—it made her want to sneeze.

The British governor's wife, Priscilla (of the Dorset Aynsworths), frequently complained of her husband's excessive hospitality toward the blockade runners, whose arrivals and departures from Nassau had been occasions last year but now had all the drama (the lady opined) of the daily post. And, she had added, the dinner guests were not exactly "our sort."

Perhaps six of the thirty guests who filled two tables in the formal dining room overlooking the harbor might have been included in "our sort." Young Trenholm's uncle, Viscount Campbell, owned estates in the Scottish Isles, and Fraser had been presented at court. Roger Bourne—one of the ship captains present—his father had been a bishop. Billings and Packwood were from good British families—out to make their fortunes in the wide world. But the pilots, so honored at these gatherings, were rude American coastal seamen, and most ship masters were little better.

Mr. Omohundru, the Wilmington shipowner, carried himself like a gentleman, but nobody knew a thing about his companion.

Marguerite's current discomfort was prompted by knowing what she'd be thinking if she were behind her chair instead of in it. She'd be wondering why the quality folks got so much to eat and how could they eat it all? She might exchange a glance with a fellow servant, one of those glances.

The young Englishman at Marguerite's elbow was describing his voyage out. ". . . cotton over the top of the wheelhouse," he said. "Bloody wonder we didn't turn turtle."

Too well Marguerite recalled her voyage from Wilmington, the blockade runner so overloaded freeboard was reduced to less than a foot, water hissing by, sidewheels churning the ship forward in an awkward powerful motion like a strong dog swimming.

"And then, not fifteen miles from safe harbor in Nassau, we spotted a Federal's smoke, and she came up so fast we escaped by tossing the deck cotton into the sea. When the Federal slowed to harvest her prize, we were saved: somewhat poorer, but better than losing the boat." He sighed deeply and drained his glass. The Englishman didn't seem to notice when his attentive servant refilled it. It was as if the black hand were invisible.

Another lesson to be learned: how to make people invisible.

"I am surprised I've not seen you in Wilmington. We have some grand affairs at the City Hotel there. We quite take over the place, myself and the other speculators. I'm part owner of the *Kestrel*. Two hundred and eighty tons, fourteen knots in a calm sea."

"We don't go out much in society." Marguerite smiled at the ruddy-faced young Englishman.

"But I say . . . aren't you . . . with . . . Omohundru?"

"With" was the all-inclusive preposition which served to describe the relationship polite whites accepted without honoring. In Nassau, a good many white captains and merchants were "with" women never addressed as "Mrs." The governor's wife spoke of "companions" and never, never asked questions. The blacks called them "outside wives."

In Wilmington, Marguerite was Mrs. Silas Omohundru.

Although Marguerite could endure gatherings like this one, she could not enjoy them. Her manners were the reverse of what she'd learned serving Stratford's parties, augmented by wit and acting skills. She watched the ladies at the head of the table, and whatever fork they used, she used, and when they dabbed with a napkin, she dabbed with hers, and when they flung it down carelessly, so did she.

"Grand boat, Omohundru's *Wild Darrell*," the British boy remarked. "What does she draw?"

Marguerite smiled. "I'm afraid I leave nautical details to my husband."

"No more than six feet, I'd wager. It's rumored she made sixteen knots on her crossing."

Marguerite flashed him a smile.

"The *Kestrel* is getting long in the tooth. Last voyage into Wilmington we were attempting the New Passage. . . ." With a swoop, the young man appropriated her wineglass. "Here, imagine this is Fort Fisher . . ." A water glass was the *Kestrel* and another portrayed the Federal blockader. "Dark of the moon, shoal water, no more than seven feet in the channel, and our dog of a pilot couldn't read the bottom. There is no sound, ma'am, more appalling to a sailor than the terrible noise as you strike . . ."

The young man went on maneuvering what became a flotilla of glass-ware as more Federal blockaders joined the fray, Fort Fisher's guns thundered reproaches, and the *Kestrel*'s crew lightened by heaving cargo into the sea.

Marguerite smiled and said "Oh, my!" but she was thinking about her son, Jacob, and his nurse, Kizzy, who was dark, dark black, and whenever Marguerite and Silas came back to the hotel, Jacob was smiling and sweet-smelling. Jacob was such a sturdy boy! Although his underpinnings were not completely reliable, Jacob explored boldly, and the other day when Silas told him to go into the other room, in his tiny voice, Jacob said, *"Not!"* and continued his play, eyeing Silas from beneath his eyelashes.

Silas simply laughed. "Then I suppose I'll have to remove myself," he said, and took his papers into the dining room.

A month ago, Marguerite had a dream where she was carrying Jacob up narrow stone stairs—stairs which circled above her forever. Though she was weary, Marguerite couldn't lay Jacob down.

Kizzy sometimes yearned for her man, Mingo—left behind to watch the Wilmington house. How could she? Kizzy had everyday care of Jacob, that precious jewel. Daily she shared in the child's ways, his amusements, his tantrums, his humors. Why would Kizzy want that fool Mingo?

"Ma'am, I'm sorry for being tedious. Our hazards were, I fear, interesting only to a seaman."

She loved Jacob so much. "Oh no! I was so fascinated by your gallant struggle. I quite forgot to eat." And Marguerite gave him a mild version of her best smile.

"The Federals were shooting flares to bring up the rest of their fleet and . . ."

Silas never asked about other men. Never inquired about the men at the Captain's House, never asked about the father of her child. Dear

Duncan Gatewood. Graceful, thoughtless, intuitive, with the playful strength of a young foal. How can white men be so fine as children and so awkward after they get their growth?

"Some plaice, madam?"

"Yes, thank you." Poor Jesse, who'd loved her all the while she was loving somebody else. Sometimes, on a still night, when she and Silas sat outdoors and the stars were specially bright, she remembered Jesse.

The evening they arrived in Nassau, Silas had insisted they dine at the Queen Victoria Hotel, where the finer owners and captains stayed. Silas marched into the hotel as if they were as truly wed as they pretended, his eyes flashing hot coals daring anyone to say a word, a single word, against his honor. Of course, there was nothing to worry about: plenty of other white captains had outside wives darker than Marguerite. In Wilmington, she was tolerated as a wealthy merchant's Bahamian wife. In Nassau, they knew better but didn't care.

"The fish doesn't please you?"

She crossed her knife and fork on her plate. "I'm afraid I haven't much appetite."

The young man set his fork down. "I am told Mr. Omohundru paid forty-three thousand for the *Wild Darrell*, that she was Clyde-built to be Fraser's boat but the purchase fell through."

"I'm afraid I do not attend to Silas's business."

"Rumor has it that Omohundru means to ship army goods exclusively: guns, powder, lead, medicines, shoes. That he refuses all luxury items."

"Silas is a patriot."

"To be sure. . . . And Confederate cargoes earn well, but, ma'am, a cargo of luxury goods is so blessed profitable that if you bring it in and lose the boat, you make money all the same. When Benson beached the *Almandine,* the goods they salvaged out of her tripled his investment. If blessed with a skilled pilot . . ." He shook his head.

"I believe Silas has engaged a pilot."

"Indeed he has. Indeed!" The young Englishman's face glowed with wine and goodwill. "Joe MacGregor. Finest pilot alive. Why, there's nobody who knows Cape Fear better than Joe MacGregor, and he's been coastering Frying Pan Shoals since he was a boy. Pilots like Mac are tolerably scarce, ma'am. You see," he confided, "when a blockade runner gets taken, you Confederates get sent to prison until exchanged. We English are neutral, so they turn us loose in short order. But the coastal pilots—the Federals clap them into Point Lookout Prison, and there they'll stay. Without a good pilot amongst shoals on a moonless night, your blockade runner hasn't much chance, don't you see?"

"But Silas has employed a pilot."

"Oh, that's the grandest story. Everyone laughs about it."

Marguerite ignored her fizzy wine. She already had drunk one glass: enough.

"Mac is a peerless pilot. But the first thing Mac does in the morning is uncork a quart of rum, and last thing he does at night is empty his second quart. He is desirous of employment—oh, most desirous. A good pilot can ask three thousand for a single voyage, and that's gold, ma'am, not your Confederate currency, and MacGregor was so desperate, he'd take half that. But Mac's a drunkard, ma'am." He shook his head. "And every skipper knew it. Until Omohundru hired him, the best pilot on the island slept under the benches of a grog shop in the Skibberdeen, where the ordinary sailors seek vice. Pardon me, ma'am . . ."

Marguerite's servant removed her fish and topped her wineglass. At the head of the table, young Trenholm was proposing another toast: "Our Confederate cousins. May they retain the freedom they so bravely defend."

Like the others, Marguerite toasted, but she did not drink.

Her tablemate assured her, "Every day our British government comes nearer to recognizing your new nation."

Marguerite said, "Surely Silas wouldn't employ a drunken pilot!"

The young man grinned. "That's the joke of it. Joe MacGregor hasn't touched a drop since Omohundru hired him.

"Mr. Omohundru invited Mac aboard the *Wild Darrell,* just to get a feel for things, no position offered, nothing definite. The *Wild Darrell* was on the west coast of Hog Island, clipping along briskly, when Mac came onto the bridge, bottle in hand. 'I do not permit drinking on my boat,' Mr. Omohundru said, and first he threw the bottle over the side and then he threw Mac after it. Well, the captain shouted, 'Man overboard!' and dashed to the wheel, but Mr. Omohundro was cool as ice and ordered him to hold course, although Mac was thrashing, hoping some shark wouldn't take an untoward interest. They sailed until they were hull down on the horizon before Mr. Omohundro gave the order to come about. The currents must have been dead quiet, because they steamed straight to Mac and dropped a ladder.

"Poor old Mac was over the rail, shivering and puking all the water he had swallowed, and Mac said he might have drowned, and Mr. Omohundro said that a reliable pilot is the best and noblest man in the world, but a drunken pilot might as well be drowned. He said he had a job for Mac at full wages if he never touched whiskey again. So Mac thought it over.

"Ma'am, this is the best part. Mac said he'd consider the offer but wanted to know if it was Mr. Omohundru's custom to drown employees who displeased him. And your husband, ma'am, he didn't blink an eye. He said Mac shouldn't have worried, there was no danger. When he threw Mac over the side he took particular note of the nearest wave. It's shape was distinctive, he said."

He laughed and took more wine to calm himself. Marguerite smiled. This was not the Silas she knew.

Duncan had been like a will-o'-the-wisp, Jesse had been awkward sullen struggle. When they made love she lay passively. Silas—Silas was like what Marguerite imagined another woman might be, delicate, subtle: as though her skin and his skin were one. Duncan liked to make love out of doors in the sunlight. Silas invariably touched her in the night.

Of all the powerful Omohundru clan, only Silas's youngest half brother had been a friend to their father's bastard. Marguerite understood that the legitimate half brother had borrowed heavily on Silas's credit and reputation (and probably considerable of Silas's money). Silas was an intuitive businessman who despised his natural skills. A bastard, he yearned to be a gentleman.

"Why did you take up with me?" Marguerite once asked him.

"I will prove you as fine as any lady in the land!" Silas said.

Marguerite learned gentle manners so quickly it seemed she had always possessed them, and from the start she knew how to bend a conversation from indiscreet inquiries.

Silas believed they could both become anything they pretended to be. Marguerite was unconvinced.

"Are you a native of these islands?" her dining partner asked.

Marguerite's smile meant the young man should have known her people, that everyone did. He flushed. Forgiving him, she said, "Do try the mango sherbet. I do not believe you have mangos in your country."

The sherbet had been chilled by ice that had been cut from Maine's Androscoggin River. Once an insignificant Caribbean trading port, the war had transformed Nassau into a mercantile capital with a hundred ships at the wharves or waiting to dock—ships from Europe, Britain, not a few from New York and Boston. King Cotton made it all possible. The Confederacy financed its purchases with cotton in hand or promised when the Confederacy won the war. Cotton drove the English and New England mills alike; cotton was better than money.

Guests were standing to leave. The young Englishman was enthusing about his portion of the *Kestrel*'s cargo. "Pins and needles, ma'am. Two full rolls of silk. Ribbons. Oh, the ladies must have their ribbons. Five cases of finest French brandy . . ."

When Silas came to her, Marguerite felt the calm she always felt in his presence.

"Mr. Billings was just telling me about silks, Silas."

"Perhaps he'll be good enough to send samples. We should have some new gowns made up for you when we get home."

The young man stood up too quickly and knocked over his chair. "Delighted," he said. And stuck out his hand and gave his name again, and his boat's name and his firm's name, all in a thundering hurry, but did not alter Silas's cool smile.

"To be sure," Silas said.

The young man was primed to continue babbling, so Marguerite smiled her goodbye and led Silas out of doors.

The trade winds blew their cinnamon breath across the brick veranda, and bay bushes flowered below. It was so gentle, this wind, that Marguerite thought, Here is a place we could live forever.

Red lantern at its masthead, a fishing smack was beating out of the harbor. It wouldn't be bothered by Federal cruisers. No blockader depended on sail. The blockade runners, lean, gray, low-freeboard sidewheelers—the *Wild Darrell, Atlantic, Kestrel, Albemarle*—rocked gently in the harbor swell, some already loaded for the voyage. They carried no armament and couldn't survive a real blow, but were the fastest boats afloat. Some had hinged funnels and flush deck cabins to reduce their silhouette. Showing no lights, with muffled paddles, exhausting excess steam underwater, in the shoal waters off the Carolina coastline they were ghosts.

"It is a beautiful night. I don't believe I've ever seen anything so beautiful. When I was a girl looking through the pictures in Miss Abigail's weeklies, I saw engravings of such places but never dreamed I'd see them. Have you thought, Silas, what we'll do after the war?"

"Darling Marguerite, the vista between now and that happy day is as impenetrable as the fog banks on Frying Pan Shoal. Have you a scheme?"

"I would assure Jacob's future."

Lanterns clustered on the wharf below. "That'll be the *Hessian,*" Silas said. "Bound for Galveston. With her centerboard up she draws less than five feet."

He paused. "Men are sometimes comforted by the notion that however much they err and sin, long after their deaths, perhaps, there will be another, a scion, who will do better, succeed where they failed. My unwed mother sometimes told me that I am the very image of Robinson Omohundru, the first Omohundru to settle in Virginia. Naturally, in her circumstance, she was wont to grasp at straws, assert the most frivolous connections to a family that offered her and her child nothing but disdain. Apparently Jacob is to be my only child. I will care for him."

Marguerite blinked back hot tears. Marguerite would not bear Silas's baby. Would not! Twice, Marguerite had sent Kizzy to the herb woman for the stinking iris. Twice she had denied Silas's dreams. How could Silas care for Jacob—another man's child—once she bore a child with Omohundru blood? Marguerite knew Silas as a generous provider and more of a gentleman than many with gentler blood. But she did not trust him to create their family. Marguerite would see to that.

The *Hessian*'s funnels were creating twin smoke banners in the light air. Silas said, "In France, I am told, they are indifferent to race. One of Napoleon's marshals was a colored man. I believe that the case also in Scandinavia. But Scandinavian winters would be insufferable."

Marguerite drew her shawl about her shoulders. "Silas, we must make do with what we have."

Starlight glistened on a silvery-black ocean.

Silas said, "Next Thursday we clear Nassau for home."

29

A BIG SCRAP

"WE ARE NOT a nation of manufacturers," Lieutenant Catesby Byrd observed, wrapping his bleeding feet in rags.

"Least our general isn't," Duncan agreed, stirring the pot. Parched corn didn't taste like coffee, but if you stirred it long enough it looked like coffee. "No sir. A man who thinks raw beef-hides will make shoes for men in the wintertime, that man isn't the sort of man you'd ask to hold your money before a fight. You know, I lost three men from those damn things? Payne slipped and broke an ankle. That plowmaker, Hebard? He fell out of ranks and never did come back. And last time I saw Ben Jones, he was sitting beside the road, weeping, holding his feet in his hands. Ben fought at Manassas and Gaines's Mill and Sharpsburg, but he'd had enough."

In that particular December twilight, the two Confederates' worldly goods consisted of:

Enfield rifles (2)
cartridge boxes (2)
bayonets (1) (Catesby's)
sabers (1) (Duncan's)
revolving pistols (1) (Duncan's)
coffeepots (1)
metal cups (2)
tobacco (1 pouch)
pipes (2)

trousers (2)
slouch hats (2)
knife, fork, and spoon set (1) (Catesby's)
Barlow knife (1) (Duncan's)
butternut-dyed overshirts (2)
blankets (2) (in which they wrapped their goods before a march)
long johns (2)
boots (1 pr.) (Duncan's)
rawhide shoes (1 pr.) (Catesby's)

Each cartridge box contained sixty bullets, because General Lee expected a big scrap.

"Those boots of yours weren't made in the Confederacy," Catesby noted gloomily.

"Blockade runners brought 'em in. My father bought 'em for me in Warm Springs. Four hundred dollars Confederate. We march anytime soon, I'll put you up on Gypsy."

"Uh-huh. Shoeless lieutenant rides while his shoeless men walk? You know better."

"You're not playin' cards tonight?" Duncan asked.

"That damned Fisher cleaned me out. Including the four bits you lent me. Do you think President Davis intends to pay his army anytime soon?"

Across the Rappahannock River, a Federal regiment was corduroying a road. They'd been at it since the 44th Virginia got here last week but weren't making much progress. One afternoon Federal gunboats steamed up the river, but Confederate batteries laid into them. The puffs of white smoke wreathing the gunboats, the near misses' colossal waterspouts, the cheers when a napoleon ball hit home: naval battles were, the foot soldiers believed, wonderfully entertaining.

Catesby and Duncan sat on doubled blankets. The ground was frozen hard, the sky darkening. One boy plunked on a banjo, others had built fires; some were cooking salt pork in their metal cups.

A gangly figure in a brand-new private's uniform and overfat haversack picked his way through the regiment. Twice he stopped and asked directions.

"I believe we know that fellow," Catesby said.

"Christ Almighty," Duncan said.

The figure made his way around campfires and apologized as he stepped across men's legs. "Hullo," Alexander Kirkpatrick said. His face was pale as a girl's.

Duncan drawled. "I'll be damned. Last time I saw you was Christmas, two years ago. I understood you were in jail."

"I'm paroled into the army. In Keeper Tyree's words, 'Few patriots would wish to linger behind bars while their new nation is imperiled.' He had a way with words, the keeper, though his tenses were not always reliable."

"How the hell did you find the 44th?"

"I am not acquainted with many men of the profession of arms, and when we replacements were sorted at Madison Courthouse, I exaggerated our previous connection."

"How so?"

Alexander smiled his thin smile. "I have become your half brother."

Duncan stood and put out his hand. "You might have done better if you'd kinned up with General Lee," he said. "Welcome to the 44th. It's a fighting regiment. Division commander's Jubal Early, and he's all right unless you get on the wrong side of him, and there's no right side. We're Colonel Walker's brigade. Walker's got more sense than he's got hair, and he'll give a man a second chance but nary a third. Walker and Old Blue Light fell afoul of each other at Sharpsburg, so our brigade usually marches last in the column and gets sent to the front soon as it comes up. I'm a captain now, which means you listen to me or if you don't I tell Catesby here, who's a mere lieutenant, to shoot you. Anything else you want to know?"

"What if I make a mistake or get confused?"

"Then he shoots you twice. Disobedient soldier's bad enough, dumb one's worse." After a long moment Duncan grinned. "Just joshing you, Alexander. Just a joke. When's the last you ate?" Duncan unwrapped a hardtack biscuit from his handkerchief.

"Not since this morning," Alexander said and bit down on the gift.

Since the parched-corn coffee was likely to be Duncan and Catesby's only meal of the day, Catesby looked away.

"I see they fitted you out proper. New uniform like that—everybody's going to think you're a staff officer. Those shoes fit all right?" Catesby asked.

"They are a little loose. . . ."

"Too loose is better than too tight. When you lie down at night, they'll serve as a pillow. Other than that, don't take them off or someone will steal them."

"Our boys aren't overparticular when it comes to shoes," Duncan added. He gestured at the rifle Alexander had laid carelessly beside him. "They show you how to use that thing?"

"No one has instructed me in my duties."

"Well then." Duncan circled Alexander like a horse buyer inspecting a horse. "What do you hear from your wife, Sallie?"

Alexander shrugged.

Duncan nudged the rifle with his foot. "Austrian," he said.

"You disapprove?"

"Oh, these muskets are allright unless they blow up. When we start to fighting, you'll do well to get yourself another one."

"Couldn't I ask your Colonel Walker for a more suitable weapon?"

"Won't be any more rifles until somebody gets killed," Duncan said. "You happen across one of those breech-loading Spencers the Federal sharpshooters carry, bring it to me." He picked up Alexander's rifle. "Meantime, let me show you how you load this thing. Pay attention now. When minié balls start snapping past your head, it's easy to get confused."

For ten minutes, Duncan instructed the new soldier in the nine-step ritual of preparing a musket. The recruit's long-fingered hands were defter than Duncan had expected, and when the final test came, the insertion of real powder and shot, they executed their task to perfection.

"Hold up with that primer, now," Duncan said. "Officer'll tell you when to prime." He paused. "You might just make a soldier."

Alexander's face brightened. "Do you think so? Although I did not seek this employment, I do hope to fulfill my duties."

The drum rattled its insistent command, and couriers rode from regiment to regiment. "Strike the bivouac! Fall in by regiment! Officers' call!"

Sergeant Fisher took Alexander in tow.

"He won't live long," Catesby said.

Duncan lifted a shoulder in a shrug.

"Whoever fights next to him will be unsupported."

Duncan said, "I'll find him duty where he can't get into trouble. For Sallie's sake."

As the last light left the sky, the gray column lined up on the frozen road and started north. The first two regiments had good footing; those behind marched through greasy mire. Ice shards and stones embedded in muck tore at bandaged feet, and some of the soldiers wished for the rawhide shoes they had discarded.

"Time I get to those bluebellies, I'm gonna be so touchy you could set me off with a squib."

"Damn, boy! Watch where you're walking!"

A mutter. "Officers got to ride while we walk. Do they got to gallop too?" Jeers slowed a young aide to a trot as foot soldiers reluctantly made room for his passage.

Although Colonel Walker was overweight with a bad heart, he marched beside his horse.

"They might have brought us up in daylight."

"Daylight and nighttime—all the same to Stonewall."

"Stonewall's 'foot cavalry.' That mean we're no smarter than a horse?"

"No smarter'n a cavalryman, anyway."

"Anybody ever see a dead cavalryman?"

"Keep it quiet back there in the ranks!"

"Who's that talkin'?"

"This is Colonel Walker talking. That you, Spottswood Bowles?"

"No sir. That was some other fellow."

"Well, you stop jabberin' and maybe that other fellow will follow your example."

"Yes, sir."

"God damn you! I hate a man who steps on my heels!"

"Baldy, you overheard the couriers. Where we goin'?"

"Fredericksburg."

"I got a cousin in Fredericksburg."

"Maybe this time we'll whip 'em for good."

"Maybe this time we'll get kilt. If I write out my testament, will you carry it for me?"

"Marse Robert won't let us get kilt."

"Lookee over there. There's the river."

"Look at them Federal bivouac fires! God Almighty!"

"Right smart of Federals."

"Got any tobacco?"

Stumbling and weaving, the sore-footed column reached its destination after midnight, and Colonel Walker passed the word to bivouac.

Duncan and Catesby saw their men settled before they bundled up themselves: Catesby's blanket on the ground, Duncan's blanket and Gypsy's horse blanket on top of them. They curled tight around each other and closed their eyes.

An eyeblink later the crash of drums brought them awake. Above the Rappahannock the sky was transparent red.

Catesby had the thought that blood is thicker than sunrises. You can't see through blood.

Some of the soldiers gobbled hardtack, some built fires. The men with soldier's disease hurried to the sinks.

Duncan saddled Gypsy while Catesby rolled their blankets.

"Quartermaster's wagons!" Men hurried to draw their issue of salt pork and hardtack, and a few even got cornmeal, which they'd boil with the salt pork.

Duncan said, "Must be expecting a scrap. This is the soonest I ever saw those wagons. Sergeant Fisher! Tell that man to go down to the sinks! This isn't a stableyard!"

"Might not see sunset this day," Catesby said quietly.

"Don't think too much. After we get to fighting and the blood gets up it's all right then."

Below the blue sky, the great plain at their feet was a fog ocean.

Colonel Walker briefed his officers. "The Federals have crossed the Rappahannock and occupy Fredericksburg. They are just there . . . underneath that, and General Lee anticipates their general attack. They have the plains, we hold the hills: Longstreet anchors our left, Jackson in the center, J.E.B. Stuart's cavalry on our right. For the moment our brigade is in reserve."

"The men will be grateful to eat and rest, sir."

"Yes, but God knows when we'll be needed. I'll require some couriers."

Duncan said, "I've a man for you, sir. He's educated. Was a schoolteacher."

Alexander sat away from the others, rifle leaned against his new haversack. He was sleepy and sore-legged—no question, prison was more agreeable than this military life. But if he could make something of this, if he could . . .

"Kirkpatrick, report to Colonel Walker." Sergeant Fisher was a crude man, with a saber scar that had quilted his forehead. Alexander supposed Roman centurions must have looked like Sergeant Fisher.

"Up the hill, new fish. Colonel's the bald man on the horse. He wants you as a courier, although I've got a dozen men better."

Staff officers clustered around the colonel, who was searching the fog with a brass telescope.

"Can't see a damn thing," Walker said. "But they're down there. J.E.B Stuart says it's Reynolds's corps."

"Pennsylvanians."

"They'll fight," Duncan Gatewood observed.

"We've a gap in our front."

"Don't worry. No troops can get through that swamp, and anyway, Firebrand Gregg's behind the swamp with his Carolinians."

"Hsst. It's the general."

Horsemen trotted down the ridgeline: Lee, Jackson, A. P. Hill, and their aides. The usually ill-dressed Jackson was in full dress uniform today, the sun glittering his epaulets.

As the party passed, soldiers rose to their feet, and many removed their hats.

Alexander Kirkpatrick wondered if he should announce his presence; he cleared his throat, but Duncan Gatewood shifted his horse and Alexander found himself facing a horse's brown rump.

"Colonel Walker, sir," Walker called out. "Early's division."

Lee nodded. Alexander had never seen such a handsome man. Beside him, Jackson looked like an ape stuffed into a uniform. Alexander stepped forward and produced a salute. General of the Army of Northern Virginia Robert E. Lee returned a puzzled glance. Through his field glasses, Jackson watched Confederate artillery unlimbering on a knoll above the plain.

When the generals moved down the ridgeline a young staff officer lingered. "Colonel Walker, good to see you. This morning, Longstreet turns to Stonewall and asks if all those Federals don't frighten him. Stonewall doesn't turn a hair. He says it'd be a wonder if we didn't frighten them." The staffer laughed and spurred his horse on.

"There'll be hell to pay," Colonel Walker said softly.

Patchy woods furred the Confederate hills. The Richmond, Fredericksburg & Potomac Railroad angled across the Federal plains below. Across the Rappahannock, bluffs stuck presumptuous heads above the fog. The dark dots on that bluff were hundreds of Federal guns.

Captain Gatewood shifted his horse to reveal Alexander and said, "Colonel, this is the man I told you about. He can read. He can write. He might have a head on his shoulders."

The colonel inspected Alexander. "Soldier, I'm told you were a schoolmaster."

"Sir, I am a graduate of Yale College, a professor of antiquities."

"Yes. Well, *tempus fugit.* I shall require you to carry messages, verbal and written, between myself, General Early, and the regiments on our flanks. Do you understand our dispositions? Atkinson on our right, Paxton on our left. Down the hill to our front are Maxcy Gregg's Carolinians. Right front, Archer—he's got Tennesseans, Georgians. Left front, Thomas's Georgians."

Briskly Alexander repeated: "Yes, sir. Atkinson, Paxton, Gregg, Archer, Thomas. Yes, sir."

"Will you remember when the shot starts flying?"

"Yes, sir. If I cannot exactly recollect an officer or position, I will make inquiry."

The colonel eyed his captain. "You vouch for him, Gatewood?"

"He'll try, Colonel. Can't ask for more than that."

The colonel extracted a leather-bound notebook from his breast pocket, scribbled, and gave the paper to Alexander. "Deliver this to Maxcy Gregg and bring me his reply."

Alexander saluted and started down the hill.

Each Confederate regiment commanded a quarter mile of hillside. Soldiers dug shallow pits or piled brush in front of their positions. Some cooked breakfast.

Alexander's stomach clenched at the smell of fatback boiling. At Virginia State Penitentiary, a man was provided for!

"Watch where you're going, sluefoot!"

"I am Colonel Walker's courier. Where might I find Colonel Gregg?"

"He's a general, Maxcy is. Find the South Carolina colors and you'll find Maxcy."

Alexander crossed a shallow ravine, memorizing landmarks for his return, ignoring curious stares and the jibes prompted by his new uniform. The sun was well up and the cloud sea was thinning from solid white to misty gray. Poets had always been inspired by war. The *Iliad*, the *Aeneid*, Caesar's terse *Commentaries*. What grand work, carrying messages between commanders, neither the originator of messages nor he who must take action upon the information contained therein. "Pardon me," he asked a soldier whittling a stick, "where can I find General Gregg?"

"Behind yonder thicket," the soldier pointed.

"Are you prepared?"

"Prepared for what?" The soldier had a decided cast to his left eye.

"The Federal assault."

"Nope." The soldier went back to his whittling. "I'm skulking to the rear plumb terrified."

The elderly figure alone in the clearing had to be General Gregg. His full black beard was streaked with gray.

"Sir! Message from Colonel Walker, 44th Virginians!"

The general was staring unhappily at the brushy swamp below him.

"Sir!" Alexander shouted.

The general was startled, "Why didn't you speak up, son? You don't want to go creepin' up on a man like that. Speak up like a man!"

As the general read Walker's message, a flush crawled up his neck. He crumpled the message and shoved it back to its messenger. "You take this back to your colonel and tell him he's a horse's ass. Tell him he's got Carolinians in his front and we'll protect you Virginians as long as we are able. Now git!"

Alexander was well away before he uncrumpled Colonel Walker's message: "General Gregg, If your damn firebrands hadn't fired on Sumter, we'd all be home with our wives and children toasting our feet by the fire. Your Obt. Serv., James A. Walker, Colonel, Walker's Brigade."

A weight lifted off Alexander's shoulders. Apparently he had misunderstood again. He had thought this a terrible war: life, death, the legions at Cannae, Caesar facing the barbarians. . . . Alexander had been willing to do his duty. But others, officers no less, thought it a joke. Alexander pasted an amused smile on his face. He dawdled and whistled and his eyes searched faces for sign that others were in on the secret.

Duncan's companies, sixty men, were in reserve, so Duncan left them and followed the ridgeline from Pickett's regiment to the knoll where artillerists had placed fourteen guns. A lieutenant Duncan knew directed men throwing up earthworks. "Hello, Elliot. What a field of fire."

"Oh, we'll hit 'em hard. But if they get amongst us, we're finished. Too many trees. Can't retire napoleons through a forest, you know. You on the line?"

"Reserves. Walker's brigade."

"We're ordered not to fire, no matter what the Federals do, not until we're told. I hope the men can stand it. I am told Burnside's got a hundred thousand men under the fog. Isn't this grand! You, there! Don't touch that gun! I want that gun pointed where I've got it, exactly."

The next time Duncan stopped, Gypsy lowered her head to graze.

The light on the fog's surface was pure white gold, painful to the eye. He wondered how the Federal soldiers felt, somewhere deep in the mist, straining to see the hills and what faced them this day. They would be taking comfort from the men beside them, from the routine preparations that preceded attack.

Gypsy lifted her head. The west wind dispersed the fog and ruffled the hair on Duncan's neck. "Good God," he whispered.

Tens of thousands of Federal soldiers in companies, brigades, regiments, divisions, each with its own banner, each with its own cluster of officers.

Their pioneers hacked down hedgerows on either side of the Richmond Stage Road, levering trees into the ditches as bridges for the artillery, while others dismantled the fences that would impede the infantry.

Confederate skirmishers retired across the railroad amid a flurry of gunpowder blossoms.

Duncan Gatewood had never imagined anything like this beautiful orderliness: the armed musculature of the great Federal army in bright array upon the mile-wide plain. Their bands struck up and Federal artillerymen raced forward with their guns and pivoted neatly, the horseholder jogging the horses to the rear while his mates wrestled their guns into place.

As one, they, It, the army, started forward, and the hairs on Duncan's neck stood erect. They were irresistible—how could mere men stand against them?

But from a thicket at the far right of the advancing ranks came a puff of smoke, another. The neatly organized Federal ranks rippled, then faltered, as a lone Confederate artillery piece, out in front of its own lines, opened fire.

The Federal artillery promptly abandoned all plans to hammer the Confederate hills and wheeled to face this crazy interloper firing where no gun should have been.

Through his glass, Duncan watched the Confederate gun crew: eight men and a single officer hopping and dancing like lunatics. The gun barked again and again, smashing the packed ranks as though men were so many dominoes.

From the bluff across the river, heavy Federal guns bellowed impotent salvos. As soon as the Federal field artillery found the range of that impertinent gun, the gunners withdrew it twenty yards and fired again, moved obliquely, and fired once more.

The massive Federal advance lost heart, and thousands of infantrymen lay down in the mud they'd created by their passage. Like an angry man trying to smash a pesky fly, the Federal artillery flailed at the lone Confederate gun. They rained tons of shot on that thicket, but wherever their deadly metal struck, the gun was elsewhere. Dismounted Confederate cavalry sallied forth to protect the gun, to interpose itself between the gun and Federal infantry. The gun was a goad, the gravest of insults. It evoked great thunderings, and so many shells descended on that thicket they briefly obliterated it, but as the smoke cleared the Confederate gun barked anew and no man among the thousands of Federal soldiers dared to raise his head. Like a bear bitten by a louse, a tycoon bedeviled by a mosquito—the offended host was too big to fight anything so small.

The Federal army hunched, flailed, stomped the earth, and bellowed. For an hour, that gun delayed the advance before it fled back to its own lines, its gunners clinging to the limber and the horses' harnesses.

The Federals reorganized. Mighty regiments countermarched. New batteries came forward and unlimbered. Soldiers who'd dropped to the mud during the artillery duel remained in the mud. Some propped haversacks under their heads and slept.

Duncan blinked. In a single hour, what had been a terrible and beautiful army had been reduced to clots of muddy men on a muddy floodplain. Duncan chucked Gypsy in the ribs. He had been too long away from his men.

Catesby Byrd's company was tucked under the trees, rested and fed. At a spring men lined up to fill their wooden canteens. Although there'd been firing, none had been directed at them. Catesby was writing Leona.

Leona had informed him of Sallie's parole into the hospital, but Catesby wasn't sure whether he should mention Alexander. Death takes a particular interest in war's novitiates, and Alexander might not survive his first battle. Leona was in deep mourning for Baby Willie, and Catesby would spare her more grief. How he wished he had seen his Willie, just once! If he'd not enlisted, things might have turned out differently. Many men of Catesby's generation had avoided the war. His neighbor James Warwick discovered pressing business in Europe. And in a Richmond newspaper Catesby read that five hundred wagons departed for the West from St. Louis every day. This war had produced many bold pioneers.

Catesby Byrd wrote: "Your brother is well and in high spirits. Though his beloved Gypsy has not been shod since Rufus shod her at Stratford, the horse has more flesh than her rider! Have Rufus and Jesse been found?"

Hurriedly, Walker's officers abandoned the ridge and skidded down the back slope. Duncan tethered Gypsy in a thick stand of white oak saplings. "Federal guns unlimbering. They mean to do us mischief."

Catesby opened his mouth to speak, but at that moment the Federal guns spoke: a stutter, a brag, a roar. Catesby clapped hands over his ears.

The Federal guns sought the Confederate guns on the hills. They hurled solid shot and explosive shell, their iron insults shearing through oak and ash, brittle hickory, chestnut and elm. Outgunned two to one, with less reliable ordnance, the Confederate gunners declined to fight. General Jackson had made too clear the fate of the impatient gunner who fired early and gave away his gun's position. In shallow pits they lay beside their gun carriages and prayed no unlucky shell would crash into a powder-filled limber box. Fire, shift a degree, fire again, shift a degree, Federal napoleons invited the Confederates to abandon this childish hide-and-seek, to play a more manly game.

Since the Federal gunners suspected Confederate batteries would be emplaced near the ridgetop, that's where they concentrated their fire. Projectiles cleared the ridge with yards to spare, and by the inexorable laws of physics, lost altitude as velocity diminished and crashed into the reserve brigades of Early's division, which, tucked behind that sheltering ridge, had not thought to dig in or otherwise protect themselves.

Metal whizzed through the trees, striking trunks that had stood for centuries with the stout whack of an axman's first blow. Shivered by the fusillade, the trees relieved themselves of dead limbs, and soldiers cowering below were deluged by falling timber of all sizes, some large enough to crack skulls. Despite this hazard, soldiers sought cover under the biggest trees they could find, and newcomers panting for safety were not always greeted hospitably.

Shells exploding among the reserve artillery behind Walker's brigade killed horses and shattered limber carriages, while frantic artillerists lashed their guns to the rear.

One horse was on its forelegs, down in the back, its neck stretched out in what Catesby knew would be a scream had the cannonade permitted hearing it. Shells flew over the ridgeline like flights of fast black crows. Solid shot thumped into heaps of autumn's fallen leaves and exhaled them so they swirled again among the trees, resurrected by the barrage. Slivers of hot metal hissed where they lay. Tattered by concussions, smoke drifted like ghost vines.

When the earth shook, Alexander was hurled off his feet and bit down on his tongue, and the blood which gushed from his mouth astonished and frightened him. How much blood did he have? Was he shot in the face? His fingers patted his face all over, but they were numbed, as if he were wearing gloves, and he could not tell if he was wounded. He looked up to ask—surely Colonel Walker would tell him—but, sheltered by a ledge, the colonel was calmly conferring with an aide. Hands clutched to his face, swallowing his own blood: so thick, so rich, so salty—Alexander couldn't say a word.

The ground heaved under Alexander again and deadly steel whisked by overhead. On hands and knees, he scurried toward the ledge where the colonel stood as if he hadn't a care in the world. His aide was barefoot and his sleeve darkened by blood, but neither man deigned to notice.

Alexander's leg was wet and hot: he had pissed himself. His haversack contained a second pair of trousers, but he could not recall, for the life of him, where he'd set it down.

The colonel's barefoot aide ran up the ridge in a low crouch as black death crows cleared his head by inches.

Alexander shivered. His wet crotch was getting cold.

Hunched over, Walker's aide duckwalked the last few terrible feet to that crest, and Alexander blinked his eyes, expecting him to become, instantly, a fine red mist. But the man was still alive, shifting to his left, seeking a better vantage point.

A shell hit ten feet from where Alexander lay. At first it was just a black something, but it took a bounce and Alexander drew himself up small so the explosion wouldn't kill him, and the dud shell stopped rolling and the colonel pointed at it and was laughing, laughing.

Duncan Gatewood thought of nothing, which was a gift he'd acquired, to think of nothing. A vague comfortable feeling suffused his bones—he was relaxed enough that he might slip into the earth beneath him, and his mind drifted, touching here and there, without comment. In a hollow formed by the roots of a tremendous white oak, Duncan lay with his cheek pressed against one root and his foot braced against another, dreaming about his childhood, the boy he'd been. He remembered Uncle Agamemnon. Years ago he'd happened on old Uncle doing his mumbo jumbo beside the river. Uncle crouched in a crossed circle outlined in white ash, chanting in a language Duncan did not know. The young master slinked away and never went near that place again. That magic spot was Stratford land the Gatewoods didn't own.

The silence, when it came, was shocking. When the Federal guns quit, blue regiments reformed across the plain. Rubbing sleep out of his eyes, Duncan joined Colonel Walker's aide on the ridgetop.

"Will you look at that!"

"Jesus Christ Almighty!"

"There! That's the Bucktails?"

"Those in the black hats. They're the Iron Brigade. They gave us unadulterated hell at Manassas."

"Your eyes are better than mine," Colonel Walker said, lifting his glasses.

A rank of infantry, two deep, at a steady step, a thousand yards wide, and a second rank, two deep, behind the first. Officers rode before their troops.

"It's a damn dress parade," Duncan breathed.

Dead silence from the Confederates on the hills. Dead silence from the advancing Federals. Not a sound, not a bird call, not the whinny of a horse nor the sharp crack of the sharpshooter's rifle—the regiments came on like something in a dream.

"Come on," Walker's barefoot aide whispered fiercely. "Bring them shoes. Bring them shoes, hyar!"

They swept over the dismantled fences.

Someone was muttering, "Fire, fire. Please God, fire." Colonel Walker's saddle creaked as he leaned forward to see better.

At exactly eight hundred yards, as per General Jackson's prior orders, the Confederate guns opened up and blew the blue soldiers into rags. Guns in the fore, guns to the left flank, guns to the right; and maybe they weren't the best guns and certainly not all their shells exploded, but there were very many guns, pre-aimed at specific targets on the plain; so Confederate guns ate men.

Some of the Federals ran, most flopped down where they stood, and some of the men who lay flat on that plain were still breathing and some had had life's breath knocked out of them.

Now they knew the Confederate guns' positions, Federal guns made their reply. Guns were rushed onto the field, quickly disconnected from their limbers, swung into place, and aimed. Now they had their targets, now they would take revenge! Federal shells tossed clods of frozen earth into the air and part-buried sweaty Confederate gunners. Federal shells disemboweled an officer's prized gray mare. Federal batteries killed gunners, smashed limbers, and hit an ammunition wagon, which blew up with a tremendous crash.

After the Confederate guns were silenced, the Federal regiments regained their feet, re-formed, and surged forward, this time at the double-quick. The Confederate riflemen had orders not to fire until the Federals were right on top of them: the railroad was their mark.

"They are not cowards," Colonel Walker remarked.

When the Federals reached the railroad, the woods erupted with musket fire, a long rolling blast. The Federal lines melted as if flesh and bone were no more substantial than theater scrims. Officers were whisked off their horses, color bearers lived scant seconds before they fell. Like great wounded beasts the federal Regiments groaned and reeled from side to side, stung, stung, stung.

One regiment howled and fired and disintegrated into individual soldiers who charged across the tracks and into the swamp at the foot of the hill.

Colonel Walker turned to Duncan. "Does Gregg know?"

"He's in reserve!"

"But there's nobody in front of him. Not a soul. Those Federals will surprise him! Courier!"

The colonel handed a note to Alexander. "Take this to General Gregg. It is no jest this time, soldier. Deliver the message into General Gregg's hands, and hurry!"

"Sir, perhaps I . . ." Duncan began.

"A man on foot will get through that tangle quicker than a horseman. Go! For God's sake, go!"

Alexander Kirkpatrick went bounding down the hill as fast as he could run, leaping shattered timber and toppled trees, the residue of battle. Alexander's heart was in the place his brain usually occupied. No one had remarked on his stained trousers! They had asked for his help! Perhaps he would be a brave Confederate soldier!

Alexander's right foot tripped on an oak staub and his left leg stretched to outrace his stumble, but he landed flat on his chest and his face slid into a blackberry thicket. His eyes went white, his breath sucked like a man shot in the chest, and he pushed his hand toward his face only to recoil from the sight. His hand was filled with thorns, a dozen of them, tips black beneath his flesh. They were so deep! He'd never had thorns so deep! When he lifted his head, more thorns scratched his pate, and in a panic Alexander writhed backward, though thorns clung as if they knew and hated him personally. He sat back on his heels staring at his hands. Tears streamed down Alexander's cheeks. He had not sought riches, or power or dominion over other men. Just a quiet corner in a library where a pale sun streamed onto oak tables in the late afternoon.

Alexander Kirkpatrick leaned sobbing against a hickory tree. For the first time in months, he missed Sallie. Sallie would have known what to do. Sallie always knew what to do. Why wasn't Sallie here?

Whimpering, sucking at his hand, Alexander watched blue-clad soldiers advancing across the plain. Confederate musketry stopped many at the railroad, but some regiments slipped sideways and entered the woods.

Those blue-clad figures would cheerfully kill Alexander. He sucked on his trembling hand. Anonymous men were coming up this hill to destroy a mechanism so intricate it could never be reconstructed. These men, flailing and cursing and fighting—they knew nothing. They fought because they knew nothing. These men, many of them, did not even know how to read! How could they comprehend a man like him?

Sallie had only pretended to understand him. The very day they arrived at her father's hovel, Sallie showed her true self: "Carry the firewood, Alexander! What will the horse do for fodder after this hay is gone?" Such questions! Such drumming, unanswerable questions!

Alexander Kirkpatrick's mind whirled like a top as he picked his way back up the hill he had so hopefully descended.

Maxcy Gregg's North Carolinians believed they were in reserve behind a full regiment of Tennessee troops, and their rifles were stacked. When bullets started whizzing through the underbrush, they ran to reclaim their weapons, but old General Gregg forbade them, cursing. "Those are our men out there, boys! Tennesseans!"

Gregg was wrong. They were Pennsylvanians, Ohioans, and New Yorkers, and although they were green regiments, they knew enough to pour fire on the flank and rear of weaponless Confederates. While exhorting his men to hold their fire, General Gregg was shot off his horse.

"The woods are swarming with Federals." Colonel Walker lowered his glass. "They have broken our line, and I fear for General Gregg."

A weaponless soldier crossed the ridgetop and started down the backside. "What regiment?" the colonel bellowed.

"Nineteenth Georgia. Ain't none of us left."

Other soldiers streamed out of the woods, some wounded, some white-faced and speechless.

A captain begged Colonel Walker to help reorganize his shattered regiment. "Thirty-seventh North Carolina. We could have whipped them, but we had no more bullets." Tears cut streaks through the powder smudges on his face.

General Early and his aides arrived just as an artillery officer lunged up the hill, his horse spewing blood from its nostrils. "Sir, there is an awful gulf before you, swarming with Federals. They will capture our guns in short order."

General Early was a dyspeptic man, a man of easy and violent temper. He exploded. "The hell with General Jackson's plans," he cried. "Colonel Atkinson, you will send your brigade forward. Colonel Walker, your brigade will follow!"

The ridgetop was transformed—officers shouted orders, the quick clattering of Atkinson's drums called his men into line of battle, and they were going forward even as they formed.

Somebody hollered, "Let's drive them hogs out of that thicket."

Hastily, Catesby Byrd finished his letter: "As I write this, dearest Leona, the brigade is forming for battle. I cannot know whether I will survive. If I post this myself, you will know the outcome. If I cannot, remember always my love for you. Catesby."

He pressed his missive on an ambulance driver, a one-armed veteran with dozens of similar letters stored in a biscuit tin under his seat.

"I hope you retrieve this yourself, Lieutenant," the driver said. "But if you have bad luck, I'll see it gets to your people. Yes, Jimmy," he said, "you too," as he tucked a gaunt young private's letter in with the rest.

"Looks pretty bad," the private said. "When will this war be over?"

"When we are all dead," Catesby said, and was shocked to realize that he meant it.

Inside the column of defeated men drifting to the rear, Alexander Kirkpatrick felt safe and anonymous. Anecdotes of ancient wars flitted through his mind: the defeat of the legions at Smyrna, the Helvetians' final desperate charge against Caesar. There is nothing new under the sun.

When they came out of the woods, they had encountered a reserve brigade, at ease, smoking and talking quietly. Officers ignored the stragglers dribbling past, but the men called out, "Getting too hot for you, boys?"

"Oh looky yonder! Is that a coward I see?"

Whistles, catcalls. A whiskered second lieutenant stepped into the road and cried, "Men, your comrades are still fighting. Nothing lies ahead but disgrace!" Though he brandished his pistol, the stragglers quietly broke around him.

A wounded man crumpled to his knees, and the soldier beside Alexander said, "Come on, friend. We're better than beasts! Take his other arm, will you?"

Their burden was just a boy, couldn't have weighed 130 pounds and touched his feet to the ground in a stumble, keeping his weight off them. "Oh, God," he said.

"You'll be all right. We get you back to the field hospital, you'll be all right."

"No. No I won't. I won't see the sun rise tomorrow." So much blood. The boy had been shot in the neck, and every time he laid his head to the right, he pumped blood over Alexander's shoulder.

The blood was briny and pungent. It smelled like the Manhattan wharves where the clerk Alexander had walked, on Sundays, so many lifetimes ago.

"I'm from Charles Town," the boy gasped. "My family has the Mercantile, not so far from the courthouse where Brown was tried. My father is Edwin Mackey, my mother is Lizbeth. I have a sister, Clara, and a brother, William. The others died as babies and are in heaven."

For a few minutes he was silent, and when he spoke again, his blood started pumping. "Did you see our napoleon?"

Alexander's helper was a grizzled, gap-toothed mountaineer. "Which napoleon was that, soldier? There was right many napoleons bangin' away."

"Pelham's. We waited until the Federals were past us, past us, the only gun out there, and then Major Pelham gave the order to fire, and we mowed 'em down like they was shocks of corn. . . ."

"Be careful how you hold him," the mountaineer warned Alexander. "Every time he flops toward me, he bleeds worse."

"I am wearied too," Alexander replied.

"We're all wearied. We're shot at and shot out and wearied. Can't you ease your brother's way?"

There was just this road, unwounded men passing on the left, wounded men on makeshift crutches moving slowly on the right. Sometimes a man stepped out of the column and lay down. An ammunition wagon hurtled toward them and they parted. The driver lashed his foaming horses through the column of broken soldiers.

"Oh, there wasn't anybody more gallant than us," the wounded boy chattered. "Didn't we plague those yankees? They were searching for us with their long arm—that's what we call artillery, you know, the long arm—and we'd shift position while they were hitting the place we'd been. And Major Pelham, oh he was jigging like a wooden puppet on a string. I couldn't help laughing, looking at him. It was the grandest fun I ever had."

"You shot?" the mountaineer asked Alexander.

"I don't know," he answered truthfully.

"I wish I could see my dear mama's face one more time," the boy said. "I have a letter for Mama in my pocket. Will you see she gets it?"

"No need for that, son. We'll get you to the field hospital and they'll patch you up and you can give your ma your letter yourself. This war's over for you, son. Don't you know it."

"My sister Clara—she's to be married next month," . . . the boy said and sagged. He became dead weight.

They laid the boy beside the road and the mountaineer pressed his thumbs over his eyes and took the bloodstained letter. "He'll fight no more," the mountaineer said. "I never wanted to be in the artillery. Every time you get in a scrap the artillery horses get killed. Me, I never could abide that. Poor beasts never ask for war. Nary one horse ever signed up to go to war. How they scream when they're hit. Many nights after a battle I stayed awake on account of their screamin'. Where you from, soldier?"

Alexander had to think. "SunRise," he finally said. "Over in the mountains."

"Powerful lot of mountains in the Confederacy."

"Western Virginia. To the west of Staunton."

"Wasn't General Jackson born in that country?"

"I wouldn't know. Sorry." Alexander stretched. Relieved of the weight of the dying boy, his body was light and free. His side was covered in gore, the boy's blood had matted his hair and plugged his ear, and his skin tautened as it dried.

"I'm Maxwell. Pine Bluff, Tennessee. After they did for Gregg's Carolinians they snuck behind our position and poured it to us. We never had no chance at all. Oh, we'll take a ribbing for that tomorrow."

"But we're going to the rear."

"Sure we are. Sure we are. Don't go thinking we'll be staying. Provost's men will send us back. We're whipped now, but we won't be whipped tomorrow."

"I'm whipped for good."

"If you ain't killed, you can fight again, and maybe this time it'll be you doing the whipping. How you called?"

"Alexander Kirkpatrick."

"I knew an Alexander once. Smallpox killed him. Only Alexander I ever knew personal. 'Course there's Alexanders aplenty, but he's the only one I knew."

"My mother hoped I would conquer all." Alexander chuckled at the notion.

"Way you talk you're educated. Me, I never got educated. All my life I worked in the fields. Oh, I'd kill a deer or a bear to keep us through the cold months, but mostly I lived by the sweat of my brow, like the Bible says. When this war started, I thought I'd see the world, and by God I have. I been to Vicksburg until we was shot out of there, and I been to Maryland, and before it's over, I expect I'll get to Richmond. We passed through Richmond on the railroad, but it was night and I couldn't see a blessed thing. How'd you come to be a soldier?"

"It was no choice of mine."

"Conscript, eh? We 'uns separated from the Union 'cause we wouldn't be told what to do, and now our Confederate government goes to conscriptin' soldiers who never asked for any part in the fight. Conscripted man ain't any better off than artillery horses, and I said so many a time."

"Full indeed is earth of woes, and full the sea . . ."

"That from the Bible?"

"Hesiod. One of the ancients."

"I never did know anything about those fellows. I can write my name, but schoolmaster quit and there never was another come to my part of the country. Always believed I'd be luckier had I got my education. Folks got respect for a man with education."

"I am expected to know what I do not know. How I wish—I wish I could be just like everyone else!"

The rough Tennessean shook his head. "Damned if that ain't somethin'. Get shot at all morning and in the afternoon meet a man who says I'm better off ignorant."

The column limped through a road cut and the sound of battle was swallowed by the shuffle of feet, the moan of wounded men, a man quietly begging to be killed.

"You got a wife?" the mountaineer asked.

"No. I thought I had one, but I did not."

"She take up with somebody else? Die on you?"

"When my Sallie wanted me, she didn't hesitate a moment, and when she was finished with me, she discarded me without regret."

"Hark that poor feller there on the roadside. Some woman'll be weepin' for him, I'll wager."

"Sallie, she never ever showed any pity for me."

"I s'pose I'm blessed. My woman's so homely nobody else'd lie with her. I ain't much maybe, but I'm what she's got."

"My Sallie was beautiful."

"Them beautiful women got the upper hand over us ordinary fellows. They can do better'n us and they know it. A homely woman like my Alice is grateful for what she's got. Never see no homely woman runnin' off."

"Do you care for her?"

The man shot him a strange look. "'Course I do. 'Course I do. It's just my manner of talkin'. I didn't know what to say when you told how your wife had left you, so I said the first thing came into my head. That's where education comes in. Educated man never says the first thing comes into his head."

"Often he doesn't know what to say."

"That's when you can say what some other educated feller said already! You got it memorized what that other feller said and can use it for your own."

"When I quote Cicero or Homer it's never appropriate and everyone stares at me and I keep smiling as if they were in the wrong."

"Well, you fought today, didn't you? Live through this scrap and you'll have something to talk about. You at Sharpsburg?"

"No."

"Father Death had his work cut out for him at Sharpsburg."

"I can't imagine worse than today."

"This wasn't so bad. Weren't for them Yankees getting around behind us today, we'd have whipped 'em." He offered a dark plug of lint-covered tobacco to Alexander.

Alexander refused the plug, and the Tennessean bit off a chew and shut his eyes in pleasure.

A vedette of cavalrymen waited where the road crossed a broader turnpike. As the defeated men arrived they were winnowed into two groups.

"Them's the provost men. They'll sort us into shot fellows and them which ain't and bring us back to the line. Way them yankees was coming at us, this scrap could go on for days. Was you at the Seven Days?"

Alexander shook his head no.

"Scrap every day of the week. See that bunch on the left? They's fellers from the 1st Tennessee. Seventh Tennessee'll be nearby. See, there's a quartermaster's wagon. I guess they'll feed us. I lost my canteen, blanket, tin cup, everything."

"I dropped my haversack. . . ."

"When you skedaddle, you got to skedaddle. Which regiment you with? You see any your people up there?"

Alexander said quietly, "I won't return. I'll not go back."

The Tennessean's jaw dropped. "But you got to go back. Just because you run don't mean you've done quit. All them boys there've run. I run myself. But you don't go back, the provost, he's gonna shoot you. Old Stonewall's provosts right keen to shoot fellows don't want to fight no more."

The line slowed to a shuffle. Officers distinguished the quick from the shot.

"It's not my fight," Alexander said.

"Why of course it is. Ain't these your people?" The Tennessean's wave encompassed unwounded and wounded men alike.

"I wish I were like other men."

"I'll be damned. Might be you have more education than a man can naturally stand. I'd be right pleased to read the newspapers and write my own letters home. But if losin' your people is the price of education, by God, I wouldn't pay it."

"I won't go back. I'll run again."

A hundred yards ahead the column divided. The Tennessean looked Alexander over as if he were one of the world's natural wonders. "Say, you ain't a coward, are you?"

"I don't know what I am. Call me coward if you must."

The Tennessean screwed up his face. "Where I come from, a man calls another man a coward, he goin' to face that man over a pistol come sunrise. Can't call a man a coward where I come from. He won't stand for it."

"Well, I don't care," Alexander said with a spark of defiance. "I just don't care! Coward, abolitionist, rebel, atheist: all the same to me. Words. Words to frighten and . . . Christ, I'm hungry. I've never been so hungry in my life."

"You . . . you ain't right. I don't mean to hurt your feelin's and such, Alexander, but you ain't right."

Alexander's shoes scuffled through the dust.

"I ain't one to tell another man what to do," the Tennessean said. "But might be this war could make you right. No offense, but there's some fellers wasn't much before this war and now they're havin' a big time. You bein' an educated man, ain't nothin' to keep you from bein' an officer. War's a mighty force for changin' a man."

"But it's crazy."

"Well of course it's crazy! Everybody knows that! But that don't mean you don't do it. If we was sensible all the time, where would we be? I don't own no niggers nor care to, but I'm fightin'. Bluebelly don't own no niggers either and don't care to, but he's fightin' too. Now you make sense of that!"

The provost's men were directing healthy stragglers to the left. "Lean against me, close your eyes, keep 'em closed," the Tennessean hissed. He fumbled at Alexander's breast pocket. "This here's that poor dead boy's letter. You post it from the hospital. Be a terrible letter for his folks, but they'd rather have it than not. Do what I say now and you'll be all right."

It wasn't hard for Alexander to sag against the other man, not hard to close his eyes. "Me, I'm fit as a fiddle," the Tennessean cried out. "And you got half my regiment here already. This here soldier's been shot in the head and I don't expect he'll live. You let me take him to the ambulances, I'll be right back. I'm Jim Maxwell, 7th Tennessee."

The provost captain said, "Sergeant, keep watch on this man. If he starts to board an ambulance himself, bring him straight to me."

"You know, sir," the Tennessean sang out as he walked Alexander toward the ambulances, "with all your ridin' back and forth behind the lines, you get to see more'n I do, since I'm only a lowly infantryman up on the line fightin' Federals. I've always wanted to know. You ever see a dead cavalryman?"

"Maxwell, 7th Tennessee. I'll remember you."

"Thank you kindly, sir. Thank you." He helped Alexander into an ambulance. Two narrow benches quickly filled with walking wounded.

Three men were laid on the floor. "You get back to Richmond, you take its measure for me." And Alexander's benefactor was gone.

The ambulance jounced south and east for the better part of a day. Men groaned, two died. At the field hospital at Guiney Station, amputations were performed. The less wounded helped the worse wounded aboard a waiting train, and Alexander sat on a wicker bench between two stunned amputees. The train chuffed along irregular track until near midnight, when it stopped behind another, even slower, train. Alexander Kirkpatrick stepped between the cars and swung down to the ground and lay in the ditch until the train was out of sight.

He followed the first road he came to. How Alexander wished he could be like the Tennessean—bluff, hearty, willing to throw life away for a lark. The man had said he had a homely wife. How Alexander yearned for a homely wife.

Alexander walked west, always picking the less traveled road, until sometime before dawn he abandoned the lane for a farmer's hayrick, and slept among faintly sour dead grasses and the bright tang of spearmint.

Earlier that afternoon, when Walker's brigade hurried toward the fighting, they bumped into Colonel Paxton's Stonewall Brigade as it was forming to charge. Officers yelled, "Go around, damn it! Go around!" But Walker's men passed right through their ranks.

"Don't be in such a hurry," one private called. "There's yanks enough for all of us."

Released from long waiting, Duncan felt the tiredness slip from his muscles, and the bile dissolved in the back of his throat. His young body took in great gulps of air, and he yelled to his men, "Let 'em know we're coming," and the men took up the terrible yip-yip-yip which was partly the cry of wolves, partly the cry of men worse than wolves. Duncan's lips lifted off his sharp young teeth in a hungry grin. The color sergeant trotting at Duncan's side wore the same grin exactly. "Dress your lines," Duncan hollered. "Dress on the man next to you!"

And the van slowed enough so that the regiment could trot through the woods as a machine, a willing machine that could concentrate its fire, could wheel, could turn. Rawhide shoes were discarded and the yelling brigade left bloody footprints on the leaf litter. Their arms grasped their Enfields, their thumbs clamped on the thick iron hammers, their elbows banged against their sides, their knees churned. Their minds were busied with soldiers' calculations: how to keep their feet on rough ground while staying precisely abreast, neither ahead of nor behind the man on their left, the man on their right. "Dress the line! Dress the line!"

The men in the second rank need only attend to the man's back in front of them, that sweat-stained butternut-dyed patch of cloth that puckered and stretched, darkened with new sweat.

The brigade's colors were somewhere in the core—the soldier's guide and identity. To the colors, the officers came, the couriers came, and there the enemy fire focused.

Their battle flag was deep gray with the seal of the Commonwealth of Virginia embroidered in the center. Around the edge were names: MC-DOWELL, CROSS KEYS, PORT REPUBLIC, GAINES'S MILL, MALVERN HILL, CEDAR MOUN-TAIN, SHARPSBURG, SECOND MANASSAS, and everywhere neat patches, each large enough to cover a .58-caliber bullet hole.

The brigade had had nine color bearers, but one might yet recover from his wounds. The present color bearer, Corporal McBride, counted 137 patches in the flag. McBride took up the colors in the west woods at Sharpsburg after his predecessor was killed. Since McBride was no hand with needle and thread, he'd had SHARPSBURG and SECOND MANASSAS stitched on by a tailor from the 13th Virginia.

The woods ahead were smoke and noise. "Dress on the colors!" Duncan's voice cracked. Gypsy sidestepped a wounded Confederate, clean jumped a dead Federal stretched out beside a fallen log. The Confederates burst into a clearing and the brigade volleyed, first the front rank, then the rear. Blue-coated troops disintegrated. Duncan yelled, "Dress on the colors!" as the Confederates advanced, walking briskly, loading, firing, loading, firing, and high-stepping over the bodies of the slain. Some bluecoats—no more than twenty—rallied behind an officer, but in a moment the Confederates whisked them away.

The officer, a major, lay dying, and as Gypsy passed, the man's agonized eyes met Duncan's. "I am slain," the major whispered, and blood bubbled at his lips and Duncan wanted to say he was sorry.

The bluecoats tumbled back onto the plain, discarding their rifles to speed their flight. Roaring like a dragon, Walker's brigade emerged above the railroad. In good order, six full Confederate regiments flowed over the railroad tracks in pursuit. The plain they crossed was littered with Federal dead and wounded.

Federal artillery blasted the advancing Confederates. Colonel Walker's aide galloped to Duncan. "Retire to the railroad! Retire! We are not supported on our left!"

The men's blood was up, and Duncan interposed his horse between them and the Federals to stop their attack. Duncan's men cheered and cheered.

Reluctantly, they withdrew behind the railroad line. "Hold your fire," Duncan cautioned. "You'll want every ball if they come at us again." He detailed men to return to the woods they'd just swept, to take ammunition from the wounded and dead.

Unlike Walker's men, Atkinson's brigade did not stop, did not hold to their order of battle, but overlapped the Federals' retreat, coming on so swiftly that their front and the Federal rear were inextricable, and men slugged and bayoneted and stabbed and bit and strangled and shot and dragged fleeing officers from their horses.

The Federals jumped down into drainage ditches and threw up their hands and white flags appeared, and Federal prisoners started for the rear, five men guarded by two, fifteen burly soldiers and their captain captured by a boy private with an unloaded rifle. When prisoners passed through the lines, none of the Confederates spoke to them—as if defeat might be catching.

One of Catesby Byrd's men had a substantial slab of roasted beef which a provident yankee no longer required. As men fought to the death on the plains before him, and fresh Federal regiments came to the aid of their battered companions, Catesby Byrd sat on the railroad bank and ate beef, washing it down with tepid water from his canteen, thinking what a wonder man is and how strange his glories.

To the west firing was furious, but on Walker's front the fighting stopped by half past two. Except for the cries of hurt men and horses, the field was quiet. Some unfortunates had fallen wounded into clumps of broom sedge set afire by the artillery. They shrieked until the fire reached their ammunition pouches. Under constant battery fire, the Confederates lay behind the railroad embankment and did not talk about it, did not talk at all. Some wept. Some tore cloth from their shirttails to stuff into their ears.

General Jackson and his young aide rode beyond the tracks to inspect the enemy depositions. A minié ball whistled past. "You must withdraw!" Jackson told the young man. "You might be shot out here!"

The sun dropped below the horizon. In the twilight, a ripple ran through the ranks, officers came to the fore, and Confederate batteries sallied onto the field. Federal guns lit up the twilight, muskets flashed like a thousand fireflies, and the Confederate guns withdrew.

The soldiers of Walker's brigade learned that General Longstreet had won a signal victory that day at Marye's Heights on the left flank of the battlefield.

Sometime after nine o'clock that night, pulsating streaks—green and purple and lavender and blue—lit the northern sky. "Catesby," Duncan said, "it is the end of the world."

Catesby said, "I believe it is the aurora borealis, though it's a rarity this far south. My friend, what marvels you and I have seen."

The pulsating light illumined the ghastly field while roving Confederates retrieved their wounded and foraged among the dead.

"Catesby," Duncan called. "I think this fellow's got your shoes."

The dead man's feet were larger than Catesby's.

"It is more difficult than one might think—untying a dead man's shoelaces," Catesby said.

"Here's a new wool overcoat. Poor bastard. He hadn't much chance to use it."

Two veterans had a Federal officer's trousers off before they dropped his legs in disgust. One fussed, "Henry, I done told you. When we're lookin' for underwear, find a man's been shot in the head. They don't foul themselves."

Kindly men cut the throats of the wounded horses. The light shimmered across the spectrum: violet, soft greeny-blue.

Two Virginians were tugging at a brigadier's coat. "I saw him first!"

"I already told you, Spottswood Bowles, I'm the one should've been a officer." The brigadier's epaulets took on the colors of the aurora; blue, purple, gold.

Litter bearers steered silently around the bodies.

A sergeant sat on a dead horse, inspecting each object he took from the saddlebags before adding to a row along the animal's neck.

Naked alabaster corpses stretched as far as Catesby Byrd could see, and a choir of lights sang as thousands of men went about the business of the living.

30

TOO COMMON COIN

EVERY NIGHT BEFORE retiring, Sallie Botkin Kirkpatrick prayed for bad weather. In deep snow, or when freezing and thawing make the roads impassable, armies do not fight and men do not maim one another. It had been not quite three months since the carnage at Sharpsburg, and the weary surgeons and matrons of Camp Winder Hospital were beginning to hope that the flood of desperately wounded men had ebbed until spring.

Jammed with wounded, puffing dense, stinking woodsmoke, the first trains rolled down Broad Street shortly after midnight. The red brick depot of the Richmond, Fredericksburg & Potomac Railroad was lit by flaring gaslight, its broad platform overflowed with people. Ambulances from all the Richmond hospitals waited at the curb. Swaddled in a heavy blanket, Sallie sat beside a convalescent, Major Sponaugle, while the train's engineer banged his bell and screeched his wheelbrakes and then there was that heartbreaking dead silence before people rushed toward the cars like an exhalation of breath.

"Come, Major," Sallie said.

Owing to his cheerfulness, the major was a great favorite among the matrons. The major had suffered his wound at Sharpsburg, and though his leg had been amputated above the knee he took his loss in good spirit. According to him, his family had been the last Unionists in his South Carolina county and had suffered opprobrium for their views. "But I have the laugh on my neighbors now," he said. "I have confuted all their arguments. For the rest of my life I am branded: PATRIOT!"

"You know what we are to do?" Sallie now asked.

"We are to assume Saint Peter's post, separate the quick from the dead. Although I am capable of ordering boys into galling fire, I defer to you tonight. And some of my sex assert that women are the weaker vessel. . . ."

"Major, you are too clever for me."

His smiling face fell. "I am sorry. I was just jesting to quiet my qualms."

"Why is it that men are so eager to make messes they cannot clean up afterward?"

Supporting one another, wounded men tottered out of the cars, while behind, its locomotive belching cinders, another train waited impatiently. Lightly wounded men and civilians rolled men onto litters. Dead men, faces uncovered, formed melancholy ranks against the depot wall. Elderly men, boys, and respectable matrons sought news of their loved ones; some carried pails of cool water, and one pretty girl had a basket of the ripest, reddest apples.

Ambulances clattered on the cobblestones, steam engines chuffed importantly. With a cry no louder than a kitten's mewl a new widow fainted.

"Careful with that officer, damn you!"

"Can you walk to the ambulance? Please do lean against me."

"No, ma'am, I've no news of the 4th Georgia. Our regiment was at Marye's Heights."

Wounded Federal prisoners were cared for without distinction and privates were loaded as quickly as officers. When one locomotive removed its reeking cars, another took its place.

Some of the ambulances were two-wheel carts, some were farm wagons, the best had been captured from the Federals.

The major, whose infirmity prevented easy passage through the crowd, stayed in the street and directed ambulances.

"My name is Daniel McClintock. Please write my father that I did my duty and look forward to seeing Jesus," one boy told Sallie. His wound, a tiny puncture in his chest, hadn't bled much; his dirty uniform was hardly bloodstained. "God bless you, ma'am," he said, and died.

The ambulance men shifted hopeless cases to the far end of the platform, where volunteer chaplains offered what comfort they could. The station tower clock struck three. The major conscripted militiamen to control the crowd. "Ambulances must have room to pass," he cried. "Please."

Most of the faces were young. Some were chalk-white with approaching death, others smeared with dirt and blood. "Will I live, ma'am?"

"Yes, yes. We will tend you."

At Sallie's direction, men were loaded on ambulances or carried to the end of the platform. She forwarded all the youngest boys to Winder, no matter how badly wounded, because she could not bear to give up hope for them.

The dawn was mild and beautiful, the sky a benefaction.

Sallie swished her bloody hands in a water bucket. Another train was pulling in.

On their return to the hospital a wounded boy moaned whenever the ambulance bumped. The major said, "I am told General Lee anticipates the Federals will renew their assault this morning."

"Perhaps General Lee will care for the new wounded," Sallie snapped. "God knows we are overwhelmed. There is no more room at Howard's or Ligon's, and they are laying boys on the floor at Mayo's warehouse. Our poor boys. Bravery is too common coin."

The major said, "Surgeon Lane's son is with Cobb's North Carolinians. I understand they took the brunt of yesterday's assault."

In the still air, smoke from Winder's morning fires formed a pall over the whitewashed ward buildings. In Sallie's ward, men lay on either side of a wide center aisle. The summer netting was rolled up and tied and potbellied stoves glowed red.

Young Jimmy perched at the foot of his cot, mending one sock. "How are you feeling today, Jimmy?"

The boy had seen just one day of war at South Mountain before canister took off his leg. He would soon be furloughed home.

"Oh, Miss Sallie, I am raring to go. I can hobble around on this stick just as good as if I had two legs. But sometimes first thing in the morning when it's specially damp I swear I can still feel that ol' leg just like I still had it."

Sallie nodded. "Others have made the same report, Jimmy."

The boy furrowed his brow. "Miss Sallie, could I ask you . . . I don't mean to be impertinent. I just thought since I was going home soon, I could ask you. I don't know another woman I might ask." The boy looked straight up at the ceiling and kept his eyes fixed there. "It ain't just me wondering. It's every man who lost an arm or a leg. We was wondering . . ."

When Sallie put her palm to his forehead it was cool.

"We was wondering if a decent girl would ever want to take up with us." He hurried on. "Corporal Rexrode says women won't have no choice, that every man in the South will have been shot up. But that Irishman, Ryan? He says a woman doesn't need a man so bad as a man needs a woman, and if they got to pick one of us, they won't pick at all. Please, Miss Sallie." He searched her eyes. "Could such a one as you care for such a one as me?"

The Georgia boy was so pale he was almost transparent, and his hand was hot parchment. "Am I to die then?" he asked.

"You will not see the morrow," Sallie replied.

"Miss Sallie, could you sit with me for a spell? I will go easier knowing you are here."

He opened his eyes twice more. The first time there was sense in his eyes and he made to say something but licked his dry lips instead, and Sallie gave him a sip of water. His fever was palpable as a stove. The second time he opened his eyes he died. Sallie covered his face.

Convalescents brought a breakfast of bread, baked at the hospital, a cupful of brown beans, fresh milk, an apple, and a hard-boiled egg. Sallie drank a glass of milk. They carried the Georgia boy to the shed out back, where he'd lie until they took him to Hollywood Cemetery or shipped him home.

"Miss Sallie!" the major said. "We are required again at the trains."

Sallie took time to splash cold water on her face.

It was such a beautiful bright winter's day they might have been on a pleasure jaunt had not their ambulance stunk so.

The trains were backed up to Henry Street, twelve blocks from the RF&P depot. There were more young women at the scene than earlier; otherwise things were much the same. The major directed ambulances to the platform, and Sallie filled them. Sometime after four o'clock, one of the colored ambulance drivers called out, "Miss Sallie! Miss Sallie! Surgeon Lane don't want you sending no more. We're full up."

"Then we shall forward them to Chimborazo."

"Chimborazo full pretty quick, too, Miss Sallie."

"Then inform Miss Semple we must release our convalescing patients to those private homes that will accommodate them. Matron Semple will make arrangements."

"Come, Sallie," the major said kindly, "you must take some nourishment."

When Sallie wiped her hands on her dress, she left streaks of blood. "Soup. Some soup would be nice."

The public rooms of the Spottswood Hotel were packed with men drinking, some to the victory, some to the death toll. One gray-faced elderly man sat on the stairs sobbing into his hands.

Before the war, the Spottswood had been Richmond's most fashionable hostelry. Important planters and visiting dignitaries called it their Richmond residence. French wallpaper still adorned the walls and chandeliers (no longer glistening) still hung overhead, but the tables had been pushed together into long rows, the manager collected his twenty dollars (Confederate) at the door, and luncheon consisted of potato soup and cornbread. The clamor was Babylonian, conversation nearly impossible.

The man on the bench beside Sallie wore a cavalryman's uniform and smelled like horse sweat and fresh manure. The backs of Sallie's hands were blood-spattered. The crosspiece of the major's crutch, a smoothed length of curved hickory padded with cloth, was propped against the table. The soup was light on potato content, but satisfactory as to broth, and the cornbread was hot and filling.

The room raised three cheers for General Lee.

What had life been like before the war? Unable to talk over those who were cheering Stonewall Jackson and intending to work through the entire Confederate command, Sallie and the major went back to work.

The last train emptied at dusk, nearly five o'clock, and when Sallie and the major left for Winder, the only men on the station platform were dead or dying.

Camp Winder's three surgeons had been cutting since yesterday midnight. Unlike smoothbore musket balls, which broke bones, the new minié ball shattered them. Sometimes when the ball struck softer bone near the joint, salvage was possible. Usually, even when flesh and muscle were intact, the bone was splintered and the shattered limb had to be amputated. Most surgery was amputations, and almost all successful surgery was. Although the surgeons did search abdominal wounds for fragments, that work was futile and they knew it: a man shot in the bowels nearly always died.

Convalescents carried a patient into the ward, and on his litter what could be done was: the cloth saturated with chloroform was clapped over the patient's dirty face, the affected limb was stripped of clothing and washed, the surgeon's knife slashed quickly and completely through muscles, exposing the bone, before the fine-toothed saw went to work. As the surgeon cut, a matron kept the tourniquet tight so the man wouldn't bleed to death.

In the pool of light the patient, a middle-aged Irish corporal, said, "And it is sorry I am to be meeting you under these circumstances. Can I keep my hand?"

A weary Surgeon Lane shook his head no.

"Well, that'll be all right then. Me mother warned me about pinchin' the girls. Religious she was."

Underneath the stink of blood was the stink of men's sweat and urine and feces and the faintest tang of gunpowder.

Men were brought to cots, laid on the floors between cots, finally in the aisles.

Cousin Molly came in and touched Surgeon Lane's shoulder. The paper she held out to him was a telegram.

Surgeon Lane made no sound but he went white and tears leaked from his eyes and he did nothing to stop them. "I am obliged to you for this news, Matron . . . Molly . . ."

"I am so sorry, James."

Tears pouring down his cheeks, Surgeon Lane amputated a left forearm, a foot, then a right arm at the shoulder. The next litter bore a Federal lieutenant. After his shirt was cut away, a bulge was apparent above his collarbone, perhaps a minié ball under the flesh or a canister ball. The lieutenant's eyes rolled in terror. Surgeon Lane dropped his knife in the filthy bucket of surgical appliances and rubbed a bloody forearm across his eyes. "Take this man to Surgeon Chambliss," he ordered. "I will not operate on this officer nor any other Federal soldier tonight. I cannot promise I will not do them harm."

At noon the next day, Surgeon Lane lay down for an hour in the room Sallie had made over for her own use. At five that evening, Surgeon Lane lost patience with a convalescent who had failed to empty the limb tub so an arm rolled under the surgeon's feet and he misstepped, slashing his patient's thigh. "We are worse than our enemies!" he shouted. "We are better killers through carelessness than they are intentionally!"

Cousin Molly Semple brought a hand basin of clean water. "Wash up, James," she said. "I have a meal for you outdoors. It's time you came away."

In the December evening surgeons and matrons ate wordlessly at a makeshift table beside the low shapes of men who awaited their ministrations. Their living breath rose from where they lay.

31

A CONTRABAND

"IT'S CHOKED UP," Cuffee announced; without, however, leaving his perch atop the honey cart.

Jesse straightened from the pump handle, set his hands in the small of his back, and stretched. Swirling snow clotted his eyelashes and melted in rivulets down his cheeks.

"Can't be much shit left," Cuffee opined helpfully.

"Less 'n there was," Jesse said. "Why is it I always go down in the pit and you always up top?"

Cuffee huffed himself up. "Because that's the way the army want it done. I drives the team, you empties out the cesspool."

The cesspool in question served one of Washington City's makeshift army hospitals. Three brownstone rowhouses had been combined to care for the wounded. The cesspool out back was Jesse's responsibility: no reason the surgeons or matrons need pay it any mind.

After the Fredericksburg fight, the hospitals had filled and Jesse and his teamster emptied cesspools every second day, but many of the wounded had died, some had been discharged as convalescent, and now Jesse worked no more than ten hours a day. His pay, twenty-five dollars a month, less the five dollars every colored worker was taxed to support frail and sickly colored the government cared for, did not vary no matter if Jesse worked ten hours or twenty. That, as the teamster had explained, was how the army did things.

Some of the city's cesspools had been constructed in George Washington's time, and stone liner walls sometimes caved in and suffocated the hapless cleaner. This was a newer one and the mortar was sound, the lid could be propped open for ventilation, but even so after a few minutes down, Jesse's head would get a little swimmy.

Jessie took a deep breath and climbed down into the sludge on the bottom. He held the mesh-covered end of the sump hose under the liquid so he wouldn't lose the prime as his hands plucked away material—most of it rotten bandages—that clogged the screen and then went up the ladder again to the light where he could take a breath. Jesse bent and coughed and coughed before he spat and began pumping again.

White men wouldn't do this work. There seemed to be plenty of work white men wouldn't do. If work got to be hard enough or dangerous enough or smelled bad enough, work got to be nigger work, and Jesse was glad of it.

Jesse had no objections to cleaning cesspools. If the Emancipation Proclamation had made him any man's equal, it had not advanced him to a state where he needn't earn bread by the labor of his hands. The work wasn't hard except when the hand pump failed (usually its leather gaskets had torn), and then Jesse was obliged to bucket ordure into the honey wagon while the cursing teamster mended the gaskets.

Twenty-five dollars a month was more money than Jesse had ever had, and he was paying for his own food and his own shelter and he had bought these clothes—wool pants and wool shirt—secondhand, and the gumboots he'd bought too.

So much in the world was new to him; sometimes Jesse felt like a child.

"I believe that has it dry." Cuffee dismounted to remove his mules' nosebags and make minor adjustment to their traces. Jesse coiled the stinking hose, hung the ladder on its pegs, and lashed the pump. He slid the pit cover closed.

When Cuffee climbed onto his perch and gee'd his mules, Jesse clambered onto the wagon and perched atop the pump. Although there was room for two men on the seat, the teamster rode alone. "You smell too bad," he explained. "I been smelling shit all day. I ain't gonna smell it on my way home."

The younger teamster who took Cuffee's place when he'd drunk too much the night before—he wasn't so fussy. "But I been a field nigger, like you," the replacement explained. "Cuffee, he was a house nigger. Cuffee come north as body servant to a Federal captain, and he's disgraced to be on a honeywagon. That top hat he wear? Same hat he used to wear when he was driving Massa and Missus to the ball."

The replacement teamster had suggested Jesse seek work on the fortifications. "You strong as a ox. You come on down there and they take you on, sure."

Men didn't stay with cesspool cleaning long. They took a cough or the soldier's disease or a fever and the army had to find another man to climb down into the pit. Jesse had been at it as long as anyone.

Jesse thought it was all right. Rufus had dared to speak up, dared to say who he was. Jesse had broken hard soil with Rufus's farrier's hammer and scooped dirt over Rufus with their battered tin cup after Rufus said who he was.

Washington City was crowded with deserters who wore civilian clothes but walked like soldiers, and when the provost's men rode by, they slipped into doorways or around corners. The provost's men never did much about them, they just rode on by. Despite their new blue uniforms, their well-fed horses and brave epaulettes, the provost's men were discouraged too.

It had been a discouraging war. General McClellan and General Pope and now General Burnside. Cheerfully, drums tapping, bands playing, they'd crossed the Potomac and headed south, "on to Richmond," and one general after another had his army killed and came back with a list of excuses as long as his casualty list.

Some coloreds—the replacement teamster was one—were talking about moving farther north. The pay was worse, but if the Federals did quit the war, a man farther north wasn't so likely to be taken back into slavery.

Jesse hadn't ever seen Father Abraham, but other coloreds told Jesse all about him. Many evenings, Father Abraham took a horseback ride along the Potomac River, and the coloreds would wait for him there, so they could see he was real and not a dream.

The honey cart paused at the C&O Canal. Jesse stepped down and gave the teamster a wave, which he didn't respond to. He walked along the wooden sidewalk—just another colored worker going home.

The sun had dropped into Virginia, gaslights were on in the shops, colored maids lined up at the bakery windows for aromatic breads and rolls. Jesse turned into an alley behind the big townhouse which had become headquarters for the Military Chaplains' Association. The first-floor curtains were drawn back and several chaplains were drinking tea, conversing, smoking cigars.

Jesse slept in the stone washhouse on the alley. The chaplains' servants did laundry on Tuesdays and Thursdays, and on those nights Jesse didn't have to buy coal.

He stripped off his trousers and washed his hands and arms. His second trousers, spare socks, brogans, knitted woolen scarf, and blanket were tucked behind a cabinet. He'd rented this sleeping space from the chaplains' houseman, after promising he'd be out of the washhouse before five in the morning and that his belongings would be hidden when he wasn't here. Jesse dunked his sodden stinking trousers and socks in the wash kettle. The amulet which hadn't protected Rufus hung from Jesse's neck.

He brushed his brogans before he went out. With a few other colored laborers, Jesse waited at the back door of a grocery on M Street, the snow falling heavier now, whitening hats and shoulders and bare heads. It was a beautiful snow, big white flakes swirling in the gaslights.

Although the little store sold a full range of provender to any white person who entered the front, its back-door fare was more limited: meat pies wrapped in cabbage leaves, slabs of rat cheese, and popskull whiskey at half a dollar the quart.

Jesse bought a pie and a half pound of cheese. As he turned into the storm, some laborers were already sharing their whiskey.

Back at his washhouse, Jesse lit his candle, wrung out trousers and socks, and hung them near the stove to dry. He emptied the wash kettle, rinsed it, and hung it up, because it was important, the houseman said, that he leave no trace. The chaplains would object to his furtive presence among their drying linens, socks, and drawers.

Jesse's rent was eight dollars a month. Another ten went for meat pies and rat cheese and his nightly candle. He had three dollars put away for new trousers when he should require them. He felt fine sitting on the stone floor beside the warm fireless stove. Sometimes, after a day's work, his back throbbed where Samuel Gatewood had whipped him, but next to that warm stove, it uncramped and eased.

He'd picked up a newspaper discarded on the street, and as he ate his meat pie he read every word, including government notices and morticians' advertisements—"Prompt, Sanitary Transportation to anywhere in the U.S."

Drying shirtfronts hung in ghostly rows on washlines over his head.

After he finished his thorough reading, Jesse rolled the paper and put it in the stove. Housing for free coloreds and runaway slaves was so scarce that hundreds were living in the old slave jail in Alexandria in the same cells where their fathers and mothers might once have been held. But here was Jesse, alone, in quiet, with clean water from a hand pump and a coal stove and the servants' necessary not fifteen feet away. He was a rich man.

He wondered what meat was in the pie tonight. Sometimes it was light meat, sometimes dark. It was always salty and always greasy, but that grease warmed his stomach. He ate the cabbage leaves which had wrapped the pie and served as his dining platter. The rat cheese would be his breakfast. His drink was water, drunk from the metal cup he'd used to bury Rufus.

Jesse touched the amulet and thought: All my friends are in the stars.

He turned to the window, but there were no stars tonight, only falling snow, fat moth flakes illuminated by lights from the house, where the Christian soldiers held their nightly discourse.

Sometimes Jesse eavesdropped. The chaplains were convinced that eternal life was assured only to soldiers who never played cards, never drank whiskey, and "suffered not from temptations of the flesh," which meant, Jesse supposed, visiting the brothels beside the canal. The notion that God would care about cardplaying or finding affection seemed strange to Jesse. There were several brothels where older colored women serviced laborers for a dime or a quarter, but Jesse wasn't tempted. Strong and young as he was, he didn't dream of women, and sometimes when he searched the stars for Maggie, he thought himself more like a child seeking his family than a grown man hunting his rightful wife.

He sipped his water with the delicacy of a white man drinking fine wine.

If he were to go for a job on the fortifications, he'd risk losing his present job. He could probably miss one day, but two days' absence and one of the new contrabands pouring into Washington City would climb on the back of the honey wagon and down the narrow ladder that was so much like the orchard ladders Jesse had once used to pick Uther Botkin's apple trees.

Jesse had been climbing down the cesspool ladder since October, and though he had plenty to eat and a roof over his head, something was gone from when he and Rufus were together. The mountains were bitter and the rivers hazardous, but now it seemed, as Jesse leaned against the washrack, warm stove and belly full, it seemed to him that all the mountains and rivers had disappeared when Rufus died.

He unfolded his blanket and crawled under the laundry table, where he slept. Tomorrow he'd go down to the fortifications and see if they had work for him.

32

MRS. OMOHUNDRU

Warm, greasy rain slid off the hood of the girl's coupe. As she passed the C&O station, she rubbed her fist against the windshield to clear the condensation. Her daddy had told her to stop wasting her time on that crazy old woman. Her supervisor wanted to know how many real ex-slaves she'd interviewed. Her uncle, who had been the girl's staunchest supporter, wondered, aloud, if Marguerite Omohundru had "a screw loose."

"Honey," he said, "she's had a long life and done some wonderful things in Richmond. Mrs. Omohundru has been a godsend to the Historical Society. But she's not herself anymore. Pretending she's a negro, and an ex-slave to boot! Why, Silas Omohundru was a hero in the war! Poor Marguerite! She must be in her nineties."

"She became a woman the year of Cox's snow," the girl said.

Letters from Phil lay on her bureau unanswered. Her mother wondered if she had "female problems."

She couldn't even pretend she was working. After her first visits she quit taking notes and stopped asking questions. Their routine was unvarying. She'd take her seat facing the sofa in that garden room and accept a cup of hot tea—just one—never a second no matter how long she stayed—and she'd listen as the ancient woman spoke about a past and a people that were as strange to her as the heathen Chinese.

Sometimes, after she parked before the overgrown front yard of what had been among the grandest homes in Richmond (so Daddy said), she sat for ten minutes before she found strength to get out of the car.

"That woman is mesmerizing you, sugar," Daddy said. "That crazy old woman has put you under a spell."

Daddy said that one night after he'd had too many drinks with the juniors from the law firm and he never repeated his theory. Nonetheless, the girl wondered if maybe it wasn't true. As the old woman talked, she seemed to grow stronger. The color returned to her cheeks, her hands moved more fluidly, she could talk for hours and never tire. In contrast, the girl sank into a curious apathy, a passive state that wasn't restful at all.

As usual, Kizzy let her in wordlessly, took her coat, and hung it on the hall tree. As usual, the girl waited alone in the garden room. As usual, the heap of histories, magazines, and dusty reminiscences seemed disturbed: different-sized stacks, different books on top. The girl wondered if every night the old woman, like Scheherazade, invented the story she told the next day.

"Again you honor us with your presence," Marguerite Omohundru said, as she made room for herself among the magazines.

"I don't know . . ." the girl said.

"We needed this rain," Marguerite observed. "See how the garden glistens."

Kizzy brought their single tray, two cups, one teapot, the cream and sugar neither used, two small silver spoons for stirring the cream and sugar neither used.

"I have been thinking about families," Marguerite said. "Are your people well?"

"They're off this weekend to open our summer place. They asked me to go. . . ."

"Richmond can be disagreeable in the summertime," Marguerite observed.

She paused for a polite moment before taking up the theme she had determined upon. "Families can only take so much hurt. When a family is injured it tries to heal, but sometimes the healing shrieks as loudly as the hurt. Thomas Gatewood, Samuel's father, owned a great competency: thousands of fertile acres, cattle, sheep, a mill. He was magistrate and postmaster. Before any civic change was initiated in the countryside near SunRise, Virginia, Thomas Gatewood was consulted. He already had what most men spend their lifetime pursuing, but Thomas was not satisfied; Thomas must also have his neighbor's wife. Perhaps he thought he was not governed by the inflexible laws that govern others. Perhaps he thought his great desire excused itself.

"I believe his son, Samuel Gatewood, tried to atone for his father's guilt, but the powerful Gatewood family—which seemed, I can assure you, more like a fact of nature than a merely human institution—had weak-

ness at its core. They were caught by surprise when their son, Duncan, took up with an ignorant little colored girl." She smiled her most charming smile.

Wistfulness transformed her face like a mask. "That Christmas, the last Christmas before the war, when Duncan held Baby Jacob for the only time he ever did, he loved his son. He could see himself, his family, his future in that boy, and his eyes glowed with love."

CHANCELLORSVILLE, VIRGINIA
MAY 2, 1863

In the spring of 1863, General Joseph Hooker, "Fighting Joe" Hooker, was a vigorous field commander and one of the hardest drinkers in the Federal army. Ambitious, he'd openly schemed to seize the Army of the Potomac from Ambrose Burnside (who hadn't wanted command in the first place, but wouldn't turn it loose once he had it). In his letter of appointment, President Lincoln warned Hooker against rashness. There was something about Fighting Joe that made Lincoln apprehensive.

Despite his Fredericksburg victory, Lee's starving army was disintegrating. Desertions were epidemic, and Stonewall Jackson had issued orders to his troops that no unwounded men were to accompany the wounded to the rear. Rations were short: regiments detailed men to forage for wild onions, sassafras buds, and poke sprouts. After a winter's use, the clothing they'd taken from the Federal dead at Fredericksburg was worn out.

When they crossed into Virginia, each man in Hooker's army carried eight days' rations and sixty rounds of ammunition. They got across the Rappahannock unopposed, passed Fredericksburg, and marched into the tangle of cutover scrub woods called the Wilderness. It was miserable country. Narrow roads connected tiny villages, clearings were small and few, and the tangled woods could conceal God knew what. The moment he struck some of Lee's troops, Joe Hooker stopped in his tracks. Hooker put his enormous army into a defensive line at a crossroads called Chancellorsville and boasted: "I have Lee in one hand and Richmond in the other."

The next morning, Robert E. Lee sent Stonewall Jackson's corps—the bulk of his army—on a twelve-mile march across Hooker's front to the Federal right flank. He urged Jackson, "Get at those people."

In Jackson's absence, Lee would hold Hooker's eighty-thousand-man army with fifteen thousand men of his own.

Hooker was as still as a bird paralyzed by a serpent. At midday on May 2, 1863, some of Hooker's men saw Jackson's great force sliding through the woods. Federal scouts and pickets sent urgent reports of masses of men moving across the army's front.

Years afterward, when someone asked Joe Hooker what he was thinking of, why he froze up the way he did, Hooker said simply, "I just lost faith in Joe Hooker."

In the late afternoon of that day, a cavalry officer accompanied Stonewall Jackson up the small hill behind Joe Hooker's lines. Thoroughly exposed and as thoroughly unnoticed, Jackson gazed on the Federal troops. The officer reported: "Jackson's expression was one of intense interest. To the remarks made to him while the unconscious line of blue was pointed out, he did not reply once during the five minutes he was on the hill, and yet his lips were moving. Oh! beware of rashness, General Hooker. Stonewall is praying in full view and in the rear of your right flank."

The butcher of the 153rd Pennsylvania and two helpers dragged the lead rope of a terrified steer; the nearer the beast came to the tripods where six of its brethren dangled, the louder it bellowed. From frying pans on nearby campfires arose the pleasant smell of liver and spring onions. The steer smelled only death. Neck extended, resisting with all its strength, it was hauled nearer while the butcher called endearments— endearments the steer knew to be lies. "Come along, *Liebchen,*" the butcher murmured. "It is not far. Soon you will rest."

Soldiers waited near the tripod with a tin washtub with which they intended to retrieve the steer's steaming liver.

"Move back, you boys. Can't you see you're scaring him?"

The butcher of the 153rd Pennsylvania was famous throughout Howard's corps for his sausages. The butcher had made sausages in Prussia, until the revolution there, when he and many other soon-to-be American immigrants had picked the losing side.

He would not make sausage of this steer. He wouldn't reserve the blood for blutwurst, nor the liver for liverwurst, and the scraps would go for soldiers' stews, not the garlic sausage, his particular specialty. In winter quarters he busied himself with savories for the ranking officers: General Howard himself was partial to liverwurst. But in the field, the butcher could do nothing so complicated. The beef would hang overnight, no more, before being produced for the 11th Corps' breakfast. He'd save the kidneys as a special breakfast for General Howard. "Move back, you boys. The little one is frightened, can't you see? He is afraid like the Confederate soldiers and would run away like they do. Ha, ha, ha."

It was a peaceful evening at the far end of the Federal line. Men played cards and cookfires glowed. The two guns aimed down the plank road were unmanned, and the infantrymen's muskets were neatly stacked. "Come on, you boys, can't you pull?"

The steer's eyes rolled. Froth dribbled in ropes from its mouth.

"You boys. Set down that tub and push. This youngster is not wishing to be your breakfast. Ha, ha, ha."

"Damn, he's filthy back here."

"First the courage fails and then the bowels. You are a soldier. You have seen it before. Push on him. You can wash up after!"

The terrible abatis—the cluster of sharpened poles—formed a man-made thicket across the plank road. The abatis was like the barricades the revolutionaries had thrown up on the streets of Berlin, which slowed the Prussian soldiers but hadn't stopped them.

Behind the abatis were the breastworks, then the plank road which connected the long line of Federal troops. General Hooker had inspected them this morning and everyone had cheered. The general said Lee's army now belonged to the Army of the Potomac.

"Push, boys. Do not be afraid, *Liebchen*. It will soon all be over. Get the hammer and the knife. Do not let the edge touch against anything. It is sharp just the way I like it."

As soon as the terrified steer was in place, the butcher swung the hammer with a solid thunk on the animal's forehead. The steer crumpled so suddenly the corporal who had complained about getting dirty fell across the animal and got a good deal dirtier. The butcher laughed while reaching for his knife. "Now," he said, "while I am cutting his throat, I wish you boys to work his leg. Work his leg and the blood all pumps out and does not taint the meat, yes. You must work his leg, just like he is walking away, ha, ha, ha."

Suddenly a deer bounded out of the woods on their right. Another. Another. Knife in hand, the butcher stared as the thickets exploded with fleeing animals. Dozens of rabbits raced from the undergrowth. More deer. Squirrels flew from tree to tree, quail whirred into the air, crows shrieked raucous objections, a fox loped into the open, and when it saw the Federal soldiers it turned and ran through the abatis, straight at where, until this moment, the Federals had supposed the Confederates to be.

Ten minutes before, Captain Duncan Gatewood had dismounted so Gypsy could make water. She didn't like to piss with him on her back, and during the long march around the Federal front, she had filled with fluid. The mare splashed gratefully, and in the woods on either side, Confederate soldiers were doing the same. Getting ready for an attack always presses the bladder.

General Rodes's division—North Carolina regiments, several from

Alabama—had already disappeared into the woods. A double battle line was swallowed in that thicket, as if it had never been.

Two months ago, Colonel Walker had taken sick, and now Duncan's brigade had a real general, J. T. Jones, and a couple of colonels too. In this outfit, captain didn't amount to much.

Sergeant Fisher gave Duncan the neatly patched regimental colors. FREDERICKSBURG had been stitched along the bottom seam with the older names. "Don't drop it now," the sergeant said. "It's bad luck, you drop it."

Men snapped and resnapped ammunition pouches. Some men counted primers into their breast pockets: other veterans counseled against the practice: "What if you get tapped in the chest by a spent round?" one said. "Primers blow up and you'll be a damn fireworks display."

J.E.B. Stuart had his horse artillery on the plank road; the horses were dancing in the traces.

When the drums sounded the charge, Duncan hoisted the 44th Virginia's colors high and moved Gypsy forward at a walk.

Rodes's division started yip-yip-yipping and their musketry destroyed the quiet and they came clear of the woods, hurtling at Federal soldiers who, until this moment, had thought that life was rather agreeable.

It had been such an ordinary spring evening. Now, unfinished letters fluttered against low bushes, were sent whirling aloft by shell concussions; playing cards were scattered, and near where slaughtered beeves dangled from tripods, a dead steer sprawled, a dead Federal soldier sprawled across his hindquarters, the man's blood as rich and red as the steer's.

Men wearing haversacks cut the straps of their haversacks and threw their rifles away to run the faster. Apron clutched around his waist, the German butcher fled for his life..

Across the wide meadow they ran, past a little church and the tavern where their officers had planned to meet that night. Scant air in their lungs, they ran, hearts bursting in their throats, young legs working like machines of panic.

Federal artillerymen unhitched guns and jump-mounted the horses and put the spurs to them, limber chests bouncing and case shot flying into the air whenever the equipage hit a rut, and other riderless horses ran wide-eyed, nostrils flaring, beside them.

Blood pounded in Duncan's ears and his perspective shortened to what was directly in front. Insensibly, the brigade's pace increased from quickstep to double-quick, and Duncan's men intertwined with Rodes's, two brigades screaming as one, killing fleeing men, point-blank. Federals dropped their swords, their guns, and threw up their hands and cried

"I surrender" and were ignored by hot-eyed Confederates streaming past.

Stuart's horse artillery dashed down the plank road ahead of columns of men, four abreast. Duncan caught up to a shirtless Federal, his braces flapping, face half-lathered with shaving soap. Duncan dipped his regimental flag, the Confederate colors crept past the man's face, into his view, and the man lowered his head and lifted his knees, pumping, pumping, and suddenly the man tripped or was shot.

A Federal line was forming ahead, and a growl rose up in Duncan's throat and he was thinking, I'll show you, I'll show you, though what he was going to show the quavering line of frightened men he never knew.

Duncan and Gypsy and Stonewall Jackson's corps, Army of Northern Virginia, cavalry, infantry, artillery, entangled in a hard knot, struck the Federal line and disintegrated it.

The Confederates were exultant murderous men who worked in a red fury and could not afterward remember how they bayoneted that gunner, the gunner's blood and the sunset the same red. Others killed coolly, fastidiously, and their memories would be cooler than the reality had been: how the bare trees looked in the sunset or the empty rocking chairs on the porch of the little tavern, waiting for Federal officers who would never sit in them. Men forgot how they loaded and fired and killed and killed and fired and killed.

Although the Confederates had marched twelve miles that day, they fought as if it were Monday morning after a day of rest. They'd eaten only salt pork and hardtack that day but fought as if they'd feasted. Some of the men were old men, some damaged in other battles: at Chancellorsville they were boys and whole. They outran the desperately fleeing Federals, and after enough butternut soldiers passed them, many Federals sat by the roadside with their hands atop their heads.

Men fell and men were blown apart and men pitched forward like bundles of rags. Black-powder smoke hung over the field, lifting and lowering like mist, and men swooped through it like raptors. The smoke made their eyes prickle and their shoulders ached from the continual slam of firing, and when their rifles got too fouled to load, they snatched new ones from the unresisting hands of the Federals.

On the road, Duncan was jammed together with infantrymen, officers on horseback, color bearers, a limber of artillery—at a pace too fast for a man, too slow for a horse. The woods hemmed them in on both sides and there were yells and shots and explosions in those woods, but the men in the road paid no heed. Around a bend, three hundred yards ahead, trotted a column of Federal cavalry, unconcerned as if on parade. Startled officers shouted urgently and the columns hurtled toward each other, one brandishing sabers, the other bayonets. They collided with a shock; a bayonet darkened itself in an officer's rib cage, a saber split a man's clavicle. A horse was shot in the chest. Another, delicately trying to avoid trampling a wounded man, crushed a bald-headed man against a tree.

Duncan shifted the colors to his left hand and wrapped Gypsy's reins around his wrist, and when a fat Federal trooper raised his saber, Duncan thumbed off two shots, the first he'd fired, and lifted the man out of his saddle. The Confederate infantry was volleying, most of the Federal cavalry was down, but here came a second Federal troop full-tilt, and the infantry's rifles were empty and a cry, half rage half despair, issued from a thousand throats as big horses crashed into them. Men clubbed Federals off their horses, horses reared and their flailing iron hooves crushed skulls. Sabers were dipped with blood as a pen nib is dipped with ink.

Duncan shot a man and the man's hands clamped his face and his fingers spurted blood. A cavalryman slashed at Duncan and missed, but cut Gypsy, opening her neck muscles, red and white striations, stretching, contracting, stretching, contracting. Duncan lowered his banner like a jousting lance and skewered the Federal cavalryman, and the sudden weight on the end of his staff almost ripped it from his hands, but Duncan stood in his stirrups until the mortally wounded man flopped into the chaos where men fought with pistols and knives and teeth.

From a low hill, backlit by the setting sun, was a tremendous flash as Federal guns opened fire, and double-shotted canister smote the men on the road like a death wall. The echoes rang into silence, replaced by the shrieking of horses and men, and Gypsy was down on her knees, and Duncan slid off and looked for someone to kill, but the Federals had fled—a few had cut their way free and those who hadn't lay in the road.

When Gypsy staggered to her feet, her intestines spilled so she was stepping on them, and with each step more gray guts slipped onto the road. The colors fell from Duncan's hand. He said calmly, "I cannot bear this," and clapped his revolver to his mare's ear and pulled the trigger, but there was no report, pulled it again, no report, and Gypsy screamed, reared clumsily, and her hooves trampled her own guts, so Duncan cut her throat.

The Confederate attack was finally halted by Federal artillery at the crossroads of the Hazel Grove Road and the old Orange Turnpike.

Blood-covered soldiers collapsed—in the woods, beside the road, on an overturned limber. With hoarse, unnatural voices, lost men sought their regiments. "Twelfth North Carolina?" "Fourth Georgia?" "Has any-damn-body seen Colquitt's brigade?"

Some picked through Federal haversacks for rations. Others counted fresh ammunition from the pouches of the dead. Some accompanied despairing Federal prisoners to the rear.

Duncan's flagstaff was cracked from butt to tip. He wiped the bloody tip clean with a blue forage cap. His eyes felt scratched by sand. He wondered where Catesby was, whether he lived.

The full moon rose smoky and red, and the entreaties of wounded men were muted as if night would heal them. A voice cried, "My God, boys! Stonewall's been shot."

33

LETTER FROM LIEUTENANT CATESBY
BYRD TO HIS WIFE, LEONA

RICHMOND, VIRGINIA
MAY 10, 1863

MY DEAREST LEONA,

I am grieved to inform you that your brother, Duncan, fell wounded on the second day of our recent battle near Chancellorsville. His left forearm was smashed by a minié ball and shell fragments have lodged in his chest near the breastbone. His left cheek and forehead were burned, though mercifully his eye was spared. Although his injuries are grave, he has a strong natural constitution and Surgeon Lane assures me that he has seen young men with worse prospects recover fully. I would have written you sooner but was waiting for the surgeon's report on the amputation of Duncan's limb, which seems to be healing as well as might be hoped. Some shell fragments were recovered, others left as too dangerous to extract.

Duncan was taken to Camp Winder, which is a hospital of some seven hundred beds beside the river to the north of the capital.

You will have heard that Stonewall died of his wounds. Here in the capital the flags are still at half-mast and weeping men as well as women are unremarkable on the street. I will always be proud that I fought under General Jackson, and wonder if his strong Christian faith, that bright moral beacon, won't be missed even more than his military skills. His last battlefield message was his prayer that Providence should bless our arms at Chancellorsville, and Almighty God answered his prayer. His dying words, we are told, were "Let us cross the river and rest under the trees."

The circumstances of your brother's wounding are as follows. On May the 2nd, we marched furiously—a march of some twelve miles across Hooker's front to his unsuspecting flank, where that evening, at four o'-clock, we assaulted his unsuspecting army. In the fury of our attack our regiment was mingled with others and I lost sight of Duncan. The Federals fled before us like sheep before wolves. It seemed almost shameful to slaughter them.

We fought until nightfall, but as we closed on the Federals' headquarters, their resistance stiffened and great gusts of artillery crashed into us. Their newfound resolution, our weariness, and the ebbing of the light brought the blood-drenched day to a close. I found your brother, face blackened, unhurt but despondent. His mare, Gypsy, had been mortally injured, and it had been Duncan's unwelcome duty to dispatch the poor creature. He could speak of nothing else. It was as if he had lost a child.

It was well after midnight before Duncan and I lay down. Alarms and tentative Federal assaults made the night bark with gunfire, but I think not much real fighting was accomplished. Duncan and I slept for a few hours.

Rations wagons had come up during the night, and we made a fine breakfast of hardtack and salt pork. Although Duncan still mourned his Gypsy, his appetite was good. Since five a.m. there had been fighting to our front: a hillock called Hazel Grove.

By half past seven we took that hill, where fifty of our guns now fired. Their noise was indescribable.

After Jackson and A. P. Hill were wounded, the gallant J.E.B. Stuart assumed command of Jackson's corps and Stuart's artillery commander, young John Pelham, directed our guns. Smoke wreathed Hazel Grove and wreathed the open ground over which our regiments were advancing through dense woods, woods so smoky that much of the time we fired at shapes rather than men. Although I could see the man to my immediate left and him on my right, everyone outside that narrow compass was invisible. When the Federal soldiers counterattacked, we withdrew past our wounded and dead, and when we counterattacked, we reacquainted ourselves with our less fortunate fellows. The fight had a ghostlike feel, as if the death we were suffering and inflicting was not quite real, and in fog and confusion, fighting might have been going on for untold centuries. Though blood darkened the waters of a small stream, thirsty men drank without qualm.

General Jones had fallen; now Colonel Garnett fell and Colonel Vandeventer replaced him. When we faltered, J.E.B. Stuart came, told a few jokes, and sang a verse of "Oh, Joe Hooker, Won't You Come to the Wilderness" to inspire us. J.E.B. Stuart has had more hairbreadth es-

capes, more bullets pass through his clothes, more horses killed under
him, than any other man in the Confederacy. He makes death seem a
lark. When finally our assaults proved irresistible and the Federal line
broke, we were issued thirty more rounds of ammunition and began the
final drive.

At such a moment there is a feeling I cannot describe. Every man is
aware of being part of something profound and terrible.

Just to the south was a once prosperous plantation: an open meadow,
house, several barns, cherry trees in full bloom. This plantation house
had been occupied by the Federal general, Hooker. From here he had
plotted the mischief our army was confounding.

Our men burst onto open ground with a shout. Dearest, I am not a
demonstrative man, but I was yelling as loudly as the rest. In my heart I
wished to murder blue-clad soldiers. Interspersed among the fleeing
Federals were horses and beef cattle and ambulances and forage wagons. When one of their regiments formed a line of battle we rushed toward that center of resistance as if pulled by magnets.

The air trembled from shot and shell, and riderless horses ran in all directions. Our rough-clad fellows fell snarling upon the Federal guns and
slaughtered the gunners. Men cheered and sobbed and yowled. Streams
of wounded men passed to the rear as if blood our army was bleeding.
Columns of dirty white smoke laid a blanket between us and the sky.
Amidst this scene, General Lee himself appeared, mounted on his gray
Traveler. Ahead, his enemy's headquarters was in flames, pouring a
black, turbulent smoke. The woods through which we had passed was
also burning.

Before his powder-blackened, underfed, weary battalions, General
Lee passed, slouch hat in his hand uncovering his magnificent gray locks
and fine features to every man's view. We raised a wild cheer—infantrymen waving overheated muskets, cavalrymen spurring their exhausted horses, even, I swear to you, dearest Leona, our wounded and
dying lying on the dirt. The man who had wrought this victory had
come to take his bow; to stand unafraid before tens of thousands of fleeing Federal soldiers with their cannonade bursting around him, to savor
his triumph and announce his mastery. I think in that moment I never
loved a man so much. Lee was in that moment all we ordinary men as-
pire to be and rightfully fear to become: the ideal Christian Warrior surveying the dreadful work his brilliance and the valor of his soldiers had
created. Darling Leona, I wept at the sight.

The Federals escaped into prepared positions, and our army pursued
no further. When the 44th Virginia regrouped, I missed Duncan and volunteered to officer those searching for our wounded.

The battle had set the woods afire, and though we dragged many men of both armies from the flames, others were overcome. Their cries and entreaties were dreadful to hear. Your brother, thank God, had suffered his wound nearby the stream aforementioned and had had the presence of mind to immerse himself and escape the heat and flames.

"I am very glad to see you." Duncan sat propped against the stream bank, a belt around his arm for a tourniquet. Litter bearers carried him to the surgeons. The flames made night bright as day while we Confederates searched thickets as yet unconsumed and rescued many a wretch who had expected the next face he saw would be an angel at Judgment Day. The only way to distinguish the dead of one army from the other was to roll blackened bodies over so that telltale scraps of butternut or blue might identify them.

I worked until rain cooled the smoking, stinking battlefield and Colonel Vandeventer ordered me to accompany our wounded officers to the field hospital.

Though the field surgeon had advised the removal of his arm, Duncan begged that the final decision be made in Richmond, and the surgeon, who was half mad with fatigue, told Duncan that he didn't have time for damn fools, not with hundreds of men awaiting his knife: he placed a poultice on Duncan's poor burned face and dismissed us. The limb heap outside that surgeon's tent was the height of a man.

Duncan and I boarded the slowest most mournful train in the Confederacy. The Richmond, Fredericksburg & Potomac is scarcely fit for the transport of cattle, let alone gravely injured men. There was an ambulance car for officers, and I laid Duncan on a bunk, his ruined arm across his chest.

The train trundled south not much more rapidly than a man can quickstep. Sometimes the railbed was so dangerous that those who could climbed down and walked beside the train, and twice the trainmen inserted iron prybars beneath suspicious rails as our cars passed over.

The ambulance car was filthy, and dark smears on the window moldings proved this was not its first engagement. A major of cavalry who had lost both his legs moaned in his delirium and cried, "Mary, beautiful Mary," over and over again.

In small towns, citizens met us on the platforms, and while the engine recharged itself with water and wood, ministering angels came aboard our car to proffer sweet water and the blessing of their tears.

The enemy's guns have taken so many of our young men, it is hard to think what our poor nation will do when the war is over. The only survivors may be the posturers and fools that inhabit Confederate statehouses. I would readily trade them all for a dozen good infantry privates!

I am sorry to seem unpatriotic, but our army sacrifices again and again and prevails, despite daunting odds. I am coming to think that we are the

Confederacy and our leaders third-rate politicos, men suitable for no other employment if governing were not so agreeable to them. If it were not for what our army captures from the Federals, we would have no means to make war. The very locomotive drawing our train, I was told, was one of those Stonewall captured.

I was last in Richmond with Duncan and his friend Spaulding, in that spring of 1861, when all things seemed possible. We were such a brave new nation! The long slow evenings after a day of drill, rich with the jests of healthy young men, full of ardor and as yet untouched by war. One morning I tugged on my boots to discover that some wag had cut away the soles the night before and my bare feet went through to the floor. To think we were so wealthy we would cut up perfectly serviceable boots!

The Richmond, Fredericksburg & Potomac station, that noble edifice, has been visibly darkened by war. In the yards a gang was removing boiler plates from a damaged engine. Two damaged engines make one whole one: that is Confederate arithmetic.

I accompanied Duncan and several other officers to Camp Winder Hospital. One begged me to notify his family of his wound. Dearest Leona, can you perform this service for me? Please write Mrs. Martin, Raleigh Springs, North Carolina. Her husband, Lewis, is shot in the knee and he hopes they will not amputate. He would be pleased if his wife could come to Richmond and bring his best trousers.

The surgeon sniffed Duncan's wound and, ignoring Duncan's protests, proceeded with the amputation. Since I was fatigued to the bone, a busy matron directed me to an empty stall in the hospital's cow barn, where I slept the clock around. The next day I walked into Richmond and procured a meal for only ten dollars! Somewhat comforted by my repast, I went into a church—St. Paul's Episcopal—and sat in a back pew. Though there were no services that morning, the pews were filled with citizens at prayer. Many were women, some dressed in mourning, but there were veterans too, some on crutches, others dandling children on their knees. I cannot describe the satisfaction I derived from sitting on a clean wooden bench in a clean place where all thoughts were of love, mercy, and forgiveness.

I was saddened by the news of Aunt Kate's sudden demise but cannot help thinking she may be better off in Paradise. Grandmother Gatewood is an all-consuming companion.

Kiss dear little Pauline for me, tell Thomas I expect him to act as a man, and know that you are the last vision in my mind before sleep and the first upon arising.

Your Loving Husband,
Catesby

34

CHEAP GLOVES

RICHMOND, VIRGINIA
MAY 23, 1863

ON SATURDAY MORNING, the ward was quiet, sunlight streaming through open windows across the floor swept by the one-armed convalescent, whisk, whisk, whisk. Mosquito netting was rolled onto frames above each narrow cot. At the far end of the room an Alabama corporal was dying while a chaplain murmured verses from the Bible. In the next bed a corpulent quartermaster major complained in a high whine about his wound, which was not particularly serious. Beside him lay a blinded drummer boy, and beside him a captain of J.E.B. Stuart's cavalry, also blinded.

The one-armed convalescent set the butt of his broomstick in his armpit and maneuvered the broom with his remaining hand. He took especial care in the corners, because he had been a machinist before the war and was meticulous by nature.

In the cot beside Stuart's captain was a Jewish colonel of artillery who was visited by his rabbi each Saturday. Both the rabbi and the Alabama boy's chaplain were elderly, called back into active service by the nation's great need.

Families were in attendance, and through the open windows came the bright noise of children at play. Next to the Jewish colonel was the cot of a fiftyish private with pneumonia who was not expected to pull through. His gray-haired, drawn-faced wife arrived at dawn, left at dusk, was never seen to take nourishment.

Samuel Gatewood stood, hat in hand. Catesby Byrd said, "Duncan's fourth on the left. I'll smoke a pipe outside."

Samuel Gatewood set down Abigail's wicker basket and laid his soft hat on the lid. Although Duncan's stump was exposed on top of the blanket, Samuel didn't look at it. His son's head was thoroughly bandaged. "Catesby said your eye . . ."

"It is saved. I'm swaddled like an Egyptian mummy until my face heals."

"Dear boy, dear boy. I . . . I was so sorry to hear about Gypsy."

"She was a fine horse." Duncan's voice was little more than a whisper.

Samuel leaned near. "What a spirited creature she was. When I bought her from Alex Seig she was so wild I did not believe you could handle her. You were only twelve. Only twelve." Samuel shook his head, wondering. "That first summer, you were just as wild as she was. We wouldn't see you from morning until night. Your mother turned gray that summer wondering what mischief you two were up to."

"Gypsy never flinched. Little Sorrel, Stonewall's horse, if she hadn't reared when those North Carolina boys fired the volley at them, likely the general'd still be alive. Oh, Stonewall was a hell of a rider. He'd been a jockey as a boy and still rode like one, forward in his stirrups."

"I see the army has not improved your language." His son turned his bandaged head. "Do you suffer?"

"It hurts like hell. My face itches terribly, but I am not to rub at it. There's nothing where my arm used to be but it hurts anyway. Sometimes I feel the bullet in an arm I don't have."

"What will we do after this war is over—so many men gone. . . ."

"There's Federals to spare. Them and their negroes can run things."

His son's bitterness was new and unwelcome.

Duncan indicated but did not touch his stump. "My injury is not without advantages. I'll save time washing hands. And that big fellow near the door, Sergeant Crenshaw, he's lost his right arm and I've lost my left. We've made an agreement to purchase gloves together. We should realize considerable savings."

After a moment, Samuel said, "Your mother sends you her love. Between her and Jack the Driver, we manage. It has been a tolerably wet spring, but we planted the oats in the river field and sowed corn on the uplands. Your mother's kitchen garden is larger than you remember it. We have our women servants still, though many of the men have run away or been taken by our government. Withal, I believe we are more fortunate than most. I am told that matters are completely desperate in the Piedmont."

A matron hurried to the Alabama boy's side.

"We were making our assault on Fairmont," his son said dreamily. "There was Hazel Grove here"—he raised a knee under the blanket—"and Fairmont here"—he raised another mound. "So we had to go down this slope and up the other. Guns on both hills, theirs and ours. First time we got within a hundred yards before they broke us. We were making our second assault when I got shot. I was still mad about Gypsy. I wasn't thinking of getting hurt."

"When you come home, you'll find changes. You'll recall that cave in Strait Creek gorge? We've taken to keeping tubs of butter and cheese and honey in the cave. It's cool there and the commissary officers aren't likely to find it. If I knew a haven for the milk cows, I'd move them too, but they need to be near for milking."

The Alabama boy's chaplain closed his Bible.

"I flopped down when I was shot. Oh, I went right down senseless. When I woke it was burning all around me and I couldn't move my limbs and I thought I must perish. A Federal dragged me into the creek. He was a redheaded fellow. I sometimes wonder about him, whether he got killed or not. Something was wrong with me. I could make my good arm go, but couldn't wiggle my legs. I thought I'd been shot in the legs too."

"Aunt Opal sent you one of her pies. She said to be sure I didn't eat it myself. I said I'd reserve that pleasure for you."

A wan smile crossed Duncan's face, and encouraged, Samuel Gatewood continued, "We make all our clothing now, honest homespun. Your sister, Leona, has made you and Catesby shirts. She did not know how long a sleeve you require, so made both regular length. Colonel Warwick suffered a similar wound at Second Manassas but is no worse a planter than he ever was."

"Did they tell you how the woods burned?" Duncan said dreamily.

"Dear son, it isn't healthy for you to dwell on such matters."

"Father, losing an arm is in some respects an enlightening experience. You do not wish to hear about the fire? Very well, I shan't speak about the fire. How are my nephew and niece? I imagine young Thomas is useful on the plantation?"

Samuel Gatewood said young Thomas was doing the work of a full-task hand—when he felt like it. He said Uther Botkin was unwell. He said Colonel Warwick believed the war would be over by year's end, and Samuel prayed so, since Thomas was almost old enough to enlist.

Samuel's son turned his head on the pillow.

Undaunted, Samuel opened the wicker basket and described the items contained therein. Blackberry preserves. Three pair of socks and Leona's shirt. A book of sermons provided by Grandmother Gatewood. A novel, *Lady Audley's Secret,* from his mother. A new treatise on common animal illnesses which, if Duncan studied it, would better prepare him for rebuilding Stratford after the war.

"Those who burned alive in the Wilderness—they had plans for after the war. They had mothers and wives they cried to as the fire transformed them. Some carried keepsakes with locks of their children's hair. . . ." Duncan touched his bandages wonderingly.

Samuel Gatewood closed the basket. "Yes, it is true that men have died horribly," he said. "In every generation some men die horribly, and we must trust that God has his purposes." He buckled the basket's strap. "Did I say that I came down the canal in the same boat that had previously transported General Jackson's mortal remains to Lexington for burial? The craft was still draped with black crepe, which the crewmen did not remove until we had passed through the lock at Big Island. General Jackson died, I am told, grateful he would go to his Maker on Sunday, for such had always been his desire. Were the men who died in the Wilderness any different from the general who commanded them? If these tragedies are not part of God's great design, reason falters."

Duncan turned his face away. "Father, I fear I have given way to melancholy. Can you forgive me?"

"I can and do, most heartily. I have brought a second basket to Catesby. Does he seem well to you?"

"He has been assigned to attend the brigade's wounded officers, and visits every second day. He's also been entrusted with the regiment's clothing monies but hasn't located what he was asked to buy."

"Catesby did not quite seem himself."

"He takes whiskey. Often when he sits where you are sitting the smell of spirits is strong enough to make me ill. He gambles more than he did—oh, there's a regular circle of cardplayers in the army, and they quickly make each other's acquaintance. Catesby is gentler than you or me, and war is no place for a gentle fellow. He will do his duty. He accepts the most dangerous post, has commanded our pickets more than any other officer in the regiment."

Samuel Gatewood said, "Some men are blessed with a sanguine disposition. Others take a thing and worry it until there's so little left it wouldn't provide a barn rat with his dinner. I am of the former disposition. When I view Stratford's depleted fields, I picture them after the war, replenished and green, workers sowing or reaping or shocking, in proper season. You will be the planter and Catesby's son, Thomas, will act the fool—as all young men must. I picture Thomas courting and marrying. I . . ."

"Father, my own son will never be welcome at Stratford."

Tears which he neither restrained nor acknowledged started from Samuel Gatewood's eyes. They ran down the furrows beside his cheeks. "My poor boy, you have not forgiven me."

"Father, what else could you have done? It is myself I can't forgive."

"We might . . . we should have spoken before."

The boy dismissed the thought. "How could we? How can we? This war has changed everything. Everything is topsy-turvy."

"We could not have acknowledged a negro grandson. How . . . ?"

"What a pity. What a pity. What have we done to ourselves? Sometimes I think that damned Lincoln is right."

"Should we surrender?"

Duncan winced. "No. Hell no! But Father, after all our suffering, what will we become?" His eyes were fluttering wearily. "I am so tired. Will you come again tomorrow?"

Catesby was on the step outside. "Samuel, another beautiful spring day. If the roads stay good our army will march again. General Lee intends to march into the North. All the men think so."

"And you?"

"I'll go with the regiment. Attending to fallen officers' needs and purchasing woolen underclothes are not duties that excuse a man from marching. General Lee thinks we can win."

"And you, Catesby?"

Catesby shrugged. "I am not a military man. Our generals have been correct in their judgments before, though I do not believe they have properly reckoned the cost. Three more great victories like Chancellorsville and we will all be dead men."

"You are in a black humor. If our western armies continue to resist Grant at Vicksburg and General Lee strikes a hard blow in the North, England may yet recognize our young nation."

Catesby's grin flashed. "I have always admired you, Samuel. Have I told you? If men like you were in charge of things, we'd never have reached this wretched impasse." Catesby rose and brushed off his trousers. "Will you take dinner with me? After two weeks in the capital I have discovered a few establishments."

The two men rode along Main Street. Catesby seemed distracted and in no mood for conversation.

How shabby it all is, Gatewood thought. Filth in the gutter, unwashed stoops, windows curtainless or shuttered. Few cabs or hackneys, not many riders and most of those in uniform.

A cavalry squadron, President Davis's honor guard, lounged in Capitol Square.

The two men turned down 12th Street and dismounted before an unpretentious two-story clapboard building with a fresh painted green door. Both passed their reins to a colored boy, and Catesby gave him a dime.

"Samuel," Catesby swung the door wide, "this is Johnny Worsham's gambling hell." He raised a hand to quell Samuel's protest. "Samuel, you needn't gamble. Though no doubt there are those doing so. Come in, I'll show you."

So early, only a few of the green baize tables were occupied. Upturned chairs rested upon the others, and the low murmur of the cardplayers seemed of a piece with the dust motes flickering in the sunlight.

"Ah, Catesby. Come to take a hand?" The inquirer was handsome on that half of his face that hadn't been scarred by a dreadful injury. His hair was black and oiled and perfumed.

"Johnny. My esteemed father-in-law, Samuel Gatewood. Planter from the mountains. A man of considerable good sense."

"Sir, my pleasure. I believe the window table is playing bezique. Do you know the game?"

"Not this morning, Johnny. We've come for some of your excellent hospitality."

The owner's smile didn't falter. "Of course. Of course. Will we be seeing you tonight, Catesby?"

"Unless I'm dining with General Lee," Catesby said and kept his solemn expression until he grinned a boy's grin and slapped the proprietor on the back. "Johnny keeps a fine buffet. The best in the Confederacy."

"We've Monopole champagne in the house," Johnny said. "The *Banshee* docked at Wilmington Thursday."

"Thanks, Johnny. Too early for me. Coffee, Samuel?"

The coffee was hot and black and good. The buffet presented two turkeys and roasts of beef and ham, as well as bread, butter, and condiments. Catesby created a large sandwich and Samuel a more modest one.

"Do take more," Catesby said. "You're accustomed to hearty fare."

"At home," Samuel said. "Where I know its provenance."

"Only the finest blockade runners supply Johnny's table. I think I will try a glass of champagne."

"You are a familiar here, I take it," Samuel said.

"It is the gayest spot in Richmond."

"I should think it one of the most dangerous," Samuel said gently.

"Lively gentlemen come to Johnny's for an evening of pleasant conversation, wagers, and a better supper than they'd get elsewhere in Richmond. Judah Benjamin, President Davis's confidant, is a regular." He put his napkin to his mouth. "On a less contentious topic, I met Sallie Kirkpatrick at Camp Winder the other day."

The murmur of voices, the clink of money, the whisk of cards. Samuel chewed his sandwich more doggedly than it deserved. "I am not satisfied that we did our best for that child. I am sure I did not. Apparently she and her husband are . . . estranged."

Catesby described Alexander Kirkpatrick's arrival at Fredericksburg and his subsequent disappearance. "He may have been killed, but he probably deserted. I do think he tried. When I spoke to Sallie the other day she said she would not have Kirkpatrick back under any circumstances. She presumes him dead."

Samuel shook his head. "These times. What times!" He set his sandwich remains on his plate. "Look here, Catesby . . ."

Catesby shook his head with a smile. "Esteemed father-in-law, I will not 'look here.' If I am willing to gamble everything in this war, I will take my relaxation as I choose."

"But you cannot afford to gamble. You are not wealthy."

Catesby's smile grew more charming. "Like General Lee, sir, I can afford it until I lose."

35

FAMILY HAPPINESS

NEAR MT. JACKSON, VIRGINIA
MAY 23, 1863

THE LAMB PRESSED its seeking head into the crevice of its mother's leg and nibbled on a tuft of wool.

"No, idiot." Alexander Kirkpatrick pushed the lamb to better align it with the teat. The ewe stood quietly eating the hay Alexander had laid down, undisturbed by either the baby creature seeking her milk or the clumsy man kneeling at her side. Seth, the eldest Danzinger boy, stood outside the perimeter of the ewe's concern, keeping an eye on things.

Early-morning light filtered through cracks between the barn boards. The door, left open when they'd led the ewe inside, was a rectangle of pale light, and along the south wall, windows opened to the new day. The dewy grass gave off a cold rich smell, the farmhouse puffed woodsmoke like a steamboat, and smoke tendrils drifted down to the barn. Alexander was very hungry. He thought he could smell bacon frying.

The lamb connected with its mother's teat.

"Tickle its behind," Seth advised. "Pretend you are a mother sheep."

When Alexander hesitated, Seth chided him, "You are too fastidious, Alex. You will never be a stockman if you are fastidious."

When Alexander tickled the top of the lamb's tail, the tail vibrated furiously and the lamb grew so enthused it butted the udder and lost the teat and searched frantically until the tail started wagging again.

"Good," Seth said. "The lamb will live. Even old Delilah here has enough milk for one lamb."

Alexander brushed straw off his trousers. "Sheep are so stupid," he said.

"So? Yet a lamb who has never nursed before can find its way to its mother's milk and eat and grow. It is a gift of God. Of course," the boy added solemnly, "this morning, you have given God a hand."

Alexander didn't say anything. The Danzingers talked all the time but never expected him to say anything. The old grandmother spoke only German and the family often spoke that language among themselves. At dinner table sometimes, conversation flowed around Alexander as if he were a bird in soft air.

"I was joking," Seth said. "I was pulling your leg."

Alexander and Seth wore the dark wool trousers and overshirt prescribed by the Brethren. Both wore stiff straw hats.

At fourteen, Seth was the oldest male Danzinger, and sometimes—assuming his murdered father's place—he seemed full-grown. But with Alexander he frequently acted younger, just a boy enjoying a fine May morning in one of God's gardens: the Shenandoah Valley of Virginia. Now, with self-conscious importance, Seth consulted his father's watch. "I have slopped the hogs and the girls have milked and Willem will have fed the horses and my stomach is growling. Come, my friend, can you smell bacon frying?"

Alexander had arrived at this small farm three months ago, not so long after Henry Danzinger's murder that the man's place had been filled nor the injury healed.

That night, Alexander had walked down the Valley Pike and slid into a haystack before dawn and was awakened after an hour's slumber by pitchfork tines and the hungry moos of cattle waiting to be fed. He crawled out backward on hands and knees, hoping those tines wouldn't poke him again, and found two puzzled boys who waited while he brushed himself.

"Are you a soldier?" Willem Danzinger had asked.

"No," Alexander said. "I am a scholar of antiquities."

The boys inspected him for a long moment before Seth Danzinger said, "The cattle must be fed," and forked a thatch of hay over the rail fence that kept the beasts from devouring this haystack at will.

"We also do not fight," Willem said with the complacent solemnity of the very young. "God forbids it. Are you hungry? Can you work?"

So the boys brought him into the house and their mother, Gretchen, promptly filled a bowl of oatmeal and set molasses beside the pitcher of fresh cream and when he had emptied the bowl scooped him another. When Alexander was finished he thanked her and she said, "We all work for our food here. There is firewood to be split. For the oven. This size." With hands apart she indicated the length, and Alexander went outside and split wood, splitting until nearly noon, reducing the mound by two-thirds, and when she came out she said, "That is good. Dinner is ready."

The wooden table had an empty seat at the head and the grandmother said grace in German, and that afternoon they set Alexander to loading the wagon with manure from the horse barn and forking it onto the wheat ground.

That evening while he washed up at the pump, Seth came to fetch him. "Pretend you are useful," he whispered. "Do not mention the antiquities."

The family was waiting in the kitchen. In her rocker nearest the fire the grandmother wasn't missing a thing.

Gretchen Danzinger coughed into her hand. She said, "We have discussed you. You have run from the army, yes?"

"I never wanted to fight. . . ."

"But you have run."

"Yes."

"We are in need of man's hands here. We will feed you and you may wear Henry's clothing. I am Henry's wife on earth and in heaven, but we need a man on this farm."

So Alexander stayed. The work took enough attention so he didn't get lost in his mind. Though all the Brethren community knew a deserter was living with the Danzinger family, no outsiders were told.

It seemed to Alexander that he had been looking all his life to find a place like this. The only books in the house were religious meditations in German and the heavy German Bible on the parlor table. Alexander had nearly forgotten his brief service with the army, nearly forgotten the penitentiary. Since it hurt him to think about such things, why think about them?

One day, shoveling corn into the hammermill, Alexander removed his shirt and young Willem saw his flogging scars and asked, "Were you a slave? I thought only the negroes were slaves."

Alexander reached behind but couldn't quite touch his old injuries. "Perhaps I was," he said.

"We do not believe in slaves," Willem said, sturdily.

Early in the war, Confederate officialdom had been outraged by Brethren pacifism and had imprisoned some of their leaders at Libby Prison, but these good farmers were too important to the war effort to stand on principle. From rich Valley farms came the salt pork, beeves, and wheat that fed the army. When slaves started running away in large numbers, the Brethren, who did not hold with slavery and whose sons were laboring at home, were less affected than the "English" farmers, and Confederate quartermasters who came to Strasburg and Edinburg Mill and Harrisonburg never left empty-handed. Some of the Brethren refused the new currency and insisted on gold (even at a discount), but they sold everything they brought.

Alas, the Shenandoah Valley was no longer the oasis of prosperous farms and tranquil prayer it had been before the war. Each of Stonewall's brilliant victories shattered humble farmers. Bivouacking soldiers pulled down rail fences for their campfires, and no chicken was safe when foragers were in the neighborhood. Partisan rangers prowled the roads by night. Henry Danzinger had gone out to speak at a meeting and was found the next morning with his throat cut, horse and coin purse taken. His new nickel-plated watch lay beside his body. "To murder a man for his few possessions . . ." Henry's widow would wonder and weep. "And to throw away his good watch as if it was nothing. . . ." Near Thornton Gap a farmhouse went up in smoke and in the ruins neighbors found the farmer, his wife, and their two daughters shot to death. Saturday evening, after he had closed his mill gate for the Sabbath, partisan rangers robbed a mill owner near Luray of the week's receipts.

"It is a wicked time," Gretchen Danzinger said. "We must pray that this scourge be lifted."

The Danzinger farm was seventy acres along the Shenandoah River, below the richer Burkeholders, above the shaley hardscrabble farms where the farmers were not Brethren.

The Danzingers owned two brood sows (when he was required, they borrowed the Burkeholders' boar), four milk cows (Gretchen Danzinger was a noted cheesemaker), twenty beehives, and a dozen ewes. They planted ten acres in wheat.

Alexander Kirkpatrick was partial to garden work, hoeing between the emerging vegetables, and when they shelled the first peas he sat with the women extracting the tiny green morsels.

Nine-year-old Lisle Danzinger was full of questions, so Alexander told her about ancient Rome, Romulus and Remus, Caesar and Scipio Africanus, while he popped new peas into a bowl. The other female Danzingers listened politely and when he paused resumed their conversation in German.

"Is this true?" Lisle demanded. "Or is it only a story?"

"I don't really know," Alexander said.

The next morning, after chores, they inspected the ripening timothy. At Seth's suggestion, Alexander knelt to inspect the tiny seed head slumbering in the boot at the base of the plant

"When it comes out of the boot, it comes all at once," Seth warned. "Then we will be glad for your help. The Burkeholders would help us, but they have their own hay to cut and Mama doesn't wish to trouble them."

Alexander's arms strengthened and his hands hardened, and in the morning the wet dew-soaked grass wet his trousers to the knee. Breakfast they ate just at daybreak, the noon meal was enormous, and there were always oatmeal or bachelor button cookies in the kitchen.

Each Sunday, when the family dressed for church, Alexander readied the buggy, curried the black horse until it shone, and hitched it to the front gate. One day he might be invited to attend worship but not yet.

After services, the Danzingers paid calls on their neighbors or received visitors at home. Alexander sat on the porch, blank-faced, as the Danzinger's friends rattled on in German. For all he knew they were discussing him! Sometimes Alexander took long walks along the river, shunning the turnpike and better-traveled roads in favor of field edges and the dark woods where wild creatures rear their young. One restless Sunday he came into the kitchen where the women were preparing the Sunday dinner and offered to help, but the discomfort on Gretchen Danzinger's face pushed Alexander out in a cloudburst of apologies.

When they sat to eat, Katrina, the eldest daughter, turned to Alexander with a smile. "Mother said you wish to become a hausfrau. It is more difficult to be a hausfrau than most men think!" The women and girls giggled while Seth and Willem pretended to find the whole business beneath their notice.

The next morning they greased hay-cart axles and sharpened scythes, and the Danzinger boys left the heaviest, dirtiest work to Alexander and weren't satisfied until he was entirely filthy and reeking of masculine sweat.

When the seed heads came out of the boot, the Danzingers cut timothy. They started as soon as the dew dried, quit for dinner (cold chicken, potato salad, buttermilk) at noon. With the sun directly overhead, they began afresh and worked without pause until the evening dew settled. They cut two acres that day. Two days later they raked and stacked the hay. Although Seth had helped his father, he'd never made haystacks himself, and instead of bright green monuments to Brethren industry and God-fearing pride, Danzinger haystacks slumped dejectedly against the poles that skewered them. That night after supper, Alexander collapsed onto his pallet in the harness room with a groan.

By the third day, his hands were calloused, he'd found a working rhythm, and near noon—Gretchen Danzinger and her mother-in-law were laying out the meal under the shade of an old elm tree—Alexander wiped sweat from his forehead and imagined the men who had harvested since ancient days. While emperors reclined sulkily, bored with the rarest wines, in their fields men toiled and drank cool water, and who was to say which was the better portion?

Alexander kept this thought close to him, turning it over and over in his mind, because it was a different sort of thought from those he had had when he was in Yale's cool library reading what scholars proposed. Could he be different? Do men change? How he hoped so!

The next day while he and Seth were honing their scythes, Alexander asked, "This work—how do the other Valley farmers do it?"

Seth was puzzled. "If they are Brethren," he said, "they work as we do. If they are rich English, their slaves do it."

"Don't they miss it? The work?"

"Oh, they are much too busy. Rich English are busy making governments and making war."

"But this is better," Alexander said.

"Why yes," Seth said, a trifle smugly. "Yes, it is."

In the evenings, they sat on the porch, and sometimes Grandmother read meditations aloud from her German prayer book. Seth whittled and Willem daydreamed. He was a dreamy boy. Alexander thought to warn the boy against dreaming, warn him that he should hold fast this world, that the distance between the self and the world should not grow too wide, that a man can lose his way and not be able to find his way back. He said nothing of this, however, because his tongue had thickened from disuse, and he spoke no more than he needed to get through each day. Alexander Kirkpatrick almost felt safe, almost happy.

One Friday evening, just at sundown, the Burkeholders arrived for a visit. The women drank tea and gossiped in the kitchen while the men sat in the parlor and talked livestock prices. As eldest Danzinger, Seth was allowed to join them. When someone asked Alexander if cattle prices were too high and would hog prices hold, Alexander shrugged and went outside. Under the watchful gaze of grandmothers from both families, stiff as porcelain dolls, young Karl Burkeholder sat in the porch glider beside Katrina Danzinger. Despite these intimidating circumstances, young Karl described his new roan colt animatedly and Katrina replied with the appropriate female interest. Alexander walked into the dooryard and sat under a tree. Would his life have been better if his mother hadn't died so young? If his uncle hadn't been so old and reclusive?

A figure crossed the yard, between him and the house. "You'll learn to talk livestock prices if you hope to be a farmer," Lewis Burkeholder said. "A farmer who can't talk about the weather or prices has little to say."

Alexander leaned back against his tree, his hands pillowing his head. Fireflies caroused through the balmy spring evening.

"You come from the war," Burkeholder said.

"Yes."

"Before they hanged him, John Brown said, 'The sins of slavery will be washed out in blood.' Were you with the Federals or Confederates?"

"Does it make any difference?"

"To a pacifist like myself, it oughtn't. But it's hard not to prefer the Confederates. Gretchen Danzinger says you're educated. Our people are not overfond of 'the learned professors.' "

"I don't care about that anymore."

"Uh-huh. I was a friend of Henry Danzinger's. He was our bishop, and traveled all over the countryside preaching. Henry wasn't the best farmer. Some of his haystacks weren't much better than yours."

"We worked hard on those haystacks! The boys and I did the best we could!"

"We kept meaning to come down and help, but we didn't get ahead of our own work until this afternoon. Not very neighborly, I fear." Burkeholder hunkered down. A bulky shadow—his eyes gleamed. "God didn't care that Henry Danzinger was only a fair farmer. While he was alive, he fed his family and they were happy. I don't believe he was killed for his money. Because of his travels the partisan rangers thought Henry was a Federal spy." Burkeholder sighed. "God moves in mysterious ways."

Alexander uncrossed his leg and recrossed it.

"Gretchen Danzinger is an upright woman," Burkeholder said. "She will make some man a good wife. It would be better if she chose among her own people."

The words banged against Alexander's ears. Was there no safe and silent place where the world wouldn't intrude on him?

Burkeholder uncoiled and stretched and yawned and called, "Karl, I believe you have told Miss Danzinger quite enough about your new colt for one night and we've got to take syrup into New Market on the morrow. A clever lad would ask Miss Danzinger if she'd like to come over on Sunday and see your colt. Fetch your mother and sisters and hitch our buggy." To Alexander, Burkeholder said, "Will you accompany us into New Market? Oh, the Saturday market is a regular Babylon: planters, Brethren, millers, drovers. And all the Confederate commissary men too."

"I believe I'll stay here."

"I thought you might. None of us will give you up to the army. We would not hurt Gretchen for all the riches of Nineveh."

The Burkeholders said their goodbyes and the boys brought the buggy around, and directly the Burkeholders' buggy lantern diminished down the road.

Afterward, Alexander took a cup of tea out onto the porch. The swing where the courting couple had sat was still warm from their bodies. Gretchen Danzinger came and sat at the extremest end of the swing. "Do not concern yourself about Lewis Burkeholder," she said. "Lewis thinks he is responsible for everything that goes on around him. His father was the same way. When our bishops are selected, it is never a Burkeholder. A Burkeholder would be more bishop than we need."

"I think . . . I think I am happy here."

"Once I was happy too," she said.

"I wish . . ." Alexander said, and a yearning filled his body, a yearning which made his body light, as a boy's body is light, so light he might fly into the night sky and companion the moon.

"You are shivering," Gretchen Danzinger said. "Behind the door is Henry's coat. Tomorrow I will lengthen the sleeves."

36

AN EVENING AT
JOHNNY WORSHAM'S
GAMBLING HELL

CATESBY SPENT THE afternoon with wounded officers, thanked the matrons, and when he left Camp Winder felt his customary relief.

It was a fine long spring evening, and the wind buffeted Richmond and whipped chimney smoke into frail banners. In some lights, war-battered Richmond was lovely. The lilacs were concluding luxuriant bloom, and every wrought-iron fence was glossy with climbing roses. Shy blossoms peeped out among the foliage. Catesby plucked a white one and tucked it through the top buttonhole of Leona's homespun shirt. The shirt had the thick comforting nap of a scarcely worn garment and gave off the faintly oily smell of the butternuts she'd used for dye. The wool had been combed and carded, spun and plied, by his dear wife before it went on the loom. Leona had worked on this shirt while she mourned for infant Willie. Sudden coolness in the air shivered Catesby.

Samuel Gatewood had assured him that Leona's health was much improved. On their remote mountain plantation, Leona and the children were safe from the ravages if not the hardships of the war. He had done all he could for them. Plus, he had two hundred dollars in poker winnings he could lose without regrets. If he were to lose every penny it would mean nothing. Catesby played for sociability. A man needed sociability.

Catesby's bundle of Confederate shin plasters had, over the course of pleasant evenings at Johnny Worsham's, grown plump as a yearling hog. Many officers came in drunk and hurled their money down upon cards that couldn't possibly support their wagers. Others played hand after hand as if dazed, scarcely more pleased when they won than when they lost.

From the first time Catesby came in, Johnny Worsham misread him, taking him for a wealthy planter or successful speculator, treating him with the special courtesy he proffered to men with deep purses.

At Johnny's front door a trio of enlisted men were kept at bay by two bouncers wearing cocky bowler hats. Catesby sometimes wondered how the young brutes had avoided conscription. "Naw, boys, you don't want to come in here. This ain't for the likes of you. Go on down to Shockoe Bottom and have yourselves a good time. Evenin', Gen'rl." The bouncer threw Catesby a mocking two-fingered salute.

Johnny was just inside. The buffet was being replenished by a colored man dressed all in white. "You know," Worsham said, "I had me a Frenchie in here last night. He said our spread was as grand as anything in Paris. What do you think of that?"

"I've never been to Paris, Johnny. You'll have to ask someone else."

"Say, I thought you were a cosmopolite."

"Johnny, I'm just a soldier who used to be a lawyer. Hoped to be circuit judge one day."

"Billy, bring out another stack of plates," Johnny Worsham called. "You gonna play tonight or you just come in to eat something?"

Catesby shrugged.

"That Fightin' Joe Hooker that General Lee whipped—they say Hooker's a poker player. I'd like to get him in here. Sit him down opposite Mr. Benjamin or Mr. Omohundru."

"The slave speculator?"

"Omohundru owns a blockade runner. Can't think what it's called—fastest boat on the Cape Fear. He's got him a first-rate pilot and a good captain, and the Federals can't catch him. Supposed to have a Bahamian wife, but I've never seen her. Not many ladies come in here. Omohundru's in Richmond for the government. He generally comes in after midnight."

"An Omohundru once frequented my country. A kinsman, perhaps."

Catesby extracted a Havana and perched on a stool at the tiny bar (Johnny didn't make it convenient to leave the gaming tables). He drew rich smoke into his lungs and was content. Catesby wondered if he'd live to see the end of the war and decided on the spot that he simply did not care. Those who worried about surviving this war joined one of the California-bound wagon trains, fled abroad, or deserted. Half of Catesby's regiment had deserted. Some returned for the important battles and then deserted again, others disappeared for good.

Catesby Byrd was an officer in Marse Robert's army. Had there ever been such a band of men under the sun? Hurrah for the bonny blue flag that bears a single star!

Catesby found a glass of champagne at his elbow, though he had not ordered it.

"That is Judah Benjamin?" Catesby asked.

Worsham nodded at a portly man whose head was too big for his body. "Yes, the Secretary of State."

"Is it not his Sabbath?'

"Mr. Benjamin's Sabbath starts when the tables close. Or when city police come through the door. Couple, three weeks ago they raided us, but the boys delayed them until the gentlemen could escape out the windows."

"I see a vacant chair."

Worsham chuckled. "No man with money to lose ever got turned away from his table. Benjamin learned his game in New Orleans. Have a care."

With his untasted glass, Catesby ambled through the crowd. "Gentlemen?"

The dealer, Johnny's houseman, managed a jerky nod. Benjamin lifted his open sunny face and one eyebrow. "I hope you won't take offense, Lieutenant. You honor us with your presence. But our game is table stakes and we require an initial investment of five hundred."

Catesby flushed. From his side pocket he extracted his own two hundred and fattened his stake with the regiment's clothing fund from his money belt. When he casually tossed the cash on the table, some slick Confederate bills slid to the floor, and stooping to gather them, Catesby felt the fool.

After Catesby was seated, Benjamin touched his arm. "I meant no offense, sir," he said. "We in government have done such a poor job of providing for our gallant armies that I worried you might play and be embarrassed, and I did not wish to compound the inadequacy for which I and my ilk are responsible."

The man's smile was so warm and charming Catesby relaxed. "Catesby Byrd of Warm Springs. I am honored to make your acquaintance, sir."

"When you gents are done bein' honored with each other," the houseman said, "I'll deal the cards." To Catesby he explained, "House rakes a dollar a pot."

Catesby looked around, smiling. It was so pleasant to be gambling. It was only scrip, not much different from the buttons they sometimes played for in camp. The Confederate dollar he laid on the baize as his ante—this week eight of them would buy a single gold dollar. Next week what would they be worth?

The players were a colonel of artillery, a cavalry captain, a naval officer, a civilian, and Judah Benjamin, who watched benignly as each man inspected his down card.

To the naval officer, Catesby said, "Have you heard news of the *Alabama?* Does she still harass Federal shipping?"

The naval officer looked up. "I have heard nothing since she took the *Hatteras* in January."

"She is our ghost." Catesby lifted his glass. "Gentlemen, the *Alabama!*"

Benjamin murmured *"Alabama"* with the others but added, "Lieutenant, I believe it is your wager. I cannot speak for these other gentlemen, but after a long week in the government, I am ready to forget the war. Surely gentlemen have more civilized topics for discourse."

Catesby flushed at Benjamin's reproof.

The naval officer ignored it. "I was gunnery officer on the ironclad *Virginia*. When we had to scuttle her because the whole Confederacy didn't have a port for her, I was transferred, and now I train Confederate naval cadets who don't have a ship to serve on. I'll raise a dollar."

Catesby felt twice insulted. First Benjamin had doubted his financial resources, then he'd implied that the war in which Catesby might die wasn't worth the attention of civilized men. "Sir," Catesby said tensely.

Benjamin lifted a placatory hand. "When Mr. Davis and I served as senators in the Federal Congress, during the course of a debate on, of all things, military procurement, I misunderstood him, he misunderstood me, I compounded my misunderstanding, and he returned the favor. Beyond some mark, invisible to each of us until we were well past it, honor and reputation became involved, and had Mr. Davis not courteously apologized, we would have fallen prey to the rigors of the Code Duello. In a conciliatory spirit, my fiery young lieutenant, I apologize if my remarks have caused offense. I had not meant them to."

And Catesby felt a worse fool but said, "You are too gracious, sir."

Mr. Benjamin said, "I believe my two queens lose to Colonel Binghamton's three sevens." He raised a finger and a waiter promised a fresh bottle of champagne.

Catesby did not play energetically. If he lost his two hundred and was reduced to the regiment's money, he'd quit. He anted, lost his ante, watched play unfold.

The naval officer and Benjamin were skilled players. The colonel of artillery had been assigned to the Army of Tennessee, would depart Richmond tomorrow, and played morosely. The cavalry captain was not yet twenty, one of J.E.B. Stuart's troopers. His uniform was finely tailored and he had a gentleman's contempt for money. At the rate he was losing it, that was fortunate.

Benjamin played an unspectacular game; sometimes he bluffed wildly with poor cards, and these rare flamboyances invited the other gamblers into subsequent traps where Benjamin's hole cards ground them up. Occasionally, Benjamin withdrew money from the table, so his visible stakes were never much larger than the others'.

The rhythms of the game became the rhythms of Catesby's blood, and when the young cavalryman angrily stood and said, "Well, I believe you have all the money I'm going to give you," his outburst was a traditional flourish within those rhythms as was the appearance of Johnny's bowler-hatted bouncers at the cavalryman's elbow and the murmur, "Sir, Mr. Worsham would be honored if you'd take a brandy with him." The captain's flustered refusal and stormy exit were reprise and diminuendo.

Benjamin glanced at his cards. "When I was a boy in Charleston, buzzards perched near the marketplace, and because they removed the market's waste, they were tolerated and a fine of five dollars was imposed for shooting one. They became so tame they walked under the merchants' feet and children fed them scraps. When I am tempted to think that we Confederate administrators are indispensable, I recall those buzzards."

Catesby's king in the hole had a twin showing and he bet ten of his dollars and ten of the regiment's dollars, and everyone folded except Mr. Benjamin with a queen.

"You are a cautious adversary, Lieutenant," Benjamin said, "but I will see another card." He paired his queen and raised Catesby's bet twenty dollars. When Catesby folded and Benjamin flicked his cards faceup to the dealer, his hole card, which Catesby had thought a queen, was a lowly seven.

Benjamin signaled the waiter. "Gentlemen, at midnight I usually eat something. If you would append your requests to mine, I'm sure this gentleman would be pleased to serve us."

The colonel said no, he didn't want food. He was going to Joe Johnston's sorry goddamned army in the morning and he'd as soon play until then. Like Benjamin, the naval officer asked for a sandwich. Catesby, who had been hungry, had no appetite now and asked for another bottle of champagne.

Benjamin specified, "Just a dash of horseradish. And the mustard with the tiny seeds Johnny has from Georgia. Did you know Georgia is Johnny's home? He came up to Richmond hoping to do something in the way of the tobacco trade but found that too much of a gamble." Benjamin's smile invited the world to join him, but Catesby didn't feel convivial. "And where, sir, did you practice law?"

"Warm Springs—in our western mountains."

Benjamin's bland smile was infuriating. "I have often dreamed that one day I would take up a less demanding practice, find some pleasant county seat, and enjoy life. I envy you, sir."

"Yes," Catesby said. He drank more champagne.

The colonel had about the same money he'd had. Benjamin and the naval officer had won the cavalry lieutenant's stake as well as Catesby's two hundred dollars.

"May I take a seat, Judah?"

"I'm sure these gentlemen won't mind. Certainly, Silas."

The man was tall, of a saturnine cast. He had long dark eyelashes and a receding hairline. "And what news of the blockade?" Benjamin inquired of him.

"The *Whippet* cleared Wilmington yesterday. The *Jane Porter* tied up at midnight with a cargo of luxury items—wines, steel needles, silk. I believe they also carried a few cases of Austrian muskets." Omohundru inspected his hole card and promptly folded. "If the government would insist on military provisions in place of civilian fripperies, our ships would carry them."

Benjamin smiled. "But to get our states to agree to regulate their maritime commerce . . ."

The colonel bet twenty dollars. "The Confederacy's peculiar obstinacies are too well known. I wish to know the identity of my next card and intend to charge you for the privilege of seeing it."

Despite his new concentration—or perhaps because of it—the colonel's luck took a turn for the worse and his stake shrank. In one hand, he lost five hundred dollars to Omohundru. By dint of cautious play, Catesby lost only two hundred in the same period.

Half an hour later, the colonel's eights lost to Benjamin's three fours. Catesby had staked nearly a thousand dollars on two aces. He had lost half the money his regiment had entrusted him with.

Benjamin inspected his watch and tsked. "Oh dear, such revelries at my age." He ordered a bottle of the best champagne for the other players, and without counting folded his money into his pocket.

"Surely you're not leaving, sir," Catesby said tensely.

"President Davis requires me first thing in the morning. My presence is not always helpful, but I do my humble best." Benjamin rose to his feet. "I thank you for a most enjoyable evening."

All the other tables were empty, and waiters were stacking chairs. A bouncer was sweeping the floor.

"What time is it?" Catesby whispered.

Laboriously, the colonel consulted his watch. "Four," he announced. "My train departs in an hour." He seemed indifferent to his losses.

The houseman flicked out three cards, facedown. Another three faceup. "Antes, gentlemen?"

The colonel stretched. "Might as well." He looked at Catesby. "Have you ever gone into a fight with the certainty you weren't coming out of it?"

Catesby's cards were a deuce and an ace.

The colonel continued, "That damned Joe Johnston tried to get me killed at Seven Pines, and he'll succeed in Tennessee. I've made my will and written a letter to my wife and young ones. Now I've naught to do but catch a train."

"Prayer?" Catesby murmured.

The colonel bet ten dollars. "There are too many damn prayers. How does God decide which get answered? When Jackson was praying for success at Chancellorsville, wasn't Hooker praying too?"

Omohundru raised fifty dollars. "I do not know that General Hooker is a Christian man."

"That doesn't mean he wasn't praying." The colonel raised back. "Imagine this big telegraph office—an office as big as Richmond. Countless instruments clattering at once, in all languages—French, Italian, Hindoo . . ."

Catesby paired his deuce in the hole. "God moves in mysterious ways," he said.

"Yes," the colonel said. He had jacks showing and an eight. "Very mysteriously. Whenever we win a victory our leaders say it is God's will. When Lee pushed McClellan away from Richmond, that was God's will. When I'm killed in Tennessee, will that be God's will?"

Omohundru had nothing showing. He doubled the pot.

The next cards helped no one.

Catesby's final card was a deuce. It was a five-hundred-dollar pot. He raised the colonel a hundred more.

"You see," the colonel said, "I have to guess whether the lieutenant has the third deuce. He must guess if I have the third jack. All mysterious. But God is standing behind the table, able to see every hand. I call."

Omohundru raised.

"You, sir," the colonel noted, "evidently believe in miracles."

Omohundru said, "Our new nation is a miracle. That we can sit here, in the capital of the Confederate States of America, is a miracle."

"So. The lieutenant has his third deuce and Mr. Omohundru might win if God decides to punish me for blasphemy and collapses the ceiling on our heads." He summoned a waiter. When told there was beef left but no bread, he said beef would be satisfactory. "It'll be salt pork in Tennessee," he added sadly.

Catesby showed his third deuce and raked in the pot. "Why do you play?"

Omohundru said, "I cannot sleep. Each time the *Wild Darrell* makes a successful passage, I am amply rewarded."

"Silks and wines?"

"No, sir. Military supplies. I carry only a few luxuries to buy swift unloading and transshipment to our armies."

"You are a patriot. Are you kin to the Omohundru who was a slave speculator in the western mountains?"

"I am he." Omohundru looked up, alert for overtones at which he might take offense.

"My home is in those mountains," Catesby said.

"Yes," Omohundru said. "A country of sublime vistas."

Catesby had another mediocre hand but won when neither player cared to contest it.

The colonel threw the last of his stake into the next pot, which again Catesby won.

A yawning waiter opened the drapes. Too-bright sunlight streamed through the windows. The houseman stretched and stood up, saying he could do with some coffee.

The colonel thanked his companions elaborately for the evening's sport.

"Good luck to you, sir," Catesby said.

"All those damn telegraphs chattering at once." The colonel marched into the new morning air.

The houseman carried his coffee to a vacant table, where he put his feet up on an empty chair.

When Catesby counted his money he had ten dollars more than the regiment had entrusted him with.

"You'll pardon me, sir, if I remark that it is unusual for a junior officer to have so much to wager. You are successful at cards?"

"It is not my money," Catesby said shortly.

Omohundru lifted an eyebrow. "Your friends place great confidence in you."

Catesby sipped at his coffee. "It was to buy underclothing. Do you know a Richmond purveyor?"

"You take me for a merchant?"

"I take you for a gentleman I have met for the first time this evening."

"Some take me to be a merchant. I am engaged in trade."

"This is real coffee. We do not often see its like in the army."

"Do you think I should be serving with the army?"

Catesby had had enough. "Sir, you are a perfect stranger. I do not presume to judge what you should or should not do. It has been a long and peculiar night—one I shall not soon forget. I am possessed of what I brought into this hell and count myself fortunate."

For the first time Omohundru smiled. "And had you lost?"

Catesby was bone-weary. "I trust I would have done the honorable thing."

"And what would that be? After all, forgiveness"—Omohundru gestured around the cavernous room, the light blazing through the window glass—"is omnipresent. As a youth Mr. Benjamin was expelled from college for cheating at cards. Yet today he occupies a position of greatest trust. I was a speculator in slaves, but I am admitted to high councils."

"If I had lost . . ." Catesby began again.

"Do I press you, sir? I have always thought money is like love. It has only the meanings we give to it. Money is like the morning light, it evanesces. A man takes a deep breath and it is gone."

"If I provide a competence for my family, I crave no more."

"And the satisfactions of your legal vocation?"

"War is wonderfully inclusive. It satisfies all vocations."

Omohundru slid back his chair. "May I fetch you another cup of Mr. Worsham's excellent coffee? It seems a waste to let it go cold."

When he set the two cups on the table, he asked, "When do you return to your regiment?"

"Tomorrow or the next day. When I have sufficient undergarments, socks, and sixteen slouch hats in various sizes, my work in Richmond is complete."

"And you did take sugar in your coffee, I recall." Omohundru paused. "You are a man of uncommon sensitivity and we will probably never meet again. Forgive me if I take liberties I might not attempt with nearer acquaintances: do you love this war?"

Catesby spoke his mind. "War is transporting but dreadful beyond imagining—and we are its willing pawns. Our lives will be used up for purposes we do not fathom by a God we imagine only at the peril of sanity. How God is served by a boy burned to death in the Wilderness I cannot imagine, but that He is served I cannot doubt. Are we tools for some grander purpose? There are those who believe so. But Mr. Darwin claims this world is more ancient than previously thought, that creatures once flourished upon our planet that no longer exist. When those creatures lost their lives in some terrible struggle, did their deaths serve some greater, nobler purpose?"

Omohundru's face bore none of that challenge which had previously characterized it. "And so you wager with money which is not yours to wager? You tempt a Providence you neither trust nor understand?"

"And sir," Catesby said softly, "what is your motive?"

Omohundru said, "I hope to see miracles."

37

WASHING THE CORPSE

NEAR SUNRISE, VIRGINIA
JULY 2, 1863

"HE SO PUNY," Aunt Opal said.

Franky Williams dipped her rag in the vinegar bowl. "There never was much to him."

"He ain't half what he was, poor baby." Opal dabbed between Uther's fingers. "He wasn't able to write nothin', not after his shakin' got so bad, but see: he still has the bump where he held that pen. His whole life he spends readin' and writin', and ever since Miss Sallie got took away, he can't read or write a solitary thing."

Uther's naked corpse was bruised. In his final months Uther often fell.

"It's a mercy," Franky said.

"Uncle Agamemnon, he older than Uncle Uther."

"He ain't got no more wits. Mumblin' about that African country he come from, that old conjurin' foolishness. If me and Sister didn't feed him, why I reckon he'd starve to death."

"Uther kept his wits to the end," Opal said. "Maybe he couldn't read no more, but that didn't keep him from talkin' about fellows he used to read, Mr. Paine, Mr. Adams, Mr. Jefferson, and them. But it was pitiful how he shook. I believe that's why Miss Abigail never come to call. She couldn't bear to see him so poorly."

"Miss Abigail 'delicate.' Master Samuel begged her go to Richmond with him, but she wouldn't. Said, 'My son Duncan he has two arms!' Between Grandmother Gatewood's prayin' and Miss Abigail bein' poorly ain't much gettin' done. Wasn't for me and Sister and Pompey, Stratford House'd fall into disgrace."

The two women rolled Uther's corpse onto his stomach, Aunt Opal gently guiding the head.

"They say the war be over soon," Franky said. "Master Samuel say that after General Lee whips the Federals again they'll leave us be."

"You think Master Abraham quit?" Opal snorted. "You think he put back into bondage all them he freed?"

"You think the Federals gonna win?"

" 'Course they is. 'Course they is."

Franky asked, "And they kill all the masters? Master Duncan, Master Catesby, Master Samuel?"

"Prolly. Master Duncan and Master Catesby been whippin' them regular. You think them Federals show 'em any mercy?"

"Master Samuel say General Lee gonna win," Franky repeated stubbornly. "He say General Lee whip the Federal army and then they gonna march on Washington, take Master Abraham prisoner, and that be the end of it."

Opal scrubbed. "His neck dirty. Just like a little boy, he never washed his neck too good." A tear trickled down her cheek. "This vinegar . . ." she said. "Powerful strong vinegar. . . ."

"Miss Leona worried to death about Master Catesby." Franky's cloth patted the old man's prominent rib cage. "He gone off to Richmond with poor Master Duncan and ain't writ Miss Leona since. Master Samuel say Master Catesby took up cardplaying again. Why that man want to do that?"

Opal snorted. "He with the army now. He have more to worry about than cardplaying." Although she'd been born Baptist, Opal's long association with Uther had softened her Baptist beliefs.

"His ankles filthy."

"He couldn't bend over so good as he did. He climb in the washtub Saturday night same as always and I'd wait outdoors, same as always. I'd have washed his ankles for him but silly old fool never wanted me to see him unless he proper."

Franky adopted an expression the primmest schoolmarm might have envied. "I always thought . . ."

Opal snapped, "Too much thinkin' sometimes. Some people see two people livin' in the same house and they think those two people might start to care for each other." Her tears started again. "It wouldn't have been proper, that's all! Drat this vinegar!"

"Can't tell about these white men. They need it worse than colored men do."

"I believe you got more knowledge of such things than I do."

"They got more too," Franky said, lifting her chin.

"How many men you washed for buryin'?"

"Right smart of them."

"Why you think you and me asked to do this job? Because we don't say what we seen. You can say what you want but whites I washed ain't no different than men of color."

They worked silently for a time, washing with vinegar, rinsing with water. When the rinse water turned gray, Franky poured it out the window and replaced it from the ewer. "What'd he do to get so dirty?"

"He just live, that's all. Old man ain't been outdoors since summer except to the necessary. All he was livin' for was Miss Sallie's letters. That Richmond must be some place to see!"

"I was in Richmond once. Filthiest slave pen you ever saw in your life. I was glad to come to Staunton to be sold. 'Course I was just a child. I was too young for the fancy trade."

Opal eyed her companion skeptically. "Maybe you got the disposition, but you ain't got the looks. When that Maggie got sold away from here I say to myself: that woman ain't gonna get her hands calloused hoeing. No, it's her backside gonna get calloused. That gal too good-lookin'!"

Franky said, "What you do next?"

"I got to clean up the house. Everybody come here this evening, and in the morning we go to the church and have the funeral and then they put . . . him . . . in his ground."

Franky said, "I meant you. What's gonna happen to you?"

Opal wiped her eyes on her sleeve. "Miss Sallie telegraphed. She can't come home for her daddy's buryin', can't leave the hospital on account of they waiting on a big fight. But she ain't been home one time since she was sent away. You ask me, she's ashamed."

"On account of Jesse?"

"That child never did have good sense. When Jesse run away and came knockin' at her door she should've told him come to us. We could've cared for him."

"Jesse—you think he livin'?"

"Nary a word. Rufus and him, they dead and buried for all we know. You gonna work on that foot? Old Uther vain about his feet. He didn't care about what shirt he wore or whether it was fresh but his shoes always brushed and good-looking. He liked to dance some in olden times."

"They have dances in them days?"

"Long as there been people they been dancin'!"

"Maybe Miss Sallie buy you and set you free."

"Don't want no more'n I got. Master Uther never once made me do what I didn't want. When I say sell a calf, we sell it. When I say keep the calf, we keep it. When I say that horse don't look too good, he needs some turpentine, he holds the horse's head while I pour the turpentine."

"You gonna shave him?"

"I never shaved no man in my life. Pompey's gonna do that."

And so it proved. The two women washed Uther Botkin's mortal remains and wrapped him neatly in his faded green blanket atop the bed where he'd slept since he'd come to this country.

A different knock. "It's me," Pompey said and waggled his eyebrows.

"Come in here and do what you come to do. And don't you go cuttin' him."

"Won't hurt him a bit. Won't no cut bother him anyways." Officiously, Pompey laid Master Samuel's Birmingham razors, a badger brush, and a shaving mug on a chair beside the bed.

"I be bothered," Opal said. "And I'm more bother than you want."

Pompey tried on a confident smile. "Shavin' a dead man—there's a trick to it. Dead man's skin don't bounce back, and they can't twist their face to help you make a pass." He whisked his razor on the strop.

At the fire, Franky bent to sniff the funeral feast, a pot of brown beans with salt pork. Last November, when Opal's neighbors brought their hogs out of the woods for slaughter, salting, and smoking, Opal had held back. When the smoke rose from the boiling fires and the tripods went up beside the meathouses, that's when the Confederate commissary men came with their train of wagons. Some of the hogs were salted, some were half smoked, some hadn't had the hair scalded off them yet, the commisary men took the hogs they found—even at Stratford. But Opal's hogs hid in the woods eating acorns, coming out only for the corn she provided when snow covered the ground. Whenever she and Uther needed meat, she asked young Thomas to go into the woods and shoot one. Dragging a dead hog through the woods was hard work, but it was a sight better than no hog at all.

The commisary men weren't mannerly: a sharp knock on the door and three or four rough-looking gents who'd already been told a thousand times how they'd do more for the Confederacy in the army 'stead of stripping poor folks' cupboards. They didn't talk much, took what they wanted, and paid on the spot with Confederate currency.

"Master Samuel gonna bring you back to Stratford, Auntie," Pompey said. "I heard him and Mistress Abigail talkin'."

"What'd I do at Stratford?"

Pompey spread lather on the dead man's cheek. "Whatever needs doin'."

"Where'd I live?"

Pompey grinned. "Live with me if you have a mind to."

Opal snapped, "I had me a jackass once and he weren't no account. Why'd I want another?"

Pompey pressed Uther's slack jaw to tighten the skin. "No matter how hot your water, dead man sucks heat right out of it. There's plenty room in the Quarters. Ain't even half of us left."

"I believe I stay right here. Miss Sallie need somebody to keep this place while she away. Otherwise it fall to rack and ruin."

"Servant without no master? Ain't natural."

Opal hefted herself onto a stool held together by twisted wire. "Old Uther, he weren't my master exactly."

"You think white folks gonna let you stay here by yourself, livin' in old Uther's house and eatin' old Uther's food and sittin' down in his chair when you've a mind to? Them partisan rangers come ridin' down the road one dark night and find you alone, what you gonna do then?"

Opal snorted. "I can shoot a shotgun same as any man."

Pompey wiped the razor on his pant leg. "Opal, you always was . . . unlikely. . . ."

"We free. We emancipated. Master Abraham's set all us free."

"Uh-huh." Pompey wiped the razor on his pant leg and leaned very close to inspect his handiwork. "Why you want be free?"

"I don't want nothin' changed! I want to lie my head down same place I been lyin' it for twenty years. I want to milk the cow and churn the butter and fork cow droppings into the garden. My German beans already comin' on."

Pompey took a step back for broader perspective. "I was wonderin' what you're gonna do with them riding boots of his."

"Boots belong to Miss Sallie."

Opal kept the boots in a locked chifforobe, the spavined horse out behind the shed, and the milk cow hobbled in the woods, though it meant carrying the milk a quarter mile. Opal feared the white folks coming to honor Uther Botkin would strip everything bare. If she couldn't defend Uther's boots from Pompey, how could she defend the furniture from any white man who wanted it? Suppose Preacher Todd said, "Old Uther promised me that mantel clock"?

"Likely Miss Sallie don't recall them boots," Pompey said. "They made by that Lexington shoemaker. They real boots."

"What you need riding boots for? You don't ride no horse."

"Because they so fine!" Pompey patted the corpse's cheek, swished his blade through the water, and dried it. "I help you dress him if you want."

Franky let the curtain fall closed. "They comin'! Master Samuel and the preacher." Pompey swiftly rolled his master's razors in the towel and scooted his parcel under the dead man's bed.

"Pompey!" Franky said accusingly.

"Mine weren't sharp." The barber flung open the door and cried, "Master Samuel, welcome to this here house of grief. Is the old Master Botkin inside, all fixed up for his funeral."

Samuel dismounted from the wagon. "Preacher, if you and my houseman here would carry in the sawbucks, you'll have somewhere to set the coffin." Before stepping inside his old friend's home, Samuel Gatewood removed his hat. Beside the deathbed in that dim light, Samuel's hair seemed too thin, too white.

Though Preacher Todd's workmanship was not so fine as could be got in Staunton or Lexington, it was adequate for a poor man's coffin. "Careful, boy," he cried. "Don't bang it on the doorframe! Pine takes dents." Once they had the coffin on the sawbucks, the preacher removed his hat and knelt to pray.

Preacher Todd's prayer was a lengthy Presbyterian prayer, during which he switched tracks several times, and he approached his terminus with a head of steam at some hazard he might roar right through the station. "All things we have are thy gift. In Jesus' name. Amen." He replaced his hat.

The preacher filled his plate and cut a substantial slice of cornbread. "Somebody in this house knows something about cornbread," he observed.

"Ain't me," Opal said. "Franky made it."

Preacher Todd rested his plate on the coffin lid. "Auntie Opal, you ordered this casket for Uther Botkin's mortal remains. . . ."

Opal blocked everybody's view while she unlocked the chifforobe. "I believe you said three dollars."

Samuel Gatewood put out his hand for the purse. "That is Sallie's money now," he said. "I shall keep it safe for her."

"I been keeping it safe!" Opal blurted.

"Of course you have. You've done your duty for old Uther and now you must do your duty for his daughter."

Opal's face slackened, but she didn't resist as Samuel took the purse. "Three dollars, sir?" Samuel said.

"Gold?" the preacher inquired.

"Oh dear, I'm sure not. Opal, what was your agreement?"

"Scrip," the woman said sullenly.

The preacher satisfied himself with a second bowl of brown beans.

Samuel asked Pompey and Franky to dress Uther in his old frock coat and best mended shirt. He and Aunt Opal stepped outside.

"I'm gonna miss that old fool. I'm gonna miss him so." Aunt Opal's eyes overflowed.

"I'm sure he is in a happier place."

Opal wiped her eyes with a rag and blew her nose into it. "Ain't gonna be the same without him. That man knew some things. People listen to him and we wouldn't be in all this trouble."

"Perhaps so. Auntie, after the burying, you'll come live at Stratford. You are getting on in years and will want someone to care for you."

"I got some good years yet. Ain't no better stockman in the county!"

Quickly she added, "I lived here twenty years. Wasn't Master Botkin takin' care of me—you know that—was me takin' care of him!"

"Once this war is over, Auntie, and Sallie returns to her home, I'm sure she'll want you. This past year Mr. Botkin was too ill to pay your rental, and I expect he failed to provide the agreed-upon shoes. Did he buy you shoes?"

"I don't need no shoes. I goes barefoot most of the time."

"You shall have shoes. Uther was a fine man, but I believe he may have been even less worldly than our good Preacher Todd."

The kitchen garden glistened in the sun, heat waves shimmered above the barn roof.

"What about this?" Auntie Opal cried. "Who's gonna milk the cow? You think somebody else gonna come in here and take care of things like I do?"

"We'll fallow the Botkin plantation. The Millboro telegraph reports a great battle is being fought outside the town of Gettysburg, in Pennsylvania. Early reports say General Lee is everywhere successful and has forty thousand Federal prisoners. If Lee destroys the Federal army, they must sue for peace. Auntie, perhaps your Sallie will come home soon—and Catesby and my poor dear Duncan. They might all be home for the harvest. . . ."

Opal shook her head slowly. She said, "Ain't ever gonna be the way it was."

38

LETTER FROM LIEUTENANT CATESBY BYRD TO HIS WIFE, LEONA,

In Camp near Culpepper, Virginia
July 25, 1863

DEAREST LEONA,

I write you in great excitement with great news! I have renounced my previous sinful ways and publicly confessed my desire to be a Christian! I cannot tell you how happy I am! I have never been a man of sanguine temperament, have oft seen the worse rather than the better, but I can today rejoice honestly and openly in the love of Christ my Savior!

I have long been contemptuous of those plain souls who found solace in their Christian beliefs. Although I gave credit to Stonewall for his military abilities, I never honored the depth of his devotion to God. Now, too late, I would sit with Stonewall Jackson at one of his prayer meetings and take comfort from his stalwart faith! If only that Christian warrior were with us today!

The army thinks that Stonewall's absence cost us the victory at Gettysburg, and I am one who believes it true. Darling Wife, we did all mortal men can do. From Pickett's division after their charge only one field officer returned to our lines; Garnett's brigade of thirteen hundred lost nine hundred and fifty; a North Carolina company which began the fight with a hundred men now numbers eight. We have done what mortal men can! My own regiment expended itself on an assault on Culp's Hill with a loss of fifty-six brave men. Our Major Cobb was wounded, and my fellow cardplaying sinner Sergeant Fisher is missing.

Our army started home through rain and clinging mud and a civilian populace which found courage to fall upon our weakened wounded stragglers. When we reached the Potomac, the river was in full flood, the only bridge destroyed, and every small boat for miles was busy ferrying our wounded. The army itself had no means to cross back into Virginia. While we awaited the arrival of the Federal host, black despair was my bosom companion.

But thanks to God, the enemy did not come! Day after day the river dropped, our engineers cobbled together a rude bridge, and while Longstreet's men crossed that, our division attempted the ford. We taller men stood chest-deep in the deepest stretch of that swirling muddy river passing our comrades from hand to hand.

When the sun came out to illuminate the far shore, our blessed garden of Virginia, I saw the Israelites fleeing Pharaoh's hordes. A frightened soldier gripped my hands until I passed him on—to a stranger of unknown rank and unknown regiment who passed him to safety.

That, Dearest Wife, was the moment God called to me.

Even before our battle at Gettysburg, many from my company had been attending prayer meetings (held almost nightly) and the services which three mornings a week have replaced routine drill in this army.

At one of these meetings, Private Henry Perkins was touched by grace and came to witness his new faith to me, though at the time I was a skeptic still. Private Perkins confessed his newfound surety of Christian salvation. "Sir," he said, "I cannot speak of the satisfaction this has given me and how my parents will delight that I have given up cards and strong drink." The boy's face shone with fervor.

Not two weeks later, below Culp's Hill, a Federal cannon ball struck him, clean removing the top of his skull, and his brain flopped, two perfect lobes, into the dirt of the road. At the time, I was horrified, appalled at the harm hot steel wreaks on mortal flesh. But today, sharing the private's Christian certainty, I believe that shot freed Private Perkins from every grief and peril in this world, and that Henry Perkins departed for heaven straightaway. I tell you, Dearest, I have seen these things.

Preachers are everywhere among us. Our regimental chaplain, Captain Nelson, invites evangelists to speak at our meetings. Nightly we have fresh testimonies of one simple story: Christ, our Savior's love for us!

As I strive to become a Christian, I have renounced cards, and I cannot understand what I ever saw in them. How contemptible we sinners are!

Although we ate well on our march through Pennsylvania (the war has hardly touched that country), here in our old camps along the Rapidan, rations are hard biscuit, a bit of beef, and the sassafras roots we dig to avoid the scurvy. Forage is so lacking for the horses most have been removed to the Valley to graze. General Lee is issuing no furloughs, and we may soon be back in the thick of it.

I cannot tell you what joy it is to gather in the evening around the campfire with other professing Christians. Leathery veterans and downy-faced boys alike entreat their Savior on one another's behalf. We pray for our leaders, for those in the regiment who have not seen the light of Christ's truth, and for the safety of our new nation. Sometimes senior officers come, standing humbly on the outside of the circle, and twice General Lee himself attended. Quietly, a Christian among Christians, the general stood, head bowed and uncovered, listening to his men's souls.

Surely God will cherish and protect His people. Surely the many ardent prayers for our brave new nation will find His Favor.

I pray daily for you and our dear, dear children. I pray things at Stratford are not too difficult and entreat you, Dearest Wife, to redouble Thomas's Christian instruction. Temptations are strongest in young men. What if calamity should strike while a boy is strayed? I shudder to think what might have befallen me had I had been slain, still wallowing in sin, a frequenter of gambling hells and drinker of wines and hard liquor. Eternity in damnation in exchange for brief years of earthly mischief! Never in heaven to embrace my beloved parents, never to see our Baby Willie thriving in the Lord's care, never to greet you, Dearest, when you cross over the River Jordan into Paradise!

As Samuel must have told you, Duncan's health continues precarious. We must trust the Lord to watch over him.

This letter to you, my Darling, is the most joyous I have ever written. I am a new man and will strive with all my heart to be a Good Christian. I trust Providence for all my needs.

Your Loving Husband,
Catesby

39

LOVE IN THE REBEL CAPITAL

THE GIRL SAT in the corner of Marguerite Omohundru's sunroom at farthest remove from her hostess. Her tea was untouched on the silver tray. She hadn't taken off her jacket.

Outdoors, red and golden leaves had been raked into hummocks; excepting the green-gray splash of rhododendron, the garden was bare. The sky had lifted—the way it always did in Richmond that time of year—and the air was so clear it snapped.

The old woman was wrapped in a fur robe, and her withered head poked out of the robe like an opossum pretending to be a bear.

The girl said, "I don't know why you tell me these things. They're not true. Everybody knows they aren't true. Daddy says if I want to know what it was like I should read Thomas Nelson Page. I should take his books out of the library."

"I never met the gentleman." The old woman brushed at a wisp of hair. "Was he in the army?"

"My supervisor says I have to get on with my work," the girl said. "If it hadn't been for Uncle Harry, I'd have lost my job."

"A summer job?"

"Well, that's how it started. Phil, he . . ."

"Started seeing someone else?"

"Some Culpepper girl he met at Monticello. Phil works for the foundation. He's a dollar-a-year man."

The old woman smiled. "Your supervisor has instructed you to interview other former servants?"

"He says . . . Daddy says . . ."

The old woman picked the lemon from her teacup and sucked on it. "Did I ever tell you why General Jackson sucked on lemons? He thought it improved his vitality. Lemons didn't save his arm. It was North Carolina boys who shot him, you know."

". . . that you're no negro! They say you've been associating with negroes at your bank for so long you've come to think you're one yourself. They say Mr. Omohundru met you in Nassua, in the Bahamas, and married you. Everybody knows it."

"Who else are you interviewing, child?"

"Nobody. I get so sick of hearing the same story over and over. If one more old fool tells me about Cox's snow, I swear I'm going to scream!"

"It happened, you know."

"I know it happened. But why must I know about it?"

"What do you do when you're not working?"

"Sometimes I go to the matinee."

"If you came here more often instead of wasting time at the movies you would be finished sooner."

The girl lifted her teacup and sipped.

"Do you go out in society?"

The girl pulled a face. "Everybody thinks I have a ridiculous job! And when I talk about you nobody believes me!"

"After General Pickett made his fatal charge, gloom settled on Richmond, a gloom the ladies tacitly agreed to alleviate. Defying the continuous processions to Hollywood Cemetery and the mourning bands on so many sleeves, theatricals and charades and levees continued, and though there were times when some new-widowed belle broke into unconsolable sobs, Confederate officers toasted feminine charms as before the war, with all the gaiety they could muster.

"Society today is dominated by Grandes dames. During the War, society was the creature of young unmarried girls. It was their parties everyone hoped to be invited to, their soirées that were attended by gallant Confederate officers.

"Richmond society had been a society of families where invitations were rarely needed because everybody knew who was welcome. But as Mattie Ould said, 'War is a great rearranger of aristocracies,' and men tramped through Richmond's parlors who never would have been admitted before the war. There was the Prussian, Von Borke, with his dreadful neck wound. General Mahone—a tavernkeeper's son. Molly Semple—who had previously been regarded as wellborn but too free a spirit—Molly was inducted into the 'Old Guard.'

"Molly Semple was likelier to attend a levee than Mrs. Kirkpatrick (her kin by marriage, Richmond believed), but when the flood of casualties dwindled, Sallie Kirkpatrick would accompany her kinswoman into society.

"Before the war, ladies prided themselves on their exquisite needlework and some notioned a lady's quality could be determined from her stitches, but fancy work had become unpatriotic. At society levees, ladies stripped lint from family underclothing for Confederate bandages. Instead of embroidery, ladies manufactured socks, woolen vests, and suspenders. Older ladies brought down spinning wheels from their attics, and as during our revolution against the English, the steady thump and whir of spinning wheels provided harmony to music produced by ensembles of house servants. Mrs. Ould's Henry was an excellent fiddler and in demand for his knowledge of French court tunes, although it was suspected that of the sheet music he so fussily arranged on his music stand Henry read not one note.

"At one time, Sallie Kirkpatrick's mouse-brown dress might have occasioned comment, but in a capital where many had sold spare clothing for food or converted the cloth into uniforms, her unvarying dress was unexceptionable. Family carriages had been requisitioned by the army, and many a dashing thoroughbred was pulling artillery limbers for General Lee.

"It was believed Sallie had come from a plantation beyond the Blue Ridge. It was known she had lost her husband at Fredericksburg, though nobody knew his regiment or rank. But many a proud scion of the Confederacy died an anonymous private, and if Mrs. Kirkpatrick preferred to keep her grief to herself so be it.

"At one gathering, several ladies inquired about the patients in Sallie's care. 'They bear the most frightful injuries with courage,' Sallie said. 'Even the youngest face death with resignation and calm.'

" 'My dear—are they in good spirits? Do they ever jest?'

"As her reply, Sallie described the young Baptist chaplain who preached to her ward one Sunday. 'I do not believe he had been long with the army, and confronting so much pain discomfited him. When his invention flagged, he embarked on themes too familiar to my patients. He was dead set against drinking and cardplaying and awfully distressed by dancing. At this last, a Georgia corporal burst into laughter, and soon the entire ward was rocking with mirth.

" ' "Sir," the chaplain cried, "are you not tempted to sin?"

" ' "No sir. I reckon I ain't," the corporal said. He flipped aside his bedclothes to reveal that both legs had been removed at the knee. That is the sort of jest our boys enjoy.'

"At subsequent soirées, the ladies made grateful noises about Mrs. Kirkpatrick's dedication, but never again troubled her for specifics."

RICHMOND, VIRGINIA
NOVEMBER 15, 1863

Sallie Botkin carried a handful of wet bandages to the wringer and Molly turned the crank. Usually Camp Winder made do with lint wound dressings, but Chancellorsville had provided a wealth of Federal linen bandages.

Earlier that day, General Lee himself had called on Cousin Molly at her home. "We had such an agreeable chat," Molly said as Sallie fed the wringer. "The general's a fifth cousin, connected through my mother's side. He was so grateful for the care we give his men. Robert Lee has the most delicate manners."

Sallie wiped her forehead on her sleeve. "Had the general troubled to call on me, I should have told him that we would not need to care for his men if he cared for them better!"

"Then perhaps, child, it is well you and the general did not make one another's acquaintance." Cousin Molly paused. "My dear, I wish you to look in on your childhood friend Duncan Gatewood."

"I cannot imagine Captain Gatewood wishes to renew our acquaintance any more than I do."

"He had recovered from his amputation and was anticipating a furlough home, but has contracted a fever, and Sallie, I fear for his life. Your familiar face would be a comfort."

Sallie hesitated. "I have been a convict," she said.

"Child," Cousin Molly said, "Duncan is dear Abigail's son."

Duncan's forehead and arms were splashed with furious red stripes, and when Sallie lifted his blanket, his chest was the palest blue-white she'd ever seen. The left side of his face, the stretched burn scar which connected jawbone to hairline, pulsed sullen red. He'd sweated through his blanket and the blanket laid under him. When he opened his eyes, they swam around the ward. "Sallie? Where are we, Sallie? Am I translated?"

Sallie touched his lips. She would not weep. She would not!

All those childhood days in Uther Botkin's sunny school: Leona, Duncan, Jesse . . . her father's intelligent, questioning voice . . . No! To recall these things would make her helpless, and Sallie would not be helpless.

In his fever, Duncan thrashed; he would not lie still. Fearing he might batter his stump or do some injury to himself, Sallie had him tied to the bed with linen strips. She bathed his body with cool water.

He muttered. He sat bolt upright in bed to shout, "Christ, the skin on her! Under her titties was the softest place on God's earth." Her patient's delirium prompted Sallie to have his bed moved into her own room, where Duncan would not distress his fellows.

Duncan raved coarsely about Midge and called her Witchy. At other times he murmured tendernesses—that Midge had given herself to him as naturally as a flower opens from the bud. Why was Midge cold? Why was poor Midge shivering? "Young Master Jacob Gatewood! Young Master!" Duncan snorted and flailed his head so furiously Sallie clamped him between her palms. All of one night, Duncan raved scripture, one verse, repeated over and over: "It would be better for him if he should have a millstone hanged about his neck and he were cast into the sea than he should cause one of these little ones to stumble." His forehead was slick with sweat. At last, almost rationally, Duncan said, "Sold south, my own son. Oh, what will they think of that?" He never said who "they" were, whether angels at the Last Judgment or men upon this earth.

The crisis came in the hour before dawn. Duncan sat upright, fever stripes writhing like snakes. "Will I perish?" he asked.

"The surgeon has hope."

"What is that you're knitting?"

"A sock."

He croaked, "Where will you find the horse that requires one?"

She laid her ungainly project across her lap. She smiled.

"Am I so amusing?"

"You have been ill."

"My soul has been sick since I lay down with Midge. Do you think she poisoned me?"

Sallie brought water to his lips. Throat spasming, he swallowed; most dribbled down his chest. "More likely I poisoned her. She was sold to another master to be used as he saw fit. I prayed she would be sold as a field worker, not a house servant, because I know her perils too well. Duncan Gatewood, obedient son! Too obedient to defend my own son, my own . . . Midge. I was a coward—a damned coward."

Sallie wrung out a cloth and wiped bristling sweat from his forehead. She touched his burn. "Few would censure you for what you have done."

"Would you censure me? You who went to prison because of principle?"

Sadness darkened Sallie's features. "Censure cannot thrive in death's presence. After enough men die, censure is confounded. I hardly recall the penitentiary. I scarcely remember Snowy Mountain or Aunt Opal or Uther or Jesse, who was more my friend than servant. How I pray Jesse has found his way to freedom, that he is not one of the anonymous corpses this war is laying up." She turned to the table. "You've a letter from your father. Shall I read it to you?"

Duncan shook his head. "He sees my lost arm as opportunity—wishes me to return to Stratford." He sank back into his pillows. "Am I so very ugly now?"

"No," she said.

His eyelids slid over his eyes. "Thank you, dear Sallie," he whispered.

Duncan slept for sixteen hours straight, and when he woke, his forehead was cool to the touch. If he ever recalled their conversation that fever-broken night, he never mentioned it. Sallie had Duncan moved back onto the ward. Even while Duncan was in death's antechamber, other matrons had complained to Cousin Molly about the impropriety of an unmarried man and widowed woman sharing the same room.

At this time, the only wounded soldier in the ward was a cavalry sergeant from Mississippi. Consumptives and pneumonias occupied the other beds.

Sallie and Duncan resumed the easy intimacy they had enjoyed as children at Uther Botkin's knee. When Duncan finally opened his father's letter, it contained Catesby's letter, forwarded without comment. Duncan smiled. "If ever a man was born to sing in the hallelujah chorus, Catesby is that man." Judiciously he added, "I hope Catesby isn't too sanctified around Samuel. Samuel won't stand for it."

"And you, Duncan. What do you think?"

He grinned. "It ain't my soul, it's Catesby's soul, and he's to have full disposition of it."

A week later Duncan was sitting up, and the next bright morning was helped outside onto a bench in the sun. Sallie kept him company.

"Lord, I feel old. I don't think I will ever be a young man again."

"Hush. Don't be sillier than you must."

"The sun . . ."

"Yes, it does feel good. Look, crows after a hawk."

Duncan shaded his eyes. "Hawk always gets the worst of it; he's more'n a match for one crow but he can't do much against four of them."

"Remember at the beginning of the war the newspapers were boasting how many Federals one Confederate could defeat?"

"We talked some prime foolishness in those days. Federal soldiers take a fair bit of licking. They just haven't had good generals. Let's not talk about the war. Please, Sallie."

"I'd thought if you were feeling better on Sunday we might attend the Davises' levee. It is their custom to open their home, and I have never been."

Duncan brushed his uniform and even polished his boots, though that was a complex task for a newly one-armed man. On the appointed day, they borrowed a hospital ambulance and, over Sallie's objections, Duncan drove. "I can drive with one hand," Duncan said. "And had better get used to it. Besides"—he flicked the leather over a horse well into his second decade—"I don't think Dobbin will run away with us."

Outside the presidential mansion, militiamen were talking strategy with some Georgians who had traveled from their home specifically to advise President Davis on his conduct of the war.

"Mr. Davis, he don't take kindly to advice," one private said dolefully. "And he's in no humor since he got home from the west. Was I you, I'd talk to Vice President Stephens. He don't care for the way things are run either, and since he's from Georgia, might be he'd know some of your kin."

Some of the crowd in the entrance hall were civilians; most, like Duncan, wounded soldiers. The hall wallpaper was the faux wood grain so fashionable before the war. "My, doesn't it look real?" Sallie said.

"Wouldn't fool me," Duncan, the onetime sawyer, grumbled.

Although it was late in the season, the mansion's paintings were still draped by insect-proof gauze.

Flanked by avuncular Judah Benjamin, President Davis bowed gracefully to each lady, extended his hand to each civilian, asked each soldier his regiment. After being received, the guests passed through French doors into the garden.

Davis's forehead was pinched with headache, and one of his eyes was milky and blind. "I am glad to make your acquaintance, Captain," Davis said. "You have suffered in our cause."

"Not so much as some, sir," Duncan replied. Then the devil took him: "Why is it, sir, that they feed us so much better in the hospital than with the army in the field?"

Davis had already grasped the next hand but swiveled his gaze crisply. "Captain, that is so we might return you to ranks as swiftly as we can."

Duncan's foolish grin fell off his face.

Varina Davis and a few of her intimates gathered in a small sitting room adjacent to the public melee. Although Varina Davis was a staunch Episcopalian, this parlor was decorated with crucifixes and rosaries, carved by Confederate prisoners of war. An elderly woman summoned Sallie with big gestures.

"Mrs. Stannard, how nice to see you . . ."

"Oh, do come in, child. You and your gallant escort. Where is your delightful Cousin Molly? Captain, so glad to see you. All we Confederate ladies are fascinated by soldiers."

In her dark green hoop skirt and green jacket, Varina Davis looked like a doll, an exuberantly energetic doll. "Which is your regiment, Captain?" she asked.

"Forty-fourth Virginia, ma'am. I lost this"—he patted his stump—"at Chancellorsville."

Almost swallowed in the upholstery of the couch, a withered old man pronounced, "Great victory. We drove 'em that day."

"Captain, let me introduce Mr. Edmund Ruffin, who had the honor of firing our first shot at Fort Sumter." Courtesy satisfied, Mrs. Davis left to pour tea for her other guests.

Ruffin said, "For years I argued secession from the northern oppressors. Years. Nobody listened to me then. Now we are seceded, nobody heeds me again."

"We met at John Brown's hanging," Duncan said.

"Don't remember you. I met too many people in those days," Ruffin said.

"I was the cadet guarding the scaffold. We talked in the moonlight."

"John Brown produced a pretty piece of work. He did more to cause this war than any man living. Tyrant Lincoln dances to John Brown's tune."

"I remember it was a beautiful night."

"Was it? What will we do without General Jackson?"

"I lost my horse Gypsy at Chancellorsville. Don't expect I'll ever find another like her."

"Do you equate your horse with the South's finest Christian general?"

Sally took Duncan's good arm. "You'll have to excuse him, sir. The captain is recovering from fever."

When Sallie had Duncan settled on a love seat in the corner, she fetched him a cup of tea.

"I'm gonna miss Gypsy a damn sight more'n I'll miss Old Blue Light," Duncan muttered.

"Yes, but perhaps this isn't just the place to say so." Sallie nodded at acquaintances across the room.

"You think I should say that every time Old Jack attacked, the Federals fell down in terror? That God and General Jackson were hitched tandem?"

The two looked everywhere but at each other. Citizens in the receiving line eyed Varina Davis's intimates with frank curiosity.

Sallie's smile was stiff. "It is so nice to taste real tea again."

"If there ever were any tea leaves in my cup they long since departed for a happier land." Duncan wanted to apologize, but his words came out wrong. He said, "Sallie, you never were so particular about pleasing other people."

"Yes," Sallie whispered. "And see what it brought me to."

Following the Davis's levee, Sallie found plenty to keep her occupied on other wards. Duncan took on orderly chores as his strength returned.

It surprised Duncan how much he had depended on having two arms. To sweep with one arm was difficult, to collect a chamber pot impossible. The cradling action of hands and arms was a ghost inside his body. Before his loss, Duncan Gatewood had faced the world head on, legs apart like a wrestler; now he turned toward life edgeways, a fencer. Simple operations—pulling on a sock, cutting a piece of beef without sending his plate skittering to the floor—taught him much about a body he had always taken for granted. How does a one-armed man open a jack-knife? By setting the haft against his hip and plucking the blade between thumb and forefinger. A one-armed man winds his watch by clamping the instrument between little finger and heel of the hand while inserting the key. Shaving his burn-scarred face was too painful, so Duncan let his beard grow.

Sometimes Duncan's missing arm ached as if he were half corporeal, half shade.

Saturday morning, Sallie arrived with a wicker basket tucked underneath her arm. "It is a lovely day," she announced.

Duncan leaned his broom against the doorframe. "Cooler at night. Won't be too long before we roll the mosquito netting."

"Yes. In our mountains they will have had hard frosts."

He took a deep breath. "Sallie, I'm sorry. I didn't mean to embarrass you before the Davises."

"I believe I have forgotten the incident. Perhaps we could picnic on the James. I know a grassy bank within easy walking distance. I have managed apples, a loaf of bread, a flask of fresh milk, even half a chicken. I hope you will accompany me. Oh, I am so bold!"

His face broke into a grin. "Oh, I don't know," he said and took her arm. "Oh, I don't know."

The river ran over the stepped falls in a soft creamy whoosh. Its bow wave broke against a green canal boat sliding upstream. An osprey flashed into the mist and emerged, wings working hard, a heavy fish in its talons.

Sallie unwrapped the cool flask. "One would never think . . ."

"This makes war seem unnatural."

"Is it not?"

Duncan grasped his knee and leaned forward. "We must need it. Else why do we fight?"

"Duncan . . . please. Would you care for chicken? Cousin Molly obtained this mustard from Mr. Worsham. It is quite famous in the city."

"Is it so important to you? This work you do?"

"I would die before I went back to . . . that place. When I add my time there to what I spent with Alexander I seem to have been imprisoned a lifetime."

Duncan wiped his fingers on the grass. "Alexander?"

"Every young girl is vulnerable to a man who promises to be her all."

A smaller osprey, a female, hung over the falls, sun flashing on her white wings.

"I miss Uther so," Sallie said. "He was the gentlest man. . . . Do you ever wonder how it must have been in those days? Men like Washington and Jefferson and Madison and Patrick Henry . . ."

Duncan laughed, "Speculators, one and all. Did you know that Washington had money in the James and Kanawha Canal? Patriotism and profit, there's a combination."

"Duncan Gatewood, you are plain as dirt!"

He said, "A simple mountain planter was all I ever wanted to be. Things don't always turn out."

They sat in silence for a long while. Sallie remembered her arrival at the Augusta Female Seminary. How excited she'd been. Jesse had driven her to the great metropolis of Staunton, Virginia; how she'd gawked. At the time Duncan was already loving Midge, but Sallie'd not known about it. Sallie said, "We have so many secrets."

"Is that unnatural? My grandfather was shot to death by the man he'd been cuckolding, and I can't recall grandfather's demise often being mentioned in the family. Candor is too blunt a tool for household usage."

"If anyone is less discreet than I am, I don't know her. First thing comes into my mind, I blurt it out."

Duncan confessed, "And I am often tongue-tied. Without means to say how dear you are to me."

Her hand stole into his and gave it a squeeze. "You must not become fond of me," she said. "For I am a felonious person."

He couldn't help himself. "You are my very favorite felon," he burst out happily.

At that Sallie did remove her hand. She searched the basket for an apple. "Surgeon Lane gets these from the river planters. They share with our wounded what they would not willingly put on the market."

"Sallie . . ."

"Hush, Duncan. I have only just learned to live alone, and it seems such a gift. Will you eat an apple?"

Held up to the sun, the apple's skin glowed like red gold. "Sallie, in your presence, I am such a fool."

Too brightly she retorted, "We will soon be apart. When you take convalescent furlough, perhaps you will write."

"If . . ."

"Surgeon Lane says you will soon be fit for travel. Young men heal wonderfully at their own homes."

"And most never come back to the army."

"Why should they? Why should you? Haven't you given enough to the Confederacy?"

He shook his head. "If you could just see Lee's army. If you could see it."

"I have seen General Lee's army. I've seen its blood and its pus and its shattered bones and its entrails more times, in greater intimacy, than I care to remember. Graybeards and boys, men who die crowded around by relatives, men who die alone . . ." Sallie covered her face.

After a time, Duncan said softly, "At night, among us, the talk is so calm. Some men pray, some sing a ditty. After Fredericksburg—oh, it was a week or so after—it was getting on to Christmas and the Federal bands were playing on the other side of the river, 'John Brown's Body,' 'Tenting Tonight,' those songs, and we crept down to the riverbank to listen.

"Not a week before, we had killed their friends, and the shoes and coats we were wearing had been taken from their dead. Come spring they'd come across the river again and we would do our damnedest to kill them. But the Federals have fine bands. Come a pause between tunes, one of our boys yelled, 'How 'bout playing some of our music now?' And damned if they didn't. They lit right into 'Dixie' and 'The Bonny Blue Flag' and they ended with 'Home Sweet Home,' and I misdoubt there was a dry eye in either army.

"If I live to be a hundred, I don't believe I'll ever do anything more important than fighting in General Lee's army," Duncan said. "Those fellows who were going to run have mostly run, and those who were truly brave, most of them have been killed. The ones of us left are just ordinary men.

"After what I did with Midge, I never thought I could hold my head up again. The army gave me back my honor." He caressed his empty sleeve. "General Mahone needs a commissary officer, and I have asked to be returned to duty. Do you—do you understand?"

Sallie averted her face so Duncan couldn't see her tears. "I have seen too much of honor," she said.

40

RECRUITERS

WASHINGTON CITY, DISTRICT OF COLUMBIA
NOVEMBER 20, 1863

THE FEDERAL COLONEL of engineers said, "We shall want two more rows of sandbags at that embrasure."

The lieutenant of engineers said, "I believe what we have is adequate."

The colonel of engineers said, "I wish it would snow. I have no quarrel with honest snow. But this drizzle penetrates my mood as readily as my overcoat. In the winter Washington City is intolerable. In the summer it is intolerable. This city has two agreeable seasons, neither more than a week in duration."

The lieutenant said, "I am told that negroes cannot survive a colder climate. This is my first experience of them. There are no negroes in Skowhegan, Maine."

"Very few in Illinois. Nevertheless, I believe some of their race have emigrated to Canada."

"The abolitionists got us into this damned war. I wonder they are not here to help us fight it."

The colonel said, "I believe the Parrot guns' muzzles will clear two more rows. Jesse!"

Jesse Burns was at the tip of the mound of sandbags that constituted the new emplacement, the latest link in the chain of forts around Washington City. "Colonel!"

"Set that surveyor's rod beside that top row of sandbags. What does it read?"

"Two foot six."

"Two more rows, Lieutenant."

"If that man has read it right."

"Jesse? He is the best man I have."

"You mean he is the best negro man you have."

The colonel lifted his pale blue eyes. "You presume to improve my diction, Lieutenant?"

The lieutenant flinched.

"These contrabands are as good workmen as any. When Haupt rebuilt that railroad bridge at Burke's Station, some called it 'the bridge made of wheatstalks,' but it got replacements to Pope's aid, and contrabands, despite sharpshooter fire, built it."

The lieutenant spoke with the precision of one who may not be on safe ground. "I think the negro emancipation a mistake. As my estimable kinsman Senator Collins put it, 'For the Union we will fight to the death. We will not fight for niggers.' "

"They are not all alike," the colonel remarked. "There are loafers and scoundrels among them, to be sure. But there are individuals who, saving the color of their skin and the ignorance due to their previous servitude, could stand comparison with any white man."

Fifty ex-slaves commanded by white officers were no unusual sight as the capital girded its loins against the Confederates. Some workers came from contraband camps, some slept in hovels and tenements in the city; for all the colonel knew, some lived here among the sandbags. Every morning, when the white officers arrived at the unfinished emplacement, their workers were waiting with Jesse.

The contrabands chanted a work song as they passed hundred-pound sandbags from man to man in a smooth flow.

Only last week there was fighting near Tysons Corner, and any day the audacious J.E.B. Stuart might appear on the outskirts of the city. Washington City reeked of defeatism, and the colonel planned to visit a friend at the War Department tomorrow and see if a case of brandy couldn't speed his transfer back to the real army. Let the lieutenant see to the city's fortifications.

The colonel had posted boys to warn when general officers appeared, and one of those boys came pelting along, arms and legs pumping, oblivious of the mounted party on his heels. "Master! Master!" he cried.

One civilian, one brand-new infantry captain, and one rumpled brigadier of heavy artillery, who returned the colonel's salute perfunctorily. "There," he said to nobody in particular. "I hate this goddamned wet. Christ! I hate this wet."

The smooth-faced civilian stood in his stirrups to examine the colonel's workers. The uniform the captain wore was new and ill-fitting, and his eyes sized up every man.

"You got your niggers building a pyramid. Who you gonna bury in there?" the brigadier laughed.

"General, from this emplacement our Parrot guns command Benning's Bridge. If Bobby Lee comes here, we'll make it hot for him."

"Oh, hell. Lee's behind the Rapidan." Suddenly, he clutched his saddle horn to contain his swaying. He uncorked a blue glass flask, and after he helped himself said, "Sorry, Colonel—my manners. Care for some comfort on this miserable day?"

"No, sir. I'm temperance," the colonel lied. "As an artilleryman, you'll be interested in our field of fire. Perhaps you'd like to inspect the embrasures?"

"Colonel, I don't give two goddamns for your field of fire. Me and this young fellow here—Wilson—we've come for your niggers. Wilson says you ran him off before, though he's got a warrant signed by Secretary Stanton saying he can sign up as many niggers as he wants. Captain Fesston here . . ."

"Fessenden, sir."

"The captain here is forming a nigger regiment, and he'll have these boys in ranks before you can spit." The brigadier essayed a slow wink. "Mr. Wilson's well connected in the War Department."

"Sir, Wilson is a scoundrel."

"Oh hell. Oh hell. They're all scoundrels. You've got good duty here, Colonel. Build pyramids all day and sleep under clean sheets at night. There's those who would trade places . . ."

"If you would facilitate my transfer to the field, I'd be grateful," the colonel came right back.

"Not so damn quick, Colonel. I can facilitate your transfer or I can make it goddamned impossible, whichever ain't what you want. You gonna let Wilson have some of your boys?"

The lieutenant of engineers touched his cap in salute, introduced himself, mentioned his connection to Senator Collins, asked how he could be of service.

The brigadier smiled benevolently. "Colonel, if you don't mind, your lieutenant and I have some nigger plucking to do. Captain Fesser . . . Fedden . . . this lieutenant will help you pick your men."

The colonel of engineers said, "No. I do not believe he will."

The brigadier's red eyes narrowed to gun slits. "Colonel . . ."

"Your Mr. Wilson has no powers of conscription. Nor, I believe, does Captain Fessenden. If they can persuade any of these men to enlist, they may do so. No doubt Mr. Wilson has great powers of persuasion."

"Thank you, Colonel. Perhaps you'd absent yourself while we get this damn business over with."

The colonel of engineers walked over to the riverbank, clamped white-knuckled hands behind his back, and kept his eyes glued to a dingy white sidewheeler steaming up the Potomac.

"The 23rd U.S. Colored Troops is a volunteer outfit." Captain Fessenden took Wilson's sleeve. "If these men won't enlist of their own accord, we don't want them. The contraband camps are filled with men."

"Filled with recruiters too." Wilson spat tobacco juice, removed his plug hat, spun it, and reset it satisfactorily on his head. "Take it easy, Captain. I'll get your volunteers." He turned to the lieutenant of engineers. "Lieutenant, who's the head man? Can't get nowhere with niggers less'n you talk to the head man."

"Jesse!"

Jesse straightened, hands hanging easily at his sides.

"You! Jesse!" Wilson said. "I want your boys to hear this."

Jesse raised his hand, and after the final sandbag journeyed from the wagon where it had been filled to the unfinished embrasure, men stretched, put hands on hips, wiped their faces.

"Boys, I'm Master Wilson, recruiter for the Grand Army of the Potomac. I ain't gonna tell you I don't get paid for men I bring in, because I do, but that ain't the reason I'm doin' it. I'm for the Union, by God, and let no man say Jimmy Wilson ain't. Now I expect you're for the Union too. Master Lincoln, he set you free, and I expect you're in favor of that. Let's have three cheers for Master Lincoln!"

The men looked at Jesse, who did nothing.

"You won't give three huzzahs for the man who set you free? By God, if you ain't a bunch of ungrateful niggers!"

"General," Captain Fessenden murmured, "Wilson is making a hash of this. Let me talk to them."

The brigadier smiled a bleary smile. "As you goddamn please."

The captain crossed his hands on his pommel and leaned forward. "I am Captain Zelotes Fessenden, from Newport, Rhode Island. What is your surname, Jesse?"

"I'm called Jesse Burns, because my grandmother once belonged to a man called Burns. My home is near SunRise, Virginia, in the mountains there."

"You know why I have come. The United States government has determined to create colored regiments. Your regimental officers are volunteers to a man. I was a postmaster myself before I stood the examination. Other officers were enlisted men who seized this opportunity to improve themselves."

"Why they want to officer niggers?" Jesse asked.

"Some from conviction. Some are abolitionists . . ."

"Like old John Brown? That Brown didn't know more about us than if we were . . . elephants."

Recruiter Wilson kneed his horse to the base of the pyramid. "Boys!" Wilson yelled. "How'd you like fifty dollars?"

The contrabands demonstrated interest.

"Fifty dollars will buy a horse like this one or five suits of clothes or a month's worth of good times. That's what this war is about: a man's natural chance to make money, and I'm offering your chance here and now. Any man put his X on this paper here, I'll hand him fifty dollars." The recruiter extracted a plump roll of bills, which he waved like a regimental flag. "He'll draw his uniform and go on the payroll just like white soldiers."

"How much he get paid?" Jesse inquired.

"Seven dollars a month, and he gets fed every day, three meals, and the army'll put him on railroad trains when it's too far to walk and steamers when it's too goddamn wet . . ."

"How much white soldiers get paid?"

"Soldiers of the Army of the Potomac get paid according to rank and experience. They . . ."

"Privates get ten dollars a month and a three-dollar uniform allowance," Captain Fessenden interrupted.

Jesse nodded. He'd thought so.

"Plus you get fifty dollars today." Wilson fluttered his currency.

Captain Fessenden continued as if Wilson hadn't said a word, "Some of you bear the marks of servitude upon your persons: the bullwhip laid upon human flesh. The men who whipped you are our enemies too."

"Yeah," Wilson jumped in. "Those rebels, look what they done. Stole you from your warm and happy land." He wrapped himself in his arms and shivered. "Stuffed you into boats like you was herrings, brought you over here in chains and worked you like . . ."

"Niggers?" Jesse suggested.

"No better'n brutes. Until you was too old and broke down to work no more." When Wilson ran out of talk, his hand was in the air, so he hastily stuck it in his pocket.

"And he made concubines of your wives," the lieutenant of engineers suggested.

"What's a concubine, Master?" Jesse drawled.

"Whore," Wilson snapped. "She's a whore."

"You say we get fifty dollars right away. How much you get?"

"Three hundred," Captain Fessenden answered.

"Then fifty dollars ain't enough. Man who signs on to maybe get killed should get paid more'n the man who signed him. That's fair."

"Don't you want to revenge yourself on those who treated you wickedly?" Wilson cried. "Don't you want to take bayonets and stuff them down their throats?"

Jesse said, "Bible says, 'Revenge is mine, saith the Lord.' Think He didn't mean it?"

Captain Fessenden dismounted and walked to the foot of the sandbag pyramid. "I am first captain of the 23rd Regiment, U.S. Colored Troops. The regiment will need good fighters. This man Wilson here is made of shoddy, but he isn't the worst recruiter in Washington City. One man's X on an enlistment paper looks no different from another's. Some recruiters will knock you on the head, some put a friendly arm around your shoulder moments before his bullies drag you away.

"It is true that United States Colored Troops are not paid as white troops. It is true that many white officers despise you and the white soldiers fighting beside you wonder if you can do your part. You know this as well as I do. You also know that no promise any white man ever made to you has ever been kept, save one: due to President Lincoln and the United States government you are now and henceforth forever free. Some of you will do worse as free men. Some will take the first steps toward being citizens. In my belief, you'll do as well in the army as anywhere. In the Army of the Potomac you can prove yourselves men."

"Why didn't you say so, Captain," Jesse said softly and slid down the sandbags, and when Captain Fessenden handed him the enlistment paper, Jesse wrote his name in large letters thereon.

41

MASTER ABRAHAM'S SERMON

ANALASTON ISLAND, DISTRICT OF COLUMBIA
NOVEMBER 23, 1863

CAPTAIN FESSENDEN SAID, "I know it isn't much."

Jesse looked around the filthy barracks. "That's right."

"You won't be here long. As soon as the regiment is filled, we join the army. We'll have training and drill before you meet the rebels."

"That'll be a comfort," Jesse said.

"And you must call all officers 'sir.' "

"Yes, sir," Jesse said too promptly.

Eight ex-contrabands, now soldiers, tested cots or poked the ashes in the cold iron stove. "Look here, Burns," Fessenden said. "These men look up to you and will take their cue from you. If you promote discipline they will be good soldiers—if not, you'll answer to me. The 23rd U.S. Colored Troops is going to be the best damn regiment in the Army of the Potomac!"

"Yes, sir," Jesse said again.

Fessenden searched Jesse's dark eyes with his own blue ones before nodding decisively. "Very well. I appoint you sergeant in charge." He rubbed his hands together. "Send a foraging party for firewood."

"What about food and blankets? It'll be cold tonight."

"Sir."

"Sir. I'll get the hang of it directly. It's like calling a man 'Master': it seems to matter more to 'Master' than it does to you, but once you get the hang of it, it ain't so hard."

The captain smiled, "Sometimes I feel sorry for those rebel slaveholders. Was I them, I'd have freed you years ago."

Jesse nodded solemnly. "That would have been best."

"I'll see to blankets and rations. Tomorrow morning, Lieutenant Seibel and I will be here for reveille, six A.M., and morning drill. We'll try you as second sergeant." The officer's eagerness glowed in the dim room. "You'll be left guide. First sergeant is right guide, and you'll line up on him. In battle, you wheel to the left and fix your eye on some feature—fence post, tree, rock, something directly in front of you—and start for it, regular step or double-quick. If you don't march straight, the regiment will bunch together, or spread until we're too thin. When you march, that's all you concentrate on, being a living guidepost so we can march straight and hit 'em hard. You get shot, the fourth sergeant will take your place. Sometimes at drill the fourth sergeant will take your place so he'll know what to do if you get shot."

"What if I don't get shot?" Jesse asked.

"Maybe you'll get promoted to first sergeant and right guide. That's a bigger job."

"What if I don't get shot doing that?"

"Aren't any colored officers. You started high on the ladder—just one rung from the top."

"Had my heart set on bein' a general one day," Jesse said.

Fessenden orated, "One day your people will attain their full potential, and it is men like you and me who are laying the foundation stones for the sublime towers that are to be built." He searched Jesse's impassive face. "How am I to know when you people are joking?"

"Looks like we both got some figuring to do."

When the captain left, Jesse said, "I been made driver. It stinks in here. You two get these shutters open. You three go on into the woods and get us some firewood. Clement Smallwood, you're in charge of them. I expect this ground's been picked clean, so look sharp. It'll be dark before long, and if you don't find some wood we gonna be cold. Git. Rest of you I want cleanin' up this hut. I don't know whether it was white soldiers here before us or colored, but they surely were dirty."

Clement Smallwood was a rangy redhead with yellowish skin. "What about you, Jesse? What you gonna do?"

"I'm the driver. Now git."

It didn't take long to clean, sweep, and air the hut, and the men were finished well before dark. "Push them cots back from the stove," Jesse said. "We got to have a place for gatherings."

Shadrach Bolden—he was young, powerfully built, and full of complaints—said, "I wish I hadn't signed my X, Jesse. I wish tomorrow morning would see me back totin' sandbags."

"If you was totin' sandbags you'd be wishing you with us. You weren't any great shakes with sandbags; maybe you can do better totin' a gun."

"When we get our guns?"

"I'm just the driver. I ain't the master."

Clement Smallwood's detail returned after dark with a small load of broken branches. "We ain't the first wood party to glean these woods," he said.

"Won't be last neither. Don't burn that newspaper!" he warned the boy filling the stove. "Give it here. Use bark. Why you think God put bark on trees if it wasn't to light fires?"

Jesse uncrumpled the paper.

"What it say, Jesse? Bet it don't say how the 23rd Colored is gonna whip Johnny Reb."

"Yeah, read it, Jesse. Maybe we forget how hungry we are."

"Don't expect this is the first night of your life you went hungry," Jesse said. "Bring that candle stub over here. I'll read to you. White children learn to read. It ain't fittin' that a colored man can't do what a child does."

"I too slow to learn how to read," Shadrach Bolden said.

Jesse looked at him.

"Many times I been told how slow I am. I got marks on my back for bein' one slow nigger."

Jesse said, "I got marks too. Hurts every time it rains. And I ain't slow."

The *Cincinnati Inquirer* was dated two days previous. "Somethin' here about a speech Master Abraham gave. Newspaper say 'it was a perfect thing in every respect' "

"Ain't too many perfect things," Clement Smallwood said. "Young girl's titties, ham gravy, drink of white liquor after you been sweatin' all day . . ."

"Shut your mouth," Jesse said. "Master Abraham was speaking at a cemetery."

"Who die? Somebody in Master Abraham's family?"

As he read ahead, Jesse lifted his hand for quiet. "No. Says here this was a cemetery where they buried Federal soldiers killed in July."

Clement Smallwood hooted. "Them white men—they ain't slow! Wait so long as that, you ain't got so much to bury!"

Jesse said, "Says they had a battle in Pennsylvania last July and was just now dedicating the cemetery. Didn't say how long it took to bury the dead soldiers."

"If they dedicatin' today, they was buryin' yesterday," Clement Smallwood observed. "You know how that goes."

Another new soldier said, "I heard about that fight. I was still with Master then—oh, Master was powerful bothered. Master say General Lee got whipped bad."

"What them Confederates doin' in Pennsylvania?" Clement Smallwood asked.

"Gettin' whipped," Jesse said.

Someone groaned, "Jesse, you readin' that newspaper or not?"

"This's Master Abraham's sermon. He says, 'Four score and seven years ago . . .' "

"When that?"

"That's a white man's way of saying four times twenty plus seven. How much is that?"

Men counted on their fingers, and Clement Smallwood's lips moved, "Eighty-seven?"

"That's right. So what year was eighty-seven years ago?"

Nobody got that right, so Jesse said, "It was in seventeen hundred and seventy-six. '. . . our fathers bro—' "

"Slave trade still goin' on in them olden days," Clement Smallwood observed.

Jesse brushed the distraction aside. "Master Abraham say, 'In seventeen and seventy-six, our forefathers brought forth upon this continent a new nation, conceived in Liberty . . .' "

"What's a continent?"

"England is a continent," Jesse ventured. "Spain, the United States, all continents."

"What this 'conceived in liberty'?" Clement Smallwood asked. "Do it mean what I think it do?"

"It don't." Jesse was annoyed. "It doesn't mean bred. What would 'bred in liberty' mean? It means settled, like when you say, 'That mare is settled.' 'In foal.' That's what it means."

"How something be 'settled' in liberty? When a stallion settle a mare there's more liberty than you can shake a stick at." Clement Smallwood's grin asserted triumph over the forces of obscurantism.

Jesse ignored him. "Listen here, this is where it gets good. Master Abraham says, that 'nation was conceived in Liberty and dedicated to the proposition that all men are created equal.' "

"How we equal?" Clement Smallwood objected. "We paid less'n white soldiers. We don't get to be officers. Let me see that newspaper, where it says about we being equal."

"You can't read it," Jesse said.

"Maybe we was equal back in seventeen and seventy-six and we got to be unequal after," someone suggested.

The boy beside the fire didn't look up, but his voice was clear. "Back on my home plantation at Aldie, old Master liked to play preacher. Young Master ain't come home yet from hell-raisin' Saturday night, but every Sunday old Master sit us down and tell us how God intended us to be good servants and if we go against God, terrible things happen. Sometimes Master preach about being equal, how coloreds was equal to white men on account of we could get sick equal, way whites could, or old and frail just like them, and we could go to heaven or hell just like white masters could. Master prayed most of us would get to heaven so his family all be together and it'd be the same as down here—white men needed servants in heaven just like on earth."

"I think Master Abraham means equal to be exactly the same as white men," Jesse said slowly. "Exactly the same." He paused for more questions, but didn't get any. "All right then, Master Abraham says, 'Now we are engaged in a great civil war, testing whether that nation or any nation so conceived and so dedicated can long endure . . .' "

"Jesse," Shadrach Bolden asked, "what's a nation?"

"Federals and Confederates—they're nations."

"How 'bout us coloreds?" Clement Smallwood asked. "How come we not a nation?"

"I don't rightly know. Listen here: it's pretty. 'We are met on a great battlefield of that war. We are met to dedicate a portion of it as the final resting place of those who here gave their lives that that nation might live. It is altogether fitting and proper that we should do this. But in a larger sense we cannot dedicate, we cannot concentrate . . . consecrate . . . we cannot hallow this ground . . .' "

"What's 'consecrate,' Jesse?"

"Don't reckon I know."

"Maybe, Jesse, you slow like me," Shadrach Bolden cackled.

"I'll ask the captain what it means. I'll learn what it means. Listen here what Master Abraham says. He says, 'The brave men, living and dead, who struggled here, have consecrated it far above our poor power to add or detract . . .' "

"Southerns too?" Clement Smallwood burst out. "Is he talkin' about the Federals or the Confederates?"

"Can't be talkin' about Confederates," the boy from Aldie said. "Confederates fighting agin the government, not for it."

"He didn't say that," Clement Smallwood objected. "He say brave men living and dead who struggled here was the ones who consecrated it. Where they bury the Confederates, Jesse? They buried in that cemetery too? If they not buried, they be stinkin', sure."

Someone chuckled.

"Hush your foolishness," Jesse said. "He says, 'The world will little note nor long remember what we say here, but . . .' "

Clement Smallwood could abide no more. Not one word. "Now what he mean by that? He President of the United States. He think nobody pay attention to what he say?"

" '. . . but it can never forget what they did here . . .' "

"What they did was get shot. Same like they got shot at Fredericksburg. Same like they got shot at Chancellorsville. Soldiers always getting shot.

Fellows who was in this hut last week, some of them already shot. People gonna remember them? You and me get shot: think anybody gonna remember us? Folks got better things to do than worry about soldiers what got shot!" Clement Smallwood hugged himself in triumph.

Steadily, Jesse continued, " 'It is for us, the living rather, to be dedicated here to the unfinished work that they have thus far so nobly carried on. It is rather for us to be here dedicated to the great task remaining before us . . .' "

"He talkin' about more killin'," Shadrach Bolden said softly. "I do believe that what he talkin' about."

" '. . . that from these honored dead we take increased devotion to that cause for which they here gave the last full measure of devotion . . .' "

The candle guttered, and Jesse turned the paper to catch the failing light. " '. . . that we here highly resolve that these dead shall not have died in vain; that the nation shall, under God, have a new birth of freedom . . .' "

Clement Smallwood opened his mouth to ask if that meant coloreds would get the same pay as white soldiers, but Shadrach elbowed him silent.

" '. . . and that government of the people, by the people and for the people shall not perish from the earth.' "

Two new colored soldiers bowed their heads and said, "Amen."

The boy from Aldie said, "Old Master was no kind of preacher at all. Master Abraham—he a real preacher!"

The candle flame shrank, sputtered, and went out. The only light in the room was the glow from cracks between the stove plates.

Clement Smallwood asked, "Jesse, are we 'the people'?"

Jesse pressed the newspaper into folds across his knee. "Not yet," he said.

42

A CHRISTMAS DINNER

CATESBY BYRD AWOKE with his arms wrapped around Private Mitchell, a diminutive farm laborer from Charles City. The snow that had fallen in the night lay atop their rubber tarp like a goose-down coverlet, cocooning the two soldiers.

Catesby was happy, warm, and slightly drowsy, and if it hadn't been for the vermin that infested his underclothes, would have been blissful. He delayed his first scratch because it would trigger more.

He closed his eyes and prayed silently for Leona, Thomas, and Pauline: picturing each in turn. He prayed that the army be worthy of the great moral charge it bore. Catesby prayed for General Lee, and General Hill and General Early and Colonel Cobb.

"You awake, Lieutenant?"

"I never thought I could be so comfortable. Between two logs, atop an armload of straw, and I am nearly in Paradise."

"Then you ain't got no rock under your butt," Mitchell said. "If I turn back this tarp toward you, we mightn't get snow on the blankets. You set?"

With a practiced motion, the private flipped their tarp beyond the halfway point so only the rim of snow broke onto their top blanket. Catesby brushed that snow away before it had time to melt.

All about, snow-covered mounds were becoming pairs of men, standing like storks on their sleep-warmed bedding.

"Mitchell, hold your water!" Catesby fussed as Private Mitchell released his stream of yellow urine into the snow and the smell wafted around him. "Where's your courtesy, man?"

"Sorry, Lieutenant, but nature wouldn't be denied." Mitchell sighed comfortably. Standing on their snow-free rectangle, Mitchell bent to his haversack (last night's pillow), drew out shirt and pants, and donned them, hopping awkwardly to get his legs through.

Catesby and Private Mitchell had been sleeping partners since the fracas at Mine Run. Although Mitchell was, to Catesby's regret, only a nominal Christian, he didn't hog the blankets or cast them off in restless slumber and was in those respects an adequate bedmate. If he smelled of old sweat, unwashed underwear, and the tang of gunpowder, Catesby smelled no better.

"Happy Christmas," Mitchell said, drawing on his shoes, which had reposed at the foot of their makeshift shelter, dry and snug. "I've got a twist of China tea that'll serve us both."

"I have bacon," Catesby said. "If we were to roast it over the fire as our water heats we will breakfast like kings."

Extracting his Enfield from the bed that had protected weapons as well as boots, clothes, and Confederates, Catesby handed his ramrod to Mitchell, and soon water boiled while the bacon, impaled on the ramrod, turned a satisfactory shade of brown.

"I have a second piece, smaller, which I intend for Christmas dinner," Catesby said. "If we are issued rations today, we shall have a Christmas feast."

Scrupulously divided into portions the size of plugs of tobacco, the bacon was greasy and scorching hot and underdone and delicious. The tea was pungent and black.

"Last summer in Richmond I ate all manner of delicacies," Catesby said. "But I can't say I ever supped on better fare than this."

Private Mitchell brushed a stump clear of snow before he took a seat. "Even a short fellow like me could have ate a mite more," he said, stuffing his pipe. He dropped a coal onto his tobacco. "Bein' as it's Christmas and all."

"I am grateful for all God's bounties," Catesby said, because he was.

The private shot him a glance. "I wish't they'd send us into winter camp," he said. "Federals ain't comin' over the Rapidan now. It'll be spring before they hit us again."

In winter quarters they could erect log huts, huts with wattle-and-daub chimneys and doors against the wind. In some of the grander huts there might be an ax-hewn bench or two. The luxurious picture made Catesby shiver.

After Catesby rolled his blanket, he visited the sinks. Although they had been bivouacked here for only two weeks, artillery horses had peeled the bark of the smaller trees as high as their necks could stretch. The country on both banks of the Rapidan had been fought over and picked over so many times there wasn't anything left for man or beast.

The regiment's most resolute foragers (among whom Private Mitchell was notable) didn't venture out anymore.

Alerted by the morning drum rattle, Catesby's company assembled under a snowy elm. Fourteen men. Nobody had slipped off during the night. Catesby wished everyone a Happy Christmas, promised no drill today, and said prayer meeting would be held behind General Early's headquarters; an evangelist from an Alabama regiment was to speak, and all were cordially invited.

Some soldiers seemed pleased, some indifferent. One veteran set his face in disdain. Catesby thought better of that man than of his lukewarm fellows. That man would attend a prayer meeting one day, and when he did, there'd be another soul saved. It was a common occurrence: a soldier would stand at the fringe of the meeting, then, gradually, ease deeper into the throng until he was indistinguishable from the other Christians. Jesus Christ knows no distinctions of rank and the poorest private is as welcome as a major general.

When chaplains petitioned General Lee that men be excused for prayer meetings, the general acquiesced, saying, "I am nothing but a poor sinner, trusting in Christ alone for salvation." Not every officer was as righteous as Lee or the deeply mourned Stonewall Jackson. A. P. Hill barely tolerated the revival in his division, but some whispered that General Hill had contracted a venereal disease as a young man and was perhaps too well acquainted with sin.

En route to the prayer meeting, Catesby was waylaid by Private Mitchell, who said, "We're gonna have better'n fatback and hard bread tonight. Special train from Richmond. Heard it from the commissary sergeant, and he don't mistake such things. They're bringing us a real Christmas dinner. Think on it."

Of course, Catesby couldn't help thinking, and while the Alabama evangelist described the humble manger where the infant Christ Child lay, adored by wise men, shepherds, and angels, Catesby was mentally savoring ham in redeye gravy. As the preacher drew parallels between those ancient days and these—likened in darkness and sinfulness but illuminated by the Christmas star—Catesby was picturing the German tree in Samuel Gatewood's parlor, a smiling Pompey hefting the platter of Christmas goose, his children, Thomas and Pauline, on the floor with their gifts, his dear Leona's tremulous, pretty smile.

The men sang "Shall We Gather by the River." The preacher spoke of the peace Jesus gave His followers, how Jesus could wash away sufferings and sorrows, and Catesby knew it was true. No, Jesus hadn't eliminated sufferings and sorrows, He had displaced them. Mere suffering was like Catesby's skin: with him every moment of the day, but unnoticed.

His loss of infant Willie, loss of messmates and friends, Armistead's death, Garnett's death, the gallant Pelham's death, Duncan Gatewood's maiming, all the other maimings—these could not affect Catesby anymore; he rested in his new faith like a babe in arms. Those were the very words that occurred to him: like a babe in arms. With his own eyes, Catesby had seen how narrow was the gap between the ferocious caterwauling Confederate and the dying boy crying out for the comfort only a mother or wife could give.

Did Catesby believe that one day, in heaven, he would meet his poor dear Willie for the first time, that the infant would coo and burble and smile and take his father's finger in his tiny fist? If he could not believe—not completely—it was only because Catesby's faith was unfledged, too young to soar into the certainties the evangelists promised.

The evangelist preached: "The Army of Northern Virginia is a Christian army—a New Model Army. Last month, five hundred tracts were distributed in Early's brigade and a captain from General Longstreet's division told me cardplaying and cursing are become practically unknown in their camps. Almighty Providence has often blessed Confederate arms, but we must be worthy of God's blessings. With a firm belief in our Savior, Jesus Christ, let us be His soldiers. Let us pray."

Catesby lowered his head but was so comfortable he forced his eyes open so he wouldn't doze off. The knuckles of his intertwined hands were reddened, and cuts cracked his fingers; the open sore at the base of his thumb was the size of a dime. A louse crept from underneath his shirt cuff, a single louse, one of the dozens that infested him. Instead of popping the louse between his thumbnails, Catesby flicked it away. Who could fathom God's purposes?

The evangelist invited the men at the fringe to come forward, confess their sins, and be welcomed into the peace Jesus could provide.

Usually some came forward, but today they hung back in the shadows under the pines, even when the Christian soldiers beckoned and called: "Joe, you all come down here. Come in with the rest of us," and "Sergeant Peters, you're a Christian in your heart. I know you are. Think of how glad your wife will be."

But they shook their heads or smiled embarrassed smiles, so the evangelist launched into "Joy to the World" and those who'd been easing away came nearer to sing, and Catesby realized with a pang that they'd come to the prayer meeting in lieu of the Christmas services they'd always attended at home, that it wasn't faith that brought them but memories of their families attending a small country church before returning home for Christmas dinner. For many this would be their final Christmas on earth, this prayer service the last opportunity the Holy Spirit would offer them. Catesby's mind backed away, recognizing a danger point, a precipice looming. He forced his mind back to Christian peace, that peace defended by his newfound faith.

After the service, Catesby told the evangelist how much he'd enjoyed the prayer meeting.

The Alabaman's sideburns framed his face. Burnsides, the style was called. "Thank you, brother," he said. "Can I offer you a tract?"

In Gothic letters, the tract asked, "Would the Lord play at cards?"

Catesby's mind shied, picturing Jesus at Johnny Worsham's. "That was my sin before I saw the light." Catesby took the tract and pocketed it before his mind could run away with him. "Cardplaying was like a sickness to me."

The evangelist's smile stretched from sideburn to sideburn. "Jesus Christ is every sinner's salvation," he said. He cocked his head. "You will have heard about the train?"

Catesby made a small gesture. "A rumor, surely."

"No, sir. I have it on the best authority. The good citizens of Richmond are providing a Christmas dinner. During the battles of the Seven Days our army divided its rations with the poor of that beleaguered city, and Richmonders have chosen this Lord's Day to reciprocate. Truly, Cast your bread upon the waters . . .' " Catesby was startled by the evangelist's wink. "The train will arrive at noon and the foodstuffs will be distributed by regiment instanter. Are you fond of yams, Lieutenant?"

Catesby envisioned the orangy-yellow tuber as it might be after it had been buried in the coals of a soldier's fire and extracted, skin blackened but yearning to burst open of its own accord. "A generous tuber," Catesby said.

"I defer to no man in my admiration for yams. My home county is second to none in its production of fine-flavored yams, and though these Virginia vegetables cannot compare, no doubt they will be delicious." He bent to his knapsack. "I have more tracts, Lieutenant, and wonder if you would consent to deliver them to others perturbed by the cardplaying vice. Set a sinner to catch a sinner, so to speak." The Alabaman enjoyed his own joke.

Although the prospect of pressing tracts on Private Mitchell and Spotswood Bowles was unappealing, Catesby took the tracts because it was his Christian duty.

A broad muddy path angled east toward the railroad, and, accompanied by other soldiers, Catesby walked that way. Last winter, whole regiments had engaged in snowball fights, but few had appetite for skylarking this year. Although most men kept to their own thoughts, a few drunks hollered to each other. Men could always find whiskey. To the north, Clark Mountain was a snowy haystack, white and smooth.

What looked to be half of Rodes's division was waiting patiently beside the Orange & Alexandria track.

Since the Federals had torn up the track between the Rapidan and the Rappahannock and the Confederates had fired the Rapidan bridge, the Orange & Alexandria was truncated, not half the railroad it had been before the war.

Catesby, who had been at the capture of Manassas Junction—was it only a year ago?—would never forget the blinding wealth of the Federal armies. There at Manassas, ragged butternut soldiers tore open railroad cars, emptied cases, gulped champagne, gobbled canned Danish hams, and smoked Havanas. When Stonewall started them marching, dozens of fine soldiers vomited into the ditches.

Since he had become a Christian, Catesby had thought a good deal about what men needed and what men wanted and how much better off they were when they didn't have everything they wanted. Was he a poor man because he owned one shirt, one pair of trousers, suspenders his wife had knit, and only one pair of shoes? Was he poor because he walked rather than rode? Was he poor because he had no importance, even to this army, as an individual, but only as part of an aggregate? Catesby was one soul in H Company, 44th Virginia Infantry, Coles's brigade, Rodes's division, General Lee's Army of Northern Virginia. Catesby was rich because General Lee commanded that army instead of Burnside or Polk or McClellan or Hooker. General Lee was coolheaded enough that Catesby's mind could follow him, and daring as a schoolboy, which captured Catesby's heart. Robert E. Lee was a Christian commander.

Far to the south, a plume of brown smoke funneled into the clear winter air. A drunk yelled, "God damn, Elliot! It's true!"

When the train came near, five thousand men jostled for a place at trackside. Mule-drawn wagons lined up where provisions were customarily unloaded, and the men gave ground with good cheer.

From its balloon stack, the big Baldwin locomotive puffed wood sparks and cinders. Behind the wood car came two cars heaped with hay, a trio of freight cars, and finally, a single passenger car.

The soldiers swarmed over the hay cars, quickly emptying the forage onto the wagons. They welcomed returning convalescents from the passenger car with cheers and shared canteens of Christmas whiskey. Then they formed a compact circle around the three freight cars: one the color of a banknote, blue-and-black; one yellow-and-red like a child's top; the third a mundane faded brown. The blue-and-black car contained barrels of powder. The yellow-and-red car held artillery shells in wooden cases. The brown car was full of shelled corn for the horses.

"Look behind that corn, Captain," one soldier cried. "Got to be hams in there somewhere."

The last man to descend from the passenger car was an army surgeon carrying a large wicker basket.

"What you got in there?"

"Where's the rest of 'em?"

"Where's our goddamn Christmas dinner?"

The surgeon climbed onto the rear platform and raised a hand until everyone got quiet. "A Richmond lady intends this Christmas dinner for General Lee," he said. "But I know Marse Robert won't take it. He never does. He'll want his men to have it."

"I'll take it," one man yelled.

"I'll want a man from Rodes's division, and one from Colston's division," the surgeon said. "Short straw out." The soldier from Colston's division drew and retired with a curse. "Now, between Early's brigade and Coles's. Step right up here. Turkey, ham, cornbread stuffing, some kind of pie—hell, every damn thing."

Men were drinking more openly and sharing their canteens less. Regiments that had lost waited beside those still in the running. The drawing continued until the basket was won by C Company of a Mississippi regiment, and the man who'd drawn the long straw claimed his prize.

Catesby's mouth was watering. He had his fatback for dinner, and perhaps Private Mitchell could scrounge more tea. Together they would make a fine Christmas dinner. A man didn't need so much when he put his mind to it.

The man who won, a sergeant, carried the basket through his fellow soldiers like an unexploded bomb. Head down, he hurried up the muddy trail, and everyone moved aside for him and his prize, but nobody looked after him once he had passed.

43

CHARADES

IT WAS TWO *days after Christmas when the girl returned to the house on Clay Street. The small package she carried was tied with thin ribbon and a bow.*

"We've not seen much of you lately," Marguerite said.

Marguerite had a woolen shawl over her frail shoulders, and her chair was drawn so near the fire the girl wondered she didn't set the shawl alight. Today the garden room's French doors looked out on snow and the bushes were bright with icicles. "Winters were colder in those days," Marguerite said.

"Well, it's cold enough for me!" The girl shivered emphatically. "The streets are filled with slush, and it's worth a girl's life to walk the sidewalk."

"You still seeing movies?"

The girl sighed. "I don't have any idea of going to a movie these days. I believe Daddy was right. What I needed was new responsibilities. That WPA was a real dead end. I'll start a new job after the holidays. I brought this for you. Miller and Rhodes has new fragrances from Paris." When the old woman didn't take her package, the girl set it on the table. She flitted her eyes like a schoolgirl ready to flee.

"Your daddy find your new job?"

"I swear—everybody in Richmond knows Daddy. One evening—I swear I have never been so blue—I was in my room crying and he knocked on my door and came in and said, 'Sugar, what's the trouble?' So I told him how I hated my job, how sick I was of asking questions of people didn't want to give me answers."

"To get answers you must ask the right questions," Marguerite said.

Her dry cough was like a sheet of paper tearing. "Who are you working for?"

"I'll be starting as a private secretary at the Ethyl Corporation. It'll be a six-month trial period."

"Yes, child. Who will you work for?"

"Billy Dunster. Billy's young but he's already a vice-president."

"I see. Is Billy married?"

"I don't see what difference that makes."

"Lots of things you don't see. 'Never underestimate the importance of propinquity'—that was in Godey's Lady's Book. I read that in Abigail Gatewood's bedroom. It's strange what a person remembers and forgets. You'll need to undo that bow. Too much arthritis in my fingers. Uncap it as well, if you would."

The girl removed the wrappings, then the tiny glass stopper, and cautiously dabbed fragrance on the old woman's wrist.

"Reminds me of the trees they had in Nassau. Big reddish-pink flowers. I wonder if they have any of those trees in France. I never did get to France. Silas, oh, he wanted to take me, but I didn't want to go. 'This is my country,' I told him, 'Same as yours.' "

"Running the blockade must have been difficult."

"Do you think the games boys play aren't difficult? They're still games."

"It's warm in here," the girl said, unbuttoning her jacket.

"Not too warm for me," Marguerite said. "My blood isn't as lively as it was. What ever happened to that boy you were seeing? That 'dollar-a-year' man?"

"Phil? I believe Phil is engaged. I wish him every happiness, of course."

"Of course. Do they pay this Dunster boy a dollar a year?"

"I believe Mr. Dunster draws a regular salary."

Marguerite nodded, "That's good. You'll want money and plenty of it to raise a family. Why don't you sit down? Kizzy'll fetch you a cup of tea. Tea was dear in those days. By January of '64 tea was twenty dollars a pound."

The girl sat. "Just one cup," she said. "I'm expected to meet Daddy later. The Dabneys . . ."

"Virginius? I haven't seen him since he was a boy. Awful boy. Nose ran constantly. This Dunster fellow going to be there?"

"I believe so."

"Your daddy sure favors 'propinquity.' "

The girl wavered between anger and laughter until a giggle slipped past her guard. "Well," she admitted, "Daddy is worried about me."

"You tell him about me? How I've been with three men and the one time I married was when I jumped the broomstick? How I've raised up my family?"

The girl looked out the window. "I tell Daddy very little about you these days. Daddy doesn't approve."

Marguerite snorted. "He wouldn't. I knew him when he was a young-ster, too. At our garden parties he wouldn't come out from behind his mother's skirt. Your mother was a handsome, well-spoken girl."

"I was just a baby. I try, but I can't remember her."

"The influenza was a terrible scourge."

Kizzy brought tea, and the girl took off her jacket. "Did you ever see Duncan Gatewood again?" she asked.

The old woman smiled. "Now you're asking the right questions."

RICHMOND, VIRGINIA
JANUARY 8, 1864

After midnight, snow began falling, and the clatter of passing carriages and horses' thudding hooves were gradually muffled until, when the mail coach passed—this at five o'clock in the morning—it slipped silent as a wraith through a snow-muted universe. Snow fell on St. Peter's and St. Paul's, on the Capitol, the Confederate Treasury, Mr. Davis's mansion, and the Lee family's rented house, where the women slept easier tonight because they had three men in the army, father, son, and nephew, and this snowfall meant there'd be no fighting along the Rapidan.

A little before seven, Cousin Molly's houseman tiptoed into Duncan's room and laid a fire atop last night's ashes. The kindling caught with a soft whoosh, and the man set a fire screen across the hearth to prevent sparks from popping onto the rug.

Beneath two comforters, Duncan closed his eyes as the houseman tiptoed from the room. The air was cold, the tip of his nose was cold, and Duncan wouldn't venture out until the room warmed. He wriggled his toes. Through the gauzy curtains, the light was a blunt white glare.

As a young man he'd wakened every morning like this. He'd thought it ordained that Pompey would come in and lay a fire while, in the kitchen house, Franky would be frying ham and baking the cornbread that would already be on the table when the boy Duncan was ready to eat.

Duncan decided that luxury was contrast and was so pleased with this reflection he rolled out of bed whistling. He had mastered dressing and could now get his clothes on as quickly with one arm as he ever had with two, except that he never wore shoes with laces or neckwear that needed to be tied.

The hall stairway was unheated, and he clattered downstairs to the dining room, where a grand fire roared behind the grate and the oatmeal pot stood on a trivet on the dark Honduran mahogany table, which, with its leaves inserted, could seat sixteen.

"A good morning to you, Cousin Molly." Duncan lifted the pot lid. "Oatmeal and maple syrup: couldn't be finer!"

Cousin Molly said, "Burnt-bread coffee isn't so awful once a person gets used to it."

"There's many a morning lately I would have been grateful for it."

In the unkind winter light pouring into the room, Cousin Molly's face looked as if the portrait of a tired and wrinkled woman had been painted over the portrait of the charmer she used to be. Cousin Molly was knitting socks of yarn unraveled from a woolen vest her father had worn to the Continental Congress.

"The attics and trunks of Richmond are emptying," Duncan observed.

"Yes, all our finery is refurbished for the army. It is no great loss. Those clothes of an earlier generation were used only for children's play and charades. Heaven knows why we kept them. Duncan, I do believe we had grown too rich, too complacent; this war is pruning us."

Duncan bent to his breakfast.

"Will you visit the War Office this morning?" Molly asked.

"Yes, but it'll be a waste of time."

"Oh, dear." Cousin Molly dipped her spoon in the syrup and tasted it. "We are invited to Senator Semmes's home for charades and a light supper tonight. If her duties permit, Sallie might accompany us."

"Sallie's too conscientious. Cousin, you will have noticed my deep feelings for her. I hate to see her so miserable."

"We have no finer matron. I had hoped Sallie would do good service, and she has exceeded my expectations, but her methods are worrisome. Somehow, Sallie persuades the wounded man that he does not suffer alone, that he and she have combined strengths and when his would fail, hers will suffice. She hurls herself into the struggle as if she could save her patients by main force. She has successes, but whenever her patient dies, Sallie is shaken to the roots."

Duncan, who was one of those Sallie had saved, made no reply.

An hour later, Molly's houseman drove Duncan to the War Office, where events unfolded much as he had predicted. For three hours, he waited in the musty anteroom with other supplicants. At first they waited in respectable silence, but before long they began making their cases— judiciously—to one other. Well-dressed gentlemen, seeking preferment, were pleased to allude to family connections and previous services performed for state and national governments. They were indeed worthy, their fellows agreed. The planters who'd come to beg the government to leave off tearing up railroad track in their county (because how could their goods get to market without a railroad?) found a sympathetic ear—wasn't the alleged military shortage of rails the grossest exaggeration? A Savannah merchant required merely a quiet office where his son could serve out the war. A delicate boy, intelligent but high-strung; completely unsuited for rough service in the field. This salon concurred: the boy deserved special consideration.

"And you, Captain? What do you seek?"

"Horse fodder," Duncan said.

Late in the day, Duncan was summoned. Secretary of War Seddon was pale-skinned, puckered, and Presbyterian. The secretary examined papers on his desk as Duncan briskly explained that the army had enough fodder for three days and enough corn for two, and that the snow could not improve matters. "Without sound horses we can't move the guns when the Federals make their next attempt upon us. Aware of this, the Federals take satisfaction in targeting horses, ignoring even infantry to do so. General Stuart's division is removed to Danville because forage is still obtainable there, and General Lee may detach Wade Hampton's cavalry for the same reason, which will leave the army without its eyes and ears."

The written reports, from Generals Hampton and Mahone, which Duncan laid on the secretary's desk confirmed his verbal report. The secretary gave them a cursory glance, signed papers he handed to his assistant, and said, "There is to be a train from Georgia tomorrow. The army's necessities will be forwarded promptly. Thank you, Captain. Next."

Duncan walked back along Main Street, past Richmond's finer homes. In the street, a single lane had been cleared of snow and traffic jingled by. It began to snow again, blowing softly off the river, fat flakes that melted on Duncan's forehead, and he was happy as a child, all duties completed, anticipating Cousin Molly's agreeable hearthside.

Duncan felt mild pleasurable guilt. Lee's army was in winter quarters near Culpepper, where they'd be warm, odorous, hungry, and lousy. There'd be no drill, few patrols, plenty of prayer meetings outdoors or in rude pole chapels the men had built.

General Mahone, Duncan's new superior, had instructed him to try the War Office first, before traveling to North Carolina. Duncan carried letters from Hampton and Mahone, whose planter friends might respond to a personal appeal sooner than an official one.

Duncan walked on, daydreaming about foals dancing in the snow.

When Duncan looked about him, the houses were unfamiliar and smaller than those in Cousin Molly's neighborhood. When he inquired of a colored man shoveling snow, the man pointed back the way he'd come.

Cousin Molly's houseman greeted him at the door. "Miss Semple say you got to hurry, sir. We got to collect Miss Sallie."

Hurriedly, Duncan washed his face, combed his hair, and brushed his uniform jacket. His boots were hopeless, blacking absent, leather too soaked to apply more. Duncan wore his dress sword. He drew on his glove with his teeth. He set his slouch hat at a rakish angle.

He waited in the parlor thirty minutes before Cousin Molly swept downstairs in a dark velvet gown fastened by a belt of gold rope.

"Ravishing." Duncan bowed and kissed her hand.

Cousin Molly said, "After our drapes are exhausted, God help Confederate society."

Cousin Molly's houseman proceeded them to the barouche. It was a moment's work to get Cousin Molly's hoops arranged satisfactorily.

Richmond's beleaguered gasworks had extinguished streetlamps six months ago. Most homes were lit by candles or oil lamps; only a few could afford illuminating gas.

House lights grew few and farther apart, and the carriage trotted through swirling white silence.

"The Davises will attend this evening," Cousin Molly said. "And General Stuart is said to be in the city. Mrs. Stannard, of course. Senator Chestnut and his wife, Mary. The Semmeses have promised chickens from their plantation and somehow obtained several barrels of oysters. I don't remember the last time I ate an oyster! The Omohundrus: he owns a blockade runner. Apparently he is contributing champagne."

"Omohundru?"

"Yes. His wife is a Bahamian—quite beautiful, I am told. Mr. Omohundru was not known here before the war but presently advises the government on matters affecting the blockade."

"The Omohundru I knew was a slave speculator."

"Omohundru is a Piedmont name, but I don't know the family,"

They passed through Camp Winder's gate and soon reached their customary destination. The air was redolent with woodsmoke.

Duncan jumped down. "I'll fetch her, cousin."

In the quiet ward, three patients lay in beds nearest the stove while a convalescent maneuvered a broom. "Evenin', Captain. Miss Sallie's in her room."

Hands folded in her lap, Sallie sat on the end of her cot. "I am not going with you, Duncan. I'm sure you will have a splendid time. The gay gossip and fine manners, dancing, charades . . ."

"It is well to find laughter where one can, Sallie."

"No doubt. Oh, I have no doubt." She had tears in her eyes.

"What's wrong, dear child?"

"I cannot get the bloodstains out of my dress." A red-brown splotch darkened the cloth she flattened across her knee.

"Sallie, there will be officers tonight at the gala whose uniforms are stained with the same material. It is an honorable blemish."

"It is Malcolm Cutler's—he vomited blood. He tried so hard not to vomit his face contorted, but he sat bolt upright and spewed and his blood splattered until he was emptied. I had sat with him for three nights. His mother and sister still live. Do the trains still run to Alabama?"

"I believe so."

"Then I must telegraph his family. Malcolm wished to be sent home. Many families cannot afford to bring their sons home, so we bury them. Imagine, Duncan, what a sight it will be when the angels sound the last trumpet and the graves open at Hollywood Cemetery: an entire Confederate army, complete in every rank, will rise up ready, once again to confront our oppressor.

"Malcolm Cutler survived Chancellorsville and Gettysburg without a scratch. But a Federal shell exploded and a piece of brass no larger than a thumbnail penetrated his chest. I have seen it! Surgeon Lane extracted the fragment! What ingenious manufactures we devise! It took seventeen years to produce Malcolm Cutler and he is removed by one ingenious manufacture."

"Sallie, you've done everything you could."

For the first time she looked directly into his eyes. "Do you believe so? Perhaps if I'd propped him with bolsters or rolled him onto his side, the blood would not have pooled inside. Had I washed him with witch hazel perhaps I would have soothed him and quelled the dreadful urge to vomit his life away.

"Only Malcolm Cutler has done everything he could. Do go on without me, Duncan. I am too morose. I could not look upon our generals without revulsion, without berating them for prolonging this conflict. I could not speak to the senators' wives without inquiring why they do not beg their husbands to quit this grisly business. I am not fit for society tonight."

Duncan lifted her unresisting hand to his lips and kissed it. "Please promise me you will rest. Your boys are resting peacefully, and you must too." He backed out the door wearing the smile men wear when leaving somewhere they perhaps should have stayed.

Cousin Molly's houseman was feeding their horse a nosebag of ambulance oats. Though Cousin Molly never dipped into the hospital provender for herself, she invariably fed her horse, explaining, as she explained now, "He is an old and faithful beast. I cannot see him starve to death."

Duncan said, "One of Sallie's boys died."

"It would be that Cutler lad. Oh, dear. He was such a fine young man, and we were hopeful. It was his lung, you know. After a battle when we are ensanguined for days we rarely mourn those we cannot save; but how we love the solitary boys who die between battles. Poor, dear Sallie." She paused to clear her throat. "Duncan, I know you well enough for an impertinent question: What are your intentions?"

"I suppose we're courting."

"Sallie is a fortunate woman. Gossip has provided her with a respectable past: widow of a gallant soldier killed at Fredericksburg. Only Governor Letcher and I know the truth, and I doubt the governor remembers the girl he pardoned so many months ago. Cousin, this war has not aged you so much as you may think. I worry you have an inconstant heart—one that flits from flower to flower."

"I've known Sallie all my life. I knew Sallie when she was a schoolgirl, and it does not astonish me that the grown woman commits herself to our wounded . . ."

She touched his arm. "Don't huff and puff, Duncan. I ask you only to remember that a lady, if she is exquisitely lucky, may survive one scandal. She can scarcely hope to survive two."

After a silence, Duncan asked, "Is that the Semmeses' mansion? They must have corralled the gasworks' entire production tonight: they are positively ablaze. I've not seen so many carriages since those Sundays before the war when families drove to the Institute to admire us cadet sons. Come, Cousin Molly, let us forget war and grimness. Let us hope. Let us hope all officers are gallant and all ladies beautiful. Let us hope the charades are amusing. Let's hope for President Davis—that he isn't smitten by one of his headaches. And, cousin, let's hope the oysters are fresh!"

The entry hall, where Mrs. Semmes greeted them, was floored with the black and white tile that so marvelously imitated marble, and Mrs. Semmes was so delighted to see them, so delighted, and her man Morgan would take their wraps, and "Molly, a new gown?"

"Next time you pass my home, do not fail to observe my second-story windows. They have rather a naked look."

Mrs. Semmes trilled laughter. Her own gown had come from Paris before the war. "Molly, we have more generals here tonight than Lee has in his army. General Preston and our Prussian, Von Borke, though it's no good trying to make conversation with him—his throat wound is not healed. Varina Davis and her daughter are present. Her daughter is to be in the final tableau tonight, and President Davis is due to arrive any moment. J.E.B. Stuart, our most gallant cavalier, is in the house, but I can't tell you more about him until later. His performance is to be our *pièce de résistance*."

The formal parlor was a rectangular room made larger by blue-gray wallpaper and the embossed plaster oval in the ceiling. Gaslights glittered from the sconces and reflected in the pier mirrors and chandeliers, whose crystal teardrops sparkled like wit. The triple-sash street windows were outlined in drapery of blue damask drawn back and tied. In the fireplace notable oak logs burned merrily. A wide arch introduced guests into the family parlor, where the table was arrayed with champagne flutes. The unfashionable long coats the servants wore might have belonged to the Semmeses' Revolutionary War forebears.

Men, mostly bearded, mostly in uniform, gossiped. Lighting cigars, they stepped outdoors onto the swept terrace, which overlooked a snowy garden.

"Good to see you, Gatewood. Good to see you." The colonel was with Hampton's cavalry. "Grand affair this, yes? Mrs. Semmes, she asks Omohundru if he couldn't bring in a few cases of champagne for her, and that gentleman says he'd see what he could do." The colonel elbowed Duncan. "Twelve cases of Monopole, and he didn't charge her a cent. This bubbly is a hundred a bottle when you can find it. Damned if I don't admire a man who knows how to make a gesture!"

"Oh, Duncan," Cousin Molly called, "come over here and greet Mrs. Davis."

"Good to see you again, Captain. Miss Semple says you come from our western highlands."

"Yes, ma'am. May I fetch you some champagne?"

"No thank you, Captain. I have promised myself only a single glass before the charades. Do you think those yankees love theatricals as we do? I cannot believe so. They are such a practical people." She waved at someone past Duncan's shoulder: "General Preston! How did you leave things in Kentucky . . ."

Duncan made his bow and withdrew. He was standing in the arch between the parlors when Midge—his Midge—arrived on a slender gentleman's arm. His Midge had never owned fine clothes. His Midge was only beautiful out of her clothes. This Midge's gown was panels of russet and tan silk, the bodice cut *à la mode*. His Midge knotted her hair. This Midge's hair was coiled in dark braids, and she moved with the easy confidence of a lady welcome wherever she might go.

Duncan felt sick. The room wobbled at the edges. When he backed away he bumped an older officer, excused himself, jostled the buffet table, poured himself a glass of water, a second.

"You all right, Master? There's chairs against the wall, if you got to sit down."

Pure cowardice assailed Duncan; his ears burned and he panted like a dog in July. Couldn't he slip out into the garden, sneak around the side of the house? Couldn't he board his cousin's carriage and be swiftly taken away from here? Oh, God, how he had loved her! Midge! Here! How? The water Duncan swallowed was painful as swallowing bones.

"Master, you sit in this chair right here. You gonna fall."

Duncan told himself he was not losing his senses. The runaway racing of his heart would slow. This urge to vanish in the cloak of night was a temptation all men felt, surely.

Midge was passing for white—here, in the battered heart of the Confederacy. Was she mad?

When Duncan opened his eyes, the room had stopped spinning. He thanked the servant, accepted champagne, and returned to the grand parlor, its thick noise and gaiety.

Midge was talking with two ladies dressed as fashionably as herself.

Duncan bowed. "Ladies, Captain Duncan Gatewood at your service. May I fetch you some champagne?"

"Monsieur, you are too kind. But my husband is presently performing that pleasant duty. I am Madame de Jarnette, and this is Lady Parker of the British consulate." Madame stood on tiptoes to wave at a friend. "How gay it is here! I so prefer Richmond to the dismal cities of the North. I am a friend of your Confederacy, and my husband urges recognition on our government at every chance. And this dear lady is Mrs. Omohundru. We were remarking how Nassau has changed since war began."

Midge's smile was calm.

"Mrs. Omohundru, you strongly resemble a woman I used to know near my home, Stratford Plantation."

"Named to honor our playwright?" Lady Parker inquired.

"No, ma'am. I believe my great-grandfather came from near that town."

Midge wore the amiable, slightly remote expression of a lady meeting an ordinary and completely forgettable stranger, and Duncan began to think he had been terribly, stupidly mistaken.

"I am pleased to make your acquaintance, Captain. You have been wounded in the struggle for independence?" She spoke with a faint unfamiliar lilt but with no trace of slave dialect.

"May I serve you, madam?"

"My lady, madame, I've enjoyed our talk. Perhaps we will meet in Nassau one day."

Smiling like strangers, the pair murmured through the crowd and out the terrace doors. En route, Midge directed a servant to fetch her wrap. "It is russet wool with a silver brocade border. Do not dally."

Excepting them, the terrace was empty. "You have learned to direct servants," Duncan said, stupidly.

"It is no wonderful skill."

"There are those who think it an art," Duncan began, stopped himself, said, "You . . . Midge . . ." She wore the tender tentative smile he knew so well, and he almost embraced her.

"I am Marguerite now. Mrs. Silas Omohundru."

"He? Is he . . ."

"At one time Silas speculated in slaves. He is a rich man. One of the richest men in the Confederacy."

"But, Midge . . ."

"I loved you so much. More than my life. I loved you as only a young girl can love. You enjoyed the best of me, Master Duncan Gatewood."

"Oh Christ!" Duncan looked out into the night, where snow was beginning to fall.

The servant brought her wrap. "Here you is, Missus. They'd took all the ladies coats upstairs into Mistress Semmes's bedroom and I looked through the heap and I feared you'd be out here freezin' to death. Why'd you go trustin' an old woolly head like me?" The man wrapped Midge in her fine cloak. "Anything else I can fetch you? They gonna start the play-actin' pretty quick."

"What is your name?" Midge inquired quietly.

"Me? I'ze Samson." Big grin.

Midge gave him a coin. "This, Samson, is for your taking trouble."

Bowing, the old servant withdrew.

"They have destroyed you," she said. "At first I did not know who you were."

"I am altered so much?"

She looked at him wonderingly. "Duncan, you were so fancy."

"Midge . . . I . . ."

"I am Marguerite Omohundru, Duncan. I have been in places that were not Stratford."

"I didn't know Father meant to sell you. How in God's name could I have prevented it?"

"It is no small advantage to southern gentlemen that they can sell their embarrassments. That circumstance has preserved many a fine family's honor." A rectangle of light streamed from the house to stop at Duncan's feet. Beyond, all was blackness. Very quietly Midge said, "Will you keep my secret?"

"Yes."

"You give the matter no great thought," she said falsely, gaily. She took a breath and shuddered. "I am truly sorry about your injuries." She inspected him for the longest moment. "My dear Duncan. My poor lost love." With her forefinger she touched the lobe of his ear.

How could anything so gentle burn so hot? In a choked voice he asked, "The child?"

"Jacob is my heart's delight. There never has been a cleverer boy."

"I . . . I never thought to see you again."

"I've always expected to meet someone who knew. I've had dreams—vivid dreams—of being denounced in some public place: a railroad station, the Exchange Hotel . . ."

"Surely it's a fearful risk."

"Wilmington is not Richmond. Even so, I seldom go out in society. I am deemed unusually shy."

"I wish . . ."

"Yes, you were so awfully good at wishes. . . ." She paused. "I suppose I was no better. Duncan, dear, I pictured us married! Me: the mistress of Stratford! Ignorant pickaninny playing the lady. Imagine!"

"And now you are a lady."

"My Jacob will be a gentleman. On my life I swear he will! Did you know one of Napoleon's marshals was a colored man? Did you know we had kings in Africa? Mighty kings!"

There were very many things Duncan should have said, but none reached his tongue. "I will keep your secret," he repeated.

And she took him in her arms and kissed him, and she said, "Silas will be anxious about me. Darling love Duncan, goodbye," and was gone.

Snow whitened Duncan Gatewood's hair.

"You still here, sir?" It was the servant, Samson. "Miss Molly, she saving a seat for you. They about to start the charades. She say you best not dawdle."

The arch to the family parlor served as proscenium for a makeshift theater. Rustlings could be heard behind the curtain, and occasionally the cloth indented or bulged. President and Varina Davis sat up front in Mrs. Semmes's best armchairs. Other guests took wooden chairs. The younger children were seated on the floor.

At the front door, Marguerite and her escort were making their excuses, leaving.

In a costume of breathtaking shabbiness, Mrs. Semmes stepped through the curtain. Duncan vaguely heard her announce that this evening's gaiety was dedicated to the unconquerable Confederate people. Mrs. Semmes begged that her guests not guess aloud the syllables of the charades as they were presented but wait until the word was presented entire. She thanked them all for coming out on such a wintery evening. On a narrow wooden chair beside Cousin Molly, Duncan wished he hadn't.

When the curtain was drawn, people acted a charade. To Duncan they were like swimmers underwater. Why had his life been destroyed?

" 'Trial,' " Cousin Molly whispered triumphantly. "They are portraying a trial. Doesn't Cooper DeLeon make a splendid criminal?"

The first syllable of the charade had been "in," the second "dust,"—the word must be "industrial." Mrs. Semmes, portraying the desperate criminal's wife, stepped out of character to glare at Cousin Molly and put her finger to her lips.

"Yes," Duncan licked his lips, " 'Trial.' "

The curtain drew back to reveal young ladies lounging about in filmy clothing few would have guessed they possessed let alone dared to wear. They lounged with surprising aptitude, guarded by fierce-looking gentlemen in turbans. "Harem," Cousin Molly opined.

Duncan wondered if pashas had as much trouble with Christian women as Virginians did with colored ones.

On the makeshift stage, children pretended to torment an old woman. " 'Scarum.' " The audience seemed dissatisfied by this "harum-scarum" charade but applauded the children, who took bow after bow.

Cousin Molly craned back in her seat to gossip with Hetty Cary. In Virginia, everybody knew everything about everybody. That's why honor was so precious: because gone, everyone knew it was gone. Duncan wished he were somewhere else.

The curtain drew back on the final charade, a sick man on his cot while an apothecary mixed nostrums, pestling until, with a flourish, he produced a pill the size of a horse bolus. He brandished this triumphantly as his patient mimed fear.

" 'Pill.' "

The second scene depicted dismal poverty, bare cupboards, a shabbily dressed man and wife. Their child was turned away from the table with an empty bowl.

Cousin Molly guessed, " 'Poor'? 'Starved'?"

Mrs. Semmes poked her head around the curtain to hush Cousin Molly again.

If this bitter scene did not prophesy the Confederate future it certainly made everyone uneasy. The word "grim" rippled through the audience.

Duncan wondered if Midge would have lain with him if he hadn't been the white young master. Innocent love. Was there anything more innocent than childish yearnings?

Duncan was a stranger inside his own body and felt acutely his missing arm, his broken gait, his whiskered ruined face. When he moved his jaw, his left cheek drew tighter than his right. He scratched his face, savagely.

In the next scene, Mrs. Semmes was transformed into a crone, her walking stick almost too heavy for her. She kept one hand in the small of her back, attempted to straighten, relapsed with a groan.

" 'Age,' " Cousin Molly guessed, briskly.

"They ought to have scenes to amuse us," an officer behind them grumbled. "Something to make us laugh under the ribs of death, because, by God, that's where we are." Despite the audience's regard for their hostess, applause was perfunctory.

It only remained to act out the complete word "pilgrimage," and commotion behind the curtain suggested that was the thespians' intent. The audience was restless, primed for oysters and more of Mr. Omohundru's champagne.

Duncan was no longer the boy he had been. He could hardly remember what it felt like to embrace Midge, to enclose her in his two arms. He was no longer the "young master," and "Captain Gatewood" was more a stranger to him than old friend. Where would Duncan's pilgrimage end?

The shrine revealed was simple and magnificent: a pine chest covered with a cloth of fine Belgian linen, ornate silver candlesticks burning bright. The crucifix was hand-carved black walnut.

Dressed in a gray nun's habit, a pilgrim crossed herself and knelt behind the altar. A friar came into kneel beside her. Even without her golden diadem Mrs. Ould would have been unmistakably a queen. Regally, she bowed her head. Her king dropped to one knee beside the friar.

As a boy, Duncan had possessed grace and thought he would always have it. From here on, as a man, as Captain Gatewood, he would want plainer, sturdier virtues.

Burton Harrison, President Davis's secretary, appeared as a red Indian chief in beaded quilled vest, leather breechclout, and moccasins and took his place beside the queen, arms crossed, expressionless.

The last pilgrim was General J.E.B. Stuart, and when the audience saw who he was, they went still. The Confederacy's beau ideal, its perfect cavalier—every line in his face was a mark laughter leaves. In full-dress Confederate uniform, high-booted, gray cape lined with shimmering red silk, Stuart removed his plumed hat. The only sound was a gentle scrape when he drew his saber and laid it tenderly on the altar of his crucified Savior.

For the first time in many months, Duncan felt light—as if he were riding Gypsy again, breathless into the wind. Come what may, he thought. Come what may.

PART FOUR

Honor

"I would die, yes I would die willingly because
I love my country. But if this war
is ever over, I'll be damned if I ever
love another country."

—*Color Sergeant D. G. Robinson,*
37th North Carolina

44

A NICKEL-PLATED WATCH

"SO," SETH DANZINGER asked, "what did you think of us? Aren't our old German hymns so sad and beautiful?"

The Brethrens' a cappella singing had been solemn and agreeable, and Alexander said so.

The horse was young and high-spirited, and with his family in the carriage, Seth kept a tight rein. The stars were very many, and a faint penumbra along the Blue Ridge limned the spot where the moon would rise.

It was the first time Alexander had been invited to their prayer service. Plainly dressed men sat on one side of the aisle, women on the other. Although the preacher ("bishop," Seth called him) must have noticed a new face in his congregation of thirty, he did not remark on it, nor did he translate any of the service into English. Since Alexander couldn't understand the words, he was free to enjoy the cadences. The preacher argued sweetly, thundered righteously, and when he smacked the podium several times with his fist, Alexander knew he was denouncing his congregation's most grievous sins.

"What was the sermon about?" Alexander now asked.

"Hoop skirts," Seth answered.

Since the two were side by side on the driver's box, Seth sensed Alexander's puzzlement. "Hoop skirts may seem a slight matter to you," Seth continued seriously. "Do you think shunning wordly vanity is easy? Why, if it were, we would shun it easily. Little things it is that bring us into sin. Do we dress better than our neighbor? Do we take too much pride in our buggies, perhaps install brass lamps and polish them? Do we begin to value man's goods more than God's promises? Are we guided by the long experience of our people, or do we let 'the learned professors' sway us from our course? Guarding against hoop skirts, Alexander, prevents worse sins. Do you listen, Katrina?"

Like all Brethren children, in her sixteenth year Katrina Danzinger received special instruction in her faith. Once a week Alexander drove her to the bishop's home (accompanied by Grandmother Danzinger as chaperon). Alexander thought Katrina's neat white cap was the most delicate thing in the world. Shy at first, the girl soon began discussing her hopes and dreams, the chest she had filled with linens she would bring to her new home when she married, the sampler she was stitching to demonstrate her housewifely skills. Because Alexander had led—by Katrina's standards—such an exotic life, Katrina sometimes tested the tenets of her faith against him. Now she leaned forward. "Alexander, do you think it is better to baptize infants or wait until a person is grown and can herself decide?"

"Oh, I don't know."

"But you must have an opinion, Alexander. You should not be afraid to voice it. On my next birthday, I must decide whether to remain in my church or choose another church or, perhaps . . ." She paused. ". . . cease to be a Christian," she added all in a rush.

"Uncle was a Congregationalist when I was young, though he became a Unitarian later."

"And what do Unitarians believe?" the young girl asked eagerly.

Alexander shook his head. "I was more interested in the ancient peoples. Did you know the Romans brought water from the Sabine Hills on aqueducts forty-four miles long?"

The girl said, "Alexander, had they no wells?"

"Rome was a big city. When you get so many people in one place, you must bring in water from outside. You must have sewers too."

"Then it is not healthy!" Katrina sat back in her seat triumphantly, having routed not only Unitarianism and infant baptism but the vices of ancient cities as well.

Alexander's uncle was neither a popular nor a successful preacher, but somewhere he had acquired an expensive edition of Piranesi's engravings of classical Rome, and the boy Alexander sat with that book for hours—its gloomy, powerful depictions of ruined grandeur, the Via Appia, the Colosseum, the aqueducts. How Alexander had envied those ancient people! What he did not understand about them, he could dream, and his dreams were every bit as satisfactory as knowledge might have been.

"No," he admitted, "Rome was not salubrious. . . ." But he scarcely heard his own words. He was wondering if ancient Rome was now as dead to him as it was to this young girl. The Brethren did not encourage converts, but if Alexander learned German and followed their rules—and the rules were not hard to understand—he might dwell with them quietly and safely.

"Such a beautiful night God has given us," Gretchen Danzinger sighed. "God has given us such a wonderful world. Why do men wish to spoil it?"

Grandmother Danzinger said something sharp in German—sarcastic, Alexander thought.

"What do you hope to accomplish?" he asked Seth.

"Oh," the young man laughed. "I wish to be *Vorsinger* at our meeting—to be trusted to keep the melody of a holy humn: 'Herr Gott! dich will ich loben.' That hymn, Alexander, a martyr wrote it in prison the night before he was burned alive." Translating as he went, in his young voice, Seth sang, "In flesh I am distrusting, it is too frail I see, In Thy word I am trusting . . ."

"Dich will ich loben," the grandmother said with satisfaction.

"We have always been persecuted for our beliefs. We do not attempt to impose our ways on the worldly people. We do not cheat them or treat them with contempt. But to them we are like the big trout in the creek— you may not wish to eat that trout, you may enjoy watching the trout, how it turns and flashes in the sun, you may even admire it, but there will always be one man who cannot rest until he kills it. And so"—Seth shrugged—"many of our hymns are about martyrs, and this one is perhaps the loveliest. But so hard to sing. If I can be *Vorsinger,* I suppose it will be an accomplishment. Is that what you mean?"

"Not quite the same, no," Alexander answered. "I mean doing something so important others would respect it, perhaps even admire you. . . ."

"All this getting admired and who is admired and who is not. What foolishness," Gretchen Danzinger snorted.

"Riders ahead," Willem noted.

"Keep driving," Gretchen Danzinger advised. "When we come abreast, I will sing out a hello."

"Mama . . ." little Lisle said.

"Hush."

In the moonlight the riders formed a clot on the pale ribbon of road.

"Slave patrollers?" Alexander said.

As the buggy closed, the riders parted, a dark gauntlet on either side. The buggy's side lamps slid over their unflinching faces.

"Beautiful evening," Gretchen Danzinger called out. "It is a beautiful evening in God's Kingdom."

The riders were roughly dressed, but without the patrollers' bullwhips. They had pistol holsters on their saddles and carbines slung across their backs or resting on their pommels.

One fat rider blocked their passage, and another man leaned to grab their horse's bridle.

The fat rider wore a tall silk hat tugged low over his brows. His eyes shone in the gleam of the side lights. "Stump's Partisan Rangers," he announced. "We're waitin' for the Danzingers."

In a breathless voice, Gretchen Danzinger said, "That will be us, sir."

His saddle creaked as he readjusted himself. "In particular, Seth Danzinger."

"I am Seth Danzinger," the young man replied.

"Then we was told right." The man hitched a leg over his saddle horn. "How come you don't do your prayin' on Sunday like Christians?"

"We have Sunday services," Gretchen Danzinger replied. "In midweek, we often meet for a prayer service. Don't you think these times require prayer?"

The fat man turned to the horse holder. "How about that, Baxter? You think prayer might help?"

The man snorted.

A very dirty man with a turkey feather in his hat said, "I never once knew no Federal cavalry run off with prayin'."

"Then, sir," Gretchen Danzinger retorted, "perhaps you haven't prayed as frequently as you ought. Or as humbly."

The fat man whooped. "She got you there, Ollie! By God, didn't she! If there's one thing in this life you ain't overdone it's prayin'. Next time those bluebellies get after us, you give prayin' a try. Can't do worse than your shootin'."

Ollie slapped his dusty hat against his knee and reset it. "Cap'n Stump, I'd be obliged to know which army they're prayin' for."

"Sir, if you'll let us pass. There are ladies in our buggy, and this night air is chill."

The fat man ignored Alexander. "You got something there, Ollie, surely you do. If they're prayin' for Jeff Davis and the success of Confederate arms, that's one thing. But suppose they were prayin' for Colonel Dahlgren . . ."

Careful with his words, Seth said, "We are not acquainted with Colonel Dahlgren. Is he Confederate?"

"Listen to him, Cap'n," the horseholder snorted. "He ain't acquainted with Dahlgren!"

Ollie whinnied his laugh.

"You haven't heard how the bluebellies tried to assassinate President

Davis? Colonel Dahlgren brought five hundred troopers to the outskirts of Richmond, and they was to slip in, murder Jeff Davis, and slip out again."

Seth said, "We do not read newspapers."

"Well, then how in the hell are you gonna get the news? Our brave boys put paid to Colonel Dahlgren. You don't read newspapers, how you learn about that?"

"If it is important," Seth said, "someone will tell us."

"And this ain't important? Bluebellies tryin' to assassinate Jeff Davis ain't important?"

Gretchen Danzinger held up her thick black book. "This is all the news we need."

"Well, Colonel Dahlgren wasn't in that Bible, but Judas Iscariot surely was. How you think them bluebellies gonna get near President Davis if Judas Iscariots ain't helping them do it?"

Seth looked straight ahead.

"Traitors," Captain Stump went on. "Oh, we Confederates, we have got vipers in our bosom. Tolerate them?" He chortled knowingly. "We embrace them. Those Federals, they know better. Some newspaper criticizes Tyrant Lincoln? They shut it down. Some traitor starts speaking against the government? Secretary Stanton writes his name, and snap!—that man is in prison. You think the Federals tolerate traitors in their midst? I should say not. But here in the Confederacy we don't tolerate traitors, no, you bet we don't." The captain groped for the right words. "We give them suck!"

Seth said, "Sir, we are citizens of the Confederate States of America. Please, let us pass."

"Why, Seth Danzinger, your citizenship was what we was wanting to talk to you about. If you don't mind stepping down, your womenfolks can continue unmolested."

"Seth, you will not," Gretchen Danzinger said firmly.

Captain Stump sighed. "Seth, there was some of my men here wanted to have our talk in your home. It ain't so far down the lane, you ain't got no near neighbors, so we wouldn't be disturbed. Now, some of these boys are rough cobs—not the sort you'd want trampin' through your parlor." He shook his head sorrowfully. "And although I don't like to admit it, some of my boys—good boys all—they have a weakness for spirituous liquors, and a few, why they'd drink anything—that brandy kept in the barn for medicinal purposes, that red wine for fortifyin' an elderly lady's blood, oh, they'd guzzle it all right."

"And glad to do it, Cap'n," Ollie sang out.

Again Captain Stump shook his head. "Sometimes I look at that turkey feather Ollie has stuck in his hat and think that feather never adorned a foolisher bird. And, if you'll pardon me for bringing it up, had we waited at your house, I wouldn't feel perfectly easy about the girls. Some of these men have been reared up pretty rough . . ."

Seth passed the reins to Alexander and stepped down into the road.

For the first time, Captain Stump noticed Alexander. "And who the hell are you?"

"I work for the Danzingers."

"Hell, I didn't know Dutchmen hired help. Thought they bred enough brats to get their work done."

"Sir, I was destitute. I believe they took me in from Christian charity."

"You talk funny. You some kind of a preacher?"

"No, sir. I was a teacher of Latin."

"Say something Latin to me."

"Veni, vidi, vici."

"Weenie, weedie, weekie? What's that?"

"It means 'I came, I saw, I conquered.' Julius Caesar said it."

"Yeah? Well, Professor. Suppose you get down in the road with your boss."

"I . . . I . . . am unwell."

"You don't look unwell to me. You look like you been bellied up to the trough. How come you ain't in the army? These Dutchmen won't fight, but that's no excuse for you."

"I will not take human life," Alexander announced.

The captain weighed Alexander with his eyes. "You won't? Boy, you *are* a babe in arms. You don't have have any notion what you will do. I seen boys like you before. Now suppose you get down beside your boss." He took the reins from Alexander's hands and passed them to Willem. "Son, you got to drive. You're the man now. Sorry, ladies"—touching a forefinger to his top hat—"but this is for the best. You wouldn't want my rogues dirtying up your parlor."

His mother pressed Seth's hand to her cheek for a moment and kissed it.

"You go on home, Mother. We'll answer these gentlemen's questions and come along directly."

Grandmother Danzinger said something in German, and Seth answered her gently. The old woman moaned and slumped against the cushions.

"I'll be damned if there aren't more funny words here than in a Creole whorehouse." Stump lifted his hat. "Scuse me, ladies. Maybe you better git."

"You will promise me you will not harm my son."

Captain Stump sighed, "I already promised your daughters will be safe. We are partisan rangers, and so long as I'm in command we ain't gonna molest no ladies."

"Mother, please. Good night! I am certain to satisfy this man."

Little Willem jigged the reins. White faces pressed to the isinglass window until the buggy disappeared around a turn.

"Well then, boys," Captain Stump said amiably. "Now we can get on with our business. Why don't you two step up on that bank there, so we can get a look at you."

The roadbank was washed from the winter rains, and Alexander and Seth couldn't get a purchase until Seth grabbed a root to pull himself up and helped Alexander.

"There now," Captain Stump said. "Ain't that better?" He eased his top hat and resettled it. "Boy, I got to tell you straight out that we're the ones killed your father and you best take us seriously."

"Why?"

"Because Henry Danzinger was workin' for the Federals, passin' information about partisan movements. Because he was a spy for them and took their gold for it. You know how much he had on him? Forty dollars in gold."

"My father had sold cattle that day!"

Captain Stump shook his head. "Cattle buyers don't pay gold. They pay Confederate scrip. But the Federals pay in gold—for value received. Oh, we was watchin' Henry a long time. Been watchin' you too. What was you doin' in Winchester last week?"

"There was guano stored in a burned warehouse. I went to see if it could be salvaged. My father . . ."

"Son, we're done talkin' about your father. We're talkin' about you."

"I am a farmer, the son of a farmer. We will harvest two hundred bushels of wheat, which will make bread for the Confederacy. We wish nothing but to be left in peace. Why do you torment those who have done you no harm?"

"Oh, hell." Ollie scratched his groin. "We already decided to kill this pup. Why you jawing?" He reached out. "Baxter, pass me that bottle. Damned if you ain't the worst bottle hog I ever see'd."

"I'm giving this boy a chance to defend himself."

Seth looked directly into his accuser's eyes. "I choose my father's defense. Innocence."

"You got money?" Baxter asked. "A watch?"

Seth unsnapped the fob and tossed it to the horseman. "No money," he said.

"This watch ain't gold," Baxter said.

"It a nickel-plate Illinois. It belonged to my father. It is a reliable timepiece."

Baxter laughed, a fox's bark. "Christ A'mighty. We already threw this away onct." He flipped the watch into the roadside ditch. "Captain Stump, we got to start catchin' these Federal spies after they visit their paymaster, 'stead of before."

Alexander cleared his throat. "I was a courier for Colonel Jones of the 44th Virginia. I was wounded."

"Oh, was you now." Captain Stump perked up. "So how come you ain't with the 44th?" Captain Stump turned to Baxter. "Pass me that jug."

"I am convalescing."

"Seem convalesced to me, way you clambered up that bank there. You was right spry."

"I am sojourning with these good people until the fighting starts in the spring."

"Plenty of fighting in the Valley. Fighting all year round. All the fighting a patriot'd want." Captain Stump took a long swig. "Danzinger—is it right what this fellow is sayin'—that he's a Confederate soldier just achin' for his chance to return to his unit?"

"And if he is?"

"Then we won't do to him what we mean to do to you. Now I know how you Dutchmen hate a lie. Lies go against your religion. Is this fellow a Confederate soldier?"

"How did my father die?"

"Henry Danzinger died game. I'll give him that. Said he wasn't no spy. Asked us to tell his family that he loved them and reckoned he'd see them in the afterlife." Captain Stump shrugged. "The usual."

"But you never told us."

"Well, we got busy. God, this whiskey is foul. Baxter, where'd you get this stuff?"

"Off that Federal sutler we hung."

"And I was thinkin' we shouldn't have hung him. Boy, you sure you ain't got any cash?"

Seth counted coins in the moonlight. "Sixty-five cents."

Captain Stump sighed. "Well, nobody ever said patriotism was gonna be prosperous." He drew a black pistol from his horse holster. When he held out his free hand, Seth laid the coins in it. "Give you time to pray, if you want."

"I have come from a prayer meeting, Captain. Our Alexander is a Confederate soldier convalescing from wounds. Many times he has said he will return to his regiment in May. Isn't that the month when Federals and Confederates begin killing each other again?" Seth's smile was steady as lantern light.

Stump said, "Don't this make you want to fight us?" In the face of Seth's silence, Stump went on, "It would me. I been fightin' all my life."

He gave the pistol to Alexander, who held it awkwardly, pointed at the ground.

Captain Stump turned to his men. "This Danzinger—is he a Federal spy?"

Ollie said, "If he weren't no spy, what was he doin' prowling around in Winchester when the Federals held it? I say we should give him the same treatment our boys gave Colonel Dahlgren."

"What do you say, Professor?" Captain Stump asked Alexander.

"Why do you ask me?"

"You're a soldier, ain't you?"

"Yes, but . . ."

"We're all soldiers 'but,' ain't we, boys?"

Somebody whined, "Baxter, what'd you do with that watch? I ain't got me no watch."

"Armstrong, you been passed out in the saddle again? Goddamned if I ever knew a man who could ride all night passed out and not fall off his horse."

"What'd you do with that watch?" It was a whine that knew it wouldn't get an answer.

"Well then, Professor, if you're a soldier, how about you show it. That fellow beside you is a convicted Federal spy. You know the penalty for spyin'."

The world spun and Alexander pressed a hand to his forehead. So this is what the world is about. This is what men do. Cows don't murder, sheep live and let others live. Just last week, Alexander was pouring whey and vegetable scraps into the hog trough, six hogs squealing and biting, and barn kittens slipped between the voracious monsters to dip their pink kitten tongues to drink and the hogs nudged them gently aside.

"Professor, I believe it is your bounden duty to shoot that man. Oh hell, don't look so pained. You don't shoot him Ollie'll have to, and Ollie's such a poor marksman he's likely to shoot him half a dozen times afore he's done for."

"I ain't so," Ollie said virtuously. "That nigger didn't want us jollyin' his wife? I popped him first shot. And that was with my pants down."

"Alexander," Seth said, "will you tell my family I died thinking of them? Tell Willem he is the man now."

"Yes," Alexander promised.

"I ask no promises of these men. You, I trust."

"Keep on insultin' us and we'll see how fast you can run tied behind a horse," Ollie said. "Gunshot's the kindliest killin' we do."

"I am grateful," Seth said without a hint of irony. "It is God's blessing my end is to be quick. I hope my father will be proud of me."

"Well," Captain Stump said amiably, "I should think he would be.

Henry didn't beg. Seth don't beg. Boy, I got to tell you, when I go out, I hope I go out as good as you."

"Christ's sake," Ollie said. "Stop the jabberin'. We was goin' on to Staunton. There's some good cathouses in Staunton."

Captain Stump said, "Well, Professor?"

Because he did not know what to do, Alexander did as bid.

45

DON'T WE LOOK LIKE MEN
A-MARCHING

THE BEAST SLID over the Long Bridge across the Potomac toward Manassas Junction, jamming the roads, overloading railroad cars. The beast sweated, sang, emptied its canteens, slathered roadside meadows with filth, drained strong wells in an hour, muddied every shallow stream it crossed. Men four abreast with officers on horseback and couriers—thoughtless young men on fine horses—racing beside the packed ranks.

The beast stopped, bulged, flowed around obstacles, stopped, rested, hurried to catch up again.

Second Sergeant Jesse Burns marched on the left of A Company, color company of the 23rd Regiment United States Colored Troops, Thomas's brigade, Ferrero's division, 9th Corps, Army of the Potomac. The horses thundering past didn't scare him, for what could hurt him now? The three men to his left dressed on Jesse and the files of men directly behind and he felt their concentrated attentions and never heard an officer cry "Close it up!" or "Dress your ranks, damn you!" without worrying that some hesitation of his, some infinitesimal swerve, had created the problem.

Ahead, First Sergeant Tubman marched with the color guard and the regimental and national colors. Some regiments had elaborate colors: one bore the motto "To prove that we are men." On another, a colored soldier bayoneted a Confederate above the motto "Sic Semper Tyrannis." The 23rd's flag was a plain government-issued banner, but Jesse would have died for it.

Riding before the color guard were Colonel Campbell, Captain Fessenden, and a bevy of couriers carrying messages from the head of the column, the rear of the column, Washington City, and General Grant, whose headquarters were somewhere ahead on the Rappahannock.

Surgeon Potts and the file closers were at the rear.

A plaintive voice from the ranks invoked the chant which had one day erupted spontaneously and had become the regiment's marching song, "Don't we look like men a-marchin' . . ."

A bass voice replied, "Don't we look like men a-marchin'."

And the regiment sang out, "Don't we look like men a-marchin'. Don't we look like men o' war!"

Some of these ex-slaves hated the endless drill; Jesse Burns gloried in it. On the drill field, the regiment swung like a gate from column of march into line of battle, and the first sergeant deployed right while Jesse marched in place, the human hinge, as the 23rd USCT (a spear) transmuted itself into the 23rd USCT (a wall) and a thousand bayonets shimmered in the sun. Precise as the machined lock of the Springfield rifle each man carried, thorough as morning muster, drill made Jesse's heart glad. It was so simple when done correctly, but let one man break step, one sergeant fail to keep alignment, and no white officer's bellowing could restore order and grace.

Since Jesse didn't drink or chew, he rarely visited the sutler's wagon and kept his worldly wealth in a brass matchbox next to his skin: thirty dollars rolled tight. He also owned a blue uniform, blue blanket, blue overcoat, haversack, bayonet, canteen, rifle, change of underwear, socks, and shoes; and these articles had been brand-new when he got them: brand-new!

When the sun was directly overhead, the colonel lifted his hand and the color bearers flourished the colors and Jesse marched backward, facing his company. "Brigade! . . ."

"Regiment! . . ."

"A Company! . . . Halt!"

Not as precisely as Jesse might have wished, the men shuffled to a halt and fell out onto a broad hillside beside the roadway for their dinner.

Jesse and Clement Smallwood were messmates, and already Smallwood was breaking up fence rails for their noon fire. Jesse was headed for the creek when Surgeon Potts rode up. "Sergeant. A word with you."

Jesse shifted his canteens to his left hand, brought his heels smartly together, and set his right hand at his forehead, a gesture which seemed mightily like a man shading his eyes against bright sunlight. The surgeon dismounted and raised a careless hand. "Ah, that's all right, Jesse. No need for that between us. Cigar?"

"No, sir. I don't smoke 'em."

"Well, if they're good enough for General Grant they're good enough for me. But I guess you coloreds are more particular than whites." Surgeon Potts had a way of putting a man in the wrong. Now he scratched a lucifer against his boot sole, puffed, and exhaled a cloud around Jesse's head. "Supposed to keep the bugs off," he said vaguely.

Jesse hadn't noticed any bugs.

The surgeon was a young man, prematurely bald, with a wispy mustache. "You're doing a good job, Burns. Was it up to me, I'd put you up for first sergeant and move that hincty Tubman back in the ranks. Man says 'Yes sir' and 'No sir' but don't mean it."

"Yes, sir," Jesse said.

"Your men don't give us any trouble, and I believe A Company could match a good many white outfits at drill. You ever been whipped?"

The ropy scars crisscrossing Jesse's back ached in wet weather, and when he changed underwear, he always found somewhere private to do it. "No, sir," he said.

"I thought them Johnnies liked to whip you boys. I heard they whipped you whenever they got bored. Lieutenant Hill, he's a Maryland boy, and he tells stories'd raise the hair on your neck. Hill says nobody cares if a white man comes into the Quarters and takes any woman he fancies."

Woodsmoke rose from hundreds of cooking fires. Private Smallwood would be waiting for his cooking water.

Dreamily, the surgeon said, "Just go into the Quarters anytime you have a mind, spot some wench, and say, 'Come over here, honey.' " He laughed. "No wonder them rebs fightin' so hard. Tell me, Sergeant, when that happens, I mean when some white man comes into the Quarters and picks out a woman, what do you colored bucks do?" He squinted into Jesse's expressionless face. "Oh hell," he said. "I'm makin' you mad and I never meant to. I can see it in your face. I'm makin' you mad, ain't I?"

"I'd like to fill my canteens, sir. Can't boil salt pork without water."

"Well, I'm sorry if I offended you. Come from De Graff, Ohio, myself, and until I joined this army I never met any of you fellows. You're a novelty to me. You tell me—how can you learn, you don't ask questions? You got any savings for me?"

"No sir. Wasn't any of my men wanted to save with you."

Surgeon Potts was the unofficial regimental banker. Every payday he stood beside the paymaster, and as quick as one of his savers received greenbacks, they passed into Surgeon Potts's keeping. Now Potts shook his head. "I don't expect you fellows to be educated. But that don't mean you got to be stupid. I don't have to do this, you know, but I hate to see a man who's making seven dollars a month lose it to some damn thief. Why, just last week, a sergeant in the 19th had six months' wages stolen. I take the men's money and I go on furlough into Washington City and I put all that money right into Mr. Rigg's bank where nobody can steal it." He patted his pocket. "I keep the names right here. Maybe First Sergeant Tubman isn't my idea of a first sergeant, but he brought me sixty-three dollars last week from B Company. Don't the men trust you?"

"Well, sir," Jesse said earnestly, "about those thieves. I already told my men that if they steal anything I'd deal with them personal before I turn 'em over to the provost. They'd be glad to go to jail when I was done with them." Jesse lifted his big black hands and cracked his knuckles loudly. "Yes, sir. They'd be glad to go. My men ain't thieves, sir."

"You think you got no thieves?"

"No sir, none in A Company."

"Damn it!" The cigar smoke made Jesse want to cough. "That money ain't gonna be safe until it's inside a bank."

"Men been askin' . . ."

"Been askin' what?"

"Been askin' what would happen to their money if something was to happen to you. What if some sharpshooter picked you off? Some say they'd like to get back the money they already gave to you."

The surgeon laughed heartily. "You tell 'em so long as they keep me alive, their money is perfectly safe. I don't mind having a few fellows watching out for me." He rubbed his fingers together. "You know why Tubman is first sergeant?"

"I expect he's a good soldier."

"You know what makes him a good soldier? He obeys orders. There's a couple boys lookin' to be second sergeant instead of you. Maybe one day I'll give another boy a try."

Jesse didn't say that Captain Fessenden had given him his rank and only Captain Fessenden could take it away. He didn't say he thought those who'd given money to Surgeon Potts had seen the last of it. He said, "Yes, sir. I'll ask the men again."

"I knew you weren't so dumb as you looked." The surgeon made to clap Jesse on the shoulder, but Jesse was already started to the creek and the gesture became a foolish swat. Surgeon Potts thought: Some niggers have rocks where their brains are supposed to be.

Clement Smallwood and Jesse ate hard crackers and salt pork and drank a cup of black coffee. Replete, the men of the 23rd found shade, pulled their forage caps down over their eyes, and dozed.

An hour later, when the regiment marched into Fairfax City, Virginia, the first woman who saw them raised her hand to her mouth. A gray-beard stepped inside and brought others out to see.

"It's niggers."

"Yankee niggers, I'll be damned."

In Fairfax City, Virginia, the paint was peeling from the houses and no horses were tied to the hitch rails and what was broken had not been fixed. The few young men in Fairfax City, Virginia, were amputees or on crutches.

Jesse snapped into alignment, the regiment settled into its perfect rhythm, and a thousand rifles bobbed on a thousand blue-clad shoulders. The flag that danced before nearly brought tears to Jesse's eyes.

Captain Fessenden doffed his cap to a pretty Confederate miss, who lifted her pert nose in a snub. Fessenden turned in his saddle to cry, "Will you, will you, fight for the Union?"

With a great growl his men answered him, "Ah ha! Ah ha! We'll fight for Uncle Sam!"

46

"DON'T WE LOOK LIKE MEN A-MARCHING . . ." (REPRISE)

Toward Germanna Ford, Virginia
May 5, 1864

NOSTRILS AND EYELIDS crusted by dust, lips cracked, shoulders chafed by knapsack straps, gaze filled entirely by the sweat-darkened shirt directly ahead, devoted to finding one less sore resting place for the rifle which lay across too thin muscle and too tender bone like a bar of fire, the regiment stumbled toward the Rappahannock. The color bearers' banners were lifeless as a poor man's laundry.

The 23rd had been called into ranks last night and marched until midnight. They'd breakfasted at three-thirty in the morning and formed in column while the sun rose in the sky. They marched as the sun burned the dew off the May leaves. Horses plodded beside marching men, riders dozing in the saddles.

The country between the Potomac and Rappahannock had been the habitat of generals: Lee and Jackson, Pope, McClellan, Hooker and Burnside. For four years, its plantations and small farms had fed marauding armies. Its rail fences had flared in ten thousand campfires, its standing corn had comforted man and beast. Confederate wives saw the blue regiments approach and locked their doors and went upstairs with a glass of water and a headache, praying someone had warned General Lee, someone. Their pale, ribby children kept to the porches of houses that had once boasted window glass.

War had improved the roads. Cow tracks and country lanes so rough they'd snap the axles of a Concord coach had been widened and leveled and planked and bridged by Federal engineers to speed men to the conflagration.

When the regiment didn't halt at noon, men began dropping out of ranks. Some marched on but so slowly their fellows overtook one rank at a time. Others reeled to the roadside, heads between their knees.

"Close it up!"

"Close it up!" Jesse called through cracked lips. He'd stopped sweating an hour ago: no more sweat in him. A courier's horse's hooves wafted new dust into the air. For a moment the courier rode beside the colonel, the two men inclined toward each other. When the colonel raised his hand, watchful officers took his signal and the bugler sounded a halt. For a second men stood stunned before drifting into the shade. Some pulled off their shoes. Some lay facedown in the grass, gasping.

Jesse uncapped his canteen and took a long swallow, which hurt his throat going down. He leaned against a shagbark hickory, looked up at the tripartite leaves, and wondered why leaves were greener on the top side than the bottom. Samuel Gatewood might know. He took an interest in such matters. Was Samuel still alive? Had the war treated Stratford as harshly as this country they were marching through? Old Uther—was he still alive? Uther wouldn't know about the leaves. His mind never turned to plants or critters. The rights and wrongs of things occupied Uther Botkin.

Jesse had concluded that two of the stars in the Federal flag were his wife, Maggie, and Jacob, his child. Since he could no longer find his family in the night skies he would follow that flag. If General Lee and the Confederate army stood in the way, why then, he'd have to fight them.

"Sergeant Burns!"

"Sir?"

"Sit down, sit down, man. I'm on my feet because I'm saddle-sore." Captain Fessenden's eyebrows were cast in dust. "Spare me your canteen? There's a clear brook ahead and I'll send a detail to fill them all." His Adam's apple bobbed. "Never thought lukewarm water could taste so good."

"Where we goin'?"

The young captain shrugged. "General Grant to General Burnside: 'Bring up your corps.' Grant must have run into Johnnies."

"Where we stoppin' today?"

"When we get as far as we're going. General Grant doesn't confide in me."

"Grant know what he's doin'?"

"I believe Grant and Lee are debating that question on the far side of the Rappahannock. Grant whipped the rebs out west."

"Him and General Lee, they fightin' now?"

"In the Wilderness again. Same place Lee broke Joe Hooker last year. Tangled brush and saplings so you can't use your guns and can't hardly see the rebs until they come shrieking at you."

"We gonna fight?"

"We're going to wait here an hour while our stragglers catch up, then we're marching on. That's what I know."

"Some white soldiers say niggers won't fight."

Captain Fessenden's eyes were blue and wet under his dusty lashes. "I never had soldiers take to drill and discipline like you men, and you're marching like veterans. We've come eighteen miles today."

"Grant's been usin' us to guard his supply trains. That's all he's been usin' us for."

"Maybe he's keeping the division fresh for an assault. Hell, I don't know. You hear the same rumors I do."

A few men were building dinner fires. Stragglers limped up the road.

"We get marching again, I want you in the rear with me to chivvy the stragglers." The captain sat with a grunt. "You'll have your share of fighting before this is over. Why are you fellows so fierce?"

"They won't let us surrender. Remember Fort Pillow? Everybody knows the Confeds murdered colored troops after they surrendered. Everybody knows it." Jesse leaned to stare up at soft green leaves. In a dreamy voice he said, "I had a friend, Rufus. One day we were crossing this long railroad bridge and Rufus said niggers couldn't build it."

"Killing Johnnies isn't the same as building bridges."

"We got to do everything—good and bad—that white men do. Come time to whip a man's back, we got to do it. Come time to kill somebody, we got to do that too. We been kindly too long."

"Your old master. What if he was with Lee's army? Would you be glad to kill him?"

"I'm not afraid of Samuel Gatewood, never was. And I'd put a ball in him as soon as any other Confederate." Jesse sighed. "I s'pose old Samuel did the best as he could."

"You have any hardtack?"

Jesse unstrapped his knapsack. The captain rapped crackers against his boot heel. "You remember that hard bread over Christmas? I swear it'd been in the storehouse since the Mexican War. Even the weevils couldn't eat it."

The regiment rested for an hour. One weary straggler caught up and sat down with a blissful expression just as the regiment fell in again. Angrily he shouted, "Master Abraham set us free!"

Some took off stiff new shoes to march barefoot. Their shoes dangled around their necks.

Jesse and the captain lagged a half mile behind, Captain Fessenden leading his horse. Soft dust covered their shoes. "You want to ride?"

"I'm too big. Horse like that needs a lightweight rider."

"Do you always do things the hard way?"

"I'm stronger than that horse. I'll be goin' when he's quit."

They marched through ankle-deep litter—blankets and overcoats shed by earlier white regiments, ripped to angry shreds.

"I'm pleased that our men aren't throwing anything away," Captain Fessenden noted.

"They're soldiers now," Jessie lied, because he couldn't admit that no sane colored man would throw away a good blanket or overcoat no matter how awkward or heavy it was. He nodded at the debris. "Some of the white children we been seeing could have made use of those blankets."

"So could Johnnie. If it wasn't for us supplying him, he would have quit two years ago. What are those people thinking of? Jeff Davis says colored troops get captured he'll put you back into slavery."

"That's the only way they know how to be. I lived in Washington City long enough to wonder if you yankees are much different."

"We pay for your work."

"There's that. Didn't Jeff Davis say there'd be no quarter for a white officer leading colored troops?"

"So I hear."

"There's that too."

Jesse thought to tell the captain about Maggie, but Fessenden was an officer and a white man.

When they came up on three stragglers sitting on a log beside the road, Jesse said, "You men got to go on. What'll the others be thinkin' of you?"

One skinny young man had enough strength for talking. "Be thinkin' they didn't sign on to be marched to death, I reckon."

Jesse attached his bayonet to his rifle.

"What you gonna do with that?"

"Goin' to stick you with it," Jesse said calmly.

"What you gonna do that for?" The man's voice broke in panic and his companions scrambled down the road.

"Soldier ain't with his regiment as good as dead." Jesse made a tentative jab. "Might as well be dead."

Hands out, retreating down the road backward, the man stumbled, turned, ran to catch up.

Captain Fessenden grinned.

"He ain't so whipped as he thought," Jesse said. "He still got sweat in him."

They were twenty miles from Germanna Ford when they heard the rumble of guns, and five miles nearer heard the musketry. The sun was setting behind a pall of smoke, and the officers were nervous. Captain Fessenden said, "Welcome to the Wilderness. Looks like Grant's got his hands full."

A breeze picked up, lifting the colors off their stands and making them pop. From the ranks a singer called, "Don't we look like men a-marchin'?"

When the singer got no response, he raised his clear tenor voice again, demanding, "Don't we look like men a-marchin'?" And though the regiment was road-weary it picked up the cadence, and its officers straightened in their saddles, and when the beast shouted it was a lion's roar: "Don't we look like men o' war?" None of the white officers sang, but they surely wanted to.

47

THE MULE SHOE

SPOTSYLVANIA COURTHOUSE, VIRGINIA
MAY 12, 1864

Take therefore no thought for the morrow:
for the morrow shall take thought for the things of itself.
Sufficient unto the day is the evil thereof.

> —Matthew 6:34, text of sermon preached at service
> confirming Generals Lee and Longstreet into
> the Episcopal Church in the spring of 1864.

"NOW WHY IN the world," Catesby Byrd asked James Fisher, "did you ever come back to the army?"

"I was missin' the high life," Sergeant Fisher said. "What's those?" He pointed at fourteen corn pones laid out on a log.

"That's supper."

"Goddamned, Catesby, if you fellows ain't been livin' high off the hog."

"I see the Federals have been feeding you well."

" 'Course they did," said Fisher, who was so emaciated his ribs resembled a washboard. "The guards were all niggers. Mean bastards. Shoot a man for thinkin' about escapin'."

After Fisher was captured at Gettysburg he had been sent to Point Lookout Prison in Maryland. When the Federals canceled all prisoner exchanges, Fisher escaped, and a sympathetic waterman ferried him across the Chesapeake Bay into Confederate territory.

"Actually," Fisher said, "I came back hoping to find a game."

"I am a Christian now," Catesby said. "I no longer play cards."

Fisher's disappointment flashed across his face. He spat. "Well, I suppose I took enough of your money anyway."

The twelve surviving soldiers of F Company, 44th Virginia, were positioned on the right-hand curve of a bulge in the Confederate line. The bulge was shaped like a mule shoe.

Private Mitchell complained, "How the hell we ever gonna get enough to eat when United States Grant leaves his sutler wagons behind? No point in drivin' Federals less'n we get somethin' to eat."

Corporal McComac scoffed, "We ain't been drivin' them. They been drivin' us."

"That is surely true," Mitchell admitted judiciously. "But that's because Grant left his sutler's wagons behind and we've got no reason for driving them."

Once they had their corn pones most of the men went off to savor them privately, but Mitchell and McComac stayed to bring the returned veteran up to date. "They don't attack with knapsacks no more either. Last night I was taking a message from General Johnson to General Gordon. And since it's a mite shorter I come in front of the lines and was slippin' along where the Federals struck the Georgians yesterday evening and I gets tangled and goes down on my hands and knees and there's racket to wake the dead and our pickets start calling for the countersign and I'd got myself hooked in the sword of this dead Federal major, and I says to myself, 'Oh-ho.' I don't want his sword. I ain't got but two boy children and they already got their Federal officer's swords. And somebody'd already got his boots. So I go through his pockets, and you know what he had? Naught but a Bible. And him a major! I figured he'd be good for hardtack, maybe a flask of whiskey. I believe that son of a bitch Grant tells his people not to carry no rations when they attack because we'll eat 'em after they gets killed. When we was fightin' with Stonewall, every Federal corpse'd have a couple days' rations somewheres on his person." He inspected his cylindrical corn pone without fondness. "This is only the third one of these since a week ago."

"Ten days," Corporal McComac told Fisher. "We left winter camp first of May and been marchin' and fighting ever since. I cannot purely count how many times we fought. I remember the first fight in the Wilderness when we was holdin' the road and they flanked us. But everything's a blue after that."

"Let Marse Robert worry about it," Catesby suggested. "It's in his and God's hands."

"Lee tries to lead any more charges his ownself, it won't be in anybody's hands. Federal sharpshooter get General Lee in his sights, that sharpshooter he'll think about going home."

"General Lee never used to lead no charges," Fisher said. "He let Stonewall do it, or Pender or Armistead or Hood."

"They're dead—except Hood—and most of Hood is shot away. Might be Marse Robert thinks he's the only one left."

Fisher shook his head. "This army's gone plumb to hell without me."

"Oh, we missed you something awful, Sergeant." Private Mitchell brushed crumbs from his lips, and his tongue darted into his palm to retrieve them. "Come over here and set." He patted a rain-slick gun carriage. "This Grant fellow ain't like them other Federal Generals," he began. "Grant don't stay whupped."

They'd whipped Grant at the Wilderness, smashed attack after attack, and they'd outmarched him here to Spotsylvania Courthouse though they'd marched all night to do it and they'd whipped him here too. Yesterday they'd beaten back a terrific attack on the mule shoe. Wagonloads of Federal dead and wounded trundled north and replacements trundled south, but Grant kept on coming.

"Oh, we been hit hard," Mitchell complained. "Many brave boys, and officers kilt. Poor Private James, a mortar cut him plumb in half. When Colonel Higginbotham took us over, they kilt him too, and Lieutenant Colonel Buckner is dyin'. Anybody know our new colonel?"

"Witcham seems a good man," Catesby said. "He says we're to get some conscripts."

"Eighteen-year-old boys . . ." That was Corporal McComac "They been eatin' too regular be any help to us. They got too much room in their gut and their feet are unblemished as a virgin's good name. How they gonna live? How they gonna march without shoes?"

"Hell," Fisher said, "good strong boy of eighteen—I've seen many a good soldier younger. Stuart's drummer, that boy's not fifteen. Remember Private Ryals? He made a soldier at Gaines's Mill. What was it killed Ryals? I disremember."

"Cholera. My son, Thomas, turned seventeen in February," Catesby said.

Private Mitchell prayed, "This Christian army is blessed in your sight, Lord. It is not ourselves we pray for, Lord, but our dearest ones at home. Amen."

"If I was a prayin' man like you," Corporal McComac replied, "I'd pray for any reinforcements the good Lord might care to send us. Shoot one bastard Federal and two more spring up to take his place."

"Don't curse," Catesby said quietly.

Corporal McComac patted the top log of the breastworks. "So long as I got a plenty of dirt and wood 'twixt me and them, I ain't awful scared. I'm a man puts his faith in a deep rifle pit."

The five-foot breastwork was dirt they'd dug from the trench they stood in and faced with logs. A spiky abatis of pointed poles paralleled the lines fifty feet in front, with small gaps where the pickets could slip through. The breastworks were topped with logs, and a man could fire underneath the top log without exposing himself. Inside the fortifications, perpendicular to the breastworks, were log traverses—walls—and should a Federal assault penetrate the line, the Confederates could retreat behind these interior walls and pour fire on the attackers.

The survivors of Company F faced a meadow and, across it, dark, dark woods.

"Here comes the rain again," Sergeant Fisher announced.

"See anything over there?" Catesby asked. "I wonder what they're up to?"

"Same as us: gettin' wet. I wish we had a fire."

Catesby closed his eyes to pray but couldn't think of anything he wanted. Thank you, Lord, he prayed in his mind, for all you have given us. May we be worthy of your grace.

"You prayin' for me?" Fisher asked.

"Nope. I don't figure to press my luck."

Fisher grinned. "Cap'n, you're a fine fellow and one hell of a soldier, but you got to learn to laugh. Man can't laugh at this"—a dribble of rain slipped from his slouch hat onto his nose—"can't laugh at anything. Think on it. There's a hundred fifty thousand of them and fifty thousand of us. The cropland around here is two inches of good soil over dead red clay. Tomorrow or day after there's gonna be two hundred thousand men willing to give their lives for ground wouldn't have fetched ten bucks the acre before the war. Now, I think that's funny."

Fisher's laugh sounded to Catesby like a mule's bray, and he said so.

Corporal McComac said, "Remember that mule our sharpshooters killed when they was trying those new English rifles? I never thought to eat roasted mule before. If we don't find ourselves some well-rationed dead Federals in the next day or so I'm gonna 'reconsider' our mules."

Artillerymen were hooking guns to the limber chests and hitching up.

Catesby splashed through the mud. "We pullin' out?"

The lieutenant of artillery shrugged. "Evenin', Captain. Can't say. I heard Grant was retreating to Fredericksburg and that Marse Robert wants to hit him before he gets away. Pull the guns back before dark— that's my orders. Maybe you'll be pulled out too."

"This rain ever going to let up?"

"Another day of it and we won't be moving anywhere. Least the guns won't. You infantry can keep going a sight longer than us."

"Fredericksburg, eh?"

Another shrug. "That's what I heard."

Warmness settled into Catesby's chest. Maybe once again Lee's ragged veterans had broken the Federals' will. Maybe another Federal general was retiring across the Rappahannock to lick his wounds. Maybe Lincoln would lose the fall election to a more reasonable man—a new northern

President who'd let the Confederate States depart in peace. Again Catesby closed his eyes and prayed his thanks.

"What'd the gunner say?" Sergeant Fisher asked.

Catesby had an aversion to spreading pleasant rumors. Life was hard enough without disappointed hopes. "Said he had orders to move his guns before sundown."

Fisher pursed his lips. "We're bare-ass naked out here without those guns. You know, I'm beginnin' to wonder if coming back to this army was the best idea I ever had."

Catesby said, "Maybe we'll be pulled out too."

"Sure thing." Fisher watched the last gun disappear in the woods before he slumped down against the traverse and cut a plug of tobacco. "You're welcome to join me," he said. "Rain don't blow so bad on this side."

Catesby unfolded his groundsheet, wrapped blankets around his legs, and tucked his ammunition pouch behind his knees to keep it dry. One fat log crossed his back just at the shoulder blades and a smaller log was exactly the right height for his pillow.

"You think any of us gonna live through this?" Fisher asked in a voice absent of its familiar acidity.

"If it is God's will," Catesby said.

"That really does comfort you, don't it? I wish to hell I had something to comfort me. My brother's got himself killed at Manassas and my nephew died in the hospital at Chattanooga. My mother and sister are tryin' to hold things together on the farm, but there's work they can't do. Our nigger Mose been with us since he was a youngster—just like a member of the family—but he run off. Might be he's guardin' Confederate prisoners somewheres. I hear Grant's got colored troops."

"I haven't seen any."

"Care for a chew? I wonder if Mose is over there with the Federals, studyin' on how to kill us. I thought I knew that boy, but I guess I didn't."

"No thanks. I smoke some tobacco when I have it."

"Night like this, man with a pipe, he's out of luck. You can chew anytime."

"See anything out there?"

"Fog's comin' off the ground. Twenty-first Virginia is pickets tonight. They'll let us know if the Federals come."

"They're good boys," Catesby said. But his eyes were closing and he was thinking the prayer he'd learned in childhood:

> Now I lay me down to sleep.
> I pray the Lord my soul to keep.

'If I should die before I wake
I pray the Lord my soul to take.

Catesby fell into sleep as a boy dives into a quarry pool; relief closed over him from top of his head to tip of his toes.

Someone shook him awake. Although it was still pitch-black, it wasn't raining. He rubbed his blurry eyes and, guided by the logs at his back, got to his feet. "Major."

"Captain Byrd, our pickets report a godalmighty rumbling out there. Come with me."

Major Anderson was officer of the day. Catesby asked, "Do you know the time?"

"It must be after midnight." The glow behind the clouds was the moon. The traverses were filled with sleeping men; none had fires.

"This rain will be good for the grass," Catesby found himself saying.

"You are a farmer then?"

"Lawyer. County-seat lawyer, hoping to be a judge."

"I was a planter before. I wonder how I can return to that patient occupation when this war is over."

Anderson was a thick young man with a flourishing beard. "Corporal Osbourne was certain he heard drums, but I heard nothing."

The moon poked a hole in the clouds and illumined the sleeping breastworks as the officers climbed on top. Ahead, the spiky man-made thicket of the abatis and beyond a stretch of meadow and beyond that fog. Catesby was still yawning.

"Do you hear that?"

"It is . . . it's like the rush of a waterfall," Catesby said.

"Or ten thousand men moving through wet grass."

They stood for a time, hoping to hear something more definite.

"Captain Byrd, inform General Johnson. He is quartered at the McCoull House."

Afraid to lose his way in the woods, Catesby trotted the inside face of the mule shoe until he struck the farm lane to old General Johnson's headquarters. Outside the double-story log house, lanterns were burning, and other officers waited on the porch. "Bad night, Captain."

"It could be worse in the morning."

"You hear the military bands?"

"Bands?"

"Yep. They're playing since midnight on our front. We're Ramsuer's brigade."

Catesby shook the other captain's hand. "Forty-fourth Virginia. Since Higginbotham was killed, we're Witcham's brigade."

"Once a man gets to be colonel, he's a goner. My wife entreats me to refuse all promotions."

General Edward "Allegheny" Johnson stood by his fireplace. "So?" he demanded. "So?" He blinked.

Catesby made his report.

Johnson was a bearded, sharp-headed man in his forties. Wounded two years ago at McDowell, he'd just come back to the army. "So?" he said, and blinked furiously.

Catesby didn't know whether to acknowledge the general's tic, perhaps blink back. "We fear the Federals are readying an assault."

Johnson pivoted. "Lieutenant Samuels, inform General Ewell that the enemy are massing outside my salient. He has removed my artillery for God knows what purposes. Tell him I must have it back." His left eye blinked while his right eye glared. "Captain. Thank you for confirming information I have received from others. Alert your command. We must be prepared to receive them at first light."

It was raining again, and the fog cocooned Catesby in soft dense white. He followed the rutted farm lane back by the feel of it under his feet.

Morning pickets from the 48th Virginia were passing silently through the breastworks. Within a few feet of the abatis they vanished in the fog, as if they had never been.

Catesby informed Major Anderson, shook his weary men awake, turned aside their hopeful rations inquiries, and told them to extract their cartridges and replace them with dry ones.

A lightening in the air promised dawn wasn't far away.

Sergeant Fisher said, "What was that?"

"I hope to Christ . . ."

Suddenly the pickets were back, clawing at the abatis, slipping through the gaps, some clambering right over the spikes. Inside the fog there was a rumble like a potato wagon rolling down a hill. A wall of blue appeared.

"We're for it now." Fisher poked his Enfield through the firing slot.

"Fire," Catesby shouted, and a ragged volley spattered. Catesby aimed his pistol through the logs and dropped a color bearer. The Federals tore at the abatis like wild men, indifferent to the bullets cutting them down. Poles and sharpened limbs were tossed aside, but Confederate fire strengthened, and Federal ranks withdrew into the fog, leaving blue flotsam behind them.

"Christ." Fisher jerked his head around. "They're behind us. The bastards've flanked us."

A blue flood poured toward them, flowing over the breastworks, as countless as the waves of the sea.

"Run!" Fisher screamed. "Or you'll rot in Point Lookout Prison!" Abandoning the breastworks, he bolted. Catesby followed him.

Federal soldiers surmounted every obstacle, and sometimes when men surrendered they were taken prisoners and sometimes they were clubbed to death.

The butternut soldiers were like breadcrusts on the tide. A swirl where General Johnson kept the Federals at bay with his walking stick. "Get away from me, you devils." Outside his flailing circumference, soldiers angled for a straight shot. "Don't shoot him, William. We got us a Johnny general!"

"Keep away from me, you devils. Leave me alone."

Sergeant Fisher was cursing—"You bastards ain't gonna take me again!"—and swung his Enfield like a felling ax.

Confederate cannons galloped up and artillerymen unfastened limbers and turned horses loose but Federal soldiers fell on them before they could load a single charge.

A loose artillery horse ran past Catesby, who grabbed at its harness and launched himself onto its back. Pressed into the neck of the terrified animal, Catesby Byrd clung to the check straps as rifle flashes lit up the world. Down the farm lane he rushed, and for a moment, charging from dawn into dark, he thought he might go on forever, that he might outrun death. His face lowered into the horse's mane, Catesby flew.

He emerged in a clearing where butternut reserves were forming. "What brigade are you?" Catesby cried.

"Georgians," one soldier answered.

"And who are you, sir?" The man on the gray horse was General Robert E. Lee.

"Captain Byrd, 44th Virginia." The calm in Lee's voice brought Catesby back to himself. "They have destroyed General Johnson's division. The general himself is taken prisoner or slain. I saw him surrounded."

"The Stonewall Brigade? The Louisiana Tigers?"

"Overwhelmed utterly."

Lee had sadness etched deep into his face. "How many of those people are there?"

"They were twenty ranks thick. Hancock's corps."

"Accompany me to General Gordon," Lee said.

Catesby and Lee rode through the Confederate troops pressing forward in the dim light and joined their officers.

"I am informed that General Johnson is lost, his division overwhelmed. General Gordon, I trust that your men will not disappoint me."

Gordon was a fiery little man, stiff with the peculiar rigidity of a man who has been often wounded. "General," he said. "I am attacking with Evans's and Hoffman's brigades."

"Can you drive them, sir?"

"My Carolinians are already engaged."

"A brigade against a Federal corps?"

"We are all we have."

Tremendous thundering racketed the woods ahead.

"Yes," Lee said. And nudged Traveler and gave him a "tsk." He removed his hat and rode bareheaded to the front.

General Gordon came quickly beside him. "General, it is too dangerous. You must retire."

Lee kept his eyes fixed to the front.

"General Lee, you shall not lead my men in a charge. Another is here for that purpose. These men are Virginians and Georgians and Carolinians. They will not fail you, will you, boys?"

"No sir!" one cried.

"Dear God, no," another groaned.

Angry, anxious, Gordon stood in his stirrups and cried, "General Lee to the rear!" Troops surrounded Traveler and began to push the horse, as if he were a stone, an insensate thing they must remove by main force.

The brigade took up the shout. "General Lee to the rear!"

Catesby gripped Traveler's bridle, and Lee offered no further resistance as the younger man led him through the cheering, weeping Confederates.

"We'll not fail you, Marse Robert!"

"Yes, sir. We'll drive them, by God we will."

"Hurrah for Marse Robert! Hurrah!"

Catesby and the general stopped where the ambulance wagons were preparing as Lee's men hurled themselves into the woods, screaming against the gunfire that drowned the yip-yip-yip of the rebel yell.

So softly Catesby could scarcely hear, Lee said, "It is sometimes easier to die for one's country than live for it. Death can become too precious to a soldier." Then, recovering himself, he said "Those are your countrymen, sir."

Catesby threw General Lee a salute, booted his artillery horse, and galloped toward the fighting.

Rain fell in torrents, the blaze of musketry and cannons outshone the sun, only a gleam through the fog. The woods were inhabited by dead and wounded Confederates, but when Catesby came into the open the Federal troops were withdrawing to the far side of the breastworks, driven by Gordon's continuous volleys. Catesby's horse lurched; Catesby loosed his hold and came off as the horse fell dead. Catesby took a revolver and ammunition pouch from a dead Federal. In another's knapsack he found hardtack and bacon and palmed them into his mouth as he trotted behind the advancing Confederates.

The Federals had been driven out of the mule shoe, but from the far side of the breastworks they poured galling fire into the Confederates. Federal artillerymen wheeled two small brass cannons into position and discharged a blast of canister that ripped the charging Confederate brigade. Holding his pistol in both hands, Catesby strode toward the guns, stopping, firing deliberately. A Federal officer was passing canister to his gunners and Catesby fired twice before the man dropped to his knees.

So much Confederate fire concentrated on those brass cannons that no man could stand near and live. Their artillery horses were killed a dozen times over.

More Confederate brigades poured into the field even as Federal reinforcements arrived on the far side of the breastworks.

Catesby fought in a three-sided fort, men firing to the front and over the south traverse. The trench was knee-deep in pink-tinted water, and men stood on their comrades' bodies to get a better shot. Men fired through the logs and over them and sometimes a Federal soldier would leap to the top of the breastwork, fire down into the upturned faces, and be shot away himself. As soon as the front rank fired, hands passed their rifles to the rear for reloading. Catesby bit open a cartridge, rammed it home, set a cap in place, and handed the rifle forward. Another gun came to him. Another.

For a moment the rain lifted and cold wind blew across the drenched bloody men. A Federal regiment rushed the breastworks and toppled onto the Confederate side. Their first volley felled fifty Confederates. In the act of handing Catesby a rifle a man was shot in the back and stumbled forward, clasping Catesby in a bloody, wearisome embrace.

Over the dying man's shoulder, Catesby watched helplessly as a Federal drew a bead, but that man was felled by a volley from South Carolina reserves coming at a run. The Carolinians swept through entangled, brawling troops and mounted the breastworks the Federals had latterly held. The Carolinians' colonel toppled, hit time and again. With his staff, the Carolinians' color bearer swept Federals into the teeming brawl at his feet until a minié ball knocked him into death.

On either side of the breastworks, Federals and Confederates fired as fast as they could reload, and bullets peeled the bark off trees.

When the Confederate dead grew too numerous, a line formed to pass bodies to a heap in the rear.

Noon came. Afternoon.

Hit by fire from two angles, the trunk of a good-sized oak tree was disintegrating. Wounded men plundered the dead for ammunition. On the breastworks, when a dead man's hand was convenient to hold cartridges, that's where cartridges were placed.

General Lee was building a new line behind them. They must hold here until the new line was done.

When men died in front of him, Catesby come forward until he was the one taking aim and squeezing the trigger and passing the empty rifle back and snatching a new one. A bayonet flicked between a gap in the logs and stuck the next man in the eye. The man grunted and blood shot forth and he fell back off the bayonet, which stabbed again and again, like a snake seeking prey. Catesby fired through the slot and the snake was stilled. The blinded man rolled back and forth across the logs, blood gushing from his socket. Someone grabbed his feet and dragged him into the trench.

It got dark. Some hours went by and more hours went by.

On the far side men stopped shooting, and an unarmed Federal officer leapt onto the breastworks.

A Confederate major cried, "What do you wish, sir?"

"Why, sir, I am awaiting your surrender. My men report you have raised a white flag."

"We are Carolinians, sir. We do not surrender."

"Why have you raised a white flag?"

"If any man has, it is without my permission."

"Well then, a mistake has been made." The officer considered the heap of dead and wounded, the group of Confederate survivors. "It is no better on your side than ours," he said before he was shot dead.

Bold Federal soldiers climbed the breastworks and fired into the massed Confederates, and they were shot down. About eleven o'clock, the oak tree was cut through by bullets and toppled onto the traverse. A branch knocked Catesby to his knees.

While Georgians kept up a determined fire, Catesby and a dozen others dragged the tree back, beside the pile of dead men. Again, Catesby loaded rifles, passed them forward, loaded, passed them forward. When men died, Catesby moved forward. One young soldier who had been firing all day and night was struck in the head and fell wordless into the mud.

Their original trench was filled to ground level with bodies. A Federal muzzle poked over the top, and Catesby directed it harmlessly aside before it fired. He pushed his rifle over the top and fired. Another. Another. His face was crusty with black powder, his hair thick with dried blood. A sudden jerk dragged him half over the breastworks and a voice hissed in his ear, "You're my prisoner, Johnny," and someone had his legs and someone else was pulling his arms until a shot blasted beside his ear and killed the Federal trying to take him prisoner and Catesby slid down his own side, over the slickness of living and dead Confederates into the ditch. When someone stepped on the small of his back, Catesby was pressed into the spongy mass of dead men. He bucked and twisted so he could breathe and another dead man fell on top of him and another, and Catesby crawled away from their embrace.

It rained. The night was lit with muzzle flashes. Men who climbed the breastworks were silhouetted by war's glare.

Catesby thought to pray but couldn't think how. He sat on a dead man who was beginning to bloat. The hand he put out to steady himself brushed a dead man who might have been Federal or Confederate, but was surely pinned to the logs by an iron bayonet. Catesby wiped his hand on the man's tunic. Someone fell at Catesby's feet and looked into Catesby's eyes and said, "Help me," in the politest way. Catesby wished he had strength but hadn't, so the wounded man slid into the ditch of the dead.

It rained. The Federals lobbed mortar shells. These exploded. The Federals kept up such rifle fire no man dared lift his head above the breastworks. Now and again snake bayonets probed.

Catesby thought that if Christ had come to this place tonight, he'd have been killed like everyone else. Death is what men truly love. All the talk of kindness and honor and decency is only talk. Children and old men are alike in death. General Lee knew why they had come here, what men are for.

At three-thirty in the morning, messengers slipped along the lines whispering they could retire, that the new line was ready, that Longstreet's fresh troops were manning it. Survivors paired up to help a wounded man to the rear. Catesby Byrd laid down the rifle he was loading and walked through the mud alone.

48

"DON'T WE LOOK LIKE MEN O' WAR?"

CATHARPIN ROAD NEAR ALRICH, VIRGINIA
MAY 15, 1864

"Is not a negro as good as a white man to stop a bullet?"
"Yes," General Sherman replied, "and a sandbag is better."

"BEST THING ABOUT this mud," Surgeon Potts joked, "covered with mud you can't tell one of them from one of us."

"Why did you cut off his head?" Colonel Campbell asked.

"He didn't object," Potts said solemnly. "Never said a word."

The rain pattered on the headquarters tent, and the smell of wet wool uniforms and unwashed men thickened the air. Since the brigade commander had criticized officers who failed to uncover in their superior's tent, the ridgepole lantern cast light on bare heads. Canvas walls were gray with the light of an overcast morning.

First Sergeant Tubman stood just outside, hands tucked behind his back, at parade rest, eyes straight ahead. No sir, he wasn't hearing a word. Second Sergeant Jesse Burns sat inside at a field desk writing things down properly.

"Potts, are you drunk?"

"Oh hell, no more'n usual. Colonel, I do my duty. I am the best sawbones in this damn division, and once we get into a scrap I'll be glad to prove it." He scoffed, "Cholera! Pneumonia! The flux! I swear these boys are the unhealthiest soldiers I ever saw. That's what I was trying to figure out. Man like Private Bolden: big strong buck, fine figure of a man, and yesterday morning he falls in for muster and drops in the mud dead as J.E.B. Stuart. And nary a mark on him. His messmates say Bolden felt fine that morning, no complaints, no soldier's disease, not a solitary damn thing wrong."

Colonel Campbell, who'd been a Presbyterian elder, said, "I'd appreciate decorum in your language, sir. Although this tent is regimental headquarters, it is also my home."

"Yes, sir. Anything you say, sir. Scientific curiosity made me autopsy the man. There he was, a buck in the prime of life, and he drops dead. Now, what do you think would happen if we was making a charge and a couple hundred niggers was to drop dead on us?" The surgeon winked. "See what I mean?"

Lieutenant Seibel, the colonel's aide, asked, "Sir, are we to understand your motives were scientific?"

Seibel, Jesse, the colonel, three senior captains, and Surgeon Potts were crowded into a tent meant to hold half their number. The air was heavy and damp and the tent's canvas walls were spattered with mud.

Potts sighed, heavily. "Finally, I got one officer to understand. Yes, I went into that boy to learn why he died. Scientific inquiry."

"I am told," Captain Fessenden said, "that having examined the man's liver, heart, and entrails, you piled them on the dispensary table."

"I had to put them someplace, didn't I?"

"And then you cut off his head."

"Captain, all the time I was sawin' on him I didn't hear one word of complaint. No sir, he just lay there, 'ready for inspection' so to speak."

"And then you replaced the head with a bottle wrapped in a blanket and removed the head to your own tent, where later that night you scalped it preliminary to extracting the man's brains."

"I got the idea to measure 'em," Potts said. "Might have weighed 'em too. Shadrach Bolden. You ever hear a white man named Shadrach? Shadrach, Meshach, and Abednego. They were in the Bible."

"They were thrown into the fiery furnace," Jesse said quietly.

"And they came out alive," Potts crowed. "You see, niggers are different. You ever watch them pour sugar into their coffee? A white man'd choke on so much sugar. White men don't fall over dead for no good reason at muster, but niggers do. I admit it, Colonel, maybe I took too many spirits that afternoon, but I meant no wrong. I wanted to find out what makes niggers different from white men."

"Captain Fessenden, you and Lieutenant Seibel will escort Surgeon Potts to corps headquarters. Dismissed."

"Colonel, I . . ." With a helpless shrug and a jerky salute, Potts and the other officers left. In terse sentences, Colonel Campbell dictated charges, had Jesse make a fair copy for the order book, and gave the original to Potts's escort.

The colonel held the tent fly open. It had stopped raining. "The men are much distressed," Colonel Campbell said.

Jesse sat at attention, his eyes straight ahead. "Yes, Colonel."

"How distressed? You may speak freely, Sergeant. What talk have you heard among them?"

"They come to fight, sir. We guarded railroads at Manassas Junction, march thirty miles in one day, which is as good as Lee's men ever did, and when we reach Germanna Ford they set us to guarding it. Rest of Burnside's men fight in the Wilderness, but not the colored troops. When the army race for Spotsylvania, it's whites doing the racing. It's white soldiers kill J.E.B. Stuart, and white soldiers braggin' about it. We coloreds guard supply trains and the beef herd. We didn't join up to guard cows. And now this business. Surgeon Potts cut Private Bolden up and piled his guts into a box and left him where anybody could take a look if they had a mind to."

"I'll see Potts out of the army for it," Colonel Campbell said quietly. "I can do no more."

"It'd help if you found a coffin for Private Bolden and put every part of him in it and buried him with everybody looking on and you said a prayer, maybe."

"Done."

"It'd help if you got us into the fightin' part of this war."

The colonel said, "I've tried. General Ferrero's tried. Burnside, he's been trying. So long as General Grant's got veteran white regiments left, he'll use them up first. Tell the men I'll do the best I can."

They were bivouacked in a meadow above the Orange Plank Road, which had seen hard fighting last year, and skulls gleamed beneath bushes and pale bones lay where the foxes had abandoned them, cleaned. Jesse passed a half-buried skull whose eye sockets were packed black with mud. Bones; just bones.

The sky was overcast, but it was a high overcast. Maybe it wouldn't rain anymore. Jesse stopped at a cookfire under a sheltering chestnut. Only good thing about guarding trains was how well they ate. For breakfast, Jesse had fresh beef, fresh crackers, and the dried vegetables they were starting to feed the army. He took a cup of coffee and stirred sugar into it. "You ever think why we always put sugar in our coffee?" Jesse asked.

Private Clement Smallwood sat on a cracker box. "Tastes better."

"I mean why is it we use sugar in our coffee and the white men don't."

"Captain Stiles, he use sugar in his coffee," someone piped up.

"Yeah. But the colonel don't. Nor Captain Fessenden. How about Lieutenant Seibel?"

Nobody knew Lieutenant Seibel's preferences. "Jesse, we gonna get our money back?" Clement Smallwood asked.

"I told you not to give it to Potts," Jesse said.

"I know you did. I know you did. But what a man gonna do when Massa says hand it over."

"Depends whether you're a servant or a soldier," Jesse said.

"You gonna stay in the army when this war over?" Private Smallwood turned the socks he'd been drying before the fire.

"Depends if we win," Jesse said.

Smallwood was shocked. "Oh, we gonna win all right," he said. "Father Abraham leadin' the way."

The commotion on the Orange Plank Road was General Ferrero himself, his staff, colors, and twenty-man cavalry escort. "Colonel Campbell!" Ferrero cried. The general was a dapper man with a fine black mustache. "Is your regiment ready for a fight?"

Jesse was running for his rifle before Campbell's reply and was fastening his bullet pouch to his belt as the drums started their roaring. "Fall in! Fall in!"

The men raced into ranks as if Gabriel had sounded his trump, and moments later were marching, tense, thrilled, every eye gleaning the countryside ahead. Ten minutes down the road, they heard musketry like big drops of rain spattering the leaves. Pap, pap, pap. The sky was dark overhead and lowering. The regimental drummers hammered the cadence while officers checked their revolvers. Nobody sang. Nobody called out a chant. The determined grim footfalls on the plank road were the only music they required. The color bearer unfurled their regimental flag. First Sergeant Tubman marched backward, eyeing the ranks for alignment and purpose. "Guide right, B Company!"

Colonel Campbell rode beside General Ferrero. Several of Ferrero's staff officers drew their swords.

The damp held the burned-powder stink close to the earth, and Jesse's nostrils filled with the peppery smell.

The 2nd Ohio Cavalry were holding the crossroads at Catharpin Road. Their colors waved on a ditchbank behind the road while dismounted troopers kept up a fire on the woods, perhaps 350 yards west. The woods blossomed with white smoke and red reports and ghostlike gray figures inside the trees. The regiment marched sharp, arms swinging in unison, feet smiting the road, and Ferrero pointed toward the woods and Colonel Campbell shouted, "Form into line of battle."

Jesse pivoted onto Catharpin Road and marked time as A Company, and each subsequent company swung from column of march into two ranks of men across the field, as if someone had laid a ruler on them. The color party joined Colonel Campbell and officers took their places. Ferrero and his flamboyant escort galloped to the rear.

Colonel Campbell lifted his sword and the drummer struck his drumhead, boom, boom, boom, and the 23rd USCT marched straight at those woods. Confederate fire got hotter and a few men fell and others stepped over or around them.

The colonel called, "Halt!" and one, two, everybody halted. The colonel called for a volley, and the front rank fired, then the second rank, and the regiment was enveloped by its own smoke. The rain came then, a torrent, as the men recharged their rifles at the count of nine and set their hammers on half cock, and the colonel ordered them forward. The firing seemed less, but more men fell, and at the treeline the 23rd poured in a volley, though with the rain dripping off his cap Jesse couldn't see a soul in there. With a hoarse cheer the regiment rushed into the woods in an extremely gratifying fashion. Colored troops stood where Confederates had been scant moments ago—they could smell them—and they dragged two wounded men out of the bushes, two gray-clad soldiers covered with twigs and dust and blood, one's left leg stuck out at a funny angle, the other shot in the thigh.

"What're you gonna do?" one of the Confederates said. He was just a boy.

"Remember Fort Pillow?" Private Clement Smallwood said.

"Why," Second Sergeant Jesse Burns said, "I guess you boys are our prisoners."

"Ha, ha, ha. Don't we look like men o' WAR!"

49

LETTER FROM MAJOR DUNCAN GATEWOOD TO LEONA BYRD

Spotsylvania Courthouse, Virginia
May 16, 1864

MY DEAREST SISTER,

I take pen in hand to report grievous news. Your husband, Captain Catesby Byrd, has given his life for his country. Since Catesby's oft-repeated wish was to return to his beloved mountains, I have had his mortal remains embalmed and shipped on the Virginia Central Railway. Their agent at Louisa promises that the melancholy consignment will arrive in Millboro Springs Tuesday if Federal marauders haven't torn up the tracks again.

Your husband perished at Spotsylvania Courthouse, where the Federals attacked our lines with forty thousand men. Although we were initially overwhelmed, our brave men rallied and retook their positions. Catesby's regiment—my beloved 44th Virginia—was among those shattered by the Federal assault, and when muster was sounded the next morning, only six soldiers of the 44th Virginia responded. Their comrades fell or were made prisoners by Federals.

On the day of the battle I was in Danville seeking forage, and I did not return to the army until yesterday. Of my old comrades in the 44th, only Sergeant Fisher was still in ranks, and he told me what he knew about the night our dear Catesby perished.

During the initial assault, a flood of Federals poured into our works, and those Confederates who did not promptly flee for their lives—like Sergeant Fisher—were overwhelmed. Fisher believes Catesby commandeered a horse to escape. After Sergeant Fisher reached the rear, he and other stragglers from our wrecked division were set to digging a new line where our desperate soldiers might retire. Through a long day and half the night they felled trees, dug trenches, and threw up breastworks. Sergeant Fisher said their last meal had been a single corn pone the previous morning. Despite hunger and fatigue, these men worked until they fell exhausted, knowing if the Federals should succeed, the army would be cut in two, and in all likelihood destroyed.

Sometime after two in the morning, the new line was finished and manned and those troops who had been fighting nearly twenty-four hours without respite were withdrawn, Catesby among them.

Catesby appeared briefly where the broken Virginia regiments were reforming. Though his appearance was ghastly, covered by gore, Catesby seemed calm. "Are you hurt, sir?" Fisher cried.

"Oh," Catesby said, with such weary indifference Fisher remarked it, "I suppose so."

"We must bring you to a surgeon."

"No surgeon can make me well."

Catesby was not unique in his appearance, dear sister. Many of the survivors of "the Bloody Angle" were literally bathed in blood and even now seem as if fires had burned too hot and too long behind their eyes. Sergeant Fisher told Catesby that the 44th was destroyed and could not be made whole.

What Catesby then said was, so far as I know, his last words on earth. He said it would make no difference in the end, that Virginians would fight until every man and boy was dead. "Death is too precious to us."

Surely Catesby uttered these bitter words from despair. Catesby's Christian faith had sustained him through terrible ordeals, but perhaps he asked too much of it. Perhaps he had simply endured more than mortal man was meant to endure. My dearest friend took his own life soon afterward.

I found your husband resting peacefully, his back to a pine tree in the shade, pistol beside his right hand and a look of profound peace on his features. With my wetted handkerchief, I washed blood and powder marks from his dear face. I shall save his watch for Thomas. He had no Testament on his person.

The battlefield where Catesby fought was the single most horrible sight I have seen. Some corpses were so shot they were but black/red jelly. Horses had taken so many bullets they were flattened to a foot thick, and wrecked cannons were splashed silver from the storm of lead bullets. Most remarkable was an oak tree some twenty-two inches in diameter, felled by rifle bullets. How can a man stand where an oak tree cannot?

I loved your husband as well as I have loved any man. Together we marched and fought and starved and many a night shared a rude bed under the stars. He was a man who felt more deeply than most men and risked more—I think to ease the pain of feeling. He was always ready with a jest to lighten the day, and whatever he had he shared with me. Though my Christian convictions were not so profound as his, that produced no breach in our affections.

Our beloved Catesby Byrd has gone to the Lord he trusted above all earthly things and he will find a loving welcome there.

Your Grieving Brother,
Duncan

50

A NEW WOMAN

WINDER HOSPITAL, RICHMOND, VIRGINIA
JUNE 3, 1864

AT DAWN, THE thunder of guns woke Sallie's wounded men. This was the first time since McClellan's ill-fated campaign that Federal armies had come so near Richmond. General Lee's provosts swept the wards of every man able to carry a gun, and Richmond's clerks and militia had been summoned to defend the city. The latest battle was being fought at the crossroads of Cold Harbor, though the guns sounded closer than that.

Lee's army had been fighting continuously since the first week of May, and the tattered creatures who arrived at Winder had not had a decent night's sleep or changed their clothes since. Men with minor wounds as well as those with mortal ones—as soon as they were laid upon their cots, they fell into sleep.

New arrivals kept the ward apprised of Lee's latest strategy and prospects. All had been gloomy after Spotsylvania, despairing at J.E.B. Stuart's death, more optimistic despite the losses at North Anna, but everyone said that if today's battle went badly it would signal the end. "If Grant breaks through he'll have Richmond in the palm of his hand." The artillery lieutenant who spoke had lost both his when a Wentworth gun blew up.

Sallie smiled at him and said that no doubt General Lee was doing his best to prevent that eventuality.

The lieutenant stared angrily at the red stumps of his wrists and said, "Lee can't do miracles, you know. He can't hold them back forever."

"We are in God's care," Sallie Kirkpatrick said.

After Surgeon Chambliss made his rounds, Sallie organized the convalescents into their routine work and stepped outdoors. It had rained all night, and the air was clear and fresh. It had become Sallie's habit, during pauses in her work, to stroll to the promontory where a flat ledgerock provided a seat overlooking the James River. She sat on the right of the blocky stone, because when Duncan Gatewood was with her, he sat on the left so his right hand could clasp hers. While seeking after provisions, Duncan often passed through Richmond.

With guns rumbling at her back, Sallie Kirkpatrick watched gulls swoop over the river and a boat's ponderous passage up the canal. The gulls caught fish and the river tumbled toward the sea, and no matter what men did to one another the world was not coming to an end.

Sallie Kirkpatrick could not number the dying men she had comforted. She had written so many letters: "He asked me to say that his last thoughts are of you," "He begged to be remembered as one who died for his country," "At the end he was at peace and relinquished his soul to the tender care of his Savior."

At boys' deathbeds, she had offered assurance and been given it too: "Don't you fret about me, Miss Sallie. I'm goin' on to a place where I can't get shot no more."

Cousin Molly Semple was as blood-smirched as Sallie, had heard as many deathbed confidences, had clasped the hands of her dearest friends' sons during their last moments on earth. But as regularly as she attended St. Paul's on Sundays, Molly Semple attended social gatherings during the week.

"Child," Molly told Sallie, "we cannot live for them and we cannot die for them either."

One midnight, during the overwhelming flood of casualties from the Wilderness, something changed inside Sallie. At first she feared she had broken. It was a coolness, an airiness, which spread from her heart to her fingertips. Sallie wasn't heavy anymore.

Although she continued to do all she had done before—comforted, nursed, encouraged—she did so more calmly. If horrors are unquenchable, death unmitigated, and all our best efforts come to naught, we must continue, because who knows God's plan?

Today the federal guns did not seem to be advancing. If Grant broke through into the city, Sallie's wounded would become Federal prisoners. If Lee won again, newly wounded Confederates would overflow Winder again and the surgeons would once more beg Richmond civilians to take hurt and dying boys into their homes.

The river tumbled at her feet. In September, Matron Sallie Kirkpatrick would be nineteen years old.

51

EARLY YELLOW TOMATOES

Stratford Plantation, Virginia
June 13, 1864

"THEY MAKE THE fattest, juiciest yellow tomatoes you ever ate. Louisa Hevener despises to let these seeds go," Abigail Gatewood said with considerable satisfaction. It was a bright morning and Abigail and Aunt Opal worked either side of the row in the kitchen garden behind Stratford House, two gray-haired women setting out tomatoes. Behind them, fourteen-year-old Pauline Byrd carried the basket of transplants. "That's if it's a good season. If it gets too wet, the skins burst. I don't know what it is about tomatoes: crows leave them alone until one bursts, and then you can't keep the crows off. Pauline, how is your mother feeling today?"

Like Abigail, Pauline wore a bonnet, and her shaded face was pale as a nun's. "She's praying with Grandmother again." Pauline's eyes were large and so golden they seemed to glow. "All day long Mama cries and prays."

Aunt Opal said, "Child, there's no tellin' how grief take a woman. Some women cry, some dance, some pray. And no tellin' how long to get through it. Some women never do get through it. When Miss Abigail's done, bring your plants over here. I like to finish this row."

Abigail said, "I can scarcely believe we won't be seeing Catesby Byrd in this world again. He had such a way about him. Honey, your poor mama has suffered about all she can bear. First dear Baby Willie and now your daddy."

The young girl's indifference was so false and so frail. When she first learned about her father she had fainted and for two days afterward stuttered so badly she couldn't be understood.

"Old Uther too." Aunt Opal put in a word for her losses. "Miss Leona was right close to that old fool. How lively they was, those children, taking lessons on our porch, Leona, Duncan, Sallie, and Jesse. Oh, they was right lively!"

"Poor Jesse." Abigail wiped her forehead. "We never wished him ill, but . . ."

"Many a colored man run good until he outrun by somebody's bullet," Aunt Opal snapped.

"Oh," Abigail said, "I pray it isn't so."

"These puny plants, something's been eating at them. I believe I'll throw them away."

"Aunt Opal, these are the last of our plants from our last seeds, and if they don't yield this summer, we'll have nothing for next year. Pray do plant them. Samuel promised Mrs. Seig some of our surplus, should we have any. I never knew weather like this—one day hot as a stovetop, next day pouring rain."

"Buggy plant draws bugs," Aunt Opal grumbled, knuckling earth firm around the suspect plant's roots. "Child, you come down this row here with the water bucket and splash 'em."

"Thomas promised he'd do the watering," the girl said, not caring much what effect this intelligence might have.

Abigail sighed. "Aunt Opal, why is that boy so contrary? Honey, you fetch the water bucket. These tomatoes can't wait on him."

"That Dinwiddie boy—same age as Master Thomas, and he's joined up. Why all the young white masters like to fight?"

Abigail covered her eyes. "I pray—I often pray—the war ends before Thomas can enlist. Were he lost too, it would kill his mother."

"Master Thomas off in the woods. He rather be ridin' around and huntin' than doin' honest work."

"Wasn't Samuel planning to bring up hay this afternoon? He'll want that horse."

"Master Thomas be back in time. 'Sides, Master Samuel don't need no horse. He gonna use milk cows pull the hay wagon. Hah!"

Any sharp reply Abigail might have made was blunted by the fact that both Stratford's milk cows/oxen had come from Uther Botkin's place and were in Aunt Opal's care, as were Stratford's remaining hogs and sheep. Every day, rain, sleet, snow, or mud, Aunt Opal slogged into the woods with feed. Sometimes she got young Thomas Byrd to help, most times she did it herself.

In the spring, the government commissary men had taken all the livestock Aunt Opal hadn't hidden away. Samuel protested that his son and son-in-law were in the army.

"Then you'll be glad to see them get fed," a commissary man said.

Samuel Gatewood's family had been reduced. In May, Uncle Agamemnon died and was buried in the servants' cemetery above Strait Creek. None of the servants the government had taken to work on Richmond's fortifications ever came home, nor had any runaways. Samuel and Jack the Driver were the fulltask hands. Thomas Byrd was so moody one day he could do a man's work, the next day it took a man to keep him working. Franky and Dinah Williams, Aunt Opal, Pompey, and Pauline Byrd did what they could. Samuel abandoned poorer ground to cedars and planted the best fields in wheat, oats, and corn. With so few animals, they had excess feed, which they sold when they could convey it to Millboro Springs. Samuel and Jack ground a little wheat and corn, but the sawmill was rusty and barn swallows nested in its rafters undisturbed.

Age had stooped Samuel Gatewood and whitened his hair. Most evenings Samuel was in bed by dark; sometimes he was too tired to eat supper or wash. These days he took little satisfaction in planter's work. Only when he got one of Duncan's infrequent letters did Samuel cheer up and act his old self.

Sallie Botkin was the more reliable correspondent and took it as her duty to report on all the county men who passed through Camp Winder and forwarded their news. Excepting Leona, who could not bear war news of any sort, all Stratford, black and white, gathered on the porch when Abigail read Sallie's letters.

"Sallie writes the whole capital turned out when they buried poor General Stuart. Sallie says General Mahone—who is Duncan's superior—is a tiny man and keeps a milk cow tethered outside his tent. Mahone can be very profane. Oh dear. I don't know why our general officers don't set a better example. . . ." Abigail turned the page to read Sallie's account of Cold Harbor. "She says Grant left his own wounded men on the field to die. Dear, dear. I don't know how Sallie can bear all that suffering."

Aunt Opal said, "That girl ain't like you and me, Miss Abigail. She a new kind of woman. Sallie ain't gonna faint every time somebody looks at her cross-eyed."

"Her hardness would come from her penitentiary experience, no doubt," said Grandmother Gatewood, who preferred to clip flights of fancy before they rose too far above the earth.

Samuel wanted to disagree, but, as was her custom, Grandmother Gatewood had passed through the brambles by a path only she could navigate and any conversationalist who ventured after her was, likely to get scratched. Mistress Abigail sighed. In her lifetime, Grandmother Gatewood had inspired a hundred thousand sighs.

Franky Williams was on the bottom step beside her sister. "How come Miss Sallie never say when this war be over?" She sniffed. "I tired of these hard times."

Jack the Driver said, "We still got cornbread and poke greens and hog meat and buttermilk. We stick together right here at Stratford—we all be fine."

"Amen," Samuel Gatewood agreed.

There had been local alarms. The Federal general Hunter had marched through Staunton and his men had been locusts on the land. Some of Samuel's neighbors feared Hunter would turn west along the Parkersburg Pike and wreak havoc in the mountain valleys. Others hoped General Lee would see to General Hunter, as he'd seen to other Federal generals before. General Hunter had torn up so much Virginia Central track, Samuel Gatewood couldn't ship what little flour he milled. Jack the Driver thought they should take a wagon to Lexington for the canal boat, but Samuel feared their old horse wouldn't survive the trip. Too, General Hunter had burned the Virginia Military Institute and Samuel was reluctant to see that devastation.

Every morning, Abigail, Aunt Opal, and Pauline gardened, starting when the dew burned off and working until the sun was high in the sky and tender leaves curled. Today, after they finished planting the early tomatoes, they retired to the porch for a glass of cool buttermilk. Abigail's old spinning wheel was handy and anyone who had a mind to could take a turn.

"I never thought to use one of these things again." Abigail plucked a rolag of unspun wool from the wooden box at her feet. "Sometimes I wonder how our forebears had any time to live, what with the getting and providing they had to do."

"Plenty niggers to help 'em," Aunt Opal sniffed.

Although Aunt Opal's manner had shocked her at first, Abigail had grown accustomed to her candor and only noticed it when neighbors dropped by. "If Grandmother Gatewood is to be believed," Abigail corrected, "the whites worked as hard and long as the coloreds."

"If Grandma Gatewood's such a worker, why we never see her in the garden?" Aunt Opal asked. "Seems all she does is pray. She gonna pray poor Miss Leona to death. It ain't healthy stay in that dark old bedroom all the time."

The wheel droned at Abigail's side. She said, "I would not dream of interfering with Leona's mourning. I am told Grandmother Gatewood was a lighter-hearted creature before her husband was killed."

"He was where he hadn't no right to be." Aunt Opal spat.

"Where was that?" Pauline asked, all ears. "I know Grandfather was shot, but nobody even tells me why."

"And you won't hear it from me," Abigail said firmly. "Silence is how we bury scandal. Aunt Opal, I would appreciate your keeping our confidence in this matter."

"Yes'm," Aunt Opal said.

Heat lay on the garden like a blanket. A few monarchs darted about, but most insects and birds had found shade.

"That spotty-face ewe got fleece maggots again," Aunt Opal said. "This is right weather for maggots: wet and hot. This evening I'll want Master Thomas come with me to lay ahold of her."

"I swear I don't know what's come over that boy. He used to be so helpful."

"Bein' a man's what's comin' over young Master. If we don't treat that sheep she'll die."

"I can help," Pauline said.

Abigail laughed merrily. "Child, that's such nasty work."

"If it's not too nasty for Aunt Opal, why's it too nasty for me?"

Aunt Opal choked and coughed and set her buttermilk down. "Went down the wrong pipe, I reckon," she said.

"Aunt Opal, did Miss Sallie help you with the stock?"

"Reckon she did. Ewes used to follow Miss Sallie like they was dogs."

Abigail adjusted the spindle. "The world won't ever be the same. But it wasn't such a bad old world, was it?"

Aunt Opal said, "I had a good life with old Uther, better than bein' his wife. I never took to that foolishness. Never wanted to let no man do with me what they want. Now you never mind, Miss Pauline." She shook a finger. "That's all I'm going to say about it."

"Like the horses and cows," Pauline said, giggling at her own comparison.

"A might too much like the horses and cows for my liking," Aunt Opal observed. "Take these glasses back to the kitchen house, and bring buttermilk up to your Grandma Gatewood and your mama. They prayin' up a thirst."

After Pauline was gone, Aunt Opal removed a rolag from between two ancient wool cards. "Don't know what we'd do, we bust one of these," she said. "No way of getting another."

"We must make do with what we have."

"Every month we havin' less to make do with," Aunt Opal said. "Next time you write Master Duncan, don't write none about the wool maggots. When he was little them things made him sick."

"I pray for Duncan. Seeking forage for horses cannot be so very dangerous. Poor Catesby. Poor dear Catesby."

"Master Duncan, he was a sunny child. Never did worry overmuch. Miss Sallie, oh, she were a fierce scholar. She'd be goin' over her readin' book and her little brow all knotted up. Master Duncan, he take one glance, learn it more or less, and Uther'd correct him and Duncan would laugh like the correction was the least thing in the world. Miss Sallie—

how she hate to be corrected. She'd scowl and lift up her head, but next time she'd get it right, sure."

"I do wish Leona would get some fresh air. No doubt Grandmother Gatewood is an admirable women, yet . . ."

"Listenin' to that woman say grace is like taking a whippin'."

The wheel droned and thumped. Aunt Opal offered to take a turn.

"I'll keep at it for a time. It is so soothing. Sometimes when I spin by myself, I am almost mesmerized."

"When you think this war be done with?"

Abigail frowned. "Samuel says that if we don't lose Richmond or Atlanta, Lincoln cannot be reelected in November. Mr. Lincoln's subjects are losing patience. Even yankees, it seems, have their limits. They say seven thousand Federals fell at Cold Harbor in just eight minutes. I can scarcely picture it. Although I suppose they deserved their losses, I am sick at heart to think of the misery General Grant has visited upon his own people."

"They's right smart Federals yet." Aunt Opal said, and her satisfaction was unmistakable.

Abigail had heard that note before and did not remark on it. If Aunt Opal had mixed loyalties in this war, what could be expected? The Federals had promised the coloreds so much! "I read in the *Richmond Examiner* that a colored body servant, Levi Miller, fought with distinction at Spotsylvania. His captain praised his courage and military prowess. His was a Texas regiment, I believe."

"Coloreds fighting with the yankees too," Aunt Opal noted. "Plenty coloreds."

Abigail sighed. "Perhaps you should take the wheel after all. I feel a headache coming on."

"This war!" Aunt Opal burst out. "I fears for Master Duncan and Miss Sallie and all our other folks. I hate that young Master Thomas is goin' to enlist. I thinks about Jesse most every night and pray he got safe somewhere. I goes up to the cemetery yesterday and put a iris on Master Catesby's grave. Why these things got to happen? Life too bitter in these times."

Abigail sniffed, blew her nose, said, "Aren't the irises beautiful this year? I believe I've never seen them so blue. And the peonies. I was thinking I might walk down by the river and gather a bouquet for my room."

Aunt Opal worked the wheel more vigorously than Miss Abigail had, and the treadle clumped the porch. "I don't like them green tomatoes fried up," she said. "I likes to wait for the first ripe one and put salt on it and bite into it when it's still warm from the sun."

52

MASTER ABRAHAM PAYS A CALL

THE PITILESS DRUM rattled its summons and the soldiers of the 23rd USCT rolled out of their blankets and rubbed their eyes praying some mistake had been made: surely that was the moon, still big in the sky. By four o'clock they'd visited the sinks, shaved in cold water, and gathered on the red clay drill field they shared with two other colored regiments. Officers checked every man's face against the muster roll. Master Lincoln's army was as afraid of a man running away as old Master had been. Once everybody'd been counted and named, they were free to boil their breakfast except for those who went to see Surgeon—Acting Surgeon—Saxton. They had the flux, soldier's disease, pneumonia, or cholera, and most who went to the big hospital at City Point never came back.

After breakfast, as the sun was peeking over the horizon, they mustered again again for work details: "Twenty men under Lieutenant Seibel to report to the engineers." "Fifty men under Captain Stiles to the wharves." Somebody had to lay track for the railroad General Grant was building from City Point to his front lines, and somebody had to unload supplies and warehouse them. Somebody had to dig the canal through a bend in the James so the navy could get upstream of the obstacles the Johnnies had sunk in the river.

Those who didn't go out on working parties drilled: "Column left oblique into line" "Change of front to the right, by companies, march!" Since green troops were still dribbling into the regiment, these maneuvers were not always perfectly executed. A man kept going straight when he should have gone oblique and the men guiding on him clumped like wet curds. Although these confusions might have seemed comical, no one laughed. Not under that Petersburg sun; not in June; not with no rain in a month and the dust from marching feet in everybody's hair and eyes and nostrils. The officers sweated and lost their tempers and in the evenings drank with officers from other colored regiments because white regiments' officers shunned them.

Jesse's company marched toward the wharves and smartened their step when they tramped past white regiments. Veterans paid colored troops no mind, but new drafts just off the steamer gawked and made remarks. Although "murmuring" was punishable under military law, it was hard to pin on anyone, so Captain Fessenden took no offense.

The James River was broad at City Point, almost a mile, and the plantations on the opposite shore had once been the best in Virginia. Side-wheelers, stern-wheelers, three-masted schooners, brigantines, and barques anchored in the channel. On busy days, two hundred ships unloaded here; General Grant's harbor was the second-busiest in the world. The harbormaster's officious little steam launch huffed among the ships waiting to unload.

Behind the wharves were rows of warehouses, sutlers' cabins, several morticians' establishments, and a village of prostitutes' cribs. Although the railroad wasn't finished, a dozen locomotives stood ready in the completed yards and rails already extended onto the wharves.

A Company marched past mounds of rations, stacks of cannonballs, a park of gun limbers, a pyramid of dismounted napoleons, their greased barrels inoffensive as lengths of sewer pipe.

Jesse's men clambered onto a powder schooner and down into the hold, where they wrestled barrels into nets, winched them onto the wharves, and rolled them into wagons, no more than two to a wagon. The cargo master stood beside the hatch eyeballing everything. "If one of your niggers elects to light up his pipe, we'll all go to tarnation," he noted.

"Yes," Captain Fessenden drawled. "I expect they know that." The moment the schooner was empty, a steam tug dragged it unceremoniously out of the way.

"That's it, then." The cargo master rubbed his hands. "Captain, what would you say to a spirituous libation?" He pointed at the river. "See that steamer?"

"Which? There must be a hundred steamers."

"The white side-wheeler, just in the channel there. You know who is aboard? Well, it is President Lincoln himself, come to inspect our dispositions. No doubt Mr. Lincoln has come to urge General Grant to take Petersburg and thus assure Mr. Lincoln's reelection. Even with all this," the man indicated the acres of military stores, "I do not believe God himself could take Petersburg unless Bobby Lee gave Him the keys."

"Cynical speech disheartens the men," Fessenden said.

"I meant no harm," the cargo master said but did not renew his offer of spirits.

The next vessel to dock had plied the China trade for twenty years but now transported conscripts from Boston to Virginia. Captain Fessenden took a step backward, the smell was so bad. Whey-faced young soldiers in vomit-stained new wool uniforms stumbled down the gangplank onto the blessedly immobile shore. Their officers and a guard of veterans formed them into an irregular column and started them toward the lines. Some of Jesse's detail grinned, some chuckled into their hands. "Johnny's gonna be glad to see you," one murmured.

General Grant's bright launch edged alongside the white steamer and tiny figures boarded her.

Jesse joined Captain Fessenden. "Men say Master Abraham's in that boat."

How swiftly they know what Grant's Pinkertons never discover, Fessenden thought. "That's what I'm told," he said. He also said, "We'll be unloading shot barges this afternoon. We'll be working with a detail from the 38th."

Commanded by a stocky, bearded sergeant, the 38th USCT detail arrived at suppertime. Captain Fessenden told the sergeant his men could take their break with the 23rd, but the sergeant said they'd eaten before starting out, and which shot barge was it they were supposed to unload?

"Have it your way." Fessenden found a seat on the warehouse steps and invited Jesse to join him. He tapped his hardbread sharply to drive the weevils out. "Grant's building us a bakery," he said. "God, how long has it been since you had fresh white bread?"

Jesse smiled but didn't say that the only time he'd had fresh white bread was twelve years ago when Mistress Abigail's children brought it to Uther Botkin's school.

The 38th's men formed a chain to pass shot from hold to wharf.

Jesse dunked his hardtack in a cup of water and shared his dried beef with the captain.

"Obliged. I hope the President doesn't hurry General Grant. When General Grant gets hurried he doesn't do well."

The cargo master poked his head out of his office window. "A word with you, Captain."

Captain Fessenden brushed his hands on his trousers before he went inside.

The sergeant from the 38th ambled over too casually and loomed over Jesse. "I was wonderin' if you was a white man," he said.

The sergeant was as black as Jesse, maybe blacker. His uniform was rumpled, and he stank powerfully for a man bivouacked between two mighty rivers.

Jesse looked him over. "I'm wonderin' what kind of officers you got in the 38th, when a sergeant's uniform look so sloppy."

" 'Cause if you ain't a white man, what you doin' takin' your ease with them?"

"I'm Second Sergeant Jesse Burns. I didn't catch your name."

"First Sergeant Edward Ratcliff, 38th United States Niggers."

"Sit for a spell, Sergeant," Jesse said. "I got more beef than I can eat."

"I ain't hungry. You and that white captain related?"

"How the hell would I know? White folks aren't particular who they lay down with. You gonna stand in the sun or you want to sit in the shade? I heard you boys did good work the other day."

The sergeant relaxed enough to lift his hands off his hips but didn't accept the shade. "We took eighteen of Johnny's guns and killed a pile of Johnnies. Took prisoners too. Jesus, they was scared of us."

"The prisoners we took in the Wilderness thought we were gonna cook and eat 'em."

The first sergeant raised his eyebrows in mock surprise. "Oh, you 23rd Regiment is fightin' niggers. I mistook you for totin' niggers."

"Rosser's cavalry was driving our Ohio boys. Colored or not, those Ohio boys were sure glad to see us. Afterward they gave us a cheer."

"What'd you do with your prisoners?"

"Turned 'em over to the provost. Some boys had sport with 'em, and one of the poor bastards pissed himself, but those two Johnnies're presently in Point Lookout Prison."

While the two sergeants talked, men drifted closer. The 38th stayed in the sunny street and Jesse's detail lined the shady walkway. Everybody just happened to be there.

First Sergeant Edward Ratcliff took a hitch in his pants. "You a house nigger?" he inquired. "Generally, any nigger loves the white man was a house nigger."

"There's good whites and bad ones. Same as us."

Edward Ratcliff laughed. "They bleed the same as us, that's sure. You don't know how it feels usin' a bayonet until you used one. Man with his hands in the air has his belly wide open!"

Jesse forced a tight grin. "We're soldiers of the Army of the Potomac."

"I was a field nigger, myself. Picked cotton until my hands bled, and when I couldn't pick no more, Master whipped me." He turned and jerked his blouse off his back so Jesse could see the web of scars. "Oh, Master cut me, he did. So now," he added philosophically, "I cut him."

"Between all this cuttin'," Jesse mused, "I wonder when folks gonna find a moment's peace."

"House nigger used to come out into the cotton, carry Master a drink of water had ice in it. I used to look up from my row and wonder how'd it be have a white man bring me a drink of water with ice in it."

"Don't reckon you'll ever find out," Jesse said.

"Only right thing you say today," the first sergeant said. "In the army, out of the army, we still niggers."

"I am a man of color, Sergeant," Jesse said, slowly rising to his feet. "Captain Fessenden is my officer and I've promised to obey all officers. Something about this arrangement seems to discomfit you."

" 'Discomfit'? Oh, you is a house nigger, indeed you is. I don't think driver's whip ever touched your black ass."

" 'Discomfit' means, sergeant, you got somethin stuck in your damn craw, spit it out."

Jesse's detail got ready to fight.

The first sergeant grinned a gap-toothed grin. "Had me a dream, the other night," he began. "Dream about the black man and the white man. I dreamed I was drivin' Johnnies until a miníe ball laid me down. Set my soul free."

"Tell it, Sergeant," one of his men said.

"And I find myself at the bottom of the golden stairs lead up to heaven, and I tell you, brothers, them stairs steep and tall. Why, you start climbin' in the morning—for that's when I got kilt—and you don't reach the first landing til evening time. Directly I get to the top, I come face to face with the gatekeeper, who is a heavenly angel, and I give my name, First Sergeant Edward Ratcliff, 38th United States Niggers. And angel, he looks at me for a long time."

"Yes!"

"A loooong time! Angel say, 'We don't 'low no trash in here.' "

"And I say, 'How you know I'm trash?' "

"And he looks me over good, and he say, 'You buckra all right.' "

"And I say, 'No I ain't.' "

"And he stick up his nose and say, 'If you ain't buckra, where's your horse? Never did let a man in here didn't have no horse.' "

"So he shut that golden gate and leave me standin'. Well, directly, who come up the stairs but old Master. He a colonel of Johnnies now and one fine morning he run into some soldiers from the 38th USCT and they promptly improve this earth by removing him from it."

Cheers, laughter. Jesse couldn't stop himself from grinning too.

"I tells him, 'Master, they ain't gonna let you in either. Where's your horse?'

"Master say to me the niggers killed him so quick he didn't have time catch his horse."

More laughter.

"Now while I was working in the sun, Master used to do right smart of thinking in the shade, so he got good at it. Directly he say he got a scheme and I say, 'Oh, no, Master. Last scheme you have was to sell a dozen niggers and buy canal bonds and the bonds went busted but them niggers gone to Texas.'

" 'No,' he say, 'this a good scheme.' Way he got it figured is, I gets down on all fours pretending I'm his horse and he ride up to the gate and they let us in and we both where we want to be.

"Well, I studies and I studies, and I say why not, and I get down on my hands and knees, and brothers, I am about wore out. I have been climbin' stairs all day, and that was after I was kilt. But I figure I can bear it a few minutes longer. Old Master ain't got much meat on him.

"We gallop up to the gate and I prance best I can and the gatekeeper angel don't even open the gate this time, he just call through it. He say, 'Who that?'

" 'Colonel John Palmer,' Master say.

" 'Is you ridin' or is you walkin'? We don't 'low no trash in here.'

" 'Ridin',' Master say.

" 'That fine,' gatekeeper say. 'Dismount, tie your horse, and come right inside.' "

Jesse couldn't help himself, he laughed aloud.

First Sergeant Ratcliff sat beside him and said, "We ain't gonna accomplish nothin', 'less we stick together. I'll take some of that beef. Jawin' makes me hungry."

That afternoon they unloaded shot barges. The mortar shells were packed in wooden cradles it took four men to lift, but most of the shot was twelve-pounders for napoleons.

"We gonna rain death and destruction on them Johnnies," Ratcliff observed.

At four o'clock, Captain Fessenden mustered the detail and promised the cargo master they'd be back tomorrow.

A mile out of City Point, a cavalry vedette trotted down the road, shouting, "Make way," and "Stand aside, there."

The men stood aside while a mounted escort clipped by, guidons fluttering.

Next came generals: Porter, Warren, Parke, Burnside, Hancock—Jesse had never seen so many generals, and if Captain Fessenden hadn't called everybody to attention and produced a salute, the 23rd USCT would have looked like fools.

Following that glut of gold braid and blue came Meade and Grant, Meade half a length ahead of Grant, as if he were in a hurry.

Abraham Lincoln rode alone behind them all. He wore a black suit and a black stovepipe, and his clothes were covered with fine dust so that he seemed a ghost.

"Steady," Captain Fessenden growled.

Lincoln was no horseman—he bounced in the saddle. And his tall hat teetered on his head as though he might lose it momentarily.

And the colored troops broke ranks and cried out, "Master Abraham," and "Thank you, Master Abraham," and "God bless Master Abraham," and they stopped the President's horse and caressed it as if the horse were the man, and tears cut through dust on the dusty man's cheeks and he reached down and touched men on a shoulder or arm or their hand.

53

BY THE DARK OF THE MOON

EVEN IN FULL SUN, the old woman wore her shawl. The trumpet creeper was in bloom, oversized red blossoms drooping from the vine. The garden was as quiet as yesteryear, Richmond's street noises muffled by thick brick walls and heavy vegetation.

The girl asked the old woman, "Did Silas Omohundru love you?"

"I believe he did. But he didn't love Jacob. Two good men wanted that child and the man who had him didn't care about him." She straightened in her wicker chair and coughed. "Did I tell you my family is coming to Richmond for my birthday? All my family is coming. They hope to see me one more time before my wits fail entirely." Her snort was frail as dry leaves in the breeze. "Silas did not enjoy my Jacob, and I don't recall one instance when he picked him up, or bent for a child's good-night kiss. Having provided Jacob's sustenance, Silas had done his entire duty, and Kizzy and I could provide whatever affection the boy required."

The girl said, "I am to start teaching in the fall."

The old woman's face showed surprise. "The employment your father found doesn't suit you?"

The girl laughed. "I'll take my courting outside the office. Probably my real job was falling in love, but I just couldn't. Billy Dunster is so darned dull! I was to be the dutiful wife. Billy'd be the dutiful husband." She shuddered. "It wouldn't have got me anywhere."

"And where do you want to go?"

"I know where I don't want to go. I want to do something with my life."

The old woman nodded. "So you'll become a schoolteacher."

"I'd like to tell the children some of what you've told me."

"How do you know I haven't lied?"

The girl faced the old woman's mocking eyes in silence.

"Will you tell them about the apples? How they were small and tart on the tongue?"

The girl shrugged.

"We had an English basement," the old woman said. *"I've not traveled to England and do not know if the English have them. These half-submerged basements were an economy measure. Ground-level windows let in light so the householder required less illuminating gas. In Wilmington, Silas, Jacob, and I occupied the first floor of our rented house. Kizzy and her husband, Mingo, lived in the English basement."* Her teacup rattled against the saucer. *"It was humid in Wilmington,"* she said distantly.

"I never bore Silas's child. I saw to that." She set her teacup on the rattan table. *"Silas Omohundru aspired to the one condition a man cannot achieve on merit—he yearned to be a gentleman. His knack—a knack he despised—was making money. And in 1864, Wilmington, North Carolina, was the best place in the world to make money. Every month, when the moon waned, cotton bales were drayed onto the wharves, speculators arrived from the countryside, prostitutes laid out ointments and powders, and the tavern keepers swept their keeping rooms and rolled casks from their cellars. When the moon shrank to a pale sliver, gaslights flared along Water Street and ruffians sharpened their knives and loaded their pistols. Wilmington was so dangerous that many of the better class had abandoned it and respectable men carried pistols when they went out at night. On those rare evenings Silas and I went to the theater, Mingo, our driver, was armed and Silas was too. After the yellow fever quarantine was lifted in '63, we attended performances at the Thalian, but by the summer of '64, the theater crowd was ruder and richer, and, as I've said, Silas had aspirations. If Wilmington's better class noticed that we, like they, now shunned theatrical entertainments, they never remarked on it.*

"Speculation in luxury goods—bonnet boards, pins, needles, brandy, silks—was the order of the day, and men and women, some of the highest birth, turned speculator.

"Silas Omohundru was uncommonly scrupulous. Let other shipowners auction luxury goods on the dock and accept payment only in gold or British government bonds; Silas never held an auction. His goods went straight from the ship into army warehouses. What luxuries he did import eased the Wild Darrell's passage through port quarantine and achieved a first-class mooring for her, and Silas always remembered to send gifts to Fortt Fisher, whose guns held the Federal fleet at bay.

"Other boats were captured offshore, sunk, or driven aground, but time after time the Wild Darrell slipped into Wilmington unscathed. The instant she was moored, Silas's stevedores would spring on her, working around the clock to empty her cargo and replace it with bales of cotton. There are but five days of certain darkness every month, and within that period the Wild Darrell must arrive, unload, and sail once again.

"The moment his ship disappeared down the Cape Fear River, Silas would board the Wilmington & Weldon for Richmond. The government so valued his advice they provided him a pass, and Silas could obtain rail transportation when most civilians could not. For the greater part of the month, he stayed at the Ballard Hotel in Richmond. He asked me to join him in the capital, but I rarely obliged.

"The grandees who'd rented us their home had removed most of their furnishings, and our house was so empty it boomed. A few Windsor chairs, a bed, a pair of mismatched settees, an old table rescued from the attic above the carriage house—after two years we were still living out of trunks. The servants came and went discreetly. Food appeared on our table, the laundry was collected and returned, floors were scrubbed. Mingo and Kizzy were 'on the town': slaves who worked for whoever they pleased and remitted most of their wages to their masters. Though this practice was commonplace, it was illegal; consequently such servants were particularly discreet.

"Little Jacob was my solace through that lonely time. For most hours in most days he and I were inseparable. The empty formal parlor was never used to entertain guests; its varnished heart-pine floors served Jacob's pudgy feet and the two-wheeled cart he pulled behind him.

"My sorrows and confusions were overwhelmed by Jacob's sweet milky breath, his embraces soft as a bird wing's underdown. Child, I tell you the greatest pleasure a woman can experience is not the marriage bed but its consequence: her own child, the delights of her child's life and curious mind. I became a child with him—seeing everything through Jacob's fresh eyes. I am a selfish woman, but I would have died for him."

"And you passed for white."

"Wilmington was the most cosmopolitan of southern cities, and after so many infusions of Caribbean blood the complexions of respectable folks were not so uniformly pale as Richmonders'. Silas's money quashed any remaining doubts. Silas had no fear of exposure. I believe he would have welcomed a challenge on the field of honor. For Silas, you see, terrible violence could settle matters.

"As for me, I dreaded pointed fingers, sniggers as we passed. I hated to go out, didn't trust the servants; I shunned those social gatherings where I might have been welcome." The old woman cackled. *"I was young and imagined that people believed their eyes."*

WILMINGTON, NORTH CAROLINA
JULY 11, 1864

Silas Omohundru's clerk dodged between carriages in that curious half trot, half walk men employ who fear losing their dignity.

Although it was well past midnight, flaring gaslights and pitch-pine torches illumined Front and Water streets. An acquaintance clutched the clerk's sleeve: "Is the *Darrell* in?"

"Yes, yes!" He dodged along the boardwalk and knocked sharply at Silas's office door: three sharp raps and, after a delay, a fourth.

At his desk, panama on his head, revolver beside his money bag, Silas Omohundru unfolded calm hands in inquiry.

"The *Wild Darrell* has crossed the bar. Fort Fisher telegraphed there was some trouble but didn't say what."

Silas gave the heavy bag to the clerk and blew out the lamp. "Stick tight," he advised.

Though it was a half hour past midnight, the boardwalks were jammed with well-dressed men and workmen, both colored and white. Every second doorway framed some painted whore.

Two other blockade runners, the *Bat* and the *Banshee,* had arrived earlier that night. A third boat had been harried into shoal waters, and apparently a party from Fort Fisher was trying to salvage her even while the Federal fleet tried to complete her destruction.

Silas paused to put a match to his long thin cigar. His tan linen suit was impeccably cut, freshly clean. His shoes gleamed, his clean-shaven face was all planes and angles.

Docks lined both banks of the murky Cape Fear River, but the moorings on the north bank, the Wilmington side, were most desirable. The wharves were still redolent of the turpentine and pine tar that had been Wilmington's chief export before the war. Stacked in front of warehouses and cramming the alleyways were cotton bales, good middling grade.

The *Bat* and the *Banshee* were tied up nose to stern. With their low freeboard and high semicircular side-wheel housings, blockade runners looked like elongated snails.

Aboard the *Bat* an auction was already in progress. The auctioneer stood on the low pilothouse as his criers passed items from the hold.

"Gold epaulets. Oh, all the officers must have their epaulets. Do I hear a thousand for a case of a hundred, left and right sides? You, sir! Do I hear eleven hundred? We accept Confederate scrip at this morning's quoted discount. I have ten-fifty for the epaulets! Mrs. DeRossette, thank you. And here, ladies and gentlemen, we have the finest pomade." He held up a jar. "Lavender scent! Six cases of forty-eight. Do I hear five hundred?"

Silas and his clerk arrived at a brick warehouse guarded by two armed bullies.

"She's passed Fort Fisher," Silas said quietly. "Knowing how MacGregor drives her, she'll moor within the half hour. Our stevedores?"

One bully nodded at the thick doors behind him. "Oh, they're inside waitin' for her, Mr. Silas. Just like you wanted. Some of 'em thought they'd find employment on the *Banshee* tonight. Christ, they was offered fifty dollars for a night's work, but me and Mr. Remington here"—he tapped his revolver—"we showed 'em the error of their ways."

Mosquitoes feasted on men and horses, thousands of swooping bats feasted on mosquitoes, and oily plumes of torch smoke pushed into the moonless night. Although not a star showed in the sky, the river was ruddy from torches and fireboxes.

A steam whistle's scream announced the *Wild Darrell*'s approach again and again, bursting as if too long suppressed. Seaman crowded the low broad prow of the boat.

The continuous hoot of the steam whistle made Silas wish—as he had often wished before—that MacGregor would leave his celebrating until he was ashore.

In a trice, the seamen tied up the seventy-foot craft fore and aft, and as swiftly abandoned her.

"Master Omohundru, sir!"

"A swift passage, sir!

Silas smiled and nodded and congratulated the young seamen and assured them that yes indeed, he would be along later.

When the bullies opened the warehouse door, a score of Silas's stevedores rushed the boat. "The usual bonuses if you empty her by first light," Silas cried. "And a hundred gold to the best worker this night."

"Mr. Omohundru."

Silas touched his hat brim. "Mrs. DeRossette. We have a busy night tonight."

Mrs. DeRossette had the tight corsets, bunched-silk hoop skirts, and pale, pale complexion of a lady, but perhaps the poor light flattered her. "Have you any special goods? I am given to understand that the demand for brandy in Richmond is very great."

"As you know, ma'am, my cargoes are destined for the army."

"How commendably patriotic." Mrs. DeRossette sniffed. "Didn't you once fetch in cases of champagne for Mrs. Semmes?"

"That was a special occasion, ma'am. She entreated me half a year in advance."

"And if I entreat you? I am told that cologne is worth, literally, its weight in gold."

"I am given to understand, ma'am, that the *Banshee* has already removed chloroform for our hospitals in favor of your shipment of cologne. Surely you cannot require more of it."

"Your people, sir. Are they the Piedmont Omohundrus?"

"I am in Wilmington tonight."

"So I see. Congratulations, Mr. Omohundru, on crossing the bar."

Silas spun on her so angrily the woman recoiled, but her expression did not falter. "I'm afraid I shall have to beg you again, Mr. Omohundru, for another small contribution to our soldiers' relief fund. I cannot tell you how it uplifts our poor wounded boys when Wilmington's finer ladies greet them at the station with coffee and cakes."

Silas extracted several coins without examining them.

"Oh, forty dollars. How generous, Mr. Omohundru. With a cargo worth tens of thousands, you find forty dollars for the brave men fighting for our new nation. You don't know my husband, Mr. Omohundru? No, I suppose not. Colonel DeRossette says all the best gentlemen are in the army."

Silas bowed a deep mocking bow. "There is no need to thank me tonight, Mrs. DeRossette. No doubt I'll be seeing you again on the morrow."

She flushed but withdrew with intact smile. Silas's clerk breathed quietly through open mouth and wished he were elsewhere.

MacGregor was the last man off the *Wild Darrell.* Deliberately, he uncorked a fresh bottle of whiskey and offered it to Silas before taking a pull. "After a dangerous voyage, that does taste good," he said.

When Silas didn't reply, MacGregor beamed satisfaction. "Not that I'd touch a drop when I'm at the wheel. No sir. I've learned my lesson." He watched the stevedores for a moment. "It's good to see the boys hard at it. I'll lift anchor Wednesday night with the tide. The Federals aren't near so sharp in the middle of the dark moon. What war news?"

"General Early's approaching Washington," the clerk said.

"Well, maybe he'll take the city and put us all out of business." MacGregor smiled.

"Fort Fisher's telegraph reported you had trouble tonight."

MacGregor held his thumb and forefinger a quarter inch apart. "A bit. We were slipping into the New Inlet when some damn fool coughed, and one of their lookouts heard and fired a flare to fetch his pals. Now, several voyages past, in Nassau, I was talking to a whaler skipper who happened to have on board a full battery of the very same signal flares our Federal blockaders employ. So, what do you think? Soon as their lookout fires his flare, I start firing mine, only off to the south, you know, like I'm signaling that the rascal blockade runner is running out to sea. They believe my flares, and within minutes half the Federal fleet is steaming south after a will-o'-the-wisp." He took another swallow. "May they continue until they strike Patagonia!"

"Patagonia," the clerk agreed.

"You'll be along?" MacGregor asked.

Silas nodded. "As soon as I'm certain of the unloading."

"Don't forget to bring our friend." MacGregor pointed at the money bag.

Every window glowed in the City Hotel, and on the second-floor landing, a seaman had a whore pressed against the wall, skirt above her waist. When Silas passed, the look she fired over the seaman's hunched shoulder was so enraged Silas recoiled.

Silas's money bag deflated like an empty pig's bladder. MacGregor got his three thousand and notioned that next voyage he'd want five hundred more. The clerk summoned up courage to ask Silas for a raise, noting that capable shipper's clerks were much in demand. MacGregor was dancing with a fat young whore, whiskey bottle pressed against her back. Several sailors recounted the ruse with the flares. Silas sipped at his glass of rum, and when one of the British seamen started undressing his whore, he left quietly by the back stairs, where Mingo was waiting with his carriage.

Outside the blazing penumbra of the riverfront, Wilmington was asleep, and the clip-clop of their hoof beats was the only sound. Silas's rented mansion had been built four years earlier, only two blocks beyond the expanding city's streetlamps.

The house was enclosed by an elaborate ironwork fence. Silas clicked the gate open quietly.

Marguerite and the child were asleep on a settee. The child lay with his face pressed against his mother's neck. Silas could see so much of Marguerite in the boy. Her dimpled cheeks, her fine high forehead, her slightly pointed chin.

He dimmed the lantern, drew the drapes, covered Marguerite with the wrap that had slid to her feet. In the basement, Kizzy had a kettle on the stove, and Silas made himself a cup of strong Jamaican coffee.

He wound his watch. It would be light in an hour.

Upstairs, he pulled a cushion into the window seat and stretched his legs out. He sipped the scalding-hot brew.

"Silas?"

"My dear, I did not mean to wake you."

"We waited for you, oh, forever. . . ."

"You know I must make an appearance at the crew's celebration. The crew must have their champagne and I must pretend to savor their merriment, although I would prefer to remain with the ship. MacGregor is drinking again. Though he does not drink on board—he knows I would not stand for that—he openly debauches in port. I pretend our earlier agreement is not breached. I nod and smile. Damn the man! He knows I cannot find another pilot."

"It was a good voyage?"

"It was a near thing. They got through New Inlet by a ruse. The boys thought it quite the best joke. If MacGregor's stratagem had failed, they would have been driven aground, and on that shore, recovering our cargo would have been hopeless. Shoes for the army. Salt for preserving meat. Lead, fourteen stands of Enfield rifles, barrels of horseshoes, two Parrot guns . . ."

"Well, it did get in safely. And while the crew celebrates, you can sleep. Silas, I wish you wouldn't worry so."

"Our new nation could use a great deal more worry! Worry is just the thing! Lee besieged by Grant in Petersburg. Sherman drives toward Altanta. I have told them in Richmond they must regulate the blockade-running, and they smile and eat peanuts and spit tobacco and do nothing. Tonight, the *Banshee* was full to its scuppers with gewgaws."

"The ladies will have their new hats."

"And they will have champagne and they will have silks. Mrs. DeRossette ships cognac-scented cologne instead of chloroform because chloroform does not return the same profit. And the DeRossettes are Wilmington's grandest family. Damn her! Tonight she had the effrontery to pun about 'the bar.' The bar at the river mouth, or the bar sinister. These fine families lack every talent save one: by God they can sniff out bastardy. Wretched woman!"

Marguerite laid Jacob in the lined trunk that served him as a bed and quelled his sleepy protest with a kiss. When she opened the drapes, faint light foretold dawn. "Will you come to bed, darling?"

"I cannot sleep." He rubbed his eyes. "I leave for Richmond Thursday. Will you accompany me?"

"Dearest heart, I wish to oblige you in every particular, but you know I cannot."

"No man would dare denounce you."

"Silas, if I am denounced, Jacob loses everything."

"And the child is your chief concern."

"Silas, do not set yourself against our son."

"Our son? Your son rather. Somehow we have not been blessed with issue."

"I . . ."

"Do you take me for a fool? Will you suggest your barrenness is my doing?"

"Please, Silas . . ."

"That damn pickaninny is not my son!"

"Yet you do not scruple, any more than his father did, to bring a colored woman to your bed! Oh, Silas, please stop. Our quarrel has awakened Jacob."

The boy clambered out of his little bed and toddled sleepily across the floor with his arms outstretched. He clutched his mother's legs.

Like heart pine that burns hot but briefly, Silas slumped, clamping one white-knuckled hand over the other. "Dearest . . . I do not know what comes over me. At every turn I encounter new obstacles. I have been ungracious to you and rude to the child. Pray comfort him as you can."

The child's tear-stained face tore at Marguerite's heart; Jacob's fear of Silas hardened it.

"I do apologize most sincerely," Silas said.

She laid her hand on the boy's warm sleepy head. "Silas, we are drawing apart. You and I can deceive the world until the last trump. But you I cannot deceive. Jacob is just a little boy, Silas. His little heart loves you. Every evening he asks, 'When Daddy come home?' in the most heartrending fashion."

Thumb in mouth, the boy squirmed around to check on the big noisy man. He buried his face in the safety of his mother's legs.

"Silas, you are a good man. You are the best of men. You have traveled a great distance to become as you are. . . ."

"But?"

"I do not believe you will ever love my son."

Silas leaned back and shut his eyes. His voice was so soft it was hard to hear. "As a boy, I was invariably invited to the Fourth of July celebration at the Omohundrus. My mother was anxious I attend, hoping, I suppose, that I might obtain preference among the family that had shunned her since my birth. On that lawn, among the gaily dressed family and guests, I was the only white bastard. My darker half brothers and sisters served punch and took coats and brought the carriages around. My father—as my legitimate brother so elegantly put it—'would jump a knothole if it'd stand still.' "

"Silas . . ."

"I always wore my best suit for the occasion—my mother brushed it scrupulously—but it was invariably out of fashion. I assumed my best manners, which were, I imagine, odd. They were always courteous to the strange boy. By no single word did they ever show less than kind awareness of my sensibilities—and inferior condition. They all had money—or had had money—or could marry money. They knew each other by first names or nicknames used only within their circle. They spoke of England as if they'd arrived on these shores last week and might return there tomorrow.

"Yet, my legitimate brother defrauded ordinary businessmen as if it were his right! What distinguishes man from gentleman if honor does not?"

"We are an impediment to you," Marguerite said softly.

He opened his eyes. "Dearest, I have never loved another woman. Before I met you, I had thought I would spend my life alone."

"I do not wish . . . I cannot accompany you to Richmond. Every moment I spend in the capital is an agony of apprehension." She lifted the boy and snuggled him into her shoulder. "My darling, I too yearn for something better. If you and I are slightly . . . peculiar, Jacob can be completely, unarguably ordinary."

"And we?"

"Silas, I am a colored woman, though I pretend otherwise and may, by the grace of God, make the pretense real. You are a man of business, respected by your government."

"But no gentleman."

"Silas, must you clutch every disappointment to your bosom? Oh, Silas—now I have hurt you."

Cold light leaked through the windows over Silas's thin shoulders. He licked his dry lips. "My word is my bond," Silas said. "I treat others fairly. I am courteous to inferiors. My fool clerk tells me I must pay him more else he will leave me, and I listen with a smile. I attend those seamen's damnable celebrations. Every one!"

"And your son will be a gentleman."

"I sometimes think I am not brave enough. That with more courage I could sweep all before me. If I bought two more blockade runners with my profits, they could not ignore me."

"Perhaps Mrs. DeRossette could not. But would she invite you into her home? Would she wish Jacob to marry into her family?"

"I dare not do it. I dare not. This business is nearly finished. Should Lincoln lose the election, the war is over, and if he is reelected, the Federals will grind us to dust. I cannot risk my fortune entirely. I cannot."

Tenderly Marguerite kissed Silas's forehead. "Your coffee is cold," she announced. "And it is dawn. I have become accustomed to our new-fangled kitchen and hot water at any hour of the day or night and will make fresh coffee. Although I wish you'd sleep, you will return to the wharves to see to the *Wild Darrell.*"

"And distribute gifts. I cannot trust my clerk to do it."

Marguerite and Jacob went downstairs to make coffee. Her head was a swirl with possibility. She hiked the boy onto the counter. "You sit for a moment, Jacob. Kizzy'll make your breakfast soon."

"Is Daddy mad at me?"

"Oh, how could he be, sweetheart? You are his dearest boy."

Wrinkling his brow, Jacob pronounced, "Father is unhappy. Why can't he get what he wants?"

Marguerite was taken aback by the boy's penetration and smiled in lieu of an answer. It was too easy forget how much the child saw. She made coffee the way Silas liked it and poured it into his favorite cup.

When she came upstairs, gold sunlight silhouetted Silas in the window seat. "How many blockade runners docked last night?"

"Three, including the *Darrell.*"

"But I understand the Federals have cut the railroad below Petersburg."

"General Lee uses wagons to bypass the severed portion."

"So nothing prevents our goods traveling where they are most in demand?"

He shrugged. "The Federal cavalry makes raids. They weren't so bold when General Stuart was alive."

"Silas, do you think me prudent?"

He smiled. "Too prudent sometimes."

"Please, do take me seriously."

"Dearest, I have always taken you with the utmost seriousness."

"Who does our household accounts? Have you ever had occasion to complain?"

He stretched. "How could I complain of perfection?"

"Silas! Please!"

"Shall we go down to the wharves and breakfast on oysters and crab cakes?"

"Of course we shall. And afterward we'll go to your office and you will instruct me in a clerk's duties. Your present clerk will remain in his post while I learn, because you will provide him with a comfortable bonus. While I do the mundane work of your business, you can stay in Richmond advising the government. Oh, do not say no. Consider, Silas. Your new clerk will be perfectly loyal, cannot be seduced away, will always have your best interests at heart. Silas, if we are condemned to be peculiar, let us be peculiar indeed."

54

JINE THE CAVALRY

NEAR BOYCE, VIRGINIA
JULY 22, 1864

> If you want to have a good time,
> If you want to have a good time,
> If you want to have a good time,
>
> *Jine the cavalry!*

THAT WAS THE tune Ollie was plucking on his banjo when the Federal courier rode into the partisan rangers' camp. Baxter was sharpening a saber, Captain Stump was smoking his pipe, Alexander was getting drunk, a dozen others were already rolled in their blankets. Perhaps from their mismatched blue uniforms the Federal courier mistook them for friends; probably he didn't expect partisan rangers to be bivouacked so near the Federal army. It was after midnight, and maybe he was tired enough to mistake their campfire's glow for comfort.

The courier had grit; credit him. When he recognized his mistake, he drew his revolver, leveled it at Baxter, and cried, "Surrender, sir!" He swiveled to call into the darkness behind him, "Sergeant Maxwell! If these rebels don't lay down their arms give them a volley!"

Baxter dove for the bush, and blankets flew as men rolled out.

Captain Stump said pleasantly, "Will somebody please shoot that boy's horse?"

Pistols cracked and the horse dropped to its knees as though somebody'd poleaxed it and the revolver flew from the courier's hand and he went over his horse's neck as the horse collapsed with a groan.

Ollie picked up his banjo. One of the rangers collected the courier's pistol. "Jack Smith, you got any use for a forty-four?"

The courier got to hands and knees. Like most of the Federal couriers he was slight, no more than 130 pounds.

"If you run for it, you'll soon be dead as your horse." Captain Stump tamped fresh tobacco into his pipe and commenced puffing white smoke. "What outfit you with, boy?"

"Vermont Brigade."

"Long way from home, ain't you?"

"Been farther. Gettysburg, Cold Harbor. Farther. What kind of outfit's this?" The courier picked up his kepi and knocked it against his leg. He was pinch-faced, fair-haired.

"We"—the captain gestured—"are Stump's Partisan Rangers. You'll find us where the fight's the hottest, where the minié balls are flying . . ."

"Where the wallets are full," Alexander Kirkpatrick added, "and the gold watches numerous. We are hell-raisers, we are." His whiskey was coarse and hot, and he gagged and belched bile.

"Always did want to shoot that boy." Ollie picked out "Cavaliers of Dixie" on his tinny banjo.

The captain smiled benevolently. "Hell, the Professor provides refinement."

The rangers who'd been rudely awakened stood just inside the campfire's circle pissing into the darkness.

Captain Stump shook his head. "Alexander, how 'bout you share your whiskey with our prisoner. It was Federal whiskey once."

Alexander made to toss the bottle, but the courier declined with a contemptuous glare.

"Baxter," Stump said, "raise up and pluck them government saddlebags from that horse and fetch them here. Vermont, don't give it a second thought. My men are crack shots and you wouldn't get ten feet. How'd you get them corporal's stripes? Didn't know the Federals were promotin' foolish boys."

The courier's face was deadpan. "Got 'em for killin' Johnnies. Was a sergeant until they busted me. I'm workin' my way back. Two, three more dead Johnnies and I'll be sergeant again."

Ollie set his banjo down.

"Naw, Ollie. You keep playin' music. We won't need you just yet." Captain Stump extracted an oilskin pouch from a saddlebag, untied a document, and crinkled his face. "Professor! My eyes are hurtin'. Tell me what this says."

"Nothing more hurtful to the eyes than the written word," Alexander remarked.

"I ain't killed you yet!" Captain Stump aimed his pipe at him.

"And I am everlastingly grateful," Alexander replied. He flipped through the dispatches: "Communications between the Federal War Office and General Crook. Two of his officers are promoted, a court-martial report, orders for Crook to move on Kernstown, da, da, da, cooperate with General Hunter, da, da, da, drive General Early's army from the Valley."

"You think Early should see that?"

"Has he got anyone with him who can read?"

"Oh hell, they're regulars. 'Course they can read!" To the courier, Captain Stump said, "He talks funny, but the Professor's all right. He's got one of your Spencer carbines. Alexander can't shoot good, but he can shoot fast. Want to bet he can't hit you before you reach the woods?"

"Only him?" The boy's eyes lit up with interest.

Stump scratched his head and inspected his discovery. "How about him and Ollie?"

The boy snorted. "Naw. He's got to shoot better'n he picks the banjo."

Ollie looked up with interest. "You pick?"

"Naw. But I heard it picked."

"Cap'n, how 'bout we kill this son of a bitch?"

"Ollie, you are meaner'n a cross dog. Suppose you carry that dispatch to General Early. Ride hard and you'll strike Early's pickets before daybreak."

Ollie wrapped his banjo and tied it behind his saddle. "I got a sister down by Woodstock," he said. "I'll be back in a couple days."

"If that girl is your sister, what you do with her is gonna get you condemned to the hottest part of hell."

"So long as you be there with me." Ollie clucked and disappeared into the night.

"Here's something in our line of work," Alexander said. "A supply train from Leesburg, small cavalry escort, rations, medical supplies, officers' dunnage. That'll be whiskey. Coffee, molasses, no mention of a payroll. They think a Federal army can fight forever without pay?"

"Speaking of pay, Vermont, I'll have your pocketbook."

Wordlessly the courier tossed it to Captain Stump, who grinned at its contents. "My, you are a thrifty lad. I'll have your watch."

The boy balked. "It was my father's."

"Is he among the living?"

"No. Last November he . . ."

"Then he'll not be needing it any longer."

The boy flipped it contemptuously, and the captain had to grab to keep it from shattering. "Is that the respect you show for your own father's possessions? Did he know you as an ungrateful son?"

"Reb, I ain't discussin' Father with the likes of you."

Captain Stump studied the boy sorrowfully. "Dear God, give me strength. I do not wish to shoot this pup. But he provokes me. . . ."

"Use him as bait," Alexander suggested. "Have him draw the Federal escort."

Alexander's new life fit him like a silk glove. He carried the afore-mentioned Spencer carbine, which fired seven bullets as fast as he worked the lever, and a foot-long butcher's knife hung from his belt. Though he goaded Captain Stump, the captain treated him with the af-fection one might have for an unusual pet, a talking crow. Alexander had found a world where mermaids swam in the sea and all things were pos-sible.

Alexander had become the partisan rangers' strategist, because his ideas were more profitable than those of Captain Stump, who had a quixotic streak and would spare a rich target for a poorer but more gal-lant one. Regular Confederate officers despised the partisan rangers, and the information the captain forwarded was not always received respect-fully. General Early had refused to meet Captain Stump, saying he had no time for men of his "ilk."

Happily, Captain Stump was made of resilient stuff and did not let snubs distress him.

The captain beamed. "Well then, Vermont, you must be hungry. Or might I offer you a libation?"

"I don't drink with traitors."

" 'Traitors,' Vermont? Harsh words for brave men who fight only to see their native land free of brutal invaders, who seek only to be let alone."

"Once we string you up we'll let you alone."

A scowl convulsed the captain's features. "Alexander. Talk to this boy. Advise him of his circumstances. Persuade him where his interests lie."

Alexander waved the boy to a seat. "What did you do before this war?"

"Farmed. Some logging."

"Are you married?"

The boy had pale blue eyes and his hair was straw-colored and his teeth were small and irregular. "Nope."

"Anybody in mind?"

"Yep."

"And . . . ?"

The boy spat. "Don't figure to talk to you about her."

"Honesta turpitudo est pro bono causa."

"That Latin?" the boy asked. "What good's a language nobody speaks anymore?"

Alexander felt a chill of relief. "Why, it's no good," he said. "Not a blessed bit of good at all." He added, "He'll kill you, you know. Anger him and Captain Stump will kill you."

The boy shrugged. "Better men than me been killed. I reckon I can stand it."

"You know," Andrew said happily, "I know exactly what you mean. Half the time I don't care whether I live or die, I . . ."

"Pass me that Spencer and I'll settle your confusion," the boy said.

A second chill, less agreeable, passed down Alexander's spine. "It's going to hurt," Alexander hissed. "It's going to hurt like hell."

"Won't hurt forever," the boy said. "What were you before the war?"

For a moment, Alexander couldn't remember. "I was . . . I was a schoolteacher," he said.

"Bet you was a dandy."

Alexander hated to think of the wretch he had been. Alexander was born for war, born for a hot life! He had been created for this war! When he drank again the fumes made him sneeze.

"God bless you," the boy said automatically.

"Well . . . well, the hell with you, you damned dunce! You would bless me? Dunce, you rode into a Confederate bivouac like a man asleep!"

"Wasn't the best idea I ever had."

"I can kill you now and dump you beside the road and the buzzards will pick your eyes. They go for the eyes first."

"If you're gonna do it, do it."

In a white heat, Alexander groped for his Spencer, but Captain Stump was there to pluck it away. "This boy provoking you, Alexander?"

"He isn't afraid of me!"

Captain Stump smiled a sad, knowing smile. "Alexander, a fair number of bluebellies probably ain't. You got to get used to it. Baxter, tie this boy to that white pine over there and keep an eye on him. Alexander, if you got any notion of going to him after we're asleep like you did that Federal we caught at New Market, I want you to think again. Baxter, you heard what I said. If Alexander comes creepin' around, put a ball in him."

"My pleasure, Captain."

"What you did to that man, Alexander, turned my stomach. I never seen such a goddamned mess in my life."

Alexander curled up. His brain was tinted red and his mental pictures were successive red washes like blood coursing down a windowpane. In Rome they knew what to do with insolent prisoners. They filled their mouths with boiling lead! Alexander pictured the ladle filled with melted-down minié balls, the rags he'd wrap around the handle so he wouldn't burn himself, the odor of the molten lead stinging his nose, and the prisoner's mouth pried open, the tilt of the ladle . . .

Cuddling the bottle to his chest, Alexander went to sleep. In the middle of the night he sat bolt upright to vomit, and as soon as his throat stopped convulsing he swallowed whiskey to kill the taste. He was awfully tired but wide awake.

Alexander was half sitting on his scabbarded knife, and the belt pulled at his stomach. Why couldn't he ever get comfortable? The campfire was sullen embers and the moon lit the clearing with pale clotted light. Head on chest, the courier was slumped against his pine tree.

How angry would Captain Stump be? If Alexander was quick, there wouldn't be much noise. Then he'd slip away, and after a week or so, after Stump had a chance to cool down, he'd return, like the Prodigal Son.

No! No place Alexander had been ever wanted him back. If Alexander had been the Prodigal Son, they never would have killed the fatted calf.

Baxter stepped out of the shadows. "What's the trouble, Professor? Lose your nerve? I kinda hoped you'd try for the boy. Ollie and me got a bet which of us kills you."

The ambush was atop a rise where the Federal mules would be pulling hard and the road too narrow to turn. Ollie and most of the rangers hid in cedars at the bottom of the hill; Captain Stump, Alexander, and Baxter waited behind a horse barn at the top. They'd lashed the Vermont courier to a locust tree beside the road and gagged him with his own shirtsleeve.

About ten that morning, the Federals came into sight, two cavalrymen at the head, another pair at the rear, outriders who drew in when the wagons started up the hill.

"I thought you said there'd be ten wagons," Captain Stump whispered hoarsely.

"Eight's plenty," Alexander said. "If that boy keeps working those ropes, he'll get loose."

Teamsters cracked whips and cursed midmorning curses.

The Federal officer's waxed black mustache was too fierce for his years. The veteran sergeant at his side kept his eyes roving.

The captured courier made no movement, but the mustachioed officer spotted him and was dismounting, even as his sergeant called, "Sir! Have a care!"

The sergeant was lifting his carbine when Captain Stump emptied his saddle. Baxter waited until the officer got one foot in the stirrup before he killed him. Partisan rangers crashed into the rear guard, those Federals who raised their hands in surrender were cut down, teamsters abandoned their wagons or whipped their teams off the road, where they upset, and Captain Stump and Baxter rode down the train shooting all those who did not flee into the brush.

Alexander killed the tied courier over and over again.

55

IN SHADY HOLLYWOOD

RICHMOND, VIRGINIA
JULY 24, 1864

" 'WITH THE ANGELS now.' " Sallie traced the blurred inscription on the sandstone tombstone. "After we are gone, will people wonder about us? Will those who come when we are gone think us quaint? Will they wonder why we wear hoops?"

"You don't," Duncan Gatewood lazily took exception.

"Like the Brethren women, I am excused from hoops. Their exemption is from religious principle, mine occupational. Perhaps my attire must be drab, but it should not billow like a sail in the wind. Duncan, will they wear hoops?"

Duncan rolled over and plucked a blade of grass. "I predict . . . they will. Yes, I'm sure of it."

Summer had been hot and dry, but vegetation which elsewhere had yellowed flourished in the deep shade of Hollywood Cemetery. Hollywood was popular with courting couples, who strolled its leafy avenues with chaperons a courteous pace behind. Duncan and Sallie reclined beside an eighteenth-century grave beneath the shade of a giant chestnut.

There weren't many trees in the new part, where dirt paths connected long rows of fresh mounds, each with its numbered unpainted wooden cross. Mourners, mostly old people and stunned children, visited there. Courting couples would rather stroll where old trees and green shade made death beautiful.

Eyes half shut, Duncan sprawled against the headstone. "You are in better spirits these days."

"It is a new thing with me, Duncan, and tender. Please do not mock me."

He leaned forward. "Oh, no, dearest girl. I am pleased beyond telling." He laid his hand upon hers.

"I think I was ashamed. To continue on when so many who were so brave have been translated." She fell silent as a cortege turned into the new section. An old man drove a rickety farmer's wagon carrying an unpainted coffin, and two women walked behind. Other mourners stepped aside incuriously.

Duncan said, "Mother writes that our Leona is failing. Her strength is less every day."

"Poor dear Leona! All she ever hoped for in this world was to be loved."

"She had Catesby for a time." Duncan forced a smile. "You look pert this morning, my Sallie. Where did you find that yellow rose for your hair?"

"I committed theft from a flowering bush on Franklin Street. Oh, Duncan, we must seize what pleasure we can. Life is in no way improved by despair!"

Duncan grinned at her. "Of course." He angled his neck to examine the leafy canopy overhead. "I go tomorrow to Scottsville. Captain Pickering's father has a plantation there, and according to the captain, his father greatly admires General Lee and possesses a thousand bushels of last season's corn. Unless we get some rain while this year's corn is tasseling, the crop will be poor."

"God will provide."

"That may be," Duncan said. "Meanwhile I put my faith in Mr. Pickering. His plantation is near the canal, so it'd be no work at all bringing it to Richmond. Although General Grant has only besieged us since May, it seems forever."

"It would be pleasant to leave Richmond. I wish I could go."

"When was the last time you were in the countryside?"

Sallie's eyes brimmed. "No, no, I'll be all right. I hate my tears! It is commendable to mourn our poor slain boys, contemptible to weep because poor Sallie hasn't lately picnicked in the countryside."

"Perhaps . . ."

"Duncan, you know I cannot. Soon Grant will make another attack, and I must be at Winder when the ambulances arrive."

"You are as much imprisoned . . ."

"Do not say that, Duncan! It is not true! I am where I wish to be. It is not uncommon for some boy to recognize me and take heart from my presence. Last week a boy was brought in shot through the neck; it is his fourth time at Winder, and though he could not speak I am sure he recognized me."

Duncan sighed. "I wish I could be as confident I am doing my duty. The feeblest militia officer could manage my job, and we lack experienced officers. I've asked General Mahone to let me go back to the lines, but he won't hear of it. Some fellows say when a man loses a limb, he loses his mettle, but I don't think that's so. Sally, consider our one-armed, one-legged generals. Our drums cannot sound attack until our generals are tightly strapped to their horses!"

Sallie covered her mouth. "I should not laugh, I should not," and her eyes widened as she giggled into her palm. "It was the image in my mind," she said, "of the flurry at army headquarters as General Hood, Ewell, and the others are attached to their steeds. I am sorry. I know it cannot be funny to you." Sallie brushed grass from her dress. "Come, let us stroll. If we stay in this bower any longer, I'll surely fall asleep."

They walked side by side, Duncan carrying their wicker picnic basket. "Duncan, what are your hopes when this war is over? Will you return to Stratford?"

"All that seems so long ago. I was a boy."

"And now that you are an ancient?"

He smiled. "It seems silly. But I'm more at ease with the graybeards of forty and fifty who command our divisions than with the youngsters enlisting today. Mother writes that Thomas Byrd is determined to join up."

"Oh dear."

"We boys all believed that war was a swift path to glory, and sometimes it's true. Pelham, the gallant Pelham, was twenty-three when he died."

"And if he hadn't died, Pelham would be twenty-four and perhaps wed!" Sallie returned hotly.

"Don't fear for me, Miss Sallie." Duncan smiled. "These days I reserve all my gallantry for the ladies. One lady, anyway."

Blushing, Sallie turned away. "The footwall of that grand tombstone will serve us as table," she said. "It is well in shade."

Duncan examined the epitaph. "This is President Monroe's grave," he announced.

Sallie spread out a napkin upon which she laid delicacies. "I believe the gentleman has quite the loveliest view in Richmond."

Duncan rummaged through the basket. "Eggs, bread, garden radishes. Few Federal generals will dine so well as this."

Sallie made a face. "Must we always refer to the war? Can we not enjoy one outing free of it?"

"Tell me, Miss Sallie, where did you get that fetching bonnet? It is new to me, I swear."

"A boy's sister gave it me in gratitude for easing his suffering."

"Yes," Duncan said. "By all means let's not talk about the war. That bird there, over the river, is that an eagle?"

Sallie giggled. "I believe it is a vulture, Duncan. But it is not a warlike vulture."

"I wonder what we'll be like when this is over. I wonder will we ask each other, 'Where were you the day of Gaines's Mill, or Chancellorsville, or Cold Harbor?'"

Sallie said, "The convalescent who boiled our eggs has a vat large enough for dozens at a time and a slotted ladle to retrieve them. One might imagine he would mistake them, but he never does. When Surgeon Lane orders eggs soft-boiled for a patient, soft-boiled is how they come. When I request hard-boiled for our picnic, they are hard-boiled. Duncan, what will become of us? I am becoming a skilled hospital matron, a skill I hope never to employ afterward. And you are becoming expert at extracting grain from reluctant patriots."

"I'll raise horses." Duncan took an egg from the basket. "Sally, I dream about horses—foals on spring pasture, horses like Gypsy, fiery horses, sulky ones, horses that never reckon the cost. Our old neighbor Andrew Seig was famous for his horses." He gave Sallie his egg. "Maybe I can break horses better than I can peel this egg."

"I could learn to do it."

"A woman horsebreaker? Sallie!"

"Who could object were I your wife?"

Duncan turned his face away. "Dearest Sallie. You could do better than me."

"You forget, I have been married to a . . . whole man, and a choice between him and you is not so difficult." She blushed. "Forgive me, Duncan, for being forward. Entranced by your dream, I forgot myself."

Duncan seized on this change of course. "Some say the grass in the western territories makes such growth cattlemen make no provision for winter—their cows can paw through snow for their forage."

"And in this new land, might not a woman become a horsebreaker?"

"Now Sallie . . ."

"Would fashion require she wear hoops?"

"Sally, you used to be such a pleasant, agreeable woman."

"La Belle Dame Sans Merci, that's me." Sallie laughed.

"Lincoln's Homestead Act allows any man to assert a claim to one hundred and sixty acres."

"But Duncan, we are not citizens of that country."

"Sometimes I forget," Duncan said.

Sallie quickly touched his hand. "Did I mock you? I did not mean to; I meant only to amuse. Yours is a beautiful dream. Nay, call it a plan. But what of Stratford? Surely, after the war, Virginia will need good horses."

He looked away. "I suppose."

Hollywood's shady silence rang in their ears. A cardinal fluffed its wings in a hemlock's branches.

"Duncan, I had come to think of my life as something that happened when I lived with Uther and Opal and Jesse: that was my Golden Age, never to be reclaimed. Though I do dearly love horses, I am joking with you, Duncan, about becoming a horsebreaker, and my forwardness is only to make you smile.

"Marry whom you will, dear Duncan. But you should have seen your face! When I proposed, your face fell into bewilderment, and when I hinted we might rear horses in the shadow of the Rocky Mountains, you turned entirely pale. Duncan"—Sallie made a grand gesture—"I release you from the promises you never quite made, those vows you have always avoided. I leave you to your own life, your undoubtedly well-mannered wife, who will think nothing of wearing hoops from sunup to sundown and may well wear them into the marital bed. I give you leave to go west, abandon friends and family, and slaughter wild Indians to your heart's content as you eke out a miserable living in the wilderness!"

Carefully Duncan folded napkins and laid them neatly at the bottom of the basket. The jug they had shared he set atop. He asked, "What shall I bring from the countryside? Pickering's father is supposed to be a great ham curer, and the peaches will be ripening."

"Nothing," she said. "Winder Hospital provides all I require."

"Some cloth, perhaps? Some mills are still operating in Scottsville."

Her look became most somber, and she lowered her eyes demurely. "A hoop?" she inquired.

"A what?"

"Since a hoop is important to you, I shall learn to wear one. I must no longer embarrass you."

"What makes you think you do?" Duncan was honestly puzzled. "Why would I give a . . . a . . . drat about women's hoops?"

"But Duncan . . ." Tears came to her eyes. "There is something wrong between us, and nothing I do seems to right it."

He took her hand. "Sallie, Sallie. There is nothing wrong, nothing at all. Will you marry me?"

"Oh, no. Oh, I don't know."

He pressed his lips to hers in token.

After more tendernesses, she drew away from him, shaken. "Oh, Duncan," she whispered, "I do not know. You must promise me you will not die."

56

MASTER AND MAN

"WHEELHORSE!" THE CAPTAIN grinned. "Blessed if you ain't a major now! Where'd you lose the wing?"

"Cadet Spaulding! What in the world?"

The former roommates grinned and shook hands vigorously. "You never know. You never know. It's got to the point where I hate to ask after old friends." Spaulding wagged his head gloomily. "Preston, Billy Smith, MacIntyre . . ."

"We lost MacIntyre in the valley in '62. How long ago it seems. But you, Spaulding . . . ?"

Dusk at General Lee's headquarters. A fine old plantation house beside an enormous magnolia tree. Couriers came, officers gossiped around a campfire before Lee's modest field tent. Bats swooped and nighthawks uttered uncanny cries.

"Dear Cousin Hill keeps me under his wing—which means we are always where it's hot. Father says my present horse is positively the last he'll contribute, that if I can't keep this one alive I will be riding a mule. I tell Pa mules won't stand up to musketry, and Pa says he had previously believed a man smarter than a mule but now has doubts. Can you loan me five hundred?"

Duncan turned his pockets inside out.

"I'm to go on furlough Monday," Spaulding said. "Papers all signed, but I've only fifty dollars to my name. You sure you don't have a gold piece squirreled away? Twenty blessed days at home, regaling the prettiest girl in the country with yarns of my derring-do. I'll pay you back one day, you know. Say, wasn't that Kernstown fight the damnedest thing? Early taught General Crook a thing or two."

"We keep teaching them and they keep not learning."

"I always did think yankees slow-witted. Now what the devil happened to you? That scraggly beard you've grown—does it conceal a wound?"

"Burn. Chancellorsville."

"Well, you used to be prettier, that's the truth. Tell me, Wheelhorse, have you heard when we'll be paid?"

"Soon as they find paper to print the money. Say, I just came in from the countryside and possess a chicken which this afternoon was clucking in a farmyard, and I have cornbread too. Have you dined?"

"Having lately feasted on hardtack and hardtack, I'd be honored to join you, sir." Spaulding bowed deeply.

Captain Spaulding's haven was beneath the magnolia's sheltering branches. His tent was torn, equipment helterskelter, and Duncan said, "It's a good thing Jackson hasn't got the inspection. Fifty, sixty demerits, sure."

"Oh hell, Wheelhorse," Spaulding said. "You were always the one who cleaned up." Under his blanket he located a frying pan, which he wiped with his sleeve. A small fire, salt pork for grease, and within half an hour, the two listened to chicken parts crackling while they whisked smoke away from their faces.

"What brings you to headquarters, Wheelhorse?"

Duncan told how Planter Pickering of Scottsville had a thousand bushels of corn he'd sell to the army, nay *give* to the army, "if'n he got a note from Marse Robert himself. It's good feed and his corn cribs are only half an hour from the canal, and I don't know how General Hill is doing, but some of General Mahone's artillery horses are too poor to shift a gun."

"General Lee going to write the note?"

"His aide, Colonel Venable, promises it in the morning. It's personal with Planter Pickering. Old man says he won't give 'ary a ear of corn to Jeff Davis, but Marse Robert ken have what he wants.'"

Spaulding lifted fork and knife in salute. "Isn't that chicken about ready? It's got me drooling."

The two didn't have much in common except the Institute, but weaker ties have cemented lifetime friendships, and without talking much as they ate, they contrived to say a great deal. Spaulding was worried about A. P. Hill. "Cousin Hill's been awfully sick. He's just skin and bones. But he comes out of bed soon as the guns start rumbling." Duncan's old roommate repeated headquarters gossip. "General Lee says the Federals are digging underneath our lines, so our boys are digging to find them."

Spaulding shivered. "If I'm to die, let me die in the sunlight. All this digging and tunneling—there's nothing gallant about it."

Duncan spoke of his dying sister, Leona, how she had lost all will to
live. "Sometimes, when I'm in a grim humor, I know how she feels."

"Don't be glum, Wheelhorse." Spaulding tapped his pipe against his
boot heel. "Die and you'll miss all the fun." He grinned, and after a
pause, Duncan grinned too.

Duncan told his old friend about Sallie, worrying her work at Winder
Hospital was so important she'd not consent to be his wife.

Spaulding said, "Wheelhorse, what would you think of a man who
shirked duty for love of a girl?"

"It's different for a woman," Duncan said.

"You're too acute a thinker for me, son."

Duncan stared into the fire. "And you? Anyone capture your fancy?"

Captain Spaulding described a neighbor's daughter, just sixteen when
he went away. "And she said she'd wait for me," he said. "For me! Can
you believe that?"

Duncan took Spaulding's tobacco for his own pipe. "Frankly I cannot,
unless she has confused conquering a Hill with surmounting a Spaulding."

Spaulding laughed. "Wheelhorse, our repast would be complete with
a single cup of real coffee. How I miss it."

"Not two weeks ago," Duncan said, "I was south of Bedford when an
aristocrat of those parts invited me into his home, where a servant
brought a cup of the finest coffee I have drunk since '61. My host was
one of these fellows untouched by the war. His plantation is prosperous
and his servants haven't run off. When I complimented him and asked
wouldn't he join me, he said he wasn't drinking coffee until the supply
was 'more reliable.' I didn't ask when he thought that would be. I believe
he expects to wake up one fine morning and find the Federal blockade
dismantled and buyers for his tobacco again."

"We've not been bothered much at home," Spaulding confessed. "A
few bucks ran off when Federal cavalry came through the country, but
they came back when they learned the Federals wouldn't feed them."
Spaulding said that since they didn't have coffee, Duncan's excellent
brandy would suffice, and when Duncan said he didn't have any brandy,
Spaulding said, "Ah well." He also said that Lincoln couldn't possibly win
reelection, that the Federals were tired of fighting and would quit.

"Brother Rat," Duncan said solemnly, "no doubt you are right. As for
me, I will not think about it."

The next morning they rose from their blankets and wished they
hadn't finished the chicken the night before. Spaulding ragged Duncan
about his beard, which he said strongly resembled a turkey gobbler's,

while Duncan named the bearded Confederate generals and claimed, "Spaulding, your sweetheart will not think you a soldier without one."

"It is of no consequence," Spaulding grumbled, "unless I find money for my leave." He jerked around. "Here, what's this!"

The courier came off his horse without hitching and ignored the sentry's salute. Officers were already assembling outside Lee's tent when, napkin tucked at his neck, Lee ordered Colonel Venable: "Ride quickly to General Mahone and have him send two brigades to Blandford Cemetery. Those people have exploded a mine beneath our lines and are attacking in strength."

Duncan was already cinching his saddle. "I am Mahone's officer, Colonel," he cried. "I will accompany you."

They galloped across the Pocahontas Bridge, through neighborhoods which had been Petersburg's finest until the Federal shelling. Roofless, punctured, abandoned mansions strewed bricks into the road. Some had been reduced to brick heaps with only an end wall or fractured chimney still standing.

Their horses kicking up red dust, they hurtled down Jerusalem Road. Venable's horse was a terrific galloper and Duncan rode hard just to keep up.

By some fluke of terrain, neither the blast of the Federal mine nor the subsequent artillery barrage had been audible in Petersburg, but just beyond Blandford Cemetery the roar of guns sucked air from Duncan's lungs. A particulate haze hung over the crater where the Confederate lines had been blown up, and the air stank of cold clay and peppery gunpowder.

Around the next bend, the Federal cannonade was silenced as abruptly as if God had dropped a blanket over it.

Just short of Lieutenant's Creek, they left the plank road and splashed through shallows into the meadow where General Billy Mahone was waiting.

Before Colonel Venable had finished delivering Lee's orders Mahone was barking commands in his high, irritable voice. Mahone extracted Weisinger's Virginians and Wright's Georgians from the Confederate positions for a counterattack on the breached one.

The brigades started along Lieutenant's Creek, keeping below the sightline of the Federal signal towers. In an orchard filled with unripe peaches they were ordered to shed their knapsacks because they were going in for a fight. Men arranged their few personal belongings where they could recover them should they live.

When Mahone and Duncan arrived at General Bushrod Johnson's headquarters, only Confederate remnants—two hundred riflemen and a few guns—stood between the Federals and Petersburg. If the Federals took Petersburg and the railroads that supplied Lee's army, the army was done for. "Only two hundred men," Bushrod Johnson said, awestruck. "Damn them! Damn them and their cowardly mine!"

"General," Mahone spoke to the immobile Johnson with careful courtesy, "perhaps you'd escort me to a vantage point where I might inspect the enemy's dispositions."

"Captain Frazier will accompany you, General," Bushrod Johnson dismissed that idea.

Because Federal artillery was hitting Jerusalem Road, the three-man party dashed for the safety of a covered way. The noise was ferocious, tooth-rattling. Mahone yelled, "What do you make it, Major? A hundred guns? Two hundred?"

Duncan shouted back, "More'n a hundred. About the same they had at Fredericksburg."

A thin stream of wounded soldiers hobbled down the covered way. "Hell is busted," one whispered.

One man had been buried alive, had lost his trousers, was smeared with earth, and dirt dribbled from his nostrils. Another had his hands clamped over his ears and was yelling loudly, "They's niggers! Thousands of niggers! They's revengin' themselves for Fort Pillow! They's givin' no quarter!"

The covered way ended in a shallow ravine angling toward the fighting. Bushrod Johnson's aide pointed. "Up there. You can see the Federals from there." The aide swallowed. "I'll hold the horses."

When Duncan and the general topped the rise, they overlooked half a mile of Confederate lines.

The Confederate trenches had been deep enough for a man to stand without being shot, narrow so an exploding shell wouldn't do much damage. Circular earthen forts anchored the line, and rations and ammunition were brought forward through covered ways, protected from sharpshooters and artillery. The soldiers lived in bombproofs, some with brick chimneys.

But after the Federal mine exploded, the only unwrecked trench was a shallow communications trench behind the crater. There the Confederate survivors had rallied.

"God Christ Almighty!" Mahone said. "Jesus Christ Crucified! The bastards! The sons of bitches!"

The crater was thirty feet deep, 150 feet across, and it steamed: raw earth, turned bottom to top—gray over red—splintered timber, wrecked gun carriages and limbers, a crumpled tin stove, an officer's leather trunk half buried, a human torso—just the torso—its wounds cauterized by dirt, human limbs, some perhaps belonging to the dislimbed torso. So many bodies were dismembered that intact corpses were a relief to the eye.

From one wall to the other, the crater swarmed with Federal attackers. Two hundred rifles pop-popped at them, but it was their own stunned horror, more than anything else, that kept the Federal soldiers in the hell they had created.

Duncan was counting. "One, two, three, four, five, six, seven, a dozen, that's two dozen, make that thirty, thirty-one, thirty-three regimental flags. General, if those boys get out of that pit the war's over."

Mahone smiled a hard smile. "It will be our duty, Major, to ensure they do not get out of that pit. Kindly invite Colonel Saunders to bring up his brigade. Ask him to come at the double-quick."

Mahone's brigades hurriedly formed in a swale below the crest. The Confederates were red-hot: life was hard enough in the Petersburg trenches without they burrowed underneath sleeping men and blew them to tarnation. Life was awful enough without they sent niggers at you.

John Brown's mad fantasy of blacks slaughtering whites filled these men's minds. They told no nervous jokes and their officers made no speeches.

When the Federals climbed out of the pit, they formed ranks two deep. At their back, in the crater, thousands more flourished like botflies in a dirty wound. Toward the pit more Federal regiments were advancing in columns, and the ridge behind was black smoke and thundering guns.

The color bearer stepped before the Federal formation and unfurled the Stars and Stripes. When the Federal army took a resolute step forward, the thin line of Confederate survivors broke and fled.

"Tell Weisinger to forward!" Mahone screeched. Screaming the rebel yell, his battle lines surged over the crest.

Federal artillery turned its grim attention to new targets, and Confederates flew apart or were scythed like grass. "Close it up! Watch your dress!" officers cried, and men who wished to rush were restrained and men who might have fled went forward obediently. Hot metal clipped them and they leaned forward and lowered their heads like men walking into a storm but kept on coming, screaming their dire yell.

As one, the Confederates halted, raised their rifles, and fired; a second volley from the second rank. Without delay, at the double-quick, bayonets extended, Mahone's furious brigades charged. "No quarter!" the Federals had shouted. Well, they'd give them no quarter.

The Federal front line tried to get behind the second line, but the second line was already breaking for the rear as the ice-cold bayonets of the Confederates dropped to the level of a man's soft parts and slid forward smooth as closing a drawer. The meeting of steel and flesh was a thud, a grunt, the yammer of curses.

Duncan took aim at a Federal captain, startled him with the first bullet, missed with the second, fired deliberately and the man dropped the flag he'd been carrying and Duncan's fourth bullet smacked him and a Confederate sideswiped Duncan's target with a rifle butt so he went down and two other Confederates invaded the man's body with triangular steel, one charging so hard he overran and when he turned to extract his bayonet he was brained by a colored sergeant swinging his rifle like a ball bat. Bone flew with brains. Duncan fired twice, point-blank, and grabbed the sergeant around the waist and they wrestled on the flag the Federal captain had defended with his life. The sergeant bucked like a wild horse and someone jerked the flag, rolling them so the sergeant was on top, and his hands grabbed Duncan's throat and he squeezed and Duncan banged at the man's back with his empty revolver—and a BLAST and powder flecks burned Duncan's cheek and the sergeant's eyes popped out of his head like soft pebbles on cords and his fingers went slack and the dead man was so suddenly weighty Duncan couldn't heave him but wiggled out from beneath. Duncan gasped thanks to the young Confederate who'd put his Enfield to the sergeant's ear, and the boy giggled and bit a fresh cartridge.

They were fighting in the shallow communications trench, jammed together so there was no room to move, no room to take a full swing or stab, and men wrestled and sometimes the bayonet that penetrated one man impaled another. Men fought with fingers and steel, knives and gun butts, and heads butted and teeth sank into the salty gristle of an Adam's apple. They tramped blood from the wounded and dead until blood rose above their shoetops. Dead men roll when you stand on them, wounded men buck. Confederates killed men who fought bravely, brained them when they turned to flee, shot them at a distance.

A colored soldier raised his hands to Duncan and said, in the softest voice, "Don't kill me, Master," and smiled a fine smile which collapsed when a Confederate officer's sword cut through his neck and lodged in the spinal cord. The officer kicked the man's head to free his sword.

Duncan tucked his pistol under his stump to reload. His left arm ached from absent hand to absent elbow. His face was stiff and sticky with blood. He'd lost his hat and the sun was drying the blood in his hair.

A Federal was using a regimental banner for a crutch and Duncan fired and the man vanished in his powder blast. A gunpowder-blackened Confederate ripped the flag from its staff, wrapped it around his chest, and high-stepped down the line crowing like a rooster.

The Federals fled from traverse to traverse, flooding into the raw smoking earth of the crater. They dove for its safety like men diving into a pond and slid and rolled down the walls in avalanches of dirt and stones.

Hammered by Federal artillery, the Confederates stalled, found cover, brought prisoners out of the trenches and started them toward the plank road. It was midmorning and desperately hot. Duncan took a canteen from a dead Federal and drank warm water that smelled of canvas and metal.

One man on each handle, Confederates lugged eighty-pound coehorn mortars into the recaptured trenches. Mortarmen measured their lightest charges to drop mortar bombs into the pit fifty feet away. Some lost Federal troops appeared and gaped at the mortar crews before they were killed.

Iron mortar bombs toppled into the pit like blackbirds and men shrieked when they exploded.

Federal guns killed the Confederates when they approached the crater rim, and Confederate bullets slathered the slope behind the crater when Federals tried to escape from it.

The sun beat down. Men pressed against the cool earth, mouths open, gasping. Mahone hurled a fresh regiment against the Federal left, and when a thousand Federal rifles spat defiance Mahone's regiment crumpled.

Kicking steps for themselves, the boldest Federals climbed the crater wall, lined its rim, and fired point-blank. Corpses were passed up to be used as sandbags. Other corpses filled a gap a Confederate gun was hitting.

In the Confederate trenches, officers sought their regiments, soldiers their friends, wounded helped wounded to the rear. The sun beat down.

Before General Mahone committed his last reserves, the six hundred rifles of Saunders's brigade, he asked Duncan, "How is it, Major? Are the bastards still coming?"

"No, sir. But if they decide to, we're not enough to stop them."

When Saunders's brigade was in line of battle, Mahone cried in his squeaky voice, "Men, the Confederacy rests on your shoulders. They burrowed under our lines and our friends were buried alive in their sleep. They collected our runaway servants, armed them, and turned them on us. They fault us for Fort Pillow and cry, 'No quarter!' " Mahone pointed forward. "God damn it to hell! I won't tell you what to do!"

"Then with your permission, General, I will," Colonel Saunders said. "Alabamians! Forward!"

The brigade rose up out of the swale like gray ghosts in gray smoke, and for a few seconds the Federals didn't notice. When the Federal guns hit, the brigade's yell of anguish and rage sent chills down Duncan's spine. That yell broke the Federals' nerve; their rifle fire became a harmless rattle and their bravest men dropped from the rim to the floor of the crater. Confederates grabbed abandoned rifles and launched them into the pit, bayonet downward. The coehorns' bombs generated screams and explosions.

"On my command, boys!" Mahone cried. Twenty seconds they waited for the order, and a man could have lived a lifetime in those seconds, might have explored all the byways of love and fear and hope.

"Forward!" Firing and yelling, graycoats toppled onto bluecoats, and Duncan strolled the crater parapet like an immortal, taking aim as if he shot straw targets. When his pistol clicked empty he dove into the melee where men wrestled and punched, bit and stabbed, and Duncan smacked a black corporal so hard with his empty pistol bone shards flew from the man's broken head. "My Jesus," the corporal murmured as he sank to his knees.

"Surrender!" a Confederate colonel demanded.

Other tongues raised the cry. "Surrender, God damn you!"

Confederates were still bayoneting and shooting blacks, and those Federals who'd surrendered recovered the weapons they'd dropped and fought again.

General Mahone yelled, "Why the hell won't you fellows surrender?"

A Federal officer turned aside a bayonet to shout, "Why the hell won't you let us?" And he stabbed his white handkerchief with his sword and jiggled it over his head and firing died and General Mahone hopped atop a broken limber and shouted, "I guarantee your safety. I give my word of honor. I will have the God Almighty ass of any son of a bitch who touches a goddamned prisoner. These men are brave bastards. They are my prisoners!"

The man beside Duncan was gasping. "Kill the damn niggers," he said.

"No! God damn it! No!."

A bareheaded Confederate snatched the hat from a Federal officer, and other Confederates followed his lead. Duncan captured an exhausted captain's black hat. The hat was too big for him and settled over his ears. Some Federal officers clamped hands over their hats, but in a flurry most Federal officers were soon bareheaded.

"No harm must come to them," Mahone cried. "I have given my word. Clear away that barricade. Let's get these prisoners out of here."

While the prisoners were gathering, Confederates raced to the back of the crater, dug firing steps, and began peppering the retreating Federals.

When Duncan reported to General Mahone, the general said, "Major, you look like hell."

"It's not my blood, sir."

"You'll draw flies. Wash and find a fresh shirt. Go tell General Bushrod Johnson we've reestablished his line—should he wish, he can quite safely inspect it."

When Duncan passed Mahone's message to Johnson, Johnson didn't turn a hair. He said, "You are welcome to wash in the springhouse." He added, "Your hat doesn't fit."

Although Federal guns had holed Johnson's headquarters, they hadn't hit the springhouse, and Duncan dragged the thick door open and came into dim coolness and the music of trickling water. The spring box was long, narrow, eight inches deep, and when Duncan dipped his hand, the water was numbingly cold and blood swirled through the clear water. When he opened and closed his fist, streamers floated away, and Duncan rubbed crusted matter from between his fingers. He knelt on the cool stone beside the spring box, removed his new hat, and plunged head and neck beneath the water. How the water plucked at him! How cold it was! If a man stayed under long enough, he might pass through to a new world, the mirror image of this, where men did not punch tempered steel into each other's bodies, where this day was only summertime.

Duncan took a breath and immersed his head again, rubbing and plucking his hair to loosen the clots of another's lifeblood. When he opened his eyes, the spring water was pink. He drank. He let water wash over his teeth. He'd been clamping his jaw, and it ached. He peeled off his shirt and dropped it into the water, and it drifted to the end of the box where an iron pipe discharged the flow.

The springhouse doorway looked out at summer, and the guns had quit. Insects buzzed but didn't come inside. Duncan set his revolver on the stone floor. The loading gate was broken and the hammer sprung. A clot of hair and something white, bone perhaps, were caught between cylinder and frame. Duncan put the pistol under water and fingered until he had the matter out. When he shook the revolver it rattled.

After he sluiced his shirt back and forth he slapped it against the wall.

His new black slouch hat had a braided leather hatband, and its silk lining was emblazoned with an eagle grasping arrows and its maker's name: "Kravitz, Fine Hats, 15 Waverly Place, New York City." The sweatband was stamped in gold: "M. M. Cannon, Capt. 40th N.Y." Duncan wondered if he'd ever visit New York. He wished Captain Cannon's head were smaller.

He drew on his damp shirt, holstered his broken revolver, and went after his horse.

At three that afternoon, Duncan met Spaulding at Lee's headquarters.

"Splendid, Wheelhorse! What a splendid hat! How I envy you."

Wordlessly, Duncan proffered it.

"Oh no! I couldn't! Wheelhorse—if you wear that hat to the next ball the ladies will flock to you. Tell me, was it a glorious fight?"

Duncan said, "I've come for my blanket and groundsheet. I never got a chance to roll them this morning."

"They tell me two divisions hit our line—and just three of our gallant brigades repulsed them into confusion. How I wish I had been there!"

"I wish I hadn't."

One of Lee's young aides told Duncan the general was inspecting the lines and hadn't signed the note for Planter Pickering.

Lee's aide said, "Sir, I admire your hat."

Duncan asked Spaulding if he had anything to eat, and Spaulding said he knew a Petersburg family with a garden. "They are only distant connections on my mother's side, but I am always welcome. We'll graze in their garden on our way to Poplar Grove."

"What's at Poplar Grove?"

"Money, Wheelhorse. Enough money to finance my furlough." Spaulding would say no more.

Of Petersburg's twenty-one churches only those on the Appomattox River side of town had undamaged steeples. The broad Augustan face of the mercantile exchange was pocked with holes. Bricks were piled neatly in the streets.

A young colored woman answered Spaulding's knock. "No sir," she said, "Master and Missus ain't home, and no sir, I can't let you into our garden on account of they say you eat like a hog. Like a hog, Master!" She slammed the door.

Spaulding shrugged. "As I said, Wheelhorse, they are distant connections. Never mind, I'll bring you a ham back from my furlough."

Before the war, Poplar Grove had been a park where bands concerted on pleasant summer evenings. Now, fifteen hundred Federal prisoners were guarded by militiamen and boys. The prisoners sat with lowered heads or lay on parched ground. Most were black and most had been robbed. The only attention they received was provided by flies.

A crude sign nailed to a tree advised: PERSONS WISHING TO RECLAIM SLAVE PROPERTY, SEE THE SERGEANT.

"Then it's true, Wheelhorse!" Spaulding rubbed his hands. "Niggers that aren't claimed will be sent to Andersonville. That is," he added, "if they aren't dispatched along the way."

A handful of Confederate officers strolled among the prisoners, asking the odd question, tilting a face for identification. "Master," one man cried, "I is Jed. Belong to Master Tom Stephens, just down the road. You remember me, don't you? I surely am homesick. Surely would like to go back to Master Tom if you could help me out."

"Wait here for me," Spaulding said.

"I thought your family hadn't any runaway servants."

"Wait here, will you? Give me your canteen."

Spaulding ignored many imploring hands before picking a young colored soldier and giving him water.

Under an old tulip poplar, Confederate officers whose former servants wore Federal soldier's uniforms waited while a cavalry sergeant wrote out receipts.

"Master Duncan."

The voice was so low Duncan couldn't identify its source. His eyes searched the disconsolate, the wounded, the dying, and the terrified. "Hello, Jesse. You hurt?"

Jesse was sitting back to a tree, hatless and shoeless; his shirt hung in shreds.

"No, Master Duncan," he whispered.

"What do you want, Jesse?" Duncan was so stunned the only words he had were simple ones.

"Don't want to go to Andersonville," Jesse said. "They kill me down there."

"I got to think," Duncan said.

Jesse whispered, "Never enough time to think, is there, Master Duncan?"

Spaulding was beelining toward them, his young negro following two steps behind. "Wheelhorse," Spaulding hissed, "do me a service."

"Spaulding, I don't . . ."

"Yes, yes! Look here. This Ethiopian and I have concocted a scheme of mutual benefit. I am to claim him as my servant and thus he avoids Andersonville and the near certainty some patriotic citizen will summarily end his life. Duncan, in the name of friendship, should yon cavalryman question my claim, you are to say that young . . . what's your name, boy?"

"Ben, Master."

"That Ben is known to you as my servant, that he was my body servant at the Institute. Can you remember?"

Duncan lifted a hand tiredly, and Spaulding led the man away.

If Duncan simply walked away, who would know? If Jesse lived to tell, what difference would it make? "He was just another Federal prisoner to me," Duncan might say. "He made his choice when he ran from Stratford."

"You'll come with me," Duncan said.

"Yes, Master."

"Those are sergeant's stripes."

"Yes, Master. Second sergeant, B Company, 23rd U.S. Colored."

"I never would have guessed you'd make a soldier. The way your generals sent you in, you didn't have a chance."

"Yes, Master," Jesse said.

"You sure you're not hurt?"

Jesse's eyes were dull. "Hurt my pride. Buckra stole my shoes."

Spaulding elaborated his yarn of runaway servants long after the cavalry sergeant ceased to care. "Yes, Captain, I don't doubt your word. You sign for him and the nigger's yours."

"Well," Spaulding said, "thank you. Ben, come along with me."

Duncan signed for Jesse of Stratford Plantation, Virginia.

The Confederates rode, the coloreds walked behind. After a few minutes, Spaulding said, "A hickory-smoked ham . . ."

"What?"

"That's what I promised you, and that's what I shall produce. It was a great comfort to know you would vouch for me. Who've you got there?"

"Jesse. Belongs to my father."

Spaulding chuckled. "How do they get up to it? Dressing them up in soldier suits, issuing them rifles, and sending 'em at us. At us!" Spaulding slapped his saddle. "Oh, I feel fine. I feel fine!" He turned. "Ben, what would you rather—go on the auction block or start that long march to Andersonville?"

Ben kept his eyes lowered, "I done told you, Master. I go with you."

Spaulding rubbed his hands together. "Prime buck like Ben. What you think he'll bring at the auction? Four thousand? Five?"

"Oh, Christ, Spaulding . . ."

"Not a word, mind you. I wouldn't want this transaction advertised."

Duncan reined in. "I never saw you today."

"Meet me at Johnny Worsham's tonight, Wheelhorse, and we'll celebrate my furlough in grand style."

Duncan said he had no heart for celebration and wished nothing so much as rest.

Spaulding rode off toward the Richmond & Petersburg railroad depot with his prize. Duncan and Jesse turned into the dooryard of a wrecked farmhouse.

Glass was out of the windows and irregular shell holes in the brick faced the Federal positions. Shade trees had been cut for firewood and the porch railings were gone. The front door hung askew.

The front parlor was empty of furnishings excepting a two-legged settee that slumped on the floor like an old dog. The mantelpiece had disappeared into somebody's cookfire, along with most of the wainscotting. Broken glass crunched under Duncan's feet. "I've got no food to give you."

"Not hungry."

"You fellows put up a hell of a scrap."

"You broke us."

"We've had considerable practice. You were green troops."

"Ain't green no more."

"Here, take this canteen to the well. Oh hell, I'll do it."

"What you think you got a servant for, Master?" Jesse said. "Sure am happy be servin' my old master. Master Gatewood always been good to me."

Duncan sat on the broken settee. He rubbed his eyes.

Jesse looked at him. "You shot someplace?"

Duncan said, "When I was young I thought everything could be made right, given time."

"You sleep. I'll keep a watch."

They did.

At dusk, when Duncan woke, his mouth was furred and his arm bloodless where he'd lain upon it. The windows were pale rectangles. A small fire burned in the fireplace. Duncan knuckled crust from his eyes and drank from the canteen. "I suppose I should see about getting us something to eat."

"Don't trouble yourself on my account."

"Jesse . . . remember those days on Uther's porch, learning our McGuffey's Reader? You and me, Leona and Sallie?"

"Like you said, some things can't be made right." He told Duncan about Rufus.

Duncan swore. After a time he said, "When you were attacking at the Crater, you yelled, 'No quarter!' For Christ's sake, why did you do that?"

Though his uniform was rags on his body, Jesse was not the servant he had been. He said, "How the hell should I know?"

"When we were young, I could have said anything to you that came into my mind. Anything at all."

"I expect that time ended for me before it ended for you. Don't take long for a nigger to learn to keep his mouth shut."

"Damn it, Jesse . . ."

"When we was tryin' to surrender back there, why did you fellows keep killing us? I saw many a colored man cut down with his hands raised."

"Some good men chose their own damnation this day," Duncan said. Wagons rolled past the house. "Christ, Jesse. You know I'm no deep thinker." A teamster's whip cracked and a mule protested. Duncan offered Jesse the canteen.

"Sallie's been a hospital matron since summer '62. I have deep feelings for Sallie. I don't know they are reciprocated."

"That can be hard. It hurts a man terrible loving a woman don't love him. Makes him feel the fool. What of the homeplace?"

Duncan was confused until he understood Jesse was asking about the Botkins. Duncan told of Uther's death and Aunt Opal's return to Stratford. They sat quietly for a while. Duncan said he'd get them something to eat.

"You gonna leave me here?"

"You going somewhere?"

It was a quick ride to Mahone's headquarters, where soldiers were enjoying Federal rations of mutton—a trainload of provisions had arrived in Petersburg.

Some men couldn't stop talking about today's fight. Others, like Duncan, couldn't speak a word, and nobody thought it remarkable when he halved a mutton ham and rode away with it.

"What time is it?" Jesse asked.

"Getting later."

The two men shared chunks of undercooked meat washed down with well water.

"You want to go home to Stratford?" Duncan asked. "If Lincoln gets reelected, the Confederacy is done. God knows you'd be a help. My sister's failing. Catesby died at the Bloody Angle."

Jesse stared out a ruined window. "I'm sorry. Mr. Byrd always seemed a good-natured man. We coloreds missed that fight. General Butler thinks niggers make good soldiers. Grant and Sherman aren't so sure."

" 'Beast' Butler—that's what we call him. When he commanded in New Orleans he threatened to treat ladies like women of the street."

"My, that's terrible. Don't know what I'd do if somebody threatened to treat my womenfolk like women of the street."

Duncan held his tongue. "If I send you back to Stratford?"

"My back still aches where your father whipped me. Sometimes Master Samuel just can't help himself."

Duncan joined Jesse at the window shell. The darkening landscape outside was treeless. Darkness pooled in the shell holes.

Duncan said, "The brothers I might have had didn't live. The twins were stillborn."

"I heard your mama took it hard."

"It won't matter who wins this war. Things will be the same—sorrow, sickness, and death."

"I s'pose it's not likely men will quit their wicked ways."

"Jesse, General Grant is a damn butcher."

"I believe General Lee has created his share of widows."

"Why . . . ?"

"Because we got to end this thing. You call me Jesse, I call you Master Duncan. Just usin' your name, 'Duncan,' comes hard to me. You are a fine white gentleman, I don't doubt. And no man can help who he falls in love with or if the woman loves him back. It'll take a hundred, two hundred years to cure this slavery mischief, and if you win this war, it'll take more time yet."

"If General Grant wins, we Virginians will be a conquered people. I don't know if I could bear that."

"Don't seem so terrible to me. 'Course I been a conquered people longer than you have."

Duncan laughed, and after a moment, Jesse laughed too.

"I never intended you harm," Duncan said.

"It ain't what a man intends," Jesse said. "It's what he does."

Although the two men talked past midnight, Duncan did not mention Maggie, nor did Jesse. At two-thirty in the morning, at a thinly manned stretch of Confederate line, Duncan passed Jesse through, explaining to an inexperienced captain of militia that the nigger was a spy carrying false information to General Grant.

57

LOSS OF THE

<u>WILD DARRELL</u>

"*I was the best clerk Silas Omohundru ever had," the old woman whispered, "although Silas employed me as proof of his positive indifference to 'trade.' Isn't it odd how eagerly the weak pick up what the strong have no more use for?"*

Although dusk was settling over the garden and lay musky in the old woman's garden room, the lamps were unlit, and the girl was drowsy. She sat up straight and asked, "Could I have another cup of tea?"

"There's a bell behind you, if Kizzy elects to answer it."

The girl yawned behind her hand. "Excuse me. It has been a trying day."

"Yes." The old woman smiled. "My family plans to come here next month. Would you care to meet them?"

"Why, yes. Thank you."

"They will try to persuade me to sell the bank. Mine was the second Virginia bank to reopen after Mr. Roosevelt's bank holiday!"

Vaguely, she added, "I just may oblige them," but then her voice strengthened. "I have been a woman of business since eighteen hundred and sixty-four!

"You cannot imagine how I loved the unsullied pages of the ledger, the clean smell of newly imprinted bills and receipts, the office at Market and Water where I executed Silas's business. Every morning I'd arrive half an hour earlier than Silas's old clerk so I could neaten my office. 'My office'—how sweet those words! Kizzy's husband, Mingo, drove me in and vanished until the end of the day. I often brought Jacob. Wilmington's

businessmen were not unaccustomed to women—Mrs. DeRossette was not the only woman speculator—but my Jacob, playing quietly or sleeping in the little bed I'd fixed for him in a corner, my Jacob discomfited them. Jacob seemed satisfied to be with me, and his seeming indifference to other children suited our circumstances, but one day ragamuffins were playing noisily on the wharf, some improvised game with stick and ball, and Jacob watched them with the forlornest expression on his little face.

" '*Why dear, are those tears I see?' I asked.*

"*Jacob rubbed his eyes but kept them fixed on the other boys. 'No, Mama.'*

" '*Then what is it? Are you unhappy?'*

"*He turned to me then and in his most earnest voice asked, 'Mama, will I always be lonely?'*

" '*Dearest, you will lack for nothing. I will always love you. You know I will.'*

" '*I am not like them, am I?'*

" '*Those boys? Why, they are street urchins of . . . of the poorest class.'*

"*In a tone of absolute conviction Jacob pronounced, 'I will always be lonely.'*

"*Though I prompted him on numerous occasions, Jacob never again spoke about the matter. Like mine, my son's will, once fixed, was unalterable.*

"*Silas left for Richmond, where he still hoped to influence government policies. His clerk thought Silas a fool to entrust his affairs to a woman. Randall, I believe the man was called. Perhaps it was Rawlins. The man did work when the Wild Darrell was in port but spent the remaining days of the month gossiping and nurturing his connections. Thus my insistence on regular hours discomfited him.*

"*Government purchase orders had to be executed perfectly. A single inadequacy in the description of a napoleon cannon—omission of the foundry name, batch number, or proof marks—would delay payment until the defective paper was corrected. In my first week, I unearthed dozens of defective unpaid purchase orders. Since our goods had, in some instances, been delivered to the army months ago and since the manifests had been discarded, I invented the details I could not provide, to the clerk's vocal dismay. Since the value of the Confederate dollar dwindled monthly and sometimes weekly, these delays were consequential, and the first improvement I made in Silas's fortunes was repairing and rebilling those purchase orders.*

"*I had never been in a bank before and will never forget my first interview with Mr. Shemwell, at the time president of the Bank of the Cape Fear. I required Silas's former clerk—was it Rendall perhaps?—to ac-*

company me to Shemwell's offices at Front and Princess streets, and after I was introduced, I dismissed the man.

"Jacob accompanied me, his little hand in mine. Jacob could be restive when we were alone, but whenever I was doing business he was extremely well behaved." She paused in her narrative. "Jacob was so young. I wonder now how much he understood of our circumstances. How I wish I could ask him now.

"Mr. Shemwell's office was a powerful male's lair. A portrait of President Jefferson Davis established Shemwell's patriotism, the enormous safe in the corner his wealth, and brass cuspidors testified to his vices. Though his desk chair had arms and cushion, his visitor's chair was poor and plain. Since the unfortunate seated in that chair would have been interrogated by the bland facade of his mahogany desk, I set Jacob in it, and when I could not locate a second chair I stood helplessly by until Shemwell himself fetched me one. I may have been the first woman to penetrate Shemwell's sanctum sanctorum, and he wasn't sure whether to be offended or ill at ease. Although he would have liked to refuse, at my request he produced Silas's accounts.

"I smiled helplessly. 'Oh dear, Mr. Shemwell. I did not expect the records to be so extensive. Please could I remove them to study at my husband's office?'

"Since he finally had something he could deny me, Shemwell did so.

" 'In that case, sir, I shall have to examine them here. I hope it will not discommode you.'

"Well, of course it did, but he was well boxed, and I spent all day deciphering Silas's accounts. When Jacob needed to visit the necessary, I enlisted Mr. Shemwell's clerk to accompany him. Finally, at four o'clock, I was finished, and when Mr. Shemwell returned to his office, I was in his chair, my ledgers spread across his desk. Thumb tucked safely in his mouth, Jacob napped in the corner. With a parental nod toward Jacob, I whispered, 'What does the Confederate dollar trade at?'

" 'Twenty-two to one, madam. That's twenty-two Confederate dollars to one dollar in gold,' Shemwell explained in a hoarse irritated murmur.

" 'I wish you to convert my husband's Confederate currency into gold. I also note that Silas has a substantial investment in Confederate nine-percent bonds.'

" 'Mr. Omohundru has subscribed to every new issue.'

" 'And what is the present discount for those bonds?'

" 'I fear, madam, buyers are not plentiful. Mr. Omohundru's cotton promissories are more negotiable. They promise payment in cotton on the Wilmington wharves one year after a peace treaty is signed, and British merchants still make a market in them.'

" 'You financial gentlemen are so clever. How I admire you. Please sell the cotton promissories.'

"Shemwell spread his hands helplessly. 'Madam, Mr. Omohundru is a patriotic gentleman. I am afraid I could not close out his position without explicit instructions.'

"Since I had anticipated this difficulty, I handed him Silas's irrevocable power of attorney.

"Shemwell wiped his glasses, tugged at his beard, and seemed as if he might wish to utilize one of his spittoons. 'Madam, I regret I cannot execute your instructions until Mr. Omohundru arrives back in the city and confirms them in person. I am so sorry.'

"Businessmen make me so angry. They are perfectly happy to sell to you but not to buy, perfectly pleased to hold your money but won't trust you to hold theirs. It is a boy's game, business, and not suitable for girls! I was furious. 'Then, sir,' I whispered, 'you must produce all of Mr. Omohundru's cash, gold, and certificates. I understand the Bank of Commerce is sound.'

"Shemwell neither wished to produce Silas's wealth nor to be seen as one who would not. He hated whispering to accommodate a child who had no business with him and shouldn't have been sleeping in his office. He said he would trade the cotton-denominated bonds, and I said I would trade the nine-percent bonds myself. Shemwell had no real choice, and deprived of the full volume of masculine speech, couldn't debate me. When he knelt before his safe, I woke Jacob and answered his little boy's questions. Yes, we were going home soon. Yes, he could ride up in the driver's box with Mingo. Yes, we'd go as soon as nice Mr. Shemwell fetched my bonds.

"Silas once told me that respectable widows made a livelihood by meeting at the Confederate Treasury to sign these bonds. The bonds are now worthless but bear signatures from the first families of Virginia.

"Fortunately, a blockade runner, the Kestrel, had been slow unloading and overstayed its safe departure. With no duties until the next dark moon, its crew took quarters at the City Hotel and determined to drink Wilmington dry. Like most blockade runners, the crew were young and reckless, and it occurred to me that young men with so much gold in their pockets might be willing to invest in nine-percent bonds, especially if approached late in the evening by a handsome but shabby young woman with charming airs. I visited the City Hotel during hours when respectable women were not abroad, and though the youths made suggestions to me that were not proper, they didn't force themselves on me, and when the Kestrel sailed its crew owned Silas's nine-percent bonds. I did not mention Silas to these young men, and if they believed me a Confederate maiden in reduced circumstances, well, they were young men, and I am certain their ownership of nine-percent bonds was no worse for them than the whiskey their money might otherwise have obtained.

"A week after my first visit, when Jacob and I again visited Mr. Shemwell, that gentleman informed me that the Confederate dollar was now trading at twenty-four to one, but he had hopes it would attain a better rate when Abraham Lincoln was defeated for reelection.

" 'How much of Silas's currency have you exchanged for gold?' I asked him.

" 'Madam, as I told you, in my considered opinion we will soon see a better rate.'

" 'And the cotton-denominated bonds?'

"Those he had managed to exchange. Some of them, he informed me, into his own account.

" 'The currency I asked you to exchange at twenty-two has not been exchanged and now trades at twenty-four?'

"He said that was unfortunate, but I had his assurances, his professional opinion, his long experience in these matters . . .

"I told Jacob that kind Mr. Shemwell was giving us a lesson in arithmetic to which he should attend, that Mr. Shemwell had proved that twenty-four to one was a better rate than twenty-two to one and he might soon demonstrate that thirty to one was better still.

"Mr. Shemwell was angry and wished to express sentiments unsuitable for the ears of a mother with a child of tender years at her side. With difficulty he restrained himself. To spare Mr. Shemwell further pain I instructed him to turn over Silas's currency and gold and the proceeds of the cotton bond sales, which were to have been, he would recall, denominated in that same precious metal.

"Mr. Shemwell was shocked. 'Madam! That is a great deal of money!'

" 'Not so much as it was, sir.'

"From his safe Shemwell produced Confederate bills, a few—too few—British government bonds denominated in sterling, and four heavy bags of gold. While I counted, Jacob clinked gold double eagles and rolled them across Mr. Shemwell's floor.

"Armed toughs accompanied me down Princess Street to the Bank of Commerce, with which I established a satisfactory relationship. The sudden appearance of so much currency on an illiquid market depressed the rate, and I exchanged the last of it at twenty-seven Confederate dollars to one gold. In my early days in trade I had more fondness for gold than the metal deserves, but I was surely correct in valuing it more highly than Confederate paper.

"Federal cavalry frequently disrupted the Wilmington & Weldon Railroad. We could not bill for military goods until they were delivered, and our connection to Petersburg and Richmond was increasingly tenuous. Every afternoon, I visited Silas's warehouse to encourage his workers, to expend every effort to get our goods to the trains. My discreet gifts to rail-

road employees ensured there were cars for them. In this manner I kept myself occupied until Silas returned, on the waning of the moon, September 12th. Silas was wornout and despondent.

"In Richmond, Silas had inventoried government warehouses which bulged with supplies while the army starved. When Secretary of War Seddon asked Silas to report on the movement of goods through Wilmington, Silas offended the man by saying what passed through Wilmington was of no consequence if it got no farther than a Richmond warehouse. The man in charge of those warehouses, Commissary General Northrup, was a distant cousin of the Secretary of War.

"After this meeting, Silas's opinions were not sought again. Without family connections, Silas had no authority beyond his experience and knowledge, neither of which impressed our government.

"When he returned to Wilmington, Silas was in a bleak humor. To raise his spirits, I detailed my accomplishments, but he was indifferent. He remarked that the railroad journey from Wilmington to Petersburg, which had once taken thirteen hours, now took twenty-four.

"The next morning, I closeted my hopes for Silas's approbation, and Jacob and I departed for the office. In the early afternoon Silas arrived at the warehouse, where Mr. Shemwell arrived soon after. Shemwell complained indignantly about my behavior and judgment. In Shemwell's opinion, the Confederate dollar would rise against gold, and cotton-denominated bonds were as good as gold. 'Your wife has extracted every penny of your money from my sound banking establishment and entrusted it to . . .'

"Silas put a finger to his lips. 'Shhhh.'

" 'She has cashed your nine-percent bonds. Exchanged . . .'

" 'Shhhh . . .'

" 'Sir!'

"Finger pressed to his lips, Silas withdrew silently into the interior of his warehouse and when Shemwell would have pursued, closed the door in his face.

"That night, the first of the dark moon, Silas, Jacob, and I dined in a private room in the City Hotel and afterward waited on the wharf for the Wild Darrell. Neither Jacob nor I had ever seen the docking of our own blockade runner, and I don't know who was more excited. Every time Pilot MacGregor sounded the Darrell's steam whistle, Jacob shrieked and covered his ears, and I knew exactly how he felt.

"The Wild Darrell was the most beautiful boat I have ever seen, low and gray and smart as a fresh-minted gold piece. Looking at her, I could have been satisfied if the war went on forever.

"As soon as the hawsers were wrapped, stevedores swarmed over her while the sailors rollicked ashore for their customary celebration. 'Come,'

Silas said quietly. 'You must see this once. It will give the child something to remember.'

"A room on the second floor of the City Hotel was reserved for the Wild Darrell's crew. In a city where many children went to bed hungry, the seamen's table was laid with hams and roasts of beef, chickens, crabs, oysters, and wooden buckets containing bottles of iced champagne. Mac-Gregor was already drunk and boldly toasted Silas, 'To him who has made our prosperity possible!'

Silas raised his own glass in salute, called for attention, and explained that I, his wife, was now clerk of the company and instructions from me were the same as instructions from himself. Silas said he was proud of their long association and glad to count such skilled seamen as friends. Silas said that words were poor thanks and proposed, as per custom, to promptly pay their wages in gold. He added—rather slyly, I thought—'If my wife should approach you with nine-percent Confederate bonds, you needn't feel positively obligated to buy them!'

"Apparently my bond dealings were news in Nassau, because the sailors found this sally amusing.

"I took no drink and Silas took only what he could not politely refuse. A glass with the drunkard macGregor was a bitter draft, but Silas downed it manfully.

"When we returned home, I warned Silas that MacGregor might have been drinking during his passage through the blockading fleet and that our ship was imperiled.

"Silas wore such a sad expression on his face. 'When I was younger, I thought success assured to those who pressed their endeavors with honesty, energy and honor. . . .'

"I was impatient with his despair and unfortunately I told him so. Without another word to me, Silas took his still packed suitcases to the railroad station, where he waited until morning for the Richmond train.

"In Silas's absence, I hoped to improve his opinion of me by attending to his business. The Wild Darrell sailed on time, but not before I told MacGregor his failings were remarked. The rogue swore he hadn't started drinking until safely across the bar in the Cape Fear River and next passage he would wait until he stepped off the Wild Darrell for his first drink. MacGregor loved that boat, and he was the finest pilot on the coast—a fact which comforted me more than it should have. In those days I over-valued talent.

"Other boat owners and speculators were surprisingly willing to share their hard-gained knowledge with a keen and flattering novice. That month was one of the happiest of my life and flew by so rapidly that Silas was back before I missed him. Silas didn't say much: they still would not listen to him in Richmond, his advice was unheeded, Lee's army starved.

"*The first night of the dark moon, our little family dined at the City Hotel, and in a desultory manner, Silas asked Jacob what he had learned at the office. When Jacob recited his child's sums, Silas was briefly interested and called him 'Marguerite's little tradesman.' That night we waited on the wharves for the Wild Darrell, until, at two-thirty in the morning, the fateful telegram was brought to us.*

"*Fort Fisher, at the mouth of the Cape Fear River, was an enormous ring of sand forts, surrounded by swamps and mosquitoes. From its parapets at dawn we could see onto Frying Pan Shoals, where the poor Wild Darrell had been driven by the blockaders. Though the crew had reached shore, the surf was too rough to salvage the cargo, and we watched as our beautiful gallant ship broke up. Silas showed no emotion, but I was sick at heart.*

"*Silas told me to pay the crew.*

"*I said, 'But I am sure MacGregor was drunk. And the crew must take the same financial risks as we do. As we have lost everything, so must they.'*

"*Silas looked at me as if he had never seen me before, never known me, never seen me nurse Jacob, never listened to my singing, never touched my skin. He nodded. 'As you prefer, madam. The company is yours. Run it as you see fit.'*

"*In silence we returned to the great house we had rented, and I took Jacob to Kizzy. Silas and I made love that day and three times that night with not one word spoken between us. In the morning Silas took the train north, and I never saw him again.*"

58

IMPROVING THE RACE

NEAR PETERSBURG, VIRGINIA
OCTOBER 9, 1864

The men who object to Sambo
Should take his place and fight.
For its better to have a nigger's hue
Than a liver that's wake and white.
Though Sambo's black as the ace of spades
His finger a trigger can pull
And his eye runs straight on the barrel sights
From under his thatch of wool!
So hear me all boys, darlings—
If he asks for rights, I won't laugh.
The right to be killed I'll divide with him
And give him the greater half!

—Poem popular in the Army of the Potomac

MOST EVENINGS WHEN the 23rd USCT was in bivouac, First Sergeant Jesse Burns held reading school, but today was Sunday and the school's texts were Testaments the Missionary Society had provided. Jesse's reading pupils had grown in number, and Jesse asked the white officers to help out. Lieutenants Seibel and Hill—who'd been abolitionists before the war—were willing, and Captain Fessenden had had a real knack for teaching.

Reading school was the one place where officers and soldiers, whites and coloreds met as men, and their manners were courteous, even delicate. For it is a delight to both races when a forty-year-old once slave whose entire name is Dempsey first writes that name and traces each letter with his forefinger, and it is memorable when he discovers that the very marks on the page before him are the precious phrase "Yea, though I walk through the valley of death."

It was a cool Sunday evening. Tomorrow, or next day, the Johnnies would try to reclaim some of the ground that had been so bloodily wrested from them, but this dusk was quiet, and around their cookfires the men talked low and a harmonica moaned.

Brass gleaming, uniform ironed, hands clasped in the small of his back, First Sergeant Jesse Burns stood at parade rest outside Lieutenant Seibel's tent and announced himself. "Sir, I'd like a pass tonight to visit the 38th. I've friends there. They were in that fight at Chaffin's Farm."

Seibel wrote out the pass. "You'll be here at reveille."

"Yes, sir."

"That was some scrap. Tell your friends some of us admire what they did."

First Sergeant Burns's pass warranted passage "within the area controlled by our forces outside Petersburg, Virginia." When Jesse was living with Uther Botkin and courting Midge, he'd ask Uther for a pass so he could walk to Stratford. This army pass was not the same thing.

On the railroad platform, Jesse showed a provost's corporal his pass.

When Jesse was courting Midge, patrollers might ask, "Goin' to visit that Midge gal, Jesse? Wish I was. She's a pert little thing."

It had shamed him, their talking about her.

Now, First Sergeant Jesse Burns stood impassively while a white corporal struggled through the document, moving his lips.

"Where you goin'?" the man finally asked.

"Anywhere within the area controlled by our forces," Jesse quoted.

"God, I hate a hincty nigger," the man said.

"Don't matter what you hate, Corporal." Jesse climbed on the train. He had a flatcar to himself. Officers rode the passenger car at the end of the train.

The country along the Richmond/Petersburg line seemed the surface of the moon. Miles of stubby tree stumps had provided abatises and bombproof timbering and cookfires. Desperate brigades had contested for these empty, meandering red clay trenches and covered ways.

General Grant's City Point & Petersburg Railroad ran from the supply wharves to the front. Where it came nearest the lines, the tracks dipped through trenches to protect trains from Confederate sharpshooters.

The upper third of the balloon stack was dotted with red bullet holes. Heat and sparks blanked out a broad band of stars directly overhead. The empty flatcar jiggled and bounced, and Jesse clung to a stanchion when the train rocketed downgrade.

Officers got on at Parke Station and Hancock Station. At Meade Station a white sergeant vaulted onto the flatcar, but moved to another after he spotted Jesse.

The train passed artillery parks, hundreds of guns gleaming in the starlight, and wagon depots where ambulances, limber carts, and supply wagons lined up side by side and head to tail in a vast silent square.

They puffed past the huge naval mortar "Dictator"; its flatcar side-tracked for tomorrow morning's bombardment. The Dictator was squat and fat, and its iron mouth was commodious enough to scald a yearling hog.

The army was a sleeping beehive. A man could almost hear the somnolent buzz.

Jesse's heartbeat expanded into the evening. Who would he be? Would he ever find Maggie and Jacob? Should he stay in the army? Should he become a schoolteacher? Some of Jesse's men expected Master Lincoln to tell them what to do with their new lives.

When he got off the train, Jesse showed his pass to another provost's man and asked for the 38th.

"They're bivouacked at Broadway Landing." The provost's man pointed to the road. "Them boys did a good job the other week. Couldn't get white brigades to make that attack. I've heard white troops are smarter than coloreds."

"Maybe coloreds got more to prove."

"Maybe so." The man coughed. "Tell 'em . . . tell 'em they did fine."

The road curved toward the landing in a slow white arc. The narrow moon was outshone by starlight, and shooting stars dove into the horizon.

A soldier informed Jesse that Sergeant Major Ratcliff was probably in his tent if he wasn't at the hymn-singing.

Ratcliff's tent was pitched on the slope above the river on sheltered level ground.

"Sergeant Major Ratcliff!" Jesse called. "First Sergeant Burns has the honor to pay a call."

Last July, when news of the Crater debacle had flashed through the army, Ratcliff had brought a company from the 38th to help the survivors, and that night when Jesse reached the Federal trenches, Ratcliff and his men had still been working. "'Bout time you come home," Ratcliff had said. "Me and my boys were thinkin' to go after you." Though the moon was bright that night and Ratcliff wasn't three feet away, he didn't remark Jesse's teary eyes. "Burns, I hope you killed some Johnnies today," he went on. "Because they surely killed a passel of niggers."

In his abraded voice, Sergeant Major Ratcliff sang out, "Burns, get in here and have a drink. I'm celebratin' promotion to the highest rank an enlisted man can get. Far as I know, the highest rank any nigger ever had."

Jesse brushed the tent flap aside. Cot, heap of unwashed clothing, a dropleaf table, one camp chair. "Now, Ratcliff, you know I don't drink."

"I know you don't. I just don't know why you don't."

"I'd like coffee," Jesse said, as always, and Ratcliff bellowed, "Private Washington, fetch Sergeant Burns a cup of your miserable coffee and get along to the singing. I'll be along directly."

The sergeant major's arm was in a sling, and a scab from a saber cut stretched from the corner of his left eye across his forehead.

"Ratcliff, you are the worst-dressed colored man in this army," Jesse said.

Ratcliff plucked at the hem of his rough field blouse as if some stranger wore it. "Hell, Burns, General Grant dresses like a mule drover, why shouldn't I?"

"I am happy for your promotion," Jesse said solemnly. "All of us are proud."

"Ain't nothin' to be proud about," Ratcliff said. "Major he gets out front a-waving his sword, so some Johnnie pots him, and the captain steps up, says, 'Follow me,' and directly a Johnnie picks him off too. Now we are down to lieutenants, and, Burns, you'd be astounded at the temporariness of white lieutenants.

"By this time we are tangled in the abatis and Johnny is cutting us up, and by God I have become acting regimental commander of the 38th United States Niggers, so I say, 'Boys, let's gut some Johnnies,' and be damned if we don't. White officers, they don't know how to talk to niggers. They say 'Follow me' or 'To the colors' when they should be saying 'Let's grab buckra by he stones.' "

"You suffered heavy losses."

Ratcliff took a drink. "I lost some friends. Next day Johnnies pushed us back where we was. You know why we attacked? Lincoln's up for relection next month and Grant wants to prove we ain't stuck in the mud."

Jesse recalled seeing Master Lincoln; Lincoln's weariness, the mightiest man in America but such a sorry damn horseman.

"Got your coffee, Sergeant Major," said a voice outside the tent.

"Leave it, Private, and go singing. Come on, Burns, let's sit outside. Maybe the night air'll improve my humor."

The James River curved wide and black, its slick current sweeping around the wrecks the Johnnies had sunk to block the Federal ironclads. Richmond was only eight miles upriver. Federal campfires dotted the riverbanks upstream and down.

The coffee in Jesse's cup was hot and sweet. "The whole army knows what you did. They think better of every colored man because of it."

Ratcliff snorted. "First Sergeant Burns, you think a white man took over command of his regiment like I done would be promoted to sergeant major? White man be captain by now, and General Grant keepin' an eye on him."

"It will be slow and hard work, improving the race . . ."

"It'll be goddamned never! Oh hell, Burns. Have a damn drink." Ratcliff leaned over and poured whiskey into Jesse's coffee. "I got this from a Johnny captain. If you wonder why they're still fightin', have a taste."

Jesse set the cup down. On the riverbank, hymn singers were gathered in a ring around a campfire, standing shoulder to shoulder. The singing began with a powerful hum, then melody, finally harmony.

"Edward, you have a wife?" Jesse asked.

"Got three, last I counted."

"We're going to win this war, Edward. General Sherman has taken Atlanta and Lincoln will win the election and before long we'll capture Richmond. I've been thinkin' what it'll be like after."

The song seemed to come from one voice, and trembled the night air.

Jesse said, "I had a wife, Maggie. Master sold her south."

"One of mine got sold. Next one it was me sold away, and the last's still down by Norfolk I reckon. Want a wife, get down to the cribs at City Point. All the wives you want."

"Never was another woman like Maggie."

Ratcliff contented himself with a snort and a drink of whiskey.

The voices were strong and clear as new honey: "We are climbing Jacob's ladder . . ."

"You teachin' reading in the 38th?"

"Hell, Burns. Readin' is for white men." He jerked his head. "Listen to that."

"I'm gonna eat at the welcome table, I'm gonna eat at the welcome table . . ." The lead was a sweet high tenor.

"That's Private Washington. He can't read, nary one word, but ain't no white man sing like him."

The chorus replied: "Yes, Lord, some of these days."

Jesse said, "You think Private Washington could lay out Grant's railroad? Fifteen miles of track laid under enemy fire. Ratcliff, our bread, when it gets to the regiment it's still hot from the ovens at City Point. Private Washington—can he do that?"

"Can't see why not."

"He can't read the damn plans!. Man can't read or write'll be the man toting rails and shoveling ballast. That's all Private Washington's good for."

Sergeant Major Ratcliff said sweetly, "You can read and write, Jesse. It be helpin' you?"

The chorus: "Yes, Lord, some of these days." Men around a fire used magic voices to drive back the night.

"It ain't gonna be different, Burns," Ratcliff said softly. "We ain't never gonna be like them. Some ways, we better."

"I've got a wife and a child . . ." Jesse said. "Master Gatewood married us, though she . . . Maggie . . . didn't want to."

"So why in hell don't you go with some woman what does? Lot of women, Jesse. Even an ugly bastard like you can find some woman put up with him."

"Maggie didn't have any choice. She was my slave same as I was Gatewood's. Ratcliff, how are we better than they are?"

Ratcliff stood up. "Sergeant, you'd talk the hair off a shoat. Let's go sing."

The moon emerged and the broad curve of the river shone colder and brighter than the campfires.

"I'm gonna sit at the welcome table."

"Yes, Lord . . . some of these days."

59

THE PROMISED LAND

THE PARTISAN RANGERS fled through a scorched land. Fields bounding the Valley Pike stank of burned corn, and burned circles marked where stooks of wheat or hayricks had been. Tangles of crusted, blackened boards memorialized pigsties, horse barns, chicken coops, cow sheds, springhouses, bank barns, corncribs, livestock scales, wool sheds, and grist mills. What livestock the Federals hadn't eaten they'd slaughtered and left to rot. When Captain Stump and his small band galloped by, black vultures groaned into flight.

Earlier, at daybreak, Stump and Ollie and Alexander Kirkpatrick had been surprised by Federal cavalry outside Harrisonburg. The partisan rangers' sentry had slept, misconduct which cost his life and the lives of three others who hadn't been quick enough from bedroll to horseback. When his comrades fled, Baxter had his hands up.

Captain Stump's band was diminished. Some men killed, some slipped away to join Colonel Mosby's more respected fighters, some gone home to wait out war's end.

Alexander, Ollie, and Stump had ridden two horses to death and Ollie had no saddle, but by three that afternoon they had put pursuit behind and paused at a stream to water. These days no sane Valley traveler would drink from a well. Ollie shuffled in circles, moaning and rubbing his buttocks. "I'm gonna kill this horse," he said. "Goddamned if I won't."

In August, the Federals had started burning the Shenandoah Valley. Though the Brethren protested the devastation of their crops and animals, they would not fight, and tens of thousands fled north to refuge with their Pennsylvania kin.

"Then you'll walk. Clever man." Alexander Kirkpatrick knelt beside his horse to drink.

After the Federals had burned most of the farms that sheltered them, the partisan rangers had ranged more widely, ridden more miles on poorer horses. Now, not far ahead, tucked into a mountain hollow on the far side of the Shenandoah River, was their safest hideout: a small farm which General Sheridan's arsonists had missed. The farmer had lost a leg at Gettysburg and a brother at Chattanooga, and there was grass for the horses, sweet water, and rest. The promised land.

"Alexander, I will shoot you one day," Ollie said. "I go to sleep at night thinking where I'm gonna shoot you and how I won't ever see your smug goddamned expression no more."

"I am grateful if I can keep your mind occupied to some useful purpose." Alexander bowed deeply.

Alexander had become a passable horseman. He carried four revolvers in saddle holsters and the seven-shot Spencer repeating carbine slung across his back. He wore a wide-brimmed, shallow-crowned black hat. Though it perched ridiculously on his head, it amused Alexander to wear the hat of the farmer he'd murdered. Alexander told time by a watch that had once belonged to a Federal cavalryman. Some evenings, when he was drunk enough, he'd open the watch back and examine the likeness of the cavalryman's wife and a lock of her black hair. How melancholy life was!

"What's that dust?" Ollie asked.

Captain Stump snatched a spyglass and scrambled up the streambank. "Christ! Don't those bastards ever give up?"

They quickly remounted. Although they flogged their weary horses, their pursuers steadily overhauled them.

"Half a mile," Captain Stump cried encouragement. Once they crossed the bridge and ducked into the piney woods, they couldn't be caught.

Ollie's horse's gait was breaking up, and the beast wouldn't have carried Ollie much farther even if the bridge had been intact.

Bridge roof, deck, pilings burned and partly submerged, clinging to the far shore. Sheridan's arsonists had visited here.

Captain Stump wheeled, peering upstream and down for a ford, but their pursuers galloped around the bend, four abreast, shooting. A bullet whipped the captain off his horse, and Alexander's mount slumped to its knees. Alexander lost his pistol when he grabbed for his pommel.

Ollie emptied three Federal saddles before a rain of bullets expunged him from this life. Alexander jerked his hands above his head. Right leg at an acute angle, Captain Stump slumped in the road, blood leaking through fingers held to his face.

Their captors were young, magnificently mounted, and skilled at their work. Without a word, they collected the rangers' guns and tossed them into the river. Several attended the survivor of Ollie's marksmanship, others tied two dead comrades to their horses. They booted Ollie into the ditch.

Not unkindly, but without speaking, they brought Captain Stump and Alexander to a square-built officer on a sorrel gelding. "Major Young," he said. "Seventeenth Pennsylvania Cavalry."

Though his nose and forehead were bleeding and his leg flopped useless as a rag doll's, Captain Stump managed a grin. "Captain Thaddeus J. Stump, Stump's Partisan Rangers. Frankly, sir, I hadn't hoped to meet you again today."

"We were delayed at your bivouac by housekeeping duties."

"Poor Baxter. You hanged him, I suppose."

"By now your man will know if Saint Peter has rebel sympathies."

Stump acknowledged the joke with a small smile. "We are Confederate prisoners and request the treatment accorded to prisoners of war."

Major Young didn't find that theory worthy of comment. "You know, Stump, that we will kill you. But we will not serve you as you have served so many of our men. We will not cut your throats but will give you a chance for your life. Ten rods start, on your own horse, with your spurs on. If you get away, so be it. But my men are dead shots."

Stump uncorked his flask, took a long swallow, and offered it to the major, who refused. Stump wiped his lips on his sleeve. "Couldn't be fairer," he said. "Fairest thing in the world."

One Federal used a dead horse's reins to tie a stick to Stump's leg as a splint. Others were gathering wood for cookfires or preparing rations. When a fellow skidded down the bank with an armload of canteens and ended up sitting in the river, his friends thought that it was pretty funny.

Two men lifted Stump onto his horse. His leg jutted to the side. Stump leaned forward to mutter in his horse's ear. When he was finished, he patted the beast distractedly, turned to the major to ask, "Say, Major, have I time for a prayer?" and at the same instant spurred his mount. Before the invisible ten-rod boundary Stump slipped over in his saddle, clinging to his horse's far side like a red Indian. The Federals fired, Stump and horse crumpled, and the horse rolled over on him. All that was visible above the horse's body was his splinted leg, sticking up like a flag. One of the Federals walked over and fired twice: once for the horse.

"Sic transit gloria," Alexander said.

"Sir?" Major Young turned his head.

"I believe the dauntless Captain Stump has been daunted."

"Are you by chance an educated man?"

"I attended two years at Yale but was an indifferent student. I knew some Latin, and phrase books easily persuaded others of my learning. I have found the world an inhospitable place and greatly prefer lies and dreams."

"I was a professor of rhetoric myself," the major noted. "In Philadelphia."

"I taught at a women's seminary in Staunton. I can't recall the name of the place. I ruined a girl and married her. It's the damnedest thing but I cannot recall her face."

"Are you one of Captain Stump's officers?"

"Do I hear you aright? Do you imagine that Captain Stump had officers?"

"Would you make Captain Stump's wager?"

"I am no horseman." Alexander paused. "Tell me, sir. Do you think there are mermaids?"

"Mermaids? I do not."

"The mermaid I saw as a boy was hideous. How is it, sir, that our dreams are so much more beautiful than anything actual?"

"Do you wish to write a letter? Is there one who would wish to know your fate?"

A trooper flung a rope over a tree limb. Another was grooming his horse. One went to the roadside to pee.

"I cannot believe there is a living soul who gives a damn about me," Alexander said.

"You are an honest man," Major Young said. "How did you fall in with these thieves?"

"I was not an honest man when I fell in with them."

60

CHRISTMAS GIFT

STRATFORD PLANTATION, VIRGINIA
DECEMBER 24, 1864

THE SECOND FLOOR of Stratford House smelled of asafetida and Grandmother Gatewood's lavender. Duncan's bed was soft and too short. That lithograph on the wall: the sword Excalibur clutched by an unearthly hand above a foggy lake—what did it mean? When Duncan stretched, his knuckles struck the headboard.

Thick walls and doors prevented his hearing the prayers offered by Grandmother and her great-granddaughter Pauline in Grandmother's room. Duncan was incurious about the content of Grandmother's prayers but suspected that had they been answered, much of the county would have been reduced to ashes.

Poor dear Leona. Duncan sat bolt upright extracting his mind from the image of his sister buried in the frozen ground.

A thought hovered at the edge of Duncan's mind that Catesby had propelled Leona to her fate, but the thought found no purchase. Catesby had been Duncan Gatewood's friend, and in some respects Duncan was (and was entirely determined to remain) simple-hearted.

Winter had frozen the armies in place, so Sallie Kirkpatrick could get leave from Camp Winder. They'd taken the canal boat to Lexington, and Duncan's horse had carried them through the Goshen Pass and over Warm Springs Mountain to Stratford.

He slipped on his shirt and buttoned it. He prepared each pant leg before he stepped into it. He wriggled socks up his ankles, started his boot, and forced his heel. When he was a boy he had flung his clothes on, buttoning his shirt as he raced down the stairs. Duncan dismissed that thought too.

Outside Grandmother's door, Duncan sang out, "Good morning, Grandmother! Pauline!" Pauline returned a muffled greeting.

His father sat at table, cup between his hands. The room was still elegant. Blue willow plates lined the shelves of the china press, its mahogany veneer doors still shone, the chair rail was recently dusted, the lithograph of Washington at Mount Vernon hung straight. His father's gray bristles were three days old and his shirt hadn't been changed recently.

Old Pompey marched in with a silver coffeepot polished until the eye winced at the glare. "I know Master Duncan be wantin' his coffee, first thing," Pompey chuckled. "This parched corn ain't so good as the old-timey coffee, but it ain't too bad. No sir! Ain't too bad." He paused. "Master Duncan, it sure good have you back home. Yes, sir. We can face all these hard times together!"

"Thank you, Pompey," Samuel Gatewood grumbled. "Will you see if you can spur Franky to alacrity?"

"I don't know if she got any of that alacrity, but that Franky! Man can never tell."

Samuel Gatewood's look meant: "See what I have to put up with?"

And old Pompey's departing chuckle meant: "Oh, these white folks too much for me."

The parched coffee wasn't worth much either.

Samuel said, "Young Thomas sleeps late. I see the army hasn't improved him in that respect."

"He's young yet. Bones still growing."

"God, how I fear for him!" Startled by his own outburst, Samuel blinked. "You'd think the government could leave us something. They are taking our seed corn."

Duncan said, "Our officers try to keep the young boys out of the worst fighting. I've spoken to Thomas's colonel."

"Institute cadets died at the fighting at New Market! Boys of fifteen!" Samuel sighed. "I begged him to stay through the spring planting, but he would enlist. He would!" Uncomfortably, Samuel shifted in his chair. "As cold as this winter has been, spring will be slow to arrive."

"Won't the government return your servants it has rented?"

His father shook his head. "Some have run away, and four fulltask hands died. Richmond's climate is not salubrious for coloreds. Along with its annual accounting of my confiscated property, our Confederate government appends a promissory note which I faithfully carry to the National Bank of Hot Springs, where it is credited to my account with the ledger notation that my deposit was scrip, not gold, and will be repaid in the same valuable consideration."

Franky backed in with a tray. "Here you is, Master Duncan. Your favorite! Probably every man's favorite! I seen many a man tuck into my ham and cornbread and never a one didn't come back for more. That Rufus, he always came back for more."

Duncan swallowed. He could not tell Franky about Rufus because he could not tell his father he'd set Jesse free.

After Franky went out, Samuel Gatewood rubbed his eyes. "Amos Hevener's son is a deserter and lives miserably in that saltpeter cave above Benson's Run. What will we think about the boy when all this is over?" Samuel eyed the lithograph of Washington as if that patriot were privy to his thoughts and announced: "Honor is neither goodness nor kindness nor Christian charity: it is honor!"

"Father . . ."

"When I did not challenge John Dinwiddie for killing my father, I believed I took the more Christian course. Father's dishonor was Father's, not mine, and could not be expunged by anything I might do. I was young, I was wrong."

Samuel looked so miserable Duncan longed to say something to help, but only perfect words would not be resented.

"My son, honor can scrub the stain of dishonor. General Lee's father was a debtor, his half brother, Harry, a wretch; has not the general's honor erased the Lee family's stain?

"And you . . ." He motioned at Duncan's arm. "Have not your terrible wounds restored our family's honor?"

At Duncan's protest, Samuel raised a hand. "Had I demanded satisfaction for my father's shabby death, I do not believe Grandmother Gatewood would have become the creature she has become. And had Grandmother not amplified Leona's grief, perhaps my dear daughter would still be with us."

"Father, fever took Leona."

Samuel Gatewood's eyes were tired and hot. Each word dripped from his tongue. "Had I behaved honorably, you would not have allowed yourself to be seduced by that jezebel Maggie . . ."

"Midge."

Samuel's headshake was a horse dislodging a fly. "At her wedding to Jesse, I named her Maggie."

"She was Midge when I knew her."

Samuel drew breath. "Duncan, I have considered these matters! I confess that all our family's problems were created by my disregard for honor."

"Yes, sir," Duncan said. After a thoughtful moment he picked up his fork, smiled, and said, "We don't get ham like this in Petersburg."

Samuel coughed and murmured, "Aunt Opal is a treasure. Her husbandry keeps all Stratford in meat."

A moment later, wan Pauline slipped in to make up Grandmother

Gatewood's tray (gruel, a single weak cup of precious tea) and tiptoe back upstairs.

When Abigail and Sallie Kirkpatrick joined them, the older woman glowed with pleasure, "Dear Duncan, it is so good to have you here. Stratford has seemed empty without you. My son . . ." She patted his hand. She beamed.

Sallie collected Pompey's brilliant coffeepot and more cups. "Sir, may I pour you another?"

"One cup is all I take. Even when we are furnished with real coffee, I only take a single cup."

Sallie said that coffee was one of the few commodities in short supply at Camp Winder. "I believe that if Surgeon Lane could find the beans, he'd swap them for medicines. Men don't understand how small comforts heal."

From her arrival just a week ago, the young woman had made herself indispensable, helping with the household work, invigorating the female side. It had been Sallie who insisted on the German tree that now adorned the parlor, she who claimed that holiday cakes made with maple syrup or honey were every bit as good as those made with sugar. "And," she'd concluded triumphantly, "we have flour! Why, if a household in Richmond had as much flour as Stratford, its neighbors would gnash their teeth in envy. And there are apples in the cellar and Kieffer pears and, oh my, everything a holiday household could desire."

So, Stratford was to celebrate Christmas despite itself. Abigail went to the attic and emerged three hours later bearing mysterious articles and a generous coating of dust. Samuel shot a deer, which hung for a week in the root cellar before he and Jack butchered it. And the day before, accompanied by Pompey, Samuel traveled to SunRise and fetched two small hogsheads of whiskey and a mysterious something which vanished into his spartan office. There were Christmas whisperings and secrecy and anticipations, and Abigail asked Sallie to help her complete the servant's annual clothing issue, since Grandmother Gatewood would not help clothe those who plotted to run away and (she was certain) had celebrated Lincoln's reelection. Hadn't Grandmother heard an uproar in the Quarters the same day the grim news reached Stratford, and hadn't two laying hens disappeared for the coloreds' victory celebration? Why should she loom for an ungrateful people?

"Oh, Grandmother," Abigail sighed.

Sallie and Abigail spent hours sewing in Abigail's bedroom and talked with the frankness of women who have decided to be friends.

Now, the morning before the celebration, Duncan said, "Sallie, you've been wanting to see your homeplace, and I'd enjoy a ride."

Samuel Gatewood checked the mantel clock. "Young Thomas would wish to accompany you. I'll see he rises."

Abigail Gatewood said, "Samuel, I'm sure that had Duncan desired Thomas's company, he would have said so."

Samuel Gatewood flushed. Although he had welcomed Sallie Kirkpatrick to his home, he had little to say to her, and in the evening when everyone gathered in the parlor, Samuel retired early. To his wife, Samuel confessed, "I like the girl—even admire her. But she calls forth memories I'd sooner suppress."

The road along the river was coated with unblemished snow, and the horse's breath plumed from his nostrils. Duncan's horse had filled out on Aunt Opal's oats and was frisky despite his double load. Signs of Stratford Plantation's wartime neglect, the flourishing crops of thistles, washouts, and depleted fields, were healed by snow. It was as it had been when Duncan was a boy.

"Can we stop at the graveyard?" Sallie asked.

The Stratford graveyard contained Uther Botkin's remains beside his beloved wife's. Leona Byrd's fresh mound was between Catesby Byrd's slightly sunken one and infant Willie's tiny grave. Sallie laid her wrap in the snow and knelt upon it to pray while Duncan stood awkwardly, hat in hand.

Fine scalloped clouds connected horizon to horizon, and Snowy Mountain seemed impossibly high. When Sallie rose to her feet, Duncan said, "Poor Catesby. God, how I miss that man."

Sallie asked about Pauline, and Duncan said she was young yet. Pauline would not grieve forever.

"But Duncan, we do grieve forever."

Aunt Opal wanted them to look for a feral sow who had taken her brood to the woods when all the other hogs were driven to Stratford. Duncan angled his horse along the logging road which Aunt Opal had said was the sow's "stamping grounds," and though they saw plenty of stamping, big tracks and little ones, they saw no sow until they neared the Botkin outbuildings, when, with two grunts and a squeal, Mama and her small porkers scurried from the empty horse barn to the safety of the woods.

Sallie laughed. "Aunt Opal will come up here every evening for a week and lay out food until she can close the barn doors on that sow. When it comes to a battle of wits between woman and pig, wager on the woman every time."

Uncut dead grass surrounded the porch of the shuttered house. Without its rocking chairs, the porch seemed too empty, naked. Duncan said, "I'll open the shutters while you start a fire," and gave Sallie the key for the brass padlock. Duncan could not remember a time when Uther Botkin's house had been locked.

He dallied with the shutters outdoors to give Sallie time to reacquaint herself with her childhood home. When she came out, she said, "Oh, it is as cold as the tomb."

"Then we'll sit outside as we did when we were Uther's prize scholars."

"You were no prize!"

He laughed, and after a time she laughed with him. He tucked Sallie's wrap around her shoulders. She said, "Leona, Jesse, you, and me: what an odd company we were. Oh, Duncan, poor Leona so hoped her prettiness would bring her happiness and so feared it might not. Thank God Jesse is safe!"

"First Sergeant Jesse Burns, if you please."

Sallie said, "Jesse was like an older brother to me."

Duncan stuffed his pipe with tobacco. "When I went with Spaulding, I didn't know what he intended and certainly didn't expect to see anyone I knew. It was a small park where they'd had band concerts before the war! The prisoners were just black faces, indistinguishable as peas in a pod. Colored Federal soldiers, that's all they were, and although I didn't wish them ill, I cannot say I wished them well. When Jesse called out from that welter of misery my heart jumped. A chill palsied me. Here, in this damnable place, was one I knew. When I recognized Jesse's face the other faces became men." Tears welled unheeded from Duncan's eyes. "My God, Sallie, what have we done?"

Sallie said, "Yes, Duncan. If you still want me, I will marry you."

The pale sun reached its zenith and drove every shadow into hiding. After the fire had warmed the house, Duncan and Sallie pulled Uther Botkin's bed near to the fire and covered the straw tick with a faded blue-and-red quilt that years ago had made the journey to this place in Sallie's mother's hope chest; and for the first time, they made love.

On Christmas eve, as was their winter custom, the white Stratford family gathered for dinner at six o'clock. Though that custom had originated in happier times when evening chores kept everyone working until dark, they had not changed the hour.

Though Samuel hadn't shaved, tonight he wore a clean shirt and a not too rumpled jacket. As another concession, instead of reading in his study, he remained in the front parlor, where Abigail and Sallie talked as they sewed. When the tall clock in the hall boomed the hour of six, Samuel wound his watch and ushered the ladies into the dining room.

Since lamp oil could not be had at any price, beeswax candles illuminated the room, their sputters magnified in crystal clusters dangling from each candlestand and chandelier. Drafts shivered the crystals and redirected dancing lights around the walls.

The front quarters of the Christmas deer had become a stew, which steamed pleasantly in its heavy tureen. Spinach, which had stayed green in the garden under a comforter of straw, heaped another bowl. A platter on the sideboard held cornbread, yellow as butter. As a centerpiece, one apple per diner formed a pyramid. Samuel Gatewood's decanter stood at his place and his glass was already filled.

Young Thomas Byrd clattered downstairs. "Sorry, sorry. Uncle Duncan, I have been reading Hardee's *Tactics* all afternoon and my head is dreadfully sore. How do soldiers understand this thick stuff?" Thomas's gray uniform was brushed, his boots neatly blacked, and he set his cap precisely on the sideboard. He adjusted his pant legs and perched on the very rim of his seat. Samuel Gatewood permitted himself a smile. He nearly said Thomas needn't "sit" on formalities here, but swallowed his jest.

Softly the door opened, softly Grandmother Gatewood took her place at the foot of the table before any of men who had jumped to their feet could seat her. Pauline slipped in silently behind and took her place at her right.

While the men were reseating themselves, Grandmother lowered her head and began, "Heavenly Father, You have set a table for us in the presence of our enemies. God bless our brave soldiers who defend us against Butcher Grant and Beast Butler and their legions. Help our soldiers, particularly those at this table, to be stalwart against the foe and ever ready to sacrifice life to honor." Though she took breath she didn't raise her bowed head nor relax her clenched hands. "Lord, today we particularly pray for the souls of men who have died in an irregular fashion and we ask You to forgive them their sins, unworthy though they may be of Your mercy."

Tears started down Pauline Byrd's cheeks. Thomas Byrd's eyes blinked open.

"We also pray for the souls of the women who loved those men, because a woman is easily deceived, Lord, and is the weaker vessel."

Abigail said, "Grandmother . . ."

Grandmother persisted. "Lord, may You see fit to visit sickness and death upon the camps of our enemy. May You blast those who oppose you." She paused to consider. "Lord, we also pray for those souls who know not repentance. Souls who have been condemned to the penitentiary yet . . ."

"You have left us behind there, Grandmother," Abigail said.

Samuel Gatewood said, "Amen."

"Lord . . ."

"Madam!" Samuel Gatewood warned.

"Grandmother Gatewood. It is Christmas," Abigail begged.

The old woman's mouth moved silently for a bit longer, but Duncan shook the bell to summon Franky.

"Pauline," Samuel said pleasantly, "I understand Abigail and Sallie will be working late tonight to complete the servants' Christmas clothing. Will you be helping them?"

"Grandmother Gatewood and I are studying Revelation. We are partway through the second chapter."

"I am sure, my dear, that Revelation can wait, but the servants will expect their socks and shirts on the morrow." Abruptly he drank, as abruptly set down his glass. "While religious studies can benefit any young woman, overmuch ardency can weaken youthful vitality and lead to sickness and sorrow. Since you are under my roof and in my care, I would have you more involved in day-to-day matters and less in the otherworldly."

Pauline's stubborn face dissolved. "But my mother . . ."

"Dear," Abigail said, "you cannot bring your parents back by following them to the grave."

Pauline crumpled her napkin on the table, "Will you please excuse me. I have lost all appetite!"

"Of course, dear," Abigail said softly. "Please wait in the parlor. Henceforth, you will sleep in my bedroom."

"But . . . !"

"Pauline. You must do as Samuel requires."

Stiff-lipped, Grandmother Gatewood also rose.

"Mother," Samuel said quietly, "that child is precious to me. In her face I see the features of my departed daughter and my dear friend Catesby, who will figure in no more prayers at my table."

"Samuel Gatewood. I am your father's wife!"

"Yes, ma'am, and my dependent. There are several smaller houses on this plantation where you might be more comfortable than in this one."

"I shall pray for you!" she said.

"Madam, I cannot prevent it. Franky, please fetch Grandmother Gatewood's dinner to her room."

After the old woman left, Samuel Gatewood replenished his glass and passed the decanter and did not object when young Thomas took a glass.

"I apologize for any distress I may have caused," he said. "Please, do enjoy your dinner."

It was a silent meal, and Abigail hardly touched her plate. After his third tumbler, Samuel Gatewood's face was flushed, but he remembered to rise slightly in his seat when each of the ladies excused herself.

•   •   •

Christmas morning, upon their return from church, Pompey greeted the carriage at the dismounting step with a smile and "Happy Christmas!" and a murmured "Christmas gift?" He collected a dime from Duncan and nickels from Sallie Kirkpatrick and young Thomas Byrd.

Later in the hall, Jack the Driver, Pompey, and Miss Abigail passed out new homespun to the servants. Each received shirt, pants, two pair of strong wool socks, and an apology for absent shoes. "Perhaps they will be available later in the spring," Abigail hoped.

There was no cash in the socks and no fireworks, but a ham and one cask of whiskey were destined for the servants and their guests.

The Heveners and Mrs. Seig arrived in Amos Hevener's buggy. Preacher Todd came on foot.

Christmas gifts were not numerous under the German tree, and every woman present wore a mourning brooch or ring. Duncan gave his mother a crucifix carved by a prisoner and the Union officer's black hat to young Thomas, who pronounced it "first rate!" From her own jewel box, Abigail gave a bracelet in the Egyptian mode to Pauline and an opal brooch to Sallie Kirkpatrick. Abigail had a cameo for Grandmother Gatewood should she came downstairs. Duncan gave a daguerreotype of General Lee to his father, and Samuel had bargained Mrs. Warwick out of a bolt of silk faille for his wife. "Samuel! It is lovely! The first new fabric I've had in so very long." She kissed him roundly.

Samuel had shaved and wore a clean jacket and foulard and had something of his old-time holiday air. He'd persuaded Mrs. Warwick to donate a nutmeg, and Stratford's eggnog was much improved by the spice.

Neighbors asked Sallie about Cousin Molly and forwarded their kindest regards. Mrs. Seig had lost her husband at Gettysburg, and Amos Hevener's son could not be mentioned, but wonderful aromas dispelled gloom. The sideboard displayed venison hams swimming in brown sauce, a ham slathered with sorghum syrup, a chicken stuffed with chestnuts, sweet potatoes, applesauce, black walnut cake, maple candies, and corn pudding. There were as many light rolls as anyone could eat and cornbread for those who preferred it.

Samuel Gatewood tapped his glass before offering his customary toast: "Our friends."

Before his father could resume his seat, Duncan rose. "Neighbors," he said, "I would like to announce that Sallie has made me the happiest man in the world by consenting to be my wife."

His father instantly turned to shake his hand, saying, "Dear son! I cannot think of anyone I would rather welcome into my family. When will it be? Duncan. I am so happy. So very happy!" Once more he raised his glass. "To the bride and groom! Sallie. So happy. I am."

Sallie invited all present to the wedding. If the Virginia Central Railroad was not repaired, why they could come by canal barge, which was, she assured them, dignified and comfortable.

Two days after Christmas, Sallie and Duncan returned to Richmond. Before they departed, Duncan informed his father that General Lee's army needed all Aunt Opal's hoarded corn and most of Stratford's hogs.

61

LETTER FROM PRIVATE
SILAS OMOHUNDRU
TO MARGUERITE OMOHUNDRU

PETERSBURG, VIRGINIA
JANUARY 8, 1865

DEAREST WIFE OF MY HEART,

I did not write to you before this moment because I was sunk in despair. My hopes were frustrated, my accomplishments ashes in my mouth. I write today as a gentleman—a soldier in the Army of Northern Virginia.

When I first came, I sought no man's company, nor did anyone seek mine. Well fed, well dressed, a man of business—to my new comrades I bore the hallmarks of the shirker. Every day our conscription laws drag shirkers to the army, many protesting that they have influential friends, that they are of more use to the Confederacy in their offices and private trade, that they are a cut above the ordinary soldier and do not intend to be mistaken for one.

Conscripts and we few volunteers were assembled in a Petersburg park and issued rifles, bullet pouches, and the other accouterments of the soldier's trade. My uniform jacket had a bullet hole in it, and I hoped—forlornly, perhaps—the jacket had been removed from a wounded man. I sought a North Carolina regiment but did not mention Wilmington. The prospect of serving in a Wilmington regiment in an inferior rank to a DeRossette or one of that circle was too painful. In the 37th Regiment I sought and found strangers.

The day I arrived, I was set to work digging. Our fortifications surround Petersburg for thirty-six miles, and we are always busy improving them. To men rained on by Federal mortars, no bombproof is ever deep enough.

As a novice at the soldier's trade I was assigned more than my proper share of pickax work. If it was a test, I suppose I passed, and after three days my hands stopped bleeding.

One day, as we were taking a five-minute rest, a portly gentleman rode up on a dappled gray gelding and addressed Lieutenant Rigler, the officer directing our efforts. "I am sorry for you fellows," the gentleman said mildly.

"Oh? Why is that, sir?"

"Because you have to work so hard." And smiling, he rode on. We resumed our work with fresh vigor, for the officer was General Lee himself! We see the general frequently, sometimes with a staff officer or two, more often alone as he inspects the lines. He rides perfectly erect in his saddle, but easily. He has none of the fiery rigidity of our General Gordon. If Gordon is a fighting cock, General Lee is a wiser bird.

I soon became acquainted with a curious substance called Nassau bacon—stuff soldiers suppose is brought through the blockade by captains anxious for unconscionable profit. Nassau bacon manages to be both gelatinous and gristly—a combination I would have thought impossible had I not tried to eat the stuff myself.

The first morning I was issued rations, I struggled manfully to dispatch the Nassau bacon, which I had boiled with cornmeal as I had seen others do. Since the food was disgusting and I supposed it an aberration, I quietly discarded the stuff in a nearby shell hole. That afternoon, when hunger pangs struck me, I inquired of Private Kissock when the next rations would be issued. He inspected me as if I were mad. "In the morning, of course." Then, as the extent of my ignorance became apparent to him, he crowed, "Boys! Conscript here thinks we eat twict a day!"

I hadn't been here long when General Hampton and three of our cavalry brigades rode around the end of the Federal lines and deep in their rear—not far from City Point—they rustled General Grant's entire beef herd: twenty-five hundred animals! Although outraged Federals tried to cut off Hampton's return to our lines, he was too quick for them. When those fat beeves arrived at Lane's brigade they were dispatched so briskly I don't believe much was thoroughly cooked, and some portions never saw the fire! Because of Hampton's audacity, we feasted on Federal rations, but such a stroke was not to be repeated, and when the last beeves were gone, the quartermasters provided us with Nassau bacon again.

I do not believe I was ever hungry before. In the mornings we collect for our issue of cornmeal mush and watch the quartermaster like hawks that he doesn't dole out to one man more than to another. If it were not for our trade with the Federals I think we must perish, and as it is, my backbone and belly button have struck up a nodding acquaintance and see fair to become friends.

Since many recent conscripts are as unaccustomed to starvation as I and see no special reason to embrace a practice they find abhorrent, they desert to the enemy, who welcomes them with the casual contempt true soldiers have for men of their kind.

I have not told my fellows that I enlisted voluntarily. Nor have I confessed I might have spent my war in Richmond advising the government. Though each veteran was a volunteer in '61 and each has reenlisted voluntarily, they would think any man who now willingly came into this army a terrible fool. They jeer at patriotic talk, and nobody dares mention "nobility" or "chivalry" in their presence. To them, such notions are "puttin' on airs." They are realistic about the war and understand that the Federals cannot win until we are destroyed. Color Sergeant Robinson said, "We are holding the key to the lock in our mouth and old Grant knows that and he is going to try and get it."

My lack of complaint did me good service with these veterans.

By General Lee's orders, we did not fell trees directly behind our lines, and their autumn colors were more beautiful than I have ever seen. The golds and reds were living things, and each leaf contained elixir. Poetry comes easily to a starving man and simple acts possess uncommon significance. Lieutenant Rigler and Sergeant Robinson were standing on top of the parapet, in full view of the enemy's sharpshooters, inspecting disputed ground as coolly as two engineers on a peacetime survey. A minié ball plucked the lieutenant's sleeve as if a breeze had ruffled the fabric.

I will never forget Corporal McCall, after receiving an unhappy letter from his wife, sitting on an ammunition box, tears streaming down his dirty cheeks.

The odor of my body has changed and become sharp and rather sweet. A starving man's eyes see everything. His concerns drop away like too abundant flesh, and he no longer has political opinions, neither whether the war can still be won or must be lost, whether the government has betrayed him, what are the merits of our cause. He clings to only one opinion, that the Army of Northern Virginia is like no army the world has ever seen and that under General Lee, the army is still capable of winning. At night, in our hut, the men read their Bibles or play cards or talk of home. By common consent, talk about grand meals is forbidden. I have heard so much about Private Kissock's twin daughters I feel I know them, their distinctions and similarities, and Sergeant Robinson so ably describes his log home in the pines I know how the sun strikes his meadow and how the water tastes from the tin cup that rests on a cool ledge inside his well.

Three broad double bunks take up the back portion of our hut. Our fireplace (built with bricks scavenged from old slave quarters) is in front, and there is room enough in the hut for one man to stand erect while feeding the fire. Two narrow windows are shuttered outside, and the floor in front of the fireplace is some inches lower than ground level so rain or melting snow that slips under our door is contained. Two of us lie on each wide platform. At the start I shared my bed with an October conscript, John Whitley. Whitley's habit of dwelling on our discomforts made him an unpleasant companion, but when Whitley deserted to the enemy, Corporal McCall took his place. McCall has been twice captured by the Federals and relates many amusing tales of prison life. By custom, the cardplayers have the bunk nearest the fire, and by everyone's consent the Bible readers take turns sitting in the firelight. Though some Bible readers can read no other book, they have little difficulty with their chosen text, because their perusal is abetted by memory. Cardplayers murmur and a Bible reader's silent lips trace each precious word. It is not quite pitch-black in my corner of the log hut, and outside the wind is blowing across ice-crusted ground and our pickets shiver in their picket holes, and those of us spared duty tonight are warmer by contrast. Conversation is quiet, mostly about home.

"What of you, Omohundru?" Color Sergeant Robinson asked. Robinson is the highest-ranking man in our hut—about my age, though toothlessness makes him seem older. At Chancellorsville a minié ball punctured one cheek, extracted his teeth (eating is difficult for him), and exited through his other cheek. "Are you going to follow Whitley over to the enemy?"

"Do they have Nassau bacon? I have become accustomed to the stuff."

This weak sally was sufficient to make Robinson chuckle. "Where is your home?"

"I lived in Wilmington until recently. My business failed and I came into the army."

I had supposed my fellows would resent the blockade runners, but no, they wanted to hear all about Wilmington, its extravagances and vices. When I described the seamen's celebrations at the City Hotel, they shook their heads disapprovingly but sought to know every detail. Although they must have guessed my business, in their delicacy they never pressed the matter. They were satisfied with lurid tales, and of those I had a good stock.

"Will you return after the war?" Private Kissock asked.

"I don't know. This war has turned everything topsy-turvy. My wife and child are there."

Politely they inquired about you, dear Marguerite, and when I said you had been born of good family in the Bahamas, they could not contain their curiosity about that island and its inhabitants' customs. I believe they had previously supposed Bahamians to be wild cannibals! Perhaps to them any foreign land (saving only Great Britain) has cannibal potential! On other nights, I elaborated on your family, your Methodist minister father, and our son, Jacob. I expressed my delight in Jacob's accomplishments and told of the night when our quarrel so upset him he wept until we reconciled.

Robinson chuckled. "I got a boy does that. Me and his momma get into it, he marches right in and gets himself in betwixt and his little face is so serious I just got to laugh, and hell, a man can't fuss when he's laughin'."

Although I do duty on the picket line and shiver in the trenches, I've not seen much fighting since October when the Federals last tried to break the railroads. Heth's and Mahone's men had the brunt of that fight while our brigade prepared for an assault which did not arrive.

Our lines face wet ground, which our engineers have made difficult of passage by damming streams, creating bogs and swamps. Our earthworks are as daunting as human ingenuity can make them. In front of the trenches are picket holes where two men go out one night and are relieved the next. Should the men be wounded by a mortar or a Federal sharpshooter they must remain until dark for relief. Behind the picket holes is our abatis, a dense tangle of wooden spears. Our earthen fortifications are fifteen feet high and surmounted with a log parapet through which we can fire with perfect safety. Provided we have the soldiers to man our defenses, any Federal assault must certainly be repelled. Our veterans actually hope we will be attacked for the opportunity to plunder Federal casualties.

At Fort Hell, up the line, the Federals are so close a man daren't raise his head, but here Confederate and Federal lines are farther apart and we are less troubled by sharpshooters. We have reached an informal truce with the Federals in our front: they will not shoot our pickets if we abstain from shooting theirs. This arrangement—entirely satisfactory to private soldiers—is deplored by general officers on both sides.

Directed by observers on signal towers we can see but cannot strike, the Federals hurl mortar bombs at us, and throughout the day their artillery blusters. In between barrages, our men comb the redoubt for spent and unexploded shells, because he who collects the greatest weight of Federal metal receives a night's furlough into Richmond, where life is, I am told, as gay as if there were no war. In their passion for a furlough, men take terrible chances and race one another to smoking Federal shells which sometimes explode. The metal so gathered is taken to Petersburg, where it is smelted, recast, and returned to the Federals via our own guns.

At dusk, we exchangers venture into the disputed land to trade. We have tobacco—plenty of tobacco—and they have plenty of everything else: coffee, federal rations, northern newspapers, needles, writing paper. Darling, I am proud to say I have become our company's chief negotiant.

My Federal counterpart (like me a private) previously owned a mercantile in Syracuse, New York, and if he was as shrewd with his customers as he is with me, I pity them.

I enjoy haggling, and though the sums involved are small (exchanging a quarter pound of plug tobacco is a major transaction), it does not diminish my pleasure in outwitting my fellow man.

Every man in General Lee's army is a gentleman. General Mahone's father kept a tavern, General Sorrel's father was a bank clerk, the mighty Stonewall was an orphan—General Robert Lee has gentility enough to cloak us all.

General Longstreet cannot use his right arm, General Gordon's face is fearfully mutilated, General Ewell has lost a leg, our own Lieutenant Dallas Rigler was first wounded at Fredericksburg and later shot through the right leg. The Army of Northern Virginia has been visited by death so many times death seems a bore, the sort of fellow one avoids because he has nothing new to say!

My darling Marguerite, in the past I have done things I now regret. A better man would have made a better husband to you and a dearer father to Baby Jacob. Does he still ask after me? How often when I returned from business he was waiting to greet me, and how often I gave him short shrift. After the war, my darling, I promise to do better. I will be a husband and father. I will be a family man and businessman—and unashamed of it.

You must give thought to where you will flee if Wilmington falls into the hands of the enemy. In good conscience I cannot suggest Richmond or Petersburg. Perhaps Goldsboro will be spared the conqueror's tread.

If God favors us we may yet prevail. I will do my duty. Everything is in God's hands.

Your Loving Husband,
Silas

62

WHY DO THEY HATE US SO?

WILMINGTON, NORTH CAROLINA
FEBRUARY 21, 1865

MUD FROM HURTLING carriages splashed the wrought-iron fence around Silas Omohundru's mansion and blunted its ornamental spears. Cartwheels squealed, teamsters yowled, mules brayed, and in handsome and makeshift conveyances, those who could flee Wilmington were doing so. "Use the best harness, Mingo," Marguerite said.

"What about the goods you leavin' behind?" Kizzy's husband inquired. Although Mingo was a fairly shrewd man, this morning his head was aswim with possibilities. The Federals were advancing on Wilmington, so Mingo was a free man, no longer required to send the better portion of his salary to his master. Would Mingo have to work at all? Coloreds had been doing the work for years while white folks gave orders, but now Master Abraham's army was turning the tables. Might Mingo live in a mansion like this one? If so, how would he furnish it?

"We'll let the Federals have our things, Mingo," Marguerite said. "After their exertions they'll require something to sit on. Unless," she hazarded, "you want the furniture?"

"No'm," he said sullenly.

"Mingo, so far as I am concerned—so far as Mr. Silas is concerned—you are a free man." She did not quite touch his arm. "The world is changing rapidly these days and it is hard to know how to proceed. Meantime, do hitch our horses. The roads are soft, but our carriage is light and our horses in good condition."

Mingo said, "Miss, what's going to happen to us? I likes it here in Wilmington." Mingo was a handsome man. Wasn't only Kizzy said he was.

"Confederate officials have ordered civilians to evacuate. Put this case in the drawer beneath my seat. Once in the countryside, we may encounter Federal patrols."

Mingo thought: This case heavy for how big it is. He said, "Yes, ma'am. They thievin' scoundrels all right." The burgundy leather case slipped under the seat like a hand into a glove.

Marguerite continued, "The silver and gold coin we possess are in the portmanteau atop the carriage. Secure that case thoroughly."

Mingo thought: I seen her put a bag of gold coins in that trunk, but that big trunk not so heavy as this little one. He said, "Yes, Missus, I rope it down."

She said, "Jacob and Kizzy will have the front seat, and Jacob's necessities will be on the seat beside me. Why haven't you gone for the horses?"

Mingo thought: Because you keep me here yakkin'.

The hubbub outside the gates excited the horses. They were young horses, bloomy horses, maybe the best horses in Wilmington. Wasn't that Mingo's doing? And the carriage, all polished up—weren't half a dozen families in the city boasted such a well-kept rig. Drive Miss Marguerite down Market Street to her place of business, perched on that seat, didn't hardly nod to the other colored drivers—they were teamsters, Mingo was a coachman.

When one of the horses pricked its ears and started trembling, Mingo went to the tack room for blinders.

A month ago, when Master Abraham's fleet captured Fort Fisher and finished the blockade-running, most speculators had left the city. When Mingo asked were they leaving too, Miss Marguerite said no, they'd stay in Wilmington in case Master Silas wanted to find them. But the Confederate general gave his order to evacuate, and that was what they were doing. Mingo thought it would have been easier a month ago.

Kizzy wouldn't quit young Master Jacob. If it was up to him, Mingo would let Mistress hitch her own damn horses and he'd march into the parlor and put his feet up and wait for Master Abraham's soldiers to come. Kizzy was big with her first baby, and if the soldiers came quick, her baby would be born free.

Mistress was dressed like she was going to a fancy ball, yellow silk hoop skirt and blouse trimmed with lace at the neck and sleeves. Mistress looked like she didn't belong to the same country as the scared refugees streaming past the house, maybe not the same religion. Young Master Jacob wore a green velveteen suit with wide lapels, and a floppy green cap covered his head.

Kizzy's dress was too tight across her belly and pulled away from the buttons. Ugly dress. Kizzy bent to wipe young Master's snotty nose.

A four-hitch wagon rumbled by filled with white people, old and young. "You better hurry, Miss," the driver cried. "Federals comin'."

Marguerite dismissed the man with a wave.

Sometimes Mingo hated Marguerite. She was so sure her money could whip troubles that took grown men by the heels and laid them low. He hated her brat and her damn fancy gown.

"Thank you, Miss," Kizzy said when Marguerite helped her into the carriage, and Mingo hated that too.

"Set out for Warsaw," Marguerite advised. "The plank road would be best."

Plank road's rotted, Mingo thought to say. Ever since the railroad built, plank road's fall to pieces. "Yes'm," he said and cut the wheelhorse with his whip.

Only a few miles out of town they began to pass the poor folks who'd prayed for luck on their journey because they had no means to prepare for it. A disabled wagon spewing plundered trunks, a cart with a crumpled wheel, spavined horses with their heads drooping and feet splayed wide apart.

Marguerite's splendid carriage split the human flood like the bow of a ship. Some white men gave Mingo the ugly eye—why was a nigger riding up so high and mighty?—but the blinds were pulled over the windows and the door panels were burnished until they shone and the carriage eased by and they said nothing though their wives had been walking since dawn and their children were whimpering.

Four hours out of Wilmington, they left the foot traffic behind. Although the road was firmer, mud from the horse's hooves dirtied Mingo and wheel splashes streaked the carriage doors, and the sun was poised on the horizon.

This was the piney woods, stands of longleaf and loblolly pine so far as the eye could see. Mingo shivered. No telling what was in those woods. Mingo was a town man, yes sir.

Miss Marguerite lifted the hatch beside him. "Take the next lane, Mingo," she said. "We'll seek hospitality for the night."

But the lane didn't lead anywhere. After a promising start, it narrowed and the ruts deepened, and Mingo couldn't find a place to turn around until they came out on the riverbank, beside a tumbledown dock and warehouse that reeked of turpentine.

"This will do." Marguerite climbed down. "This will do wonderfully. We have come far enough today, and Kizzy is tired. Isn't the river beautiful, Jacob? Hear the chirping? That's frogs talking to each other. Mingo, the wicker basket contains our supper. Brush and feed the horses, and if you fetch kindling, I'll make a fire."

They'd packed a week's provisions: a beef roast, two cooked hams, and canned vegetables whose tins bore the labels of British firms.

As the woods darkened, Mingo collected firewood. In his hurry to be back with the others, he brought punky wood, which was hard to get alight and smoked. Marguerite was annoyed when smoke got in her eyes but made no complaint. The boy Jacob asleep in his mother's lap, they sat until their fire was a dim glow and more stars than Mingo ever wished to see washed the sky white.

The women and boy slept in the coach. Mingo climbed up on the roof and curled among the trunks and baskets.

Next thing Mingo knew, Mistress was yanking at his elbow, saying it was light enough to move on. "Yes'm," he said. He had never been so stiff or so cold. When he went into the woods his manhood was so cold and shrunk he could hardly pee. Kizzy wasn't far away, being sick.

They were traveling north, more or less paralleling the Weldon railroad. The tracks were silent; no trains came. They spotted one other traveler, but he spurred his mount into the woods.

At noon, Mingo wanted to make a fire, eat, and rest a spell, but Mistress Marguerite didn't want to stop, so they made up sandwiches. Young Master Jacob asked to ride up top, and Mistress said he could. "If you pester Mingo or ask too many questions, you'll come back inside."

Usually the boy jabbered like a young crow, but today he was quiet and pressed close to Mingo.

All morning, intermittently, the road had touched the railroad, whose shiny rails and sturdy wooden sleepers seemed to promise that despite present fears, they would eventually find a town and civilized, hospitable people. Around a bend they entered a broad empty valley where the Wilmington & Weldon Railroad had been wrecked.

Bonfire circles stretched along the roadbed for a mile. Fires had been built beneath trees and rails heated and wrapped around the trees like shoestrings. Some fires still smoldered.

The boy had been humming to himself but quit. "Mingo," he asked, "why do they hate us so?"

"Well, honey, they don't hate everybody."

"Are they going to make a new railroad?"

"Don't reckon."

"Look, there's a boxcar they burnt up, too. Mingo, were those horses inside?"

"Appear to be."

"Why would they burn up horses?"

"Honey, if I knew about these things, reckon I'd be somebody instead of drivin' your mother's carriage."

"Look, there's a locomotive lying on its side."

"Uh-huh."

Guidon fluttering, the blue column came at them in a hurry and surrounded the carriage before Mingo had time to do a thing, and a trooper grabbed Mingo's lines and carbines leveled at his head.

"Please, Masters, don't shoot! We ain't done nothin'!"

One trooper jerked the window blind out of its sash. "Two women. One of 'em's white."

Marguerite poked her head through the window. "My servant is heavy with child," she said. "Do you intend to terrify her into having her baby here and now?"

The troopers were commanded by a beefy sergeant. "Just who the hell are you?"

"Mrs. Silas Omohundru, lately of Wilmington. And who are you, sir, to interrupt a respectable woman on the turnpike? Are you highwaymen?"

The sergeant grinned. "Now, ma'am. I expect you know better'n that. We're the fellows drivin' the rebel armies from the field."

"Then shouldn't you be at your work? I understand that General Lee does not drive easily."

"Oh, there's plenty fellows takin' care of Bobby Lee. Bixby, see what's in those trunks."

Before anyone could protest, a soldier was on top of the carriage tossing trunks to the ground and two others were doing similar mischief at the boot. Little Jacob clutched Mingo's arm. "You leave my momma's things alone!" he demanded.

"You raisin' you a little rebel, ma'am? Already defyin' lawful authority."

"If my husband were here, he would reintroduce you to lawful authority!"

"Oh, I'll just bet he would. Bixby, pry open that portmanteau."

Marguerite's clothes were dragged from the luggage, her petticoats sabered and flaunted like banners. Business records were dumped, and invoices and ledger sheets fluttered across the burned landscape like hungry birds.

"Lookee here, a silver teapot. I believe we have got ourselves a rich lady here, Sergeant. A rich rebel lady."

"Ma'am, why don't you and the nigger gal step out of the carriage. You, driver. Step down with the boy."

"Got me some gold, Sergeant. Twenty, forty, sixty, eighty, hundred twenty, hundred forty dollars' worth!"

The sergeant tsked. "Rebel property is forfeit to Federal seizure."

In her yellow gown, Marguerite was as bold as the first rose of summer. "I am unacquainted with uniformed highwaymen. Are soldiers' uniforms now the fashion among thieves?"

"Ma'am," the sergeant replied, "I'll bet you are one hell of a fine lady. I'll venture you got a big white house with columns in front. . . . Bixby, you know those houses we been burnin'? She lives in one of them. And you got niggers to do your wash and tote your pisspot. Your husband an officer?"

"My husband's rank is no concern of yours. Were he in your place, however, he would not be waylaying your wife nor vandalizing her belongings."

"I suppose that means he's better'n us."

Startled, Marguerite said, "Why certainly he is!"

"Lady, that insult just cost you your horses. Bixby, cut 'em out of the traces. You there, nigger!"

"Yes, Master," Mingo said.

"You and your woman can come with us. Big contraband camp at New Bern. Roof over your head, food every day, and nobody whip you. Your mistress got money we ain't found?"

The blue-clad sergeant was watching him like a hawk, and Mingo licked dry lips. "Some of it mine?"

The man roared his laughter: "Nigger, one hand washes the other."

Kizzy clutched at her husband. "Mingo, don't . . ."

But Mingo hid behind the sergeant's horse. "It's under her seat," he mumbled.

A soldier was at the seat in a flash and dragged the heavy burgundy leather case out and popped it open. "Jehoshaphat!"

Marguerite cried, "Sergeant, that is all the money we have in the world. It was got honestly!"

"I don't doubt that for a minute. Bixby, how much you got there?"

"Must be a thousand damn dollars, and not a nickel in scrip. Just what we have been searchin' for all these weary days: a hoard of Confederate gold."

"If you steal our horses and our money, you leave my family destitute," Marguerite said.

"Climb on the coach horse, nigger. Leave the wench."

"Mingo!" Kizzy's despairing cry.

"A man . . ." Mingo said. "Kizzy, a man's got to better himself!"

The sergeant spurred his horse, and when the horse reared, Marguerite crumpled against the coach and Jacob lifted his tiny fist to defend her and all the world was dust and rioting horses until they became a dust cloud far down the road.

"Please, Kizzy, sit down and take deep breaths. Jacob, fetch her water. Kizzy, do not waste your tears on him. Mingo is not worth your tears. These hoops are so inconvenient! Our respectability was less protection than I had hoped. Kizzy, you may remain with the carriage while Jacob and I go seek help."

"No, please, ma'am. I can walk. Just don't walk so fast."

"Jacob, I believe that is your waterproof beside that ruined trunk.

Since we can carry no change of attire, it will be more practical than your dress jacket. Please, dear, turn your back while I remove my hoop. Perhaps, Kizzy, you will pass me one of my hats. No, not the bonnet, the wide brim. From the look of those dark clouds, I fancy we can expect rain."

"Oh, Mistress, we lost now."

"Then we shall have to get ourselves found. Can't we carry the smaller ham? Perhaps I can make a sling of my petticoats. I had not thought to see men take such pleasure slaughtering a harmless woman's underthings."

Jacob lifted his tiny face. "Mama, where are we going now?"

"Are you strong enough to carry that canteen? What a brave boy! Oh dear, I believe these are raindrops. I do not know exactly where we are going, darling. But I am certain it will be better than here."

63

LETTER FROM MRS. DUNCAN
GATEWOOD TO ABIGAIL GATEWOOD

RICHMOND, VIRGINIA
MARCH 21, 1865

DEAREST, DEAREST ABIGAIL,

Duncan and I were sorely disappointed you and Samuel and dear
Aunt Opal could not attend our nuptials. I cannot thank you enough for
the gown you provided, and your own mother's ring was a precious gift.
Your own new daughter shall cherish it!

Dear Cousin Molly had hoped for a gala wedding. We were to have a
reception in her parlor, and Molly had located three jeroboams of French
wine (she has the most amazing resources). After Wicked General Sheridan wrecked the James River Canal and cut Richmond off, our guest list
shrank to nothing, and Molly's jeroboams vanished into her cellar to
await another event. Happy events for your cousin Molly are not "few
and far between." Hers is a sanguine disposition and she finds goodness
even in these dark days. "After all, child," she reassures me, "God does
not give us burdens we are unable to bear." Though I know that is true,
I am sometimes unable to believe it. In the past, I was subject to much
melancholy. Usefulness keeps my sadder humors in check.

Since General Sheridan fulfilled his martial ambitions (why must the
Federals make war on civilians?) we are isolated from the world excepting the rattletrap Southside Railroad, which makes its hesitant, painful
way up from Danville carrying necessities which keep our army and capital from starvation. Since Wilmington fell, we can obtain no medicines,
and gravely wounded men rely on what succor nursing can provide.
Each battle produces more wounded, and our patients were weak from

hunger and exhausted even before the enemy's minié ball or case shot tore their flesh! How they endure it, I do not know! Rumors abound that General Lee must soon abandon the city, and if that is defeat, in our present circumstance defeat seems something to be envied!

The pure contrariness of Confederate nature has pitched the capital into a matrimonial humor, and young girls and brave soldier swains hurry to Richmond's altars to pledge vows that may endure a single day but are vowed for a lifetime!

Like so many well-wishers, I was in the gallery at St. Paul's when Hetty Cary married the North Carolinian General John Pegram. I had met the indomitable Miss Cary in society, and her sister Constance sometimes helps at Camp Winder. Three weeks to the day after the wedding, General Pegram took a minié ball in his breast and fell dead, the watch his lovely bride had wound for him that morning still ticking in his pocket. A second service, much graver, was held in St. Paul's, with her who had been so radiant in white dressed in somberest black, scarcely able to stand upright beside her young husband's bier. It is whispered that omens (a broken mirror, a normally reliable horse—President Davis's own—that refused the wedding carriage) foretold disaster, but what is one to do with such portents? Shun every worthy enterprise? Even knowing Hetty Cary Pegram's fate, had a mirror shattered on my wedding day it would have given me a start, but I should have proceeded willingly to the ceremony. If we cannot be broken by Grant's army, starvation, and the direst poverty, why should we shudder at omens?

When it was certain Duncan's dear family could not pass through General Sheridan's ring of destruction for our wedding, we decided to act "on the spur of the moment."

When Molly consulted the rector he could not "fit us in," but promised to marry us should any previously scheduled couple cancel. St. Paul's rector, Dr. Minnegerode, has a homely face that has seen much joy and too much sorrow. During Stoneman's raid on our capital, he was officiating at his altar when news arrived that his son was among the fallen lying at the railway station. The rector blanched, gave his duties over to his assistant, and made the sorrowful journey so many parents made that day, only to learn that it was all a mistake, the poor dead boy was not his son. How gratefully he celebrated Vespers that evening!

The very next Sunday, at breakfast, Dr. Minnegerode sent word that Duncan and I could be wed if we could be at St. Paul's at two o'clock sharp! Cousin Molly dispatched her servant to General Mahone's headquarters with a note begging Duncan's presence. Not only did General Mahone grant Duncan a furlough, he insisted on attending himself with two staff officers previously unknown to Duncan. Duncan confided afterward the general required these gentlemen's attendance because they were West Point. Apparently there is rivalry between West Point officers and those who attended VMI. Since General Mahone and my dear new husband were Institute men, the general thought to humble these grand officers by requiring attendance at an affair beneath their station. Are men sillier than women? What is your honest opinion?

Though the general's motives were not the noblest, these officers added dignity to what was, after all, a "makeshift" affair. At the reception in Cousin Molly's unready parlor (as we arrived, her houseman was whisking dust covers off the settees), after some awkward conversation, brilliant Cousin Molly bethought herself of the jeroboams, and petty rivalries were swiftly dissolved in pleasant gossip and laughter.

Camp Winder is presently "between battles," so Surgeons Lane and Chambliss were able to attend our nuptials. Surgeon Lane lost his only son at Fredericksburg and speaks too frankly about the deathbeds he has attended. I have heard him damn our own officers with the same vigor he damns our enemies and feared a contretemps. Thankfully, Cousin Molly's jeroboams worked their magic, and the ruddy glow of comradeship replaced the divisive intercourse I dreaded.

As you know, I have married before, and that marriage was unhappy. After that experience I confess I was hostile to an institution so blessed by universal approbation. If my first marriage had caused me such pain, surely all marriages were suspect.

Duncan's kindness, forgetfulness of self, quiet courage, and steady good humor have so captured my heart that my mind must follow! Dearest Abigail, your son has conquered a proud woman and subjugated her with love. If, God forbid, he should fall before this dreadful war is over, my days of happiness with him will linger in my heart forever. I am made for joy, not sorrow!

We are humbled and privileged to have exchanged our precious vows in Confederate St. Paul's. The church is a model of graceful rectitude. The Virginia gentlefolk who have worshiped here have imbued it with their own delicacy and consideration. Its stained-glass windows light the interior with lambent joy.

"To love, honor and obey"—how beautiful those words! How they must have comforted you and Samuel through the years! Oh, I know that Duncan and I will have our "disagreements"! But I promise to you now, in the fullness of my joy, that I shall never forget that he is the author of all my happiness!

Can a mortal woman be so happy? A month ago, even a week ago, I should have said no! Doubts persisted even as I donned your beautiful gown and brushed my cheek with the humble daffodils which were to be my bridal bouquet. As Cousin Molly's carriage clattered toward Capitol Square, I chattered nervously. I do not know what I said! When we arrived at St. Paul's and I saw the gallant officers in the vestibule, breath left my body and I feared I would disgrace Duncan and myself by fainting away! Dear new mother, I am no coward. Some have said I exhibit too much spirit for my own good! But those beaming gentlemen were as frightening as the Horsemen of the Apocalypse! If, at that moment, without disgracing Duncan, I could have bolted, I should have done so. I would have run straight into General Grant's lines and claimed the comforts offered other deserters!

General Mahone greeted me, his famous hat swept low, and I ventured a trembling smile as he took my arm. "Miss Sallie," the general said, "Major Gatewood is one of my most trusted officers, a gallant patriot. And you have devoted yourself to the care of our wounded. The major informs me there is no kinsman to accompany you to the altar. If you would deem me suitable to perform such a service, I would be greatly honored."

I blushed. The gentle courtesy of a man who has risked so much for his country—when will we ever see such men again?

Duncan awaited me at the altar before the beaming Dr. Minnegerode. The rest was as a dream. My voice perhaps tremored as I made my vows, but I was not ashamed. A woman has a right to quake on that occasion! And when Duncan turned to put the ring on my finger, his own hand was not perfectly steady. I steadied his hand as he slipped his love upon my finger. Such joy!

Our nuptial home is in the back of a Petersburg house. Though it is on the Appomattox River side of the city, in October a Federal shell struck the house, and parlor and upstairs bedrooms are without roof. Our two small rooms look out on the garden, where, yesterday, I planted peas and lettuces. The door between our cozy home and the ruined portion is kept closed tight, and since we enter and leave through the garden, it is easy for me to pretend that our two rooms are the whole of the world! The larger room serves as dining room, parlor, and kitchen (there is no kitchen house). The patented cookstove is still warm when we emerge from our cocoon to face another dawn. Duncan must be with General Mahone at four, but his departure is routine, since most habitable houses on our street are occupied by officers and their families, who have endured dawn separations since this siege began.

My devoted husband accompanies me to the Richmond & Petersburg station, where I board a train with our wounded into Richmond. Duncan did ask that I resign my post, but I refused. "If I am to stay alone, all day long, listening to Federal guns, waiting for the furor that signals another attack, worrying about you, I shall go mad. At Camp Winder I am too busy to give you a thought!" I sealed my words with a kiss, and this, as much as my poor argument, carried his position, captured his colors, and occasioned his manly surrender!

I sometimes believe I am the only woman in the world who is so blessed! But so many women are married, so many have dear children, so many love their husbands no less than I. How is it that we can have loving marriages and war? How is it we women permit it?

Dearest Mother, I thank you for the gift of your son. I shall cherish him, I promise, to your maternal satisfaction.

Your Obedient Daughter,
Mrs. Duncan Gatewood

64

THE LANYARD

PETERSBURG, VIRGINIA
APRIL 2, 1865

"Whatever God in His Providence has laid down, that we must believe in and obey. Yet often we murmur against God's Providence, not knowing that His Providence is all for the best. It's like if we look on a leaf of this Bible; if we only reads what is on one side without looking underneath, on the other side, we can't understand its meaning; so we can't see through the ways of His Providence. For instance, take death! If every man had to say when he should die, he would live on to a hundred, a thousand years—he never would die. But you all has to go! And when Providence calls you! Death am universal!"
— *Sermon preached by the Reverend John Jasper, 6th Mount Zion Colored Baptist Church, Richmond, Virginia*

WHEN THE FEDERALS struck, Silas was dreaming about the river. He'd been relieved from the picket line at dusk, heard rumors of a disastrous fight to the south of them at Five Forks Junction, eaten his biscuit and salt pork, decided to save his precious coffee for morning, crawled onto his platform, laid his shoes for a pillow, and tugged his blanket over him, and though Federal guns complained through the night and firing on the picket line was fevered, Silas slept like a blessed baby.

In his dream he was sitting on a hogshead beside the river while stevedores unloaded a blockade runner. The ship might have been his own but might have been someone else's. Silas wasn't watching the work, he was watching the river. It was dawn and the river might have been two or a hundred feet deep. Softly, the silver river flowed past while silent men moved goods. In a moment Silas would understand everything . . .

Bam! Bam! A musket butt slammed the hut door and drums were yammering and officers were shouting, "I Company!" "K Company, to the works!" and Silas rolled off the platform part-awake and the floorspace was jumbled with men; through the door, grab his Enfield from the stand, loop the cartridge box over his shoulder, barefoot in the spring mud, into the works, onto the firing step and prime his rifle and poke it through the slot and pickets slipping through the jag in the earthworks and Silas blinked his eyes clear of sleep and drew the hammer back and someone was yelling, "On my command, boys! Give 'em a volley!" and Silas still couldn't see anything except musket flashes where pickets were being overrun and some Federal was yelling, "Christ! Watch out for Johnny's shitpits!" and an officer shouted, "Ready . . . fire!" and Silas pulled the trigger and a lance of flame shot from his muzzle and he twisted to reload and a horde of blue men came out of the blackness and struck the earthworks and started to climb and Silas jabbed his rifle muzzle into somebody's gut and somebody said, "Oooff," and disappeared back where he'd come from and Silas clubbed his rifle at a Federal and something flashed over his head SWORD! and Silas blocked a terrible downward slash and his rifle butt punched the Federal officer but blue men were cheering, hurting Silas's ears with their hurrahs and he stepped off the firing step back from the works, jammed a load into his rifle, whipped his ramrod across a Federal's face, thumbed a primer into place, and kept backing until Confederates appeared at his elbow and then Silas aimed his rifle at the blue wave pouring over their works, fired, and reloaded.

Color Sergeant Robinson rallied a handful to the regimental colors and was shouting something Silas couldn't hear over Federal cheers and the racket of musketry. A bulge of blue licked out and enveloped Robinson and the colors briefly waved above the blueness but were sucked under. Musket flashes and Silas backed into a tree which knocked the wind out of him and he thought he'd been shot as he gagged and gasped for air. Rifle fire lit the North Carolinians as they retreated through the woods. Silas loaded, shot, loaded, shot, loaded, shot. A calm voice said, "Oh, I am slain."

As the darkness started lightening, Silas broke out of the trees into cutover ground with a hundred other gray-clad figures, some walking backward.

Silas wondered why he was thirsty when he had to piss so bad. He unbuttoned himself, passed water as he stepped back, his urine splattering bare earth and grass grazed to stubble.

His left eye stung so he rubbed it clean of blood and patted his head to find the wound he hadn't felt, maybe the sword had cut him, something had. He pawed bloodflow away from his eyes.

On the Federal side of the woods, the huzzahs were continuous and moved south as the Federals rolled up the Confederate line.

A Confederate two-gun battery unlimbered long enough to fire, to no particular effect. Their lieutenant was vowing, "We took these damn guns at Gettysburg and we ain't givin' 'em back."

His anger attracted stragglers, and Silas and other Carolinians rallied on the guns. Lieutenant Rigler had a battle flag. "Thirty-seventh! Fall in on me! Thirty-seventh!"

"Ain't many of us, is there?" Private Kissock noted.

"Never has been many of us," Corporal McCall snapped back. "Only enough to do the job! Shut your damn mouth."

Lieutenant Rigler wanted to know who had ammunition and how much. Men searched their pouches. One man complained, "Hell, I skedaddled so quick I didn't bring my gun."

More stragglers joined them. Like Silas, many were barefoot. Most seemed dazed.

"Never saw so many bluebellies in my life," one private said. "More'n at Sharpsburg, more'n at Gettysburg. That damn Grant must have a million men!"

Officers arrived on lathered horses and counted heads and galloped off. Men who had rations ate them. Private Kissock shared hardtack with Silas. Those with canteens passed them around; most knelt at puddles and drank. As the sun came up, clots of Confederates drifted north toward the thinly manned inner line, Petersburg's final defense.

Lieutenant Rigler hoped, "General Lee will rally us."

"Rally who?" Private Kissock spat. "Our regiment is Federal prisoners, or dead."

The sun was warm on their backs. Guns trundled alongside. Here and there, calm officers reformed broken regiments. A thousand yards behind them, somewhat uncertainly, Federal soldiers came out of the woods, their bayonets shimmering.

"We're done for, Omohundru," Private Kissock said. "I reckon they can drive us through Petersburg plumb into the Appomattox River."

"They aren't doing much now."

"They come on too quick. Probably didn't expect to have it so damned easy."

When the guns halted, the remnants of the 37th Carolina stopped too. A wagon clattered up, distributed ammunition, and raced away.

They trudged toward Petersburg.

A courier—he was an older captain with a white streak in his black beard—had orders for them. The two guns and hundred stragglers were to hold Fort Gregg.

When he pointed they could see it: a child's mud fort in the middle of a bleak treeless plain. The captain said, "Good luck," and whistled tunelessly.

Inside the semicircular earthworks, the Confederates wrestled their guns onto earthen platforms. On three sides, Fort Gregg was protected by a shallow moat.

It was noon on a pleasant spring day. Stragglers in no particular hurry trudged past, and some waved. White smoke rose from where the old line had been, and men wondered if it was their huts burning.

With their colonel, two understrength Mississippi regiments came into the fort.

When Lieutenant Rigler returned from talking to the other officers he said, "The Federals have broken our lines all to hell and General Lee is withdrawing to the inner lines." Petersburg's church steeples lifted over the hillocks behind them. It was Sunday. The churches would be bursting with prayers. "Longstreet's coming, but he hasn't got here yet."

A flustered brigadier general rode into the the fort and cried, "Men, the salvation of the army is in your keep. General Lee asks you not surrender this fort. If you can hold out for two hours, Longstreet will be up!"

The crash of Federal artillery drowned out anything more he had to say.

Private Kissock yelled, "Tell General Lee we'll hold 'em!"

Between explosions, Lieutenant Rigler said, "Private Kissock, you in your right mind?"

Kissock scuffed the ground and mumbled, "Well, hell. Well, hell."

Though the Confederate guns cracked defiance, Federal artillery began hitting the fort, and wood splinters and hot metal zinged through the air. Silas crouched on the firing parapet, his face pressed against a barky log. When the Federal guns stopped, Silas's ears rang.

Lieutenant Rigler put a glass to his eye. Three columns of Federal infantry were coming at them, bayonets sharp as spite.

"How many?" Silas croaked.

The lieutenant counted regimental flags for an unpleasantly long time. "Private Omohundru, I believe we are to be honored by the attentions of a full Federal division. I doubt that so few Confederates have ever been so honored before."

Men lined up on the firing step, shoulder to shoulder.

"Six thousand men in a Federal division," Private Kissock observed. "And every damn one of 'em ate breakfast this morning."

Men laid spare cartridges and ramrods in the chinks. Bayonets were stabbed into logtops like a picket fence.

"Got a chaw?" Private Kissock asked.

Someone tossed him a plug, which he bit with some satisfaction. "Now if we'd had the troops and the Federals had the tobacco we'd have surrendered four years ago," he noted. "Of course, if they'd had the whiskey and we'd had the tobacco . . ."

"Kissock, quit yarnin'." Corporal McCall was drawing a bead. The three Federal columns were melting together.

"You will fire on my order," Rigler said. "One volley, then reload. Steady now, steady!"

The Federals broke into double-quick, a blunt fist of men.

"You think General Grant wants us out of here?" Private Kissock drawled, but his voice was shriller than usual.

"Fire!"

The volley smashed the Federal attack, then a second volley and a third while they were reeling. Loaded with double canister, the two Confederate guns snarled and snapped. Hundreds of iron balls whizzed through the Federal ranks.

Leaving a carpet of blue behind, the Federals sullenly withdrew. Once again they formed and came forward at the double-quick, again volleys flamed from the walls of Fort Gregg, and again the Federal legions withdrew. Fort Gregg raised a triumphant rebel yell.

"Less of 'em every time." Private Kissock upended a canteen and water splashed down his chin onto his filthy powder-blackened shirtfront.

This time the first volley did not check them, nor the second, and as the Federals neared they returned fire and Confederates started falling from the firing steps. A dip in the terrain funneled the Federals across the front of the fort.

Wounded Confederates loaded rifles and passed them to the firing step, and Silas could see faces of the men he was killing—old men, young men, fathers and boys who never would live to be fathers—spume of a great blue wave that should it break over the fort would drown them. In the blossom of smoke at the end of his muzzle Silas couldn't see if his aim was true but knew it was.

The two guns roared hot defiance but Federals waded into the shallow moat and with Confederate defenders silhouetted against the afternoon sky, took the advantage, and their volley swept the parapets clean. When one of the Confederate guns blew up, the gun layer clamped hands to his face and shrieked.

Inside the fort, men reloaded while wounded men crawled from corpse to corpse retrieving ammunition. The parapet was defended only by the dead.

The Mississippi colonel was down, wounded. "Steady," he croaked. "Steady, boys."

On the other side of the parapet invisible Federal soldiers caught their breath and ramrods clattered against rifles and men coughed. The faint splashing everyone heard was them coming through the shallow moat, wading, row on row.

"Steady!"

Terror clamped Silas's gut like an iron knot.

The Federal hurrah was louder than guns. In a lunge their banners spurted over the parapet, another lunge and men stood on top. The lone Confederate cannon blasted them and musketry tore at them. Color bearers fell with their colors. Soldiers poured over the parapet, and some paused to fire and some jumped onto waiting Confederate bayonets. Out of bullets, one Confederate hurled bricks.

The Federals concentrated fire on the sole remaining gun, and the gun captain set his primer before they shot him down.

In a soft voice, Silas said, "Would a gentleman be afraid?" He had a picture in his mind: Jacob, tearful but smiling, clinging to Marguerite's knees. Silas so wished things could have been different.

The hubbub was awful.

Although a Federal officer sabered the Confederate ramrodder, the gun was loaded and primed and a living wall of men fronted its spout. Silas snatched the lanyard cord and wrapped it around his fist.

"Surrender!" The officer lifted his bloody saber.

A small earthen fort on the plains outside Petersburg, Virginia, caught the attention of God's appalled angels. It was the silence that drew them; the quietude where a dozen Federals leveled rifles at a middle-aged, barefoot Confederate who held a lanyard in his hand. Some aimed at his belly. Some aimed at his head. The farthest wasn't twelve steps away.

"Surrender!"

"Let go that lanyard or we'll shoot!"

"Shoot and be damned!" Silas Omohundru yanked the cord and put paid to it.

65

A BURIAL PARTY

THE ARMY OF Northern Virginia began to die. Federals smashed its lines below Petersburg and rolled over its supply roads and railroads until, by day's end, only the Richmond & Danville Railroad was in Confederate hands. President Davis was at worship in St. Paul's when he received Lee's message that he could no longer protect Richmond and might not be able to save the army. Davis's face went pale but the President left the church with his customary composure.

Grant's army surrounded the capital on the north, east, and now the south, but Mahone fought on, Gordon held them at bay, Fort Gregg broke their heart, and the soldiers of Grant's army halted, knowing that tomorrow morning all the plums would drop into their hands.

Duncan Gatewood carried a message from Mahone to Lee.

Lee, his staff, and some of A. P. Hill's officers were mounted outside the farmhouse that had served as army headquarters until this morning. Federal guns were finding the range, and explosions made hearing difficult.

Robert E. Lee was dressed in an uncharacteristically fine uniform, complete with dress sword, and Duncan Gatewood wondered if Lee had prepared to be taken prisoner. Lines of Federal skirmishers crossed the field below, almost within rifle range, and the battery of Confederate cannon behind the farmhouse wouldn't detain them much longer.

Lee had just learned of General A. P. Hill's death and made no attempt to hide the tears in his eyes. In a choked voice he said, "He is now at rest, and we who are left are the ones to suffer."

A. P. Hill's officers wept openly.

"Someone must inform General Hill's widow," Lee said. "Captain Spaulding, I recall you are his kinsman."

"Sir, I have the honor to be General Hill's cousin."

"Break the news as gently as you can."

A little desperately, Spaulding searched the officers' faces. "Sir, may I have the services of Major Gatewood here?"

Colonel Venable looked up from Duncan's dispatch. "Mahone is holding them, General. He will require no reply."

"Very well then."

When a shell crashed into the farmhouse the telegrapher bolted out the door, his instrument tucked under his arm, and flung himself upon a horse, which made a dozen startled jumps toward Petersburg before a shell burst directly beneath, amputating the animal's legs and dropping its rider onto the dirt. The telegrapher rolled, scooped up his precious machine, and ran down the road as fast as his feet would take him.

"General," Venable warned.

Smoke poured out the farmhouse windows. Lee said distractedly, "They fire upon it because I stayed there. I should not occupy a private house." Lee and his staff started toward Petersburg.

"Oh Christ, Wheelhorse, I'm glad you're here," Spaulding said. "I'd rather lead a charge against Sheridan's repeating rifles than face Dolly Hill with this news."

Third Corps headquarters was well inside the lines, and General Hill's wife and two children occupied a modest frame house across the road. Yellow tulips bloomed beside the doorstep, and they could hear a woman singing inside. There is no lovelier sound on earth than a woman singing in her home.

General A. P. Hill was brought to his headquarters, draped over his saddle, the back of his shirt bloodied, his cloak almost touching the ground. "For Christ's sake!" Spaulding said. "Find an ambulance to lay him in." When he turned to Duncan, his eyes were desperate with appeal. "Wheelhorse . . ."

"No, Spaulding. I will not," Duncan said. "You are Hill's kinsman."

After Spaulding had been in the house a minute or so, a woman screamed. It was the shriek of a woman suddenly broken. When she quieted, the silence was almost worse.

Pale, Spaulding came outdoors. "Poor dear Dolly. She will be so unhappy now." He mopped his brow. "She wishes her husband buried in Hollywood. 'The Place of Heroes,' she calls it. When our ambulance . . . ah, there . . . but what in the hell is this?"

The horses were gaunt from starvation, and the ambulance's wheels had served previous wagons: one green, one blue, one red; and the near front was taller than the off-wheel.

Every sound wagon in the army was in use.

"Every one?" Duncan asked.

"We's skedaddlin'," the soldier/driver said. "It weren't easy gettin' this 'un."

Hill's veterans laid his body on the ambulance floor and folded their general's cape over his face. Awkwardly, they removed their slouch hats. "Weren't he a fighter though?"

"Remember when we come up at Sharpsburg to save Longstreet's butt? We marched seventeen goddamned miles that day and I was ready to lay down by the roadside, but the genr'l poked me with his damn sword and I was so hot I kept on marchin'. We whipped 'em too."

"Oh, when A. P. Hill hit, he hit hard."

"He's out of it now. Lucky bastard."

The soldiers replaced their hats and stood indecisive until a bare-foot sergeant said, "Let's go back and hit us some Federals. It's what the genr'l would have wanted." They started toward the nearest gunfire.

"Dear God, Wheelhorse," Spaulding said. "Lee's told the government to evacuate Richmond, and our navy is to blow up ships and stores and the sailors are to be soldiers now. . . ." When the new widow came down the walk, both men uncovered. Dolly Hill's face was bloated by grief. Her daughters clung to her and wanted to wail but were afraid to.

"My husband . . . ?" the widow asked.

"Dollie, the general is not disfigured. . . ."

She lifted the cape. "His poor mangled hand still wears his wedding ring."

Duncan boosted the girls into the ambulance, and they perched side by side on a narrow wooden bench, feet tucked, not quite touching their father's body.

Downtown Petersburg was bedlam. At the railroad station Longstreet's troops were coming out of the trains and double-quicked toward the fighting; a gray-haired woman begged a surgeon to come attend her wounded son even as the distracted man was directing badly wounded men into the train which would carry them to Richmond. With sheaves of currency, civilians tried to buy their way aboard any train.

The lop-wheeled ambulance creaked across Pocahontas Bridge and climbed into the heights where General Lee had his headquarters during the battle of the Crater. Closed up now, the mansion was shuttered, but the great magnolia was furry with new leaves.

For an hour or two, the ambulance made good progress, but outside the suburb of Manchester the first refugees appeared, those few who could afford sound horses and good carriages. Soon, fleeing civilians jammed the turnpike from ditch to ditch. Many were junior government officials in their Sunday best, respectable men with respectable wives, shepherding their straggling children. One man propelled a wheelbarrow carrying a large trunk set sideways. Pouring sweat, his best coat draped over the trunk, he did not speak to his wife beside him.

Two oncoming riders spotted the ambulance, and the younger stood in his stirrups to wave. "Spaulding! This is too bad. Oh, this is too, too bad!"

"Powell! Henry! Dear cousins, thank God you got our telegram," Spaulding cried. "How is the way ahead?"

It was dark before the burial party reached the bridge into the Confederate capital, where it stalled. Mayo Bridge was clogged with fleeing citizens and infantry brigades, all coming one way. The ambulance stopped beside the esplanade where bridge traffic debouched.

Mrs. Hill was faint, her girls exhausted and hungry. Henry Hill suggested the family repair to his father's plantation, not far upriver. "You will be safe there while we cross into Richmond. Dolly, we shall bring our poor dear general to Hollywood. Will you take my horse? Cousin Spaulding will be your escort. Please, Dolly, for the sake of the children."

Feet shuffled off the bridge, teamsters monotonously cursed; wheels creaked, military accouterments jangled. Spaulding helped Dolly Hill into the saddle.

"Spaulding—a word?"

They stepped behind the ambulance, and Spaulding's hands shook when he unscrewed his flask. "So this is how it ends. Grieving women and fear." He touched the ambulance. "The general didn't wish to outlive the Confederacy. General Lee warned Hill this morning to be more careful. Lee himself warned him."

"I should return to General Mahone."

Spaulding clutched him. "Oh Jesus, Wheelhorse. You've got to accompany General Hill into Richmond. What chance do two civilians have of getting through that? Duncan Gatewood, you have always been a damn stickler. A stickler! Must I have Dolly Hill beg you?"

One of the general's daughters began to wail. The people crossing the bridge were irresistible and anonymous as the tide. Duncan thought the older of the two Hill girls would be about the same age as his lost son, Jacob. "I will accompany them."

A quick handshake and Spaulding was lifting the girls onto the horses.

The moon punched through smoke and mist while the ambulance waited for traffic to ease. Upriver, two railroad bridges crossed the James. The Richmond & Petersburg was busy with trains shuttling troops to the fighting and wounded to the city; the Richmond & Danville had been (as Powell Hill told Duncan) commandeered by the Confederate government to carry its records, bullion, and officials out of the city. When the last Richmond & Danville train left, shortly after midnight, its lights illuminated the bridge's latticework like a line drawn across the river.

"That'll be Jeff Davis's train," Powell Hill said. "Davis and his cabinet.

If the Federals catch up to them, they'll hang them sure." He paused. "They should douse those lanterns."

"They can't hang all of us," Henry Hill observed.

"They can hang us till their arms get tired. We're rebel traitors, aren't we?"

On the far side of the river, President Davis's engineer blew his whistle, and the echoes rang.

Although they provoked inventive cursing and were pressed hard against the railing by a regiment of Alabama troops, General Hill's burial party crossed Mayo Bridge into the capital of the Confederate States of America. When they came off the bridge, cavalrymen were rolling turpentine barrels under the bridge timbers.

The city pulsed like a heart at its limits. Gunshots, smashing glass, laughter more like howling than laughter. Glass crunched under the ambulance wheels, and Duncan clamped the reins under his stump to draw his revolver. The cortege rolled past shops burst wide open. Somewhere ahead a mob was in full cry.

They arrived behind the Confederate offices on Franklin Street and carried the body up the back stairs. Henry Hill's office was a wasteland of discarded papers, and the desk they laid the general's body on was littered with them. "They wouldn't take all my records," Henry fussed.

One of the general's fine yellow gauntlets was black with dried blood. His shirtfront was stiff with blood. There was dirt in his eyebrows and beard.

"Look, cousin. They haven't washed his face."

When Henry Hill unbuttoned the dead man's shirt and peeled it away from his chest, Duncan turned away. He was not kin and did not need to know the details of this hurt. Windows faced Capitol Square, where hundreds of convalescent soldiers, many on crutches, waited. Tomorrow they would be Federal prisoners. Behind the statehouse a dull red glow lit up the sky.

Henry Hill murmured, "The ball struck him through the heart. It passed through his thumb and then his heart." He added, "Oh, dear brave kinsman."

On the statehouse the Confederate flag drooped against the flagstaff.

While Powell Hill washed the general, Duncan and Henry Hill went after a coffin. They rattled down 10th Street onto Main, past Corinthian Hall and Crawford's, the saloon that had been turned into a hospital. Although the bronze front door of the Farmers Bank was bolted, the street was ankle-deep in Confederate currency and bonds. Their horses' hooves stirred paper into the air, and the ambulance was pursued by a blizzard which reddened when it fluttered into the firelight above the rooftops. Blevin's furniture store had disgorged its contents into the street: a broken gateleg table, a velvet ottoman upset in the gutter.

The interior was illumined by square holes where windows had been and rectangles which had previously framed doors. The coffins had not been disturbed, and they took the nearest. Henry Hill sincerely promised Duncan he would reimburse Mr. Blevin for his merchandise at some later date.

When the two men got the coffin back to the office, they discovered it was too small, so they laid General Hill on his side and bent his legs.

Having come so far, they could go no further. There was no official to grant permission for burial, so they decided to take Hill to the plantation where his wife, Dolly, had already gone. They would bury the general temporarily.

A. P. Hill's distraught cousins thanked Duncan volubly and shook his hand. They said when this dreadful war was over perhaps they would meet again, and Duncan said he was sure of it.

Duncan was mounting his horse when an explosion slapped him. Window glass shattered over his head, papers shot into the air like frightened quail. Rockets soared from the heart of the explosion like lines of fire, red, yellow, red, white, red. Duncan lay against his horse's neck, arm over his head, while glass rained onto the cobblestones.

In Capitol Square convalescent soldiers turned toward the explosions, their faces ruddied by fire.

Duncan's horse shivered but stood stock-still. It was a good horse, a very good horse, and it was not its fault it wasn't Gypsy. Duncan patted it and said soothing things as they trotted along Cary Street while rockets lit the sky.

Gangs of men and women were in the streets, drunk, swearing, weeping. One woman carried a hatstand; one man's trophy was an empty parrot cage. Columns of weary Confederate soldiers marched down the middle of the street toward Mayo bridge, ignoring the an anarchy on both sides of them.

Militiamen broke into a warehouse to destroy the whiskey stored there. They stove in barrels and dropped cases of bottles from the second story, but men (and a few women) knelt to drink from the gutters. They scooped whiskey with pans, drank the dregs from broken bottles, and a crowd formed below a window where whiskey poured out and washed their upturned faces like rain.

The Richmond & Petersburg depot was situated near the river, near the tobacco warehouses the militia had fired. Ambulances lined up outside the depot, and as soon as one was loaded, it hurried away. One of the convalescents at the door carried an old-fashioned horse pistol, the other a musket. The man with the musket said, "Everybody in Richmond is mad as a hatter tonight. We've turned away ruffians who thought they could steal something here."

The station platform was a mat of wounded soldiers. A dismounted door across waiting-room benches served for an operating table. When the surgeon finished sawing, his assistant kicked the amputated limb into the railyard.

A young matron wiped a wounded man's brow.

"Sallie!"

"Oh God, Duncan! How . . . ?"

"My dearest heart. Please come with me!"

"Oh, Duncan, I cannot abandon them. We are all they have."

In the shadows of a brick arch the couple embraced. Ruddy light from the burning city played over recumbent wounded. Richmond's women, many in mourning clothes, provided what comfort they could. Another great explosion shook the ground. "Duncan, they are blowing up our navy. What shall we do, oh, what shall we do?"

He said, "Hush now." He said, "It will be all right."

"Is the war over?"

"General Lee is retreating south to join with General Johnson in North Carolina. If our two armies combine, we may fight on."

She examined him gravely and steadily. She said, "Dear husband, is duty always so exacting a master?"

On the riverbank, turpentine barrels flared under the Richmond & Petersburg Railroad bridge.

Sallie shaded her eyes. "Thank God no more trains will come tonight. Duncan, I am so wearied of dying."

Another explosion. A shriek that went on and on. The staccato of exploding munitions. Along the riverfront, two-hundred-foot walls of flame made night bright as day.

She took his face in her hands. "Must you go, my dear new husband? We have had so little time."

Duncan turned and kissed her hand, just where the web connects thumb to index finger.

Though her eyes brimmed, Sallie smiled. "Of course you must. Yes, of course. Shall I ever see you again, my heart's delight?"

"Darling Sallie, I promise you shall. I promise. In this life or the next."

Out front, men slid wounded men into ambulances. Some of the ambulances dripped blood. Tobacco smoke rolled down the slope toward the river and clotted Duncan's nostrils and made him dizzy. Fire had jumped from the burning warehouse to the depot, but no men fought the blaze.

Cary and Main streets were impassable. A church steeple flowered like an aspirant candle. A well-dressed elderly woman sat upon a trunk, gloved hands in lap, portmanteau at her feet, watching intently as fire lit up the second story of a grand home across the street. Duncan touched his hat in a salute. "Madam, a dreadful night."

"Yes, Major," the elderly woman said. "I comfort myself with the thought that I shall not live to see another like it. Do you ride to join General Lee?"

"Yes, ma'am."

"Do give him Mrs. Stannard's best regards."

Duncan got beyond the fire and fell in with a cavalry regiment. On the curbs, deserters, many still in uniform, watched in silence. The cavalrymen ignored them as if they were dead.

Outside her shack a blowzy washerwoman howled: "Four years you been fightin'. And now you're runnin' like dawgs!

"Dawgs," she repeated wistfully.

It was daybreak when Major Duncan Gatewood crossed Mayo Bridge after Robert E. Lee's retreating army. A Georgia battalion marched at his heels. All Richmond's waterfront was blazing, and the pale blue sky was punctuated with black pillars of smoke. The bridge was already afire. A flotilla of small boats sailed down the James River reach into the April sunrise. All the boats were burning.

65

UNTIL DEATH OR DISTANCE
US DO PART

RICHMOND, VIRGINIA
APRIL 4, 1865

THE 23RD USCT fought fires all day and half the night, blowing up those buildings they couldn't save. They were sore-eyed, coughing, and weary to the bone when they left Richmond across the pontoon bridge Federal engineers had thrown across the James.

The regiment bivouacked in a cow pasture on the outskirts of Manchester, and most men slept where they halted.

First Sergeant Jesse Burns's back and shoulders ached; the bullwhip scars knotted and throbbed. Before he slept, Jesse brushed his uniform pants and blouse free of soot, blacked his boots, and polished his brass. Then he said a prayer for Maggie.

At morning muster, the sun lay red and smoky on the eastern horizon and the air smelled burned.

Five men overcome by smoke on the sick list, and four absent. "They've got family near," Corporal Smallwood explained. "S'pose they figure Lee's on the run, they can quit and go home."

"They're absent without leave," Jesse said.

After breakfast, the regiment sent out working parties. Fifty men into Richmond to guard against looters. A hundred would report to the engineers to pull down ruins.

Some of those picked to distribute rations to Confederate civilians balked at the job. Jesse said, "I believe you men were raised as Christians. You do as you're told." Special orders arrived for First Sergeant Burns. "I recognize that signature, sir," Jesse said. "Sergeant Major Ratcliff is coming up in the world. General Weitzel's headquarters, oh my."

It was nine o'clock before Jesse finished his paperwork and borrowed Lieutenant Seibel's horse to ride into Richmond.

If there were people living in the shacks Jesse passed, they kept indoors, away from the windows.

Jesse had been imagining his future as a free man, but Maggie wouldn't stand still in his mind. For a time she'd been his guiding star, literally all he had to live for. But before that time she'd been his reluctant wife who did her marital duty when she couldn't avoid it. As a star, Maggie'd been beautiful, but his wife had been angry and plain.

Were they still married? Did a slave marriage matter now they were free? If Jacob lived, he'd be five in August.

Not far from the pontoon bridge, Jesse came on four boys, the eldest perhaps ten years old, chopping the hind leg off a dead mule.

The eldest, towheaded and pale, laid his hatchet on the mule's rump and wiped hair out of his eyes. His eyes were flat blue. "My daddy's with Genr'l Lee," he said. "You done killed my brother, but Genr'l Lee's gonna whup you yet."

Jesse dug into his saddlebags for his rations and tossed the parcel to the boy. "Maybe so," he said, "but until he does, you've got to keep your strength up." He sniffed. "That mule you're whittlin' on been dead for a time."

The other boys formed a circle when the towhead picked up the parcel, and one made to snatch it but the towhead held it out of reach. He deliberately emptied the parcel into the dirt and ground it under his foot. "It's nigger food," he explained. "Mule ain't been dead but three days."

On the narrow pontoon bridge, blue-clad soldiers crossed into the city as ragged civilians passed silently out. Jesse wasn't sure he remembered Maggie, not exactly. That skinny light-skinned pickaninny; she'd be older now, different. Time wouldn't have stood still for Maggie either.

No whole building stood along the riverbank. Corner walls, chimneys, nothing behind the window arches but air which smelled faintly of tobacco smoke. The clip-clop of Jesse's horse's hooves seemed the loudest sound in Richmond.

Here and there Federal sentries stood guard over looted shops until their owners could board them up. The coloreds on the streets were as quiet as their former masters. Yesterday when Federal troops came into Richmond they'd been wild with joy, but today they were wondering what came next.

Richmond was smaller than Washington City, and shabbier. How many months had they tried to take it? When General McClellan first marched up the Peninsula, Jesse had still lived at Stratford.

Number 110 East Franklin was a narrow three-story brownstone with a tiny front lawn behind a wrought-iron fence. The fires had stopped on the other side of the street and an avenue of ruins stretched downtown, brick hulks smoldering as if campfires burned within. Directly across, the window arches had been the worshipful curves of a church.

Sergeant Major Ratcliff uncoiled himself from the brownstone's front steps. His uniform was new, but his brass was tarnished and his blouse hung carelessly outside his trousers. "First Sergeant Burns."

"Sergeant Major, I congratulate you on your assignment."

"Oh, I am one prime buck nigger," Ratcliff said. "Anytime General Weitzel wants a nigger to show to some congressman, front and center Sergeant Major Ratcliff." He spat. "Makes me yearn to serve under Grant. Nigger's better off under generals what don't like niggers."

Jesse grinned. "Nothing ever be right for you, will it?"

Ratcliff shook his head. "Boy, once you've been whipped bad as I have, it crimps your jollitude. You ever think to see Richmond surrendered? And half of it burnt crispy? Ain't it fetchin'?"

Jesse tied his horse to the fence. "They're starving, Sergeant Major."

"How long we been starving, First Sergeant? Since we first set our fettered feet in this land." But he grinned and clapped Jesse on the shoulder. "Oh, hell, Burns. Why we fussin'?" He gestured at the broken walls across the street. "Ain't this one beautiful day? Richmond in our hands and Lee on the run? You heard about my medal?"

Jesse hadn't.

"That scrap on New Market Heights where I took over the regiment after Johnny killed all our officers—General Weitzel wants to give me a Congressional Medal for it. Day after tomorrow. Me and five other colored heroes, all at one time. Afterward we goin' have us a grand celebration. You know Corporal Stuart? Stuart's the best hand with greens and brown beans in the whole damn army, and our foragers found an unemancipated hog. Can you get a pass?"

"I expect I can. I'd be proud . . ."

Ratcliff cut him short. "It's foolishness, but I mean to stay in the army, and that medal might help." He jerked a thumb over his shoulder. "This's what you guard," he said. "This house here. If looters come this way, put a bullet into them, white or black. And watch out for reporters. They comin' round now the shooting has stopped, and they sneaky. Nobody can pester the family without they is kin or has a note from General Weitzel."

"Which family? Who am I guarding?"

Ratcliff grinned. "Family of Robert E. Lee."

For a time, Jesse sat on the stoop. Then he paced the tiny yard inspecting the borders where tulips were blossoming. Would the master of the house ever see them again? Jesse sat down. Directly he got up and inspected the window boxes hanging from the porch rails: more tulips.

The front window curtain fluttered. Someone inside was looking Jesse over.

Might be they'd let a few coloreds stay in the army. If so, they'd station them at the poorest, most remote post they had: Indian territory, probably. Jesse could bear it, but what would Maggie think? Jesse had a mental picture—a rough sketch—of himself courting Maggie again. They were sitting on a porch somewhere. Though the locale was outside the sketch's outline, the two of them were seated in a porch swing talking and holding hands. He had no idea what they were saying.

When they married again it'd be by a real preacher in a real church. No broomstick.

A colored auntie came outdoors wielding a broom so vigorously that Jesse retreated first from the stoop, then down the walk, and finally beyond the front gate while she suppressed all sidewalk dirt. Auntie rattled the gate latch and engaged it with a click and marched back inside. Jesse came back, easing the latch closed behind him.

Jesse was hungry. He recalled with regret the ration parcel that rebel boy had squashed.

The crash/tinkle of breaking glass and a laughing shout. The coloreds coming down the street were attired in rags and finery. A silk hat, a homespun vest with more holes than cloth.

"Oh, ain't he pretty!" a blowzy female breathed. "Always did yearn to see a nigger with a gun."

Jesse stood at attention.

"Ain't this their place? Ain't this the rebel general's home?"

An old colored man assured her, Adam's apple bobbing, that yes, he'd seen General Lee at this house many a time, and other rebel generals too—Hill, Longstreet, Stuart, all the Confederate generals, he'd swear to it. "This the place all right," the informant repeated. "Henry, you hoggin' that bottle." Henry passed a brown bottle and winked at Jesse. "Oh, we havin' us a time today," he said. " 'Tis the day of Jubilo."

Jesse said, "We all been waitin' for this day."

Henry waited until Jesse's words completed the perilous journey into his brain before he groped for the gate latch.

"You stay outside and we be all right," Jesse said.

"I never thought I'd live to see it," the female observed. "A nigger with a gun." She cupped her hands to shout at the house, "Master! Master! Come see what we got here!"

Her shout alarmed her friends, and some looked over their shoulders.

Pleased with this result, she cried louder, "General Lee! General Lee! There's a nigger in your dooryard and he got a gun!"

Jesse said, "That's enough. People inside this house never done you no harm."

Instantly furious, the woman produced her hands, which were raw, cracked, and covered with sores. "No harm? I been rented out to the laundry of the Exchange Hotel since I was big enough to look into the tubs. I never said that's how I wanted to spend my life. I never asked to wash white men's dirty linen. Look at my hands!"

"Auntie, you can't come here. This isn't your house. Might be you should go to your own place, take your friends, have a good time."

"Exchange Hotel it burned," she said wistfully. "Nothing left but chimleys."

"Any of you fine folks gonna invite Auntie home?" Jesse asked.

"I want to sit in the general's parlor!" the woman wailed. "I am a free nigger woman and I want to sit in the general's parlor. I don't want to steal nothin', I just want to take my ease!"

Jesse shook his head no, and when her hand snuck toward the gate latch he said no again.

"I ain't never gonna have nothing," she said. "Woman live her whole life and work every day and never be any account and never have anything call her own."

The old man said, "Auntie, you can come with me. I got me a shack down by Tredegar's, back in the weeds where nobody can see. It ain't much, but it's mine."

The woman dropped her eyes and her hand stole into the old man's. Continuing their vague pilgrimage, the party weaved down the street.

The sun had traversed more than half the sky. A smoky haze hung over the ruined city.

The lady who came out of the house was big-boned and thoroughbred. Her eyes were red and her pleasant face was slack with fatigue. She looked down the street where the coloreds had vanished and in a not unfriendly voice asked, "Boy, who is your master?" The lady was Jesse's age.

"Twenty-third Regiment USCT, Miss."

She waved the past four years away. "I mean before all this, this . . ."

Jesse said, "I was with Uther Botkin. And the Gatewoods. In the western mountains."

"I am Mary Custis Lee, General Lee's eldest daughter."

"Yes, Missus. None of my white folks were fancy. I misdoubt you'd know 'em."

"I thank you for preventing that . . . unpleasantness. My mother is in poor health, and I would not have her distressed. Mother wishes you to go away. Your presence at our gate is . . . unacceptable."

"Missus, I can't do what you say. I'm a soldier."

For the first time Mary Custis looked at Jesse, really looked at him. Now, she could have picked him out of a crowd. She blinked tired eyes. "I am not unacquainted with soldiers." She gazed over the blackened ruins as if the calamity were an interesting curiosity that had little to do with her. "I believe that J.E.B. Stuart was the handsomest man ever turned a poor girl's head. You killed him, of course. You people have killed everything that was fine or gentle or beautiful."

"Missus, I . . ."

"At home, at Arlington, when our rose garden was blossoming the scent would quite take breath away. You people sowed our garden with corpses. You have made a necropolis of my childhood home."

Mary Custis Lee gestured at the stoop. "I sat here, right here, with a bucket of water while our capital burned. I don't know what I might have done." She smiled at herself. "But I was certainly resolute. I thought we should go into the countryside. Your General Weitzel offered to pass us through the lines, but Mother refused to leave this house. We have nowhere to go."

"I'm sorry, Missus," Jesse said politely.

"Tell me," Mary Custis asked, "when you were with your master, didn't you take pride in his plantation, his crops, in his children?"

"Old Uther's crops weren't much to brag on. He was too dreamy to be much of a planter. But I was proud of his daughter, yes I was. Miss Sallie, she was a natural wonder."

"And didn't Master Uther take care of you?"

"Yes, Missus, best he could."

"When I was small, whenever I'd come home to Arlington I'd run straight to the Quarters and greet everybody with hugs: Little George, Mical, Cassy . . . How I missed them. I loved them so." She paused. "We will always be connected. No matter what. We need each other."

Jesse thought that was so, but not exactly the way Mary Lee meant it. "Them coloreds you used to hug when you was a child. They with our army now?"

Mary Custis winced. "I do not believe you can conceive the misery of 'free blacks' in the North. Life for them is far worse than servitude. Those wretched abolitionists, promising so much and delivering nothing but starvation, contempt, and disease." She inspected Jesse. "What would your master say if he saw you in that costume? I believe it would just break his heart."

"Master Uther, he was fond of Thomas Jefferson. You married, Missus?"

"I have not had that honor."

"Since June of 1860, I been thinking of myself as a married man because me and Maggie jumped the broomstick—we promised 'until death or distance us do part.' Master wanted us married, on account of, well . . . and Maggie was so fine. I plain couldn't get enough of her. Maggie, she didn't want to be married but didn't have her choice in the matter." Jesse looked away. "It was wrong," he said. "And I don't know if it can be made right. I'll look for Maggie and ask her does she want to be my wife again. I pray she'll say yes and I'll try to persuade her, but I can't make Maggie love me. Unless Maggie's free to not love me, she can't love me either. Missus, I believe you love your coloreds. I believe that. But how could they love you unless they're free not to?"

In a soft almost dreamy voice, Mary Custis said, "Every night I pray Father is not killed on the battlefield. You people would kill my father if you could." And she went back into the house.

A half hour later the old auntie came out with a small wicker basket. The checkered napkin that covered it had been washed so many times the checks were ghosts. She set it on the stoop. "Nigger, if you hasn't et, Miss Mary says you should."

Jesse lifted the napkin. A leg of chicken and some warm cornbread. "I thought the Johnnies was starved," he said.

"People take care of Marse Robert's family," she said.

"Uh-huh. Well, he's runnin' now."

"You'uns better pray he don't stop."

When Jesse was finished with the meat, he gnawed on the bone.

The colored houseman came out a side door and passed by Jesse as if he were invisible. The houseman walked downtown toward Capitol Square.

The afternoon lingered. Two white men went into the ruin of the church across the street and shifted burned timbers and extracted blackened objects they heaped on the curb. It was hard to make out what the objects had been, but Jesse thought he recognized a crucifix and a candlestick. After a time, the two men went away.

It was dark when a detail of white soldiers marched down 7th Street, a white corporal counting cadence, "Hup, hup, hup."

Sergeant Major Ratcliff strolled along behind. "You relieved, First Sergeant Burns." Ratcliff took out his pipe and fussily stuffed it. "Corporal, take some men around back. Be sure all the doors are locked. No telling what some crazy nigger might elect to do."

With a clatter of equipage the corporal's men did his bidding.

Ratcliff tried and failed to get his pipe lit. "It's enough to make a man chew," he said. "You dip snuff?"

Jesse shook his head no.

With his second match, Ratcliff puffed smoke. "I don't know about you, Burns. I give you this job to increase your understanding of who you are, which is a nigger, and what you are, which is a nigger with authority which you had better enjoy while you got it because you ain't gonna keep it, and what do you do? You offend the Lee family. General Grant, he sends a message to General Butler, and Butler, he climbs on Weitzel, and General Weitzel says to me, 'What kind of a damn fool you post at Mrs. Lee's? Mrs. Lee has complained that we posted a nigger cavalryman outside her home as a deliberate insult.'

"I say, 'Jesse Burns ain't no cavalryman,' and General Weitzel gets that look on his face. So I say I posted the best man I know in front of General Lee's house. I say my man can read and write and is a fine soldier. General says he's nobody to be trifled with and a medal can be took away as easy as given and there are plenty men hopin' to wear sergeant major's stripes, if I took his meanin'. I said I did. I told him, Jesse, that you was just a country boy who never been whipped and you were so trusting that it would never cross your simple mind that guarding the Lees was different from guarding any other white family."

Jesse said, "They gave me supper."

Ratcliff nodded. "Horse won't work if it ain't fed, nigger won't either."

Jesse said, "They didn't cause this war."

"Well, one thing for certain: ain't no nigger caused it. Gonna be white men get the credit for fightin' it and nobody ever remember the U.S. Colored Troops. Jesse, you and me forgot already."

67

SPRING OATS

STRATFORD PLANTATION, VIRGINIA
APRIL 8, 1865

FRANKY HAD A platter of buckwheat cakes in her hand. "Mistress Grandmother ain't eatin' it, Master Samuel. Says so long as Marster Lee's army ain't eatin', she ain't eatin' neither." Her hoarse confidential whisper echoed to the farthest corners of Stratford House. "She tired of buckwheat cakes and syrup. She'd eat allright if we was to bring her a mess of ham. She eats eggs when we has 'em and makes speeches when we hasn't. Anyway, she says she is prayin' for Master Duncan and Master Thomas and asks me tell you you be prayin' too."

Samuel Gatewood managed a smile. "Thank you, Franky. If you don't want Grandmother's plate, you may carry it down to Agamemnon."

"Can't." Franky raised her eyebrows.

"Oh dear. Of course—I had forgotten. Feed it to the pullets, then. I won't have them reheated for my supper. If we are to do planting work, we'll need meat, and as I recall there are a few scraps of sidemeat in the smokehouse." Samuel went on, "If you see me before supper I'll entrust you with the key."

"Yes, Master. I sure wish Auntie Opal had stayed here with us."

"As do I. I'm afraid she thought more of those hogs than she did of most people." He mocked, " 'These ain't Jeff Davis' hogs, these is my hogs, and I ain't givin' 'em up.' "

"There was justice in what she said," Abigail said from the doorway.

Samuel Gatewood got to his feet and poured Abigail's cup of sassafras tea. "Alas, justice is the least honored of the virtues. If justice were well served, Richmond would still be our capital and Mr. Davis would not be a fugitive."

"Have you any news?"

He folded his hands in front of him. "Amos Hansel stopped at day-break. Oh, he was so hungry and tired it wrenched my heart. He said he had 'left the army.' When the lines were broken at Petersburg, he lost hope. Amos said the army is in deplorable condition, without food or ammunition, the merest ghost of an army."

"Had he . . . is there any news of . . ."

Samuel Gatewood shook his head. "Amos was with Pickett's division. He said Pickett was thoroughly smashed. Hansel was an artilleryman: how could he persist when the Federals had captured all his guns?"

"General Lee persists."

"Yes."

"Then we all must. I pray every morning for Duncan and Thomas."

"My mother has loosed such a barrage of prayers in their behalf, God cannot ignore them."

"Oh dear. I do hope they are kindly prayers."

Samuel smiled. "Mother's is the God of Battles, a jealous and angry God. If any God can interpose Himself between our boys and General Grant, Grandmother Gatewood's God is surely He."

"Please, Samuel . . ."

"Yes. I shouldn't mock. Anything that will bring those boys home, honor intact . . ."

"General Grant has so many men, so many guns. His army is rested and well fed. I fear an Armageddon!"

"Come, dear." Samuel took his wife's hand. "Let us consider how fine it will be when they do come home. Our servants will return to Stratford, and Duncan and Thomas—it will be just as it was before."

"Samuel, why do you think the servants will return?"

"Where else have they to go? Who will care for them?"

She patted his hand. "Husband. Dear husband . . ."

"Jack and I are making plans. We'll repair the old harness, split new shakes for the barn roof. We'll get the mill turning again. Virginia will need all its mills when our boys come home. If our servants do not come home, we will hire new servants."

"And how will we pay them?"

"Oh, dearest, we will sell the silver. We shall become hard-trading yankees, and won't give a damn for anyone. Perhaps we will purchase one of Mr. McCormick's machines and be shut of servants forever."

"It will be so much lonelier, Samuel."

"Yes, I suppose."

Abigail smiled. "You might hire those runaways presently abiding with Aunt Opal at the Botkin place."

"When the boys come back from the army we'll clear those scalawags out of there."

"Oh, Samuel, what harm do they do?"

"They are runaways. I've known some of them since they were children. Billy from Warwick, Yellow Jim from Dinwiddie's, Pompey, and our Dinah . . . I never would have thought . . ."

"Hush, Samuel. Franky will hear."

Samuel started to say he didn't care if Franky did hear but restrained himself. "The Botkin place belongs to Duncan now."

"Sallie wouldn't mind Opal living there. You know she wouldn't."

"She'd mind every scamp in the county abiding with her. There must be a dozen people in that house."

"And as many hogs in the woods."

"She didn't have to take all we had."

"Aunt Opal said since you'd given half her hogs to the government, if we wanted hogmeat, we could just ask Jeff Davis for it."

Samuel sighed. "We'll deal with that after the boys come home. I hope Duncan's horse survives. We have work for that horse."

"Samuel, what if General Lee breaks through?"

Samuel Gatewood's eyes unfocused. "I fear for our people. The Federals burn our crops and barns, slaughter our livestock, and leave our dead unburied. Though at home they may be God-fearing citizens, here in the Confederacy, they have become thieves, and arsonists. Their generals incite excesses. We have made them doubt their virtue, and each time they despaired and nearly quit—they hold those moments against our account. Only Mr. Lincoln's influence restrains them. If Lee eludes them again, I cannot imagine what they will do. I dread their revenge."

Abigail shuddered. "I feel as if someone just walked across my grave."

Samuel smiled and patted her hand. "My dear, I am so sorry. My gloomy notions should be confined to the nightbed that engendered them. Come, let us step onto the porch."

Man and wife took the air on a fine spring morning. It had rained the previous night and the grass was wet and sparkling; a thrush gurgled from the fire-in-the-bush. Early crocuses had been succeeded by white and yellow jonquils with their brave stalks and fragile transparent heads.

The Quarters were swallowed by unmowed thatch. Only Jack the Driver's cabin was neat, only his garden had been opened, and his path to Stratford's back door was the only path cleared.

The big meadow was yellow with dead bluestem. When the tall grass died back and lodged it provided shelter for rabbits and groundhogs and raccoons, foxes and moles. Deer dropped their fawns in that tangle with perfect safety.

No path led to either of the barns, and an unfriendly wind had peeled twenty feet of cedar shakes from the smaller one. Franky had collected the broken shakes and used them for kindling.

Stratford's millrace was choked with joe-pye weed.

Abigail said, "I love the way spring grass shimmers in the wind. It reminds me of the ocean. Did I ever tell you, Samuel, about Cousin Molly's plantation on Carter's Creek? When I was a child we'd go there in the summer and gig for crabs and the water was that peculiar milky shade of gray . . ."

"I trust Cousin Molly will endure the Federal occupation."

His wife sighed. "She may welcome it. Her last letter said that even the hospitals were low on food and medicines were unobtainable. I do suppose the Federals will share provisions with our wounded, won't they?"

Samuel Gatewood shrugged. "They are such a bitter people. And what have we done to them? We did not wish to be a part of their country. We wished to freely leave a union our own fathers had formed. Why . . ."

"Hush, Samuel. We must look to the future and hope we can bear it. Our son is still living—I daily pray—and our grandson too. Pauline is in the milking barn with poor old Rosey, who produces what milk she can. Compared to so many, Samuel Gatewood, we are blessed."

"I suppose . . ."

"Come now, Samuel. Our task today is novel and we will not master it with words. While you and Jack make ready, I'll go indoors and put on my old dress and high shoes. Do you think I'll ever learn to go barefoot? I went barefoot as a child—at Carter's Creek I was invariably barefoot."

In his neat but clumsily patched work clothes, Jack the Driver was waiting outside his cabin's front door. "Mornin', Master Samuel. It looks to be a fine cool day."

"It does."

"I said a prayer for Mr. Duncan, this morning. Prayed he'd come home soon."

"Thank you."

Jack rolled his head to get a crick out of his neck. "Those scamps over at the Botkin home place—some of those boys are fulltask hands. They living on rabbits up there. Rabbits! While mighty plantations going to rack and ruin!"

Samuel Gatewood spoke softly. "Miss Abigail suggested we might hire them. We couldn't pay them a full year's wage—unless they'd take Confederate . . ."

Jack boomed out his laugh.

"But we could pay two men for six months. We'd pay them the same as what we used to rent servants for."

"Maybe you could let 'em stay right here in the Quarters," Jack suggested. "Mr. Samuel, since Agamemnon died, it gets awful quiet here at night. Everybody gone!"

"Rent them their homes?"

"Mr. Samuel, I don't care how you does it."

"And you, Jack. How shall I treat you?"

"Why, just the same as you has been."

"I mean, now you're . . ." Samuel Gatewood coughed. ". . . free."

Jack the Driver's slow smile. "Master?"

"You and I, Jack, we'll want to do things differently."

"But I likes things just the way they is—or was—before this foolishness got started. I want a young gang and an old gang in the woods. I want fulltask hands in the fields and half task milking the cows and slopping the hogs and tending the horses. This my home, Master, and I want Stratford be the finest plantation in the Jackson River Valley, all its babies and horses *fat!*"

Samuel Gatewood turned from the look in his driver's eyes. "Yes," he said softly.

"We ever be happy again, the way we was?"

Sam'l Gatewood put out his hand. "Shake my hand on it."

For the first time in his life, Jack the Driver shook a white man's hand.

Cleaned and oiled, the old-fashioned shovel plow shone like silver on the floor of the barn. The two men dragged it onto the stoneboat and laid the harness they'd modified beside it.

"I never thought . . ." Samuel Gatewood laughed.

"Me neither," Jack said glumly. "Not in this world."

The two dragged the stoneboat into the river field and set the plow on the ground.

"You've set the coulter properly?" Samuel said.

"Took a file to it yesterday afternoon." Jack attached the harness to the plow. He was less sure about the hitch end and flipped straps and buckles first one way and then the other.

"It'll come right in the end," Samuel said. "Here's Abigail now."

Abigail Gatewood wore a straw hat fastened around her chin with a pale yellow scarf and gloves of the same color.

"Dearest," Samuel said. "I don't believe I've ever seen a more charming field hand."

"Never mind about that, Samuel. Just tell me what I'm supposed to do."

"We have seed oats for three acres," Samuel said. "I estimate we can prepare a half acre each day."

"You always were clever with figures, Samuel," Abigail said. "What do I do?"

"You'll steer toward that cedar tree. When you come parallel to the millrace, that'll be your headland—where we'll turn around."

The men set the plow upright and balanced it, and Jack showed Abigail how to grip the handles. "Keep the plowsole flat, Missus. Don't let it dig in. It starts to dig, sing out."

The field was flat, and there was plenty of bare earth under the stubble. Moss grew here and there, and Jack vowed to put lime on the field soon as the mill was running. Frilly clouds slipped by overhead, and a raven cawed from the fenceline.

Jack buckled Samuel Gatewood into the adapted harness. "It'll be our legs what pushes and our shoulders what pulls, same as if we was horses," he advised. "We got to step out like a team—smartly." When Jack buckled himself in, the thick traces ran up his back and looped over his shoulders.

"You ready, Jack?"

"Ready."

"Madam?"

"Yes, I am prepared."

"Then suppose we get this crop into the ground!"

68

LOOKAWAY, DIXIELAND

Appomattox Courthouse, Virginia
April 12, 1865

"I WILL NOT surrender to those people," Thomas Byrd said. The camp-fire lit his dirty, determined face. "I'll Indian through their lines and join General Johnson."

They'd been sitting by that fire all night. On the sedgy creek banks other fires burned and men stared into the coals. On the eastern horizon, a sullen red band beneath roiling black clouds.

"It'll be daylight soon," Duncan observed. "All that Union beef I ate last night made me feel like hell. Damned if I don't think my stomach's ru-ined."

"Fellows in the Washington Artillery buried their guns in the woods. Just dug a pit and buried them."

"Did they say any words over them?" Duncan asked. " 'Rust you were and to rust you must return?' "

"Don't go funnin' me," the boy said sullenly. "I can't stand it."

Patiently Duncan said, "General Longstreet says to surrender. And General Mahone agrees with him. General Lee says surrender, and our generals got together with the Union generals and worked it all out, so we quit fighting and go home. You see something wrong with that?"

"We could still break through!"

"We tried to break through and we couldn't. Didn't even come near to breaking through. We hadn't had rations in four days and they outnum-bered us two to one and they held the high ground. We were caught in a slaughter pen. At least that's what Lee thought. He might have been wrong, but that's what he thought."

"Then the Confederacy is dead!"

"Likely so."

"My father died for this country!"

"Yes, and so did General Jackson and J.E.B. Stuart and Pettigrew and Armistead and Pegram and Garnett, and A. P. Hill—Christ, I hope they found him a bigger coffin—and little Johnny Pelham—the gallant Pelham—what a wonder he was—and several hundred thousand other men who thought it'd be grand to live in their own new nation."

The boy was filthy: he'd lost the better part of his jacket, and a blood-blackened handkerchief was bound around his wrist. "Uncle Duncan, why are you mocking me?"

"Because I don't want to surrender either."

The sky was lightening but it was going to be a gray day.

Duncan said softly, "You think General Lee wanted to surrender? You think that old man wouldn't rather have died?"

"Then it was all for nothing. We were fools to try. Stuart, Jackson, my father—they died for nothing."

Duncan sipped scalding hot coffee. The Union soldiers had brought coffee last night. It was good of them. From here on they'd be able to drink coffee anytime they wanted. They'd eat anytime they wanted. They'd wear shoes. It was unlikely they'd ever be so tired or so frightened again in their entire lives. "We've been some places," Duncan said. "We've seen some things."

On the hill where the Union army camped, a bugle sounded reveille, and other bugles took it up.

"Last time we'll be hearing that particular tune," Duncan said. "Can't say I am overfond of it."

Men stood and stretched. Some made water or wandered down to the sinks.

"We are General Lee's Army of Northern Virginia!" the boy said. "God damn it, if we aren't that, what are we?" He snuffled and wiped his nose on his sleeve. "God, how I miss him!"

"In all the years I knew your father I never heard him say anything hard about another man. He could be hard on himself, but he was easy on everyone else. That sorry Alexander Kirkpatrick—one day I was carrying on about him and Catesby said, 'Alexander has his own cross to bear.' I never forgot that. A lot of fellows have taken to religion, but I misdoubt most will keep at it. Catesby would have. When he went for a thing he went for it whole hog."

"But he took his life . . ."

"Thomas, you weren't there. I saw that battlefield after the fighting was over and thanked God I hadn't been in it."

"But what does that leave me and Pauline?"

"Because your father is dead? Boy, look around this army and you'll see thousands whose fathers and brothers and sons are dead as Catesby Byrd."

Breakfast fires sprang up, and Duncan could smell the bacon cooking. The rich greasy odor made his stomach jump. Maybe from now on he wouldn't eat so much. "A man can get used to most anything," he said.

"What?"

"When I was your age, if you'd told me I'd have starved as much as I have or fought so desperately or put myself so often in harm's way, I'd have laughed at you."

Men were drawing water. Others went about camp duties in a lackadaisical manner. Duncan thought to say the Army of Northern Virginia wouldn't die today, it had died three days ago when General Grant and General Lee sat down and talked surrender. Duncan thought to say something about that but instead said, "You want some of this coffee?"

The boy shook his head.

"Look, I don't know," Duncan tried. "I mean, I've been following General Lee for four years and he's never led me wrong and he says we should quit and go home and be citizens of the United States. I suppose I'll follow him one last time. You think the general wasn't tempted to die? Before he went off to talk to Grant, Marse Robert said how easy it would be for him to ride along the lines and when the Union sharpshooters spotted him it'd be over. Marse Robert wanted to take that ride but didn't. He said, 'Our duty is to live.' "

"Damn me if that ain't a different song than he has been singing." The boy's face was ugly with anger.

Some were striking their shelter tents. Some were feeding horses. The Union soldiers had provided fodder and corn too.

"You seen to your horse?" Duncan asked.

"That all you can think of, your damned horse?" The boy was snuffling and mad at himself for snuffling.

Duncan grinned. "Well, I used to think about the glories of war and chivalric knights, but I haven't thought about chivalry in some time. These days mostly I think about horses."

"I'm sorry, I . . ."

"That's all right, boy. It isn't an easy thing. Those boys who buried their guns, the officers who broke their swords, the fellows who smashed their rifles against a tree—I know why they did it. We already signed our paroles, so now we'll turn in our guns and cartridges and then we'll go home. I believe I'll march with the 44th. That's where me and Catesby started. You'd better look after your horse. She won't be getting any of General Grant's corn tomorrow."

The boy shivered.

Duncan's horse was cropping streamside grasses. Most of the horses were starved; some could hardly lift their heads. But let a gun be fired or the drums start jabbering and they'd snort and flare their eyes: General Lee's warhorses. Duncan rubbed the horse down with broom sedge and saddled her.

Division after division, the Army of Northern Virginia would march before the Union ranks, stack their rifles, loop cartridge boxes over the rifles, and lay down their flags. After each division was disarmed, its weapons and flags would be hauled away in wagons, its cartridges dumped in heaps upon the ground.

Duncan didn't recognize many of the twelve men who were what remained of the 44th Virginia Infantry Regiment. A bald-headed private with a wispy gray beard was color bearer. "I'm Johnson, Major. Samuel Ryals's uncle, sir. That boy which was took by the cholera."

Duncan remembered the boy he'd shown how to load a rifle. You didn't tousle a soldier's hair, not even a fourteen-year-old soldier's hair.

"His mother never got over it," the man said. "She pined away."

"It's been a hard war. You'll carry the colors?"

"I been carryin' 'em since John Lilly fell at Fort Stedman."

"Then you'll carry them today. Some men are tearing up their flags or hiding them, but you won't do that."

"Oh hell," the man said. "I got no regrets puttin' her down. She was a good old flag, but she's a mite heavy and when them Union boys see her coming they always try to shoot whoever's carrying her. Color sergeants got less chance of living than you officers do."

Duncan grinned. "Well, you seem to have survived."

"Yes, sir, I have. And better men'n me are buried beside the road. I got some Union whiskey in my canteen if you'd like a taste."

Gordon's division fell into marching order, General Gordon himself in the van. There were many flags for so few men. The turnpike bristled with Confederate battle flags.

"Division! Forward!" They'd never marched smarter, and Duncan's horse picked up her feet and snorted against the bit thinking she was heading for a fight.

They passed the village courthouse and the house where the surrender had been signed, and swung along before the Union ranks. Blue soldiers, neatly dressed, neatly groomed, some of them plump.

Suddenly, on a command from their general, the Union soldiers snapped to attention and presented arms, and the sudden salute, so unexpected, startled the Confederates. General Gordon stood in his stirrups, drew his saber and touched it to his boot tip, and ordered a return salute. The men of Gordon's division snapped their hands to their rifle stocks.

Eyes left, Duncan passed rows of anonymous blue-clad men saluting, and Duncan could scarcely see through his tears.

"Division! . . ."

"Brigade! . . ."

"Regiment! . . ."

"Halt!"

Their officers dressed the ranks as if on parade, two armies, gray and blue, twelve feet apart, the width of a country road.

When the barefoot ranks were correct, every bit as straight as the Union divisions facing them, Confederate officers gave the command to fix bayonets before each regiment stacked its bright weapons and one at a time, each regiment laid down its flag.

Some color bearers wept. Some acted as if it was nothing to them. Some prayed.

And when they were done they stood for a time, no longer in ranks, each man lost in his own privacy, becoming the man he would be for the rest of his life.

A little later, Thomas Byrd and Duncan Gatewood started toward home.

69

ADVERTISEMENT IN THE
RICHMOND WHIG

RICHMOND, VIRGINIA
SEPTEMBER 12, 1865

MAGGIE BURNS FORMERLY MITCHELL Any person having information of the whereabouts or fate of my wife, Maggie Burns, formerly a slave on the Gatewood Plantation near SunRise, Virginia, is urged to communicate with 1st Sergeant Jesse Burns, 23rd USCT, Camp Sam Houston, Galveston, Texas. Maggie Burns was sold south in the winter of 1861. She is a comely light-skinned mulatto of slight stature, twenty or twenty-one years of age, and, with God's mercy, Maggie has a male child at her side.

70

REUNION

"AND DID YOU reply?" the girl asked.

Marguerite replaced the disintegrating clipping in her scrapbook. "I'd had my fill of being a nigger. No matter what I'd asked Jesse—begged him—Jesse would have come to Richmond to see me and Baby Jacob, and that would have ruined everything. I never loved Jesse, never promised him a thing. What right had he to ruin our life? When the government disbanded the U.S. Colored Troops, a few coloreds were allowed to enlist in the regular army. Perhaps Jesse was among them."

"He had such high hopes."

"Am I to be shackled to another's hopes?" In a softer voice she added, "The history of colored people in America is the history of hopes. Jesse wished to head a black family. Do you have any notion what powerful hope that requires?"

Outside the old woman's bedroom it was early summer; inside was last century's furniture, expensive, carelessly polished, musty. The girl could not think how anyone ever thought this stuff attractive.

A timid rap at the door. "We're ready for you to come out, Grannie M!"—a child's voice.

"I'll be with you in a minute, honey."

An older voice, a woman's: "Do you need help, Grannie M? We're all anxious to see you."

In a whisper, "All morning they've been shopping Thallmeier's, and they're dining at the Jefferson Hotel tonight. Let them stew." The old woman was so light she scarcely indented the bed she sat on. "I knew Catesby's son, Thomas, when he became senator. Thomas Byrd inherited his father's brains but his mother's nerves. He wasn't a notable senator.

"It didn't take the ex-soldiers long to restore order in the countryside. They terrified or hung every black man who stood up to them. Night riders shot that fool Pompey dead. Pompey had been Samuel Gatewood's houseman so long he thought he was somebody."

"Grannie M!"

"Yes, sweetheart. I'm coming." To the girl: "The gentry were whispering about Sallie, and 'convict' was the nicest name they called her. Virginians never forget. You may think they've forgotten but they've just put it out of their mind for courtesy's sake, and they'll recollect everything soon as they need to. Duncan and Sallie Gatewood hitched up Stratford's best wagon and headed west. Did I tell you about their advertisement?"

"Ma'am?"

"Well, it must have been twenty years later, '84 or '85, I can't recall. I was at a garden party, one of the river plantations. They were a horsey set, and if you didn't talk horses, they didn't have much to say. Of course I'd been invited because of the bank. The horsey people were chattering away on the lawn and I was reading periodicals on the veranda and came across an advertisement for a SunRise Ranch. Duncan and Sallie Gatewood's Wyoming plantation offered stud service and colts and could outfit eastern sportsmen. 'SunRise Ranch'—can you imagine? At the bottom of the ad were Duncan's and Sallie's names and three children— Samuel was one child, the others' names escape me. Aunt Opal was identified as 'Chief Horse Wrangler'—an honorific title, I assume.

"When Richmond resumed commercial activities, I found a white man willing to act as my president and opened my bank's doors. I was now and forever Mrs. Silas Omohundru, and it did me no harm to be a Confederate widow, particularly one whose husband died as Silas did. People argued whether Fort Gregg saved Lee's army or whether it was another useless sacrifice. They are arguing today. I only believe Silas died a happy man. I pray he did." Marguerite tottered to her feet. "Now, child, let us enter the lion's den."

The garden room was full of sun, and a jumble of kinfolk greeted Grannie M and hugged her and asked blessings for children large and small. Dressed in her Sunday best, Kizzy dozed at the end of the couch.

The girl had expected more negritude. Hair was brown and light blond—only one woman's was dark straight black. Some skins were brown, tanned by the California sun. Noses were aquiline or fat, lips thick or thin. The girl could not distinguish Marguerite's blood kin from her in-laws.

The man who approached was more casually dressed than a Virginian would have been. Though his linen sport coat was unexceptionable, his shirt was unbuttoned and he wore no tie. "I'm Josh Omohundru. So you're the girl Kizzy has been telling us about." He winked at the snoring old woman. "We spent every summer in this old house, me, brother Bill, and my sister, Selah—the pack of us. What a tyrant Kizzy was! We swore she had eyes in the back of her head. Grannie M was always downtown at the bank and what 'raisin' we got, Kizzy gave us. You're with the WPA?"

"For a time I was, yes." The girl couldn't determine if the hair that fringed Josh's balding pate was kinky or curly.

"Kizzy says you are interviewing ex-slaves. Fascinating, just fascinating. Kizzy was Grannie's house slave in Wilmington. Get Kizzy in the right mood and she'll talk your ear off."

Leading a parade of children, a thin handsome woman brought in a candle-bedecked cake. "Birthday-cake time, everyone. Children, it's apple cake, Grannie's favorite!"

"Hurrah for Grannie M!" a fair youth of eleven or twelve called.

"Bill's wife, Evelyn," Josh identified the woman. "Selah's boy, Jacob."

"What a handsome child! He's like a faun."

When Marguerite sat beside her ancient servitor, Kizzy woke and mumbled and rubbed her eyes. With his aunt's cigarette lighter, the fair youth cautiously lit the candles.

"That's a fine job, son, thank you." Marguerite eyed the blazing candles skeptically. "It's discomfiting to celebrate my birthday without knowing the exact date or, for that matter, the year. I was born . . ."

"Oh, Grannie M," Evelyn burst out. "Please don't tell us about Cox's snow."

The old woman stiffened. "I have not told you everything about Cox's snow," she snapped.

"Happy birthday, Grandmother." A plump beaming man hurried into the breach. "And many many more."

"That's Bill Omohundru," Josh identified his brother. "When the Volstead Act was repealed, Bill went on a tear, and I'm afraid he's still on it. Right now he's with MGM Pictures. The business end." Josh put his hand to his heart and struck an exaggerated pose, "All true Omohundrus have a theatrical bent. Bill's met Gable and Lombard—all of them."

"Your father, Jacob—that boy is his namesake?"

Sorrow creased Josh's face. "Yes. I suppose we all thought Father would go on forever. Jacob Omohundru died last August. Heart attack."

"I'm sorry."

"I miss him terribly. He was Harvard Law, you know—clerked for Justice Holmes. Has Grannie M told you about fleeing Wilmington with Jacob? It's a wonderful yarn. She'd sewn her husband's money—in English bearer bonds—into her skirt. Six months later, the war ended, she exchanged the bonds, and *voilà!*—a national bank is born!"

"I thought Federal soldiers found her gold."

"They found what gold she meant them to. Grannie M is a clever woman."

"Why hello—you must be the girl we've been hearing about." The woman who took the girl's hand had an amiable face and gentle grasp. "I'm Selah Omohundru, and this dope is my brother, Josh."

Excepting Kizzy, Selah was the darkest-skinned person here. Jet-black braids were coiled on top of her head.

"Whatever happened to Kizzy's child?"

Selah knitted her brows. "Years ago, here in this house—I suppose I must have been my Jacob's age at the time—I asked Kizzy why she didn't have children of her own. Kizzy said, 'My baby buried down in Goldsboro.' There was terrible grief in her voice.

"Kizzy and my father were very close. He phoned her on each birthday and they chattered for an hour. After the war, Kizzy was as much my father's mother as Granny M. Father used to joke about it—said he was extra lucky because he had an extra mother. Granny M makes her business success seem inevitable, but I gather failure was a real possibility on more than one occasion. Did you know hers was the first Richmond bank to reopen after Mr. Roosevelt's bank holiday?"

"She's a remarkable woman."

"Yes," Selah said. "She is, though sometimes not entirely likable."

"Mama?" It was the boy, Jacob. "Can we go out to the garden and play? Cousin Elliot wants to play too."

With Selah's approval the children slipped through the French doors into the sunlight. Kizzy had wakened and was sharing her cake with two of the youngest children, very much on their party manners.

"It's Kizzy's gift," Selah said. "Children trust her."

Josh said, "Marguerite sits on the board of the Historical Society. Last night, we were at a dinner party at this wonderfully photogenic plantation and everyone was talking about the biography Dr. Freeman is preparing of Robert E. Lee. Don't you think it strange to make heroes of men who tried to break up our nation?"

Selah winced, but the girl smiled courteously. "It seems less strange to a Virginian."

Selah said, "Josh, would you mix me a daiquiri?"

"Sister, are you sure . . ."

"Please, Josh, we've discussed this." Selah steered the girl to a quiet corner. "I gather Marguerite has told you?"

The girl took a deep breath and said, "Marguerite has spoken about her life as a slave, if that's what you mean."

Selah looked her straight in the eyes. "Yes, I thought she might. Well, you're the first outsider in on the Omohundru family secret."

"You knew?"

"Oh yes. As soon as we were old enough to keep a confidence we were told. I can't speak for Josh and Bill, but I found the news of our racial makeup horrifying. You know how much young girls wish to be indistinguishable from their friends. And it turned out I was different—hopelessly, everlastingly different. Oh, I cried and wailed and said hateful things, but Marguerite simply replied that willful innocence tempts Providence. Have you been to Europe recently?"

The girl, who had never been, said as much.

"I was in Hamburg in March and—I'm an art historian, you see—and the Warburg Library—we fear that if that wonderful library isn't relocated outside Germany, the damn brownshirts will burn the books. Burn the books!"

"One reads about such things . . ."

Fiercely, "They are true! It is worse than you read! We Americans are hiding our heads in the sand." When Josh arrived with Selah's daiquiri, she said, "I'm sorry Josh, but I've changed my mind. Could you fetch me a glass of water?" To the girl, "Marguerite is so proud of her water. Hers is probably the last private well in Richmond. When she passes on . . ."

"Is your husband here today?"

Selah's look was a challenge. "We are divorced."

"I am sorry."

"I am not. I suppose I've inherited my realism from Marguerite. No Omohundru is likely to be ruined by dreams."

"Your father . . ."

"Jacob Omohundru was the sanest man I've ever known. Because he was so calm, some thought him meek, but once Jacob set his course, no power on earth could dissuade him from it. Father didn't make friends. He was ill at ease in society and turned down most invitations. Mother was killed in a trolley accident when we were quite young, and Father never remarried. I cannot tell you how much I miss him. My father was one of those men who carry on the honorable daily business of the world and never make a fuss about it. People trusted him. Do you find us ordinary?"

Startled, the girl said, "I . . ."

"I'm sure you must. Brother Bill is the kindest man alive, but he drinks too much. Joshua is forever saying the slightly wrong thing and loves his children to distraction. And I, divorced woman with child, junior professor of art history. People trusted my father. Is that so negligible?"

"And Marguerite?"

With a flourish, Josh presented Selah with her glass of well water and solemnly intoned, " 'I've been living beside the James too long to wish to drink of it.' "

Selah's smile was fleeting, and she continued as if she'd not been interrupted. "Those who create a family are never ordinary. Marguerite may be many things, but ordinary she is not."

Josh's grin became a grimace—somewhat like Edward G. Robinson's. "You gonna rat on us, sister? I mean—if this got out, Christ! I'm with the water authority, you know."

The girl said, "I supposed things were different in California."

Selah said, "I don't think my university would mind. Bill's studio wouldn't turn a hair. But some of Josh's political enemies might use it—this mixed-race business—against him."

"There are several prominent negro families in Richmond."

"Yes, but there are no prominent families that are negro. When I was young, Kizzy told me how the slaves prayed for the day of Jubilo. I have no doubt that day will come. But not now. Not yet."

"So you think Marguerite did the right thing?"

"You must ask Marguerite." Selah's flashing grin was so pleased with herself and so mischievous the girl knew what little Midge must have looked like so many years ago.

Josh went to help Kizzy scrub apple cake from good children's faces.

"Will I see you again?" Selah asked. "I am between terms and plan to stay in Richmond for a while."

"Meeting you," the girl said, "all of you, today. I wish I could have known your father."

Selah smiled. "Like every ordinary man, my father had his glimpse of heaven. Just one glimpse."

Marguerite faced the remnants of apple cake, a mound of sticky candles. The girl came to sit beside her.

The human voice is the last thing to age. Marguerite chuckled. "I see you've met our Selah."

"Yes."

"She reminds me of myself. As I might have been. Do you think I might have done better? Don't patronize me. No one but a fool reaches the end of her life without regrets." Her eyes followed the boys playing in the garden. Her great-grandson, Jacob, broad-jumped a low boxwood planting and covered his ears, giggling with pleasure.

"After Silas was killed, I was never with another man. I was then twenty-one years old. It is difficult to remember how it felt to be twenty-one years old."

Sentimental tears glistening his cheeks, Bill leaned to give his grandmother a boozy embrace. He said that he had a train to catch, that they were starting a new picture, that Sam Goldwyn spent money like water. "We'll be back for your hundredth!"

"Not if you don't stop drinking," Marguerite said.

Bill beamed, "Same old Marguerite! Promise you'll never change!" He went to hug Kizzy.

Marguerite sighed. "That is the hardest thing: that I can no longer protect them." She nodded at the children in the garden. "I am thoroughly ready to die, but to see that boy grow up, I would almost be willing to live forever. If you wonder what Duncan Gatewood looked like, look at Jacob: his ears, how he holds his head. Lord, how I loved him. I love him still." Softly she said, "That boy is right fancy."

Oblivious to the old eyes which beheld him so tenderly, young Jacob tossed his head, laughing with the delight of being alive.

ACKNOWLEDGMENTS

IN 1990, WHILE researching county records for a book which became *An American Homeplace,* I found an evocative court case. Samuel Gatewood was a prosperous mountain planter who owned a large plantation, a mill, and twenty-eight slaves. In February of 1861, Gatewood accompanied slave patrollers to the modest Kirkpatrick cabin seeking Jesse, Gatewood's runaway slave. When Jesse was discovered, the Kirkpatricks might easily have disclaimed knowledge of his fugitive status, and surely that would have been the wiser course. (The record hinted such may have been Gatewood's preference.) Instead, the Kirkpatricks were defiant. When Jesse was asked if he'd run again, he was unusually bold. "It's a mighty big mountain up there," he replied.

It was a terrifying/thrilling time. Men of good reputation reported hearing cannon fire deep in the mountains. Fort Sumter was besieged by the new Confederacy, and though Virginia was still in the Union, its sympathies were with those states already seceded.

In those days, when malefactors weren't hanged outright, prison sentences were relatively light: two years for burglary, three for robbery and assault. Both Kirkpatricks were found guilty of felony (Jesse was Samuel Gatewood's property) and sentenced to five years in the state penitentiary in Richmond.

Kirkpatrick was not a local name. Apparently the land they lived on once belonged to Mrs. Kirkpatrick's father. There is more known about the Gatewoods (which I did not pursue), but nothing more about Jesse or the Kirkpatricks. Penitentiary records were burned in the evacuation fire of 1865.

You now know what I do about the real Jesse, the real Gatewoods and Kirkpatricks. In the pages of *Jacob's Ladder* they are wholly fictions.

The Confederate surrender at Appomattox disturbed U. S. Grant, who wrote, "I felt like anything rather than rejoicing at the downfall of a foe who had fought so long and so valiantly for a cause though that cause was, I believe, one of the worst for which a people ever fought and one for which there was the least excuse." As a liberal, reared in the North, I shared U. S. Grant's view—as I suppose most Americans do—and my first working title was "The Worst Cause." I was off on the wrong foot, my research perplexed me, and several times I nearly abandoned the project. It was impossible to understand the Confederates who fought so gallantly. For what? The right to oppress another people? And given the disparity in military forces, population, even farmland (in 1860, the North grew more tobacco than the South, had three times as many horses, four times the wheat production), it was hard to understand what the southerners were thinking of, why'd they'd chance lives, fortunes, and honor in such a forlorn struggle.

Twenty-five years ago, my wife, Anne, and I moved from New York City to a farm in the Virginia mountains. Though we cannot be natives, we have become Virginians, and this farm is our only home. During summer months, irregularly, my young neighbors hold what they call "deer/beer parties." On the riverbank, deer steaks are barbecued while good old boys spin yarns and drink Old Milwaukee and Willy Nelson tunes blare from a pickup truck. My neighbors are proud, poor, crack shots, honest to a fault, the best of friends and least forgiving of enemies. At one such party while the southern stars slid overhead, I understood that if the year were 1861 we Virginians would be fighting for Robert E. Lee.

But if by accident of birthplace I might have been a Confederate soldier, by accident of race I might just as well have been my or one of my neighbor's slaves.

The attempt to understand both experiences, Confederate and African-American, is the soul of *Jacob's Ladder.*

I determined to write these people's stories as they understood matters at the time, before historians decided what actually happened and moralists determined what it all meant. My liveliest information came from memoirs, diaries, newspapers, sermons, and letters written before and during the war. I could not read these letters, so full of hope, fear, and vows to be better people, without admiring the men and women who endured the most terrible and consequential of American wars.

The Civil War is the single most important event in African-American history, and the ex-slaves who became Union soldiers knew that perfectly well and resolved to standards of courage, dignity, and faith few of their white fellow soldiers could equal. As Medal of Honor winner Sergeant Major Christian Fleetwood, 4th USCT, wrote, "Here the negro stood in the glare of the greatest search light, part and parcel of the grandest armies ever mustered upon this continent, competing side by side with the best and bravest of the Union army against the flower of the Confederacy and losing nothing in the contrast."

These are happy times for researching the war. New southern historians are uninterested in justifying horrid racial practices and busy themselves revising our understanding of the lives and beliefs of ordinary southerners, blacks and whites alike. In July 1991, the definitive exhibition of antebellum slave life, "Before Freedom Came," opened at the Museum of the Confederacy in Richmond. For many black schoolteachers who brought their young charges to that exhibition, it was the first time they had ever set foot inside a museum that represented for them all that had been most hurtful in the South.

Research is the historical novelist's map, constraint, and purest energy. The events of the Civil War are so odd, ferocious, and poignant that fictional characters do well simply to inhabit them. I am no historian but have tried to stick tight to the facts.

Throughout I've given the names of real soldiers to my fictional characters. Had you been in Silas Omohundru's hut during the bitter winter of 1864, you would have met Color Sergeant Robinson, though the real Color Sergeant Robinson may have been morose and gray where my fictional Robinson is undaunted. If you'd attended a hymn sing with First Sergeant (and Medal of Honor winner) Edward Ratcliffe you might have encountered a man less an angry realist than I've made him out. Robinson and Ratcliffe survived the war and may have descendants who honor them in memory or possess letters or their ancestor's battered diary. I owe their descendants this apology for fictionalizing their family story. I also ask pardon of the family of Private Lawrence Barry of the Washington (Louisiana) Artillery, whose defiance symbolized the battle for Fort Gregg.

Memoirs, diaries, and letters have provided insights and language. Chapter 12 is lifted in its entirety from an anonymous article in the *Southern Planter* of 1857.

Not producing a bibliography is a novelist's privilege I gratefully exercise. However, since they are not widely known sources, scholars may wish to examine master's theses compiled by students of Dr. Eslie Lewis, at the Moorland Springarn Research Center, Howard University, and

"From the Wilderness to Appomatox: Life in Lee's Army of Northern Virginia, May 1864–April 1865," a doctoral dissertation by J. Tracy Power, University of South Carolina. The former are the only regimental histories for U.S. Colored Troops recruited from Virginia and Maryland, and the latter is invaluable for anyone seeking to know what Lee's soldiers were thinking near the end of their bitter struggle.

I am deeply indebted to those who have abetted my research and ask those I've neglected to name to forgive me. Whatever I got right I owe to them, every misunderstanding is my own.

Jack Ackerly, Richmond, Virginia

Rick Armstrong, Millboro Springs, Virginia

Charles Ballou,MD., Clifton Forge, Virginia

Mary and David Britt, Reynolds Homestead, Critz, Virginia

Dr. Chris Calkins, Historian, Petersburg National Battlefield

Mary C. Coulling, Lexington, Virginia

Shelby Foote, Memphis, Tennessee

Dr. Warren R. Hofstra, Shenandoah University

Professor Ervin Jordan, Curator of Technical Services, Special Collections, Alderman Library, University of Virginia

Dr. Ken Koons, Virginia Military Institute

Dr. Stephen L. Longenecker, Bridgewater College

David Nicholson, Washington, D.C.

Judge Oliver Pollard, Petersburg, Virginia

Dr. James I. Robertson, Virginia Polytechnic Institute

J. Susanne Simmons, Fort Defiance High School

Nancy Sorrells, Research Librarian, Museum of American Frontier Culture

Lucinda Stanton, Historian, Monticello

E. Gehrig Spencer, Historic Site Manager, Fort Fisher, North Carolina

Evelyn Timberlake, Research Librarian, Library of Congress

Tom Word, Richmond, Virginia

My wife, poet Anne Ashley McCaig, weighed every sentence and denounced each shabby word, every mangled attitude. While I am deeply grateful for her months of hard work, I love her for that morning when things looked most bleak and she said, "We had to take this risk. It was the right thing to do."

Knox Burger has been my mentor, editor, and friend for as long as I've been writing prose. *Jacob's Ladder* would not exist without him.

Starling Lawrence found the warmth in Cox's snow.

I am grateful for the tangible confidence of Merle M. Dodson of Planter's Bank and Trust Company of Virginia and M. Scott Glenn of Staunton Farm Credit.

Finally, I'd like to thank the staffs of the Antietam, Manassas, Fredericksburg, and Spotsylvania National Battlefields; the Richmond National Battlefield Museum; the Petersburg National Battlefield; the Cape Fear Museum; Warwick House, Bath County, Virginia; the Bellamy Mansion, Wilmington, North Carolina; the Bath County Historical Society; Hollywood Cemetery; the Bath County Clerk's Office; the National Archives of the United States; the Southern History Collection at the University of North Carolina; the Historical Collection, University of Michigan at Lansing; the Valentine Museum; and the Museum of the Confederacy. I thank the librarians at Washington and Lee University, the Alderman Library of the University of Virginia, the Charles Town Public Library, the Virginia Military Institute, the Virginia Polytechnic Institute, Howard University, the Wilmington (North Carolina) Public Library, the Virginia State Library and Archives, and the Virginia Historical Society. And last but by no means least, my thanks to the redoubtable ladies of the Junior League of Richmond, who got me into the old Virginia State Penitentiary after it was closed but before it was torn down.

Donald McCaig, 18 March 1997

AFTERWORD

"So far from engaging in a war to perpetuate slavery,
I am rejoiced that slavery is abolished. I believe it will
be greatly for the interests of the south. So fully am I
satisfied of this, as regards Virginia especially, that I
would cheerfully have lost all I have lost by the war
and suffered all I have suffered to have this object attained."

—Robert E. Lee,
Baltimore, Maryland, April 28, 1869